LIMANORA

LIMANORA

LIMANORA

THE ISLAND OF PROGRESS

GODFREY SWEVEN

INTRODUCTION BY
KARL WURF

WILDSIDE PRESS

LIMANORA

THE ISLAND OF PROGRESS

GODFREY SWEVEN

INTRODUCTION BY
KARL WURF

WILDSIDE PRESS

INTRODUCTION

KARL WURF

Though lesser known than *Brave New World* or *1984*, *Limanora* (1903) occupies a fascinating corner of the early utopian-dystopian tradition in speculative fiction. Written by Godfrey Sweven (the pseudonym of New Zealand academic John Macmillan Brown), the novel imagines a remote island where an advanced post-human society has eliminated war, religion, and moral compromise in favor of rational perfection, eugenics, and technological transcendence. Unlike the grim warnings of Orwell or Huxley, Sweven offers a vision of relentless, even chilling progress, where individuality is sacrificed for species-wide ethical evolution.

Limanora follows a castaway's journey through this surgically improved society, blending spiritual mysticism with hard science, telepathy, and dream-based education. The novel is dense, philosophical, and idiosyncratic—closer in tone to Samuel Butler's *Erewhon* or Francis Bacon's *New Atlantis* than to modern dystopias. Sweven's influences include Victorian science, spiritualism, Darwinian evolution, and the rising faith in technocratic utopias at the turn of the 20th century.

While *Limanora* never gained the widespread influence of its successors, it has attracted modern scholarly attention for its proto-transhumanist ideas and for anticipating ethical themes in science fiction. Its closest literary kin may be Olaf Stapledon, whose *Last and First Men* echoes Sweven's concern with species-level destiny. Though rarely cited directly, *Limanora* stands as a precursor to the genre's enduring fascination with engineered societies, idealism pushed to extremity, and the costs of perfection.

PREFACE

It was long before our strange guest could be induced to continue his narrative. He had seemed to hesitate as he approached the close of his sojourn in the outer islets of the archipelago. He several times postponed the story of his exit from it in the projectile. And for months he left his history hanging in air, and the strange coffin in which he had been confined executing its parabola from his yacht.

There was some excuse for his delay, for the winter had fled, and the birds and the flowering trees around us gloried again in song and colour. He grew restless as the days lengthened, and could not bear to settle in our shelter by the fiord. All that we saw of him for months was his occasional flight from precipice to precipice above the sombre green of the bush. It was as easy for him to flit from knoll to knoll as it was for us to leap a ditch. He had regained his old bird-like gait, that to us was noiseless. What he fed on came to be a puzzle, for he seldom joined us now in our meals; and the old semi-transparency came into his face.

Weeks and weeks together none of us would see him. Where he went we knew not, nor had we the heart to follow him and trace his whereabouts. Now and again he would join one or another of us at our work, and indicate the direction in which we should tunnel or dig for the richer layers of wash-dirt. His instinctive sense of the presence of gold beneath the surface of the earth seemed to us in our blind groping miraculous. We never found him mistaken in his indications. But we felt it a kind of desecration to ask him to condescend to such base and trivial pursuits as the research for wealth. At times his absence was so prolonged that we thought he had vanished back to the ring of mist, whence he had come. But a great storm always brought him to our huts again.

The summer waned into autumn, and the days began to narrow down. Blasts from the south grew keener; and his flight from us was more circumscribed. We saw him almost daily. When the winter nights began, he gave himself up again to memory. He drew towards us in sympathy, and there were in his narrative fewer and fewer reserves. His English became fuller and more exact, though time and again he stumbled over thoughts too subtle to transfuse into so rough and materialistic a language. Our own interpretations of his descriptions must often have been mistaken, we are certain, and many passages we have had to omit because of manifest ambiguity or mistiness of expression.

—GODFREY SWEVEN.

GLOSSARY

AILOMO—The astrobiological families.

AIROLAN—A sensometer, or instrument for finding the personal equation of a man.

ALCLIROLAN—Radiographic cinematograph; an instrument combining microscope, camera in vacuo, and electric power.

ALFARENE—Oxygen shrub.

AMMERLIN—Historoscope.

CIRALAISON—Museum of terrors.

CLEVAMOLAN—Combination of telescope and makrakoust, or distance-hearer.

CLIMOLAN—Earth-sensor.

CLIROLAN—Instrument that combines electro-microscopy and photography.

CLIROLANIC—Infinitesimally microscopic.

CORFALEENA—Vacuum-engine car.

DOOMALONA—The hill of farewells.

DUOMOVAMOLAN—Instrument that interprets the music of the cosmos.

ERFALEENA—Anti-gravitation flight-car.

FALEENA—Ship of the air.

FARFALEENA—Electric faleena.

FAROSAN—Aroma-recorder.

FIALUME—The valley of memories.

FILAMMU—The will-telegraph.

FIRLA—The electric sense.

FIRLALAIN—The firlamaic department of Oomalefa.

FIRLAMAI—The arts of the electric sense.

FIRLAMAIC—Belonging to the arts of the firla.

FIRLAMAN—A musical instrument that appeals to the firla.

FLORAMO—The botanical families.

FLORONAL—The tree of life.

FRALOOMIAMO—The families of pioneers that imagine and represent the distant future.

GERMABELL—A tree with fruit that makes the muscles and cartilage more elastic.

IDLUMIAN—Electric steriliser.

IDROLAN—Observer and magnifier of electric impulses.

IDROLINASAN—Machine-reporter of the thoughts and feelings and words of an assembly.

IDROSAN—Recorder of electric impulses and sensations.

IDROVAMOLAN—Instrument for at once seeing and hearing at great distances.

ILARIME—Edifice devoted to the arts of smell, taste, and sound combined.

IMANORA—Centennial review of the civilisation and its progress.

IMATARAN—The focusser of history.

INAMAR—Instrument for splitting up light into its constituents.

INASAN—Recorder of luminous impressions.

INOLAN—Measurer of light.

IRELIUM—Iridescent metal applicable to all manner of purposes by the Limanorans.

LABRAMOR—Alloy of irelium that sponges up and retains electricity.

LABROLAN—Instrument for drawing electricity from the air and the clouds.

LAVIDROLAN—Camera-telescope.

LAVOLAN—Revealer of the inner tissues and mechanism.

LEOMARIE—The science and art of earth-seeing.

LEOMO—The families of earth-seers.

LEOMORAN—The earth-perforator.

LENTA—The minutest division of time in Limanora.

LILAMO—The families that watch the security of the island.

LILARAN—The storm-cone.

LILARIE—The science and art of island-security.

LINAMAR—The analyst of sounds.

LINASAN—Recorder and reproducer of sounds.

LINOKLAR—Spectroscopic analyst and recorder of vapours.

LOOMIAMO—Families of pioneers who imagine and represent the links that connect the present with the distant future.

LOOMIEFA—The theatre of futurition.

MANORA—Decennial review of the progress made by the people.

MARGOL—Electric instrument for blending or reducing the strength of perfumes, flavours, and sounds.

MINELLA—Edifice for formula-machines.

MIRLAN—Life-lamp for revealing and recording internal processes for the use of the eye, the ear, and the electric sense.

MOLTA—The Limanoran measure of infinitesimal length.

MONALAN—Electrical distance-analyst.

MORNALAN—Time-telescope.

NAROLLA—Dream-stimulants.

OOARAN—Psychometer.

OOAROMO—Psycho-physiological families.

OOLORAN—The sonarchitect.

OOLOREFA—The hall of sonarchitecture.

OOMALEFA—Halls of nutrition and medication.

OOROLAN—Instrument for transforming form and colour into melody.

PIRAKNO—Machine for drawing electricity from space.

PIRAMO—The meteorological families.

RIMLA—The centre of force.

SALOSAN—The gustagraph.

SARIFOLAN—Instrument that interprets for sight, hearing, and the electric sense the graphic records of the mirlan.

SARMOLAN—Cosmic barometer.

SIDRALAN—Biometer.

SIDRALMO—Bio-chemical families.

SIDRAMO—The chemical families.

TERRALONA—The edifice of outlook into heaven and hell.

THINAMAR—Visualiser of sound.

TIRLEOMORAN—Electric earth-perforator.

TREMOLAN—Electric clock indicating the changes of electricity in various parts of the island.

TREVAMOLAN—Graduated modifier of sound.

VAMOLAN—Makro-mikrakoust.

VIMOLAN—Photo-electric analyser.

BOOK I

THE OUTER OR MATERIAL CIVILISATION

CHAPTER I

MY AWAKENING

I OPENED my eyes in a world no feature of which I could recognise. Everything around me was of the most dazzling beauty. The walls and vaulted roof of the room where I lay gleamed like mosaic-work of lit jewellery. The floors were duller, and yet shone with a coloured radiance like that in a dew-belled meadow under the light of the slant-rayed forenoon sun. The light broke up in innumerable points and corners of the roof into a magnificent display of prismatic colours, moving and changing every minute. Yet, with all the marvellous iridescence, there was sufficient shade in the vault and walls to check the fiery oppression of the sun. I had dreamt of such fairy palaces; but the dream had ever been abortive or glanced off into something hideous or appalling. Here was architecture as unlike anything I had seen upon earth as a dream, and yet it had a grace that no dream had ever caught.

Nor did I know the material of which this room was formed. It seemed like ice, yet was never changed by the fire of the sun. It was capable of being moulded into the most delicate lace-work, and yet could be made as massive as marble walls of Eastern palaces that were built for both pleasure and siege. It was in portions as transparent as glass, and in others frosted with wondrous pictures. And how were those countless domes and arches and arborescent columns produced with such ease? How were those airy galleries hung? How were those fragrant fountains poised so nicely that an infant's finger seemed capable of overturning them? Even the gently moving curtains had the same crystalline character as the walls, now frosted as by the artist of our winter-mornings, again goldenly dim, or rainbow-hued.

There was a spaciousness that reminded me of the colonnaded aisles of our great cathedrals. Was I resting in one of the temples of the island? Was I being consecrated for sacrifice? And yet the dainty warm nooks, the close-hung curtains, and graceful tapestries so broke the awe and loneliness of the place as to make me feel that it was a chamber for a solitary. And I could look out upon the fields and forests and the far-stretching sea; for every foot of wall had in it some transparency that with its landscape stood like a picture framed in the frosted tracery around it. I seemed never to reach the limit of these varied perspectives and distances. I sank back exhausted on my perfumed couch, then slowly recovered by aid of the sweetness that met my every sense. The fragrance that filled the room was like that of finest garden flowers, and kept changing from one lovely variety to another, never cloying the sense. Around, too, from unseen sources, floated sweet music, that now swelled into a chorus, and again fell into angelic softness. Then a new sensation came to me; with every breath I seemed to draw in a subtle nourishment and stimulation to my senses; every minute added to the renewal of my strength. And, to increase my delighted bewilderment, I gradually felt a new sense appealed to; every nerve in my body seemed exhilarated, and I felt capable of heroic actions. Some magnetic influence was raying towards me through the atmosphere, and a dormant electric faculty seemed to be awakened in my mind and in my body, producing the effect of intoxication without its stupor or the numbing of the moral powers. It was like a beautiful dream without the helplessness of the dreamer. I felt no delirium or voluptuous languor from the excitement of the senses. It all led to spiritual vigour, that would have made the body its prompt ally.

My renewed energies turned my mind to my strange surroundings. I wondered where the beings were who had built this wondrous palace, and were now doubtless playing upon my senses. Was it all a dream? And had I never been shot into the sea with Noola? It seemed as if my inmost thoughts were at once communicated to my watchers; for from some direction, out of some niche or doorway I had not noticed, moved softly a figure, that, in its muscular breadth, large head, and springy gait, reminded me of Noola. Upon the face a smile shone out of unfathomed depths of thought and sympathy, and yet the lips were close as if to forbid speech. It was enough to rest and gaze at the beautiful expression of the face with its intensity of love and pity in the eyes. But the features had not that symmetry of outline which we call beauty in Europe; and the form was not "divinely tall." The whole of the attraction lay in the upraying of the soul into the face. It was like gazing into the limpid waters of a lake; I tried to give speech to my emotions, but the hand rose gently to the lips in a gesture that commanded silence, then waved over me, and, as I looked, I fell into a deep and dreamless sleep.

I knew not how long I had been unconscious; for when I woke I seemed to be a new man; every faculty tingled with energy; health glowed through my tissues; I wandered from niche to niche, from arcade to recess; I climbed the lofty galleries and raised the curtains, shaking the sweet perfumes from them as they swung in the air; I ran from transparency to transparency with the delight of a child, and gazed through each at the ever-varying landscapes that stretched outwards to the sea. Music, distant and entrancing, floated around me in the air, with variations and cooling bars of silence, so that it made a subtle ether circumambient rather than a definite impression on the senses. Under such conditions what could not I do in life? I remembered the old weariness and despair that used to cling around me like a shirt of Nessus even in the morning when I was refreshed with sleep, and the clogging humours that used to retard my most generous or most energetic action. In my former life I had moved in a clammy viscous medium that dragged back my most eager faculties. Now I was built of air, and stirred lightly as air.

What was it that had accomplished this strange transformation? I had not felt so in the other islands of the archipelago or even on its seas. I had not been so exhilarated at my first awaking. How had this great change come about? Or was it but momentary, to pass away like other intoxications and leave exhaustion and ache? I began to be puzzled and to feel the return of the thought that it was perhaps only a dream after all. How was I to test the matter?

Surely I could not have thought aloud. Yet here from somewhere or other was moving across the floor the figure that had appeared after my first trance. I was so awestruck by the noiseless flash of the approach that I could make no sign of welcome. What could I say to a being who came so near to what we consider in the old world the supernatural? As soon as my thoughts touched upon the state of my mind and the circumstances that surrounded me, my host (should I call him so?) appeared. And, though my senses, I thought, had acquired preternatural acuteness, not a sound had I heard of his entrance or of his footsteps across the chamber.

He seemed to know the perplexity of my thoughts again, for he advanced with so airy a grace that my eyes were fascinated by the ease of the motion. And his words came almost like music; I scarcely considered what he was saying, so beautiful were the tones and manner in which it was said. "Come, and I shall tell you what has occurred," was what I understood. It was in the primary or simplest vocabulary of Limanora, the vocabulary that Noola had taught me.

He led me by a covered but transparent way into a vaulted chamber, that seemed to the other as a cathedral to a chapel; for it was pillared and galleried and aisled with the most transcendent art. But I was too interested in the story he had to tell to give way to my passive enjoyment of the scene. He motioned me to ascend with him a platform that rose above us in a lofty recess at one brightly sunlit corner of the building. I saw him lean back, and feared that he would fall to the floor; but with his motion the rich mosaic of the platform opened, and a rest rose to meet his body which was of the same alabaster-like texture as the curtains and seemed to shape itself to every curve and bend of his figure. He stretched out his hand towards me, and before I knew what he had done I was resting, in an attitude not far from the upright, on a soft machine like his own. He showed me how to control this by a knob under my right hand, and then together we flew to the ceiling and back, wheeled round, swung gently in the air, or remained still. It moved like a thing of life in sympathy with every desire; a slight change of the position would relieve any part of the body and yet leave all the rest supported; any kind of motion was accomplished on changing the screw that lay in the knob. I afterwards investigated the mechanism, and was amazed at its simplicity; a few levers, cunningly mastering all the various combinations of motion, turned on or off the force needed for the necessary changes. After a few hours' experience of it, I could find no comparison in nature but the couch of air on which the albatross seems to rest as it moves. I afterwards found that a nice management of compressed air was the secret of this wonderful rest that was neither couch nor chair. As soon as we ceased to use it, it disappeared as suddenly as it had risen. This accounted for the complete absence of the furniture that impedes free motion in our European houses and made me think as I awoke in my chamber of our great cathedrals with their free floor space.

There in mid-air we lightly hung as if resting on wings; he seemed to know my anatomy and the points of greatest pressure in any attitude, and controlled both machine-rests with such adroitness that we swung hither and thither, changing slowly from the recumbent to the erect attitude or back again, finding every few minutes a different point of view of the chamber or of the landscapes that could be seen through the walls. But I soon grew oblivious to the beauty that stole through every sense; my whole consciousness was absorbed in watching the play of the intelligence on his face and listening to his narrative. I missed many of the links in his story, even though he contrived to put most of it into the primary and secondary vocabularies, and, where he was compelled to go beyond them, put so much of his thoughts into his features that I could almost have gathered it from them. But I saw the drift of the story, and, when it was over, pieced the fragments together and found, when afterwards I knew the language and the civilisation better, I had missed little of the real meaning. I give it, then, as if it were in his own words, although my intelligence seemed to stumble at every step in it.

"You wonder at your hospitable reception. But you will not wonder when you know the change in the condition of our knowledge since Noola was exiled. He was unhurt by the ricochet of the missiles on the beach. In the darkness they were ill-aimed, and, though they struck in sand, they were shattered by the impact and recoiled from the shingle underneath. He disentangled himself from the wreck and rescued you. But soon the watchers by the storm-cone were down on the beach and carried you to our house, whilst they led your comrade to another. You were each examined by the wise men and the medical families. Your faculties and emotions and tendencies were all tested, and their various strengths measured by means of the different kinds of cerebrometers whilst you slept. Since Noola was exiled a hundred years ago, our knowledge of the brain and the nerves and their various functions has been applied in the most practical way to the art of living. Every curve and convolution of the controlling instrument of the body has its value and meaning tabulated. Every action, thought, and emotion has had its physical symbol and locality fixed; and the minutest change in the strength of any one of these points in the brain or in the nervous system can be discovered by applying one of the cerebrometers. You will know what these are some day; but it is enough to say that they can measure, by means of a delicate apparatus controlled by electricity, the amount of force that exists in any living tissue; there is a separate kind for each portion of the brain and each nerve section of the trunk, and it will move only when near that portion or any living tissue that has similar properties and powers. Our own magnetic sense, which has greatly developed since Noola's banishment, can roughly gauge the relative strengths of the various faculties and emotions in any man; and it is deeply thrilled when any thought or passion is energising in his nature. But it cannot accurately measure the strength, as these instruments can. We can absolutely trust them, in testing the character of any human being.

"Noola fully expected to be thrust back, unless he came across his own relations and friends, to whose pity and sympathy he might appeal. He trembled in alarm when he was led to the chamber in which he was to be tested. But it was found that, though his humanity had not progressed in the lines or with the rapidity that the Limanorans have developed since his departure, all the atavistic taint had disappeared from his nature, and the weak elements of his system, love, pity, tenderness, sympathy, had greatly strengthened. He could no longer by any possibility side with the warlike and revengeful in human nature.

"But even if he had only kept the evil qualities in abeyance, in the state they showed before his exile, we should have let him return; for with his strong desire to keep pace with our advance and his regret for his retrogression, he would have gladly submitted himself to our new creative surgery. Our increased knowledge of the functions and constitution of the brain and nervous system enables us to reduce or excise any portion that interferes with the development of the individual. And we can also stimulate or retard the activity of any part by placing the patient in any of our medicated atmospheres specially adapted to his circumstances, and making him breathe in the element required by his system.

"Noola is now supremely happy in the confidence that he is to be allowed to remain. Every defect in his system has been tested and measured, and he knows how far he has fallen behind our race. He would have accepted any conditions, and in order to overtake us is willing to enter upon a new education——the abbreviation of the slow and painful advance of many ages into the hurried pace of a few years. He wishes, though three hundred years of age, to become a child again and return to his first century. But his long and painful self-discipline in Broolyi has shortened the process; and he will soon be able to keep step with his old comrades. He will be aided in every way by the wise men, some of whom will give their best wisdom and energies to him. All the physical arts we have will be brought into play to shorten his term of probation, our creative surgery and medicine, our arts for the development of tissue and nerve, our magnetic arts for the development of the senses, and our ethical arts for the development of the spiritual sensitiveness.

"For yourself he has pleaded, and, though our wise men have recognised that you are thousands of years in the rear of our civilisation, and have confirmed their recognition by scientific measurement of the forces and elements in you, they have consented to let you remain and to take your education in hand. It seems an almost impossible task to contract thousands of years into tens; but they do not despair; for our system of education has already accomplished this for children born amongst us, and you have a nature peculiarly open to our educational influences. You have first of all the passion for progress as strongly in you as in any of ourselves; and this is the prime essential of our ethics and civilisation; to it all other passions must yield; from it flows all that subdues the material world and gives dominance to the spirit, and makes for righteousness. But with it often go pride and arrogance. In you was found strongly developed the desire to treat all good men as equals, whatever difference of capacity or position or possessions might seem to separate them from you. Had you had even the slightest tinge of contemptuousness or hauteur in you, you would have been sternly repelled. To contemn is the mark of an incurably savage nature, a nature incapable of true knowledge of itself and of its relations to life. From these two desires come purity of thought and life, the love of peace, respect for the rights of others and reverence for what is fine in their personality, and absolute transparency of nature. This last we ever take to be the shortest and truest test of a progressive character, the love of truth and simplicity, complete harmony of word and act with the inmost thought. As long as a man or a nation lacks this, there can be no real advance; what seems advance is but a mirage of fame or glory. Accuracy of vision and of prevision is the first condition of true progress. It was one of the first things that Noola saw in you, and the first reason he urged for your retention; you had no desire to conceal your thoughts, so closely did they tally with your life; you had an overwhelming passion for truth and for the truthful.

"There was no need to distrust his assertions for we all felt how genuine he had become; and even sick and unconscious as you were, our magnetic sense told us that his description of you was correct. But it has become the custom to test scientifically the nature of every inhabitant of our island every week, and also at every crisis in his nature or in the history of the community, in order that any incipient defect may be at once remedied, and that drastic applications may never be needed. A complete survey of your character and faculties and corporeal system was the first step towards your admission into the community. Everything had to be known, in order that your education should be mapped out. And the cerebrometers gave us a favourable report of you. Your body and your working faculties are far in the rear of ours; you lack transparency of tissue, ethereality of motion; the material side of you is earthy and ponderous. These elements of retrogression we shall never be able to eject wholly from your system; but we shall be able to modify them, and in your children and your children's children the body will keep pace with the spirit. The forwardness of your emotions, of your soul, is what has drawn us to you; you love the ideal and imaginative more than any but one section of our community; and you have an intermixture of the finer spiritual elements such as we have either lost or never had amongst us. We hope to graft your nature upon one of the divisions or castes of our race and so produce in the next generation a variety that we need. Your retention has thus been justified by the highest morality of our civilisation. We never take any step without reference to the ultimate aims of our progress: so to improve the breed that our posterity may feel nearer to the highest life in the universe.

"Your education has indeed already begun. We have assumed from your highly disciplined and progressive spirit that you would be willing to submit to those medical methods that shorten the already abbreviative process of education. It is true that these make an enormous drain upon the physical strength for a time; and we prefer the ordinary spiritual methods of training. But you have gained from the open-air employments in which you have passed your life great stores of bodily health and vigour. You are still but a child. The period of childhood and tutelage extends with us to the thirtieth, sometimes to the fiftieth, year, that of youth to beyond the hundredth. At the time that other men are preparing to die the natural death of old age, we are just beginning to feel what it is to live.

"And from some ancestral cause you are developed beyond your years in some of our ethical lines. You have reached a humility before the living forces of the universe which is the primary mark of the true governor of the world. How you have attained so rare a virtue amidst the pretentious barbarity of civilisation it is not easy to conceive. There worldliness and arrogance inherit the earth, though there are not signs wanting that they feel the approaching triumph of its true heirs and mask as the meeker virtues. In older times they were not ashamed to show themselves as they really were; for those were the days of glorified highwaymen who seized the throne of the world. Conquest is nothing but successful brigandage on a large scale, veneer it over with diplomacy and historical fame as you will. But for centuries there has been an uneasy feeling abroad that the humble must come to their rights some day; and so the gilded brigands have allied themselves with a religion of the meek and despised, that they may hoodwink mankind into acquiescence in their ancient dishonesty.

"We banished all the makings of monarchs, aristocracies, and great men at the purifications of our people. We could see no difference between these and the worst criminals except one of degree. We measured their skulls and brains by the rough, unscientific methods we used to have, and found in them almost no difference from those of murderers and thieves; and comparing them with the skulls of savages and of our own far-back ancestry, we found that in the case of both heroes and criminals the cause of their likeness to each other was their recoil upon the footsteps of the past, and away from the line of human progress which leads towards harmony with the higher laws of the universe.

"Happily for you every trace of such arrogance and contempt and ambition is absent from your system. You have nothing merely mimetic in you; you live unashamed and truthful in presence of all that the world is capable of being. It is one of the surest signs of fear of threatening annihilation that a species has to simulate the appearance or the modes of life of another. Hypocrisy in the human race, like mimicry in the kinds of animals and plants, is the brand of feebleness and the omen of coming decay and subjugation. We use truth and sincerity as one of the most inward of tests of a strong and healthy nature. In the olden days, as in all large and mixed civilisations, it was difficult to distinguish the imitation virtue from the real, and when it was discovered it was easy to pardon it and even accept it as a virtue amid the universal effort at simulation. But when we had swept out the survivals of primitive and savage times and the atavistic returns to them, we found that every need of mimetic virtue had disappeared. The slightest taint of unreality or falsehood in any of our community is as offensive as carrion; we rise in a body and have it removed. And we have as keen an enjoyment of sincerity and truthfulness. Your loyal character at once attracted us to you; we felt that all germs of moral disease would lose their virulence within its influence, as germs of physical disease lose theirs in sunshine."

CHAPTER II

MY EDUCATION

THE strain on my attention had been extreme as I tried to follow his explanations. It was not merely the words that were unfamiliar, but the very manner of the thoughts. I had not felt how exhausted my tissues were growing, or how soothing was the influence of the perfumes and soft music. I had been deeply moved by the joy of my acceptance by this strange community and by the profound truths woven into the fabric of its civilisation. Imperceptibly the mist of dreams stole over me. I was not even conscious of the gesture of his hand. I thought that I had fallen back again into the darkness of Western civilisation, and yet that my Limanoran guardian was silently hovering round me, protecting me amid the horrors of the reality. I seemed to be present at a court scene, where the monarch and his ablest statesmen and soldiers were welcoming a hero back from a victorious campaign that had added a great province to the kingdom. There were shoutings and huzzas without, whilst within strains of triumphant music alternated with bowings and ceremonies from the gorgeously robed officials. In some strange way I thought that it was I who was being lauded. Conscious of the tens of thousands left dead upon my battle-fields, I loathed it all; for by some soul-magic, perchance my Limanoran influence, the hearts of eulogists and courtiers were laid bare before my eyes, all (there was not an exception) black with envy and designings; the king himself was sick of me and my honours, even as he showered them on me. I knew the pitfalls and intrigues prepared for me; I saw the whole mass of humanity, both lacquered and tattered, that was now cheering, hiss and groan at me as I fell; and I turned away from the applauding crowd and looked into the homes of my dead soldiers, and I heard the weeping and despair of the widow with her orphans and the mother bereft of her children in their prime. Here the depths of sorrow were its surface too. What was there to my credit in the book of time?

Then with sudden transformation I saw the crowd swaying like billows before the wind; every inch of space on the floor of the vast cathedral was filled with an adoring multitude, tears falling from the eyes of every upturned face. What could not be done with a mass of humanity so filled with passion for the highest! None too large were the vaulted aisles and nave for the tremulous thunder of the anthem. It seemed as if the dome of the sanctuary would open and the Deity would reveal Himself to His rapt suppliants. Then the music died away and silence magnetised the people and drew down the influence of heaven upon them. And it was I that was in the pulpit, seeming a feeble and sinful thing beside this divinely inspired multitude. Could I do aught but still their quivering hearts?

With sudden impulse my voice rang out in the cadences of the great organ as I raised their thoughts to the cross over the altar where hung the One who was rejected and despised of men. I painted the poverty and neglect and scorn of the life of the Man of Sorrows. They wept as I bent their thoughts to the weary mission of this lofty spirit amongst men, and His despair as He saw them turn in contempt from Him. The death of torture that marked the close of His sojourn here was as nothing to the crucifixion of the spirit that He bore each day from the cold neglect or the supercilious sneer with which His message was met. None but lowly fishermen would accept His divine teachings. And never a murmur issued from His lips. Heart-broken and martyred in soul, the crown of thorns was a fit close to His career. I seemed to hold the great assemblage in the hollow of my hand. The sound of weeping rose, while with love and adoration they gazed on the crowned agony as it hung on the cross.

Then I blessed the people and left the pulpit, my heart hard and dry within me, when an alien sound broke upon my ear from the farther end of the great aisle. A commotion arose, and before many minutes the whole mass of worshippers had joined in the passionate discord. There was a conflict about some centre that was moving upwards from the door. Before I could regain the pulpit, a bruised and bleeding body had been raised above the sea of heads upon a cross against one of the huge pillars. A cry of execration rose from the whole church. It was useless to attempt interference, for my voice could not be heard in the tumult. In a few minutes the insults and buffetings had accomplished their work; the wounded, bleeding head sank upon the breast of the figure on the cross; his spirit had fled. It was a preaching reformer of the town, who was accounted a madman for his enthusiasm. He had fallen into some controversy and had shown his opponents the gross and material nature of their worship, insulting to a Deity who was pure spirit; he had prophesied the downfall of all their gorgeous churches and ceremonials, and the substitution of silent reverence within the temple of the heart. They had taken his prophesy as an insult to the Christ and His church. Fleeing to the sanctuary to be safe from the furious attack of the crowd, they had followed him and with a few hurried words had enlisted the worshippers within against the blasphemer. And this had been the result.

As I looked at the blood-stained features, there seemed to gather round the head a halo of light as of a crown of thorns. I was struck with a strange resemblance and glancing back at the altar, saw the faces were the same. This passionate devotion to a dead Christ had found Him in living form and had crucified Him again.

I was appalled at the thought of all the centuries having passed for naught. Not one step upward had been made. No nearer were the multitude to recognising their Saviour when He came in the form of living man. There seemed to be nothing to live for, if this were the end of the agonising toil of the ages.

How sweet it was when I awoke to find it was but a dream, and that I was not in Christendom but in Limanora! I was alone, but there was the sense of comradeship around me. I found afterwards that the wise men of the medical caste had been electrising portions of my brain as I lay asleep. It was the beginning of my education, which was to go on even in sleep, moulding dreams that should modify my whole nature. Perhaps the most important part of the growth of the spirit is during the hours of rest, when the past or future may enter the vacant mind. My imagination had been sent out on its travels into my past and had found its way into the heart of Western ambitions and hypocrisies. Thus the wise men had perceived by their electric sense the dreams that had oppressed me, and they drew from them the master-sorrows of my past.

Half of the success of education depends upon the most intimate knowledge of the history of the soul to be educated, a knowledge more intimate than the soul itself can have; else the educator will be alarmed and defeated by the surprises of survivals or resurrections. It is not the history of the mere incidents of life, of even spiritual life, from birth that is needed, but the unrecorded history of the mental and emotional tissues of a countless ancestry. And no annals could reveal this so well as the dream-flashes of the night. They are brief as the tremors of lightning, but they illuminate a midnight world, a glimpse of which is as great as an inspiration. "Night is the confessional of the unknown"; "Sleep unburies the dead"; "Dreams kaleidoscope the vanished past." These are three of their world-old sayings, which were striking at first, but after I knew their exact science of somnology, became as commonplace to me as they were to the Limanorans.

This science, like all their sciences, was practical and but the other side of an art; it was one of the most helpful auxiliaries of education. It had classified all types of dreams, and found the inner test of truth in them. Though seemingly capricious, to these medical wise men not a dream occurred but had its significance in the life of the individual. They could touch any section of the brain tissue into dream-activity during sleep by means of their magnetic and electric probes and stimulators; they could feel by their own electric sense all that was flashing through the corridors of sleep; and, with their electrographs could take an exact image of every portion of the dream.

Dreams, they held, made men children again, with their souls upon their skins, so absolutely transparent did they render the nature, so free from convention and the mask of policy. And what was best of all, the shadows of the past, at times of the primeval past, answered to their call and played upon the mind during sleep. "We are such stuff as dreams are made of" was a saying of our own far-seeing dramatist's which often came into my mind as I looked into their somnology. Into the making of our bodies and our brain-tissues go elements from all the ages of our human and animal past, ages buried beyond the reach of history or speculation. They enter subtly into the tissue of our life, though we are all unconscious of the process. And these elements are the stuff that goes to the making of dreams as well. But in the dream-world there is no central personality, no will to control or transform, no mask to wear, no power to conceal. We are ofttimes ashamed of our dreams because they are so unconsciously naked in their savagery or even animality.

Nor is it an uncommon or unnatural thing that dreams foreshadow incidents in the after-life of the individual; for they bring into play elements in his nature that he has never been conscious of and whose existence he would stoutly deny. Then, when the favouring circumstance or set of conditions brings these elements into action, he is startled to remember how close the long-forgotten dream had come to the unimagined reality. If only he had known how much it had meant, as it entered on the theatre of sleep and then vanished, he might have been forewarned and have avoided the opportunity for its reappearance on the stage of life.

And the Limanoran medical sages had taken advantage of this prophetic provision of nature. They systematically tested every fibre and cell of the brain of each individual they had to educate and develop, and without hesitation or error found out every possibility of his nature. They tested and tabulated the results of every electric stimulus and every dream that followed it, and by this means had a complete natural history of all his ancestral past. No revolution could happen in the state of any Limanoran, nothing of what we mean by conversion. It has sometimes been said in the science of the West that there are two brains or physical organs of soul in every man, and this explains the strange actions and reactions, conversions and recoils that so often occur in life. But it is far truer that there are a hundred brains in every man, and that his brain is composed of elements out of all his ancestry, even his far-back animal ancestry; and it all depends on the stimulus which of those brains or ancestral brain-elements will come uppermost. The Limanorans had millions of sun pictures of their own exiles and of the various peoples of the rest of the world in innumerable attitudes and situations, and with expressions on their faces unconsciously worn; and they could point out in each the predominating animal. In going over the memories of the men and women I had known I could recall times when the look of some animal had come out strongly on their faces. I had had, to my misfortune, much acquaintance with the serpent nature, the most predominant in an unwisely progressive civilisation like that of Western Europe where convention and custom and law become the opportunity and the mask of characters fallen far into the rear of progress. When laggard natures are not monasticised and prevented from breeding, a progressive people get overrun with hypocrisy; under convention and custom and law they take shelter and there is no power that can drive them out; the finer phases of civilisation, industry, art, learning, speculation, morality, religion, become their nesting-ground. At last the serpent nature is accepted as the type, provided there is not too fatal a sting in it. The religious legends mirror this serpent-like development. The serpent is the spirit of evil which caused their degeneration from the godlike. The serpent they see everywhere, even when it has disappeared from their own land. Their greatest successes in any sphere are by means of serpent-like subtlety, whilst they still profess to worship the ideal of truth and candour abandoned by them in the far past. In practice it is the qualities of the serpent they embody and develop; in theory they worship its foe and conqueror.

The Limanoran sages explain this reappearance of animal natures in human civilisations and individuals by showing how the elements of all exist in infinitesimal germ in the most primitive form of animal life; as this crept up the scale, certain elements grew stronger and led to new species still retaining the others in subordination; at each higher and higher division of the vital way the elements became more vigorous and more distinct in their characteristics; it is therefore traces of the higher animals that are most apt to appear in man. And the only means of ridding these of their retrogressive influence is to make the newer and higher spiritual qualities more dominant. The first rule of a civilisation that means to advance in reality and not in mere appearance is to monasticise all atavistic natures and prevent them from handing on their retrogression to a posterity; the second is to encourage only the higher and more spiritual features of those that remain.

It took many months to examine and catalogue my powers and tendencies. I often awoke unconscious or with a confused recollection of the dreams they had stimulated and recorded. The first few were most distinct, and seemed to follow me when I waked with the reality and perspective of life. But I could not interpret them; they seemed fanciful and capricious, and when I puzzled over them, yielded nothing. And yet, when I saw my dream-confession and autobiography, I was startled with the truth of its great features; thoughts that I had never uttered to mortal ear were there; words that had been spoken in the secrecy of confidence far off in my village home were recorded; actions light and insignificant had their due place, and seemed to have new and infinite meaning in their new setting. So circumstantial were the details of much of my past life and character that I could not but accept the rest as absolute truth. And what a strange array of facts it was! Parts of my immediate ancestral history I knew, more I had conjectured, some I could never have guessed at; but here it was spread out as on a map, with every new advance or retrogression any progenitor had accomplished or suffered. I seemed to see my inner nature photographed and by the light of a magic-lantern.

At first, when I saw it stand out detail after detail in lifelike truthfulness, I felt in the presence of some supernatural power. But when I came to know the methods they had employed, it seemed as simple as a child's puzzle. Every conclusion had been reached in the most scientific way. All the minutiæ of every dream had been faithfully recorded and microscopically examined. Then they were tabulated and compared with the most untiring industry. And out of the shapeless mass had come by the aid of their logical methods or dream-tests the clear, unquestionable truth. Their brilliant, but by no means reckless, imaginations did the rest, evolving order and lifelikeness out of seemingly barren and confused facts. It is true, they did not make any attempt at the chronology of the past; they had been able only to group the facts in great spaces of time, and in a certain order of development. Their minute knowledge of the evolution of life, and especially of human life, gave them the framework for this grouping. I was astonished at the quickness of their work, when I considered the fulness of the natural history of my mind and character; it seemed as if they should have taken years and not months to investigate with such care every atom and cell of the tissue of my brain.

CHAPTER III

SLEEP, REST, AND FLIGHT

I COULD not but surrender myself into the hands of men whose wisdom seemed to me to approach omniscience; and this I was the more inclined to do that I felt, instead of exhaustion from their operations on my brain during sleep, the greatest sense of exhilaration I had ever experienced in my life. They acted on the principle of giving complete rest to one set of nerves and tissues by stimulating the others. They could produce the deepest sleep in all the brain- and nerve-centres by gathering the life-energy that remains during sleep into one minute point, which they stimulated by magnetism.

They smiled at the clumsy methods of resting that Western civilisation had adopted, the awkward, unyielding beds and chairs and sofas, and the wasteful and futile attempts at exercise that were meant to give rest. Ages ago they had banished dancing and all corybantic amusements as extravagant waste of tissue, destroying a hundred cells or nerves for every one that they saved or invigorated. All frantic and violent exercise encouraged the animal part at the expense of the progressive: it mangled and rent the delicate tissues of the brain and heart, and sent the currents of sustenance into the muscles and bones of the legs and arms. The riding and hunting and athletics of the aristocracies only helped the animal to persist, and clearly identified their ancestry with the conquering nomad hordes that swept down on the peaceful plains and destroyed primitive civilisations. Exercise, they held, should help, on the one hand, to increase the store of energy to be transformed into the higher elements, and on the other to rest the spiritual forces and faculties.

Rational rest was one of the great secrets of the prolongation of life. There was a latent passion in living things for rest: and this rose to its highest in man. To balk it was to shorten the career of all the powers. And they had set themselves to understand this passion and the methods for its satisfaction as one of the first duties of an advancing people. They knew that there never could be any complete rest for a living system short of death. Even in the soundest sleep the functions proceeded, though feebly, and there was a misty consciousness of existence; else it would lapse into annihilation. They realised that they must provide for many gradations of rest between the edge of death and the borderland of full activity. Nor should any portion or element of the human system go long without its period of rest and its period of exercise.

On these principles they built their methods of alternating rest and activity, all duly subordinated to their great aim—the advance of the higher nature. The only reason for muscular pursuits was that the intellect and the imagination might be relaxed and the higher energy reinforced. Even the loftiest thought resulted in certain waste products, that, if left to accumulate, would soon clog and stifle it. This waste must be carried off by reposeful exercise of the lower and more physical organs. All the lower elements which remain to mingle with those of a higher plane after they cease to be needed as regenerators of energy grow at once poisonous and must be removed by exercise.

For many months I occupied one of their beds, half hammock, half framework, made of soft, flexible stuff that looked like metal, yet yielded like down. These beds were hung not only at the four corners, but along the two sides, so that the body lay in a kind of groove; yet, by a second series of rests, the material was kept from contact with the sides of the body or from any pressure upon it. Within this groove was laid an air-cushion of still softer and more elastic material, which fitted itself to every irregularity of the body and to its various changes of position. The pillow was of the same soft network, and so shaped as to fit the head. I afterwards found that through the whole fabric of the pillow passed a mild current of positive electricity, that drew the energy from the nerve-centres of the head, and soothed every tissue to rest. The framework of the lower portion of the bed was charged with the mildest currents of negative electricity, and thus the circulation and the life were kept up, however deep might be the sleep. The sense of exhilaration and replenished stores of energy with which I rose each morning was enough to make me enamoured of life. Day by day I grew lighter in step, and seemed to walk and rest on air. It was the grosser particles of my system that were being withdrawn from it by this nightly process of rest. I gained energy and lost weight till I felt that I could soon rise on wings. I noticed before long that I had acquired the tripping, elastic gait that I had remarked in Noola. My movements and footfall came to leave almost no impression on my senses, and I could have played the ghost with appalling effect in the superstitious atmospheres of my native land. I did not seem to grow much smaller in bulk; yet in a year or more I must have weighed one half what I did when I arrived. Whether they applied some other degravitating process to my bones and tissues besides the magnetic sleep I never ascertained. But they had the power of reducing their own weight considerably in a few moments. It seemed as if their bones were hollow like those of birds; for I could lift even the largest of them with my one hand; and they had some reserve store of an element lighter than air in their bodies, which they could increase and distribute over their system at will. When they were asleep I found I could raise them as lightly as a feather, but when awake they could, whether by muscular effort or by some other process of their bodies, prevent me lifting them even the fraction of an inch from the ground. They seemed able at a thought to increase their weight tenfold, and though they had wonderful strength of muscle, I am certain that was not all, for I observed they made little use of it on such occasions.

It can be easily imagined then how little friction of the body there was during sleep; indeed, they never moved whilst resting, for there was no need of relieving the tension of any part. I enjoyed still more another kind of rest they had; it was half chair, half bed, and consisted of an incline of the softest netting made out of their usual metal and in such a way that the body could not collapse when loosed in sleep. Even pleasanter was the swing-sleep; here a huge magnet kept the supple incline gently swaying whilst at the same time it drew the blood from the head. The float-rest was as pleasing; in this the head rested on a floating pillow whilst two air-cushions stretched along one side of the body and supported it on a network held between them. But the most complete of all rests was that in which the Limanorans were supported in the air by a cloud of sweet-scented and wholesome gas blown from innumerable jets with steady power; electric fences kept it from spreading into the atmosphere around. I never reached that power of reducing myself in weight so that I could enjoy this rest. It needed fine skill of poise to climb to this bed and remain there, and I was ever afraid of falling.

The same physical incapacity prevented me from reaching the most graceful and soothing of all their combinations of exercise and repose. This was the wing-rest. I had often seen the albatross, as it followed in the wake of our yacht, swoop down and float up the curves of the wind without apparent effort, its broad wings motionless but for occasional adaptation, like sails, to the changes in the strength or direction of the breeze. I had never expected to see human beings master this bird-power over the air; but it became the commonest sight in the breezes of the dawn and the sunset to see old and young of both sexes in Limanora fasten great wings to their arms and feet, and, charging their small wing-engines with new stores of energy, sail up underneath the chameleon clouds, and float hither and thither like spirits of the storm. This was part of their night's rest and their morning's exercise; and they used to descend from it with heightened colour in their cheeks and the look of profound repose in their eyes. The long training they had had from youth in the management of their wings and in gauging the force and current of the winds had made their skill and knowledge habitual, if not instinctive. They could shut their eyes and rest their intelligence as they floated up and down the levels of the breeze; their wings seemed to be at peace. I can find no analogy in my own experience for their delight in the swift-curving movement but my youthful enjoyment of skating before the wind for miles over clear ice. It was a gladness merely to watch them sport amid the rays of the growing or lessening sun. Often would they time their movements to some rhythm, and flash through intricate evolutions like rooks in the evening air. Again half of them would fold their wings and be borne by the other half with a speed and lightness almost as great as when flight was unburdened. All mere earthly amusements and exercise had ceased when the secret of flight had been mastered.

For generations their biologists, anatomists, and physicists had studied the wing-power of animals with a view to the practical mastery of it for the Limanorans themselves. Their chief guide towards the analysis was the study, not of birds or insects, but of the bat. They measured the force of the strong chest muscles that enabled it to move its wings with such rapidity; this could be done to a nicety by means of their refined instruments for gauging latent power, whether in tissue or nerve or muscle. They calculated the number of beats it could make in a minute. They measured the spread of the wings and the weight of the body. Thus they came to an almost constant equation of wing-power to size and weight. The physicist and mechanic were then called in; but they would have been helpless without the new metal, irelium, and their power of concentrating great power into small space. This metal was extracted by a process from common earth, but could also be found pure some miles down in the earth. It was perhaps the first essential to the rapid advance of their civilisation because of its extreme lightness and strength, and still more its wonderful flexibility and elasticity when mixed with certain proportions of other substances. It could be made into the most delicate membrane, fine as gauze and yet tough and resistant as leather. It formed the material of their most massive engineering works, and of their lightest draperies and garments. Nothing could surpass its adaptability to all purposes of civilisation.

It was out of this that they were able to make their wings which seemed so fragile and yet could bear the force of the wildest storms. It would stand stiffly on its framework against the strongest pressure, and yet could be expanded balloon-wise from within. The only means of disabling these wings was perforation by a hard, sharp point. This could never occur in the air except from the beak of a bird; and then they could still use their spread as a parachute to break their descent. Another quality this metal had was its transparency, and their flight was somewhat concealed from the sight of gazers below by the colour they took from their atmospheric surroundings; it was difficult to distinguish them from a floating cloud or a darker patch of grey or blue sky. The wings could be easily folded or expanded, so flexible was the material; and, when the Limanorans landed from their flight, scarcely a minute elapsed before the huge sails, framework and all, had been furled and had disappeared in the ordinary outline of their bodies.

And these bodies differed as much as their natures from those I had been accustomed to see. They were short and squat; and this, with their broad chests, great heads, and long arms, would have led Europeans to call the Limanorans gnomes. Muscles and bones that in other men had been of little importance had grown into what we should have called abnormal size and strength. But after I had met the power of their eyes and felt the beauty of the natures that shone in their faces, their bodies seemed to me the normal garment of the highest human spirits; and I came to understand the high purpose of every change they had brought about in their forms and features. Without their broad chests they could never have had such expansible lungs or such powerful heart-action essential to easy flight, as well as to the lightning sweep of their thoughts and energies and the rapid advance of their civilisation. The pulse could be seen in many parts of the body, it was so strong; and its beats were twice as frequent as in my own. The great heat of summer was to them little inconvenience; they could thrust their arms into what seemed to be boiling water without shrinking; and they could bear a degree of cold far below the lowest temperature I had ever felt, for the high temperature of their bodies made them capable of enduring far greater extremes of climate than any race I had ever known or heard of. But their breathing was much less frequent than mine; they seemed to take in enormous draughts of air at each inspiration and to retain stores of it in their system. They continued at their ease in difficult atmospheres and exertions long after I had begun to pant and gasp for breath. The spaces within their bodies that had once been wholly filled with the organs of digestion and discharge had evidently been largely utilised for their marvellous expansion of lungs and heart.

Another purpose that their huge chests served was to bear the strain of the great muscles that controlled their arms, and of the powerful engines that, strapped on to them, gave the strong and swift beat to their wings. Their arms were moulded on lines of similar strength; for they had to bear the strain of the forward stroke of the wing, whilst also having to manipulate by means of the long and sinewy fingers its great folds in the backward sweep; and, when more expanse was needed during calmer weather or when resting in the sky, the arms had to thrust out and to bear long rods that in their turn bore expansions of the wings like the studding-sails of a ship. The thumb of each hand was kept free for the management of their breast and shoulder-engines; and it had become by exercise more vigorous and more flexible than the ordinary human thumb. In each armpit was carried a small engine that could be used either as subsidiary to the great breast-engine or for the partial or complete furling of the wings. Beside it was a storage-battery, in which could be generated by the movements of the arm more electricity to supply the central power, thus enabling them to extend their flight through long periods. If they became tired they could expand and inflate their wings with a gas made much warmer by the heat of their bodies than the surrounding atmosphere; then throwing themselves on their backs they could rest or rise in the air as on a balloon.

In slow or ordinary flight, or when the wind was not high, they could steer themselves rudely by manipulating the outer folds of their wings with their fingers. But if they wished to fly swiftly, or in some other direction than the wind would bear them, they could push out a tail-like membrane of irelium from between the feet and move it hither and thither by the sinewy power of the heels. The great toe of each foot was also much developed by long use for stretching out and managing the wings; it had become more like a thumb, capable of seizing and manipulating cords or membranes. It was this, added to the lightness of their bodies, that gave them their springy gait, and made them seem when they walked as if they scarcely touched the ground; they could skim like a bird close to the earth by using only the outer folds of their wings and the tip of the great toe for propulsion.

Much though my weight was reduced, and ardent though I was in my attempts to come up with their mastery over the air, I was seldom able to do more than quicken my pace in running and rise in short, clumsy, laboured flights on their wings like a callow nestling fallen from its nest. I was soon exhausted by my efforts, even when aided by my ultimately deft management of the breast-engine and the shoulder-engines; for my lungs were short of compass, my heart soon beat too rapidly for the strength of its tissue, and my arms and fingers and great toe soon grew weary of the work they had to do. Nothing but the selection and adaptation of my ancestry could have made me capable of progressing physically to their level. Their past had been a rapid and deliberate process of adjustment to new and higher ideas of life, one of the main aims being this new mode of locomotion in order to give them command of a sphere that other men had abandoned to the birds and insects; for it was but one of the corollaries of the great purpose of their existence, which was to master or eject the grosser elements of their system, that they might rise into a more ethereal or spiritual life. By the power of flight they seemed to gain independence of the earth, greater freedom of movement, and an approach to that frictionless, untrammelled motion through limitless space which thought gives a foretaste of.

CHAPTER IV

HERMITRY

FLIGHT was one of their best methods too of achieving complete solitude. One of the early discoveries of this people in the art of progress was that, where men are too much or too long together, they confirm each other's faults and clog advance; the weaker and more superficial ambitions get the mastery and force energy into mistaken directions. The risk of this grew less as the individual grew older; for he receded farther and farther from the ancestral stages of life through which he must pass in youth and early manhood; and he came to have less desire and less need for intercourse with his fellows. Complete love of solitude and capacity for solitude were two of the signs of the perfecting of the individual life; thereafter death, the rending of the veil that divides the seen from the unseen, was the most natural step in development, and scarcely needed effort. They held solitude as much one of the essentials of noble life as society; and the latter needed no stimulus; by nature and beginnings man was a social animal, but only some strong impulse would make him seek the companionship of his own thoughts. The final triumph of life was to be able to be confidently alone, to stand with the highest man can think and feel against the herded universe. Under the stimulus of the more physical and primary passions it is the universal instinct to flock together. The baser, the more destructive feelings are gregarious.

To ensure periods of solitude for each member of the community, every man and every woman had a separate house, as soon as the powers were mature. One of the horrors of the past out of which they had come was the intrusion of friends and relatives every hour of the day, and the irritating sense of the continually watchful eyes of servants or slaves. Only by seeking the wilds could one find real solitude. In all human communities there are endless opportunities for social intercourse; opportunities for solitude are artificial. Life was arranged in Limanora with a view to allowing and securing as frequent and as long solitudes as were consonant with the progress of the race. On the most prominent point of every house there was the representation of two climbing flowers; and if these hung drooping, colourless, and apart, everyone knew that the occupant desired seclusion; if they flushed with rose, stood up to the sun, and twined round each other, then was it known that human converse was permissible, if not desired.

There was indeed sufficient magnetic communion of spirit among all the people to touch into life at intervals the love of that definite and open intercourse so native to the human system. This inborn social faculty might be trusted to prevent the love of loneliness from severing all ties. There were daily public duties that brought everyone into the knowledge and sight of his fellow-men, the rota of physical exercise at the centre of force, the flight-drill, the general meeting of the community, and the medical review. And every day and almost every hour of the day communion of spirit could go on in the magnificent baths, in the halls of recuperation, and in the valley of memories. There was no lack of occasion to draw the Limanorans together.

But the other duty to the higher self was sacredly guarded and fostered, especially in the earlier stages of life. One of the greatest blunders they had to correct in their former civilisation had been gregarious education. Large families had been one of the consequences of a half-developed humanity, more kin to the animal world than to the spiritual. The lower a living thing is in the scale of life the more prolific it is, the more devoted to the mere function of keeping its species alive. Unicellular organisms perpetuate their existence by continual fission. Microbes become massive in their effects by the countless myriads each is capable of producing. The higher the organisation, the less is the energy that can be spared for generation, and the more capable is the offspring when matured of ensuring its own survival, of rising above and managing the laws of nature. Civilisation has not advanced far when it acts by masses and needs masses to keep it going. Then mere subsistence and procreation are the only purposes and functions of most life. To feed, to reproduce, to die, that is their history.

The Limanorans looked back to that stage of their development with a shudder, so far in the mists and darkness of animalism did it seem. Now one man of them was more able to do battle with nature and her fecundity and her catastrophes than a hundred thousand of that olden time, and not one hundred-thousandth of the generative power was needed. Then but a poor fraction of the life-energy could be given up to education. The offspring had to be trained in masses or have no training at all. The parents were too busy earning the means of life to mould their families, and had too many children to give heed to the character of the individual. All the offspring were handed over to professional trainers, who managed them in the mass, and who had to work by the methods of nature with its myriad children through the law of the survival of the fittest. They had to be handled like armies, and the stricter the discipline, the better the result was supposed to be; and where the people were counted in masses and moved in masses the better it undoubtedly was for the survival of the state. Schools and universities were a necessity of that far-back stage of civilisation; they were the drill-sergeants of civil life, dragooning the young and their ideas into accordance with the prevailing and accepted type. Too much independence of character or thought or manner would have broken the ranks and endangered the existence of the commonweal. But the chief purpose of life on the world, the progress of the species, was ignored in this devotion to mere persistence of the species. All variant germs and elements that nature supplies in every individual it brings forth were smoothed down or annihilated into uniformity. The type persisted from century to century unchanged. Only by stealth or by audacity did any new or alien element succeed in modifying the species; and when it did succeed the modification was as often retrograde as progressive. Therefore, in order to be secure from variation, public opinion punished all habits that would lead to independence of character or thought or feeling.

As soon as the great exilings had been completed, the Limanorans recognised that the best chance of swift progress was the selection and preservation of the finest variants in their character and thoughts. They therefore abolished the profession of teacher, that manufacturer of uniformity, and all schools and universities, hot-beds of convention, worship of antiquity, and retrogression. They by no means abolished education; they recreated it, intensified it, and made it the chief function of the community. The whole time and energies of the parents, or, as the case might be, of the proparents, were given up for a period of from fifty to seventy years to the training and moulding of each child. Nothing was left to nature or haphazard. And every new tendency or faculty that was discovered in the pupil was recorded and reported to the council of sages. It was discussed by them, and, if judged to be hostile to the progress of the race, the parents were assisted in eradicating it; if manifestly progressive, every means was taken to make it grow; if doubtful in its results, it was submitted to the community, and their instincts soon brought them to a decision. Thus it was that their world was being continually renovated. Never was an idea or method of action rejected simply because it was new. Every opportunity of advance was seized and tested. Every suggestion of a new direction of progress was investigated and followed out till it was seen to be impracticable.

And, to prevent emphasising the old and outworn or reviving the past, the young were isolated from one another; for, as the embryo records in its growth the stages of animalism through which terrestrial life passed upwards from the unicellular to the complex human organisation, so the immature periods that come between infancy and full manhood record human development, prehistoric as well as historic. The long ages of primitive futility in presence of the powers of nature are abbreviated into the helpless years of infancy. Prehistoric savagery shows itself in various traces in the rebellious, adventure-loving, omnivorous phase of boyhood. The first stages of civilisation appear in the early years of puberty; its later stages in the approach to full manhood. The imperfect past ever springs up like weeds amid the growth of the new life, and will choke it if encouraged. And nothing, they held, gave such persistence to the evils and imperfections of the past, thus appearing in early life, as the gregariousness of youth. Nothing had done so great a wrong to the race, or had so hindered its progress, as their former education system with its schools and universities. To throw men in the immature stages of their life into close intercourse was to confirm their immaturities, to encourage atavism, to make the past tyrannise over the future. As long as their old system continued, their civilisation was enslaved to the times that were gone, and imagination deified the world as it had been.

Next to their exiling policy, their educational reform was one of the most important starting-points of their new and swiftly progressive civilisation. I was astonished at the length and frequency of my isolations during the period of my training. For years I saw few or none but the two proparents to whose care I had been handed over, even after I had been introduced to other sections of the community. In the process of my advance towards Limanoran habits and powers, I was often left for days together to my own thoughts, and yet in the presence of some supervising power that seldom made itself definite to any of my senses or even to my mind. Throughout these intervals of solitude, I felt continual suggestion of noble thought and emotion come to me from my surroundings, the divine music that rang so softly and variedly amid the silences, the deep meaning of the arts that filled every corner of my life, the magnetic energy that rayed forth from unknown centres upon my spirit. The finest impulses of my nature became dominant in me at these times and grew in strength. I came to recognise the power that such solitude gave to character. Without it I should have inclined to become the echo of my tutors, even though they were ever impressing upon me the necessity of thinking and acting for myself. They were so noble, so far above the men and women I had met or heard of or read of that it was a hard task not to fall down and worship them.

Once I had the misfortune to question the benefits of prolonged seclusion. I urged the praises of friendship so common in the literature of my country, and spoke with great fervour of the pleasures of social intercourse, the keen emulation on the path of development it stirred, and the wide influence which the finest characters had. I painted in glowing colours all that refined society might become—the witty Parisian salons of the eighteenth century, the artistic circles in the fifteenth-century Italian republics, the brilliant association of thoughtful men in some of the London literary sets of the nineteenth century. What could be nobler than such intellectual brilliancy of intercourse as is recorded in the biographies of the great men and beautiful and refined women of the West! Then I turned to the happiness of children and youth together in the gardens or woods or on the shores of the ocean, and their sadness when they moped alone in their rooms or at their books. Companionship was the very life of childhood and youth. Did not solitary musings even in maturity produce morbid self-introspection? The intercourse, even with superiors and elders, was somewhat unwholesome for the young spirit—it crushed spontaneity and naturalness and confidence in one's inner self.

I worked myself up to a climax of eloquence, and thought that I had demolished all possibility of defence of their system. But I had succeeded only by ignoring the vices and weaknesses of society. These wise men quietly and almost unconcernedly took me behind the gaudy theatrical curtain of the world, and smiled to think how like their old social ideals had been to those I had described, and to see the same vanity and posturing in European refinement as in their own evil past. They mourned over my blindness of mind in failing to look through the gorgeous transparency at the tawdry vulgarities behind. Following it through many forms and stages of life, animal and human, they showed me the law of social intercourse; not the highest but the lowest emotional and moral level of a herd or circle do the natures and minds of its members ultimately reach, however lofty the aspirations of some of them may be. A company in which free utterance is the rule is soon mastered by base interpretation of the noblest lives, and it is to guard against the effects of this hydrostatic law of ethics that churches and temples have been erected. There the awe of a higher power and the conventions of worship conceal the inevitability of the law, and save the shyer natures for brief periods from the evil influence of the bold. The most masterful religions have always provided permanent refuges for the finer spirits who dread conflict with the unscrupulous wit or power of the world, and who know how in a struggle of speech or action or even pure thought the wielder of the fouler weapons wins. It has been the rule throughout civilised history that the greatest characters, if they cling to moral principle, at last withdraw into solitude partial or complete, and become the sages of the world; if they remain in action and succeed, the necessity for further success drives them to accept the moral level of the lowest they have to struggle with; for if immoral men of less intellectual power overcome them, defeat means to them ultimate exhaustion of the soul; nothing bleaches the faculties and reduces them to the common level like failure after failure. However great a hero may be to begin with, success in action closes his moral career, whilst failure closes his intellectual. To die in his first great victory is the truest happiness that can befall him.

In fact the Limanorans came ages before to see that all public life with its competitions and ambitions, social, artistic, political, military, meant the triumph of cunning or force; it meant the retrogression to the nakedest savagery hidden underneath the gewgaws of civilisation. No real advance could be made by any form of humanity so long as its ablest spirits were drawn into the furious struggle for glory, in which the cruellest and most audacious cunning was bound to win. The founders of new religions and new philosophies have been strong spirits who saw the foul imbroglio before them in public life and shrank back from it. The first aim of the Limanorans, when once they had rid themselves of their more degenerate brethren, was to abolish this contest of might and cunning, and turn their stronger spirits to the true progress of themselves and their race. And little difficulty was experienced in accomplishing this most fundamental reform; the island had been purged of the furiously ambitious, of all who longed for the naked palæstra of civilised savagery. They knew better than most men how much of the essence of life was competition, how necessary to all progress was the struggle for existence, how fundamental was the law of the survival of the fittest. But they realised vividly that nature unguided often chose false directions, that the struggle may be in a myriad various arenas that differ greatly from one another in nobleness or baseness, that the law if left to itself might lead to the survival of the fiercest or cunningest or basest according to the conditions that were to be fitted. The will of man could work on the conditions, so elevating the struggle and leading the law to a nobler issue. They did not, they could not, put an end to the struggle. What they did was to withdraw it from false grounds and false aims, and guard it from any appearance of the lower nature, sensuality, cunning, or force. The competitive energy in every Limanoran's nature was bent towards his own future and the future of his race, and strove to surpass the past, if it were great and noble, and to cast it out, if it were base and threatened to reappear. To strive upwards, to help the whole people to progress, these were the aims that transformed the everlasting struggle and the ever-working law.

This revolution in existence accomplished, and public life having in consequence vanished, there ceased all need of social display, of conversational fireworks, and of tact in managing men either singly or in masses. The object of gregarious education disappeared at once. As long as the coarse and selfish struggle called public life was the highest sphere, they knew the youth had to be trained for it, its methods and aims had to be adopted, and schools and universities were a necessity, as miniature reflections of the greater world. In order to succeed in life they had to be rolled together and tumbled against one another like pebbles in a stream till they had taken the conventional smoothness of outline and similarity of sheen; they had to learn to keep the wild beast in their hearts and the silken courtier in their manners, to cloak untruth and hypocrisy in an appearance of brilliancy or wisdom, to make grasping selfishness seem almost divine love, and brutal cruelty and arrogance the most dazzling refinement. It was painful to read the flashy lies and stabs in the dark that went for wit, and the cruel intrigue and showy falsehood that went to the making of history, in those old times. Even the friendship of the foremost was but a piece of acting; little trust could be put in it; it served its purpose and was abandoned as soon as it failed to impress the dupes. And solitaries then seemed useless, moping self-analysers; they made no history and they were soon forgotten. No parents could afford to let any one of their children thus lose his life; and, however gentle and meditative he might be by nature, he must be thrust into the cruel struggle of school and university in order to acquire hardness and brilliancy; however virtuous and noble in purpose, he had to prepare for the arena of polished scoundrelism.

As soon as these conditions of competition ceased, education in masses had to cease too, it must be a miniature of the general life and a preparation for it. At a distance and in a haze it seems as if the immature in their sports were leading a life of primitive and happy innocence; but innocence often accompanies untamed passion and fierce emulation. The appearance of simplicity comes from their ignorance of the advance of the world. Nothing did the Limanorans so shudder at as the chance of perpetuating the methods and habits of this early and undeveloped stage throughout later life. What their associative education in former times had done for them was to confirm the vices of savagery under the gloved conventions that civilised life demanded, and to destroy the simplicity forever. Solitary training under the supervision of sages, they soon found, had the reverse effect; it confirmed the naturalness and spontaneity, and swept out the inclination to intrigue and arrogance and cruelty.

There was a childlikeness in their natures that gave great beauty to their faces; and this they retained through the longest life and the most absorbing work. If there was one quality more than others which marked them as a race, it was their gentle and trustful outlook upon life, their naïve candour and transparency of character, their simple wonder and delight over any new discovery or invention. They never grudged the quiet admiration any word or action deserved. They never assumed that tone of superiority or sophistication, which, coming as it does from envy, jealousy, or malice, mars all praise or blame. They were children to one another in the limpidity of their life. And so their features, which had not often the attractions of regularity, had come to be transfigured by this single-heartedness; however old and experienced and wise they might be, all possessed this divine beauty of childhood. Sailors and backwoodsmen, men who have to spend long periods of their lives in comparative solitude, away from the sophistications of crowded life, often reveal traces of this childlike beauty of nature and expression. And it was this peculiar educational system and its long intervals of solitary meditation that kept the Limanorans children, simple and ingenuous, till the day each vanished in the ether.

What deprived these isolations of bitterness was that one never felt lonely nor abandoned by his fellows during them. In a moment, there could be communication in thought or magnetic sympathy with his dearest friends, and within a brief space they would be at his side. They often resisted the associative impulse, through fear that it might be but the return of the old immaturity in disguise; and they knew that friendship was ever at call, and that all true solitudes deepened the current of life.

As I came to feel the spirit of their existence, these arguments grew self-evident; I saw how all-important to progress were these intervals of isolation. They had studied with the minutest care and ultimate shuddering the features of their old civilisation, and they had found that the worst of them came from the associative principle in the training of youth. Atavism became their greatest horror; in the breast of every child born into civilised life an embryo savage is born, and this had been vitalised and fostered by sympathy with what was savage in companions and schoolmates. Under their old school and university systems the age of training was that which corresponded to the military stage in the development of man; and boys were forever fighting, girls ever encouraging to fight; emulation became fierce rivalry and hatred. A crude stage of the past was confirmed and perpetuated through life by constant association in the time of life that stood for it. That was why their leisured classes had so devoted themselves during peace to the wilder sports of the hunting stage of mankind, whilst they were ever itching for war that their sons might distinguish themselves. That was why they had indulged so often in breaches of the marriage bond, and outraged the monogamy that they professed to revere; the minds of the youth had been inflamed by the free proximity of the sexes before the passions had been mastered, before the polygamous and unmoral stage of their career had been passed through. And education, instead of checking the perpetuation of these immaturities, encouraged it. Teachers had come to pride themselves in the development of these savage stages of boyhood and girlhood, and called the weaknesses by euphemistic names, pluck, pride, grace. The young men and women were taught to glory in them. And thus evil became eternal. In more primitive life, there had been of necessity a wiser method of training. There were no large centres of population where their youth was massed in schools and universities. Families wandered or rested by themselves; and the hardships of existence ensured the survival of the few that were fittest. These few had from their earliest years to join their elders in their pursuits, and they learned in such society to pass rapidly through the primitive stages of man's development, emulating the skill of their betters and following them with modesty and reverence. In the later industrial and centralistic ages the youth had to be massed educationally, and by the mutual encouragement of sympathy came to glory in their immaturities as perfections, and desired to prolong the savage stage of their life into later years. They judged their elders by false and atavistic standards and so lost their modesty and reverence. It was only an occasional wave of lofty feeling issuing from some inspired poet or prophet that raised one generation above the preceding. For centuries and centuries they stood still or retrograded. Crimes were sanctified in war and politics; the evil past became a fetich; impetuosity, anger, hatred, revenge, falsehood, lust, were tricked out in the apparel of virtues, and made the aims and the glories of the leisured. It was the associative method of education that produced such results. And, after the great purgation of the race, they were amazed to see how blind they had been. Would any civilised parents agree to send out their child into the wilderness there to spend the educable period of life amongst savages, primitive in their instincts and habits, even if the savages had the most persuasive and influential missionaries amongst them who would change them in a few years into civilised beings? Yet this was what their ancestors had been doing when they concentrated youth in schools and universities.

Never before the age of twenty-five were the Limanoran youth allowed any freedom of social intercourse, and then only for brief periods and under the supervision of sages. And if there was any sign of atavism apparent in them at their first draught of social life, back they were sent into isolation, that their character might be strengthened, and the stage of peril passed. Even when socially enfranchised, their first companions had lived beyond their fiftieth year. By that boundary-line, it was held, all the risk of atavism had passed, and all the chances and possibilities of the character had been discovered and provided for. It was not till the seventy-fifth year that anyone was supposed to be fit for parenthood; for then, though the faculties and powers still went on improving even till death, most of them had reached the maturity of self-control and intersubordination; then reason had begun to be master, and all the stages of the development of man before the final purgation of the race had been traversed.

Only a few years before this epoch in their lives were they permitted to look into the deeper mysteries of existence. They thought it one of the strangest pieces of inversion, if not desecration, to place religious ideas, as we did, before the youngest. Nothing but evil could come of such an attempt. With the Limanorans it was the final initiation into life to acquaint their grown men and women with the sublimest thoughts and doubts and emotions on the purpose of existence; it was the copestone of their education; after all the field of knowledge had been traversed by them and all the reverences had been instilled into them, the last reverence was revealed to them. Then and not till then were they capable of realising its fulness. Communicated in childhood or early youth, before the powers were mature, before the animal and savage stages of development had been gone through, it could end only in gross familiarity or gross superstition; the noblest and most inward of thoughts and emotions would be misunderstood. What was it that had made their old religions so stagnant, so obstructive to all advance, but this mistaken principle of attempting to teach the holiest and deepest ideas to the young! It made their ancestors cleave to crude superstitions as if divine and refuse to give up any item of their childish ideas of them. So thoroughly are the sources of our youthful impressions lost in the mists of the past that any connected with reverence seem to come from the divine eternity beyond birth.

CHAPTER V

JOURNEY TO THE VALLEY OF MEMORIES

ONE of the things this people feared most was enslavement to the past; and I was encouraged to strip my mind of all sentiment connected with the life I had led before my arrival and all superstitious devotion to the historic. Bury the dead past, was one of their primary maxims. Nor would they permit religion or any other conservative element to hallow tradition. The world is well quit of what it has been, was another of their sayings. They seemed to look upon the past as a fierce pursuer ever ready to overtake and strangle them. Out and away from it were they ever hurrying. It was the dark shadow over existence. And into the future, into the future and the sunshine, they cut their way through the thick tangle of life.

I was much surprised, then, after I had been admitted to the full confidence of my proparents, to hear them refer with pleasure, if not joy, to what seemed nothing but a glorification of the past. The name Fialume came repeatedly into their conversations with each other till at last it roused my curiosity. There was something imaginative in the ideas connected with it; it never rose to their lips without bringing into their eyes a beautifully piteous expression that bordered almost on the ecstasy of joy. They saw that they had piqued my curiosity; and before I had asked them they gave me the information I desired. The word, Fialume, translated, meant "the valley of memories." It was the great library and university of the island. There the second stage of education was largely passed. If by the age of fifty all superstitious veneration of the past had been eradicated from the nature of the new citizen, he was led to this valley day after day, month after month, until he had seen the career of the race, and had grown familiar with the steps of its development; he learned to shudder at the darkness out of which it had come, and to watch with joy the growing light and the fleeing shadows as it neared the present. Thus did he learn true gratitude for what he was, and true reverence for the future towards which they were all striving. I was not yet fit to enter the precincts of the valley. I had still too much of that anguished yet exquisite homesickness for my own past to be trusted with insight into a past that might seem great to me. And yet my probation would be shorter, as my buried world was so different from theirs; there would be less danger of superstitious reverence awaking in me for any of their old stages or antiquated institutions, and no danger of Ayala stirring my idolatrous devotion. This new word puzzled me, they saw. And they explained that it was but the older name for the same valley; it meant "the resting-place of the untrammelled." In fact, their great library and university was their graveyard too.

Years passed in happy renovation of my whole being, body and soul. As I looked back I began to shudder at the past out of which I had come, its low ideals, and its still lower planes of living; it seemed centuries behind me and not mere years; it had grown into a murky cloud on the far horizon. I could see how often I had been on the verge of despair or disease and began to know the blindness and ignorance that had been almost the air I breathed. I shrank in horror from all I had been; for I could examine the poor fabric of it almost microscopically now. There was little fear indeed of my ever longing for what I had left behind me.

Thus at last there came the supreme moment that I had laboured for. I was to be permitted to visit Fialume. I shall never forget the day. I had swept out of my mind analogies for their great graveyard from the doleful surroundings of death to which I had been accustomed in my native land, the long train of mourners, the ghastly hearse with its burden of mortality, the unkempt grass of the place of tombs, the dreary wait beneath the un-sympathetic sky; and then the rattle of the clods upon the coffin-lid, and the frantic effort to drive from the soul the thought of the gradual corruption of the body and the final residue of skull and bones. Years though I had been in Limanora, I had never heard of a funeral. Indeed deaths were as rare as births in a community that had striven to avoid the lavish waste of nature, and had so studied the human frame as to know how to arrest decay of its powers and to give every individual full possibility of developing himself and through himself his race. The reckless and indiscriminate bearings and dyings of the old world were no advance on the course of the animal or even the vegetable sphere; the higher the organisation the fewer the young and the greater the care of them. But man in other lands had still, with all his thought and fore-sight, the extravagant method of nature, and had increased and multiplied without stint in order that an occasional exception might help by favouring conditions to lead the race onwards and perhaps upwards. Thousands of Al-exanders and Cromwells, of Mahomets and Socrates, of Homers and Dantes and Shakespeares had lived and died unknown, because they had not been born into the circumstances which fitted their peculiar faculties. This people had seen that the method of nature was haphazard, if not heartless, that the rate of progress could be indefinitely accelerated if every child that was born were born with a definite purpose, and his life were guarded and extended till that purpose was fulfilled. They meant every act of generation for a definite advance. Birth and death were in the hands of the race and not of chance, and thus it was that I had never seen or heard of obsequies during the many years of my probation.

So my difficulties were solved by my guardians before we set out for the national place of tombs. Yet my curiosity was as active as before. This was the beginning of a new epoch in my new life. How could its wonders surpass those of the past years! And I was all eagerness to study the past history of this noble race, to study the gradual ascent to the height they had now reached.

The whole atmosphere was jubilant as we rose into its upper levels and thrilled with light and electricity; even unseen living forms from other stars mingled with the sunlight that supplied so much for the support of our being. There was not a cloud to mar the purity of the ether, inspired with wandering breaths of wind. We rose joyous and bright under the gleam of the sun, I alone having my exhilaration somewhat dashed by the consciousness of my laggard gait; for my limbs were not yet light enough, my arm and leg muscles not strong enough, to accomplish any but the briefest journey upon wings, and that in the most awkward and shambling way. I was borne in one of their faleenas or weight-transference flies; it was one of the smallest, yet I had room to move about freely in the car in spite of the baggage of the troop. It was not unlike a huge tropical butterfly that I had admired in a case in one of our museums; the car was long and narrow and pointed like a boat at either end; from each side stretched out wings that were enormous beside the body they carried; and these, rainbow-hued, seemed to fill the whole air through which we passed with a solid gleam, so quickly did they shuttle up and down; aft extended slantwise two great antennae-like shafts that moved hither and thither to defeat the baffling puffs of wind and so direct our flight; along the keel lay the engine that produced the beat of the wings, silent and motionless as if it were but a shaft that strengthened the framework. There was no vibration, in spite of the great speed of the faleena. A huge awning, so high above us as to be out of reach of the wings at their fullest stretch, seemed to hold us easily aloft at whatever level we desired, and to let us gently down whenever the wings beat slowly enough to be seen as they moved up and down. It was in one of these slow movements that I discovered the principle of these sails; they were made of the wonderful metal, irelium, and had its properties of lightness, tenuity, and strength; I had noticed as they flashed solidly through the air that there was an alternation in the flash of greater or less sheen; I now saw that each wing consisted of two fine plates of open scroll-work sliding over one another back and forth; in the upward stroke the holes were open so that the air passed easily through, and the whole expanse looked like a delicately reticulated fan; in the downward stroke the upper plate so slid over the lower that the apertures of both were completely closed, and the wing formed a solid sheet of metal. I afterwards saw how simply this was accomplished.

The under irelium network had but one motion, that on the hinges attached to the side of the car, but it had grooves on its fore and aft edges; into these, corresponding projections on the upper network fitted, moving in them easily by means of small half-hidden wheels; this upper plate was attached to independent hinges on a long rod that was drawn back and forth about half an inch by a connection with the driving engine; its motion, however, was completely controlled by the ligatures that drew the wing upwards and downwards, so that they should ever be in harmony, and the closing of the pores should occur only at the beginning of the downward beat, and their opening only at the beginning of the upward beat. The effect to the eye was very beautiful; the transparency of the metal let the coloured light of the sky shine through it even when solid; but when reticulated the azure seemed to form into a flashing loom of the finest lace. I could not cease gazing at the ever-shifting lights that played through the embroidery of the wings. It was pleasing to the ear as well: for the whirr and creak that usually accompany the flight of great birds and the movement of machinery were used up as undertones to a grand but simple musical march that seemed the very spirit of the beat of the wings.

For a time these sights and sounds held me entranced, so that I was scarcely conscious of our ascent. When the power of the charm had freed my senses, I looked down, and my heart leapt into my mouth; eagles being swept from the island by the blast of the storm-cone appeared to me as flies crawling over the sun-glitter of the houses below or on the snows of Lilaroma. I shrank back breathless at the sight, and imagined myself falling down this heart-sickening distance. Then the almost irresistible desire to throw myself into this abyss came over me, and I clutched at the framework of the car that I might not yield to this feeling.

I had forgotten my companion for the time: one glance at her drove the terror from my mind. I saw the beauty of the benignance that shone upon her face, and my spirit nestled in her protecting smile that had interpreted aright the horrors of my thoughts. I was not merely thankful that I had not been alone with my terrible longing: I could almost give my life up to this being who swept out my fear by the loving-kindness of her glance. My guardians had been unwilling to trust me alone in the faleena, even though the engine and the machinery were simple enough to have been managed by a child. So they sent with me Thyriel, who, I long afterwards found, had been selected by the sages as my spiritual twin as soon as they had tested my past history, my faculties, and my possibilities. None other in the whole community was so fitted to stimulate my best qualities, to be preferred by me as intimate friend and comrade or, if passionate emotions followed the same direction as friendship, to mate with me as parent or proparent, when full maturity had been reached. This I came to know only when all had fallen out as they had anticipated and desired. We were both allowed our full option and free will in our spiritual approaches and agreements: we were not forced into each other's company, only when opportunity for mutual protection or confidence came were we paired for the venture. Everything issued as they had planned just as if we had had no free choice in the matter, and yet our impulses felt as free as if we had been the only living organisms in the universe. We chose with a passion that would not be denied; we were willing in our freedom of attraction to surrender life and all to each other.

This flight was one of the first great adventures on which we were together, and it is graven upon my very heart. Thyriel, O Thyriel, I await thee with soul weary of waiting! What are the years now but centuries without thee? I am alone but for God and thee. It is the only consolation of my soul that thou risest ever towards God and livest in God, and that I rise and live with thee.

It is exquisite pain (and delight too) for me to tell of that flight into the ether; for then I first realised how incomplete was the sum of my existence without this being. She was so gentle and yet so strong, so full of eager sympathy and yet so vigorous of character. She knew every weak point in my system, and bent herself to correct its weakness or protect me from its effects without making me conscious of her sacrifice. With power that I could not but acknowledge as the superior of mine, she played the companion and equal. I could have worshipped her almost as a divinity; but she modestly bent herself to my level, and veiled her superiority in her childlike playfulness. I shrank in fear from the implied familiarity, and could not bring myself to recognise except intellectually the common humanity and the difference of sex. For years I felt too much adoration to pass into love. It was indeed long before I could admit myself capable of her friendship. But gradually she led me to put more confidence in my powers, and to recognise the superiority of some of them. My intellectual admiration took a warmer glow that soon fused our intercourse into the most devoted friendship. So braced were we by our mutual help in our common pursuits that we seemed helpless, the one without the other. Yet the sense of sex was not stirred for years after the bond between us had grown inseverable.

It was this flight that first awakened me to the wealth of her nature and her immeasurable power and desire of self-sacrifice. Like her people, she had none of the statuesque beauty or moulded regularity of feature that has swayed the thoughts and passions of European sex; but the spirit that shone through made the face divine. I rested almost as in a dream, as I felt the benignance of her soul; and before long I was able to look calmly over with her at the increasing depths of light through which we had come. Below us we saw valley and hill pearled with the gleam of wide-scattered houses; we could see the flash of streams and rivers as they broke through the darkness of forests or fell in snowy cascades; and around the coast the sea spun for the black fringe of rock a moving thread of surf. Around us rose the carol-ling of many voices to the gates of heaven. Song after song, anthem after anthem, burst forth from the various groups of our comrades. Buoyant were they as thistledown, revelling in the pure serenity of the upper air. For very joy I could have thrown myself among them and joined the harmony of their flight; but her glance was upon me, and I returned to thoughts of prudence.

She showed me why we had risen so high into upper air far above most of the Limanorans who were flying with us. These faleenas could not adapt themselves to the varying winds as the human figure and arms could when managing wings. They had to rise into the regions of calms or of steady winds, in order that they might float by power of sail down to their destina-tion. What seemed a mere awning acted in two ways; it served as aëroplane to steady the whole structure in the air and as parachute when it began to descend; and could be inflated with heated air, to help the wings in raising the faleena upwards. She pointed out in the far distance below us a gleaming line that marked the valley towards which we were voyaging, and then look-ing at a height-gauge that hung beside her steering-seat and at a wind-gauge that stretched over the side of the car, she decided by a brief calculation that we had reached the proper key-place of the arch we were making in our journey, and that we should by changing our course wing our way with ease down to the desired goal. She touched a notch in the side of the car and above there sounded a flute-like note, that, varying in strength and pitch, made no disharmony with the music of the wings. I looked up and there I could see the awning gradually collapse; it had bulged downwards, I had noticed, in a strange way; the tenseness of its curves disappeared, and as we began to fall, it became concave, and broke the velocity of our descent.

The wings still plied with bewildering swiftness of beat, and forced us onwards as we shortened our distance from the earth. We still could hear the music of our comrades, but so softened by the long space between that I could have imagined it the spheral harmony of orbs which circle round the throne of God. But I could see them, dim flakes of light in the azure as they outdistanced us, the few laggards that had skimmed above us for a short time still showing the outlines of their forms, yet rapidly lessening into star-specks. I was gazing out at them with the exhilaration of the outlook and of the ether in my blood, when the wings suddenly began to labour with short, irregular beat. I glanced at Thyriel. She kept her face unmoved, as she ex-amined the engine beside her and the various keys and wheels and hinges of the machinery. I took courage, for she looked quite unconcerned, yet I could see that she had not discovered the cause for the uneasy motion of the wings. She told me that she would have to examine the outside, but that I might keep my mind at peace, for there was no danger. She adjusted her wings and dived from the side, then rose to our swiftly descending faleena, and by the strength of her muscles seemed to stay the descent, while she looked at all the gearing of the sails from below. Then she climbed into the car, and began to work at a small pump in the forepart. I ran to help her, and in a few minutes I felt the faleena buoyant again and holding its own against gravitation; we had refilled the balloon of the awning enough to keep her afloat. Thyriel stopped the engines and let the sails lie lazily out on the same plane as the car, then she fastened a cord to the bow and, having adjusted her wings again, seized the cord and leapt over. I saw her purpose: she was towing the maimed faleena through the air, still at a great height from the earth. We were near enough, however, for me to see as I looked over the danger we had escaped. We had been falling upon a group of pinnacled and serrated rocks that would have gored our vehicle and endangered my life. Moreover, we were still a long way from Fialume.

Thanks to the cessation of our music, the attention of the distant aëronauts was drawn to our laboured flight. It was not half an hour before we saw them hastening back to meet us like a swarm of butterflies; and in a few minutes more they were beside us. I watched their evolutions in the air with absorbed delight; and ere I knew what they were about, they each held a cord from the bow of our faleena, and Thyriel was on board with me directing our flight. How loud their chorus sounded now that they were near! They timed the beat of their wings and the straining of their cords to it, and we sped on our downward way even more quickly than before. I did not know till long after how great was the danger out of which I had escaped. Yet I was conscious of my comrade's courage and that to her I owed much. It brought us closer together in spiritual friendship, and we seemed to feel ourselves singled out of mankind for mutual confidence.

CHAPTER VI

FIALUME

I WAS revelling in the thought of our comradeship and in the exhilaration of the motion through the air, when the chorus began to soften. It sounded far off, like the echo of an echo, and out of the distance rang notes of welcome. Our company burst out of their low tones of pleading into loud triumph and joy. Then came the whispered softness of their former song; answered softly as if from the hollows of the earth. This swelled again into welcome, and the air rang with notes of joy.

My eyes followed our route; and beneath us I saw a huge valley forested to the ridge on either side and spanned with a glittering roof that turned the light of the sun into myriads of many-coloured gems. Over the cliffs or in through the olive-green or blossoming trees swept streams with rainbowed cascades, covering the vast dome with spray till it seemed an arch of ice that melted in the sun. We made for the entrance of the gorge, out of which fumed and fretted through gates of pinnacled rock a milky torrent. Borne on mighty pillars of limpid metal rose a great archway; and this enclosed lesser semicircles spanning the various roads that led into the wild tropical scenery of the dale. I never saw such an impressive spectacle beneath human roof. Cataract rose above cataract in the centre. On all sides fell miniature cascades, or rose fountains that sent in wayward clouds their breaking water-spears and flags. The flowers and shrubs and trees of every climate under heaven seemed to be collected here, and to blend in marvellous harmony of colour. Cool winds blew from hidden sources wafting the fountain-spray or the odours of the flowers about us. The beating rays of the sun were softened by the stream-cooled dome; and out of some cave or hollow in the far distance came the murmur of entrancing music.

We had descended and passed far within the wondrous structure before I could recall my senses from their bewildered enjoyment of the scene. Then I saw that our company had parted in various directions, vanishing in groups or pairs, round a verdant cliff or into some overarching bower. I was left alone with Thyriel. The sudden loneliness of the vast valley-hall made me feel the delight of having her spirit to lean upon. In spite of the companionship of the flowers and the close ranks of the forest, I felt the great spaces of the valley solitary because of the loftiness of the roof, like the arch of night making space seem more vast than under the warm, indefinite sky of noonday. Bewildered and alone, my thoughts sought the shelter of friendship.

Not long had I felt this consolation when both of us were in the shadow of a nobler and more mature personality. He came I knew not whence, and the suddenness of his appearance added to the awe I felt at once for his character. He was, I was certain, one of the sages of the community, so deeply had the centuries engraved their experience upon his face and spirit. There seemed to come from him even before he spoke or recognised our presence a benign and godlike influence, and I knew at once the greatness of his soul. There were the lines of long struggle and complete self-mastery upon the countenance like the curved stratification and cleavage of the older rocks. He had not to speak before I had surrendered myself entirely to his guidance. He who had seen so many hundreds of years pass over the earth and learned all the lessons they had to teach was the natural master of two such novices in life as we were. For I now felt that, however superior Thyriel was to myself in instincts and development and beauty of soul, she was completely overshadowed by this spirit of centuries.

Yet when he spoke to us we felt that he had still the elasticity of youth about him; he had in his words and actions the rapid recoil of healthy tissues that have a long career before them yet, and in his faculties and ideas there was still the unlimited capacity of development. After explaining that he was to be the interpreter of this house beautiful for us, he led us by a maze of paths through the blossom and the verdure to an open space, from the centre of which rose a noble flight of steps flanked by porticoes and colonnades. These we ascended, resting at times on broad platforms, and looking out on the fairy scene that more and more unfolded itself to our eyes.

At last we stood on the highest platform, not many hundred feet from the gleaming roof. He touched a spring here and there, and out of the tessellated floor came rests that moved automatically with the movements of the head and eyes; wherever I gazed as I reclined thither my rest wheeled round. This I afterwards discovered was managed by hidden springs in the groove in which the head rested. These were rests of observation, and the purpose was to allow of the whole energy and consciousness being directed into one channel, that of vision. The numberless easy methods of rest and motion that this people used would have certainly induced sloth and luxury but for their inherent energy of nature. To them these methods were but economisers of the time and power which might be spent on less routine work.

I soon saw that the valley ran more than a score of miles into the heart of the mountains, its deepest hollows rising now by easy gradations, again by bold platforms of rock far above the level on which we rested. For the dome, I could now see, consisted not of one span whose top ran horizontally along the ridges of the valley, but of hundreds of spans that rose arch above arch up the slope of the mountain. There was something in the terracing of the valley, too, that suggested the hand of man. Nature's work had been supplemented and rounded by noble art. There was regularity in irregularity, statuesque beauty amid wild grandeur. Human thought had utilised the massive ideas of nature. The scene would have overawed the spirit and made it solitary, but for the familiarity of minor features moulded by human imagination that had not geological ages and forces at its disposal.

In amongst the greenery of the forest stood on lofty pedestals what I took for memorial statues of the dead, with features so like to life in every minute line and curve and even graining of the skin, that I marvelled at such waste of human energy and imagination. My guide soon saw my mental question, and showed me that they were the dead themselves. The moment after every trace of life had gone from the body it was ireliumised by an ingenious process; for every atom of tissue and cell there was substituted one of irelium, and thus no decay could approach it; it would retain for untold centuries the form and expression of the vanished man down to the minutest detail. As we passed farther back into the valley I noticed a difference in the appearance of the statuesque dead; they had not the hues and expression of the living, but were leprous white, as if hewn out of marble with infinite care. I appealed to Oolmo, my guide, and he told me that these were their dead as they had been preserved before the age of irelium and the discovery of the process that rapidly changed living tissue into this metal. At that period the body used to be buried for years in stalactitic caves, where the percolation of the liquid gypsum turned it after a time into a calcareous statue.

These caves ran into the mountain at the head of Fialume, and were now used for converting traceries and forms too delicate to work in marble into white stone. They made a beautiful contrast in ornamentation to the rainbow-hued limpidity of irelium. The process had been too long and slow for the petrifaction of the dead. And about the same time as the method of extracting irelium from the rocks had been discovered, the careful study of the petrifactive methods of nature had led to the new and rapid process of immortalising the form and features of those who had passed from life.

From our movable rests I could never have seen what all these statues were. I would have said that this was the island's great gallery of sculpture. But there were other things that Oolmo pointed out to us before he led us round this vast hall of his ancestry. He showed us far back in the recesses of the valley up the slope of the mountain what looked in the distance like a great settlement of some burrowing animal. This was the oldest burying-place of the island, where had been laid in apertures in the rock the urns that contained the ashes of the dead; for they had brought the practice of cremation with them in their primitive migration from the south. Then followed a period of superstition and recession, in which the priests taught the sacred-ness of the human form and its final resurrection and when they buried the bodies deep in the earth beneath the urned rock recesses. A period of reaction against religion followed, and sanitation became one of the first essentials of the new scientific era. It was feared that plagues would come from this old burying-place on the side of the mountain, if the percolating waters brought the corruption of the rotting corpses down into the valley. It was resolved that the remains of their ancestors should be dug up and removed to a mound made for them on a level with the sea. Then it was found that almost all the bodies had become stone white as snow, for the calcareous percolations that came along the surface of the rock down the hill had done their work, and an accident in digging up one of the lower row of graves revealed the marvel-lous stalactitic caves underneath. There had been a movement towards a re-turn to the practice of cremation, but it was stopped at once by this discovery. The caves became the natural burying-place, and out of them the dead were brought and erected in the valley when they had turned into stone.

After we had viewed the whole scene from our platform under Oolmo's direction, he bade us enter a car that had sprung up at his touch. It seemed made of gossamer, and I was afraid to enter it, till I felt the toughness and strength of its material. It floated rather than ran round the valley above the tops of the tall trees. I could see no wheels, and there were no rails for them to travel on if it had had them, nor had it any wings or sails like our faleena. At last I saw that it was hung by a transparent cord of metal from some mov-ing force in the dome that to me was invisible. It was an electric car, and electric currents bore it aloft and swept it along with lightning rapidity. But a touch of Oolmo's finger broke the circuit and stopped it in a moment.

I was not long held by this new wonder, for beneath and around stretched the great graveyard, that seemed a harmony of forest, wild, and garden. We rested at intervals of a few miles on the lofty platforms, descending the flights of steps at times to view the statuesque dead and their surroundings. Here and there we came across groups of young men and young women intently listening to strange voices that seemed to issue from some hidden being within the statued dead. These were students, and the sounds were the voices of the dead, treasured up on fine tablets of irelium, which could either be read or made to re-utter their recorded words. To me the silent bowed figures of the living seemed the lifeless, the whispering dead seemed the liv-ing. It was a piece of necromancy, I felt at first; and, but for my questioning intellect, I should have shrunk back in fear. It is true, I could not see the lips of the erect figure move, and when I gazed long enough some tremor of the eyelid would betray the life of the listener; but for the first few minutes the illusion was complete, and all the surroundings, the stillness, the far echo of wailing music, the sombre trees, seemed to confirm it. Every new group we encountered produced the same eerie feeling.

But we passed on; and the joy which filled the spaces of the great valley buried the sense of death. It was the least funereal scene I had ever witnessed; for along the paths and wide tree-arched avenues went bands of carollers singing songs of triumph and gladness, the air was sweet with the perfume of flowers, and masses of varied colour broke the olive darkness of the groves. The world was at once jubilant and harmonious.

Farther and farther into the valley we flashed in our lightning car, and even my inexperienced eye could see the change in the erect dead. Many of the figures were taller; the attitude was often overbearing and arrogant, and the expression was generally mean or cunning or truculent like so many European faces when surprised in unconscious repose. The farther we receded, the more familiar the forms and features seemed to become, so like were they to the normal human beings of our Western world. Animalism, sensuousness, rapacity, vindictiveness, cruelty, fanaticism grew more and more frequent, the nearer to the primitive graveyard we approached. At last on the faces of the dead that had been dug out of their old tombs there was the manifest touch of the ape, the tiger, the wolf, or the snake. I shuddered to see withal the regularity of the features and the stature and grace of the figures. They came nearest of all to the ideal beauty and the haughty bearing of aristocratic Europe. It scarcely needed the explanation of Oolmo to see that the body had then been developed at the expense of the soul. Underneath the handsome and generous outlines lurked the beast that had entered into the making of ancestry. Splendid animals they had been; and, as our interpreter explained, given up to war and field sports and at intervals debauchery, or to the overreaching of trade and money-making, or to the subtleties and falsehoods of political life. They belonged to the age just before the great emigrations. As we took our way back on the other side of the valley, I could notice how rapidly these lordly animal forms disappeared, and yielded to the compact little figures, irregular features, and divine expression of face I had grown accustomed to in the Limanorans.

The dead were grouped in families and in order of time after the epoch of exiling, and a student could trace the growth of a talent or virtue. But many of the family groups were small; the line had suddenly ceased. In these I could see after a time an occasional evidence of atavism in the size or the sensuousness of the form, and the interpreter explained how on the appearance of this recession the right of having posterity had ceased, or expatriation had occurred. The general sense of the unfitness of an individual for fatherhood or motherhood was too strong in the community to need any expression in public resolve. Those who felt this great misfortune fall upon them knew that their race must be cut off; and they set themselves to eradicate the desire of family life. If they could not eradicate it and at the same time make effort to subdue their retrogressive tendency, they had to go into exile. At first action on the part of the community had been needed. Now this expurgative policy worked almost automatically and without friction.

When we had taken a comprehensive view of Fialume, we entered another faleena, which had been substituted for our disabled car. We shot farewell glances at Oolmo and were off in the air before I had well disentangled my thoughts from the last sight. Below us receded the massive archways of the door and the foaming streams at the entrance of the valley. The jubilant music began to grow dim, and the dome shone softly in the colours of the sunset. I thought we were to be alone on our return journey, and began to question Thyriel on some of the mysteries of the day. She had not much light to throw on them, for she was herself a novice in life. But of a sudden like a flock of homing pigeons a band of our comrades broke out into the level sunlight from the mouth of Fialume; and along with them other bands that streamed east and north and south. Before long the western train had overtaken us, and their voices rang like carolling at heaven's gate. They saw our faleena land in safety at the house of my proparents, and then, joined by Thyriel, they streamed away through the twilight sky, ever breaking off into more and more widely separated groups till they were lost across the horizon, or in the darkness of some distant valley.

Week after week, and at last day after day, we took our path through the azure to Fialume. For several years under the direction of Oolmo we became acquainted with the history of Limanora, and saw the gradual development of the civilisation and of the human form and faculty. We came to feel how naturally ends followed means chosen in the mind and frame of man, as in the plant creation and in the other animals. We saw how creative had been this community, not in the arts merely, but in that art of all arts, human nature. They had moulded generation after generation to higher and ever higher purpose. How poor and subsidiary seemed all the sciences when compared with this great practical science, the knowledge to mould man into any required form, to bend his energies ever upwards! Every week there grew upon us the consciousness that there was no more plastic material in the whole world than the human soul, when it had reached a certain stage of development.

Oolmo traced for us each new faculty and power and virtue to its starting-point, and showed us how feeble it was to begin with, and how rapidly it grew when once artificial effort was turned upon it. At first it was the physical powers that he drew our attention to; in family after family, for example, he showed us how the capacity of flight had been acquired, and how the human frame had gradually become adapted to it; the body grew lighter, the shoulder and breast muscles stronger, the bones hollower, the arms longer, and the legs shorter, with greater strength at the heels.

He acknowledged that there was something peculiar in Limanora that made this adaptation easier; a magnetism seemed to come from the earth that made the force of gravitation less; there was also something more exhilarating in the atmosphere and climate that differentiated it from all other lands. This explained why I had so rapidly acquired the tripping, noiseless gait I had so admired when first I saw Noola. There had been a time in the history of the earth when the human body was so light and agile in proportion to its size that a few coincidences in nature, as, for example, the increase of swift land and tree enemies, would have made it ultimately winged. That was the geological epoch, when, after a period of great contraction and increase of density (the period of the huge saurians and other monsters of the prime), the orb had, through volcanic explosions within it and the impact of myriads of aërolites on its crust, expanded its texture and partially volatilised its internal elements. Since then it has been cooling down within, and thus growing less in size, though losing none of its mass; this can be seen in the twistings and foldings of the rocks and the enormous wrinkles on its surface. The result has been that animals, and men with them, have been growing heavier for their size. The possibility of man becoming a flying race has passed away. Land and sea animals have no longer the chance of developing into birds of the air; and even some of the tribes of winged things have almost surrendered their prerogative of flight; nothing but embryo and unused wings remain to them. It is only in exceptional spots like Limanora, where the magnetic conditions and the spongy nature of the interior of the earth lessen the force of gravitation, that men could ever acquire the power of artificial flight with any ease. By dint of the application of enormous force, and of inventive mechanical power, men in other lands may master the art of aërial voyaging; but it will never become an accomplishment of the individual; there will be too much strain and stress for it ever to grow a pleasant mode of travel.

Thus Oolmo flashed light upon the past and the future as we traversed the groves of Fialume. We grew familiar with the great forces of the universe, and their bearing upon the problems of mankind, and gained the true perspective of existence. I felt that Europe was but standing still, reform herself and advance in science and art and civilisation as quickly as she might. European man himself was not progressing, but only the external results of his individual efforts. It would take ten thousand years for the huge nations of Europe to make the step upwards that these islanders made in a day. Material progress meant nothing to the Limanorans unless it meant also the progress of the men themselves in capacity, in power of attaining higher and higher goals.

Year by year I came nearer to the special purpose of my education. As we passed over the family groups of the island, and learned their sciences and arts, both Thyriel and myself began to feel drawn to one branch of investigation above all others. Every family had a special department of the civilisation assigned to it, and for generations it had cultivated this. To prevent narrowness of view in its members, and to enable all to understand the value and purpose of the work of each, a long tract of their youth was devoted to a bird's-eye view of the departments of human knowledge and progress. And, that no section of life might be left at the mercy of accident, there worked with the representatives of every family one or two supernumeraries. Thus new blood was introduced, for the alien was generally chosen from a family not even distantly connected, and had such a nature and temperament as would be likely to lead to marriage and to the best results in posterity.

There was one family grove to which I was specially drawn. The faces of the dead seemed to me exquisitely beautiful; the natures that shone through their petrified bodies attracted me with tenfold power. Every day as I entered Fialume I felt inclined to bend my steps thither, and the close of the day generally found me amongst them. Oolmo tried with some amusement to himself to break me of the habit, which yet grew stronger and stronger. And Thyriel showed the same tendency. Perhaps one feature which gave great attraction to the place was its seclusion; it was almost the only family grove that had not two or three studying the records. Here we were generally left to our own companionship; for Oolmo had often to go when we arrived there; and, with our common tastes, we found the time far too short.

At last I came upon the explanation. We were studying the growth of some feature through the generations, and I had remarked to Thyriel how like she was to this family in character and appearance, when suddenly the foliage parted near where we stood and disclosed three figures, two of whom seemed to my undiscriminative eyes facsimiles of the last of the group which had been ireliumised. The feeling of worship was aroused in me, for I felt in them the beautiful nature of Thyriel, and besides this the atmosphere of years and experience mellowing it and making it seem loftier and more divine. The third was different and yet as noble, and when I gazed into her face I found the solution of a problem that had begun to perplex me, the source of those characteristics of Thyriel which made her different from the two others and from the family group. The last was her mother; the other two were her father and aunt. This was the treasure-house and sleeping place of her ancestry. Her own relationship had instinctively drawn her to it, and my natural kinship with her had attracted me there.

We were now to begin the special study which was to make us useful working members of the community, filling our own places in it, and serving its great and final purpose with our own labour and thought. Many years would we have to spend in this secluded grove mastering the knowledge and achievements of this family. Its distinctive name was Leomo, which meant earth-seers, and its department was the study of the crust and inner movements of our orb. It was one of the peculiarities of all Limanoran science that it was art too; nothing was lost; every investigation or discovery or law had practical issue; and it was the duty of the investigator to find out how his work bore upon the progress of the race to its final aim. As I saw farther and got deeper into this study I discovered that much which had seemed purely speculative was most practical and relevant to the purpose of the race. A shallow view would have rejected nine tenths of it as useless application of the energies, as mere fancy thinking. The wider my knowledge, the more my admiration of the far-sight of these investigators grew. They seemed to me to have almost the gift of prophecy as they looked at the facts they accumulated and the conclusions they tried to draw.

It was easy to follow them for every generation had reduced the ancestral writings and thoughts and achievements to the briefest available form, and indexed all that previous generations had done. It was the duty of every new student of a family, after he had finished his general education and seen the advances made in other branches, to bring all his ancestors' researches and suggestions into relation to these, and to place a brief account of them on record in the latest phraseology and scientific light, so that any alien student might read or hear with understanding. There was thus in every family grove a summary of all that was known or achieved in its department of science or life. And this great graveyard was also the library of the race, so classified and summarised and indexed that any man could take a complete survey of its contents in a few years. There was the living index, too, available in every grove. Anything that was obscure could be at once explained by the representatives of the family. Besides these there were families whose duty it was to supervise the relationships of the various sciences and branches; they could point out to the investigators how far their work tended to overlap or interfere, what was futile in their efforts, what directions had still to be taken and what paths to be traversed. They permitted no piece of work to be wasted; everything was correlated by them to the purpose of the race and to its contemporary efforts. The boundary-lines of the various departments were defined and mapped by them. They were the organisers of research, the dividers and economisers of intellectual labour.

But they themselves had their separate functions and duties. Some had the faculty of order exceptionally developed; and they were the classifiers of the community and of the work of the community. Others had the logical powers in especial vigour; and they followed out the philosophy of the race, the correlation of the ideas and of the lines of reasoning. A third group consisted of those with a dominant imagination; these looked into the future; they performed some of the functions of imaginative writers in Europe, sketching out imaginary routes for the race and for each family into the unknown; but they also covered a much wider field; they put into form and expression schemes and projects such as European men of action of the most romantic careers have often attempted to carry out, but have seldom been able to put into words; these were not allowed to interfere with action, but the ideas, plans, and romances they invented and put into shape were tested and accepted or rejected by the practical men whose sphere they touched. Imagination, it was held by the Limanorans, was apt to be a futile, if not mischievous, faculty through want of its being ranged on the side of utility; and yet, if trammelled and yoked to the necessity of practice in the individual, it came to be stifled. They specially cultivated it in these families in order that it should have full scope and development, but took care, by ranging these families with those that superintend the purpose and progress of the race, that their romances should have full relevancy to the goal of all their efforts. Many of the projects and ideas which seemed at first the most fantastic were found after many generations to be sound and most possible of realisation.

One of the striking features of the civilisation was the complete absence of a literary class or profession or group of families. They smiled at the "pure frippery" of European literature, which used imagination as a mere means of entertainment. It seemed a complete inversion of the natural order of things to make that faculty which was the prerogative of everyone who could speak, and the servant of the highest purpose of life, into a special art to suit the pleasure of the idler hours. They held that the man who had thought a thing out could express it best. So they trained up every citizen to the fullest power of lucid and final expression. In their language, so perfect was it, there was one best way of saying a thing; and everyone who knew the language aright and understood the thing could find this best way. Style as a matter of mere expression they laughed at as linguistic trickery; the force and life of everything lay in the idea, and the expression grew out of that and was a part of it, as the colour was a part of the flower. It was only a clumsy and inchoate language that could admit of style or literature as a special art; and it was trifling with one of the most divine faculties to prostitute it to the entertainment of leisure hours; it was to class imagination with the arts of the mimic, the buffoon, and the juggler.

Art for art's sake, one of the latest creeds of the writers of Europe, was to them almost blasphemy. It made the garment of ideas, the garb of human progress, into a separate entity, and the servants of God into the tailors of human folly, the dress more than the figure it clothed and the body more than the soul. Literature without the intensity of the loftiest purpose of the race was but a tinkling cymbal. Expression was the gift of nature to every civilised man, and woe to the race that neglected it in any of its individuals, the race that should divorce it from its ideas, that let the men who write filch the glory of those who think!

Like strong beliefs had they about the profession of teaching as separate from parenthood and investigation. It meant disloyalty on the part of most citizens to their most immediate duties. Who could develop the instincts of youth and be so deeply interested in his future welfare as those who were bound to him by the ties of nature? And then, when he had matured and needed the wider education, who could give it him so well as those who were most familiar with its special objects and themes? If he was to follow the art and knowledge of some other family, the sooner he went under the tutelage of its representatives after his intellectual life began the better. The only portion of their youth that the young men and women could spend with profit under others than their parents or proparents was the period of general knowledge, of summarising the results of the whole past. The representative of one of the supervising families alone could give with ease a survey of the whole field of knowledge and art and action. They and they alone were in any way an approach to the profession of teaching, and they were saved from the petrifying influence of pedagogy by their wider duties in correlating the sciences and arts, the fields of knowledge and action. Thus reason and the emotions were kept from getting benumbed by the vanity of a too easy superiority. The beings they pitied most in the world were the despot and the professional teacher; for these get buried in unreality before the life is out of them, and are so unquestionably supreme that nothing but what is pleasing to their minds dare approach them. They fall out of relation to truth, and it is difficult for them ever to regain that wholesome fear of contradiction and that shyness before destiny which constitute the essence of sanity; they have to become intolerant. The schoolmaster soon becomes intellectually barren; the despot soon falls the victim of luxury and of illusion. For the sake of the grown men and women who might be sacrificed to it, as well as of the children and youth, they abolished the profession of teacher. Individual training was the only true foundation of a sound progress. Two might be permitted to form a companionship in education and study, just as two might form the friendship of marriage; but that was only when the periods of possible atavism had been safely traversed. Nor must they be wholly given up to their comradeship; the parental influence and solitude must continue to govern their lives.

Thyriel and I had become educational companions and friends; but every item of our education was supervised without our noticing or feeling galled by it. There was no prying into details; but every change in our character and every stage in our training was tested at the periodical investigation of the citizens. Our parents or proparents took the keenest interest in all that we did and all that we tended to become.

Now, that our specialisation had begun, we were put wholly under the care of Thyriel's parents and family. I still returned to the home of my proparents, but spent the hours of training with the Leomo. There had evidently been discovered in the preliminary investigation of my faculties some especially suited to the pursuit of earth-seeing. From the beginning of my journeys to Fialume I had been attached to this family of earth-seers, and the result confirmed the decision; my tastes all developed in this same direction, and the more I penetrated into the mysteries of the science and craft, the more deeply interested in it I became. Every day, under the guidance of my new friends, I listened to the voices of their ancestors stored up on irelium tablets; for these tablets, when placed in a voice instrument, reproduced the exact sounds which had engraved the letters upon them. Their written alphabet was in fact a natural one; the letters were the forms produced by the sounds themselves when uttered by an instrument that blew upon loose particles of irelium arranged on a vibrating disc of the same metal. By a simple process the particles, when they took their form, were permanently fixed to the disc, which then became an everlasting record, easily read by any Limanoran; or, when placed in the voice instrument, speaking the words into his ear. This voice instrument was a kind of organ, whose minute keys and stops were easily controlled by the ridge of letters.

I ever preferred to listen to the records of the past instead of reading them; for I never attained great facility in deciphering the letters because of my own long familiarity with the English alphabet and writing. But Thyriel could read the tablets with great ease; I came to prefer her reading to the sound of her ancestors' voices although these gave fuller meaning to the ideas they communicated, and it was pleasant to feel that she was listening with me and not tiring her throat. Our minds seemed to become one, as we sat silent and motionless with ears intent on the statue of some one of her forefathers. There was a strong magnetism from the dead minds gradually welding our souls together.

Yet there was nothing personal or emotional in our studies. For years they were chiefly historical, watching the growth of earth-science through the generations, seeing the share that each member had in its development. How little they knew of it even up to the time of the exilings! The earliest ancestors groped amongst barren facts and their classifications. They named the rocks and the elements of the rocks, and speculated on the order of their formation; they told the story of the growth of glaciers in the original Antarctic land from which their ancestors had migrated, and tried to explain the origin and development of the strange archipelago in which they lived. But they saw no practical application of the resulting theories: even when they knew the stratum and its trend, they often failed in their directions as to where certain minerals would be found in it.

Still the strides made by the family both in the knowledge and its application were marvellous, since the island had been purified and the true purpose of their civilisation was known. An instrument that I had grown accustomed to during the previous or general stage of my education enabled me now to see at a glance the improvements of each age or generation. It was the ammerlin, which might be translated historoscope. It focussed for the eye and ear any periods of the past. The whole pageant of some section of the history of any man, science, or object could be flashed stereoscopically in a few minutes on a dark surface, whilst all the sounds that accompanied the scenes would be reproduced in any required pitch and tone. It was one of the duties of the students and representatives to take numberless sun pictures and sound pictures of all the important scenes in the life of the family and in the development of their science and art and instruments. In order to reproduce any scene, the two long strips of irelium that contained the series of momentary pictures of it were made to rotate as swiftly as they had rotated when receiving the impressions, and the sun pictures being transparent, light and magnifying glasses threw them life-size on a wall opposite the spectator; the lightning movement produced the full effect of action in life; and, as all the tints of the scene had also been impressed on the strips, there was nothing wanting to produce the illusion of life but the voices and the sounds. These, too, had been taken on an irelium strip and this, when placed in a voice instrument, added all that was needed to make the whole scene live. It was the duty of the students in each generation to single out the most striking and representative series and have them ready mounted in the instruments, that any new scholar might in a few days take a bird's-eye view of the whole development of the family. Thus was I enabled to sit and study the past as if I had been a contemporary and eye-witness of it. The very music that accompanied and harmonised each act and scene was faithfully reproduced as loud or as low as I desired. I had but to touch a certain spring in the historoscope, and raise or lower the tone.

It was little wonder that we so rapidly covered the history of the family and its achievements. By means of the work of former students we were able to avoid all the mistakes and unessential details of the route they had traversed; and Thyriel's friends pointed out every pitfall that edged the road, every by-path that led only into the darkness or into some inextricable labyrinth. Our steps were watched with infinite care; for, with all the knowledge and skill we had already acquired, we were but infants on the threshold of a universe of darkness. What was twilight in the future to our guides was to us midnight blackness. That was no science, they held, which did not flash light upon the gloom before us; and their whole efforts were bent on turning every fact and law into a prophecy and every student into a foreseer as well as a seer in his own science. The limited faculties of man fenced in by narrow bounds the future into which it was possible for them to see; but they were ever extending these bounds and creeping towards the infinite.

It took but a few years to master the recorded lore of the Leomo, the work of our predecessors had made it so easy, and it was an epoch in our existence when we began the practical part of our training. We were by no means done with Fialume, but less time was now devoted to its historical and theoretical studies. I well remember the morning when our guardians and guides informed us we were fit to see the practical applications of the science throughout the island. Taking some new apparatus, they embarked me in a kind of faleena which had been invented since I came to the island. The families of imagination had long ago suggested it, and one of the families engaged in the development of methods of flight had just succeeded in perfecting its mechanism and making it easy to manage. This aërial car had no wings, but rose by means of the many vacuum tubes which were the most important part of its impelling machinery. A powerful electric engine created and destroyed the vacuums many hundred times a minute. Each tube sucked in the air ahead and expelled it with great violence at the stern of the car. Both actions aided in propelling the faleena. The result was that, though not so graceful as the old winged car, it went with much greater swiftness. Indeed, laden though we were, we kept pace easily with the flight of my companions and guides through the air; and its parachute attachments obviated any risk, even if all the tubes should by accident become ineffective. Its chief disadvantage was that it could not rise out of the denser air of the lower atmosphere, and at the same time keep up its great speed. The old style of faleena, or farfaleena, as it was called, to distinguish it from its new rival, the corfaleena, was still kept in use for higher journeys, and the flight-families set themselves the problem of inventing a means of propulsion through space without the aid of air. One dealt with the possibilities of electric currents, and experimented on the method of alternating attraction and repulsion, using the repulsion in the rear of the car and the attraction in front. Another dealt with the possibilities of the rays of light that were ever traversing space, experimenting on their power of starting machinery *in vacuo* and keeping it in rotation. A third made effort to test the capacities of the ether, which was the basis and medium of all things, a more difficult and problematical path of investigation, yet one not to be abandoned without certain proof of its impossibility; for many apparently insoluble problems had been solved in a manner that made incredulity hide its head.

CHAPTER VII

LEOMARIE

AS I was attached to Leomarie or the science of earth-seeing, I did not follow up their experiments in the building of air-cars; I only saw the results when at last they came out perfect from their hands, and greatly admired the easy and swift action of their corfaleena. Over the hills and valleys and plains we flew close enough to see what was going on upon the earth below. Again and again we passed over long wisps of steam or columns of dense smoke. I conjectured that the steam indicated the heat wells like that which penetrated the rock near the house of my proparents, and supplied every chamber with heat or power as required. It went down some miles into the crust of the earth, and could be closed or opened at will by a huge lever worked by the steam it emitted itself. The denser brooms of smoke I took to indicate the sinking of their artesian power wells by the leomoran.

For I had seen ours being mined; I had seen the entrance of the great irelium tube into the earth, ring within ring, and its slow but inevitable work from day to day and week to week. The principle of this leomoran or earth perforator had been found by investigation of the anatomy and method of work of the pholas or rock-boring shell, partly chemical, partly mechanical. The edge of the lowest ring was like a sharp-toothed file that, as it rotated by means of power applied from the centre of force, wore its way gradually into the rock, the ridges of the file being as hard as the diamond. An inner ring-file was attached to it on the inside, and between the two was let down a certain chemical compound, which by the friction of the files produced little explosions in the rock below and thus quickened the process. Other ring-files followed in the same way. Another chemical compound, differing according to the character of the rock to be attacked, was let down in the space within the concentric rings, and rapidly decayed the rock so that it ascended like a column of thick black smoke. After all the ring-files were at work, the leomoran needed little guidance; for by an application of the principle of the spectroscope, its use of the chemicals according to the nature of the rock became automatic. As soon as the volatilised mineral that ascended out of the rings changed its character, the beams of light that passed through it changed the spectrum; and the new spectrum influenced a certain solution that controlled a thread, and this thread set free a stream of the proper chemical compound down the leomoran.

A still more striking use of the spectrum was the linoklar or spectroscope analyst and recorder. It analysed the vapours that ascended from the tubes, and recorded their spectra on a moving strip of irelium that was guided by the descent of the leomoran into the earth. Thus anyone could see what strata were passed through in any given time and the extent of the strata. But the linoklar did much more than this; whenever it struck any vein that had the much-desired irelium in it in any quantity, its spectrum released a spring which opened a small tube; through this streamed the irelium vapour into a cavity of the earth, where by means of a purifier it deposited only the pure metal. There was less demand for the other metals, gold, silver, platinum, tin, copper, iron. But there was also an arrangement for separating and depositing their volatilised forms in other cavities. Thus they were able to have more than they required of the metals, and especially of irelium, the most precious because the most adaptable of all.

I was now to see a further development of these mining instruments. We winged our way to a part of the coast which was farthest from the surrounding islands and most easily protected from invaders by the storm-cone. I noticed the exceptional lowness of the sandy beach, as shelving as that on which I had originally landed; there were none of the great bastions of rock which, moulded with such symmetry of terrace and escarpment, barred off all landing on the island. We directed our course far up the mountain and alighted on a rocky platform overlooking the sea. The new apparatus had been sent after us in a faleena and was now placed in position. A cylinder was erected on the ground and attached by machinery to wires and pipes that had been laid from the centre of force. But this was unlike the old leomoran in having the mouth tightly closed, and I soon saw the principle on which the new perforator was to work. The air was exhausted in the cylinder, and then a powerful stream of electricity was made to pass through a piston constructed of innumerable wires which kept moving with lightning rapidity over the surface of the rock at the bottom. The success of the experiment soon manifested itself; for, as soon as a spring was touched, a valve that separated the end of a projecting tube from the air-tight cylinder was opened, and out streamed a dense column into the atmosphere above. The spring was afterwards managed automatically so that as soon as the red-hot electric piston had eroded enough of the rock and volatilised it, the valve sprang open, and the moment the vapour and smoke had all escaped, it was shut, and the air was immediately exhausted.

We returned day after day to the place and found that the new perforator, or tirleomoran as it was called, worked with ten times the swiftness of the old instrument. The chief objections to it were that the metal vapours were denser and more offensive, and that the irelium cylinders had to be oftener renewed because of the great friction and the intensity of the electric heat. The one was obviated by a longer smoke-tube and an application of a vent of wind from the storm-cone; the other was obviated by longer cylinders and refrigerative packing between two of their layers of irelium. But the strangest result—strangest for me at least—was to come. The tirleomoran descended miles beyond the usual force well into the crust of the earth, at a great rate of speed, and I soon saw preparations for some change. Great channels of their usual metal were laid down to the beach, and irelium barriers erected in the sea along the shelving shore from bastion to bastion. By the greater rapidity of the descent, the increase of the proportion of their favourite metal, and the ease with which the electric current volatilised the material below, our guides judged that they had reached rock that was already molten. Before long there began to ooze out of the smoke-tube a red-hot stream, that trickled its way down the slope. Then the air-tight lid was burst off the cylinder, out of it came the electric piston on a wave of red-hot lava, and down the channels the thick stream of molten rock flowed till it reached the barriers in the sea. There with vast columns of steam it cooled and solidified, forming a new and stronger rampart to check the inflowing fire. Day after day we found that the beach was disappearing, and in its place, when the steam cleared, we could see that the great gap in the bastion-works of the island was filled up.

This was the first of their lava wells I had seen. Its operations explained to me the massive symmetry of the rocky shores and the cyclopean terraces and shoots down the mountain-sides, that had, I thought, been either chiselled by tens of thousands of years of slavish labour, or laid by the hands of a race of giants now vanished from the earth. This little people was itself the Vulcan that turned the bowels of the world into smelting-works and used the mighty forces lying underneath the crust of our orb with the ease of a smith at his forge. What had the Limanorans to fear from invaders with even the mightiest war-engines that had ever been invented? They had made themselves fortifications which would outlast the attacks of any human invention. When the beetling circle of precipices was complete around their island who could land troops, even if they evaded the blast of the storm-cone? To the Limanorans themselves the height of their shores was no disadvantage; in fact it gave them easy starting-points for their wing expeditions; they could plunge from the jutting cliffs into the air and so gain impetus for their flight.

Thus had they been able to destroy that spirit of militarism which, after a certain stage, is the implacable foe of true progress. It is based on two of the most childish and most primitive of forces in the human breast, combativeness and the passion for display. Hence the impossibility of stamping out the contagion. Ever and anon in the former history of the island the age of peace seemed to have begun; but marauders from abroad would land and stir the instinct of brigandage and make an army and a military leader necessary. Thenceforward again all the arrangements of the community were made subordinate to the ambition of the soldier. An intrusion of savagery and brute force, however veiled in glory and the panoplies of civilisation, is irresistible by the powers of peace. Only slow and silent conquest of the armed power brought back progress in peaceful arts again, again to be maimed and thrown back from some external accident. Not that they ever pretended that they could eject struggle out of their life, but they did aim to raise the plane of conflict and competition. Never could this people have entered on the rapid development of their powers without their lava ramparts and their storm-cone to keep off all occasions of militarism.

These lava wells had still other uses. Out of their flow were made the rock foundations on which the houses of this people were built. It puzzled me for years to know how they succeeded in making their immense platforms and terraces out of the hardest trap. Their mansions stood out from the precipices and cliffy sides of the mountain on isolated plateaus that gave the inmates free view on every side and free circulation of air around. They rose picturesque and romantic from the top of lonely rocks, like the castles of the Rhine, dominating the whole locality. Down the rocky foundations poured at times torrents of water from the sluice-gates of the mountain, cleansing or cooling the surroundings; yet never was there any danger for these everlasting ramparts.

Another use to which these lava wells were put was to modify the temperature. They were generally opened and let flow in the coolest months of winter, and the red-hot cascades falling into the sea heated it to such an extent that the climate of the whole island was mellowed and tempered. From the wells far up the slope of the mountain the lava flow had been so guided and moulded that immense channels had been made down to the edge of the cliffs, with sides as lofty as the precipitous shores themselves. Down these were shot in summer great avalanches of mountain snow right into the ocean, so tempering the strength of the summer heat.

But these were only subsidiary uses of the tappings of the central earth fires. Their main and original purpose was to relieve the perturbations of Lilaroma. It was one of the chief duties of the Leomo to watch over the destiny of their island, which was volcanic in its origin, though it had been greatly added to in former ages by the coral insect. Lava-streams had overspread the coral, and then the myriads of minute architects had thrust out their structures farther and farther into the sea and thus the lowlands had been broadly extended, while the red-hot layers of lava added massiveness to the body of the island. Yet it was continually shaken by earthquakes and threatened with partial if not complete disaster. It was the function of Leomarie to watch the approach of these earthquakes and guard against them. The Leomo had the most delicate instruments for recording every tremor of the earth's crust. They had also thermometers and electrometers down their heat wells and lava wells, and these automatically recorded at the surface every variation of the heat and magnetism of the earth. They had classified through many centuries all the preliminary and concomitant circumstances of earthquakes, and had found and formulated certain causal relations amongst them. Thus the minutest symptom of change in the records made by their instruments roused them to watchfulness. They were soon able to tell in what direction the explosive materials were accumulating and how far below the surface of the earth; then, when they had fixed with more or less definiteness the time they had to spare, they began sinking lava wells right into the perturbed lake of fire. The vent acted as safety-valve; the shakings of the island ceased as the steam roared forth, and the molten rock began to yeast down the side of the mountain. All danger was past for another period of time. Again and again throughout the past ages the Leomo had saved the island from the ravages of earthquake and uncontrolled lava-streams from the crater of Lilaroma. Never did they intermit their vigilance or cease to advance their knowledge of the earth and its habits and laws. It seemed to me at first that nothing could occur in the crust of our planet which they would not foresee. I came afterwards to know the limits of Leomarie, and the reasons why they pushed almost feverishly forward to further knowledge. They were ever afraid that something unforeseen might occur and threaten the stability of their land and the progress towards the nobler life.

Once in the dark ages before the great exilings an appalling disaster had occurred which ploughed deep into the consciousness of the people the necessity for the development of this earth science. Their central city stood upon a great plateau up the slope of Lilaroma. Within recorded memory there had been no great outburst from the mountain; and the inhabitants travelled fearlessly up to its rim and down the bowl of its crater. At times there had been slight spittings of ashes and once or twice a new fumarole or hot spring or even lava fountain had opened at some point on the mountain slope; but these were all at a distance from the bustling, luxurious city; and most of them had awakened slight notice. The volcano indeed had been practically quiescent since the great migration from the Antarctic regions and the sealing of the archipelago by the circle of fog. The citizens were keeping one of their annual feasts, and were lapped in luxurious ease and pleasure. They had been exhilarated by a long period of prosperity and a recent victory over the savage clan that inhabited one of the adjacent islands. The country people and a number of hermits living in lonely parts of Limanora had been alarmed by various premonitory symptoms, sultry clouds turbaning the head of Lilaroma, tremors in the earth more and more threateningly repeated, great and unaccountable disturbances in the sea, and a hot, heavy, brooding atmosphere around the whole island. Some of them came to the city and warned the revellers to be prepared for some catastrophe; but they were waved aside as dreamers, mere superstitious disturbers of life and its traffic. Half the city was gathered together in the central market-place to see a great spectacle, when the earth shook beneath them. They fell on their faces and cried to their gods; but it was in vain. The market stood upon a plateau high above the rest of the city, overlooking the ocean. Like a cap this platform was blown into the air, and all the pleasure-seekers vanished like smoke. Out on the sea and here and there on the land a rain of dust fell mingled with minute pieces of human flesh, but never was any one of the gathered thousands found; and as if to obliterate the traces of her ghastly work, the mountain sent down a broad stream of lava, which filled up the gulf where the market-place had been, and sealed up the dust-buried city, preserving it for after-ages like a fly in amber. Those who escaped destruction fled, some to distant parts of Limanora, some to other islands; but all were buried for centuries in grovelling superstition. It was out of the hermits and the country people that a new nation was built up, which set itself as a first duty to establish Leomarie, that it should not be taken unawares by any repetition of this great catastrophe. Nor has it ever recurred, although there have been many premonitory symptoms. The lava wells or vents eased the labours of the internal fires and saved the island.

Their new and deeper wells, driven by the tirleomoran, and reaching the internal fires, gave them greater sense of security. Irelium floats were let down which would not be injured by the great heat, and these, communicating with an indicator at the mouth, told of every disturbance in the surface of the lake of fire. All the indicators were connected with the centre of force, and automatically recorded there all they had to tell. The same system of centralised record placed the various indications of the climolans or earth-sensors at every moment ready to the hand of the Leomo. These climolans were down every force-well and told every variation in the heat, the density of the air, the kind of vapour, the magnetism, and the movement of the crust of the earth. No change in the earth below the island down to a distance of thirty or forty miles (the latter the greatest depth they had reached) was neglected. Every indication was properly tabulated and classified, and year was compared with year and month with month, till the meaning and importance of every change were exactly known. The furthest records of the past, as well as those more recent, were daily consulted in order to find the generalisation that would fit any new symptom. The Leomo felt daily the pulse of Lilaroma as a doctor would that of his most valued fever patient. They knew that they had the fate of the race in their hands, and no indication was of too little importance for them to consider. What would all the strivings and labours of the nation come to if any laxity on their part should allow such a volcanic catastrophe to recur as had destroyed the capital of old?

CHAPTER VIII

RIMLA

IN studying the practical aims and issues of earth science, I was taught to manage their apparatus, and to interpret every tremor in the earth's crust and every indication of the instruments. I had already been taught to make their apparatus, for my physical discipline had begun several years before I was admitted to Fialume. It was in fact one of their primary maxims that muscular exercises should go on contemporaneously with intellectual and spiritual pursuits, that nol citizen should be allowed to neglect for even a day the development of the body, intimately as the soul was interwoven with it. As soon as I was thoroughly tested and put through my course of probation, the training of my muscles was begun, and along with the magnetic moulding of my brain-tissues went the development of the force-tissues of the body and the powers of my senses. But no one was permitted to enter their great practical university or workshop till he had become a certain devotee of the race. The mysteries and arts and crafts which gave the nation its peculiar powers could not be communicated to anyone who might by some change become an alien. It was thus that many years of residence in Limanora passed before I was admitted to one of the marvels of the island, the great valley of Rimla.

I well remember the evening of my initiation. The night work was as a rule done by the younger men and women of the community; the elders took their turn at the machinery by day, as they had to husband sleep during the hours of darkness and silence. I had often wondered whither went my proparents at a fixed hour every day; they vanished in the distance as the sun began to wester, and they returned at evening with high colour in their cheeks and the look of having used their muscles with a will. Their physical life seemed to take new impetus from these expeditions.

One day on their return they told me that I was to be admitted to Rimla, which they explained to mean the centre of force. The mature judgment of the community had decided that I could now be fully trusted. My practical and muscular education was to begin. I was to set out that evening with a band of young workmen who kept the first watch of the night.

The sun had scarcely set when my escort arrived; and, as with my slow powers of locomotion I could not be expected to keep up with them, I was placed in one of their flight-cars. I had no companion, for the whole band flew in front and drew the car by some magnetic power unseen; and it was so light-hung and so balanced by wings and domes and parachutes that it seemed capable of being the sport of every wind. Over the central ridge of the island we swept towards a distant slope of Lilaroma. Suddenly underneath me in the growing darkness there shone out in a deep broad valley a vast dome of light, transparent enough to reveal the flitting shadows underneath it. It seemed the laboratory of a world. Innumerable streams flashed under its upper edge; they sped from the summits of the surrounding hills, or across the gorges from other and more distant ranges. I had seen as we flew hundreds of noble aqueducts spanning the valleys with their arches and columns, some of them thousands of feet up the slopes of Lilaroma. All the waters which the great mountain gathered from the clouds of heaven made their way towards this marvellous domed valley. At its mouth there was a deep gorge, whether artificial or natural was not clear to me then; and through the chasm leaped a river mightier than any I had ever seen; it seemed to be on its way to the sea, but I could not trace its course farther than its massive gateway out of the valley. Underneath the dome I could see vast wheels of irelium move at all levels; they seemed so fragile that a pebble thrown at them would break them; yet each turned spindles of enormous power, which moved swifter than lightning. I soon saw that all the intricate machinery was sheathed in casings of their translucent metal, along which flowed a slow, glutinous stream of some liquid that dripped through perforations on all points of friction.

As we alighted, night fell, and the titanic crystal workshop gleamed with a soft radiance that seemed to come from no centres, but was diffused everywhere in the manner of the sunlight or the atmosphere. It was like a vast ice cave of the Arctic circle lit by brief and splendid summer. Fairy-like yet vast, it seemed a fabric of some dream-world; but the splash and hiss of the forceful waters and the unresting motion of the machinery made it all real enough. The noises were by no means deafening; they were subdued and musical with a halo of mysterious whisper like the sounds of nature on a bright day of summer. Nor was the sight bewildering to the eyes; there was too much symmetry in it to perplex and dazzle.

My guides and companions tripped lightly and fearlessly through the labyrinth of movement till they reached an edifice underneath the dome more elaborate and majestic in its beauty than the noblest of Gothic cathedrals; its towers and spires and pinnacles seemed to aspire to the very stars as we looked up, and yet the loftiest of them failed to reach the zenith of the vast diaphanous roof. Towards this building radiated the moving network of spindles and axles that the flashing water-wheels turned, and out from it passed great transparent tubes of metal, woven together fantastically into a forest of gigantic trees and flowers. Nothing of this arabesque of movement marred the colossal symmetry of all beneath the crystal canopy. The church-like building was the shrine of force. In it we found one of the wise men of the elders seated on a high throne; and beside him stood muscular forms ready to do his behests. He laid his hand on a key-board of innumerable keys, each of which was marked with some hieroglyphic. The attendants scattered to various points along the mosaic floor, and watched the working of the labyrinth of wires and tubes. At the touch of the master the whole edifice vibrated, and a sound as of the most sublime orchestration filled the vault. We saw countless wheels and pistons move and flash beneath their transparent metal sheaths, and along each tube, now lit as with starlight, we could watch the rush of vapours or liquids towards their destination in the various factories and houses in the valley and along the mountain-side.

It was one of the masters of physical force who manipulated the keys. He was controlling and harmonising the vast power that was concentrated in Rimla, and, instead of the demoniac jarring of the engines and machinery which I had been accustomed to in the industrial centres of other lands, the sounds of the marvellous vault made sweet concord that ever varied with the transference of power from purpose to purpose. He was the pointsman of the numberless railroads of energy, and at the same time the musician of the titanic workshop. His will disciplined and guided both the generation and the distribution of all the force of the island. Our troop took the place of that which had been on guard through the sunset and twilight, and separated in pairs throughout the valley, each pair taking under its charge one section of the labyrinthine movement. My comrade, Ooriel, the cousin of Thyriel, was a youth of splendid build, the strength of his upper limbs seeming almost bovine, his shoulders and arms not too large for his size, yet giving the impression of gigantic power. I soon saw how much he could do. We were to inspect the generators of force underneath the dome. He first led me to the various streams which came leaping down the slopes and cliffs. One of them from some cause only to be ascertained at the cone of Lilaroma was swollen into a yellow torrent that threatened to overflow its lava banks and flood the valley. In a moment he saw the danger, and rushed to the wing-dam dividing the upper course and controlling the amount of water which should flow down to its various wheels and the amount which unused should find its way to the great exit. He found that the separating barrier had lost its automatic motion through the sudden increase of the overflow and the intrusion of a huge boulder that had come down like a battering-ram upon it. He set me to guide the machinery and power that moved the dam to suit the strength of the current, and then, fixing a narrow irelium shield in the bottom of the channel, he leapt into the torrent. The shield, I could see, keeping erect just above him, shed the stones and boulders to this side and that. Thus protected he raised a huge hammer which he had taken with him and by three or four well-directed blows split the obstacle into half a dozen pieces; he then bent down and removed them out of the way, and suddenly I felt the steering-gear begin to work, and saw the dam swing round into the channel leading to the centre of force, whilst the bulk of the torrent found its way into the exit, which was deeper and broader. The danger was past; but a moment's hesitation, either in order to bring up the heavier tools or to call other assistance, would have ruined many of the great works upon the levels below and stopped the whole of the operations of Rimla for several days.

Ooriel shook the water from his garments as he leapt out, and in a few minutes he was on his way with me to the other brooks, cascades, and conduits which gathered the aqueous forces of Lilaroma into this valley of power. Not a drop that fell from the tributary clouds about the head of the mountain but did its work for this singular people; the moisture-lifting power of the sun, and the force of gravitation that fought with it were alike made the servants and yoke-fellows of the Limanorans.

They refused to waste the energy that nature gave them so freely. This I saw more fully illustrated as I followed Ooriel. Having inspected all the forms of stream-power, he sped round to the side of the valley nearest to the western shore of the island; there in a great cave or hollow in the rock, brilliantly lit, I saw myriads of wires and cables concentrating from all westward directions on an immense block of labramor or irelium alloy. This, he explained to me, was the great electric storage-battery of the waves. From the north-west and the south-west came the chief storms and currents that broke on the shores of the island; and underneath the beetling cliffs of lava erected on the western shores they had a line of long, lofty caves running some hundreds of feet underneath into the land; in these huge vanes and water-wheels were hung from the roofs and the higher portions of the sides; and the waves as they ran in and out beat their paddles and made them whirl with lightning swiftness. The motion thus communicated was turned by their electro-generators into currents of electric force which found its way by the network of wires and cables that I saw into this enormous storage-battery. In another series of caves they cooped up the water of the full tides by means of gigantic dams and sluice-gates, and this during ebb drove huge wheels and turbines and thus sent the power of the moon into their treasure-house of power. Every storm that ruffled the surface of the ocean, every current that swept past their shores, every ebb or flow of their tides added its quota to the energy accumulated in their electric treasury, a far more wonderful concentration of wealth than any Sindbad's valley or Golconda. Here was ready to the hand of man power greater than all that the nations and the generations had ever been capable of.

And the winds had been made as much the slaves of this people as the waves; for another great cavern that we visited was the storehouse of the energy of the winds. In every gorge and pass and gully around Lilaroma up almost to its crater had been erected immense windmills, which as they revolved generated electricity; this found its way from all points by massive cables buried in the earth to the conservator of energy in this second cave. Ooriel tested the wires to see that they were not leaking anywhere and tested the batteries for faults, and finding everything in good order, we passed into a third power treasury in the rock. This was vastest of all; for into it there poured the energy of the power-wells which was not needed by the private houses spread over the face of the island. As soon as the head of steam was shut off from the machinery or the tubes of any mansion, its whole force was turned upon an engine near the mouth of the well, which kept generating electric force day and night. The accumulation of energy in this cave of the wells would have been enough to supply ten times the power that Europe had ever used in her industries.

In order to round off our tour of inspection, Ooriel led me to another but smaller cave which had just been fitted up with storage-batteries. This was the cave of the sun. For generations it had been contended that most of the power from the sun's rays was lost, even when they reached the earth; and the inventors had at last worked out the problem of its utilisation. I had noticed as I flew over the country in a faleena vast gleaming spaces sparkling like gigantic diamonds in the sunlight. These were the reflectors which collected the sunbeams and concentrated their heat and light into power. Upon the slope of Lilaroma they utilised the miles of snow surface and gathered their gleam into a few heat-engines that sent the generated electricity into Rimla.

Vast as the force was which in these various ways was bent into the service of this people, there seemed still to be the need of increasing it. Never a week passed without some facilitation of the collection and distribution of energy by an improvement in the machinery. The mechanic families were ever busy competing with one another in invention and practical application of some principle or idea, and the pioneering families who rode imagination to the verge of practicability marched ahead of them, mapping tracks and highways into the unknown future. One proposal was to utilise the magnetism of the earth as a new source of energy, and already one of the mechanical families was far on the way to its realisation. Another that was near at hand was the use of the expansion of their liquefied and solidified air for purposes of power. One plan somewhat farther off from the realm of practicability was the utilisation of the primal ether by means of its compression and expansion. Yet they were working at it in full hope of finding a solution of the problem at some unexpected turn of their imaginative road into the darkness. They had achieved so much that they had almost boundless faith in their ultimate power to solve all problems presented to their minds. They would face the death of the whole race sooner than the thought of ceasing to push forward into the night that encircled life.

My mind was almost paralysed at the thought of the vastness of the power controlled in this centre of force; but it explained to me the ease with which they could drive their leomorans miles and miles through the solid crust of the earth, the power they had over the volcanic fires of Lilaroma, the strength of the blast they could send far out to sea from their storm-cone, and the general facility with which they could control and use even the most titanic forces of nature. I did not wonder now that they were the masters rather than the servants of nature, especially when I saw that by the strength and nicety of their machines they could concentrate all this tremendous force upon any single point or distribute it over a wide area at the striking of a key on the great key-board of forces. I have seen one of the masters of energy turn the whole current from the ten thousand services it was doing through-out the island upon the making of a diamond; so enormous was the tempera-ture it generated in a few moments that a piece of carbon, submitted to the heat and pressure, came forth a magnificent jewel, gleaming and sheening in the light. But this was for no silly purpose of personal ornamentation; it was meant for the friction edge of a leomoran down where it bit into the rock. It was the easiest thing in the world for this people with all the concentration of power they had at their call to follow nature in her most occult or tremen-dous processes. There was not a metal they could not produce with their high temperatures and enormous pressures. It is true that all other operations had to be stopped in order to transmute rapidly common materials into gold, ire-lium, or diamonds; but it could be done, and they had no need to dig into the bowels of the earth like other men for the more precious metals and crystals which had accumulated there in the volcanic or chemical past.

It was one of their commonest sayings that no science which was not creative was worthy of the name. True, there were often long tracts of scien-tific investigation that seemed entirely barren; and many of their researches seemed to lead nowhither. But when I inquired more minutely I found that the investigators had realised many of the practical applications of the dis-covery when once they should reach it. They regarded as futile all abstract inquiries which had only a distant and unforeseen chance of ending in some-thing useful. Even their astronomy had a keen eye to the possibilities of their future; it led not only to a deeper knowledge of the living heart of creation, and to a wider enjoyment of the pleasures of imagination and faith, but to the purposes of the immediate life; it gave them immortal forms for their art and especially their architecture; it moulded or suggested their divinest music; it brought into even their physical life influences unlike those of the earth, and they hoped with full faith that through this they might catch the wandering thoughts or voices of the beings of other worlds and at last reach the power of emigration from star to star.

Their most creative science was chemistry; for this had reached the secrets of nature's most mysterious processes, and had imitated and generally abbreviated the workings of her great laboratory. The Limanorans did not need to grow the plants and trees that used to produce their food. Agriculture had ceased to be necessary for them except as a part of landscape-gardening. The elements and combinations that used to be extracted from their harvests in order to support and exhilarate life could be created directly in the chemical laboratories. Everything needed as diet was drawn straight from the earth without the long process of growth and culmination. They had the prime factors of sustenance in unlimited quantity and purest form with the minimum of labour, and they could give to these the exact quality and refinement which would bear them straight to the various tissues or cells of the body without the need of its offensive chemical processes. Most of the chemistry of life-sustenance was accomplished before the food entered the human system, and the space and energy of the body that had before gone to the alimentary processes of life were now free for other and higher functions. Pharmacy and chemical science combined to create all that the constitution required not only for its support and frictionless continuance, but for its progress towards longer life and more ethereal texture. Their medicine had ages before passed the crude stage of mere cure of disease. They laughed at the idea of the science as merely therapeutic: it must be creative. The inter-relations of the higher and lower elements of the nature were unremittingly studied in the case of every member of the community, and every means of change in them that would lead to the ennobling of Limanoran humanity was carefully prescribed.

I was led through their food factories and grew deeply interested in their processes of analysis and combination. They seemed never to have any hesitation about the exact quantity of each element and the exact temperature and pressure needed to produce any given kind of sustenance. One of the most singular departments of these factories was that in which they had yoked the infinitesimal plant and animal life of the universe to the chemicalisation of their food and medicine. They knew how to utilise all the life they could come across, however microscopic, and here under their marvellously powerful magnifying instruments I could see the minutest of all life enslaved to their purposes. Nothing could surpass the exactitude with which they had defined the functions and spheres of these mysterious beings invisible to the naked eye. Each had its own department of industry. No one of them interfered with the other. It was life put to its best purpose of sustaining the noblest life. When I saw the huge irelium tubes bearing out the results in aërial or vaporous form, I grew anxious to test the effects at the other end of them. At my own request I was taken one day to Oomalefa, the great series of public halls and baths which formed the chief centre of associative life in the island. I had not known of the institution before; for I was still too little advanced in physical nature to be clear of the inner chemical processes needed for nutrition, and it had not been thought necessary to show me a section of their public life in which I could have no special share. But, now that my own eagerness for knowledge had brought me to the stage of education which demanded insight into this institution, they were willing that I should inspect it and see all its peculiar features.

CHAPTER IX

OOMALEFA

THESE halls of nutrition and medication were situated on a great promontory extending miles into the sea. It had been ledged and bastioned with lava walls, and round the gleaming edifice ran a balcony or rocky platform, which broke the fury of any ambitious billows that might threaten the crystal translucence of the walls. Here, overlooking the sea, the Limanorans could drink in its medicating breath; here in the vast hall could they take that restful exercise which is the first essential of all life; here they could commune with their own souls or with the stars and listen to the ever-changing rhythm of the waves as they broke into spray or climbed to the rocky wall beneath. They considered this chamber of the ocean and the stars as more medicant and alimentary than any they could make with human hands; hence it was that they had thrown out this great projection into the sea, where they could spend most of their hours of nutrition.

Along its highest ridge ran a series of the noblest buildings that ever met my eye, unlike all other edifices I had ever heard of in style of architecture and method of grouping, but resembling in their bewildering variety and inherent symmetry the gleaming clusters of night. Countless points of fire aimed at the heavens from spires and towers which shone with rainbow fluctuation in the sun. There was a milky way of jewelled pinnacles; and around were strewn fire-flashing constellations of jewel minarets and domes. Innumerable centres of varied roof and aspiring form led the eye by their incompleteness to some great centre; and soon it rested calmly on the vast yet ever-broken and changing dome that like a snow-clad mountain-ridge mastered every spirit that was drawn to it. Alone this galaxy of clustered starry forms stood out above the sea, undwarfed by any neighbouring land and masterful over the billows below it. A true temple was it even in the presence of the universe of suns that stretched out into endless night. Within it surely might the spirit of man feel no unholy doubts of its immortal destiny or of its kinship with the divine. Pure and noble orison might here be raised to the Maker of the makers of this shrine; all trivial and mean thoughts would here be sacrilege. When night fell, the stars in the heavens held spirit communion with this their brother. This was Oomalefa, or the jewel of immortal longings.

My first visit to Oomalefa is engraved upon the record of my past, for it was one of my first expeditions under the guidance of Thyriel. The beauty of her spirit dawned upon me as the day passed; afterwards I came to see that it was everything that my own needed, but at the time I could not reason out the nature of my feelings. She grew upon me as the day upon the night, and when we parted it was as if my sun had set; helpless and stumbling, my spirit groped for the guiding dawn again; I was forlorn, reaching out for my other half in a lonely universe.

Her presence doubtless coloured all the scenes through which I passed, yet they were enough of themselves to impress my mind. We alighted on the mainland and made our way out towards the archway which spanned the root of the promontory. The weight of our bodies as we stood upon a certain spot swung up the transparent portcullis, and we found ourselves in a spacious entrance hall, its roof a moving orrery of the sky of night, its walls lit pictures of the ocean around framed in living sections of the sea alive with sea-denizens, its floor a tidal beach of sand, soft yet firm, whereon the sea ever seemed to cream and retreat. It had all the beauty and the freshness of the shore beneath the starred night when the tide is making.

The next chamber we entered was as vast, and was as many-coloured as the rainbow. It was the index hall; for here were marked the name and number and situation of every chamber in Oomalefa, and underneath each name was shown in graphic experiment the effect of the different medicated atmospheres upon the various tissues of the human body. Complete reproductions of the bones and muscles, the flesh and blood, the cells and nerves and coatings were here enclosed and the transformations pictured in the transparent sections of the walls. An expert from the family having the manufacture of each atmosphere under its charge stood by and guided and explained the process. It was a physiological laboratory, in which every Limanoran might see with his own eyes and hear explained by one who knew, every modification in the tissues that a longer or shorter time spent in any chamber would produce.

Twin with this hall was that of measurement and consultation. Here every entrant had all his important organs and tissues tested scientifically, and was then told the atmospheres which would best suit the development of any or all of his parts and faculties. He stated the chief purpose of his existence, and consulted the experts on the directions that would best lead to it. He was told of any defect in his organic functions and advised how it could be remedied. After this consultation he could return to the hall of experiment and see with his own eyes the effect of the various atmospheres upon the unseen portions of his system. Then he was permitted to enter the halls of nutrition and medication, and choosing those which he specially needed that day spent the time required in each. He found exit again by the hall of measurement, and there another testing revealed whether he had been successful in his alimentary sojourn in Oomalefa, and whether he would have to remain longer or have a certain atmosphere introduced into his sleeping-chamber in his own mansion.

Every Limanoran except the young and undeveloped had as the result of attention to health in past ages what they called the conscience of the health. This put them on the alert the moment any function was disordered, and off they went to Oomalefa to consult the medical families on the exact nature of the derangement, its locality, and the diet or treatment that would restore to complete health. Few or none of full maturity but would feel this sanitary sense within them like a whip or goad which would not let them rest till the evil element was swept out. It was a daily occurrence to meet some islander hurrying post-haste for consultation and medication, and I came at last to be ashamed of the lethargy which would let me remain inert under some decay of nerve or tissue in its primary stages until it had resulted in ache or pain. The feeling of lassitude or the absence of the sense of the full tide of life made me rush in fear and trembling to the hall of consultation. In my former existence I had had the embryo of this sanitary conscience in the pains or prostration accompanying disease, but then the warning generally came too late. Now I was sensitive to the slightest derangement of any tissue or part of my system and without the goad of ache flew to Oomalefa to find the remedy; otherwise I felt that I was doing wrong to my future and my posterity and to the future of the whole race. Even the actual present of the people was affected; the slightest disorder of my constitution seemed to weigh upon the spirits of my companions and friends, for they believed there was contagion in every disease. As strongly did they hold that there was a contagion of health, and would not allow any member of their medical families or council to approach a citizen even in consultation unless the healer was himself whole in every atom of his constitution. To be sound in body and spirit was as sanative of the derangements of others as any active remedy.

Every citizen was taught enough of the medical science of the island to know what was wrong in himself or his neighbour; for every citizen was a possible father or mother; and for parenthood a thorough and practical acquaintance with the laws of health and the causes and cures of the commonest diseases was a first essential. The Limanorans laughed at the absurdity of Western civilisation in allowing men and women to generate and bring up children with no more knowledge of their constitution than if they were mere animals. Still oftener they mourned that so much human generation in the world was left to the chance dictates of caprice, and that most medicine and education were only blind groping in the dark. That nothing should be done on mere authority was one of the first principles of their civilisation.

The medical councillor knew that he had a keen critic in every citizen; and he had to justify and make clear every process he recommended, in order that faith in him might remain clear. His sole advantage was his fuller and deeper knowledge and the faculty he had acquired from long familiarity with the questions and problems he had to deal with. Each member of the medical families and council had a special section of the human system to explore, besides having a mastery of the whole. It was this division of labour that caused their science of the human tissues to advance so swiftly. Not a moment of their work was lost.

I had thought at first that a people so healthy and vigorous and devoted to such wholesome ways of life had no need of medical science; but I soon saw that their general sanativeness demanded a more advanced science and art than the rude quackery of Western medicine. All the worst diseases of maturity in Europe, fevers, consumption, diphtheria, rheumatism, indigestion, and the rest, were relegated in Limanora to childhood, and were then as mild and innocuous as scarlatina or measles or whooping-cough; they had become the enemies of unformed tissues, and found little to batten upon even in them. Generally they were checked in their first stage by the medical knowledge of the parents or proparents, and it was the rarest occurrence to have to resort to the deeper knowledge of the medical council, rarest of all where childhood was concerned.

I rushed to the conclusion that the medical families would have nothing to investigate but the development of the tissues and organs and faculties as they existed in Limanora; but I was disabused of this idea by the occurrence of an epidemic in the island not long after I arrived there. It took the form of dream-disturbed sleep, which held the faculties in its grasp beyond the usual number of hours of rest. The patients tossed and moaned and imagined horrors of the past of humanity and animalhood as still occurring in their lives. It abridged the hours of consciousness, and left the sufferers spent and un-exhilarated. It was no fever, but only a languor that attacked the imaginative faculties and made them morbid and secretive in their activities. My brain-tissues were perhaps not fine enough to be attacked by it, and I escaped; but I was greatly distressed to find that Thyriel had been touched by the epidemic. My anxiety led me to know all that the specialists discovered concerning it. It could not be fatal, they assured me; for no epidemic had been fatal to Limanorans for many centuries. It only meant the loss of a valuable portion of the time of working. In the other islands, the winged scouts brought the news, it had swept half the populations into the grave; but so vigorous and healthy were the various tissues of our people that no disease could produce anything but a temporary derangement.

By means of their skilful surgery they soon isolated under the microscope some specimens of the living organisms that produced the disease; they experimented with all the elements and their combinations and saw what encouraged them, what attenuated them, and what killed them. It was not long before every trace of the microscopic creature had vanished from the island; there remained only the knowledge and the antidote that would enable their outposts or messengers through the sky to resist its attacks, should they ever encounter it again. Limanorans who were sent on missions out of the country had to be made epidemic-proof by inoculation against known diseases before setting out. But it sometimes happened, especially to scouts into the higher regions on the outskirts of the earth's atmosphere, that they brought back with them symptoms that were new, and a new disease and a new microbe had to be added to their medical lists. It was explained to me that our solar system was travelling every moment of its existence into new regions of space; and as it moved it passed from time to time through swarms of minute and attenuated life which had been left myriads of ages before in its tracks by some diseased member of another system. This microscopic life was in its own special way immortal, and could subsist on the scattered material life that floated though the ether unclaimed by any planetary centre. It was out of such waifs of life peopling space that a new world made a new beginning in vital history; as soon as it cooled down sufficiently, after creative collision and separation, to allow of individual existence upon it, myriads of these microscopic inhabitants of space took possession of it, and began again the struggle of life which was the universal law of infinity, and meant the ascension of all energy through higher and higher circles.

Disease was but a form of this eternal struggle for existence; it was the attempt of invisible lower forms to master the higher human tissues and make them their feeding-ground. The original enemies of man, the wild beasts, were subdued or tamed or driven forth into the deserts as soon as savage life was passed. Then began the fiercer contest for the possession of his own cells and tissues and organs. Enemies that he could not see migrated out of the surrounding elements into his system as soon as it became delicate enough to stir their appetite, and for ages there were no weapons against them; chance now and again offered one; but generally he groped about in his frantic ignorance for anything that would ease the pain from these gnawing foes within him. Out of this rose by slow steps a kind of quackery they called the science of medicine; but the conflict still remained unequal; the invisible enemies had the best of it, and they were ever being recruited by new enemies out of space, which bred new and more appalling plagues. Not till it was found that the newer these settlers were the more virulent were their ravages was there any chance of a real science of medicine arising from this everlasting agonism.

The first beginnings of a true science appeared in the attempts to deplete the soil by setting tamed and exhausted specimens of their foes to feed on it. A soil once reft of the elements that invited and fitted any disease germs seldom suffered in any serious degree from them again. Soon by their new electro-microscopes or clirolans they were able to classify the infinitely minute foods of these infinitely minute pasturers on the human tissue. Their microscopes, enormously though they had added to the power of human vision into the atomic world, had been unable to advance beyond the discovery and complete classification of the invisible organisms. Their clirolans combined photography with electro-microscopy in such a way that every change in the systems of their minute foes was recorded; they were able to see the elements taken from the human system absorbed and sifted of their nutritive powers, and the débris or manure ejected and left to poison the human tissues; it was not the presence of the organisms themselves, or even their destruction of essential elements that generally produced the disease, but the accumulation of the exhausted excreta, clogging the various functions. At first medical science satisfied itself with cultivating feeble and underbred germs, and turning them loose on the human body in order to make them exhaust the elements which attracted their kin. Next they discovered the chemical combination that, introduced into the body, would neutralise the poisonous qualities of the bacterial débris. Last of all by their vimolans or photo-electric analysers they found the exact food which attracted each form of microbe to the tissue and nourished them there; and they experimented electro-chemically till they knew the element that, combining with this bacterial food, would neutralise its attraction and yet leave the body as efficient and healthy as before; in short, they could prescribe the antidote to every disease that had ever enfeebled any portion of their system. Diseases were nothing else than the infinitesimal life of space fixing itself, after an eternity of detachment and attenuation, upon a living soil fat with the elements of attraction and nourishment and yet too feeble to hold out against its ravages. They drew an analogy from their old agriculture; weeds were nothing but plants finding at last the conditions which would give them the victory in the struggle for existence and would enable them to grow so rapidly and luxuriantly as to choke all neighbours; and their old science of earth culture set them on the way to a true medical science. They had watched with their clirolans the selective processes of the roots of each weed, and by various analysers had found the combination of elements in the soil and air by which it overcame its rivals; they then discovered the special component which, uniting with its food, would deprive the weed of its nutritive powers. Thus were they able to encourage or discourage on any soil any growth they might select. But agriculture had been completely superseded by their later chemistry. The best thing it had left to their civilisation was the cue it gave by analogy to their true science of therapeutics.

How minute and detailed was their study of the infinitesimal life of the universe, I could not have imagined without having seen it in practice. They had advanced so far with their clirolans and vimolans that they were now discovering a still more infinitesimal world which was parasitic on microscopic life. There had been elements and effects at times discoverable in their therapeutic problems that disturbed the certainty of their conclusions and solutions. Again and again their foresights had been mistaken, their calculations thrown out. Most often was this the case on the borderland of the moral world. They had known in their own far past history, and in the more recent history of the other islands of the archipelago, the demoralising effect of epidemics and plagues, especially of a new and vigorous type. For a time the people who came within the influence of the disease seemed to return almost to savagery. And yet every plague differed slightly from every other in its moral results. One made the whole population thieves; another made them liars; a third stirred up a fury of lust; a fourth delivered over the soul to despair of life, and a fifth to disloyalty and intrigue. When once their attention was called to this widespread demoralisation after an epidemic, they began to watch the effect of individual illnesses on the mind; and in every case there were results, emotional, moral, or intellectual, that were not to be accounted for by mere weakness of the body or irritation of the nerves, or by the poisonous débris that the minute organisms threw off.

They invented still more powerful clirolans, which revealed an intensity of life they had not imagined. The disease germs brought into the human system still more minute parasites that at once attacked the brain and the nerve-centres. In one disease these invisible vermin preferred one set of brain-cells, in another they preferred another. The therapeutic families engaged in the investigations were only just coming to classify these moral and intellectual parasites of the disease germs. Nor had they yet been able to discover any cure for these but the sympathetic proximity of strong and noble minds. The look from the eyes of some of their greatest doctors, even the touch of their hands, seemed to drive the living evil forth, or at least to attenuate and enfeeble it. The mind of the patient rose triumphant in the presence of one of these wise and healing personalities. It had been for ages the traditional maxim of polity that only the loftiest and most advanced, as well as most sympathetic natures should be allowed to specialise for the medical castes, or marry into the medical families. None were allowed to nurse the sick but the beautiful souls of the community; their mere presence seemed to strengthen the fainting heart in the struggle for life. As the mind grew strong, the ravages of the disease lessened. For now with their more powerful clirolans they found that, as the brain or nerve-centres acquired strength, the parasitic, invisible life took its way back to its original hosts and preyed on them. It was indeed one of the maxims of their community to keep the system of every individual at its highest point of vitality. A loss of exhilaration in any citizen was marked at once by his neighbours, just like a lapse into criminality in Western civilisation. It was the symptom of possible disease with all its power of contagion. The sense of active vitalisation (what we call the spirits) was the barometer of the sanitary, moral, and intellectual atmosphere, and every Limanoran was keenly sensitive to all its changes.

In Oomalefa it was impossible to conceal the source of the degeneration. The specialised families of the medical council knew where to apply their investigatory instruments. Even with their own eyes and ears and electric sense they could often detect the exact nesting-place of the intrusive microbes; for though to my muddy senses their bodies were as opaque as my own, except for a certain pellucid light which illuminated the skin and made the complexion so beautiful, the processes of life seemed an open book to their acute observation. Their hearing could detect any change in the normal beat of the heart and even the passage of the blood in the veins, which, Thyriel has told me, sounded like the liquid rhythm of mountain-rills. Their eyes could see through the skin the delicate veinings underneath and detect every nervous or muscular effort. Their magnetic sense could tell them whether thought or emotion was developing in the centres or passing along the nerves. The very casing of the brain seemed to them to be semi-transparent, and they were conscious, though dimly, of the movements of even the finer tissues, non-existent to my senses except under the microscope. Hence it was that each Limanoran had an isolated dwelling-place for himself. It would have been impossible for him to find rest or sleep close to the living and unresting functions of another human system; and it was only the rhythm of the movements and sounds of all the organs and processes which made proximity to one another tolerable. I have often seen Thyriel in raptures over the noble harmony of a healthy and virtuous personality; to her ear the pulsations and other sounds were like a majestic piece of music; to her eye the rush and hurry of the vital processes were not unlike the motions of the starry system of night; whilst the exhilaration through the electric sense from the speeding thoughts and emotions of a sound mind in a sound body was at times ecstatic. The nobler the soul that she was conscious of in her neighbour, the keener was her enjoyment of proximity. It was this that made only the purest and greatest minds in the healthiest bodies admissible to the medical families or council. There was a curative power in their very presence.

With their clirolans and vimolans and other aids to the senses the medical sages could detect the slightest jar in the rhythm of the system and locate it with the greatest ease. Having located it, they knew the parasite that had begun to multiply and clog the organ or tissue or function, and the treatment that it required. Every moral fault had its corresponding disease and infinitesimal parasite they held; and so rapidly could the minute organisms increase and so impalpably and easily could they migrate from human being to human being that the contagion of vice was a thousand times more appalling in its ravages than that of mere physical disease. There was great trepidation when any ailment attacked the body of a Limanoran, and he was heartily ashamed of its appearance and alarmed lest it should spread, or lead to its natural consequence, moral degeneracy; but, if the parasitic attack was found to be on one of the higher centres of life, the alarm was great and wide, for it was far more subtle in its insidiousness and omnipotence. The patient was at once quarantined and only the noblest of medical sages could break his isolation. All the powers of his mind and of the minds of his nurses and medical attendants were concentrated on the offending tissue, and strong thermoelectric aids were applied to it, so that it should soon regain its old vitality and drive the intruders out. In the chamber was kept up an atmosphere of the special elements which would nourish the degenerate cells and also of those that would destroy the microbes; only as a last resort was surgery used and the part laid open to the local application of re-agents against the hostile organisms. The ruder and older forms of evil—passion, envy, malice, hatred, jealousy, contempt, vanity—rarely appeared in grown men and women at that advanced stage of their civilisation. They had become diseases of the immature periods of life, when the soul was passing through the primitive phases of the development of mankind. They were the ailments of childhood and youth; and hundreds of the Limanorans now grew up without once experiencing any one of them. When they did appear, isolation was the first step; and the parents or proparents could generally cope with the moral disease without having recourse to a medical family or to Oomalefa. Every traditional method of cure was applied most vigorously, for they shrank from the thought of leaving any seed of the contagion in the system to germinate at some later and more dangerous period of life.

When the home circle was unable to detect the exact character of the disturbing influence, the young patient was brought under the gaze and the tests of the medical families. If their clirolans and vimolans failed to identify the parasitic evil, they tried their magnetometers, which were so delicate as to indicate the first beginnings of mental or moral disorder. By means of another magnetic instrument they were able to extract portions of the microbic débris, and then with their photo-electric analysers or vimolans they separated its various elements and saw what moral evils had entered into the system. They had the physical equivalents and results of every form of guilt and crime, and thus in its very inception a moral taint could be detected and cured before it had time to appear in the words or conduct of the patient. Most often this taint was due to some ancestral weakness of tissue inviting the swarms of parasitic microbes through which the earth is forever passing. On the first signs of lowering vitality the pedigree of the patient was consulted for the record of the retrogressive tendencies of his forefathers, and not till the possibilities of atavism were exhausted were the other tests resorted to.

It was on the basis of these two coincident causes, degeneration of tissue and microbic life in the atmosphere, that they were able to explain the strange contemporaneity of revolutions, panics, wars, religious revivals, and widespread outbreaks of crime or immorality in various parts of the earth. The planetary system as it sweeps through space cannot help passing through vast oceans of living microscopic matter which have drifted from other universes geological ages before in their unresting migration from infinity to infinity, and which lead a feeble death-in-life till they meet with fit atmospheres, such as will make them strong and teeming. For new-born worlds, just ready for the settlement of life upon them, this is a blessing; but for those having upon them highly developed organised life it is too often a curse. Every nation or tribe where civilisation has become enfeebled by luxury or immoral systems of polity or domestic manners becomes the prey of the new swarm, which multiplies and spreads itself on a fat and unexhausted soil with the swiftness of a long unsated appetite. The people rise in epidemic fury, and every institution suffers from the madness. In different ages the frenzy takes different forms, but there is a striking simultaneity in these outbreaks all over history; and only this intrusion of cosmic infinitesimal life on the weakened higher centres of the human system can explain it fully. None but the peoples who have ordered their existence on the moral laws of the universe and thus kept the tissues strong, solid, and unyielding can resist the plague-like mania. The result of these epidemics was in the end, they held, a benefit to humanity; for they swept away most of the tainted life from the earth and left the healthier constitutions able for another advance in intellectual power or in morality. The Limanoran medicists were ever testing and analysing the atmosphere of the earth for these intrusive emigrants from other worlds; vigorous and healthy though their systems were, some chance minute stranger might find a lodgment in them, and cause much derangement before he could be got rid of. Ethics, psychology, history, and ethnology were as important to their medical investigations as physiology, anatomy, and chemistry.

With all this extension of medicine into regions that seemed to me, a man of Western civilisation, the most remote from it, there had been a gradual contraction of the sphere of surgery. The hacking and hewing of the human frame to get rid of some intrusive organism seemed to them as barbarous as the butchering of animals for food. Brilliant operations they thought the confession of failure in previsional and preventive medicine. They would have considered it a disaster, if not a crime, to let any disease proceed so far unobserved as to need the excision of the part affected. Even when, by an accident, a bone was fractured, they could light up the whole sphere of the accident and see exactly how to get the sections or fragments to meet again.

Then, keeping the limb or organ at rest, they concentrated all the energy of the patient's body and mind and the curative influence of their own presence upon it. They sent the nutritive powers of circulation and nerve-energy into it by application of their various electric instruments, some of which combined the effect of exercise and the effect of heat. In a few days, sometimes in a few hours, the junction was complete, and only rest and a medicated and nutritive atmosphere were needed to make the tissue as sound as before.

One of their newest instruments and the most effective for the avoidance of surgical operations was the alclirolan, a combination of microscope, camera in vacuo, and electric power. It could by means of a swiftly moving film, on which fell electric light through a vacuum, take a picture of the life-processes within the living body, however minute. Then by means of magnifiers and brilliant light they could throw from this film a moving picture on a screen, so enormously enlarging the process of any part of the body that even a novice could see at a glance what was healthy and what was diseased or obstructed. It was this alclirolan that made the study of physiology in the living body simple enough for the very youngest. It was by this that they were able to supplement the experimental hall at the entrance to Oomalefa, and to show in process the effect in actual human bodies of disease, microbes, and remedies. Every minute process of the various organs and tissues of the body and of the brain was reproduced marvellously magnified on the walls. There was no new medicine but was tested and had its effects on the various parts of the body revealed by this new method. There was no new disease or microbe but gave up its secrets to this instrument.

The only surgery they had was creative, like all their other sciences and arts. It had to do chiefly with the capacity of the skull. The appearance of epilepsy in some of their ablest men and families ages before had pointed the way. Their knowledge of the localities and tissues of the brain, along with the semi-transparency of their skulls and the advantages their alclirolan had introduced, gave them complete command of everything that was proceeding within the head. They could by their electric apparatus light up the tissues and see what part was growing and pressing upon the containing bone. They therefore learned to trephine the epileptic sufferers and thus relieve the oppressed locality of the brain. From this practice and the growing knowledge of the great purpose of life they passed into the stage of creative surgery. For imperfect tissue perfect was substituted. Man-grafting had become the most important branch of surgery. They could modify and even create new faculty or organ or tissue by grafting what they had made on to the part of the infantile system which needed it. A child to be devoted to a special pursuit which needed some faculty exceptionally developed had his skull enlarged in its early and plastic stage over the portion of the brain that was the material equivalent and instrument of the faculty; and when most of the energies of life began to pour into his pursuit the tissue had room to grow. If a combination of exceptional faculties were needed in any profession or pursuit, protuberances in various parts under the hair or even on the brow could be perceived on looking closely. So nice had this creative art become that the most delicate and minute trephining could be accomplished without the patient knowing much about it; the operation was generally finished and the wound healed whilst he slept. Their bodies had great recuperative powers, and the means applied were wonderful in their rapidity of working. The hand of the operator, too, manipulated the part under a huge microscope that magnified the tissues ten thousand-fold. In fact they had all kinds of modifications of the microscope that would fit even internal investigations; one reflected the part in the manner of the reflecting telescope, and turned microscopes of great power on the reflected image. They had surgical modifications of their clirolans and vimolans so that they could examine permanent moving pictures or analyses of the tissues to be investigated. Nothing could escape their methods of finding out defects in the human system. However deep the organ or tissue to be examined might be in the body, it flashed out its forms and processes upon their irelium sheets as they moved. By moving these photographic records rapidly underneath their microscopes the physiological processes of life could be reproduced and examined; stationary, each moment of the processes could be slowly investigated. Their photo-electric instruments could light up and make transparent any stratum of tissue desired, whilst keeping the rest in shadow or dark outline.

CHAPTER X

THE FIRLA, OR ELECTRIC SENSE

THEIR physiology had no longer any need of anatomy or vivisection as its foundation and starting-point. Besides the alclirolans, they had their mirlans or life-lamps, as they called them; and these enabled them to watch any process of the human body and see how it changed under the treatment they applied. These life-lamps appealed not only to their eyes and ears, but to their electric sense. They isolated the magnetic force as well as the sounds and appearance of any section of tissue, and took graphic and permanent record of it, as they did of the changes in form or texture or sound. Every kind of tissue in any organ or limb had its normal magnetic equivalent measured in terms of the personal equation of force and beat of the heart. The slightest deviation from this at any time of the day or month would at once challenge attention and lead to microscopic investigation. They enlarged the electrograph, the phonograph, and the photograph of the point indicated and were thus able to examine under the sarifolan every infinitesimal atom of it in all the aspects which appealed to their sight, hearing, and electric sense. Their sarifolan magnified and interpreted for these investigative senses the graphic record of their mirlans, as the microscope magnifies for the sight. I could see and hear the movements and processes in the tissue, but the electric effect was to me as general as a shock from a galvanic battery; I could not detect anything definite or measurable. But the Limanorans, though they had something of our diffusion of electric sense, had also in the back of their necks a localised sense that responded to the faintest magnetic influence and measured roughly its amount and its changes in kind and degree. The delicate nerve-centre there, which might have been the remains of a backward-looking eye, had developed with them into a most sensitive collector of electric vibration in the air or in any section of matter; and in every atom, whether organic or inorganic, they declared there was ever some electric wave motion; in some it was too faint to affect their firla or electric sense, but then their delicate instruments for magnifying it, like their mirlans, made it manifest to their senses and definable. It was to my general feeling of magnetism what the muscular sense in my fingers was to my diffused sense of touch. It had taken many generations to develop, and in their children it never appeared till they had reached the close of youth; but part of their education was directed towards making it more sensitive and useful as a power for measuring force. A former generation of their medical investigators had long noticed and studied the effect of the concentration of will-power through the eye upon the back of the neck of one who sat in front of them; although the patient could tell nothing by means of his five senses of such an effort being made behind him, he generally turned round. Experiment after experiment proved that there was a force communicated through the intervening space to some sensitive spot on the back of the head or neck, and they knew that relics existed of what seemed once to have been an eye in that region. They came to the conclusion that this must have a closer connection with the higher brain-centres than any part of the body except the eye, and bent their whole attention upon its nature. They soon defined it as a localised electric sense and by practice made it as keen at least as the sense of touch in the fingers. They were at last able to define the direction of an electric influence and to note its changes of force, and, after several generations, their firla, as they called it, came to rank next to sight and equal to hearing in the analysis and investigation of the phenomena of the universe.

Corresponding to this electro-receptive sense, they had also cultivated the magnetic force of the eye. They had long known and investigated the exact relationship of light and electricity, and they could at any moment and place transform the one into the other. They had also observed ages before that even the commonest and weakest human eye had a faint luminosity in absolute darkness, and that any exertion of the will or passing wave of passion greatly increased it. Beside this fact they put the open secret that men of strong will and character differed from their fellows in the power of the eye, not only over human beings but over animals, and also the fact that the long-known plaything, mesmerism, had the eye as its chief organ. They came to the conclusion that the will was on its physical side a magnetic force, and that though most of its play was through the sense of touch, the muscular energies, and the voice, the eye was its highest and best channel. This inference was strengthened by noticing that amongst animals the fiercest-willed and most predatory could paralyse their victims by the exercise of some optic power, and as they prowled through the night, they had a perceptible glitter in their eyes that shone in the dark like lamps. They applied themselves to a minute and systematic investigation of the subject, and soon had instruments which would respond to the faintest ocular exercise of the will. They could measure any increase in the magnetic power of the eye; and before long it was observed that the subjects they experimented on grew rapidly in optic magnetism as they practised, and came to have a perceptible sheen in their eyes when they stood in the darkness. These men and women were found to have rapidly increasing power of sending anyone to sleep by gazing at him. At last all doubt vanished as to the new latent faculty which lay in the eye.

They set themselves vigorously to turn this new knowledge into art, and trained themselves, and still more their children, in eye-power till it became an instinctive habit to use it. After a time they came to see that the power was not one but manifold; the sleep-inducing effect was only an elementary application of it. A further development was a soothing influence upon the nerves that never went as far as sleep. Then the medicative powers of the eye were raised in the families of medicists into capacities which seemed to me almost preternatural. A more widely diffused specialisation of the new function was eye-language. Long-continued emotional dialogues would proceed in companies where I could not hear a sound, and at the end Thyriel would tell me the intricacies of the interplay of thought and emotion. It is true they could not easily communicate any unspiritual fact, needing some concrete image, unless they employed the code of eye-signals which every Limanoran learned; this combined the motions of either eye and magnetic impulses of various kinds and degrees, and contained several thousand words and phrases. I had so much to learn in the island that I had not time to master more than a few of the simpler combinations, so that I was often bewildered in their silent assemblies. But for a long time what seemed to me most marvellous was that intimate and facile converse went on when the two friends were at considerable distances from each other; when occupied in this they kept alternately turning the back and the face. This was due to the receptive magnetic faculty being in the back of the neck and the active one being in the eye. The eye was receptive in only a secondary degree, so that when the magnetic impulse was weakened by distance, the eye could not interpret it, and the back had to be turned in order to catch its full force. To see two men or women standing a mile or two apart and wheeling back and front every minute, and that, too, in alternating harmony as if they had been two sympathetic toys, at first would have made me laugh but for my wonder; and when the intercourse was rapid they looked like two whirling dervishes; but I grew accustomed to the sight, and soon began to feel with the people themselves that it was a most dignified feature of their life. For a time it seemed almost beyond nature that they could communicate even emotions and impulses at such a distance; for it was only emotions and impulses, and not facts, that passed, as the motions of the eye were not apparent except within comparatively short spaces. Yet there were electro-magnifiers which, affixed to their firla on the back of the neck, enabled them to feel the faintest impulse from a distance and interpret it, and a modification of the vimolan, used like spectacles, reduced the sense-numbing power of distance a thousand-fold; they could see by means of these electro-optical instruments the minutest movement many miles off.

The most striking manifestation of their active electric faculty was to be seen only in a few Limanorans, who would have been in the primitive ages leaders of masses either as orators or as warriors. These had such power of eye that they could bend others to their purpose without the utterance of a word. It was not greater genius or nobility of thought or strength of character that made them so much more influential than their fellows, but sheer magnetic force of will. With evil motives or depraved minds, they would have been dangerous to the whole community: as mere war leaders or beasts of prey they would have been exiled; but with beneficent purpose and a deep-ingrained sense of the ultimate aim of their whole civilisation, they were of great power on the side of progress. They were the organisers of the community, the captains of industry. They managed and directed the various services in which all the citizens had to take part so that there should be no superfluous issue of commands, no friction, or even consciousness of direction. They were in complete sympathy with all the people, binding them into a unity of discipline; and their magnetism of will, applied through the eye, served but to stir the love of service and duty to enthusiasm. In an age of semi-savagery, or of revised savagery such as the military ages of Europe were, some of them would have been great conquerors, combining many peoples and vast territories for a few years in order to sate their ambition or love of glory. As it was, the equal development of their other powers and the universal dominance of the moral aim of the race made their wills innocuous.

It was the same with the other manifestations of human magnetism, which in defective or half-developed civilisations played so maleficent a part. That power of voice and speech which could sway mobs to evil in such communities was in Limanora the endowment of every citizen. The electric tone quivered and rang in every voice I heard; it was like the sweetest music, drawing the soul to it. The fascination of personality, which so often in Western women, even where they have no beauty or grace, proves the ruin of dozens of men, belonged to both sexes in Limanora and to every citizen. It was a powerful, diffused magnetism ever attracting its opposite without revealing its secret even to its possessor. There was to me something very winsome in most of them, even when saying and doing nothing; and in Thyriel, although my intellect told me she was not what Europeans call beautiful, this became ravishing. Her personal magnetism was overpowering, even when she was silent and stood at a distance, and in rude times of ignorance would have been set down to witchcraft.

All these investigations and results I learned as clearly as if I saw them with the eye, in the firlamai or division of the electric sense, one of the vast halls of Oomalefa. Here were all the instruments needed to develop the firla or aid it, and all those by which it sought deeper into the secrets of nature. Off the hall ran corridors and arcades, which were to the firla what picture and sculpture galleries are to the ocular imagination, supplying it with noble and pleasurable excitation, as the music domes touched the aural imagination. They had their passive firlamaic arts of beauty as well as their active. In one vast arcade they could sit and feel with their firlas the electric harmonies of any given tract of air or earth or ocean, the harmonies that play as it were on the surface; this was equivalent to gazing at landscapes, real or pictured, with the eye. In another there was firlamaic sculpture; in this were gathered the noblest achievements of their electric artists, who strove to concentrate into some definite form varied magnetic materials so as to stir the imagination through the firla to thoughts of the titanic harmonies of the universe. They gave this form beauty for the eye as well; but that was not the primary aim; the gazers, as they sat, preferred to turn their backs to the work; for then through the firla their imagination was thrown into an attitude of placid meditation which seemed to have before it some great spheral harmony of the stars. In a third series of lofty corridors there was continually proceeding what might be called firlamaic music. In two or three it was entirely instrumental. Great firlamans or electric organs, at each end of one corridor I entered, flashed out what was to me the most appalling medley of lightnings; the gleams crossed and interwove and changed mass and form as if it were a dance of meteors, now slow and stately like a minuet, again swift and brilliant and dazzling as if the stars of heaven had joined the lightnings in a bewildering yet harmonious ballet. At first I was stunned and blinded; but soon I felt dimly the ecstasy apparent in my neighbours. Their eyes gleamed with joy; to me some of them seemed almost in a delirium; they were unconscious of their immediate surroundings, for I spoke to Thyriel and received no answer, and her motion through the hall as we started to leave it was somnambulous. She told me afterwards that, though her firla was only in its infancy, she felt drawn up into the heavens as in a trance; she seemed to feel the worlds move around her and attract her into their spheral chant; her imagination dealt with interastral forces as with playmates from eternity; she leapt vast ages every moment, and spanned in a stride spaces which seemed to her common powers infinite. She would not rest till she could enjoy this macrocosmic orchestra to the full as her parents did; she would not let a day pass without such practice as would develop her firla to the utmost. I felt solitary and forlorn as I heard her ecstatic descriptions and resolves, and thought upon my incapacity to understand them. In a moment she knew my dejection, and realised how forgetful she had been of me and of her surroundings. She at once threw off her imaginative trance of magnetic enjoyment, and determined to keep pace with my advance. It was a slow and weary path I had to travel; but her cheerful encouragement prevented despair. Through the years between I was able by dint of constant and vigorous practice to concentrate into my eyes and into the back of my head much of the magnetic power and receptiveness that had existed before in my body, but in a diffused condition. I was at last able to go with her and appreciate the stellar imaginings which the flashing firlamans excited.

There was another majestic arcade, in which Limanoran artists themselves joined in sublime firlamaic music. On my first visit to it, many years after my introduction to Oomalefa, I was appalled to see human beings stand like Joves flashing long tongues of lightning or flame from their eyes or fingers; they seemed to stand unscathed in a fiery furnace, or rather to weave and plait and mould the flames as if they had been threads of some plastic material. Had I come here during my early novitiate in the island, I should have fled in terror as from dreams of hell realised. There in the midst passed the artist like a dark shuttle through a loom of lightnings as he wove them into an ever-changing web of living colour. For a time I could not control my terror, as I looked to see him shrivelled to ashes. At last through my reason I managed to calm myself into feeling that he was the master and creator of this display and that the dreadful tongues of flame and swift meteors which rose and vanished around him were unstinged and innocuous. Then began to creep into me a sweet sense of some magnetic harmony, stirring my mind to contemplation of the mighty forces of the world. I seemed to know the voiceless majesty of time, as if vast ages were crushed into moments; I followed our orb as it swept away from the immense concentric circles of flame wheeling round the core of whirling fire; I saw it mass into an eye of passion fixed in gaze upon the mother star it had left; alone it travelled into space tied like an infant still by magnetic threads to the parent sun; out into the infinite it yearned to rush seeking life and souls to nestle in its bosom; yet never would the unseen mother cord give way. Out and out flamed the earth into immeasurable space and the wild longing was calmed; the tempests of fire lulled and fell; the luminous billows ceased to rear their crests or toss their fiery spindrift; a dull, still-glimmering crust imprisoned her torrid heart; the conflagrations burst forth in wider and wider intervals. At last she wooed the germs of life from the wandering infinities to rest for brief spaces on her bosom. Night brought peace to her, and the stars with their cool and unimpassioned rays bred within her through the ages gentle thoughts and a love of teeming life; they quenched her superficial fires, and, binding chains of magnetic power around her, drew her out into spaces of infinity beyond the scorching flame tongues of her fervid mother. Life born and nursed in the cold interstellar tracts teemed on her breast. Back she sprang again into the warmer rays of the mother orb, breaking the stellar bonds, and life leapt from sea to air and crawled upon the new-won lands in monstrous forms. Last came the strangest monster of all, erect like a bird, yet wingless, first swinging from tree to tree, then skimming the plains upon the backs of fellow-beasts he had mastered: man, the portent of God, had come. Slowly he grew and slowly sloughed off his beast habits. Prehistoric time focussed into a moment. First came tyranny and war as moulders of his spirit; then they became monsters, barring his way to the divine. Great monarchies and empires flew by like a lightning flash; thousands of years with their events or somnolences passed swift as a dream. Stronger grew reason in man's brain, the love in his heart; divine influences surrounded him, watching the dawn of the new power of thought and nursing the growth of the spirit in him. Then out of the darkness came the historic ages of this island's progress towards diviner light, and rushed in a flash across my brain.

Then I awoke from this ennobling dream, swift and beautiful as a trance made up of moments, each of which contained an eternity. The electric song of the history of our world had ceased, and my spirit fell like a meteor from heaven, out of the exhilaration and the ecstasy. Never before had I felt as if my life was that of a god watching from above the flight of time. I scarcely knew that the darkness around me had suddenly turned into daylight and the web of lightning flashes had vanished; I was led from the arcade by Thyriel as in a dream. When we reached the gallery which overlooked the ocean and I turned my eyes to the dome of heaven, I was conscious that a new glory had come into my life. Dim though my conception of the electric song of creation had been, I realised with joy what a vast universe had been added to the possibilities of my life by the discovery of this new sense and of the sublime things I might perceive through it. I would not be behind Thyriel in the cultivation of the magnetism in my system, but would enter with redoubled ardour on the practice of my firla.

It was thus too I came to understand the passion they had for Firlalain, as this section of Oomalefa was called. The young were not allowed to enter it, lest it should act as a narcotic on their sense of duty to the ultimate aim of their civilisation. Not till they had gained full mastery of themselves, and especially of their appetites and passions, were they admitted, and even then it was with a caution which showed the greatness of the risk they incurred. The delights of the new sense were apt to grow intoxicating, and there had been at one time a fear of some becoming magnetic drunkards, who would spend their days in Firlalain besotted with indolent enjoyment of the exhilarating flight through the realms of fancy, and heedless of the health and interests of their other tissues. Once they had reached maturity, there was no such fear; and no curb was then set upon their liberty to enter these halls of electric harmony.

After they had come to that stage of life when the walls of their blood-vessels began to lose flexibility, it became almost a duty to frequent Firlalain. The stimulus given to the currents of life by the mere physical influence of the electricity was enough to overcome the growing rigidity of cell and tissue; but the rush of thought and fancy gave the whole nature such impetus that the torrent of the blood through its channels induced the plasticity of youth again. They had other methods of postponing the approach of old age; they could withdraw from the walls of the various vessels of the body the accumulation of lime and other hardening elements; there were several chambers of diet the atmosphere of which neutralised the increase of salts and carbons in the body, and other medicinal chambers which could bring off by the pores any deleterious or obstructive matters forming in any of the tissues; but Firlalain was the most effective postponer of that stage of life when yearnings come into the heart for final and complete rest, for it flooded the whole being with new impulse and new energy. Most of all was the great stellar arcade frequented by the old in order to drive off the ennui of existence; a feeling which indicated the gradual calcarescence or induration of the brain and heart-tissues. Here any region of the starry night they chose could be made to concentrate its magnetic influence upon their firla. A man might take a new tract and new blending of imaginative impulse every day of life for centuries and yet not exhaust the limit of variety; for the stars moved through infinite space as the earth moved, but in different directions, and ever new universes or worlds were coming within the range of the Limanoran electric sense.

I shall not easily forget my first experience of this astral gallery. Along it at intervals were placed great electroscopes and magnetic magnifiers, that gathered in electric influences from various portions of the heavens. Almost every seat was occupied by one of the older inhabitants of the island, and as they sat with the focus of the huge instrument resting on their neck their faces seemed almost to have a halo round them, so brightly did they beam with ecstasy. Their eyes were closed, and I would have said that each was dreaming some dream of glory which inundated his being, had I not seen their eyes open for a moment as we passed, in consciousness of the world around; the vision came to their waking imagination. Then I looked up through the great magnifying domes and saw the stars and constellations mass upon the face of heaven, and huge spheres concentrating upon themselves the sheen of some starry circle.

Thyriel led me to one vacant seat, and before I turned my back to the magnetic lens, I gazed upwards and saw the Southern Cross pouring down its silver arrows. I had not sat there long before a thrill came upon me which spread throughout my system; my pulse fluttered like a bird in contending storms; every nerve began to throb with expectation and delight; I could have created worlds in my ardour; sublime thoughts swam in from eternity upon my soul; I had the mother passion within me which would have moulded nobler spirits than my own. At last I felt the currents of my existence centre upon one realm of space and was conscious of countless life around me which struggled and mounted upwards. I felt my nature drawn to higher levels than any terrene existence I had ever known. I seemed to breathe with difficulty the diviner airs of greater purpose, and yet there were strains of discord from lower types of being revealing gradations in the new universe. Some orbs were already on the path of decay; and on them the higher life was succumbing to the weakened vitality. Others had just attained to life; and on them had settled migrants from other spheres, whose elevating powers they had exhausted. Some were flitting like ghosts about their mother suns with but a thin ethereal life now darting between atmosphere and solid crust. Only one planet in each system was passing through the climax in its history, and near it my rapture became too great to bear; my veins seemed on the point of bursting with the fulness of life; my soul was dragged above my natural level, till the physical bonds which fettered me were about to break, and I was glad to be attracted to other circling orbs that with coarser but stronger magnetism drew me to them. The median point of balanced joy was reached when, resting between two spheres, I felt their magnetic currents neutralise each other, and yet the higher influence of the new system raise the pulsing of my spirit. As full bliss was it when, darting from system to system, I experienced the power of life that dwelt in each, and felt the varied types of existence mingling their magnetic thought with mine; I could feel the struggling of worlds up to their goal thrill through my spirit; on the underside it was like the wail of one who has abandoned the upward conflict and plunged into the waters of oblivion; on its upper side it was like the fervour of souls who see through mists of life the elysium they have yearned for. I was conscious of the infinite tragedy being enacted upon each orb, and yet not near enough to see what destiny awaited it. I was drawn within the eddy of a new and loftier ambition; my spirit perceived stages of being within its reach, yet beyond all it had known; and it throbbed with new eagerness to rise above itself. Nothing could be more rapturous than the consciousness of this system beyond system, each with its own type of life and stage of spiritual aim, each with its peculiar medley of magnetic influence, each drawn into its own vortex of emotion and energy.

A touch on my hand broke the spell, and I was down on earth again, exalted, yet knowing the contrast. It was Thyriel, who would remind me of my duty to my own being and to the state. I arose and moved out with her but she knew the ecstasy too well to break in on my dream, and led me out to the sea arcade, where I could hear the low rippling melody of the waves beneath and the faint music of the world of air. I turned my eyes up to the azure, and seemed to tread amongst the orbs that veiled their silver radiance in the blaze of noon. Out of my life, I am sure, the exaltation never wholly vanished. I had been among the living fountains of eternity. I had moved conscious of the birth of worlds, and known the throb that is a myriad of ages. Was this not to be kin with God, to know the all-grasping passion of a moment of divine life? Ever and again the greatness of the memory flamed out into conflagration within me, and I was then in the mood to make or conquer worlds; and never wholly out of my blood died the exaltation I had felt.

CHAPTER XI

A CATASTROPHE

BUT long years divided my first visit to Oomalefa and my admission to Firlalain. I saw that there were certain vast sections of Oomalefa that I was led past; massive portals showed their rank, but the number on them defining the age at which entrance was possible warned us off, and allegorical pictures adorning their arches figured the decay of tissue and cell that would result in the youthful body from too early admittance. Any curiosity Thyriel or I could have felt was repressed by these ominous symbols; for this people never relied on mere authority. Their strongest prohibitions were in the form of graphic appeals to the reason, and only where these could not impress youthful natures sufficiently were the emotions involved; the influences of any special indulgence upon the human system were represented in living form, which, looked at through a medium magnifying them ten thousand-fold, stirred the heart of all the more deeply.

We saw in a moment that we were unfit to enter Firlalain, and we passed on into the vast series of baths wherein the Limanorans could rid their bodies of obstructive or noxious elements. Here was every grade of temperature endurable by their tissues: for every grade there was a separate swimming-pool in which they could exercise themselves; and every hour automatic machinery driven by force from Rimla sent the contents of each pool into one of the lava wells, where in a few moments the water and all the débris thrown off from the bathers' bodies vanished in fire. These baths were so arranged that not more than two should be empty together, and at the general entrance were seated two medical counsellors, who measured and tested the state and temperature of the body, and showed graphically what would be the effect of entering each bath of the series to which the state of the bather restricted him.

Far more important than these water baths were the baths of ether, baths of magnetism, and solar baths, in which any portion of the body or the whole of it could be submitted to the purified forces of the world. From the ethereal baths all terrene elements were exhausted, and there remained the pure medium of life beyond our atmosphere, the divine air which spiritual beings breathe. Nothing so raised the power of the mind over the body or the part of the body immersed in this. It partially and for the time being dematerialised the part, withdrawing its earthy tendencies, and giving it an exhilarant atmosphere in which it acquired new life and energy, and resisted the encroachments of lower parasitic life. The two other kinds of baths had somewhat the same effect, but were less powerful than this. Magnetism allowed the ether a more direct influence than either water or air; it concentrated the force of the purer medium on any point. The solar baths had been used from time immemorial. It had been one of the earliest discoveries of their science that the lower organisations and microscopic forms of life that battened on the human frame lost vitality in the full beams of the sun. Later their investigators had found that solar radiance dispelled the vapours and terrene elements which floated in the air, clinging invisibly to bodies and forming the feeding-ground of quickly generative microbes. It purified by its energy all that it came into contact with, and in short allowed the ether which was its medium freer play. For generations sunshine had been one of their most successful curative agencies and was now used to reinforce and stimulate human life and energy. The rays of the sun, blanched to some extent of their heat and excessive force, were concentrated in rooms made wholly of transparent irelium, or upon irelium glasses of various shapes and forms to suit the part of the body to be subjected to their influence. These were their solar baths; but their whole system of life was one continuous solar bath: for every corner of their houses both public and private was laid open to the sun's influence from dawn to twilight, and this stored up in the atmosphere of the rooms and halls forms of energy which during the night gave ease and exhilaration to those who slept. They fully realised that it was not merely heat and light they got from the sun, but subtle energies, a fine aroma from the diviner medium that filled the interstellar spaces.

Every Limanoran of an age to be admitted to Oomalefa resorted several times a day to each of these three kinds of baths. First came a magnetic bath, in which every organ and tissue was stimulated to throw off its débris towards the pores. Then came the swim in one or more of the pools, in order that all this rejected part might be washed off. After this came the solar bath, which penetrated into the superficial channels of the body and swept away all bacterial life that might be nocuous. The last stage was the ethereal bath, which was enjoyed in solitude and could be endured by any but the mature for only a few minutes; the exhilaration and tenuity of atmosphere were too great for unaccustomed lungs, and I could see the heads of the bathers thrust out at short intervals to take a breath. But long practice made the older Limanorans enjoy the buoyancy of the pure medium for hours. It was indeed one of the hopes of the race that they would be able at last to breathe the interstellar ether with greater ease than the air surrounding their own earth.

It was in these baths I first came to see the marvellous grace and plasticity of their garments. They were outside of all my previous experiences and conceptions, and seemed so natural that I took them for a part of their material outfit like their hair. It had never entered into my mind to question whether they laid them aside in sleep or not. Perhaps it was owing to the beauty and animation of the countenance, when they spoke or even looked, that I had not paid any attention to their dress except to see how it never impeded their movements either in flight or in work, and how it varied with the individual, and never with the sex or age or profession; it belonged to the childhood of the world to regiment men in the minor details of life. Now I saw in the baths that the vesture did not need to be laid aside in other elements than air. It was made of some fine and flexible stuff woven out of irelium threads, plastic to the shape, yet capable of stiffening out when the wearer sent an electric wave through it from the electro-generator he always bore under his right arm. This process at once shook out every drop of water from it, when he issued from the bath or the sea. It was so porous that it seemed fragile, and yet it could bear great strains. Through its pores passed with ease the water or air or ether that was to influence the body underneath; and along its threads passed with ease any magnetism the wearer wished to feel. In certain lights it was almost transparent, yet with such a play of rainbow colors that it seemed a living fence against lights and shadows. In the darkness it shone with dazzling radiance as soon as the electric current flowed into it. At the will of the wearer it could be, like a magic garment of invisibility, black as midnight, yet in daylight could reveal every grace and tint of the limbs it covered, clinging closely like an outer epidermis to the body. Nor was it ever laid aside except to be replaced by a new vesture, and that was every few days; for all germs and débris that adhered to it or obstructed its pores could be destroyed and got rid of by the electric current the wearer had control of. It was on my first visit to Oomalefa that I came to know these things, as it was then that I first donned a like vesture, and was taught its properties and the ways of managing it and the minute electro-generator that went with it.

There were alternative garments, that they wore under different conditions. One, almost as plastic as the ordinary vesture, but armoured by electricity against the inroads of excessive cold, was worn when they ventured up into the higher regions of the air or beyond; for it enabled them to keep up the natural temperature of the body as they flew. Another was as well suited for protection against extreme heat. It consisted of an asbestine double wall of irelium, within which was kept up a constant current of cold air by means of a minute apparatus worked by their wings and arms; and, if they could get moisture from the atmosphere to run between the two textile folds, it was at once frozen. Such an arrangement was necessary in their adventurous experiments in the bowels of the earth or under the blazing eye of the sun. The most beautiful and most convenient of all their vestures was one which looked and felt like a film of white cloud; I would have said that it was woven of the misty fleeces that caught and rent themselves on the lesser peaks of Lilaroma. It was indeed no distant mimicry of this; for though it could be thrown loosely round the figure in the most graceful forms like a toga, and seemed as thin and fragile as gossamer, it consisted of a treble fabric: between two transparent films, fairly delicate as if woven by a spider on a windless dawn, moved in cloud-like purity and dimness the airy vapour of some liquid that shone as silvery and warm as moonlight. Its purpose was to conceal and yet to reveal the general contour and movements of the body; to sift the strength of the sun's rays as they fell in their purity from heaven, and yet to pass as much of their curative power through it as the skin needed; to cling to the limbs, and yet to impede them no more than a fleece of cloud would.

It was as I was studying the texture and the beauty of these garments that there happened the first approach to panic I had yet witnessed among this calm-eyed people. There had been a stillness as of ill-bridled tumult in the atmosphere all day. My proparents had moved restlessly abroad from daybreak, and all the Leomo were on the wing husbanding every minute with feverish clutch. We were sent in squadrons to different parts of the island, and many new leomorans were set to work in unaccustomed corners of the mountain, yet there was a look of baffled intelligence in every face. I had felt there was an undeciphered portent overshadowing their life. Thyriel and I had worked at two new leomorans and watched them till they wielded their brush of smoke across the sky. We had done all that we could and were sent out to Oomalefa to uncloud our troubled minds.

The excitement of this new sphere had removed from our thoughts all ominous shadows and we were as innocently absorbed as primitive men of the woodlands in the wonders now opened to us; but silence had fallen upon the gambolling swimmers, and the hush awakened us from our new dream. We felt the foundations of the building tremble and quiver like a panic-stricken beast. Up the translucent walls clicked a huge rent, and slowly the liquid in the baths hissed and vanished. A tumultuous muffled cannonade rolled beneath us. The crystal roof crackled and snapped like ice-rafts that groan and toss before a sudden flood. The chink widened into a chasm, and through it we could see the ocean seethe in turbulence and revolution. Up through the roof whizzed the wings of the alarmed bathers, and as the jarring and detonation grew, I stood knowing not whither to turn. All I could do was to bid Thyriel follow her mates. More awful came back the reverberations from the domes, and Thyriel's face was pale and her lips set, but she did not move. Finally she bade me follow her to that end of the gallery farthest from the chasm in the walls, a raised platform whence the swimmers dived. There she placed me with my back to hers, and ran a rope under my arms. Before I knew what she was about, I was off my feet; she was running at full speed up the rising platform and with a sudden jerk we were in the air. I heard the beating of her wings, and lay still lest I should baffle her purpose. I lay on my back between her wings, and shuddered as I saw their points broken against the lips of the chasm. A deep-mouthed clangour filled my ears; and for a moment my eyelids fell in palsied terror. When I raised them and looked down, the vast crystal of Oomalefa had vanished and the great promontory stood gaping, with the surf hissing and baying as it leapt over the upper surface.

I felt that Thyriel was almost exhausted, and thought of detaching myself from the rope which bound me and leaping into the ocean; but the idea had not quite grown into resolve when I saw her wings beat slower and knew that we were hovering over the solid land. In a moment we were standing side by side, she exhausted, I supporting her with my arms. It was not long before she recovered herself, for her attention had been awakened by a startling appearance out in mid-ocean. A high peak rose beyond the cleft and scarred promontory where there had been only waves before, its head turbaned with steam and smoke. It was still shouldering the sea to right and left with hiss of lava tongue and splash of cinder shower. We could not speak for alarmed wonder, and mingling with mine there was deep sorrow over Oomalefa vanished. What had become of it I could not tell. Thyriel roused herself and, divining my thoughts, led me to the steps which had once given entrance to the starry portal. She stooped and lifted in her hand some of what seemed to me fine-sprinkled snow, that covered every inch of rock. It was irelium dust. Once the cohesion of the great edifice had been overcome by the shocks of the earthquake, it fell not into fragments or huge blocks, but into its constituent atoms. Nothing, I thought, could ever replace the wondrous palace of delights that I had only begun to know.

I felt saddened beyond recovery, as we turned homewards, over the ruin of such magnificence and so great hopes. Thyriel's dejection, I discovered, was retrospective. She mourned over the failure of Leomarie, the earthquake art of her family and friends. They had thought that they could anticipate and prevent all the grumblings and revolutions of Lilaroma, and this outbreak had shown the imperfection of their knowledge and the limits of their art. Though but a novice, I could see that something was yet wanting to make them masters of the crust of the earth. For the first time for many generations their foresight had failed. They had known that there was disturbance beneath the mountain, but they had been unable to fix its centre, which was far out at sea. The inflow of the waters had baffled the power of their mountain-cupping instruments, and the rapidly generated steam had rent the crust in the line of Oomalefa; and until the slow-trickling lavas and the swift-belched ashes had sealed the lips of the chasm again, there was danger, they knew, of the whole island exploding. How they were to prevent or even anticipate such cataclysms was a problem that weighed upon every member of the family and saddened every leisure moment.

For some days the Leomo were busy with the wreckage of the outbreak. I was attached to the section that had to inspect the lava wells, gauge the amount of molten matter which had oozed from each, repair every clirolan or other instrument that had been deranged, and replace those submerged. The urgency of the occasion excused us from the regular duties and pleasures of the day. All our ablutions and essential exercises were performed in the private mansions. Most of the hours not spent in sleep were devoted to the tasks made for us by the new exigency. The excitement removed the monotony and burden of the work, and almost before we knew that there was so much to do it was done. New wells were sunk and new clirolans fixed wherever the overflow had choked or sealed the old. The instruments of even the most distant section of the island were put into their best working order.

Then we were free to scatter to the winds and to follow our old delights. Thyriel set herself with renewed eagerness to teach me the art of flight, and I attained the power of describing an easy curve from a shoulder of Lilaroma down to the plain. Again and again in her new desire to master flight with me seated between her wings, she carried me up to some jutting platform of the mountain: and then she showed me how to work the wing-engine with ease. I could keep level with my starting-point for a few minutes, but after that I had to let myself glide down the parabola of the air. I was too heavily weighted by gravity and the inertia of my muscles to rise as she did.

There were many secrets of their flight that I soon understood. The curious construction of the wings, formed as they were of two sliding membranes, I have already described. What I had taken for a mere rudder was a large series of small screws that gave forward motion to the flight. The engine that whirled them round as they churned the air was of great power, and without them the flight would have been but slow and clumsy. It was through inability to manage this engine that I was so long in mastering even the rudiments of the art.

I progressed greatly that day, and would have progressed more but that the lesson was abruptly broken off. In each new air voyage to a higher sally-point she bore me farther round the mountain towards the great plain that stretched to the south. When we reached our last flight platform, and I had descended, my glance shot over the countless centres of industry and investigation that stippled the rolling downs. It was a noble sight, and I could have long rested in the gaze: but an unwonted gleam drew my eyes to the precipitous coast. There on a vast new promontory which ran out miles into the sea was gathered such a galaxy of jewelled domes rainbow-lit by the sun as I could not have conceived even from my remembrance of Oomalefa and its marvellous architecture. Thyriel's eyes had also been riveted by the spectacle. "It is a new Oomalefa," she burst forth. I could not believe it; how could such a palace of wonders be reconstructed in so short a time?

There were only a few thousand mature Limanorans; and if they had been all engaged on such a structure night and day it would have taken many busy years to rear it. I took it for a mere illusion. The position of the sun and some unusual commotion in the sea had produced it by reflection and refraction. It was but a bubble of the imagination bred by some abnormality in our eyes upon our memory of Oomalefa and the grief of our minds at its evanishment.

So I argued. But Thyriel was silently decided in her dissent. We could take no more interest in our aëronautics, nothing could keep our gaze from that radiant orb resting, gigantic, on the beach. As the sun declined the facets of the new jewel shimmered with living sheen: now it was a city of burnished gold, again it was a myriad of lambent flames aspiring to the centre of fire: now a thousand rainbows weaving and unweaving themselves, again uncounted stars clustered and heaped in restless silver, or wintry thistledown of swarming snow. Surely it was but an army of will-o'-the-wisps lit in the marsh fumes that the gaping sea had sent forth. Yet as I gazed it grew in my mind that this sparkling halo had a fixed centre; there was symmetry in the refulgence and in the recurrence of colour and sheen. It could not be illusion; we were both transfixed like sculptures in eternal gaze.

The flash of wings broke the completeness of the glory and our spell. Above the transplendent spectacle fluttered a snow-storm of ariels; the sun shot a fiery gleam through a rent cloud, and across his silvery beams danced and played these winged motes. The beauty of the sight moved us almost to tears. We knew that this was no phantom joy; our fellows were aloft in the air hymning the glory of a new creation. Soon Thyriel had persuaded me to start with her towards the new palace of wonders. We had not got half-way when I felt my arms weary and my flight dragging towards the plain. She would not leave me to trudge across the uneven earth; before I could argue she had me safely nestling between her wings as they beat the air upwards from the low knoll on which we had alighted. She no longer laboured under her burden, as she had done in her first attempt some days before; yet I felt that she grew tired, and made her land upon a hill a few miles from the new Oomalefa. After a rest I was able on my own wings to curve down towards its flight of new-rocked steps and its scintillant portal.

We entered, and all was joy and music. Up underneath the new domes flitted the happy artists putting the final touches on the tinted translucence of the irelium walls. The plan was more elaborate and yet simpler than the old Oomalefa. The beauty of it was more overwhelming to the imagination of the eyes. I could not have conceived two structures more unlike from their larger architecture down to their minutest detail of ornament, and yet so adapted to the one purpose. The halls of medication and sustenance, the galleries of the magnetic sense, the baths, the arcades, and the sea balconies were all complete, yet as different from those that had gone to dust as Western architecture from Oriental. New instruments and apparatus, new indexes and tests were there at work. Not a detail had been neglected; but the rocky platforms over the sea were broader, and when we flew into the air and looked at it from above we could see that the promontory stretched farther into the sea and was broader both on its surface and at its base; and strange to say, it had as its outermost point the new peak that the eruption had thrown up in the ocean. It was conjectured by the Leomo, I soon knew, that this line, now sealed up as it was and with its lava vent at its outer extremity, would be freer from terrene paroxysms than any other portion of the island marge. This was where my proparents and the rest of the earth artisans had been engaged so busily during these days; they had been guiding the lava flow along the line of rent out through the sea to the great beacon which the outburst had raised; and the dash of the waves had cooled and congealed each layer as it flowed and curdled from the new peak to the shore of the island.

CHAPTER XII

OOLOREFA

BUT by what magic had this wondrous jewel group of domes and spires and minarets grown upon the platform within these few alternations of sun and dark? From my own experience of bastioning the shore I was able to understand the rapidity with which the foundations had been laid. My wonder grew all the more at the marvellous piece of art that now stood upon them; every detail was so complete and so beautiful. The giant forest aisle of Cologne Cathedral, the mosaic splendour that had overawed me within St. Peter's, the statued frost-work of Milan, seemed to me tawdry beside the colossal domes with their jewelled magnificence and the infinite variety in simplicity of the labyrinth of arcades and galleries and arches. Yet those were the fruits of a thousand years' faith and work; this was the product of a few days. The more I thought of it, the more bewildered I was.

Thyriel divined my thoughts and saved me from my perplexity. "You have never seen the Ooloran," she exclaimed. I asked her what it was. I could see that the word might be translated sonarchitect. Her description of it, though lucid as usual, did not convey to my slow thoughts a full idea of the instrument; and we got permission to visit Oolorefa, or the hall of architecture, the following day.

In the multiplicity of wonders throughout Limanora I had failed to notice this great edifice, although it stood on a level, symmetrically cut plateau, commanding all the region in which were gathered most of the exceptionally great and magnificent structures of the island, and was but one of a series of gleaming palaces which crowned the points of the rocky spurs of Lilaroma. In each palace was concentrated some one of the services that the new civilisation had to offer to the progress of the race. I had visited a few of them, and it was part of the programme of my education to make me spend such space and time in each as the desire or the necessity arose in my life; but it had never struck me to inquire how the marvellous buildings had arisen. Nor, though I had noticed the frequent change of outward shape and ornamentation of parts of the mansion of my proparents, had I ever had leisure or curiosity to find out the reason or source of the transformations. It was delightful to see the growth of the building and to remove into the new parts; and as silently and invisibly the sections we had left vanished. I had never time to grow tired of one chamber or set of chambers before another was ready for me. It was like the growth of a palace of dreams; but I soon accepted it as one of the magic habits of the island, a natural feature of my life, never rousing query and seldom awakening even thought. So much of new and striking was crowded into the days and months and years that large portions of the civilisation had to pass uncommented on and ultimately unnoticed.

With the same wonder with which in later life we begin to watch the marvellous workings of the functions of our bodies I entered on my new investigation. As we approached Oolorefa it seemed to me that we had made a mistake and come to the wrong building; for it rang with the most entrancing music and I thought that it must be the cathedral of the island. It had one vast central dome surrounded by countless cupolas, and as we skirted the edifice I heard underneath each of these smaller roofs sweet melodies sounding too low to be heard beyond its partition walls and almost drowned in the thunderous diapason of the central dome. These I took for chapels and fanes subsidiary to the great temple, round which they clustered.

We entered and I was amazed to find under what I had thought to be the temple of the island a great mansion, but dwarfed by the height and size of the temple roof. The fence enclosing it had just been shaken to dust by their new electric process for the atomising of irelium. What was to be done with the new structure? It was walled in by the giant cupola, and could not possibly be removed. The thought was beating about in my mind, but ceased before a sudden crash; I looked up and there, one complete and evenly cut quadrant of the dome had vanished, and the bright sun shone in undimmed by any medium. I again noticed something going on around us. Great flanks like the sides of a ship were fitted to the bottom of the new building, and along them underneath were adjusted huge floats. Wings were then attached to either side, and a strong wing-engine was placed in the body and two rudder-engines in the after-part of the raft. They were rapidly charged with electricity, the floats were exhausted of their heavier air, and up rose the whole structure through the huge aperture in the dome; and I could see its pilots guide it this way and that through the air to fit the unequal and varying wind that blew, till at last it disappeared round a shoulder of Lilaroma. I had run out of Oolorefa to watch the flight of the great mansion on its aërial raft, and when it went out of sight I returned, reflecting with a sigh of relief that this explained the magic growth of the house in which I lived; the additions had arrived and been fixed and adapted to the purposes of human habitation while I was sleeping or absent on my daily pursuits.

I was startled when I got back to find the dome complete again and preparation being made for constructing some other irelium shell. The fence-work had been raised. By its wall stood the key-board of a gigantic organ-like musical instrument, the other half of which was so arranged within the new framework that the whole volume of its sound should bear upon whatever the fence enclosed. A huge bell mouth opened out into the chamber; and I soon saw that out of this issued a snow-storm of irelium particles which floated lightly in the air. A peal of music rang out from the instrument, and I saw the dust motes settle rapidly into a symmetrical figure, that minute by minute grew into a gigantic nautilus shell. The musician who sat at the key-board watched the snow-whirl within and the magical rise of the walls. I perceived that the bar of music was repeated again and again, with gradual ingrafting of variation as the shell-like walls bent over. At a certain point where the whorl began to incurve backwards the strain completely changed and reminded me of a fugue. Back and forth it shot its monotonous shuttle of sound. I was spellbound by the cradling melody and the sinuous flexure of the vast conch. The completion of the process and the cessation of the music broke the spell, and I pressed near to ask explanations and to see the result. Some enchanter's power must surely have drawn in the floating particles to the thin curves of the structure and held them there; for the motes continued to float unattracted, but in sparse and sparser cloud; and at last they ceased to move, and settled on the fence, dimming its translucence. I felt the metal floor grow first hotter and hotter, and then cooler and cooler till it was ice-cold. Within a fraction of an hour the whole process was complete; the fencing walls were shaken to dust, and there stood the gigantic nautilus perfect in its grace, clear as crystal but for the frostwork of nautilus patterns all over its surface. It was a new experiment in form for a winged ship of the air, and as I stood the wings were added and the engines put on board. The navigators embarked; a smaller quadrant of the dome crashed aside; and out by the aperture floated this huge air-bubble rainbow-lustrous in the sun.

Thyriel led me to the vacant space whence the airship had been launched; and there I was shown how powerful magnets made the snow-storm sweep so rapidly downwards and held the irelium dust in position, once it had taken shape. Then the alternate floors were exhibited to me, one emanating heat which melted the new structure into a permanency, and another that reduced the temperature below freezing-point and completed the architectural process by chilling the metal. There were other floors easy of substitution by means of leverage and the application of great force; as one was withdrawn, another was run into its place. One was suited for one chemical process, another for another. A second set were for applying to the walls of the new structure different forms or grades of electricity. A third set could infuse into them various kinds of concreting fluids to make them cohere when the heating and chilling process was likely to fail. This was the great Ooloran that I had come to see, and only the most skilled musician and architect was allowed to sit down at the key-board.

In order to show me the part that music took in this swift architecture, I was led round the circle of sub-chapels, that I had seen surrounding the great dome. In these were employed the various draughtsmen of Oolorefa. In the first we entered the experimenter was engaged in seeking the most beautiful form for a new mansion which was to be placed up amongst the snows of Lilaroma; it would have to withstand great gusts of wind and at times heavy drifts of snow; it would also have to bear a variety of high temperatures within in order to protect the dwellers from the bitterness of the night. The building was meant for those who had to watch the storm-cone and keep it in perfect working order. The draughtsman was using a miniature Ooloran, and deftly sounding various musical notes, and sometimes songs into its irelium dust whirlwind; but there was always one predominating note, meant to introduce into each experiment a feature that had been before tested and found suitable. He fixed his experiments by means of his small movable floors, and then placed the resulting forms in order along a shelf, attaching to each the score of music which had produced it. It was like a collection of toy observatories. Within a neighbouring compartment of like transparent walls another artisan submitted each of the models to the influences of stress and strain, of heat and cold, of snow pressure and tornado violence that the ultimate and full-sized mansion would have to undergo. One succumbed to the heat, another to the severe cold, a third to an avalanche from above, a fourth to a gust of wind. He marked the flaw in each and the influence that had brought it out, and handed the model back to the draughtsman, who at once corrected the note or notes in the score of music which symbolised the flaw. When the result of the experimentation was complete, the score of the music and the miniature fabric were sent to the central dome; and in less than an hour the huge mansion was on its winged raft speeding towards its destination far up the great mountain-slope.

I was led through the whole series of experimenting chapels; in each was there a miniature sonarchitect producing test forms for special purposes under the skilled hands of creative workmen and their pupils. In most of them new designs were being produced for private houses; for of these was needed the greatest variety, as each islander had his home renewed so frequently. I could not have conceived that so many different forms could be created for the same purpose; indeed the number seemed to be limited only by the possible combination of notes of music and the need of adapting each design to habitation and the habits of the dwellers. The skill of the artist lay in the selection of the proper forms out of the multitude he daily evolved, and in their adaptation to the necessities of Limanoran life. It was in these designs that the younger members of the architect families were engaged; thus they learned their art and developed their creative instincts.

Under some cupolas which we visited we found experiments on new designs for the large public buildings, and to these the wisest members of the families were applying their century-tried skill. As we approached any such chapel, we could hear the most elaborate and entrancing music, for the design in such cases was labyrinthine, and needed the noblest artistic faculties to select and develop it. The executive musical talent displayed and the talent of extemporaneous composition and modification would have been called genius in European communities; but this people had no word corresponding to the quicksand of meaning this word covers in Christendom. They knew the origin and growth of each faculty, even when exceptionally developed, too well to attribute it to an indefinable something which nature had somehow conferred upon a chance-chosen individual. They knew as exactly the causes that produced given effects in the human system as they could calculate the forces of the inanimate world, and had no belief in the power of nature to give to human work by some caprice more value than it deserved and that deranged all calculation. This criticism I brought down on me from my guide when I expressed amazement at the beauty of the music and the resulting design in one chapel, and attempted to translate the word "genius" into Limanoran. Such expressions, he persuaded me, are but the half-articulate escape-valves of wide-mouthed ignorance; they mean no more than a confession of blindness and incapacity, and should be rapidly rejected by every progressive civilisation. The musical and designing power of this particular Limanoran belonged to most in his family of his own age, and was merely the stage the art of sonarchitecture had reached in its development on the island. Wherever a nature especially adapted to the double art was found it was imported into the family to reinforce it.

In spite of the dissertation, I could not but listen, entranced by the intricate splendour of the music; and my eyes were riveted on the growing design within the receiver of the Ooloran. Yet when finished and tested it was found inadequate to the artist's new conception of the utilities of the ultimate edifice. It was shaken again into dust before I left the workman, and its faults were noted and corrected in the score of music which he had before him. He had been years on this single design, which he had been moulding and improving every day; and he hoped soon to find a form that would be strikingly new and in every feature adapted to the purpose of the building.

I could well understand now that the new Oomalefa was no work of magic; but I was still unable to see how its vast proportions could have been shifted from its place of fabrication to its ultimate site. Thyriel led me to a new structure which had just issued from the central sonarchitect; and the master-workman bade me lean upon it; huge though it was, it shifted before my weight and I fell. It was as light as if made of silk, and we two could lift it from the floor. This explained the ease of rafting the great edifices through the air; but how did they resist the winds that blew, or the impact of wave and storm? I was led to a wall of Oolorefa itself; and I was bidden to raise one low parapet of it; not the application of my greatest strength could move it. My guide then waved what seemed to be a magnet above it, and bade me try again; it rose in my hands and my muscular effort landed me on my back. He showed me how the foundations of their buildings were powerful magnets, and how the fabric would be torn to pieces before it could be hoisted off them unless an equally powerful magnet was applied in another direction. I now understood the strength of their structures before winds and the rapid disappearance of Oomalefa after the earthquake.

But I had seen only one department of Oolorefa, that which consummated the work of the rest. One branch of the sonarchitect families was specially charged with experimentation on the materials for building. Irelium was the general name for the metallic combination of elements best suited to the state of civilisation they had reached; but there were innumerable modifications and grades of it, and there were more being discovered every day. We entered one magnificent building, and there found a dozen or more workmen, each isolated in a transparent chamber and busy with some combination of irelium and one or other of the stellar metals. Every star or series of stars had its own predominant and characteristic element or amalgam of elements; and it was a main duty of one of the chemical families of the island to examine every star for its new element and to find something corresponding to it in terrene matter. This section of the people studied with the most anxious care the products and the results of the leomorans; they visited almost hourly the mouths of the lava wells and watched the spectroscopic recorders of the fumes that rose out of them; for they seldom failed to find at one time or another some constituent of the interior of the earth corresponding to any new stellar element or metal recently discovered. Whenever it was found in any leomoran a chamber for its deposition was constructed and the clirolan was specially adapted to the preservation of all of it that issued out of the bowels of the earth. These new metallic constituents were called by the name of the stars in which they predominated, and were at once put into the hands of the sonarchitect families to be tested for structural utilities. It was thus irelium had been discovered, and thus they hoped to find materials still more plastic to their purposes. Already they had so modified their new metal by amalgamation with other stellar metals that they had fitted it to functions no metal had served before; it could be made flexible or tough, light or heavy, transparent or opaque, malleable or brittle, soluble before heat or water or electricity, or resistant to any or all of them; it was difficult to say what quality they could not impart to it; and here I could see the workmen testing new combinations in order to find new qualities or new grades of a quality already found. I stood and watched one who was trying an amalgam of a new stellar metal called vanelium with gold; he had already attempted to combine it with iron, silver, copper, irelium, and found it in each case either impossible or useless; but the reactions had pointed him to gold as its natural ally; and now, having found the two combine with ease, he was exhausting the various possibilities of combination in different proportions, and after submitting the new amalgam to his tests, was recording the results. It gave a marvellous toughness and elasticity to gold, so that, when beaten thin enough for a breath to raise it in the air, it could not be torn except by sudden and great mechanical force. Another workman near him was testing the effect of electricity on the various grades of the new amalgam and recording the results minutely. In each of the crystal chambers there were at hand supplies of all the forms of energy that might be needed, such as heat, cold, pressure, electricity. Each workman was isolated in order that the elements he used might not interfere with the experiments of his neighbour; but his workshop was transparent, that he might beckon for help at any moment, or exhibit to his fellows the result of any experiment without modifying the conditions or breaking the continuity.

A third branch of these families dealt with the adaptation of the new amalgams to the various structural necessities of the community; they found out which form or grade would resist the disintegrating influence or the power of water or of electric force; they tested what shape would best suit each grade, solid or hollow, cylindrical or spheral, cubic or rectangular, thin or thick, curved or rectilinear. Another branch devoted itself to the means of making the various metals or amalgams cohere either temporarily or permanently. A fifth studied the adaptation of the new discoveries to tools and machines and to the invention of new mechanical forms that would bring out their greatest utilities. To go through all the departments of this vast architectural workshop would need a week's rehearsal. To my first view it seemed bewildering in its complexity of specialisation; but after closer acquaintance it became simplicity itself, in fact the only plan that nature itself could have pointed out.

CHAPTER XIII

THE LILARAN

HAVING finished our survey of Oolorefa, my mind returned to the observatory for Lilaroma, which I had seen growing in miniature under the modeller's hand and music. It seemed to me a strange romance that citizens of this beautiful island lived amid everlasting snow and ice tens of thousands of feet above their fellows. How could those who were accustomed to the conditions and privileges I saw around me bring themselves to surrender it all and live the lives of hermits amid antarctic rigours? Thyriel reminded me of the glacial cold of the southern land from which their ancestry had come; but this did not wholly satisfy me. The long centuries of life in a new zone had changed their powers and tastes, and it must be a great sacrifice to live in a climate so different as was the glacier region of a mountain. My curiosity was roused, and I resolved to observe and know for myself at the earliest opportunity. I could see the observatory now perched on the gleaming shoulder of the mountain above the circle of the storm-cone, and every day I turned my eyes upwards I grew more eager to inquire into the conditions of life in so different a temperature.

It happened that the next department of the civilisation of the island that had to be studied by me in our educational development was Lilarie, or the science of island-security. We were handed over to one who belonged to the Lilamo, or families specially absorbed in this section of practical knowledge, and were told to choose our mode of ascent, car flight or wing flight, or either of the two instantaneous methods of transit. We preferred one of the two last, so he decided on the wire-line or aërial method for our first ascent. We were enclosed in a casing, shaped like a shuttle and rounded and sharpened to a point at each end; it lay slightly inclined on a close web of wires, which sloped up to the mountain-top. The door was closed and made secure, but, as our shuttle car was made of transparent irelium, we could see on all sides. It was then drawn slightly upwards into a complete enclosure of wires, each of which touched it at some point. When our guide saw that we were all ready, he pressed a button, and we shot up at incredible speed. The whole sky and earth and sea fell from us in an instant. I closed my eyes in alarm. No sooner had I done so than the whizzing sound which accompanied our flight ceased and in a moment we were at our destination, close to the peak of Lilaroma. Our shuttle car slid into another groove and rested; the door opened, and I stood amid the eternal snows. I could see the great buildings of Rimla and Oomalefa and Oolorefa like minute soap-bubbles gleaming in the sun far below. We had travelled these tens of thousands of feet with the ease and swiftness of lightning; for it had indeed been the lightning that had borne us up. Along this cylinder of wires so great an electric power could be sent that it seemed to undo the force of gravitation. Distance was almost annihilated by this mode of transit. It outdistanced sound, if not light too, in its magic motion.

As soon as I began to reflect, I was astounded to find the cold not merely bearable, but deprived of its bitter penetrativeness. My heart bounded with exhilaration; every tissue of my body seemed elastic and full of spring. I could account for these sensations by the atmosphere of these heights, but how was I to explain the mild temperature of this snow region? When puzzling over the problem, I began to notice a haze of half-glowing light like the shimmer of heat over the surface of the earth at blazing noon. It seemed at first to be an optical illusion coming, I thought, from the suddenness of my transference from the plain to such a height, but its unsteady gleam moved so uniformly that I soon saw it was outside of me. Yet it did not intercept my view of the snow and ice around. They fascinated me by their splendour of whiteness, but there was a warmth, a pallid glow over them that was quite unwonted. Our guide felt my mental interrogation, and pointed out that we had stepped from the shuttle car on to a movable platform, which would soon bring us to the observatory; over this platform was an electric covering, that protected us from the outer air and radiated heat in all directions. He showed us the snow melting on all sides of our platform in form corresponding to it, and, as it moved along the steep, the dark honeycombed square of snow moved with us. There was above and on every side of us an electric field produced by unseen circuits of wires; and these fields gave out heat falling short of light.

This was how they modified the climate up in these glacial regions and made it even sweeter and healthier than the purified atmosphere of the Limanoran plateaux below. They had done much for the climate of the lower levels; by daily casting their electric shuttles through the atmosphere they brought its impurities to the earth, its particles of dust and minute living organisms; but as more of these crowded in again from the outlying regions of air, the electric shuttles would have to ply ceaselessly in all directions in order to keep the lower strata pure. In those mountain altitudes the air was naturally sterilised to a large extent; few organisms could persist in so keen a medium; and the constant use of electric walls and roof for modifying the bitterness of the cold swept every trace of bacterial life into the snow. Hence the purity of the air we breathed up there and the buoyancy of the soul. The body seemed no clog upon the spiritual functions, and the magnetism that came from the heavenly bodies uniting with that of the earth had free play upon our minds, stimulating them to lofty flight. I no longer wondered why the Lilamo had no aversion to life at this altitude. They passionately loved it. It was, indeed, being drunk without wine, without self-abandonment, without waste of tissue.

They kept strict rein on this intoxication, ethereal though it was; for, like all their race, they had severe practical issues before them. Daily each of them returned to the less volatile and less pure air of the lower levels in order to check excess of buoyancy and to reinforce the graver purposes of life by consultation with the elders and wise men. They had in their hands an important phase of the well-being and continuance of their race. They had all the foes of human life, as it existed amongst the Limanorans, to fight off, whether seen or unseen. The tornadoes that swept across these subtropical regions, the climatic strata that drifted from other lands or realms of space, the bacterial swarms bringing plague in their train, the lower-planed human life which might swoop down on their shores from the archipelago around them—all these had to be watched and directed past Limanora. Any one of these evils might in a few hours or days sweep out the civilisation that had taken long centuries to develop and leave them all their steps to retrace. Eye-tense vigilance was needed to watch for any sign of their approach, and the keenest invention to prevent their advance when observed.

I had not long to wait for evidences of the great services the Lilamo did to their country. Thyriel and I were led by our guide into the various divisions of the observatory. We inspected the innumerable testing and controlling machines without fully understanding their intricate and often subtle arrangements. Had we not been acquainted with Rimla and Oomalefa and Oolorefa, we should have been bewildered or even awestruck. As it was we were amazed at the refinement of purpose in the apparatus, approaching almost to human intelligence; but we saw that a mere novice would have deranged most of it, so nice were the adjustments.

Our attention had been especially arrested by the electric indicator or tremolan. It contained a complete chart of the electric variations of every point of the island throughout every day in the year. This had been compiled and drawn up from the observations of several centuries, and marked the differences between periodical and temporary, regional and narrowly local, terrestrial and planetary variations. Every day the instrument was set like a clock to all the electric changes which they expected to occur periodically on that day. Each of these, indicated at every point of the map, represented an electrically uniform locality of the island with which it was connected. The superintendent of the tremolan for any section of the day specially studied all the unclassified variations which had occurred at the corresponding hour of the same day and period of time. He knew every change in the position of the earth or in the movements of the stars that might affect the electricity of the atmosphere at any moment during his watch. Along with him there was a sky-watcher, who used one of their marvellous reducers of distance and magnifiers to scan the sky and the whole horizon, and reported every new appearance which broke the uniformity of the sky-line. In an adjoining chamber with transparent partitions a third observer was stationed with his ear at a makro-mikrakoust or vamolan, that gathered in the slightest sounds at the distance of even hundreds of miles and magnified them for the listening sense applied to it; it also indicated approximately the distance of the source of the sound by an automatic calculator. This was a kind of eaves-dropper that could pick up whispers on the orb of the earth, just as their astronomical instruments could catch the faintest gleam in space myriads of miles beyond the scope of the eye. In another crystal-walled apartment stood a fourth watcher, who used an instrument that was to his electric sense what the telescope is to the eye and their vamolan was to their ear. With this idrolan he swept the sky for new and unclassified electric impulses; and the faintest and most distant indication, quite unrecognisable by his unaided sense, was magnified ten thousand-fold; at the same time the distance of the source was roughly measured and indicated.

This was by far the most attractive group of chambers for us. Not only could we test the wonderful instruments for ourselves; but we could examine by aid of magnifiers the graphic results of their observations automatically recorded as if by photography. We could minutely study the flight of sea birds not visible to the naked eye. The babel of sounds that went on in the cities of the archipelago quite beneath the horizon we could hear like a great roar beside us when we placed the sonoscripts in the sound-magnifier; and with the aid of its analyst we could unravel the sounds by repeating them slowly. Though I had not my electric sense sufficiently developed to feel the differences in the starry impulses when the electrographs were placed in the electro-magnifier, I could distinguish their differing degrees of force, and I could see how much Thyriel appreciated the fine shades of variety in the impulses.

We were engaged in testing the electric records, when we could see the observer of the tremolan bustling from table to table and map to map, whilst his pupil watched the indicator. His excitement spread into the adjoining chambers, and their occupants, leaving their instruments to assistants, came to his aid. There was an inexplicable electric disturbance on the north-east shore of the island; the field in that direction was agitated. They ran to the idrolan and turned it to the north-east; at once they knew that some seven or eight hundred miles off there was advancing at a rapid rate a great wave of electric disturbance. We all recognised a growing sultriness of heat in the profound calm of the atmosphere even at those icy heights. No time was to be lost. All the members of the Lilamo were called up, and in a few minutes were assembled in the observatory.

It was resolved to turn the whole force available in the island into the storm-cone, and especially into that part of it which could shoot masses and streamers of electric energy out to great distances in the atmosphere. Other indications of an approaching tornado soon appeared. The great telescope discovered a vast cloud of birds on the horizon, and the sea greatly agitated by shoals of fish beneath them. The vamolan analysed the sounds made by the birds and revealed that they were not all of one species; sea birds small and great were predominant; but there was no lack of land birds, insect-eaters chiefly, and a few great flesh-eaters, vultures, hawks, and falcons. The Lilamo knew in a moment what this meant. Myriads of microbes were afloat in the air in front of the storm, and the sky in the van of the cloud of birds was obscured by the mass of insect life battening on the unseen plague. The fish had gathered to eat the clotted life that dropped into the ocean, and the sea birds had assembled in pursuit of the fish. It was a striking sight, this great moving internecine slaughter and feast. Seated at a clevamolan, or combination of telescope and makrakoust, we were present at the scene, though hundreds of miles off. We could see the swoop of the vultures down on the land birds, too busy with their banquet of insects to foresee their own fate, the water boiling with the leap of the fish and the dive of the sea birds, and the air turbid with the flash and glimmer of wings; at the same time we could hear the war of jubilance and dismay, the wild cry of foretasting appetite, and the still wilder death-shriek; and round and through the clangour like an atmosphere moved the dull hum of happy glutted insect life. It sickened us and we had to cover our eyes and ears to shut out the carnage. We had forgotten that we had been using the clevamolan, and were glad to find that we could leave it and return to the ordinary powers of our senses; there was a speck on the horizon, which might be a boat at sea for anything our eyes could make out; whilst to our hearing there was the profoundest calm.

Everything was ready for the concentration of our millions of horsepower in the direction of the north-east, when a new but by no means unexpected phase of the phenomenon occurred. Word came up from the northeast shore that a plague had broken out amongst the dwellers in the district, and that the medical wise men had been summoned to their help. The Lilamo had already given warning that something of this kind might be expected in that quarter, and the physicians were by this time removing all the Limanorans in the north-east to Oomalefa. So dense a cloud of insects was not there without the attraction of superfluous bacterial life. Not always was a tornado thus heralded and vanguarded by a winged army, but when it was, it meant the migration under magnetic impulse of clirolanic plague-swarms from some favourite breeding area.

As soon as it was thus known that the bacterial couriers of the storm had reached the shores of Limanora, the electric forces of the lilaran were brought into play, and we could see lightnings belch forth which seemed to make the north-east atmosphere and ocean glow. Swiftly the shoals of fish were gathered close to the bastions of the coast, for masses of insects were falling every moment into the water. Soon we could see our lightnings reach as far as the insect darkness and the bird cloud. The air cleared and the surface of the sea was covered with death. Away to the west screamed and shrieked the survivors of the winged army. Then could we see the pitchy midnight of the coming tempest moving stealthily towards us; and its heralds howled and shrieked through every crevice of our mansion. It was bearing right on Lilaroma.

How could that battering-ram of heaven's fury be turned aside or evaded? It seemed to me that nothing but death and destruction were before us. I had already seen a tropical cyclone level a gigantic forest clean as a mower would clear his swath in his breast-high corn. What could man do in presence of so terrific a force but hide in holes of the rocks? The thought of those noble buildings levelled with the dust mingled sadness with my fear and shook all cowardice from it. What was the immolation of animal existence which I had just witnessed compared to the destruction of all this people had done? I felt as if the torch of the world's salvation were about to be extinguished.

There was no sadness or languid inaction of despair about the other inmates of the observatory. All was bustle and joyous effort for a time as in veterans quivering with the passion of battle. Every man had his duty and place; and every woman was there, too, in the ranks of champions. We could now see the nucleus of the storm just above the horizon, a mass raven-black. At once the whole power of the island was concentrated in the electric charge of the lilaran; and a long tongue of flame shot straight for the dense cloud. As if by magic the whole atmosphere was in a moment ablaze with lightnings. The sea was cloven into billows of raging foam, and seemed itself to aid in the hellish pyrotechny. It shot forth great tongues of purple flame, yet fled with reared crest from the strokes of the storm-flail. Slowly the lilaran moved its lightning-thrust away to the east. Then half the island power was put into the blast of the storm-cone; and we could see the war of elements and the thunderous scowl of the tempest shift round the circle of the horizon, instead of bearing down on us. For hours the roar of the lilaran went on. The edge of the tornado struck us, and the building shook and swayed. Hail pelted its sides; rain and snow blinded our outlook; we could see not one inch outside for the gloom. Yet within, all was radiant and calm. They knew that the centre of the tornado had passed many miles to the east, and that its trailing skirts could do no harm to anything in the island. Even if it had come straight on Lilaroma, they had given a vent to its fury so many leagues out to sea that its force would have been largely spent before it reached the shore. It was a yearly occurrence, this throttling of a tornado from the tropics; for these great electric disturbances made straight for the loftiest peak within their reach, drawn by their polar complement, the masses of electric energy which played within the heart of Lilaroma.

One of the ordinary duties of the Lilamo was to milk the great mountain of its electricity, in order that it should offer less attraction to cloud and storm. Every night, especially during the season of tempests, I could hear the roar of the energy out of the earth, and, if I looked up to the shoulders of the mountain, I could see at a hundred points the purple streamers flicker in the wind like living, moving flame-flowers growing out of the soil. When needed, this escaping energy was collected and sent down to Rimla for storage and was another of the numerous sources of power that that treasury of force drew upon.

When the tornado had passed and left its huge contribution to the snows of the peak, the lilaran was stopped, and the electric energy used in it was rapidly run over the white slopes that now obliterated every trace of the great groove and railway on which the storm-cone moved. In a few minutes the outline appeared, and soon the whole circlet was cleared of its encumbering snows. So the weight that pressed on the roofs of the observatory and the drifts that kept the light from its walls melted before the electric snowplough. The storm had not vanished an hour before all on the peak of Lilaroma was as it had been when we arrived, except for the greater purity of the snow on its shoulders. Beneath, the brush of the tempest had swept out all traces of the plague that the physicians had not got rid of, and the atmosphere was clearer and more exhilarating.

So calmly and fearlessly had the whole danger been met that there had even been leisure in the midst of the turmoil to discuss this great waste of natural power. It took them as many days as the tornado lasted hours to generate and store in Rimla all this energy which was now falling useless, or rather mischievous, upon the face of the ocean. Could they not yoke the cyclone as they had yoked the billows and the winds, the rivers and the snows, the lightnings and the central fires of the earth? There was nothing impossible to a people who had tamed the raging of the volcano and the earthquake. The difficulty was the very greatness of the force. Any machinery they might erect would be trampled to pieces by the brute power of the giant they yoked. Here was a problem worthy of their most imaginative men, of their most inventive faculties.

Not a year had passed before a trial was made, and within a decade the machinery was complete for storing the energy of the tempests. An immense cave was hollowed out in the rocks of Lilaroma, and its mouth was extended out into the ocean for miles by means of lava bastions. In it was placed enough of the alloy called labramor, or electricity sponge, to take in trillions of horse-power of electric force. At first cables containing millions of wires were floated out towards the coming tornado and electric fields were raised in the air to tap the energy of the blackness. This was continued afterwards to some extent; but it was found that, if only the clouds were electrically tapped, most of the current transmitted itself to the receivers in the cave by means of the water of the ocean. It was thus unnecessary to float out towards the storm more than one cable, so binding to the shore a great raft which held up many labrolans or electricity milkers towards the blackening sky. They acknowledged that they lost by this water-transmission much of the energy emitted from the clouds; for the ocean bore it away in all directions; but they got as much of it as they needed to fill their storehouse, and they killed the cloud monster; at least it floated away across the horizon blowing a mere gale that could do no havoc except upon the careless and unforethinking.

One of the most singular effects of this new contrivance was to rid the sea in the neighbourhood of the island of its teeming life and to precipitate to the bottom the matter that floated in the water. For weeks after, we could see the rocks or streaming weeds in the depths as clearly as if it were an ocean of air. Its emerald or azure had vanished, and white light poured down into the hitherto unfathomed hollows and valleys. There could we see the dead denizens sway idly with the forests of marine vegetation and here and there the bulk of some monster lay tangled in the herbage. Only by degrees and after some months did the colour and opacity return to the waves and the myriad life stream from other regions into the void. The currents that swept past the coasts bore down the suspended particles from other seas; and with them came new fish and their parasites.

Until these came a new danger to the health of Limanora threatened. A few days after the tornado, the precipitated organisms began to rise to the surface of the water and underneath the hot sun to form breeding-grounds for the dangerous microbes of the air. Up against the bastions of rock beat the stench of the living death. A plague threatened for a brief time; but they were not a people to remain passive in presence of such a danger, even though they could easily prevent its worst results by remedial measures. They sank the dead organic masses again by means of a charge of electricity, and then the deeper currents that brushed their shores swept the corruption into the great valleys of the ocean-bed, there to be embalmed for geological ages hence.

They regretted that they should be the instruments of this great waste of life before it had fulfilled the purpose of its stage of development; but their regret was tempered by the thought that it was a low and feeble stage, that an infinity of such existence would not weigh in the balance with one day's advance of a single Limanoran, and that the energy set free by this wholesale dissolution of organisms was still ready for other embodiments in the universe. The worst effect they feared was upon their own natures; to destroy life or deal with it frivolously was one of the worst offences against their humanity, for it introduced into the mind a brutalising element. Respect for life in all its forms was one of the truest tests of a civilisation, they held.

And the Lilamo were, almost as much as the physicians, imbued with reverence for human life and with the sense of the importance of preserving it and giving it the longest opportunity in the individual to gain its highest possibility. They had to protect their race from all external foes. They had therefore to study climatic changes and watch the sanitary conditions of the island. Sanitation meant primarily the expulsion of all hostile clirolanic life and the prevention of all conditions that would attract it or form its breeding-ground. They were especially interested in the magnetic and electric peculiarities of Limanora and of the section of the globe in which they lived; for these affected not only the health and spirits of the people, but the amount of minute life that harboured in the earth or floated in the atmosphere. They could by an increase of these elements rid an unwholesome district of its unhealthy conditions; and yet the inhabitants of it could not remain whilst the process of purification was going on. Too much magnetism or electricity in the earth or air would endanger the nervous balance of the human frame. The test instruments in the lava wells were frequently examined to find the electric state of any section of the island; and one central electrometer was constantly recording the electric state of the atmosphere in all parts of it. Thus were they able to recharge by means of their apparatus whatever localities were found defective, and tap those that had a superfluity; and over the country at night the flame-like streamers lit up the darkness here and there. But this occurred at rare intervals, for it was only in certain conditions of the sun that the earth sponged up more electricity than was good for the highest life upon its surface.

The storm-cone as a rule was enough for sanitation. By its wind force it could drift all dangerous clouds of moisture or of bacterial life past Limanora. By its electric-darting powers the heart could be squeezed out of storms before they struck the shores. It regulated the rainfall, depositing the contents of clouds by day far out upon the sea and by night upon the thirsting land. Sultry blacknesses that would otherwise float past with only stifling effect were tapped, first for their electricity and then for their rain. Storms of dust that now and again darkened over the circle of fog could be precipitated into the ocean partly by electricity, partly by the blasts of the storm-cone. The atmosphere was kept singularly pure and free from deleterious germs or particles, and few nights passed without a drenching shower cleansing the whole lower portion of the island. The peak of Lilaroma drew to it like a magnet all the masses of moisture that collected within many hundred miles of it; and a little manipulation would break these up into refreshing night showers that swept its slopes and the plateaux and levels below; and, in order to prevent the destructive floods that this might produce in the rivers, the shoulders of the mountain and its deep valleys bristled with great forests which sponged up the falling moisture and let it down gently from hour to hour into the bastioned channels.

Climate was to this people as much a matter of management as food and its production. They could modify it to fit any change in the conditions or necessities or purposes of life. To be at the mercy of the forces of nature was a state of existence in what they now considered their barbarous past. It was only the unforeseen that had them at a disadvantage; and the unforeseen was to them now only the cosmic. As the planetary system shifted through space, it had to encounter conditions and modes and degrees of energy and life that nothing short of omniscience could anticipate; but they were beginning to master the secret of many of those unexpected changes of condition. The astro-sciential families had been classifying for centuries the symptoms that accompanied these in the appearance of the sun or of one or other of the planets. With their innumerable delicate instruments for recording and analysing the electric, magnetic, luminous, and heat-vaporous state of distant space, they could see afar off the beginnings of cosmic disturbances and anticipate their ultimate direction; and in many cases they could guard Limanora against the more patent and destructive effects of magnetic and electric storms and of great waves of heat or light.

Yet there was much to master in the new cosmic conditions that from time to time beset the earth or the planetary system. Some seemed to arise so suddenly that no observation could have anticipated them. Especially was this the case with living drift, into shoals of which the universe struck, the spawn of undeveloped worlds. Hence came new diseases so widespread as to be plagues. These generally evaded the fine instruments of the astro-scientist, till they had reached the very atmosphere of the earth; for in the interstellar spaces they led so meagre a life and were spread so thinly and widely that they scarcely intercepted the light or other forms of energy from the sun or other systems. Yet the imaginative families and the inventors were struggling towards some more delicate instrument, which would observe and record the presence of interstellar material life.

CHAPTER XIV

CHOKTROO

THE Lilamo were usually occupied in these sanitary duties, but at times the other section of their defence of Limanora claimed their attention. I had had good reason to know the force of the lilaran, or storm-cone, in my attempt to arrive in the island. Had it not been decided to permit our entrance, our perseverance would have failed of the attainment of our object.

I was soon to witness a marvellous display of the defensive and repulsive powers of the storm-cone. For some years after the first period of my novitiate and my partial admission to privileges as a citizen with which this period ended, there had been observed throughout the archipelago a movement which spread with considerable rapidity. It was one of the amusements of the Limanorans to watch the comedy of life upon the other islands through the idrovamolan, or instrument for distance seeing and hearing, which they had fixed high up the mountain. On a floating strip of irelium, that could be projected far into the sky, scenes beneath the horizon could be mirrored and watched through this instrument and through other instruments for reducing distance. The sounds, too, that rose from the scene re-echoed from the under-surface of the floating mirror, and could be magnified by the makrakoustic part of the idrovamolan into their original volume. A rarer and more difficult instrument was one which combined with this power of seeing and hearing at a great distance that of noting the magnetism working in a community even under the horizon.

Recently they had found that they could dispense with the floating mirror and reflector. The ether was their transmitter of all they wished to see or hear at a distance. Through it passed electric waves from even immeasurable distances, whilst the sky itself formed a sufficiently complete mirror for reflecting whatever was occurring under the horizon. By recent discoveries and inventions they were enabled to transform electric impulses into the scene or sound that gave them out into the surrounding air. Their new instruments would tap the occurrences at any point on any given line or in any given direction. They were now independent of any artificial medium for their knowledge of the outside world. The receivers of their new idrovamolan were every moment recording and analysing whatsoever occurred along the line in which it was directed; and its transformers were constantly translating the electric records into the forms or sounds which originally sent out the impulses; it was so constructed as to prevent the confusion of waves that came from different points on the route, for it moved with the swiftness of light or, if required, with that of electricity. These new modifications gave them hope that they would soon be able to see and hear much of what goes on in universes which, though invisible, yet transmit luminous and electric waves sufficiently strong to affect their telescopic instruments, and that the straggling rays of light or electricity might be transformed into the scenes and sounds which gave them birth.

As it was, the Limanorans were able to watch all that was going on in the islands around them. During their leisure hours, when it was their duty as well as their pleasure to relax the mind, they would sit and observe the life of what they called their menagerie. To them, indeed, the whirling eddy of existence with its ambitions and crimes, its luxury and misery, in the archipelago around seemed little more than the antics of monkeys or the internecine appetites of wild beasts. The scenes were generally amusing in the ape-like vanities and mimicries they exhibited. Sometimes they were offensive and even repulsive in their filth or brutalities. How beings formed like themselves could endure the grossness of their luxuries and the falsity and hollowness of their most admired social displays was to them a bewildering problem. Even the best of these islanders were as far behind the Limanorans in true human qualities as they thought themselves in advance of apes. The daily observation of these creatures so humanly endowed and yet so foul and blind in act was often too much to bear for any length of time; the most repulsive scenes were those of what was considered high life, of courts and courtly circles, of rulers and leaders of act and thought. "Who can bear the horror of their intrigues and hypocrisies, their cruel trampling of the fallen, their hideous fawning on the successful, their insolent pride and intolerance of the weak!" I often heard exclamations like this from the lips of the watchers as they turned away from the idrovamolan with a shudder. The combination of ape and bully, of reptile and vapourer was, in the thoughts of this people, the lowest depth to which human nature could fall; and it was the usual and most envied form in the high social life of most of these islands. The barbarism and ignorance of the poor and downtrodden marked a less retrograde phase of humanity. The sight of the posturings and scrapings, the insolence and spaniel manners of the higher classes served every day to deepen the horror of exile and to frighten every Limanoran from anything that would lead even to the slightest retrogression. Had it not been for this wholesome effect upon their minds, they would have long ago abandoned the custom of watching this beast spectacle of retrograde and showy civilisation, so much pain mingled with their amusement at it. They knew that their pity was vain; for it would take unremitting effort for thousands of years to raise these peoples to the Limanoran level, if the Limanoran missionaries had not in the meantime been dragged down to the lower level; and these thousands of years could be better spent in attaining higher and higher ideals in their own life. The task, they knew, was as hopeless as if these descendants of their degenerate exiles should attempt to drag the lower animals up to their stage of human development, and this irremediable nature of their state added to the pain of the observers.

Had the habit of watching the comedy of their menagerie been given up, the Lilamo would have still had to observe the enactment of history in the surrounding islands. It was part of their duty of defence to anticipate all armaments against Limanora; and they had discovered that there was unusual excitement amongst the various peoples since the arrival of the *Daydream* in their waters. It was evident that this formed an epoch in the history of the archipelago. The Lilamo reported the movements of the portentous smoke-pennoned ship which sailed in the teeth of all winds like their own ships of the air. What was to prevent it approaching Limanora in spite of the force of the storm-cone? The thought brought the first trace of fear into the breasts of this people; for, once a foreign element had been able to force its way into their midst, how could they prevent moral contamination and swift retrogression? Their advance would crumble away in a few centuries, nothing but their material progress being likely to survive the incursion of barbarism.

It was imperative that new measures of defence be adopted. It was then that the forces of Rimla had been enormously increased, thus making it possible for most of its energy to take the electric form in the storm-cone. With this they would be able to repel the new monster with so much metal in its bosom; they would play with it as with a toy on the water. All my wanderings had been narrowly watched, my landing in Aleofane, my escape from it, my sojourn in Tirralaria and ascent of Klimarol, my companionship with Sneekape and my scorn of him, my sympathy with the refugees in Nookoo, and my friendship with Noola. Nothing escaped their attention, and my character was analysed in the most minute way by deductions from the details of my conduct. It was decided that, if I showed eagerness and persistence enough, I should be allowed to land with Noola; but that my fire-ship and my men should be blown off from the coast.

Since then the affairs of the archipelago had been observed as narrowly as before, and especially the wanderings and history of the *Daydream*. As I expected, it passed finally into the possession of Broolyi, and the new ideas and methods it brought into the warfare of this isolated zone of the world made an era in its history. A great military organiser had arisen; and he had by the potency of his will moulded Broolyi into a unity which with the help of new fire-ships built on the model of my yacht had brought the other islands into subjection. Even the aristocratic and refined Aleofane with its subtle government and all-powerful central institutions had to bow its neck to the yoke. This strange romance had been enacting for more than a decade; and the Limanorans had been watching it, at first with amusement, and afterwards with resolution and clear purpose. They knew the whole of this subjugative process was based on hypocrisy and injustice and bloodshed, but it was not worse than the methods of political existence it displaced; it only meant the substitution of one vicious ideal for others as vicious. There would be more movement and activity for a time, but as soon as the masterful will had vanished, there would be a quick return to the old lazy luxury in the few and lazy misery in the many. It had cost multitudes of lives, and would cost many more before the military mania had burned itself out; but of what worth were most of those lives to themselves or to the world? They succeeded, where they did succeed, only in sustaining themselves wretchedly and perpetuating a strain of existence that was, if changed at all, tending downwards. The new spectacle was more sanguinary, but not one whit more dismal than the ones the Limanorans had witnessed for many generations. The misery was irremediable, the standard of existence was so low. To fence it off like a plague was all that could be done.

When I sat down to the idrovamolan I soon discovered the master of this transformation scene. I heard in Broolyi from all the entrenched camps and the towns loud huzzas and cries of "Long live Choktroo!" Turning the line of sight to the capital, the conflagration of cries which swept the crowded streets soon led my eye to the centre of the far-reaching magnetic thrill, the square of the imperial palace. There I saw step out on a balcony and bow to the enthusiastic populace a little firm-set figure that seemed to awaken memories in me. I strengthened the power of vision in order to examine the face more keenly, and, as a great burst of "Long live our emperor! Long live Choktroo!" kindled and blazed athwart the city, the identity of the little conqueror broke upon my consciousness.

It was my cabin-boy, Jock Drew, whom I had rescued from a life of degradation, if not ultimate infamy, in his native village. His father, the local chimney-sweep, a man of vigorous but small physique, had succumbed to the fate of so many of his trade, and swept his throat hourly with the fiercest of whiskey. His mother, a brave, strong little peasant girl, had died early of the effort to master this thirsty piece of humanity that had been tied to her, and his vice. The boy had the maternal lines in his nature, strong will, great courage, and fiery passion. It stirred my pity to see him struggle with such a mean destiny, doubtless to sink hopelessly into the ditch. He had been shielding himself from the temptation that his drunken father set before him by living in a world of penny romance. His imagination was strung to its highest pitch by the gory pages of his hard-won treasures. When he heard of my proposed expedition to the other side of the world, he came and pleaded for even the most menial position on board the *Daydream*. I was only too eager to rescue him from the hideous fate before him, and engaged him as cabin-boy.

After he came on board, some of the men were inclined to patronise him, and, when he resisted their approaches and grew sulky, to apply a rope's end to him. I had to stand between him and them, even though I saw that in the end he would have the best of the quarrel; for he was strong of build and violent in temper, and only controlled himself, I could see, that he might have the surer and more complete revenge. He was a solitary, musing boy, and I thought to draw him from his solitude by interesting him in scientific and philosophical books; but he returned with the greater gusto to his penny series of lives of the great pirates, robbers, warriors, and conquerors. The only section of the *Daydream's* library which could seduce him from his loved studies was that containing history and adventures. The crew, as was natural, held the studious little recluse too cheap; and occasionally felt the sting of his tongue when they bantered him; but his melodramatic manners and attitude, copied from the coloured representations of his heroes in his favourite series, laid him open again to their laughter and scorn. His mind was unwholesome with brooding over gory achievements and tremendous ambitions. He often uttered absurd boasts and gave himself airs that were incongruous with his minute figure and menial position, and Jock Drew ceased to be the butt of the ship only when I was present; but he never ceased to read and meditate. The laughter of his shipmates drove him more and more into his books and into himself. Later on in the voyage he extended his reading to books on naval architecture and the management of the steam-engine, and at last would spend hours assisting the engineer below. He came to know every part of the machinery and every secret of its construction and management. Indeed, the chief engineer acknowledged that in case of his illness he had an able successor on board. The guns and all the ironwork of the ship drew his attention next, and he came to be respected for his practical knowledge of every part; when anything needed mending, it was he who was ultimately called in to give advice or aid. Slowly he rose to be the real master of the *Daydream*, even though he continued to be laughed at for his heromimic airs and his occasional boasts. He had by his reading and studies made himself essential to every man on board, and his strong will exacted outward respect, if not obedience to him, in return. It was strange to see the revolution in the ship's crew during their voyaging about the archipelago. When I came on board again, I saw that, though they continued a semblance of their old bantering, they had in their hearts begun to bow before the boy of twenty. The very gall of their scorn and of his menial position had driven him into this slow but striking revolt.

And here I saw the result. His boyhood, neglected and beaten, had given the cunning and worldly wisdom and concentration of power that belong in most to late maturity. The strength that had lain dormant for so many centuries in his mother's peasant race had gathered in him like a torrent. The hard conditions of his youth had reined in the wildness and animality which had run riot in his father's debauchery. Hundreds of such masterful natures, finding no sphere in their native locality to give scope to the long-dammed-up powers of their race, waste themselves in chafing against their petty surroundings and die with the reputation of miniature devils. The focussed energy of two long-suppressed races had in this case found its career and scope, and a diabolic conflagration was the consequence in this isolated region of the world. The race of Jock Drew had never before blossomed; now that it had found the fit soil, it had flowered portentously.

The misfortune was that his ill-moulded youth and his favourite reading had left him naked of morality. He was not in this respect much worse than the people whom he misled into war or than those whom he subjugated. He had only more concentrated will and energy and a keener appreciation of the means that would best satisfy his appetite for power. The complete suppression of the desire through thousands of years of his peasant ancestry made its ultimate manifestation on finding freedom of action all the more tremendous. It grew with growing self-confidence; and confidence grew with success. His bearing wholly altered during the wanderings of the *Daydream* before I had abandoned her. He had grown erect and threw his great chest out and held his large head up till he overawed his persecutors. Seeing him only in a sitting position or looking only at his bust one would have guessed him to be of lofty stature. Yet like his father and mother he never rose above five feet in height; and as his face filled up with good fare and the knowledge of his own powers it grew handsome and calm, seldom showing the fierce brute slumbering underneath. His wonderful self-control and reserve held him silent in circumstances where speech or action would have revealed his innate folly or animality, and he learned the power of such reserve, allied with sudden and decisive action, over the wills of others; he saw that it throws an air of mystery round the individuality. So he refrained from action till he had complete control of the circumstances and had gathered such resources into his hands as would astonish his rivals or enemies; silently, unscrupulously, he got to know the cards they held in their hands, whilst he concealed his own under seeming inaction; then with a sudden and unnerving move he threw all his forces upon them and demoralised them. I had watched the method in the little intrigues and conspiracies on shipboard, and I knew when I observed him through the idrovamolan that he was the same Jock Drew, only more developed by his astonishing successes.

He had found his opportunity when the *Daydream* finally anchored in the chief harbour of Broolyi. There was much need of government after the plague; the monarch and his family had fled and finally perished; and the two rivals for the position were almost equally matched. There was prospect of a long civil war. The wiser and stronger counsellors set up a republic, but this was only a feeble stop-gap. The flames of civil war burst out in spite of it.

Jock arrived at this stage of their history, and joined the staff of the competitor for the throne who held the capital and the key of the public treasury. He rapidly became prime adviser in the camp, and as soon as he had attracted confidence in himself and his character he set his method to work. He led an army out to attack the enemy, and completely routed them by the suddenness of his action; he had led one half of his troops straight out to meet the forces opposed to him, but he had sent the others round by a secret path into their rear, and they burst simultaneously upon the enemy. The surprise broke the spirit of the attacked and they fled in rout.

With wily stratagem he incited other officers to rival him, and took care that they went out under disadvantageous conditions. They failed, and their failures led to loud demands for Choktroo, as he came to be called. He now got command of the whole of the resources of the state, and used them for the making of guns and other surprises for the enemy. Meanwhile he allowed the enemy to think that his party was wholly demoralised by defeats, and they crept up towards the walls of the city in their excess of confidence. He knew by his spies in their camp how vainglorious they had become; but he allowed their bravado to rise to the pitch of foolhardiness, and then, his preparations being made, he opened fire upon them, from all sides. So complete was the rout, that the enemy disappeared from the country around and took refuge in distant castles and forts.

His name grew into a power of itself, rousing enthusiasm wherever he appeared and greatly terrifying his opponents. It was then that there began the most striking part of his career. All the brave and able generals who during the civil war had come up from the ranks were completely in his power. He sent them out to master castles or detachments of the enemy, but with such imperfect forces or supplies as would render them inactive. Their individual talents snatched occasional small victories, but as a rule they only prepared for ultimate victory by raising entrenchments and scouring the country around. Whenever he discovered that in any part a general was about to be successful in spite of his disadvantages, he hurried thither and led the troops to victory. If the feebleness of an officer anywhere seemed about to ensure defeat he marched reinforcements to his aid and turned it into success. Whenever he suffered defeat himself, he always managed to represent it as a brilliant success marred by the incompetence of some other general. At last he grew weary of the guerrilla warfare and resolved that it should end. So he withdrew his troops from siege-work and allowed the rebels to gather confidence and to mass again. He sent several generals against them with small armies. Their defeats gave the enemy still greater boldness. They ventured nearer to the capital; and when they were defiling through a pass he appeared on the heights with his guns. The two sections of his army closed the mouths of the pass, and the finest array the rebels had ever shown was shattered. The castles and forts soon surrendered. With one acclaim Choktroo was elected emperor, and the candidate whom he was supposed to be helping vanished from the scene.

His boyish reading had made him as much of an actor as he was by nature an organiser. Before long the whole people of Broolyi were adoring him as a god. Their passion was glory; and in him they had found the incarnation of glory. No piece of work in the state so minute but, if successful, he claimed as his own, even should it have been centuries old. No act of his own but, if unsuccessful, he found a scapegoat for. He was mean enough to steal and eavesdrop in his own household; he was bold enough to outlie the foulest of his minions, to outface the most manifest exposure of his crimes. He even dared to assume the rôle of divinity. He ringed himself round with mystery and ceremonial, and when he did appear in public made the appearance impressive by its display. He knew the effect of silence, and cheapened neither himself nor his words. He organised the state on military lines and made it centre in his personality.

He soon had exhausted the treasury and the resources of the country in the civil war and in his public displays. Nor could he keep up his glory long in inaction, even though it was an inaction of mystery. He must soon go to war beyond the bounds of the island. There he could shine, there he could get all the supplies he needed; but he had to keep up the farce the nation had played for centuries of professing to keep the peace, for he had adopted the title of the Prince of Peace. He had to make it appear that his wars were forced on him by his neighbours, and for this invented an elaborate system of diplomacies which enabled him to pick a quarrel and yet seem to have it thrust upon him.

His first quarry was Aleofane; for it was the wealthiest island in the archipelago. For years he kept up a show of alliance with it, till he had his fire-ships ready, built under his direction on the model of the *Daydream*. He racked his dominion to make guns and all kinds of firearms. When the expedition was complete, he made a demand of Aleofane that had show of reason and yet could not be complied with. It was refused, and his fleet was outside the capital before it could make preparation. He sent some of his ships to the other side of the island to land troops, and as these marched up by land he disembarked the rest under protection of his guns. The first battle decided the war. He dethroned the monarch of Aleofane and annexed the island to his dominions, setting up a viceroy, with a strong force to support him.

He drew new troops from the ranks of the people for service in other islands. He impoverished those nobles who refused to join his court or his staff. He broke the spirit of all who would not adore him, and he drained by taxation the resources of the country.

With still larger armies and larger fleets he swept conquering over the whole archipelago, till every people bowed before him. Those who distinguished themselves in his wars or in his service he elevated to new distinctions and titles. Those who died in his wars he beatified. With great ceremony he would raise all the dead on one of his battle-fields to the rank of sub-divinities, till his heaven was as crowded as his court. He did not obliterate the old religions; but he overshadowed them, and his policy kept subject to him the passion for glory in life and deification after death that lurks in every human bosom. The active and the romantic were strung up to enthusiasm by the magnetism of his name. Most thought it was his personality which set their blood throbbing, but it was only that his deeds and his histrionic power of magnifying them worked on their imaginations. How wild their fervour I could scarcely have realised had I not observed it with my own senses.

He had to keep moving and victoriously moving if his magnetism were not to vanish. When his empire included all the islands in the archipelago but the Isle of Devils in the centre, there was nothing for it but to attempt its conquest. We heard him bluster out his favourite bombastic phrases, learned from his penny romances and biographies. "Heaven is our ally, and who on earth can stand against us? Is it not our mission, the mission of a god, to chase all devils from the earth? Our last conquest shall be hell, and its denizens shall die by fire and sword." Utterances and proclamations like this fired the imaginations of his soldiers, and they would have laid their lives down at the moment for this fire-eater. What he had boasted or threatened before, he had done, or had by astute fiction persuaded his followers that he had done; and what limit was there to his deeds? If he said that he would scale the heavens, they were certain he would do it. The thought fused them into a unity and chased out of their breasts the panic which the mere mention of the central isle produced.

He had not the traditional and hereditary ague-fit to overcome in his blood, yet there was a new sinking of the heart when he thought of his task. He had to reassure himself by wild rhodomontade, as he superintended the building and armament of an enormous fleet and the concentration of the largest army the archipelago had ever seen. He could not pick a diplomatic quarrel with his new victim; yet he must have at least the semblance of a cause in order to put heart into his followers. He announced that he had sent envoys to the Isle of Devils to open intercourse with it, but they were not allowed to approach. Again and again had he tried this pacific measure, but no heed had been given to him. Let vengeance be upon the heads of so churlish and unjust a people! How could such poltroons and men-haters be allowed to cumber the earth?

I watched the great fleet put out from Broolyi with its streamers of smoke. We could have heard the acclamations almost with the unaided ear; they rent the sky when Choktroo went on board his own fire-ship, which was thrice the size of the largest of the others, and thrice more brilliantly caparisoned. He passed with his favourite silent and self-absorbed look on his face through the applauding crowds on to a raised platform in the stern, reserved for him and his staff. Arrived there he paced silently with his chin resting on his folded arms. He knew what an impression of godlikeness this made on the crowd. Small though he was in stature, he doubtless seemed to his followers and the people on the shore to take gigantic proportions.

I was amazed to see so little perturbation amongst the Limanorans. They seemed to watch the whole scene as if it were a comedy. On the fleet steamed, and yet there was perfect calm in the community; only the Lilamo were at their posts on the peak of Lilaroma. The rest were peacefully seated at the idrovamolans or busy with their usual avocations. I knew the destructiveness of the great cannon that Choktroo had prepared, and the distance they would carry. On this point indeed I had been consulted some months before. I knew, too, how this people shrank from every act that would involve the loss of a human life. How were they to repel this great armament without whelming it in the ocean and drowning a large proportion of those in the ships? Thyriel could throw no light on the problem; we were both too young to be taken into the confidence of the wise men or to know their designs. I could do nothing but watch the fleet and then pass to my daily duties.

A night passed, and at dawn we could see the islands of smoke lie black on the horizon; the ships themselves had not appeared. Choktroo evidently knew that it was useless to conceal the expedition or its object from this far-seeing people under the darkness of night. It was too well known throughout the archipelago how penetrative was their gaze. He meant to make his attack by day. Soon the funnels and the masts broke the sky-line. Yet there was not a sound from the storm-cone. The slight wind had fallen; everything favoured the invader. He could see through the translucent air every feature of our island and almost every movement of its inhabitants as soon as we could discern the human beings on board his ships with the naked eye. Were they getting drawn into some gigantic trap? This thought evidently occurred to the leader of the armament, as it occurred to me, for the fleet lessened speed. I could see Choktroo, at a loss what to do, on his poop consulting with his officers, who could help him little. Still the storm-cone stood silent on the mountain-peak.

The bold step had to be taken; the order was given for advance. The smoke again streamed in the rear of the fleet, and I could see the gunners prepare for action and the sailors and soldiers set the boats ready for launching. What had happened to the Lilamo? Were they all asleep? Was the progress of the island at last to be trampled under the feet of this brutal soldier and his forces? The fire-ships were almost within cannon-shot of the shore; there puffed out the preliminary whiff from the side of Choktroo's steamer and the ball fell with a roar into the ocean between. Another five minutes and matters would be past remedy. Yet there was perfect calm among the Limanorans. I controlled my excitement and watched the fleet. Everything was bustle on board, and when I sat down to the idrovamolan all sounds were jubilant and boasting. This Isle of Devils was at last to have her master. This proud isolation was at last to be broken. Such exclamations I could hear from the gunners as they loaded and ran out their guns.

All was silence, for all was ready for the word of command. Choktroo paced his poop in scarce-controllable glee. His thoughts were doubtless stretching out beyond the fog circle to the countries he had left behind him with his boyhood, other worlds for him to conquer. His arms were folded and his eye was turned inward; he knew that the whole expedition was awaiting his nod. Soon he stopped stone-silent and stiff, as if to give the decisive word. I waited the action, but he still stood moveless. I looked over the ship; there was his staff awaiting his beck as if petrified. Every man was at his post, but not a muscle moved; the eyes stared as if they belonged to the dead. My glance took in the other ships; all were as silent and still as the grave. The whole armament seemed turned to stone.

Then there fluttered down upon the vessels human figures that I recognised as of the Lilamo. In a moment a Limanoran pilot stood at the helm of each fire-ship; and as if by nature the whole fleet turned majestically round and made for the shelving beach of a low uninhabited island underneath the horizon. On and on they sped straight for the shore, round whose margin not the least fringe of surf whitened. Through the idrovamolan I could hear the grating keels as they struck the sand and pebbles at full speed. The crash seemed to awaken the crews and the soldiers, who rubbed their eyes as if roused from a dream. Before them the bows of their ships were burrowing themselves in the blown sand of the beach; but already I could see the pilots winging their way through the sky back to Limanora.

There was a silent power in the lilaran which I had not investigated: its power of magnetism. This it could exercise several miles off; but it grew feebler with the distance. In this aspect, then, the lilaran could not be used as a weapon of defence far from the shore of Limanora. If, however, there was a mass of iron or like magnetisable metal in the ship that contained its victims, its power had been discovered to be as great far as near. It was only recently that they had so far developed their personal power of arresting the consciousness by sudden sleep-petrifaction as to be able to exercise it at a distance. This they accomplished by material aids to the magnetic faculty. The sudden flashing of brilliant objects before the eyes and the use of powerful magnets had been found to intensify the somnifactive power of the eye and the magnetic sense. This led them to make experiments with the concentrated power of magnets all brilliant with irelium jewels. The result was that they found the somnifactive power to reside even more in things than in persons. They tried it through the lilaran on Limanorans of the most powerful will at the farthest corner of the island, and found it to be the more effective the more power they concentrated and the more iron or metals of similar quality were near the patient.

This result had been reached about the time they had come to see that the invasion of their island by Choktroo was inevitable without some other than the mere wind-power of the lilaran. Step by step the Lilamo brought their new weapon to perfection; at any moment they could concentrate the forces of Rimla into this faculty of the lilaran. They experimented on Limanorans in boats out at sea, and finally could tabulate the magnetic powers at various distances. This explained to me the flashings I had often seen on the horizon and had taken for an effect of the idrovamolan; but they were too near the surface of the sea for that. This explained the perfect calm with which the Limanorans watched the approach of Choktroo's expedition and the thrilling keenness of the flashes that swept over his fire-ships.

I watched for many days the effect of this great blow upon the nature and fortunes of my old cabin-boy. Over his immediate staff and army he was able to regain his full sway as soon as they recovered from the shock; but his power over the other islanders was completely shaken. Bodies of them launched the boats from the steamers and made off for their own islands before the leaders were aware of their intentions. The moment Choktroo realised the position he turned his still uninjured guns in the direction of the sea and commanded all issue from the beach where his ships were buried. For wholesome example he sank several boats which had almost got out of his reach. Then he set his army to dig canals around one of his fire-ships; but no sooner was she ready for floating than the whole force of the lilaran was turned in her direction; the waves rose and a single night's surf completely undid the labour of days. The ship was as deeply embedded as ever; and her sisters had almost disappeared beneath the sand-dunes. The weight of metal in them shortened the process of burial.

It was clear that nothing could be done to save the expedition or bring its material back to Broolyi. Before many days we saw the soldiers embark somewhat sadly in the boats and find their way across the ocean to the adjacent islands. Piecemeal the whole army retraced its steps to Broolyi.

It was not likely that Choktroo would allow this slur to rest on his fame and eat into his power like rust, for there was clear evidence that his influence over even the Broolyians had greatly suffered. By means of his advertising and his histrionic abilities he had brought them to believe that he was invincible; they now began to feel that he had the same limitations as themselves: he was powerless against the magic of the Isle of Devils. All his wiles were needed to check the spread of panic and distrust. He first of all minimised the defeat in his proclamations, and before many months were over he had come to speak of it as a victory marred by the invincible powers of nature. He had been quick to recognise the similarity of the phenomenon to that we had experienced in the *Daydream* when running the gauntlet of the fog circle, and he sent out party after party to explore the ring of mystery and to come back with tales of its magical powers of inducing sleep. Thus was he soon able to convince the archipelago that the failure of his great expedition was due, not to the inhabitants of the Isle of Devils, but to the forces of nature. He had in his own eye and will great mesmeric power, and by practice was able to develop it into something that he could exercise at pleasure. Then he made public exhibition of his capacity in the various islands. He threw numbers into mesmeric sleep, nor would he or could he release them from its thrall. They became his willing slaves and lived only to please him. A milder form of mesmeric fascination he used in order to rivet his despotism on his armies. He would address sections of them with bombastic self-glorification of his deeds and powers and with flatteries of them and their glorious courage. His personal magnetism worked upon them as they gazed at him, and by the close of his speech he had them enthralled to his will.

It was not long before he was feared as a magician by all who did not mesmerically worship him; and tens of thousands were eager to do the most wicked and shameful deeds, if only he bade them. Yet he dared not shrink from another fall with the inhabitants of the Isle of Devils; else even this preternatural fascination that he exercised might vanish. For years he racked the wealth of the islands and built an enormous fleet of still more powerful fire-ships, and armed it with still more powerful guns. To supply the funds for the expedition, those who were not trained fighting men became slaves, who toiled for him all but their few hours of sleep. Rebellion against this galling and impoverishing despotism was slowly forming in the breasts of the people. Many of them were disappearing mysteriously. They had betaken themselves to unapproachable caverns like Nookoo, and my dreamer of Swoonarie was arming them with his plague-pellets. A few more months and revolution would have broken out against the despot, and he at least would have perished; but the expedition sailed in all its pomp, again deeply impressing the imaginations of the islanders. This time he had taken precautions against the somnifaction of his army by means of a sleep-expelling drug. Every man was furnished with a dose of it to take as soon as they came near the dreaded isle. The Lilamo had been busy for some time, I had seen; but the Limanorans were as unconcerned at this approach as at the former one. What new defence had they? I could see no more preparation than there had been on the previous occasion. The calm which prevailed reassured me; yet soon I grew restless with the fear that this fire-eating cabin-boy with the mystery in his eyes would sully the shores of Limanora with his vulgar ambitions.

My fear became alarm as I saw on the horizon the smoke of the fleet and heard through the idrovamolan the shout of triumph rise from the army when the peak of Lilaroma had burst on their view. I could see each man drink his drug; and I thought that all was lost. Suddenly there came a roar from every ship; and I could see that it accompanied a plume of steam that escaped from the sides. The boiler of every fire-ship had evidently been punctured; and soon I could see that it cost those on board unceasing effort to keep afloat. The soldiers were about to take to the boats when a deeper-mouthed roar numbed every other sound. It was the lilaran at work, and the whole fleet soon vanished over the horizon before its compulsive blast.

The puncturing had been accomplished by submarine action. The Lilamo had sent through the waters their floating batteries, which by nicely adjusted weights lay beneath the surface right on the track of the fleet. The electric cables by which they were secured could shift them hither and thither; and through them immense force could be applied, sending a volley of keen darts up towards whatever iron there was above them. These darts had entered the hulls of the ships just beneath the water-line and made their way into the iron of the engines; one or other told on the boilers and disabled the ships. The electric floats were unseen by the expedition, and the wounding of the fleet was as mysterious and magical as the sleep had been on the previous attempt. Panic seized on every soldier and sailor, and they thanked their gods when the blast of the lilaran hurried them to the shelving beach of a low island and they heard the keels grate on shingle and sand. They scrambled on shore through the surf and found shelter from the wind behind the mounds that covered the former fleet or under their gaunt ribs or sides.

But a new panic overcame them when they discovered that their leader was gone and could nowhere be found. Then it was remembered that in the worst of the storm which blew from Lilaroma a giant bird had swooped down towards his ship and rested for a moment on the platform, where he stood in solitary meditation, and as suddenly soared up again. It was two messengers of the Lilamo who had been sent in one of their bird-shaped airships to make an end of these warlike expeditions. They had alighted beside Choktroo, and by the powerful means they commanded had sent him into a deep sleep in spite of his drug; they tossed him into their airship and in a few moments were high in the azure rushing before the blast of the lilaran. Away they fled with him all day and all night across the belt of fog, and having reached the outer world they let him down still tranced on the shore of a lonely coral islet of the Pacific close to a group inhabited by a savage and warlike tribe. Choktroo had their instincts and ambitions; let him master the savages when he awakened. A wild beast could do no harm amongst wild beasts.

His memory and example haunted the archipelago like an evil dream for generations. Some thought that he had been borne aloft to heaven by a messenger of the gods, and worshipped him as divine; his cruel tyranny and wars goaded on his worshippers to wild fury of injustice and slaughter. Others who were keener of brain and had perceived the earthly character of their leader and his purposes were incited to like ambitions. The romance of his life was glorified in verse and prose by every new school of literature and fired the imaginations of boyhood to warlike exploits. War, piracy, plunder came to be the favourite forms of dishonesty in the archipelago. It was marvellous how much the peaceful and obscure suffered from the romance of this cabin-boy's adventures.

But no man of the islands dared again to approach the Isle of Devils. Even he whom so many of them reputed a god had been unable to break in; and the mishap to the last fleet had been more bewildering than that to the first. Magical powers were possessed by the inhabitants of this island without a doubt; there seemed to be no limit to their transcendence of the order of nature. Evil they were, and the fear of them the Broolyians had to endure in patience. Nor did it grow less from generation to generation. Fancy never let the stories of the defeat of the great Choktroo rest; they gathered to them features more and more terrible to contemplate. A halo of dread and mystery is far more effective as a fence against human intrusion than a halo of sanctity or even divinity. It cows the miscreant and the brute in the human breast. The duties of the Lilamo in repelling the attacks of men would vanish for hundreds of generations.

For Choktroo, his fate was a romantic contrast to that of his fame. Reports were brought in by the idrovamolan or by flying messengers who had ventured over the belt of fog. He was rescued by the neighbouring tribe before he starved on the barren islet, only to be threatened with sacrifice to one of their gods. A missionary who had some influence over the heathen arrived at the moment of sacrifice and saved him. After learning their language he worked his way by intrigues and assassinations and what they thought magic up to the headship of the tribe. When he had made himself secure in his power over them, he built a great fleet of war-canoes, and, after mastering the groups of islands within range and enlisting their warriors and canoes in his service, he set sail southward for some land they knew not of. South and then east the fleet made way, his followers still unalarmed. At last appeared the circle of mystery on the horizon. He gave the word to row forward into it; but, before the command had reached the outermost of the canoes, he was hurled from his platform into the sea, and, as he rose to the surface, he was promptly speared by his own immediate staff. Round swung the heads of the canoes by one simultaneous impulse. Their chief had become a madman to think of entering that belt of mystery; and away they paddled for very life; nor did they cease their frantic efforts till the dark cloud had sunk beneath the horizon.

CHAPTER XV

THE DUOMOVAMOLAN OR COSMOPHONE

THOUGH the Limanorans calmly pursued their regular employments during these attempts at invasion, I had myself felt the uneasy spiritual atmosphere that precedes and presages turmoil. None but the Lilamo were engaged in preparation for defence; yet during all the years every spirit was tense and giving out its energy in sympathy to this section of the people. There was a palpable loss of nervous power in the community, for they knew that by accident some joint in the arrangements might fail to work and all the defence miscarry. Not till the bold disturber of their progress was finally disposed of did the tension or the leakage of nerve-energy cease. To be absorbed in mere war was to them the hades of human society, and to have again sealed up their island from the intrusion of degenerate souls was a happy epoch in their history.

While the whole community quivered with inward jubilance, two momentary dangers threatened it: it might take some time to recover its equilibrium; and its thoughts and interests, narrowed by the necessity of defence against this threat from below, might be long in rising to the true cosmic level. Some exceptional stimulus was needed to raise their lives and aims, some appeal to the spirit, which would set them free from the trammels of earth and all deteriorative excitement. Such liberation had been by no means uncommon in their past, but no occasion for it had occurred since I had entered on my novitiate, except in the case of individuals and families; then I had been too busy with my training or too distant from the household concerned to notice it.

Now it was to be a national purification of the nature, and I was to share in it. Would this be a religious ceremony, a day of humiliation and prayer, such as I had often witnessed in my old home after great national disasters or during plague or famine? I had seen no churches or temples, no signs of religious service, no acts of private worship. I had never heard anyone speak of gods or priests or expiations. Was this at last to be the revelation of the inner shrine, into which I had never been able to penetrate?

I had not long to wait for the solution of my problems. Purposes here moved to conclusions with lightning swiftness, and when one impulse stirred the people, there was needed no heralding to mass them in the desired place. I found myself drawn with my proparents and Thyriel and her household towards a massive building that stood upon a peak far up the slopes of Lilaroma. There was no need of road or steps to it; wings made the wide air the highway. Yet were there great terraces ramparting the sides of the peak, and from the highest seawards there was a marvellous flight of steps which, when the clouds hid Lilaroma, seemed to lead up into heaven. I had often seen the edifice gleam high in the setting sun, yet there were so many temple-like structures on the shoulders and peaks of the giant mountain that it had ceased to excite inquiry. Now as we flew towards it its titanic proportions and jewelled beauty seemed to dominate all the lower world. The building, the most striking that I had ever seen, raised an enormous circular dome of crystal to the sky, and around this were innumerable smaller structures, which elsewhere would have bulked huge to the eye. As we drew nearer, I saw that each crystal cupola, instead of crouching low upon the terrace as I had thought at first, rose upon a lofty and massive tower of great strength. What I had taken for smaller and higher terraces and bastions were the walls of towers and square citadels that seemed built to outlast the wars of Titans. Solid lava they were of extraordinary thickness. There was nothing here of that slenderness and delicacy which had made me compare their other buildings to lace-work. The terraces and flight of steps I had seen from below were but the outer flanks of the layer on layer of foundations laid upon the plateau to save the structure from all but the deepest-sourced tremors.

As we entered the mighty portal, I felt that no storm or earthquake could move it. It seemed a city sculptured out of the solid rock; but, as soon as we were in, the sense of this massiveness vanished and the whole appeared as we looked up fairy-like and gossamer. In any one of the vast temples nothing but a film seemed to separate us from the azure sky. In the smaller towers we gazed up a dark shaft roofed by a circle of sky, and the very stars shone out upon our vision by day, so palpable was the column of darkness above us.

We soon settled in our hanging rests under the great central dome. Around us were thousands hung in mid-air in different attitudes of rest. Yet the building sounded empty, so vast was it and so silent were all. The slightest whisper rang across its great untrammelled spaces with the sharpness of a word beside us. Not a column or beam or ornament broke the harmonious simplicity of the spacious circle from vault to floor, from side to side. Everyone by instinct kept still; for the mere rustle of a wing appalled by its far-reaching effect. We even held our breath lest the sound should break the colossal stillness. To me it seemed for a time frozen silence.

I soon perceived that there was no effort in the self-repression of my neighbours' movements. They were entranced, their heads erect as if catching the echo of some far-off music. To me there was as deep stillness as before. I listened intently, but felt no change except a slight exhilaration; an electric influence was pulsing around. To the electric sense in them some great harmony was appealing. Yet there was more than this; for their eyes were fixed intently on the dome. I looked up and felt awestruck. There on a scale that seemed to match the sky of night I saw enacting the evolution of a universe. In the blue vault a great sphere of glowing vapour was whirling round; from it sprang off huge concentric rings, that one after the other, themselves became whirling spheres ablaze with the intensity of white heat. Step by step a system of earths revolving round a central sun was developed. On one as it cooled we could see life appear and grow varied, then fade away and finally vanish. Before the last tragedy had closed, another had taken up the strain of existence, had run its course upon the globe, and a third had stepped into the ranks of life-bearers. The torch of generation was passed on from orbit to orbit, the central luminary ever dimming its fires, till at last the system wheeled on through darkness, seeming to have no purpose in the universe; but just as the last light flickered and began to vanish from the surface of the sun, out of the darkness seemed to rush another dead universe; through the eternities the two had been approaching nearer and nearer, drawn by their common doom. In a moment they had crashed together and out of the collision came a mist of fire, that soon by whirling in space became again another and a larger sphere of glowing vapour.

How impressive was this reincarnation of worlds! Deeper and deeper the scene sank into the spirit, as the electric thrill which accompanied the earlier steps of the process passed into dim-echoing music, translating all we saw into sounds. A singular feature of their music was that it was never produced in the same room in which it was to be listened to. The machinery and the orchestra drown by their clack and clamour the soft footfalls of harmony that are the only true spirit of music; this was their reason. They had a contrivance in every large room, a huge-mouthed tube by which inflowing music was softened or strengthened and which could if need be raise a whisper into a thunder-peal; in this was a series of keys or stops, by which any sound coming through it could be modulated. One key could make the apparatus soundproof by filling its throat with a pledget of a peculiar fibrous metal they had. One series could wring out the harshness of any sound till it became soft as a much-reverberated echo. A second magnified any sound, however soft, to the required loudness and volume, and the whole was controlled by a minute key-board which could be held in the hand and moved to any part of the room.

In this vast auditorium I could not see where the key-board was managed; but he must have been a poet-musician who manipulated it, so delicately did the volume of sound adapt itself to the mood of those who watched the growth and decay of worlds. Now it swelled with the collision into thunderous harmony; again as a crisis approached in the tragedy it fell to the low music of far-echoing nature-sounds. At times this marvellous opera of universes died away to my hearing; yet my neighbours lay in trance as if still catching harmonies that mastered the soul. I knew nothing but the vague electric thrill that passes through the nature at some great thought. Harmonies as colossal touched their electric sense as those which before had come through their hearing. I longed to follow them into those spheres of melodious being that were still beyond me.

I came afterwards to know the astronomic family that had arranged these wonderful effects upon the soul through the various senses, and I saw the mechanism by which they were contrived. Its simplicity was what struck me most, when I remembered how complicated were the sensuous modes of appeal to the spirit. Out of innumerable sonoscripts and electrographs impressed by the world of stars upon their records, they had selected those that would fit together and raise the souls of the listeners to the sublimity of seeing the infinite cosmos.

This daylight representation of the music of the spheres was but a prelude to a more impressive effect as night fell. By some ingenious mechanism the immense dome was changed; instead of a semi-opaque crystal, on which could be enacted a mimic evolution of systems, there slid into its place an enormous lens, which gathered the sky ten thousand thousand times magnified into the focus of a smaller lens; and upon this was turned another magnifier, which threw upon some light-bearing film in front of us a picture of the sky a million million times the size of what appeared to the unaided eye. Here we saw enacting the infinite tragedy of the cosmos. We could turn aside and view the azure above us strewn with its silver eyes, and the contrast raised the soul to unknown heights of sublimity. In the picture the worlds lived and moved, and the number of those that filled the spaces behind was past all counting; we seemed to have drawn as near to some of the golden centres of systems as lightning flight from the beginning of our earth would have brought us.

And what gave transcendent sublimity to the scene was the strange music that accompanied it. By means of the duomovamolan, a marvellous instrument which reversed the processes of Oolorefa, we heard the harmony that the worlds made in their motions. As they moved across our lens and round and across one another, their movements, enormously magnified, awakened such harmony of sounds as never embodied soul had heard. Their flight and their magnetism affected an irelium film in such a way that the complicated lines and curves and figures produced upon it translated themselves into the music which would have produced these figures in the ooloran. This people had long practised architecture by music in Oolorefa before they thought of attempting the reverse process and converting form and colour into melody;

but once thought of, it was soon accomplished, and the oorolan was the result. The shadowy figures which any melody produced could be made themselves to reproduce it.

From the use of this little instrument it came to be seen that their telescopes could by a little modification and addition be made to tell out in music the scenes they witnessed and recorded. Step by step the astronomic families advanced till at last they reached the wonderful duomovamolan, or cosmophone, which, facing the heavens unbrokenly for generations, stored up the music of the spheres in their various changes. It was this instrument we heard as we gazed into the hitherto unfathomed depths of night. The worlds themselves in their motion played upon it, and through it upon our souls. No human thought could have conceived the marvels of harmony that rang through the great auditorium. We felt as if we had been present at the creation of the universe and our thoughts ranged through infinite space. A dream of the most tremendous kind was being enacted before our waking senses. How poor seemed the whole long history of life upon our earth! Thought was the only element in us akin with infinity or like to last through eternity, the thought that could thus span the abysses between the systems of worlds and comprehend these cosmic melodies still ringing in our ears.

When the treasured-up music of the spheric movements of the past ceased, the night itself, the very sky we were contemplating began to stir fresh harmonies through the lenses of the subsidiary towers. We gazed, and the stars in their silver motions, motions unnoticed by the naked eye, told their tale in sweet harmony. These new symphonies were simpler than the operas of creation and decadence that we had been listening to and, after those titanic effects, seemed almost monotonous, so few complications had they. They soothed the souls lost in the sublimities of infinite space and time and we came gentlier down to the earth on which our life was cast. We still trod on air, our heads were still amongst the stars, but the earth was near us and counted as one of the myriad worlds.

As night swung towards the mid-vault, the music faded and seemed to sound from far valleys. At last it sank into a lullaby, the lullaby of slow-moving constellations. Sleep came on me by unconscious, scarce-heard footfalls, and through its magic portal the universe of dreams appeared. Amongst the stars I flew, never-resting, eager to visit and know all. Here I communed with beings so like me and yet so far above me that I yearned to remain with them; but on I had to speed. Then I rested on a world still dominated by the rudimentary stages of life-energy, and so repulsive were the sights and sounds there that I fled shrieking from it. Next came a sphere so filmy and translucent I scarcely knew how it persisted in tiding the storms of space; yet here, too, was life, life so noble, so immaterial, that I felt ashamed of my body and its sensuous methods of knowledge; so ethereal were the beings there that the common forces of gravitation and attraction seemed to have no power over them; so far below them did I feel myself to be in the process of evolution that I had not the heart to remain. Away into space I winged, till a dark orb drew me towards it, shone on by suns of the most fantastic and ill-omened colours. Here, too, was a manhood not unlike that of earth, yet so sinister that it seemed an orb of devils; the forms were graceful; the faces had a beauty of their own, but shone with such evil meaning that they fascinated like snakes; amongst them I could recognise the great conquerors and monarchs and warriors and colossal criminals whose faces or the representations of whose faces I had seen upon earth; war and pillage were their occupations; cunning and force, hypocrisy and arrogance, were their weapons. In horror I fled from the sight of their internecine passions and into the depths of the night I sped on. So varied was the constitution of the orbs that I approached, so marvellous the range of the kinds of beings inhabiting them, that my mind seemed to sink under the task of imagining them. Everything was in transition, there was no rest for any form of energy in the cosmos. On it must sweep towards a higher transformation or a lower. I saw beings that seemed to be the very acme of creation, so beautiful and noble were they, so purged of all grossness and materiality; yet ever beyond them I found some form they looked up to and yearned to reach. Below me I could see on endless orbs lower and lower kinds of energy receding into darker night, yet ever pressing upwards, step by step. What an eternity of ascent was before them! Looking up, my soul was drawn to some great centre my eyes could not discern; the exhilarant force seemed to give me wings finer and nobler than those of my body. With infinite longing I left my material part behind floating slowly in space. A trance came upon me as I flew upwards with lightning speed and I swooned with the ecstasy of final achievement.

Then I awoke, still lying in my pendulous rest. Morning had broken and the cosmic strains had died away. This dream-flight had been but the climax of the purification. Such music, such electric impulse had been poured about us as we slept, that our spirits could not but accomplish these imaginary voyages through space and time. Without this sublime uplifting into the diviner realms of ether our souls might have fallen back to the mean purposes and ambitions of earth induced by the fears of the invasion and the necessities of its repulse. Now we walked like angels amongst men, a wall of eternity separating us from the gross needs of war and defence. We were again on the upward path that leads towards the highest, and, purified and ennobled, were eager again for the immediate duties of life.

Such purifications of the soul occurred amongst the community as a whole whenever any influence tended to drag it down to a lower plane. Their eyes were drawn downwards; they had again to be turned to the goal of all energy. Victory over such a conqueror as Choktroo had to be given its due insignificant proportion in the results and aims of life, else it might atavise some of their spirits and bring to life ambitions buried for long ages. One night's voyage amongst the infinities was enough to throw human conquests, however great they might seem, into pettiness and oblivion. Thus the evil spirit such events might raise was exorcised, and yet the sensuous power of the music by which the exorcism was achieved was evaded. Mere music, such as I had been accustomed to hear with luxurious passion in my old home, would have let our spirits, after raising them to the heights of ecstasy, fall crashing into the world of commonplace as soon as it ceased; but this cosmophonic harmony permanently soothed and elevated the embruted soul. It implanted thoughts so high that it seemed sacrilege to return to any lower plane.

CHAPTER XVI

THEIR HEAVEN AND THEIR HELL

THE race returned to its daily life, purified and elevated. The danger of intrusion upon their upward struggle had called out unwonted vigour; and the expulsion of the grosser elements and ambitions which threatened to accompany this had resulted in clear gain for their progress. The pace at which they developed greatly quickened; and we felt the pulses of the race beat with the eagerness of prevision. Every new age had accelerated its advance till it seemed to have breasted all possibility, yet as the step grew swifter and swifter the lightning swiftness of a far past seemed to them but a snail's pace. Back the darkness of the future was pushed, and new vistas opened where the black wall of fate had seemed to face them.

One of the most striking proofs of their advancement was to them the rapidly developing love and power of foreseeing. They seemed to live in the future, and that future was an ever-receding circle like the horizon ahead of them, widening and widening as they rose above mere earth necessities. A considerable section of their community was devoted to pioneering for the race, exploring the possibilities of the future; and whenever there was a danger that the energy of development would slacken the imaginations of the youth were fired by a sight of all that they might be.

One of the chief duties of the imaginative pioneers of the race was to prepare a vision of the time to come that would at once appeal to the youthful fancy and fire it to renewed effort; for often in a generation a family or individual would become so absorbed in a special pursuit that the idea of the whole was obscured; and to prevent or obviate this false perspective imaginative prevision was ever and again needed. An easy bird's-eye view of all that the race might become was the best means of attaining this.

Another magnificent edifice was set apart for this purpose, again on the slopes of Lilaroma, not to give outlook, but merely to draw all eyes. It was perhaps the most impressive of the great buildings of Limanora; so vast were its proportions that it seemed almost a city in itself; for in huge subsidiary halls every phase of the possibilities of their civilisation was represented. These were dwarfed by the central hall, which seemed large enough to contain the whole of them. In it all the phases of the future were focussed in what they called the mornalan, or time-telescope. This made the pictures of what they might become live and move before the eyes of the gazers, who as they gazed through one of the many thousand eye-pieces seemed to look upon life itself in its noblest ideals.

My first visit to the great building, which they called Terralona, or mille-narium, was not long after the final repulse of Choktroo. Into the younger and less purified hearts of the community the idea of warlike glory had returned with some force, even though we realised intellectually how shallow and false and retrograde it was. The introduction to what I might call the heaven of the race ought to have come naturally later in life, when we had passed completely out of pupilage and assumed the full duties and privileges of ma-turity; but it seemed necessary to erase from our emotions this atavistic taint that the appearance of Choktroo and his expeditions had begotten in us. The national purification had succeeded in making earthly ambitions seem insig-nificant, but as we settled down again to our pursuits the awe that the cosmo-phone had bred in us grew fainter. The world narrowed into a prison-house, and our daily duties forced a recoil to a wider sphere of ambitions, such as we had seen out in the archipelago in the masterful wars so lately witnessed. It was time, indeed, that some of us were brought into the presence of the immediate ideals of the race towards which they were as a whole struggling.

We were now to enter upon a new epoch of our existence and to know the wider heaven in which our own special pursuits took their orbit. We were thereafter to drink at the purer fountains of inspiration, to know the rewards of all our struggles, the possibilities that lay within the reach of a measurable number of years.

Up through the morning air we flew, exhilarate with the wine of healthy life, joyous in anticipation. My proparents were with us, and explained in answer to our inquiries the character of the building we were to visit. It ab-sorbed the best energies of some of the most imaginative and artistic families of the island. They were ever forging ahead of their own work. Like life, their art never rested. What they imagined today grew familiar or even tame tomorrow. The consequence was that the inside of the edifice was never two days alike, and the most frequent visitor never found it monotonous. There was no such thing as a fixed paradise for any race; it varied, it must vary, with every development or retrogression of its members. Heaven was merely the brightest ideal that a people could imagine for itself; and the heaven of a highly progressive race was rapidly antiquated, and in the long flight of ages came to neighbour their hell. It is like climbing a mountain; the shining peak we long to attain as we start from the plains at dawn is found to be but a lower ridge of plateau which conceals the gleam of higher snows; these again when reached are found to be overtopped by still higher peaks. The difference is that in truly advancing human life the process seems unending. There is no spiritual ambition, no ideal, no creed, no ethical code, but when realised in practice is found to reveal something higher still to long for and realise. A stationary heaven means a stagnant civilisation.

Onwards we sped as we discussed or listened, ever nearer to the vast pile of buildings that was our goal. We who had never been inside or known its purpose tingled with expectation. Even our elders, we could see, were eager and alert with anticipated pleasure. They were sure to see some new and striking features in the fore-picture.

It was with great awe that we found ourselves within Terralona; for we had entered the great central hall at once, without any attempt to study the separate sections of the experiments in progress depicted in the subsidiary halls. It was more impressive in its proportions and size than any I had yet seen, and was dimly lit with that strange, diffusive, centreless light of which they had command. In no one part was the light brightest, so that it was impossible to say whence it came or how it was produced. The roof rose so high and the walls were so far apart that we found flight easy inside; and there were platforms all round for leaping into the air and taking flight. Along the farther wall we could see many Limanorans hovering, like butterflies that alight for a moment and then flit to another flower. There were also rising to the roof hundreds of tiers of different kinds of rests.

What these were for I could not conjecture, unless they were placed for easy flight. At length we reached that end of the building and saw that every rest was placed so as to bring the eyes level with a large lens set in the wall. We each mounted into one of them, and I set my face against the smooth transparency. The sight that met me I cannot even at this distance describe. There seemed to be miles and miles of space beyond filled with a representation of an island which I soon recognised as Limanora; but it seemed to be afloat in the azure of the sky, and from it a pathway of silken threads of light led upwards to the stars, which floated within neighbourly distance of it. Busy travellers sped up and down the climbing flightway with a swiftness that almost obscured their form and size. It was only when they rested at either goal that I could see their features or study their nature. They were Limanorans, yet completely transformed. The tissue of their bodies seemed like light itself, so transparent and filmy was it. Their wings seemed a part of themselves, and their flight was as easy as a swallow's. They moved through the air like shreds of sunlight or animated snowflakes, with power to fly up or down, often at lightning speed. In their faces were none of the deep shadows of baffled thought or blind emotion, but they seemed supremely happy in their enfranchisement from earth. Yet they were but human, only a few steps removed from the humanity I saw around me. They had still upon their faces the look of pity so frequent amongst the Limanorans when they gazed out on the men and life of other lands; but it was only when they gazed or travelled downwards that this took the place of the serene calm which marked them out as sages. At times an agitation marked their gait as they set out on the gauzy pathway of the stars. I could feel that there was still a world beyond that which they had reached, and that towards this they must progress with eager thought and effort.

It was the inhabitants of other stars that they were trying to emulate or gain as friends. They could live in the intervening ether and found movement through it rapid as thought. Their highest wishes, the subjects of their imagination, encountered little obstacle or friction in the accomplishment. They were evidently nearer omnipotence over the forces around them than they had ever been. Their bodies were so much dematerialised that they were not far from the state and texture of their souls. Thought was not clogged with an earthy matter so different from itself as to hold it down till freed by death. Yet I could see that there were limits to their actions. The forces of other worlds and the conditions of interstellar space narrowed and checked their activity. They could not yet create; they could only transform what already existed, for there I saw one pair, moulding a creature perfect according to their ideals and trying to breathe life into it, and not yet could they know the centre of all being. The path was still upwards and onwards.

Their activity was no longer restricted to the immediate confines of the earth. Beyond and above it they soared till it became an insignificant speck of light in the azure, busily exploring the universes that strewed infinity and finding out the higher and ever higher life that inhabited them. I could see them marking on their itineraries of the sky the orbs to be avoided for their degenerate or degraded forms of life or energy. Every grade of existence was found and indicated by brighter light or deeper shadow. They loved to linger over those orbs whose dwellers were but a step above them, watching their actions and thoughts and learning their higher ambitions. At a distance they hovered over the worlds of beings many stages beyond them in the evolution of energy, afraid lest they might be repulsed as degenerate. As they watched, their longing study helped them to rise more rapidly in the scale of being, and back they would come to Limanora with new thoughts and methods and set themselves thus equipped to work out with increasing pace their own evolution.

This vast widening of their horizon was evidently an era in their history, it added such lightning swiftness to their rise in the scale of existence, it gave them such power of fulfilling whatever they designed or even imagined. Nobler and nobler ideals remained to be discovered in every corner of the cosmos. They had only to sail out and investigate, and then, returning with higher thoughts and ways of life, mould their being to them. And to die— what was it now but to slough off a trammelling form? Death was to them an ecstasy. Every moment of advance was to them a death, a death of the old, a realisation of the nobler and higher.

Such was the representation I watched through my optic glass; for my proparents interpreted what I saw, and showed me the spiritual meaning of this cosmorama of the future. The details of the living picture I had not time to mark; nor were my guardians willing that these should distract my attention from the central ideas; they emphasised the guiding principles of the new life we might perhaps soon lead, and the glory of it overcame my earth-born ambitions. What a pitiful figure did Choktroo and his armies and fleets seem in comparison with such a life! All the great conquerors and heroes of earth were pigmies seen in a light like this, slaves to brute longings and ambitions. I grew ashamed of ever having harboured anything but contempt for even the greatest career of mortal upon earth.

Nor yet were we done with our cure. The imaginative artists had filled another and complementary edifice with living pictures of all that by means of horror could drive us forward on the path of progress. It was called Ciralaison, or the museum of terrors. I had often heard of it and had imagined it as a place of unending torture, a Limanoran and rationalised version of the hell of Christendom, and looked forward with much loathing and curiosity to the sight of it. We were taught that this was no imaginary place, but the too real result of all retrogression and encouragement of atavism, and that there was nothing supernatural in it, but that it was the natural outcome of all lapses from the existing ethical path of advance. It was the contrivance of nature herself to prevent degeneration.

As I had read Dante's *Inferno*, it was easy for me to map out the features of Ciralaison. I knew the vices and faults they most shrank from, and these would define their own natural punishments. As we winged our way towards the sombre edifice, perched, strangely enough, upon one of the most prominent spurs of Lilaroma that beetled over the sea, I let my mind wander over what was soon to meet my eyes; pictured a place of intense woe, full of the horrors of a mediæval place of torture: I could almost imagine I heard the weeping and wailing and gnashing of teeth.

We entered the gloomy porch and passed into the central hall; it was almost the exact counterpart of Terralona, except that there was no brilliant suggestion of all that was beautiful and noble. There was the same dim suffusion of light, the same lofty wall of lenses with rests, the same series of flight platforms round the other walls. With some precipitancy I made for one of the optic rounds in the wall, and the first sight I saw struck me as the most commonplace and familiar. It was a representation of one of the foul lanes of our Western cities. There were the gutter children, the reeling drunkards issuing from the gin palaces, the cursing drabs behind them, the tatters, the filth, the dilapidated buildings. It was but an unending series of instantaneous photographs moving with great speed under stereoscopic glasses, whilst the sounds accompanying the scene, having impressed themselves similarly on long strips of irelium, were in one of their sound machines reproducing themselves. It was indeed the commonest and most repulsive of sights in the east end of any of our large towns. What astonished me was that it should have been taken from European life; and yet, when I gazed more attentively at it and put the sound-magnifier to my ears, I knew that it was not European. The words spoken were in a language I did not know, and the rags of the men and women were the rags of a national costume I did not recognise.

I shifted my rest and lens, and I saw a rustic village, such as I had known in my boyhood, with the toilers busy at their work. At a distance it was a happy scene; for the men and women were absorbed in occupation and seemed to have forgotten the evils of mankind. They were much in the open air, which was bright with the colours of the sunlight; and the children's voices sounded merry at play or humming like bees from the window of the school-house. It was a picture such as city poets had often painted as ideal and primitive happiness, yet some contrivance seemed to analyse it all for my mind and reveal to me that it was even more repulsive than that of the foul city lane. Not to my hearing or my eyes did this come; but to my magnetic sense, ill-developed though it was. I felt a deadly stupor over the whole pressing out the higher life of every rustic. Not the diseases which often overtook them unprovided, not the poverty leaving no outlook for their old age except reluctant and hated charity, not the constant slavery of toil, or the meagre assuagement of its woes by a weekly booze in the tavern, weighed upon my spirit and made me sad to look at the scene. It was the stagnant spiritual level on which they and their children to the thousandth generation must live, without power of perceiving the nobleness that was above them and around them, without the chance of ever developing the spiritual energy that was in them, without one approach to the line of infinite progress going on throughout the universe. To stand still or recede was the true inferno of the Limanorans.

Again I changed my optic glass and a greater sadness came to me through my magnetic sense. I saw men and women such as I used to envy for their respectable life, their serene comfort, and their sure grasp of both worlds trooping into buildings for religious worship. They bowed and sang, they genuflected and prayed, they raised their eyes to the ceiling, they groaned and professed to pity themselves as miserable sinners; yet I could feel they had an inner consciousness that these performances were superfluous on their part, so comfortably worldly, so charitably godly were they. As they rose to leave the temple, they seemed to purr and pat their sleek stomachs in supreme self-content. Yet through the magnetic magnifier I knew that they were in a lower circle of the inferno than the rustic slaves. Their past stood out through many generations of ancestors exactly the same as their present or better. Never a chance had they of progressing; they thought they had reached perfection as far as earthly conditions would allow. They prayed that they might be made better; but that was only as they prayed that their sins might be forgiven when they were certain that they had committed none, or as they prayed for guidance in their daily duties when they knew that no one could manage them better than they. Stagnancy was written on every feature of their faces and of their lives, fatty degeneration of every faculty and organ necessary to development. Their ethics, their religion, their business, their habits of life had all reached a stage that made criticism superfluous and that knew no higher outlook.

The next scene that came through the lens was one of the most envied of Christendom. Men and women of the highest birth and best breeding were moving to and fro in brilliantly lit and decorated rooms, in the largest of which the dance was proceeding. In another room a luxurious supper was laid, varied and fine enough to tempt the eye and palate of the most fastidious gourmand. Voluptuous music and scents filled the air; witty conversation was stirring even the most languid faces to smiles. What could be more perfect on earth than the enjoyment of such a scene? Yet this was a deeper slough of hell than any I had yet viewed. The whole of life was concentrated in the senses, the least progressive of all the organs of human nature, the organs soonest sated with what they desire. And what a horror of life was revealed beneath all this brilliancy! A crescendo of such pleasures was needed to drive off ennui; and such a crescendo was not to be found. The young still lived in hopeful mirage. The middle-aged were sick of it all. The old sneered cynically over everything or babbled the senility of second childhood. The vulgar consequences of vice or the entanglements of crime, the surfeit of pleasure or the tedium of life kept most of them within one step of suicide. Their course was ever downwards. I pitied these magnificent voluptuaries, in all their ephemeral pursuits and aims. The brilliancy was only an attempt to hide the ghastly grinning of death and corruption in the reality underneath.

Another change of the point of view, and the world of fame revealed itself in its gilded horrors. I watched the struggling poet trampled beneath the foot of luxury and contempt, happy if only he died early in the hateful wrestle for glory. I saw the drowning agonies of the novices in the sea of literature, appealing in vain for help to the wealthy as they passed in barges lulled by the rich music of flattery; here and there a frantic swimmer clutched at help, and out again he was thrust into the depths by the minions of literary fame. How little the rejected knew of the reality that they strove after! I looked into the hearts of the famous and saw corrupt masses of jealousy and hate, or hollow shells echoing the misery of life. The most appalling sight was, not the failures in art and learning, science and commerce, but the successes. Behind a mask of smiling prosperity and conventional enjoyment of the world there was but a handful of dust that bore the weary load of existence in agony.

Generation after generation came and passed through this torturing fire, knowing not why they bore the pangs for threescore years and ten, or whither they were borne. They seemed to improve, but only sank deeper into the original barbarism. Here and there they picked out a name of one long dead and worshipped it; but the shrine was empty; it was only a name, and not the personality for which it had once stood. Behind I could hear the spirit wailing and cursing its fate and the falsehood and hypocrisy of his adorers. He knew the hollowness and pretence of the whole performance; he knew that the name had become a weapon for offending and maiming those who in their innocence were struggling for fame, as he had done, in vain.

The deepest circle of hell was still to meet my eyes. I thought, as I was guided to it, that it must be that of murderers and furious criminals. My amazement grew, as I looked into the lens and saw that the actors, or I should more truly say the sufferers, were the great of the earth, the monarchs and statesmen and warriors, who drew all men's eyes to them as the masters of life. A movement on the part of my guide touched some key, and a strange gleam of unearthly light threw out into relief the hidden mechanism of their existence. Round everyone was a network of threads like a spider's web, and the controlling ends of the threads led up obscurely into the hands of a crowd of miscreants, who lay out of sight of the applauding mobs; when a limb or a lip or an eye seemed to move of its own accord to the music of huzzas, it was jerked by a thread in the control of some scowling villain who worked the movement for his own murderous purpose. These gorgeous figures were but puppets playing a marionette-play upon the stage of life. One or two of the strongest seemed instinct with the breath of originality, but a still stronger light revealed adamantine chains woven around them, and attached to these one master-chain which disappeared into infinity; they were in the spider-web of fate. Still more awful was the sight of their own hearts; each had a crimson-taloned vulture gnawing the vitals, and each saw every detail of the agonising sight; nor could he move to the right or left except to clutch at the bared heart of his rival and torture him. Who could imagine hell more appalling than this? Yet up the giddy approach to the seats of the mighty climbed eager competitors for any place in this torture-chamber death or defeat might empty.

Then behind all stretched the curtain of infinity; and as it rose the ranks of worlds and universes appeared, dwarfing into pettiness the sights that had racked my eyes. Life and the ideals of life rose higher and higher up through the regimented worlds, and the little inferno I had watched became a microscopic speck on the round of existence. The shadow of their heaven fell over their heads. The agony I had seen became but an atom in infinity.

CHAPTER XVII

MY EDUCATION CONTINUED

THE gaze into the probabilities of the future and into the realities of the past ejected from my system whatever of dangerous admiration I might have felt for the career of such a military adventurer as Choktroo. In spite of my self-control and rapidly developing reasoning faculty, there lurked in me the same longing for power that had been so evident in my cabin-boy. Though he had fallen so wretchedly there was a romance about his career which appealed to something deep-seated in my spirit. I knew what a hypocrite and scoundrel he had become in order to make his success, yet the success seemed to condone his offences against the progress of humanity. The lust of rule that lies in the hearts of all men had not yet been eradicated from mine. I had advanced so far as to be ashamed of it; and I tried to reason it down or to conceal even from myself the fact of its existence; but my guardians knew that it was there, and they took the necessary precautions against its growth. Thus did I pass with the whole people through the national purification ending with a glimpse of their heaven and their hell.

And now I was ready to re-enter on my process of education. The more spiritual portions of my nature had been remoulded or confirmed to follow in the true path of Limanoran development. The last purificatory process had revealed in me the virtuous or progressive balance that ensured success in the island. The minds of my guardians were now at rest with regard to my spiritual future, and I was on the fair way to become one of the community.

Still my physical constitution lagged far behind the race. Nor had I any hope of ever making up this lost time, so much had the education of generations and the accumulations of heredity done for them. My senses were but feebly developed compared with those of the Limanorans; and though they gave sensuous faculties a far lower place than the most advanced thinkers I had ever known of in Europe, they by no means neglected them, but considered them important instruments of progress in the material conditions of their life.

My proparents thought it necessary that I should be brought in the development of my sensuous perceptions nearer to their own level, now that my love of reason was so strong as to preclude the possibility of being overwhelmed by sensuous energy. They began with the most intellectual of the senses, the eyesight, and by the help of magnetism, hypnotic suggestion, and constant practice under their tuition, they soon brought me to see farther afield and more keenly into the structure of things around me than I had in Europe thought it possible for the human eye to accomplish. I could perceive with the naked eye stars that I had been able to see before only through the telescope. I began to note the changes of tissue underneath the skull of my neighbours when any great thought or emotion stirred in them, and could use their wonderful instruments of far and near research with appreciation. Through these instruments faint stars appeared moons, and the nearer planets revealed many of the secrets of their surface; whilst the elements resolved themselves into even simpler constituents. What still lay beyond I could not imagine, yet there were manifestly worlds, intensive and extensive, still to be explored beyond the limits of these aids to sight.

In the life of an individual I could not expect to approach the development of optic faculty attained by this people. This impressed itself more deeply upon me when my guardians tried to evolve in me the magnetic power of eye which every Limanoran had by nature. When any one of them turned his full glance upon me, it was like encountering the direct beams of the sun; I had to drop my eyelids in self-defence. It was this that gave them such hypnotic power over Choktroo and his followers. Their eye was an active exponent of the soul within as well as a passive recipient of messages from the world without, and could concentrate into its glance the energy of their powerful wills. Any one of these Limanorans amongst the feebler-eyed millions of the rest of the world would have proved himself a master-spirit. He would, with his unhesitating will and the magnetism of his eye, have kept masses of men in check and moulded them into a unity, and the great commanders of history would have blenched before his gaze.

From the first I had felt uneasy under the full glance of my island friends, in spite of its kindliness and benevolence. Before I left England, I had been supposed to have the mesmeric faculty to an exceptional degree. Now I found it pale before those marvellous Limanoran eyes, and all the training and physical aid my proparents could give me in this direction, though they added greatly to my energy of will and eye, only brought out my hopeless inferiority. I was able at last to bear their glances with ease, and even to raise my eyes to theirs for a few seconds; but I ceased to hope for the attainment of their ocular command or their magnetic power.

Even their passive electric sense was far beyond my possibility in many of its ramifications. For years I had wondered why their couriers into far regions of the sky could without any chart or landmarks find their way back to their island home with such ease. It could not be by means of vision; for they often went flying above the clouds to the antipodes; nor could it be by smell; for that sense was not nearly so much developed as the others. In some of my now more distant flights with Thyriel I discovered that they homed by the electric sense. It had become keen in the measurements of amounts of electricity; and every locality had its own electric possibilities, not to speak of a certain peculiar quality in its electricity which differentiated it from all others. One of the most important branches of their education was the magnetography of the earth and sky. Although I never got beyond a vague perception of differences in the degrees of electricity, it was of some use to me in my flights to have learned the elements of this great descriptive science. I could tell with fair accuracy how high I was above the earth and whether I was drifting away from Limanora or towards it; for the amount of electricity in any region varied within certain definite limits and the conditions governing it were constant for long periods of time; these were, roughly, the metals beneath the surface of the earth, the differences in temperature of the strata of air above, the evaporation and chemical changes on the earth below, and the periodicity of the influence of the sun and the stars. Their electric charts of the sky and air were ever in process of correction, but so slightly and gradually in each region that it was only after long periods that the Limanoran couriers had to revise their magnetographic knowledge; indeed it was their reports after long flights which generally led to the minute corrections of their charts. It was the work of a few minutes only to learn the new modifications, for their charts were exact miniature models of that which they were intended to represent; the learner had only to touch a spring and by the inner mechanism of the globe out would ray to each point of it the electricities that in degree and quality belonged to the region indicated; the member of the electric family who guided him would explain the changes that had occurred since he last consulted the instrument, and his own electric sense would tell him the rest.

Nor was this magnetographic training useful merely for the purpose of pilotage through the heavenly vault. It enabled any courier to seek the region where he would most easily recharge the little engines which he bore with him under his arms to aid in his wing journey. Although he could prevent the complete exhaustion of these power auxiliaries by supplying them with some of the magnetism in his own body, it was only in emergencies that he did this; for his own system needed electric recuperation as well. Whenever this was required, he made for some region of the air that he knew to be highly electric; and there he floated, whilst with his receptive sense he drew in new stores for his own system and for his little armpit engines. Then he went on his way rejoicing, exhilarated by his new energy. One of the purposes of their frequent flight into atmospheric spheres other than their own was to drink in new magnetism from one of the great sky fountains.

When a Limanoran returned from an aërial flight there was renewed life in him. His eyes glowed with a heightened radiancy; I could see a soft light play about them in the dark, and this, if needed, he could make even piercing in its brilliancy. He required no light to guide him in the deepest night. His electric sense gathered in from the atmosphere the scattered radiance that was hidden from my sight; and from his eyes he could emit this electricity in the form of light. For me, who, under all their training, was never able to develop such power over the unseen forces of the air, the eyes of Thyriel were a guide in our flight through the night sky; and by day so gentle a brilliance played around them it was little wonder they fascinated and drew me ever to them. After experiencing their power, I was not surprised at the hypnotic influence Limanoran eyes had had over the leaders of the hostile expedition.

It did not astonish me to find that by means of their electric energy they could move vast masses which no mere muscular force could have touched. I had a constitution that seemed to be physically far stronger than Thyriel's; yet, if she had time to reinforce her store of magnetism, she could accomplish feats of strength I could not approach. In her fragile system there seemed to reside a giant's energy; but this was only at times, and especially after she had made some long journey into the regions of the air. The tissues and fibres of her body seemed to grow tenfold stronger when the new electric energy tingled along her nerves. In only the faintest way was I ever able to develop my electric-receptive sense so far as to realise what a new store meant to their physical powers.

Yet my guardians set themselves to bring out my latent electric sense or firla. After much practice and the application of many stimuli I began to feel impulses more keenly even when they came from a distance: the back of my neck grew more and more sensitive, so that I would wheel round instinctively when anyone looked at me from behind. There was almost hope that I should, after many years' practice, come to distinguish the different kinds of emotion with which anyone, though unseen, might look at me; and I could produce by a concentration of will-force in the eyes a certain luminosity, noticeable when I stood in deep darkness.

My power of sight was greatly strengthened by this new electric faculty that the eyes acquired. I began to raise my eyelids before the penetrative glance of a Limanoran, or even the full majesty of the sun; but never could I hope to reach their analytic power of vision. Their senses were distinguished from those of the rest of mankind by intellectuality, and were, I thought, not merely the observers and reporters of the mind, but its outlying parts or functions. The eye especially seemed to do what through its means reason and experiment might have done. At a glance a Limanoran would tell to an inch the distance of any object and was not far wrong in his estimate of the space between the earth and any star when its rays reached his eye. He could distinguish one ray from another by its colour or colour-constituents and by its magnetic affinities. What he had learned in the use of the inamar or spectroscope in the lava wells and in the fusion of metals in Rimla had come to be a visual instinct. With scarcely a minute's hesitation he would tell the predominant elements in any one of the heavenly bodies. Doubtless the firla had something to do with this analytic power. One of their imaginative pioneering books held out the by no means remote possibility of catching symptoms of the life which, they knew well, filled the dim worlds above.

Their auditory powers had been far less developed than their visual, and gave but faint hope of transcending interstellar space, and my training soon brought me within easy distance of their hearing capacity. The range of this faculty both at its upper and its lower limit had been considerably extended. Sounds dangerous on account of their loudness to the inner mechanism of ordinary ears were by means partly of strengthening the protective cartilages and partly of a trevamolan or graduated modifier of sound, which they constantly wore, made harmless and even gentle and enjoyable. Those that were too faint to reach any human ear became audible to me after some training in the use of their vamolans or makro-mikrakousts. So greatly had these been improved along with the power of hearing that they could discriminate the different noises of microscopic life. These vamolans in their application of electricity to hearing could make the buzzing of an insect sound like the roar of thunder. By modifications of them any of the sounds heard through them could be recorded forever.

Thus had been formed a library and museum of the phonology of animal life. They had been able to study the records of sounds emitted by the various species of animals and had come to know the meaning of each sound before they had driven all but microscopic life from the island; thus they had learned by means of the recording vamolans the language of animals. The birds of the air I have seen follow the cries of Thyriel, gathering around her in clouds, as she flew, until by a sudden change of tone she would scatter the fluttering masses to the four winds. Even the fish of the sea would rise and leap above the waves to her notes; ferocious, devouring monsters would leave their prey and follow gently in her train. Most of this power over the undeveloped creation was due to the record and study of their cries; but not all. The magnetism of her personality had a strange effect upon the wildest birds of prey: it seemed to bear with it tacitly the lesson of Limanoran civilisation that no life was to be destroyed by those who meant to make the best of life; there was a gentle, merciful spirit in the glow of the eyes. I have seen her take a wounded bird to her bosom as she flew, and, putting new life into it by the stroke of her fingers, set it free, strong and happy.

There was a life-giving power in the tips of Limanoran fingers that puzzled me at first. Why the mere touch should so soothe the lower creation that the agony of their wounds would soon vanish and their cries cease bewildered me for a time. My own pains rapidly disappeared under the touch of my proparents. I afterwards knew that part of the active magnetism of their system came through their fingers and they helped me to develop this channel of influence in myself. I could at last by passing my fingers over Thyriel's hair or face relieve any tension of her nerves which might have produced pain; nay, I could hear her hair crackle under my touch when I had charged my system with much electricity. Once or twice I was able to draw a wounded bird to me, and change by my stroke on the feathers its cries of pain into low notes of content; but I could never draw the winged creation to me in clouds as Thyriel did.

It was all the more surprising to me that they fenced off animal life from their island. What might they not have done with such powers over the lower creation? When I put my question into words, the answer was unhesitating and unanswerable. All failures in development had to be thrust from the path of progress; they could do nothing but clog it. If the Limanorans had little hesitation in the case of their own flesh and blood, they had still less when they had to deal with animals. It was quite true that many of the more highly developed of the servants of man had nobler natures than most of their masters, deeper loyalty, greater sincerity, truer and more lasting courage; much might and did come from companionship with their primitive and guilt-proof natures; but the fact that when associated with man they were destined to serve, made such good impracticable and rather brought out the mean and brutal tyranny of man than helped to implant in his nature their own virtues. Even with such noble qualities as they had it was impossible for them to overleap the many ages their systems had lagged behind in other respects, the open offensiveness of their grosser animal appetites and needs, their lack of that great instrument and teacher of the brain, a fully developed hand, and the inability to foresee beyond a few hours, days, or months. Nor could any human process prolong their period of life and postpone their day of dissolution. It was not a good thing for these pioneers of the human race to see the approach of death and its agonies in a being that could not assuage or postpone it. Still less beneficial was it to touch the carcases and reduce them to harmless atoms. The presence of animals meant the daily obtrusion of offensive sights that would either shock or degrade their natures. All that animals could do for them was already done by their science or their machinery. Nothing that had fallen so far behind in the race of life was worth the trouble of missionaryism; for the energy that was in it had a better chance of rising swiftly in the scale of existence by dissolution and entrance into some other form.

None the less had they studied the language of animals when they had had the opportunity. It belonged to the orchestration of the world, and all the sounds of nature were of interest to them. They were in the habit of visualising what they heard by a refined and complicated instrument which they called a thinamar, and had long been able to translate into its appropriate form and colour every sound, inarticulate as well as articulate. Through long use of this instrument the tones of nature bore with them something that appealed to their eye. I never grew expert enough in its use to make the visualisation of sound an instinct; still less could I reverse the process. A modification of their thinamar had enabled them to translate sights into the symbols of sound, and by skill in using it they had come to attach certain notes to certain sights. Thus a noble landscape would appeal to their imagination not only through the eye, but in the form of music, and they spoke of hearing the beauty of a star or a flower. A section of this instrument did for complicated sounds what the spectroscope, or inamar as they called it, did for light. Every substance, every individual living thing, had its natural and peculiar note; and the linamar analysed what seemed to me the simplest sound into its constituent primary notes, each of which revealed its source. Aided by their mikrakousts and makrakousts, it enabled the Limanorans to analyse the chemical elements of any object, whether at a great distance from them or too minute to appeal to their senses.

Their makrakousts were instruments which by means of electric currents and magnetism could make a beam of light transmit any sound to its source, or make the ear gather in the same way whatsoever sounds were filling the air at any point on its course. I knew when I saw a steady flash in any direction that the sound of some point was getting tapped by one of these instruments. Each had an apparatus for laying and keeping fixed its luminous telegraph-wire along which it received and transmitted. An application of this in the gossip-telegraph enabled them to listen to the comedy of life as it went on in any one of the adjacent islands of the archipelago. Their mikrakousts used the same means for gathering the faint sounds which echoed from the clouds or through the upper regions of the atmosphere and turning them into loud notes, which might be recorded, analysed, and interpreted. Their magnifying power was quite equal to that of the clirolan. Faint buzzings of insects at vast distances could be collected and made as loud as thunder. It was even applied to cosmic sounds that impinged on the atmospheric envelope of the earth. Mikrakoustic balloons rose into the upper air, and after gathering whatever faint sounds wandered thither from outside the world, were drawn back again to divulge their secrets; eavesdroppers of the cosmos they were, and perchance in some future age they would enable the Limanoran to listen to voices from other worlds or even to communicate with the dwellers there. A more immediate and practical advantage of these instruments was found in medicine. They told in clear accents the unexpected or dangerous changes in the tissues or organs of any man's system. They were used in the weekly medical inspection, which every member of the commonwealth underwent. When the keen eye, aided by the camera-microscope, could detect nothing abnormal in the body, the mikrakoust would tell the examiner's ear of some obstruction or deleterious change; he knew the normal sounds of healthy action in every part when they were magnified thousands of times by this instrument, and every departure from them readily caught the ear. All the citizens were trained to use it as an aid in diagnosis, so that they might be able to locate in the system any beginning of disease. It was part of the training of my ear to use the mikrakoust and to interpret its physiological revelations.

But these instruments were getting antiquated by the rapid development of the electric sense that could, by the aid of their various electro-magnifiers and analysers, gather in cosmic news from distances which the sense of hearing and its aids would count infinite. Magnetic kites and balloons rose to the uttermost fringe of our atmosphere, whither common terrestrial influences could reach only in such faint waves as to be neutralised; there they gathered the electric impressions and impulses coming from other planets and even other systems. On them were recorded the varying strengths of the waves and their direction. From these records the astronomical families could tell what was happening of a cosmic character in universes far out of the reach of even their lavidrolans or camera-telescopes—perturbations in the atmospheres of great unseen suns, collisions between worlds that circled round them, births of new universes from these lost systems, periodic disturbances of the routine revolutions through the approach of some meteoric wanderer, the settlement of life on worlds grown ripe for it, and the death of outworn stars. For many generations had they kept and classified these reports of cosmic history and were beginning to recognise a wide periodicity in many of them and to draw conclusions as to the path of our universe through infinite space. It seemed to them that there was some point far distant in the cosmos, round which our sun and its satellites with innumerable other systems of stars revolved, and that this point, with its satellites, had its own independent movement. Age by age, with the aid of their idrolans or electric telescopes, and other electric instruments, they felt that they were getting nearer and nearer to the centre of this interwoven epicycloidal movement and were almost convinced that it did not proceed infinitely, but that there was some ultimate centre which had no movement round another. Their instincts told them that this was the divine consciousness towards which all things rose in the scale of being. They never remitted their ardour and diligence in the development of their electric sense and of the instruments that aided it to become a receiver of cosmic news and a recorder of cosmic history, for they were confident that this was one of the tracks that led up through the intricacy of the cosmos to God.

One of my greatest regrets was that my electric sense could not follow the footsteps of these pioneers in the infinite; it had but a dim consciousness of the reports of their instruments, and train it as eagerly and diligently as I would, it lagged behind my power of vision and even my sense of hearing. On this account I preferred to learn the results of their researches through these two senses, for the electric reports were carefully translated into appeals to the eye and the ear. I could see their wonderful discoveries in the unknown, as they worked them into picture and mechanism, and I could listen from day to day to the orchestration of their newly discovered spaces and movements. What seemed at the moment an intolerable discord chimed in with the notes which preceded or followed and formed marvellous harmony. Not the least part of my education lay in this cosmic stimulus to my imagination. Out of my terrestrial conditions and limits I daily rose into spheres which seemed to me more and more divine. Sight and hearing became noble channels of the influences of infinity, instead of gross senses. I struggled to bring my firla up to the enjoyment of their labours, but ever fell back hopeless.

This was especially the case when I was brought to examine and test their monalan or electrical distance-analyst, for a fully developed electric sense was needed to appreciate its refined analysis of impulses from far distances. It was an ingenious application of an alloy called by them labramor, or electricity sponge, and had the power of splitting up any electric wave or impulse into its constituent movements. Each of these had its own clear and distinct effect upon the firla and varied with the substance from which the impulse came or through which it passed. All substances and elements in the terrestrial system were classified according to their electric impulses. Even before the Limanorans brought the firla to its high state of sensitiveness and efficiency, they had been able to examine the stars and other distant bodies and analyse their elements by means of this classification and the application of their alloy, labramor. Every substance or element had its place in their tables according as it was positive or negative in its electric impulse towards some other substance or element; and all its affinities, strong or weak, were tabulated. Thus when they turned their monalan upon any distant body like a star they were able to analyse its elements by means of these tables. Even now that their firla interpreted the analysis of the monalan without the intervention of classifications and tables, they had another electrically analystic instrument which appealed to the eye; this turned the electric impulse into a flash or glow, which at once revealed in the inamar or spectroscope the substances or elements whence it had come.

Their lower or more material senses I was more nearly able to approach, even though they too were highly intellectualised and were more the servants of the spirit than of the animal part. In developing mine I had more hope of raising myself to the Limanoran level, and yet there was less stimulus; for I felt that they looked down upon these senses of smell, taste, and touch because of their need of close contact with their objects; they were the primitive senses; they were narrow and bound down to immediate matter, and seemed poor gropers in the finite and the dark compared with those rangers of infinity, the ear, the eye, and the electric sense. It was then with a feeling of humiliation that I saw those lower and more finite senses in me develop so quickly, proving me a being of a more primitive and material type.

Yet there was no neglect of these in their education and no contempt for them and their uses; in fact contempt was one of the vices that they had with most pains weeded out of their systems and civilisation. They had not merely considered that nothing in creation, if looked into scientifically, was worthy of contempt, but that contempt was the truest symptom of crudity of character and ignorance of reality and nature. Even if they had had any remains of this primal savagery, they would not have felt it towards those finite-seeking senses. They only set themselves to make them more and more the servants of the soul, the instruments of the imagination. They rejected the idea that the arts belonged only to sight and hearing. Their arts of the firla were far more important and striking than any sculpture or painting or music could be. Not merely as a variation on these and a relief from them did they have arts that brought in the senses of smell and taste and touch; these had their own special uses in their civilisation. All of them, but especially smell and taste, were closely linked with memory, and through memory with imagination. A special perfume and even a special taste would flash before the mind a scene or fact with more vividness than even a piece of music would.

The perfumes and tastes had been classified according to their affinity to certain virtues and ideas and to the great deeds and scenes which best represented them. The island was one vast flower-garden at all seasons of the year, arranged not alone to please the eye, but to bring by the suggestion of their perfumes the noblest virtues and deeds constantly into the mind. For example, wherever a child or youth was being trained, the flowers possessing certain well-known scents which were closely connected with the finest qualities and ideas of the race shone profusely yet with striking art. The art of the gardening family did not consist merely in arrangement of the landscape and the varied coloration of it. The scent of every flower had to be taken into consideration and the faint flavour or taste the seed or fruit might produce in the air when sent adrift or bruised. The problem of no science or art was so complicated as that of gardening in this island, it had to take account of so many senses, seasons, and conditions of growth. They were never done with creating and selecting new variations of flowers and plants, and colour, scent, and taste in the vegetable world were as adaptable in their hands as tones in the hands of their musical composers. Their task was made comparatively easy by the great development of methods and appliances for rapid growth and decay. They had not only complete command of the weather and clouds and sunshine; but they could bring up and perfect flowers in a few nights over vast areas by the use of their streams and watering platforms and of artificial light. When the Limanorans slept, wonders were being accomplished in colouring the landscape; for first some of their great rivers would pour refreshing rain all over the plains; and then the electric glow, brought close over the plants, would develop their bloom-producing capacity. As careful were the gardeners that no withering or dead vegetable matter should ever taint the air of the island; the moment one set of blossoms had perfected and shown traces of decay, an electric pruner ran in a few minutes over the whole area, and not merely cut them off, but burnt them to dust that fell on the roots to stimulate the new growth of the plants. As soon as the plants had passed their bloom-productive point, an electric life-destroyer ploughed lightly through the soil in all directions; and by the morning what had been profusely flower-coloured the day before was brown earth, ready for the new plant-growth of next day. The slow-growing perennials and bushes and trees occupied separate and fixed quarters at a distance from the residences and the great centres of intercourse, and all rampant vegetation and rotting boughs and leaves were daily turned into good soil by the electric weed-destroyer. No decay was ever allowed to approach the senses. Their knowledge of the secrets of the soil made them independent of rotting or offensive manures. The particular elements of which any kind of plant or flower robbed the soil were accurately ascertained, and their chemistry enabled them with ease to supply the deficiency after a crop had been removed.

The gardening family had to be familiar on the one hand with the innermost secrets of psychology, and on the other with the last discoveries of the more material sciences; for no one could avoid the effects of the flowers and trees, as he could painting and sculpture, music and firlamai. Gardening, in short, was the most public of all the arts and the most pervasive in its results. A garden (and in Limanora there was only one vast garden) was a great mnemonic instrument, which could play upon the souls of the whole community at once. That it should not be in the hands of novices, or of unwise or wrong-thoughted men and women, was one of the prime cares of the people. Of all families those that managed the garden of the island had to be most simple-hearted and true, most sure in their knowledge of the human heart, and most eager to stir to what is great and noble and humane. They were the lords of the sense of smell, one of the most immediate portals to memory and to imagination. To have the complete command of one out of the six dominant sense-entrances to the soul was, they considered, the greatest of responsibilities, and no care was neglected in selecting, purifying, and training the families of gardeners.

They, too, had the superintendence of Ilarime, a structure devoted to the arts of smell, taste, and sound combined. Aided by the musicians and the chemists, they produced symphonies which appealed to all three senses and roused the imagination to exceptional flights. The imaginative or pioneering families frequented the halls of this great building daily in pursuit of new stimulus to their faculty. Every chamber in it had special emotions to rouse. A garden could have only a mingled effect upon the memory and mnemonic imagination; Ilarime separated the effects and classified the emotions and imaginative ideas which were to be stimulated. Anyone entering could find out at the porch, either by looking in the index-chamber or by consulting one of the superintendents, what hall or halls he ought to rest in. I had often during my education to take refuge in Ilarime, when clogged in my endeavours to advance by dulness of memory or imagination or by the weakness of some emotion. After a time I did not need to consult a guide; I knew what element in my soul was deficient and what emotion or memory would stir it to activity, and by aid of the index-hall and its graphic representation of the effect of every chamber upon the spirit I could choose what symphony I needed. As soon as I had entered the hall that I had chosen, I lay down on one of their hanging rests and shut my eyes. At once the medicated atmosphere began to affect my palate, whilst the delicate perfume entered my nostrils and my ears drank in the sweet-sounding music. Before many minutes had passed memories of striking scents I had witnessed or heard of or seen represented in the island began to rise in my mind, and the emotion I needed thrilled me through; if it was heroism or courage, I felt myself urged to deeds of valour; if it was benevolence, I was soon inclined to rush to the help of the suffering and the poor; if it was hope, I saw bright visions of the future.

But this exercise was too passive to be allowed for any length of time. The imagination and emotions were apt to gain at the expense of the will and the nervous energy by too frequent resort to Ilarime. Strenuous endeavour was held to be one of the prime essentials of progress, not only in the race, but even more in the individual. And, though all the prevailing odours and tastes and sounds of the island were agreeable, the Limanorans carried with them a small instrument, called margol, that by an adaptation of electricity could blunt at will the acuteness of smelling and tasting and hearing, and, on the other hand, reduce the powers of perfumes and flavours and sounds; it acted by drying the air around the head and drawing the moisture and heat from the nostrils, the tongue, and the ears. It was partly to mitigate the force of smells and tastes and sounds that they always kept the atmosphere dry and cool by day. In the margol, too, there was a combination of chemicals and electricity which would modify any odour or flavour to suit the taste; but if they wished to increase the strength of any perfume or taste, they applied electric heat to the source of it, and moistened the nostrils and the mouth. It was one of the new peculiarities of the race that the mucous and salivary flow was under the command of the will, and they could smell and taste with satisfaction to themselves without the aid of moisture on the organs.

Their senses of smell and taste had become by means of their acuteness what they were originally meant to be, the guardians of the throat and the digestion. They told with accuracy the nature of the substances brought to the mouth; whatsoever would be deleterious to the system was offensive. In most civilised peoples what is grateful to the palate and the olfactory nerves is often pernicious to some tissue of the body or some faculty of the mind. Here the two senses were the true friends and protectors of both body and soul; there was no seducing them or bribing them into evil or irrational reports, so completely had they been saturated with reason.

In the medical, chemical, and alimentary families these senses were trained to a pitch that seemed to me marvellous. By either smell or taste a member of these families could tell the constituent elements of any compound. A medical sage, if a man, could distinguish by the faint odour that marked each human body whether it was losing energy or expending it, making progress or decaying; if a woman, the sage, in order to make this decision, had as a rule to bring in the help of taste; for it had remained from the primitive animal stage of man's development one of the differentiating marks of sex that the male had more energy of smell, the female more energy of taste; now that they had so spiritualised their senses, perfumes formed the quickest stimulus of the masculine imagination and flavours of the feminine. At the food vats it was always the Limanoran women who superintended the flavouring of any compound; whilst it was the men who had most to do with medicating the atmospheres of the chambers, and men presided in the chemical laboratories. The historical origin of this distinction, they thought, was on the one hand the development of the acuteness of smell in male animals at rutting time, and on the other the power in dams of recognising their own offspring by licking it with the tongue. And it was a well-known maxim in their medical families that every individual had a distinctive odour and taste. They could tell one man from another in the dark, and even at a considerable distance; and to touch him with the tongue was to make assurance doubly sure. The kissing that was so common in the West as a symbol of friendship and love, like the rubbing of noses amongst less civilised peoples, had as its origin and basis the recognition of the individual by the taste or smell. They did not need so close or material an investigation of the individual to have pleasant memories of friendship aroused. Their methods and symbols of companionship and love had become more and more spiritual with the passion itself.

But, preternaturally acute though their senses seemed to me to be, they would rely upon their decisions no more than the modern scientist of the West would rely upon his. Error, they held, was ever maiming the conclusions from reports of the senses, and they took every precaution in recording or using their own perceptions. Accurate though their sense-memory was, they had instruments which kept a permanent record of any report of the senses they meant to use again. Not merely sounds and sights did they automatically record, but perfumes, and flavours, and electric impressions. Ages before, the inasan or recorder of light and the linasan or recorder of sound had been brought to a high pitch of perfection; all the colours and forms seen in nature, at whatever distance, could be kept in permanence on irelium-plates and reproduced to the eye by the insertion of the plates in the inasan and the reversal of the instrument. So was it with sounds, however loud or faint; the linasan would tell out to the ear music or speeches recorded hundreds of years before down to the minutest tone. By a modification of these two instruments they took record of the inner structure of things even at cosmic distances, and of sounds which seemed to be intercepted by vast material obstructions. The development of the recorders of the other senses had been more recent; not till perfumes and tastes and electricity had begun to enter largely into education and the stimulance of memory did the necessity for such instruments arise. In the earlier times before the purgation of the race these instruments would have been a temptation to new and epicurean vices. Now they were nothing if not educational aids. The farosan or aromagraph enabled the gardeners to arrange the mnemonic harmonies of flowers as mere sense-memory could never have done; it could reproduce any subtle perfume or mixture of perfumes that had ever been experienced in the island. The salosan or gustagraph gave incalculable aid to the chemical and alimentary families; without its permanencies of flavour they would have fallen into daily errors in mingling the atmospheres of the halls of sustenance and medication and those of Ilarime. By its aid they could recall any of the tastes which had made substances or compounds pleasing to the palate. But it was the idrosan or electrograph that was most needed; for the firla or electric sense had been so recently developed that its reports as to the amount and quality of any electric impulse were most untrustworthy. Without the aid of this recorder they could never have compared the electric impulses of the past with those of the present, nor could they have been so accurate in measuring the electric powers of various substances.

They knew that the basis of all scientific advance was accurate measurement. Their old measuring instruments had gradually been overtaken by their own senses, and had to be replaced by others more and more refined. In order to make sure that their senses introduced no personal element into the reports and representations of their various delicate measurers, they had invented an instrument which for fine adjustment surpassed all of these. It was the airolan or sensometer, and by it the medical families in their weekly review of every system in the community were enabled to find the exact personal equation of each. It recorded the upper and lower limit of the various sensations, the limit of endurance, and the vanishing point. Although there was a great evenness

in the development of the senses in the community, there was yet considerable variation in the delicacy of perception. One man was keenest in sight,
another in hearing, a third in the electric sense, yet there was a certain constancy or proportion in all the senses of every man, a proportion varying according to well-ascertained laws with the hour and the season, the man's age,
and the temperature and health of his body. The airolan tested, measured, and
recorded the regular variations of each Limanoran's senses, and thus he was
able to know how far he judged accurately anything he perceived. By its aid
he was able to know the exact point at which he would need to call in any
one of the various mechanical aids to the senses, the magnifiers, or modi-
fiers, or distance-reducers. By its means they were able to gauge the proper
mixture of colours and proper size in architecture that would please at certain
distances. By its means, too, they could accurately measure the distance from
which any electric or luminous or somniferous impulse had come, when it
struck on the senses.

It was one of the commonplaces of their policy that whatever could be
done by machinery it was waste of skill and energy to do by human labour
and thought; and instruments were generally more exact and reliable than
the senses and active powers of man, however delicately developed and refined. Of course man's brain and hand must still guide and superintend all
instruments and machinery, but his interference with their automatic working
was reduced to a minimum, in order that the discount for personal equation
should be as little as possible. It was not, however, so much for the sake of
accuracy of result that mechanism was substituted for human work, as for
the sake of progress. Every operation and function which could be performed
mechanically it was a slur upon human dignity to do; and at once Limanoran
humanity was relieved from the necessity, and the freed energy was applied
to other and nobler efforts towards progress.

During my education I had noticed again and again with surprise that
mathematics took no part in it. Not once had I heard the subject mentioned by
any of my guides or companions. I remembered the important place it held
in Western curriculums, and wondered how the various scientific families
could manage their abstruse formulæ and calculations without that science.
A people that laid so much stress on exactitude of research as an essential of
all scientific progress were surely lax to a degree in failing to train their youth
in the various branches of mathematics.

On having my senses tested by the airolan, the thought came uppermost
in my mind again; and my proparents at last took notice of it, perhaps as the
time had arrived for enlightening me on the subject. They led me to a vast
museum-like building, crammed with all kinds of small and intricate machines, not unlike a kind of patent office, where the models of new inventions
are deposited for examination and comparison. There was evident in the ar-

rangement a careful classification according to elaboration and delicacy. In the first section we entered there were the simplest of machines, having a few levers and cog-wheels, and a few keys set in a key-board; these were meant for the easier rules of calculation—addition, subtraction, multiplication, and division. We tested most of them and I saw that they were infallibly accurate; never once even in the longest and most intricate calculation was there any error. In fact, these machines had been first invented to avoid the constant errors that vitiated important results when novices were set to work them out. It was then found that not only did they rid calculations of fallibility and the youth of heartless drudgery, but they enabled the race to advance more rapidly. They set free years of life, especially in the formative stage, that had been wasted on mere routine and mechanical work; and, best of all, they allowed the tissues of young brains to be less rigid. It was noted that, after the calculating machines were set to work, the youth grew in mental and especially in imaginative power at twice the old rate. The elders of the state were amazed at the result, prizing as they had done the effect of arithmetic in the discipline and education of the young; indeed, it had been with great regret that they saw the youth relieved of so disciplinary an exercise; and they even thought of making an exception to their usual utilitarian state-principle, and training the boys and girls in rapid calculation, although it would be of so little use to them in their after-lives. But a few years convinced them of the serious mistake they had made. The pace of development so suddenly and greatly quickened in the new generation that the result could be set down to nothing else than the new freedom from calculations. Their own faculties and imagination seemed stiff and almost ossified compared to the ease and flexibility of those of their sons and daughters. Invention and discovery struck out with unprecedented energy, and the ethical and emotional phase of imagination grew at a marvellous pace; new ideal realms were opened out for morality and practical thought.

The experience threw a remarkable light upon a phenomenon which had puzzled them for generations. After the period of youth the members of the community had to specialise; and for some undiscoverable reason those who devoted themselves to mathematics and the working of abstruse formulæ had been found, able though most of them were, to be the most rigidly unreasonable in the community; they refused to admit that they could be mistaken in any of their judgments or even opinions; nothing would move them—neither logical argument nor emotional appeal; they assumed that they had found absolute truth, and refused to have compromise. In one generation in the far past the mathematical families had to be exiled, so serious an obstruction had they become to progress. Again they had been completely renewed, children of the most noble-minded, freest, and most imaginative families being substituted for the old members, and trained to fulfil their functions; within a generation the result was the same; these scions of the finest of the race became as narrow-minded and obstructive as their predecessors had been. It seemed to be useless to change the stock, and for some generations the community accepted their conservatism and obstinacy as inevitable; they grew accustomed to smiling at the mathematical families as "the omniscients."

Why the true cause of this degeneracy had not occurred to such a shrewd and logical people it is hard to say; probably because they were so wedded by long tradition and practice to the idea that mathematics was one of the loftiest of sciences and one of the most essential elements in education. They doubtless refused to reconsider its claims or to abandon their inherited reverence for it. But the discovery of the effect of the calculative habit on the tissues of the brain at last forced them to face the true cause of the infallibility of the mathematical families. It was their occupation that caused their degeneracy. Men began to pity them for the slavery in which they had been so long held and to devise means for their liberating. The old habitual smile at the mention of their name became sadness at the thought of what these members of the race might have accomplished for its civilisation had they not been so frozen in their tissues by the perpetual use of formulæ. They were amazed at their own dulness in failing to see that men who dealt in such mechanical methods and exact results could not but be mechanical themselves and easily fall into the fixed mental attitude of the omniscient, and dealing with a world so unreal in its stiff, skeleton-like outlines could not but fail in a world of conditions and compromises.

At first the prevailing idea was that all the studies and sciences needing exactitude of formulæ and result should be neglected by the community. On consideration it was felt that some of the most valuable stepping-stones to the loftier ideals of the future would be sacrificed if this were done. The other alternative was chosen. The inventors who had made the calculating machines were set on to find instruments which would accomplish what the mathematicians had had to do for the community. And, one after the other, the years had produced them. Even differential and integral calculus had been superseded by a series of machines that with little guidance worked out all the applications of their intricate formulæ to the sciences. As we advanced from department to department we watched these machines at work confirming the imaginative results of the physicists, the chemists, and the astronomers. The mathematical families were relieved of their duties and distributed, and every member of the scientific families was taught to use all these formulating instruments. Their brain-energy was not monopolised by calculations; the use of the machines was but a routine detail in their wider intellectual life, and absorbed so little of their energy that it seemed to have no effect on their faculties.

I was not many days in mastering the details of the formula-machines; for I had paid some attention to mathematics in my buried life and the memory of the subject rapidly revived. I soon came to see the wisdom of the Limanorans in eliminating the study from their scheme of education. It would have been the height of extravagance to waste long periods of their lives in studying and doing what a machine could do better. It was exactly the kind of work best done by a machine, for it had to do with a world rid of all conditions and, mathematically speaking, perfect. The inventors were still busy making new and simpler machines for the use of the scientists; and, though they had to know the new mathematical formulæ needed, they busied their brains rather with their practical application and with the machinery that would use them. It was imagination in the practice of mechanics rather than the mechanical use of methods and formulæ that they were engaged on. Hence it was that they avoided the old unpracticality of the mathematical families, and stood in no danger of thinking themselves infallible and the only treasuries of absolute truth.

One of the most interesting departments of Minella, as this great building was called, was that which contained the measurers of time. I was somewhat surprised that this department should exist, for I had admired every day the power the Limanorans had of telling to a minute fraction the passage of time. Their sense of time seemed to me to make watches and clocks superfluous. Even when the sky was clouded over and no heavenly body or light to be perceived, they could tell the exact fraction of the day or night that had passed, as I tested again and again by the watch I had brought with me. Their knowledge of the natural signs of the time of day or year had become instinctive and automatic through long centuries of daily use. The position and state of the petals of flowers would at any moment by day or night, by shine or cloud, reveal to them the time. So would the temperature of anything they touched, or, if it were highly contractile, its size. But these external signs were quite unnecessary. They had not to go beyond the sensations of their own bodies to tell the time or season. They knew by the intensity of the magnetism in them, by the acuteness of their senses, by the amount of energy they could command.

But their experiments needed far more exactness than even their senses could afford. Time had to be counted in their science not by mere seconds, but by the hundred-thousandth, or even the millionth, part of a second. One old-fashioned measurer of time was based on the length of a wave of sound as it passed through a vessel of water. The length of the vessel contained a round number of moltas (their smallest measure of length, perhaps about the millionth part of an inch); the vibration in the water reflected a bright light through a microscope and camera combined; and a photograph of the pulsations imprinted itself on a strip of irelium that kept moving with lightning swiftness across the focus; this strip was divided into minute sections, each of them corresponding to a lenta or millionth part of a second and numbered in order up to a million. A newer clock had its principle based on the length of a wave of light in a vacuum. Another and more convenient clock, or rather watch, consisted of an electric battery that kept a light irelium tongue vibrating; this latter controlled a graduated mechanism which pointed out on a face the exact lenta in the time of day that it was. It was small enough to be carried about on the person like a watch.

A similar microscopic minuteness of division appeared in all their weights and measures. They could weigh in their balances down to the million-millionth part of an ounce. So with their measurement of heat and cold; their thermometers could test ten thousand times the range of temperature that their senses could bear, although their power of endurance of fire and frost was to me something miraculous; their furnaces were able to volatilise the most refractory of metals and earths; they could reproduce the conditions of the most glowing suns, and also the temperature of the coldest interstellar space, which, age by age, they were bringing their frames gradually to bear with the aid of certain foods and combinations of elements. Thus did they hope in some future age to subsist, even when they ventured outside of the atmosphere of the earth.

All their measures were based on the decimal system, the fundamental unit for microscopic measurements being the amount of energy in an atom of one of their elements, and that for cosmic measurements the energy that would bring a beam of light from the sun's surface to the earth's. They were able to see at a glance the exact amount of energy in any phenomenon, to whatever sense it might appeal, and in their minds there was ever a common measure for all types of force. Their electrometers and magnetometers told not merely the amount of electricity or magnetism in any machine, material, or phenomenon, but the motive-power it would have when applied to any purpose. They could compare at a glance, without any elaborate calculations, the advantages to be obtained from any substance when using it as a force, whether through the electricity or the heat or the gravitational power to be obtained from it.

Especially useful was this common measure in dealing with the power of light as separate from that of heat. It was of great importance to them to know the exact amount of energy even in a beam of light which their eyes could not perceive. For they used sunshine as one of their great curative agencies, and the medical families were constantly experimenting on the effect of more or less light upon the microscopic life existing in and around the human body. One of their own new developments had been the consciousness of light all over their skin; they could tell with eyes shut whether it was the light of sun, stars, or moon, or an artificial light which was falling on any part of their body; the effect, even on the mind, differed completely in the four; the sunlight, or at least a certain amount of it, gave exhilaration or even joy; the starshine brought contemplative melancholy; the moonbeam mildly stirred the passions; whilst artificial light varied in its power of exhausting brain and nerve energy with the material or element that produced it.

Sunlight deprived of the intensity of its heat was to them one of the essentials of life. Its bactericidal power had been scientifically proved ages before, and a family had been set apart for testing its effects both qualitatively and quantitatively. It was not merely a loose knowledge that they had acquired of the antiseptic influence of sunshine. They had measured exactly its power of depriving microbes of their deadliness in the case of every disease; and they knew to a nicety how strong or weak it would be needed in order to check their ravages in any constitution, whether concentrated on a spot or diluted and spread as in a bath, how long daily its application would be required, and how many days. It was this family that superintended the sunbaths in their halls of medication, and assisted the medical sages in advising as to their use. It was true that daylight, and especially that of a sunny day, swept one third of the noxious life out of all water open to its influence, whilst the rays of the sun bleached most bacteria of their pestiferous tendency. Yet used indiscriminately sunshine became itself unwholesome, because of the other forms of energy besides light that it brought with it from the sun and the intervening spaces. If not used with caution, it would destroy the microscopic allies of human life in the body, rendering feeble the phagocytes that devour the virulent microbes; it would by its great heat injure the delicate tissues of the brain, and by its magnetism and weight press heavily on the nerves and the circulation. It was the duty of the solometric family to rid it of its unwholesome elements, and to indicate the exact amount and use of it that would be beneficial in every state of the body. Another of the duties of this family was to cultivate colonies of microbes of the various diseases and make them harmless by means of sunlight for use in inoculations against their own unmodified bacterial kin. One of their greatest aids in this process was the use of the water of the sea; wherever it did not kill the bacteria completely, it emphasised the bleaching power of sunlight over them and rendered them the allies of the human system in its struggle against all disease and decay. This sterilisation of disease was one of the most important functions of the family. It was they who led the flight-gambols of the Limanorans into the outer fringe of the atmosphere, where they might drink in the elixir of unadulterated sunshine; their guidance and contrivances were needed even there, in order to prevent the action of the other energies in the light growing deleterious. Even moonlight and starshine had their uses in the hands of this skilled family. They could separate the deadly or poisonous elements of moonbeams to help them in destroying bacterial life, and leave only their healthy and inspiring tendencies; thus dealt with, the rays of the moon gave a stimulus to the brain-tissues which worked up imaginative materials. And every star had, in their science, its own peculiar influence, sometimes malign, more commonly beneficial, when treated according to their wise discoveries.

Little of all this would have been possible without the inolan or measurer of light, one of the most delicate instruments they possessed. This was but a modification of the human eye as it had been developed in their bodies. It magnified the impression made on the lens so that it should move a small mirror delicately hung *in vacuo*; the reflection of this mirror ran along a graduated scale on which it recorded by bleaching a point of colour, the energy of light in the beam producing the movement. This recorded not merely the strength of the rays of which their eyes were conscious, but that of many octaves of light outside of the range of all human eyes. A more modern and delicate form of the inolan used a microscopic camera as the medium of measurement; this had accomplished new wonders in the way of measuring the power of rays from stars out of reach of the human eye. A third photometer, recently invented and still untested when I visited the collection of measurers, had made use of electricity in collecting and testing the quality and energy of beams of light.

In all of these forms of the inolan there was an arrangement for ridding each ray of its heat and of other forms of energy before it entered the lens; a thermometer measured the heat; and the other elements were absorbed and analysed by a subsidiary apparatus as the beam approached the inolan. Another modification of the apparatus had a prismatic arrangement attached to it, not unlike their inamar, and this broke up the beam of light into its colour components; the inolan measured each separate component, the length of its wave, and the energy required to produce it, its camera also recording in photographic form the metallic elements through which the beam had passed. A more recent modification, promising great results, was one which by means of a vacuum-lens recorded the dark beams that shone from unseen stellar bodies through the corona of our own or other suns. When fully developed they expected this to reveal the secrets of the darker depths of the heavens; the systems revolving round the stars would stand out clearly with all their elements for the investigation of the astronomic families.

Nor did the extraordinary refinement of these instruments, that were constantly being discovered, interfere in any way with the development of Limanoran senses. On the contrary they stimulated advance. Every new aid to any sense pointed the way to its improvement; and in a few years or generations this aid was rendered almost superfluous and a new and more delicate machine must be invented; for the combination of so many functions in the living body rendered the observations of any one sense less exact and trustworthy than those of a machine which had but one purpose.

Thus the evolution of the senses kept up an unending race with the evolution of fine machinery to aid them. Even the roughest, most material, and least specialised of all the senses, touch, had grown into something that was most delicate in its manipulation; and one of the most important parts of the education of my senses was to refine and develop it. They had specialised it to an astonishing degree. The lips, especially the outer edges of them, were able to distinguish the latent energy in any substance applied to them; whilst a delicate fringe of hair upon the upper lip, too minute to be seen by ordinary eyes, revealed to them the movements and character of gases and vapours that were so faint in their impulse as to be unrecognisable by the other senses. The measurement of force had been raised to a high point of exactness in their huge chests and shoulders. Their hands, within certain limits, felt temperature with the accuracy and minuteness of a thermometer. And the prehensile and manipulative skill of their fingers far surpassed that of the ablest European conjuror I had ever seen. Without any intention to outwit my senses, they would do things with their hands so swiftly that I could not follow the movements. It seemed to me at first as if they had more joints in their fingers than other human beings, so nimble were they; but this was not the case, although the arm had greater scope of movement than mine; in fact it seemed to move in the shoulder socket as in a universal joint, so freely could it revolve in all directions. Their joints were really more padded with cartilage than mine, so that there was more flexibility in the limbs along with greater firmness and strength.

Their nerves were also more magnetic than those of other men, conveying the messages to and from the brain and will-centres with far more swiftness and certitude. Indeed, if I were to find any one point in their systems which most differentiated them from European humanity, it was this increased and accelerated nerve-energy. For a long time their rapidity and ease of movement and action bewildered me; whilst I was deliberating what was to be done, they had done all that was needed. They had instruments for measuring the flash of thought from brain to hand and of sensation from hand to brain, and when tested at first, the swiftness of the message along my nerves was not one tithe of theirs, but when my education had somewhat advanced, this disparity was reduced by half. This advance was accomplished, not merely by practice, but by variety of diet and medication, and by living in a more magnetic atmosphere. I was often borne aloft into the purer air that fringes the envelope of our earth, and there, half-asleep, I drew into my system the electric elements which went to the quickening of my nerves. Down in the island everything that would excite me was avoided; the muscles and the other tissues of the body were exercised, whilst the nerves completely rested. Then they would be given gentle exercise of their own, to strengthen and make them supple, without unduly stimulating them. I soon began to feel the difference in the increasing nimbleness of my limbs and could move with more celerity and ease. The fingers were quicker to follow the eye. I grew what my old companions would have thought unerring in my aim and would have made a deadly shot with bullet or arrow in the wars of my native country. What was still better, the tips of my fingers came to be powerfully magnetic both in their appreciation of the electricity in any body they touched, and in actively producing magnetic currents. I was even able to cause a faint flash in the darkness by concentrating my will-power in my fingers, and waving them in the air.

POSTSCRIPT TO LIMANORA

When he had reached this point in his narrative, a striking instance of the result of his education occurred. It was getting towards the end of winter, and we who had our rules of thumb for the changes in the weather were looking for the equinoctial gales that harbinger the approach of spring. The days were lengthening, and the light of the sun was growing clear and strong upon our high-perched huts.

We had noticed a certain distraction in his manner, an absence of thought or of consciousness, when he was describing the development of his magnetic sense. And when he ceased for the night he could not rest but paced uneasily along our platform of cliff which overlooked the waters of the sound. The moon had begun to wane, and our weather lore bade us look out for storms at the beginning of her next phase. I could not go myself to rest for thinking of his strange narrative and the wonderful people he had sojourned amongst. I sat up many hours writing out what I could remember of his conversations and descriptions while it was still clear in my mind.

Some time after midnight I looked out and saw the silver moonshine on the still waters below and was attracted by the beauty of the scene. I had thought that he had retired, but I had scarcely seated myself on a projecting boss of rock that took in one of our widest views, when his musical voice startled me out of my reverie.

We fell into such sympathetic intercourse as the beauty of night often stimulates in two sleepless spirits meeting under the moon. He told me that the earth was then tremulous with suppressed passion, and that far off in his old home in the Pacific her heart was about to break. He felt waves of magnetic feeling pass through him, and they drew his soul back to Limanora. He knew that the spirits he loved there were yearning for him. For his heart quivered and throbbed with full memories of all he had known and experienced. There was anguish in the magnetic undulance vibrating across his being. It was not merely that a great storm was approaching; that he had known for some days. There were human pulsations in the ether which beat like an ocean upon his brain. That was why he could not rest. If only he could have his wings again, he would try to respond to the call. But it was useless with the recrudescence of his muddier humanity to attempt return by such aërial means. I offered to go with him on the morrow to the nearest city and charter a ship to carry us to his former home. But he would not listen to my proposal, and bade me seek rest and sleep.

I began to feel that I was intruding on the privacy of an agonised soul, and I bade him good-night and left him to his own thoughts.

The exhaustion of overcharged emotion soon let me drift into troubled unconsciousness. Dream followed dream like hurrying clouds over the moon. At dawn I woke in nightmare. The hut was shaking. I thought that I was still dreaming. But the swish of the rain and the lashing of the tree-branches on the roof soon made me understand. The calm of the night before had given way to tempest; and the earth was suffering rupture.

I remembered the prediction of our guest, and rushed to his hut. He was not there; nor could I conjecture whither he had gone. I thought he had taken shelter in the bush from the storm. Three days it lasted, and then we were able to go out and search the drenched forest. We followed up every track that he had been accustomed to take. We went to all his favourite haunts. But no trace could we find of him, though days were spent on the search. Then we forced our way through the dense undergrowth in several directions we had never seen him take; and at last we came upon a yawning chasm, which had every appearance of being newly opened. The precipitous side of the mountain had split, and a vast landslip had swept down it and filled the bottom of the gulf. We could not resist the natural conclusion; this was the tomb of our guest. After all his wanderings he had found appropriate resting-place. The earth he knew so well had taken him to her bosom.

BOOK II

THE LIMANORANS
The Inner Life of a Self-Selected People

PREFACE

LATE in the autumn, when the memory of the stranger who had told us so many wonderful things had begun to lose its sharpness and we had almost ceased to talk of him, we were startled by his reappearance.

We were in our tunnels, taking advantage of the dry weather to get piles of our wash dirt out ready for sluicing in the wet season, and were working till nightfall. On a still, fair evening, which reminded me of the night he vanished, we were returning jaded from our long work and had just issued from the belt of bush that fringed our clearing when the moon rose above the peaks on the other side of the fiord and flashed a shuttle of gold across the waters. Raising our eyes to our huts, we stopped thunderstruck. Was that but a lunar effect on the throne-like cliff in front of them? It could not be a spirit; we had never heard of ghosts in these new lands, nor could the belief in them seize hold of minds so accustomed as ours were to deal with the rougher and more material elements of nature. We shook off our trance, and stepped forward. The sound of our footsteps made the figure move and as he turned in the moonlight we recognised our lost friend (his apparition, we first supposed). But he rose with his old quiet and dignified salute of welcome, and joining us as we sat at our evening meal, we talked as if he had parted with us only that morning. We had not the hardihood to ask him what had become of him these long months. But I noticed that he had more of his old semi-transparency of tissue and ethereality of hue, and in his eyes, as he ceased from talking, there was a baffled look I had never seen before in them. He would lapse more frequently into deep reverie. He seemed to have gone through a lifetime of effort and suffering, and his spirit was, I could see, weary and sore within him.

He shrank at first from all reference to his life within the circle of mist out on the Pacific. It seemed now to be a painful memory. There was a pathos in his tone as he spoke far keener than I had noted in it before. But gradually I drew him into reminiscence of it when we were alone in the bush, and he seemed after a time to find consolation in thinking and speaking about it, especially when he talked of the spiritual side of the civilisation in the midst of which he had lived for so many years.

In the long nights of that last winter he resumed his narrative again. He seemed to have difficulty in finding English expression for what he had to tell, but I encouraged him in our wanderings around the fiord to repeat and interpret and explain what he had told us. Gradually the narrative found a more intelligible language, and I was able to jot down notes that I understood. I have done my best to throw them together into the form that they ultimately found in his story as he told it to us sitting together in our hut. But I am still puzzled and sometimes confused by many of the ideas and feel that they have baffled my best skill to put them into our tongue. Some of his descriptions awakened in us a sense of incredulity, and others shook our old world of beliefs to its foundations. But we were drawn to him by the noble and ingenuous way in which he told us all; indeed, were often fascinated and blinded as we listened. We could not but accept his story as the highest truth we could hear in this world, and yet we were struck dumb by its strangeness. Much of our bewilderment we attributed to the difficulty of understanding his strange speech, and more to our own ignorance of the intricate problems that have troubled sages. We have kept back this latter part of his story for a time in order that by study and care we might make it more intelligible and more suited to the thoughts of Christendom. But we have to acknowledge ourselves still baffled by the impossible task of making this road through difficult regions plain and easy, and so have resolved to issue the narrative with all its faults upon it.

—GODFREY SWEVEN.

GLOSSARY

AILOMO—The astrobiological families.

AIROLAN—A sensometer, or instrument for finding the personal equation of a man.

ALCLIROLAN—Radiographic cinematograph; an instrument combining microscope, camera in vacuo, and electric power.

ALFARENE—Oxygen shrub.

AMMERLIN—Historoscope.

CIRALAISON—Museum of terrors.

CLEVAMOLAN—Combination of telescope and makrakoust, or distance-hearer.

CLIMOLAN—Earth-sensor.

CLIROLAN—Instrument that combines electro-microscopy and photography.

CLIROLANIC—Infinitesimally microscopic.

CORFALEENA—Vacuum-engine car.

DOOMALONA—The hill of farewells.

DUOMOVAMOLAN—Instrument that interprets the music of the cosmos.

ERFALEENA—Anti-gravitation flight-car.

FALEENA—Ship of the air.

FARFALEENA—Electric faleena.

FAROSAN—Aroma-recorder.

FIALUME—The valley of memories.

FILAMMU—The will-telegraph.

FIRLA—The electric sense.

FIRLALAIN—The firlamaic department of Oomalefa.

FIRLAMAI—The arts of the electric sense.

FIRLAMAIC—Belonging to the arts of the firla.

FIRLAMAN—A musical instrument that appeals to the firla.

FLORAMO—The botanical families.

FLORONAL—The tree of life.

FRALOOMIAMO—The families of pioneers that imagine and represent the distant future.

GERMABELL—A tree with fruit that makes the muscles and cartilage more elastic.

IDLUMIAN—Electric steriliser.

IDROLAN—Observer and magnifier of electric impulses.

IDROLINASAN—Machine-reporter of the thoughts and feelings and words of a council.

IDROSAN—Recorder of electric impulses and sensations.

IDROVAMOLAN—Instrument for at once seeing and hearing at great distances.

ILARIME—Edifice devoted to the arts of smell, taste, and sound combined.

IMANORA—Centennial review of the civilisation and its progress.

IMATARAN—The focusser of history.

INAMAR—Instrument for splitting up light into its constituents.

INASAN—Recorder of luminous impressions.

INOLAN—Measurer of light.

IRELIUM—Iridescent metal applicable to all manner of purposes by the Limanorans.

LABRAMOR—Alloy of irelium that sponges up and retains electricity.

LABROLAN—Instrument for drawing electricity from the air and the clouds.

LAVIDROLAN—Camera-telescope.

LAVOLAN—Revealer of the inner tissues and mechanism.

LENTA—The minutest division of time in Limanora.

LEOMARIE—The science and art of earth-seeing.

LEOMO—The families of earth-seers.

LEOMORAN—The earth-perforator.

LILAMO—The families that watch the security of the island.

LILARAN—The storm-cone.

LILARIE—The science and art of island-security.

LINAMAR—The analyst of sounds.

LINASAN—Recorder and reproducer of sounds.

LINOKLAR—Spectroscopic analyst and recorder of vapours.

LOOMIAMO—Families of pioneers who imagine and represent the links that connect the present with the distant future.

LOOMIEFA—The theatre of futurition.

MANORA—Decennial review of the progress made by the people.

MARGOL—Electric instrument for blending or reducing the strength of perfumes, flavours, and sounds.

MINELLA—Edifice for formula-machines.

MIRLAN—Life-lamp for revealing and recording internal processes for the use of the eye, the ear, and the electric sense.

MOLTA—The Limanoran measure of infinitesimal length.

MONALAN—Electrical distance-analyst.

MORNALAN—Time-telescope.

NAROLLA—Dream-stimulants.

OOARAN—Psychometer.

OOAROMO—Psycho-physiological families.

OOLORAN—The sonarchitect.

OOLOREFA—The hall of sonarchitecture.

OOMALEFA—Halls of nutrition and medication.

OOROLAN—Instrument for transforming form and colour into melody.

PIRAKNO—Machine for drawing electricity from space.

PIRAMO—The meteorological families.

RIMLA—The centre of force.

SALOSAN—The gustagraph.

SARIFOLAN—Instrument that interprets for sight, hearing, and the electric sense the graphic records of the mirlan.

SARMOLAN—Cosmic barometer.

SIDRALAN—Biometer.

SIDRALMO—Bio-chemical families.

SIDRAMO—The chemical families.

TERRALONA—The edifice of outlook into heaven and hell.

THINAMAR—Visualiser of sound.

TIRLEOMORAN—Electric earth-perforator.

TREMOLAN—Electric clock indicating the changes of electricity in various parts of the island.

TREVAMOLAN—Graduated modifier of sound.

VAMOLAN—Makro-mikrakoust.

VIMOLAN—Photo-electric analyser.GLOSSARY

AILOMO—The astrobiological families.

AIROLAN—A sensometer, or instrument for finding the personal equation of a man.

ALCLIROLAN—Radiographic cinematograph; an instrument combining microscope, camera in vacuo, and electric power.

ALFARENE—Oxygen shrub.

AMMERLIN—Historoscope.

CIRALAISON—Museum of terrors.

CLEVAMOLAN—Combination of telescope and makrakoust, or distance-hearer.

CLIMOLAN—Earth-sensor.

CLIROLAN—Instrument that combines electro-microscopy and photography.

CLIROLANIC—Infinitesimally microscopic.

CORFALEENA—Vacuum-engine car.

DOOMALONA—The hill of farewells.

DUOMOVAMOLAN—Instrument that interprets the music of the cosmos.

ERFALEENA—Anti-gravitation flight-car.

FALEENA—Ship of the air.

FARFALEENA—Electric faleena.

FAROSAN—Aroma-recorder.

FIALUME—The valley of memories.

FILAMMU—The will-telegraph.

FIRLA—The electric sense.

FIRLALAIN—The firlamaic department of Oomalefa.

FIRLAMAI—The arts of the electric sense.

FIRLAMAIC—Belonging to the arts of the firla.

FIRLAMAN—A musical instrument that appeals to the firla.

FLORAMO—The botanical families.

FLORONAL—The tree of life.

FRALOOMIAMO—The families of pioneers that imagine and represent the distant future.

GERMABELL—A tree with fruit that makes the muscles and cartilage more elastic.

IDLUMIAN—Electric steriliser.

IDROLAN—Observer and magnifier of electric impulses.

IDROLINASAN—Machine-reporter of the thoughts and feelings and words of a council.

IDROSAN—Recorder of electric impulses and sensations.

IDROVAMOLAN—Instrument for at once seeing and hearing at great distances.

ILARIME—Edifice devoted to the arts of smell, taste, and sound combined.

IMANORA—Centennial review of the civilisation and its progress.

IMATARAN—The focusser of history.

INAMAR—Instrument for splitting up light into its constituents.

INASAN—Recorder of luminous impressions.

INOLAN—Measurer of light.

IRELIUM—Iridescent metal applicable to all manner of purposes by the Limanorans.

LABRAMOR—Alloy of irelium that sponges up and retains electricity.

LABROLAN—Instrument for drawing electricity from the air and the clouds.

LAVIDROLAN—Camera-telescope.

LAVOLAN—Revealer of the inner tissues and mechanism.

LENTA—The minutest division of time in Limanora.

LEOMARIE—The science and art of earth-seeing.

LEOMO—The families of earth-seers.

LEOMORAN—The earth-perforator.

LILAMO—The families that watch the security of the island.

LILARAN—The storm-cone.

LILARIE—The science and art of island-security.

LINAMAR—The analyst of sounds.

LINASAN—Recorder and reproducer of sounds.

LINOKLAR—Spectroscopic analyst and recorder of vapours.

LOOMIAMO—Families of pioneers who imagine and represent the links that connect the present with the distant future.

LOOMIEFA—The theatre of futurition.

MANORA—Decennial review of the progress made by the people.

MARGOL—Electric instrument for blending or reducing the strength of perfumes, flavours, and sounds.

MINELLA—Edifice for formula-machines.

MIRLAN—Life-lamp for revealing and recording internal processes for the use of the eye, the ear, and the electric sense.

MOLTA—The Limanoran measure of infinitesimal length.

MONALAN—Electrical distance-analyst.

MORNALAN—Time-telescope.

NAROLLA—Dream-stimulants.

OOARAN—Psychometer.

OOAROMO—Psycho-physiological families.

OOLORAN—The sonarchitect.

OOLOREFA—The hall of sonarchitecture.

OOMALEFA—Halls of nutrition and medication.

OOROLAN—Instrument for transforming form and colour into melody.

PIRAKNO—Machine for drawing electricity from space.

PIRAMO—The meteorological families.

RIMLA—The centre of force.

SALOSAN—The gustagraph.

SARIFOLAN—Instrument that interprets for sight, hearing, and the electric sense the graphic records of the mirlan.

SARMOLAN—Cosmic barometer.

SIDRALAN—Biometer.

SIDRALMO—Bio-chemical families.

SIDRAMO—The chemical families.

TERRALONA—The edifice of outlook into heaven and hell.

THINAMAR—Visualiser of sound.
TIRLEOMORAN—Electric earth-perforator.
TREMOLAN—Electric clock indicating the changes of electricity
    in various parts of the island.
TREVAMOLAN—Graduated modifier of sound.
VAMOLAN—Makro-mikrakoust.
VIMOLAN—Photo-electric analyser.

•

CHAPTER I

DISCOVERIES

WHAT I rejoiced over most of all was the growth of my sympathetic magnetism. Not merely was my firla or electric sense developing more satisfactorily; but I was becoming rapidly conscious of the impulses of the race. I no longer walked amongst this refined people like a blind man amongst men who see. I began to feel the enthusiasms that stirred them as a body, like a wind across a cornfield. I seemed to know whatsoever of public concern was occurring without having it directly communicated to me. I remembered in the buried life of my boyhood and youth, the lightning-spread of a new impulse through an assembly or a crowd; the most rational members of the mass were unable to resist it, even though it might be irrational or vile. How like a tornado the war-impulse bursts through a nation is one of the commonest observations in the study of history; statesmen and kings and heroes have to bow before it, and are swept along with it in spite of their better judgments. And as swift and widespread is the coward-impulse that sends a defeated people cowering to their homes. It is this unspoken magnetism, giving vent as it too often does to the evil in the human heart, that makes the cause of progress in even civilised races so hopeless. Through its all-leavening power success inspires and often consecrates the diabolic, and failure damns the noblest and most divine.

And this it was that made progress so easy amongst the Limanorans; it became the instrument of the highest elements and thoughts in them. The whole weight of their humanity was on the side of advance, and it was to the better future that they ever gravitated. Everything that made for a higher plane was an inspiration to this people.

This personal magnetism had been developed in them into a definite faculty of their souls. They had recognised for many ages the close affinity of mass-inspiration and the power of the individual will. It was the same energy working along the nerves, and even, though with some dissipation, through the space intervening between individualities. They had investigated its nature, conditions, and methods of action in their exact scientific way, and had identified it, as far at least as its form of energy was concerned, with electricity. It was even less dependent on material contact than that universal force.

As they developed it in their frames, they were able to send more and more definite impulses through considerable distances. This was their filammu or will-telegraph, one of their most remarkable faculties, drawn with deliberate purpose by the elders of the race out of the chaos of mere vague influence and tendency.

Though making use of the active electric sense as channel, it was not the same as the firla, for it implied a greater effort and outwelling of the whole spirit. Only exceptional impulses and enthusiasms set it into full efficiency, such impulses as entangled the whole soul in their issue. It was no mere toy to be used for the amusement of the passing moment; dormant it lay, if ever summoned to such a purpose. It was the faculty that in other races and periods of history had set up men as heroes and leaders; not that these had even been conscious of its existence in them when they began their career; success and gathering enthusiasm in their followers gave it strength and issue, till their mere glance seemed to command. But when failure came, and the glamour or magnetic atmosphere rarefied about them, their faculty vanished; for it had no means of communicating its meaning or power.

In certain periods of exaltation every Limanoran was conscious of the filammu or will-telegraph; he could not only receive but send emotional impulses through long distances. The intervening air was magnetised by their great enthusiasm or sympathy, and became a medium for transmitting emotional or imaginative thought from mind to mind. Not yet had they been able to send a definite piece of information by this means, unless it represented the spiritual crisis through which the sender was passing. But in movements that shook the whole race to its core, like Choktroo's threat of invasion, even those who were still in pupillage seemed to feel the beginnings of the faculty, at least on its receptive side; secluded though they were far from the scene of deliberation, they knew the magnitude of the danger that threatened the life of the commonweal; the air seemed to tingle with it, and their embryonic filammu could not help responding to the vibration. Once awakened they were eager to bring out its latent power, that they might feel and know the impulses which sped the race onwards as a whole. They soon discovered that it ceased to grow or even work except under certain conditions; they must keep step with the people, and fix their eyes steadily on the future: they must never swerve from uprightness or candour, never let the perfect transparency of their lives be clouded.

Such had been the conditions of the development of the filammu in the race. In fact its indications had become unmistakable as soon as candour and truth had become the primary virtues, and progress the watchword. And it grew as the ideal of the nation became clearer and more imperative, and their character more uniformly strong and noble. They also found that something depended on the physical conditions; the atmosphere must be free from all impurity, and the body must be supremely healthy, whilst the magnetism of the will must have free course along the nerves. As my nature clarified under their training and my spirit grew more at one with the purpose of the race, I grew more sure of the stirrings of the filammu within me. At first its indications might be explained by other and more patent causes; I had been in an attitude of expectancy, or my reason had been following up certain trains of thought from previous events. But after a time there came to me thrills of emotion that were out of the range of my immediate surroundings and thoughts. I followed them out and found that they originated far from the locality in which I was working at the time.

* * * *

Once a sudden tremor passed through my system as of some great fear; I had not been thinking of anything but the work before me; no cloud had come over my sky; no danger that I knew of threatened. As I was trying to explain the emotion, it suddenly passed into longing to see Thyriel. I knew where she had gone that day and my work had almost reached a finish, so I adjusted a faleena, and flew quickly over the country in her direction. I soon knew why I had come. She was pinioned by a huge rock that had just tumbled from Lilaroma. Happily only her wings had been caught, but they had been caught in such a way that she was wedged tightly between them and could not free her arms and legs nor move her hands; and the boulder was too large for her to heave up by the strength of her body, even when magnetised by her will. When she saw this, she withdrew the magnetism from the effort, and turned it in its full power into her filammu as she thought of me. I was not long in disentangling her wings from their prison. But, before I was done, her family were beside us; they too had experienced the thrill, though more feebly than I had and at a greater distance.

Another time I had not seen Thyriel for some days; we were both busy at our own pursuits in different parts of the island. She, as I learned afterwards, had been set to account for a new and somewhat peculiar odour that had recently begun to accompany the issue of vapour from a distant lava-well. I was engaged in timing a new and intermittent disturbance on the surface of the sea off the eastern shore, and trying to find whether it had any relationship to an intermittent fumarole which had recently broken out on the eastern slope of Lilaroma. I had kept watch for several days, and could find no synchronism in their periods, although I was convinced that there was a close connection between them, if there was not a common cause. I was feeling baffled and somewhat downcast; when suddenly there sprang up in me a sense of elation, if not of triumph, which continued for the rest of the day, although I still failed to discover the connection between the two phenomena. When I set out next day for the scene of my observations, I was joined by Thyriel, who explained that she had finished her task the day before and had now been detailed to assist me in mine. I then knew the cause of my thrill of joy, and told her of it. She had at that very hour not only discovered the source of the fumes in a new mineral that the leomoran had touched, but found that this new deposit was extraordinarily generative of electricity. It was this that had made her heart leap for joy and go out towards me. She had longed for my sympathy in her rejoicing, and unconsciously her filammu had energised in my direction. Between us we soon saw that there was a complicated periodicity in the alternations of my two phenomena; it needed several days' observation to catch the rhythm, and for that reason I had been baffled at first. Before long I discovered the cause; as soon as a lava-well farther north had ceased to flow, they also ceased; it was the viscous intermittance of its stream opening and then closing two apertures below tide-line into the subterraneous fires that had regulated the rhythm of these new vents; the break in the lava-current, the rise and fall of the tide, and the rush of the breakers had made it complex. And the lava had finally closed both before it had ceased to flow.

* * * *

It was at the same period that the whole race breasted back the darkness. There came at times in their history an age of exceptional advance, that made the preceding era seem almost stationary. Nor had they yet been able to explain its appearance satisfactorily. It was easy enough to say that such and such exceptional men lived then, and that they produced the phenomenon. But that was only reasoning in a circle; they were as much a product of the time as their fellows; whence did they get the inspiration which spurred them on, or the plastic material in which they could work? They would have been nothing without their conditions and circumstances. They surprised themselves with their powers and successes, as they strode forth into the primeval darkness and illuminated it. It all appeared very simple when once accomplished. They had been gazing for generations into the darkness, where now there was a blaze of light.

An imaginative pioneering book had long ago suggested that the impulse came from outside the round of the earth. And one of the most brilliant discoveries of this newest period of advance was a scientific proof of this hypothesis. The great development of the filammu or will-telegraph had made it easy, by localising the new thrill of expectation, and revealing that it came from no terrene source. Out of what seemed the profound inane such inspirations issued, and if they found a soil prepared for them by long self-denial and patient outlook and industrious collection of materials, they fertilised the period into exceptional efflorescence and fruition. Many an impulse comes out of the blue and falls unavailing in that no nation or race or period is fit to receive it. The profound inane, they came to see, was one of the falsest of ideas; because no matter patent to the human sight fills it, the interstellar space was believed to be the wilderness of the universe, cold, bleak, inhospitable, lifeless. Now it was felt to be the home of all supersensuous life, crowded with an energy that needed no stellar matter or atmosphere to support it, that never appealed to any but the highest and latest-developed senses of man. The Limanoran couriers out on the verge of the earth's atmosphere had been the first to feel this new flash that lit up such a vast region of the infinite darkness; they came back inspired with new resolution and made the first of the discoveries; they gave a magnetism to their fellow-workers in the same line, and soon the leaven spread through the whole people. The fervour of originality became the order of the day. To decipher the unknown handwritings on the wall of life, to solve its hardest problems, to make new inventions and discoveries, to push out into the darkness that surrounds the world—these became the ambitions of all.

Nor did the filammu of any in the island fail to thrill to the influence. Thyriel felt before I did that there was something exceptional in the atmosphere. But even my will-telegraph seemed to respond. I longed to go out and conquer the unknown, to outpace the slow movements of human discovery. At first I thought the impulse had come from Thyriel, and then from my pro-parents or my teachers. And so it was with every Limanoran; his first thought ran to his closest friend as the source of the magnetic thrill. But after much consultation and report, the conclusion appeared that no one in the island had originated the impulse, that all in the air had felt it simultaneously in their filammus, and after them all down in the island had felt it simultaneously. The truth gradually forced itself home on the investigating families that the magnetic vibration had had its source far beyond the limits of the earth; for they knew that from no other country or race upon the surface of the globe could it have come.

Ages before, they had abandoned the belief in what seemed supra-terrene influence as unscientific and leading to superstition. Faith had been in the past so often the cue and basis of the worst of tyrannies, the inspiration of the grossest immoralities and irrationalities, the impulse to most retrogression. It had also, it is true, been the nurse of gentle and just spirits. But it made them so timid that they were afraid to go forward; it wound round the soul such a network of fears and observances that its life was useless to the race. As soon as the final purgation of the people had been accomplished, it was found that every citizen ceased to speak of faith, or to use it as the basis of any work or practical step. They did not thrust it out by any public act, nor consciously reject it, they only left off giving weight to any of its commands or suggestions; not that they might not be true or on the side of all that was best; but that it had so often discredited its authority by prompting, or allowing itself to be used as the pretext for, retrogression or baseness. They preferred to take every step in life on ground made sure by investigation and proof that appealed to reason.

And here they were again on the limits of the unknown and vague. This sense that was closest to the portal of the soul, their filammu, had brought them to face an intelligence that came they knew not whence, and to stand in the presence of an infinite darkness that flashed out at times the lightning of noble impulse. They were by no means unwilling to listen to its report, but gladly received it as a sure and trustworthy revelation; however dim the region into which it was about to lead them, they were eager to follow, if only they set each step upon solid fact. If there was anything unverifiable in this new leading, they would soon be done with it. It now became one of the duties of the astrobiological families to watch for these extra-terrene vibrations of the will-telegraph, and to investigate the circumstances and conditions.

These families had been the first to feel the new impetus to discovery, for they were the couriers who went out to the borders of the atmosphere and watched for signs of energy and life in the infinite beyond. Again and again had they brought back specimens of microscopic and attenuated life, which seemed to float in interstellar space. Again and again had they analysed the beams of light shooting through it, but without much result. Now they were to be rewarded for their patience. They had taken out with them one of the new faleenas made of transparent and colourless irelium like glass; and as an experiment they sent it up by means of electricity far above themselves. As it rose above the limit of the earth's atmosphere, they saw all over its surface a strange fluorescence, which grew unearthly in its beauty and brilliance. Rainbow colours played through its texture as if they were threads thrown by the shuttle of some hand out of heaven. Its wings moved at lightning pace, and yet soon it began to fall towards the earth. Again it struck upwards, and again the prismatic weavings gave it more brilliant life. They watched it as it rose and fell between the denser and the rarer medium. And when finally they caught it and brought it down to earth, upon its wings both within and without there was imprinted, not the iridescent web that had been weaving over it, but a hieroglyph of faint, half-distinguishable forms, some familiar, some strange, inextricably mingled.

They investigated the phenomenon, and came to the conclusion that the faleena, in the comparative vacuum which lies on the borders of our atmosphere, had acted with its electric motors like the lavolan, one of their medical instruments for the inspection of the inner tissues, whilst the wings acted like the films of a photographic apparatus, and retained a shadowed impress of the inner structure of all the beings or forms coming between them and the body of the car. A new world was opened up to them beyond even their electric sense. Outside of the denser envelope of our orb the rarefaction of space meant no longer lifeless desolation traversed only by beams of light, electric impulses from other worlds, and the flight of occasional meteors. Now they knew that there were ethereal beings living in infinite space, and that their inner structure differed in density from their enveloping material. Some of this life was manifestly minute and attenuated, unsuited to the medium in which it floated, waiting for some fit orb to land on. But under their powerful clirolans it was as clear that there were highly developed organisms fitted to this element in which they swam, organisms probably higher than any to be found on the earth, yet too ethereal and shadowy to touch any of even the latest-evolved senses of the Limanorans.

What possibilities this glimpse into the vast unknown opened up for them they shrank for a time from imagining, lest they should again enslave themselves to superstition and absurd fancy. For astrobiology they saw at a glance there was begun a new and lofty career. Soon would they modify and improve the lavolan to fit the conditions of interstellar space, and the faleena, if not their own organs, for venturing far into the rarest ether. And then what reports, what pictures of the invisible universes would they bring before the eyes and the firlas of their fellow-islanders! How would they ever have time to investigate and classify the genera and species that inhabited the ether? What limit was there to the ambitions and ideals they would be able to set before the race?

Another investigation that followed from this discovery had as its object the nature of the new forms of energy that evidently filled interstellar space. This was the province of the families devoted to astrophysics. They produced apparatus for isolating each type of energy which seemed to have full action only in a vacuum, and they experimented with it in an innumerable variety of ways so as to find out its characteristics. The force of gravitation had been familiar to them even in primitive ages, and had long been investigated so as to reveal many of the qualities of its action that were unperceived by ordinary senses. Electricity had been one of the commonest of their phenomena, and recently a vast unknown region had been opened up by them, lying between the verge of eye-awakening light and the verge of firla-awakening electricity which their machines had made plain even to untrained senses. For generations they had passed with ease in their inamars or spectroscopes beyond the bands of colour that affected their eye, and the unseen rays had yielded most of their secrets to them. In their lavolans or vacuum-energy mirrors they had traced the characteristics of the torrents of energy which tore away from the negative pole of their batteries. And now they had to face a new form of radiant energy, the product of these negative streams and of the irelium which they struck. Experimenting with it in their lavolans they found it different from its parent energy; by passing through the irelium it had grown indifferent to the power of magnetism. This peculiarity enabled them to investigate the inner nature of magnetism; for on the two sides of an irelium sheet they had the same electric rays acting differently towards a magnet; on the one side they could be deflected by it, on the other they went on their way as if it were not there. The difference was also used in producing a new kind of electric motor, governed by an irelium film which closed or opened a channel of magnetic influence. A third useful application of the discovery was a new irelium-covering for the head and the body, that milked the east wind of its deleterious qualities. And a fourth was an apparatus for finding by the aid of a magnet the stuff of irelium with greater certainty in their lava-wells.

But the discoveries that flowed from this were still more important. By further experimentation they found another type of radiant energy that behaved in a similar way towards gravitation. In a vacuum formed within a vessel of an alloy of irelium it ceased to obey the force of gravity; but as soon as it had passed through the side of the vessel, it gave full heed to the force. Within a few months after this had been discovered, there had been invented a faleena that fell or rose according as the new rays were intercepted by a film of the irelium-alloy or were allowed free passage *in vacuo*. The energy in mass drove the car on indifferent to the earth's influence, or at the will of the guide brought the erfaleena, as they called it, gently sloping downwards at any angle required to the surface of the globe. A pioneering book at once developed the results of this discovery and invention. It showed how a way was now opened to other stars. For this new radiant energy was found to stream in and past the earth's atmosphere in vast currents. The denser the medium, the more was it absorbed and lost, so that in the earth and the atmosphere it seldom or never manifested itself. Hence the long ages of scientific investigation before it was discovered. By means of these currents, which evidently set through space in definite directions, they would be able to guide their new anti-gravitation faleena to any point in the interstellar ether, and be able to keep up the supply of force that would drive it. And when they approached a new world they could by means of their new machinery bring its force of gravitation to bear on the car and so hasten its flight; and they would be able to hover over the atmosphere by means of the alternating movements of their engine, till they could find out its conditions, and see whether it would be safe to land on it or not. What they wanted yet was the evolution of their physical system in the direction of living in ether or in various atmospheres indifferently. It pointed out to the physiological families the way that would lead in this direction; and it showed how, though it would take countless ages, it was yet within the scope of their humanity.

For their knowledge of the constitution of the universe the discovery of these two forms of radiant energy proved to be of great importance. They were able to find out the relationships of gravitation, electricity, the dark rays of the inamar, the negative rays of the lavolan, light, heat, and the two new types of energy. And by means of the similarities and differences found to exist between any two of them they were enabled to resolve the molecules of any element into their constituent atoms, and thus to reveal the characteristics of the fundamental ether. They felt that they were at last in the immediate presence of the medium which filled space, and they invented an apparatus isolating the ether from all the forms it enters into, so that it became manifest under their magnifiers to several of their senses. In it they were able to make any one of the forms of energy move and play. From it they were able to mould many of the terrene forms of latent energy, and they hoped to mould most of the others with which they were familiar.

One of the most immediately practical results that came from the discovery of these two modes of energy was another kind of engine, which almost doubled their store of force in Rimla. The main form of it took advantage of the radiant energy that showed indifference or obedience to gravitation according as it played in a vacuum or through an alloy of irelium into the air. The new rays lifted a piston *in vacuo*, and by an automatic arrangement they passed through a film of the alloy and then allowed gravitation to pull them and the piston with them back into its first position; the rapid alternations drove magnetic machinery which produced and stored up electricity. Another form of the new engine used the difference between the conduct the other newly discovered radiant energy displayed towards magnets when it played in a vacuum vessel of irelium, and when it had issued through the vessel's filmy side.

The increase and concentration of force in their island was one of the great subordinate aims of their civilisation. For they knew that the greater the power they had command of the more rapidly could they advance towards higher and higher goals. Greater force meant greater dominion over nature and her secrets and laws; and this implied accelerated speed in progress. It had been one of the primitive blunders of their civilisation, as it still was of all other civilisations, to imagine that extended empire over men meant a true development of humanity; wide sovereignty was mere artificial change of the locality and application of the forces of mankind, without increasing them; it was but a reshuffling of the cards (to use your similes), with all the honours in one hand instead of being distributed over all; it was merely political and not real. Any gain that might come from the concentration of power and wealth was wasted on increased war-material and military expeditions for retaining or subduing territories and peoples, on futile and routine administration, and on growth of court splendour and luxury. The pursuit of the sanguinary phantom of power over other men had to be forever abandoned before any real human advance could be made. Empire over the powers of nature was the primary condition of full development of human possibilities, and every tissue of their wonderful brains was strained to its utmost for the rapid extension of this sway. A new addition to the stores of the centre of force, a new source of energy, was therefore ever hailed by them as the warranty of a leap upward and onward into the future.

The invention of these new engines, then, had no slight significance as events in their history. And the assurance of more and more rapid progress was increased by a discovery of the chemic families in the same direction. They had used coal for the generation of heat before they had left their primeval home around the south pole. But in their more tropical archipelago they found no coal-beds, the islands having originated in volcanic and coral formation; and the climate made the use of such a concentrated fuel unnecessary; it was warm even in winter, and it supplied fruits and cereals which needed little cooking. The forests of the islands had furnished whatever fuel had been required for hundreds of generations, and outside of Limanora they were still sufficient for all purposes. But the centre of force had recalled the great heat they used to have from coal, and the Leomo, in their probings of the earth, had ever been on the outlook for beds of the old fuel. Recently they had found thin strata of it, but so deep in the earth that it was of little value to them.

But a discovery by the Sidramo, or chemic families, made them reconsider this decision and try to invent some form of the leomoran, which would cut and send with ease to the surface of the earth the coal they had found. The Sidramo had experimented with it in various lines. They had made the steam from it give power as they had seen it give power to the *Daydream* and her Broolyian imitations. But so large a proportion of the latent energy in it had been lost in the process that they turned their researches in other directions. Before long they found that, when the coal was placed in a chemical solution containing comparatively common and cheap elements, electric power was largely generated. And following up their discovery the Sidramo were soon able to draw electricity from any of the rocks of the island. Once having had their attention applied to such problems, they made a number of them surrender their secret; by surrounding one common rock, *e. g.*, with a certain solution they brought from it heat alone. But the discovery most important for the development of the race was that which brought electric power directly from the rocks and even from the earth. For this increased the possible store of force in Rimla enormously. And there was no limit to what they might use there for the advancement of civilisation.

Within a few days of this discovery the Piramo or meteorological families had applied the lavolan to one of their long-unsolved problems, the extraction of magnetic power in large quantities from the air. They had been already able to draw from the thunder-clouds their electricity, and make them pass harmless. And by means of personal effort and the magnetism of the body they were able when high up in the rarer regions of the atmosphere to recharge their little shoulder-engines for driving their wings. But in the lower air they had failed to draw electricity from any but thunder-clouds in any quantity. They based a new apparatus called pirakno on the lavolan and its discoveries, and with this they were able to draw magnetism from even the gentlest breeze. They increased its size and capacity, and soon could give a daily supply of new power to the centre of force. Nor did this deprive the air of the island of its exhilarant quality; for the more they took from it, the more seemed to flow in from surrounding space. But, when the east wind blew, they found the inflow of magnetism too much for their smaller piraknos; only the larger could cope with it; and then the store of power in Rimla received enormous additions.

For ages they had been testing the amount of magnetism in the air at various heights and temperatures and various times of day, month, and year, and recording the results of their investigations. They were now able to decide from these and from their experiences of the pirakno that irregular changes in the weather were due chiefly to magnetic influence. They saw that the tremendous storms which every few years swept the earth had their origin in exceptional inflows of cosmic magnetism. During the history of man since he had come to self-consciousness and to the habit of recording his own movements, there had been many sudden and temporary climatic changes, that had led to vast displacements of the inhabitants of the earth. A series of severe winters in the north and in the temperate zone would strip the trees and fields of all frugiferous qualities, and drive the animals of the chase away to the south in search of food. And the races of man had to follow them. So in the tropics a series of droughts would destroy half the chances of life, and exterminate one-third of the dwellers inland. As a rule the agony there led to no displacement of nations, so passive and fatalistic are they by nature near the equator; but in times when some new religious idea had broken the spell of fatalism, the first goad of starvation drove hordes to search for food in other zones. Oftentimes there has been a simultaneity in the meteorological severity, partly due to a universal influx of interstellar magnetism, but still more to the fact that the earth and the planetary system to which it belongs have swung into a region of space that is exceptionally barren of all life-impetus. At such periods came those wide-spread migrations of the dwellers on the globe that made new eras in history. It was one of those cosmic disturbances of climate that sent the Arabs out of their deserts, a flaming portent along the shores of the Mediterranean with their newly reformed religion, the creed of Mahomet, and at the same moment flung the Saxons against the northern frontier of Charlemagne's empire, and the Danes on the coast of Britain. So, earlier, in the fourth and fifth centuries of the Christian era, the Huns burst from the east like a torrent, and again and again swept all before them in the west, whilst simultaneously the Goths broke in from the north across the boundaries of the Roman empire. Later, in the ninth century, the Danes and Normans broke away from the north again and again, and plagued Europe with their piratical energy in the very period when the Magyars were migrating from the east to the west. And it was only the closer packing of the continents, and the consequent military organisation of European nations that checked these displacements in later centuries, though there were refluxes towards the east, as in the crusades. But the cosmic meteorology of the earth took different effect in the same direction, when plagues mowed down their millions of victims from east to west; where wide-spread displacements are impossible, there must be decimation by some cosmic means in order to let the light into the overpopulated regions. Another escape-valve was found for the pressure of those periods of temporary climatic change, when the western peoples were driven over the oceans to find a home. Emigration then came to mean transference of masses across the sea, at first to America, where there were other but weaker civilisations to be overcome, afterwards to lands and islands that were either empty or occupied by a few scattered savages. It was their circle of mist that saved the archipelago of Riallaro from the effect of these vast displacements of population. When every acre of land on the earth shall have been filled with its complement, and human forethought and ingenuity are still unequal to the sudden changes of cosmic meteorology, then famine and plague will be the only means of relieving the pressure.

The Limanorans had no fear of such effects in their own island, except indirectly. For they had complete command of their own birth-rate and death-rate, and kept the numbers commensurate with all the purposes of their existence. Climate was to them as plastic as any material or force of nature, and the unexpected in meteorology was gradually becoming unknown. But they had a strong indirect interest in all inbursts of the cosmic. For the peoples of the other islands, the descendants of their ancient exiles, were as ready victims as ever to what seemed the caprices of the seasons and the years. And the frustration of the consequent movements involving the interests of the Limanorans absorbed more of their time and reserve energy than they desired. A violent tornado would obliterate the products of a year over the whole archipelago, and the fear of starvation would goad the inhabitants into expeditions in search of food, sometimes even towards the isle of devils. Again, hungry microbes, the spawn of some plague-stricken world, would float into the earth's atmosphere and find new soil on the islands; and the dwellers would die so quickly that there was no time or room on their circles of earth for sepulture. Into the sea the festering dead would be thrown by the thousand, each bearing its myriad germs of contagion; the very fish that fed on them would die of the plague and bear its microbes to every shore; the currents and the winds, if left to their own bent, would sweep down the foul nests of contagion on the Limanorans; and it would take them weeks of superhuman effort to prevent the bacterial spawn from settling in their systems, and to cleanse the adjacent seas of all taint. The effort to prevent these disasters often wasted their store of force and checked their advance. It seemed to them therefore more economical of their energy to help in dispelling the original evil or making it swerve towards other oceans. For a time they considered it to the interests of their progress to save the whole archipelago from the irruptions of interstellar magnetism or bacterial life. But even this was found to have serious disadvantages. Unbroken prosperity surcharged the leaders of the other islands with conceit, and made them lose their fear of the central isle and resume their projects for its conquest; or it deluged them with population, which, whenever nature grew economical again, was driven to foreign means for its sustenance, and, at times, goaded by hunger, made in military wise for the isle of devils.

Yet these alarms and dangers were more infrequent and more easily repelled than when the more ambitious of the archipelago were driven by the spur of famine and disaster to incursion. And, though for a brief period the Limanorans allowed an occasional tornado or plague to devastate the islands of hostile neighbours, they came to the conclusion that it needed less of their energy to repel an occasional hive of enemies impelled by narrowing limits or the lessening generosity of nature than to beat off vast bodies of embattled peoples frantic with hunger and reckless of life, led by the keenest skill and fieriest ambition of the archipelago. They could better avoid all destruction of life in the one case than in the other—one of the duties of their civilisation, even though a subsidiary one.

The Piramo were thus essential to the progress of the race; their growing knowledge of the conditions that governed the climate as well as the passing weather saved in a day as much power as the use of such an instrument as the pirakno at first could add to Rimla in a year. And the scene of the labours of the Piramo was every year more and more extended to the extra-terrene; meteorology became in its investigatory and experimental department more and more cosmic, and often overlapped astronomy, astrobiology, and astrophysics, and aided them; more and more did they find their problems questions of magnetism or electricity. In the interstellar spaces must be sought the sources of the greater disturbances of season and climate and the pirakno grew every year of more and more importance, as they traced the magnetic influences around the earth back into the infinite fields of space.

About this very time they invented an instrument of great delicacy, which foretold the vaster tracts of magnetism into which the earth was swinging, and measured the increase. It depended for its principle and basis on the intimate relationship between electricity and light, on the effect of magnetism upon light and upon electric radiation from the negative pole in a vacuum. They had noticed for some time that the light from any meteor or luminous body outside the sphere of influence of the earth never reached the instruments of the observers on the edge of the atmosphere quite true, and that the aberration differed at different times. By means of various experiments they came to the conclusion that the aberration was due to magnetism in the extra-terrene spaces. Their new instrument, which they called a sarmolan, they sent out into the ether beyond the earth's atmosphere and beyond the influence of terrestrial magnetism; and, as it received beams of light from any one heavenly body towards which it had been directed, it recorded the amount of this body's deflection from the straight course. They preferred to turn it to the moon or to Venus or Mars; for then they were sure that the deflecting masses of magnetism lay within immediate range of the earth. This sarmolan turned out to be for cosmic changes of climate what the barometer is for daily or hourly changes of weather. Whenever it recorded violent deflection, it meant that the earth was approaching an exceptionally vast tract of magnetic influence, and that there would be great and frequent disturbances for months, if not for years, in the regularity of the earth's seasons and climates, or at least of those of one zone. It warned the Limanorans to get ready their piraknos and all other instruments they had for drawing and imprisoning for their own use the electricity from the atmosphere and the spaces above it. It was in short their cosmic barometer foretelling changes in climate years ahead. It eased the minds of the Piramo and set free half their energies for other investigations, as soon as it had proved itself a true prophet. Later improvements in it measured the distance of the supermagnetised region of space from the earth, and thus indicated the exact year and sometimes even the month and the day when the series of climatic perturbations were likely to begin. What had been guesswork before, made just before meeting the phenomenon itself, was now reduced to predictive law; and they looked forward to the time when by recording, classifying, and mapping the variations and regions of cosmic magnetism they would be able to get at the cause of its unequal distribution in interstellar space. Nay, when they had charted the great drifts and currents of varied energy that the earth encountered as its universe swung through space, they might have ready for their future voyagers to other worlds a full cosmography, which would instruct them in the kind of oceans and torrents they would have to breast, the types of energy they would have to accustom their systems to, and all the risks and dangers they would have to meet. And, when their knowledge of the conditions and regions and tracks in the boundless space they might have to traverse was fairly rounded and complete, then some slight adaptation of their sarmolan would be to them their cosmic compass.

There was evidence in other discoveries too that this hope was not so utopian as it seemed at first, that at least not countless centuries would pass before they might be able to fulfil it. One especially, that of the Floramo or botanical families, quickened their expectation far beyond the mere flight of fancy. It was a new sublimation of a vegetable extract, which seemed to give their lungs free play when there was little or no air to breathe. They had used for ages the fruit of what they called the floronal or tree of life for giving new vigour to the organs and especially to the nerve-tissues; they still continued to use it, even though the chemical families had analysed it and found all its constituents, and then reproduced a mixture that had most of the revivifying qualities of the fruit. The tree grew only in marshy districts, and they had reserved an obscure and rarely visited corner of the island for its culture and for the culture of plants and trees like it. There was another tree growing only in the cooler zone half-way up the mountain, and preferring shallow and poor soil to root in, whose fruit gave extreme flexibility to the more muscular and cartilaginous tissues, and especially to those in the chest; if taken inwardly or through the pores, muscular exercise became more easy, and breathing became deeper and slower or quicker as the will directed. A third low plant or shrub, which grew only on the highest altitudes of Lilaroma, and had its roots generally in the soil underneath a layer of snow, had been found recently to have in its tissues, and in a concentrated form in its nuts, great stores of oxygen. For ages it had been considered a poisonous plant, and avoided; for within a considerable radius of it breathing had always been more difficult than at a distance from it; it had therefore been eradicated from all parts of the cone frequented by the Limanorans. It had no beauty of form, often grew low like a lichen or moss, and could remain under the snow for years without perishing. It had thus been neglected and in fact seldom observed in its growth; whilst its nuts had been thought to be as poisonous as the plant itself. But recently an avalanche from one of the little-visited slopes of Lilaroma had uncovered a hollow, in which one of the Floramo had found a bird, emaciated and unable to fly, yet still alive; and beside it were the remains of a number of these poison plants and particles of many of their nuts. It had evidently been imprisoned many weeks, if not months, and its only food had been the obscure and offensive snow-bush, stunted, scabrous, and without green or leaf.

The Floramo became deeply interested in the phenomenon, and gathered many specimens of the shrub from the top of the mountain. They fed the bird till it became plump, and then shut it up in one of their irelium vacuum-chambers with only the nuts to peck. There they watched it from day to day, and saw that as long as it fed on the nuts it continued vigorous and lively, even though it began to lose its rounded outlines again. They soon closed their experiment, and set the winged creature free to fly whither it would, satisfied that there could be only one logical conclusion with regard to the plant. They saw that its nature was to lay up stores of oxygen in all its tissues, and they called it alfarene or the oxygen-shrub. It was this treasure in it that enabled it to live so long beneath vast accumulations of snow and ice; it was this feature of its life that made it when open to the air so exhaust the oxygen for yards around it that men found it difficult to breathe beside it; it was this that, when it became the food of the bird, enabled it to live and breathe so long away from the air. It was the outcome of long ages of selection up in those difficult altitudes, where nothing could live under the snow without this power of storing up oxygen. And its nuts, too hard and innutritious except for hunger-driven birds to attack, concentrated round the seeds an extraordinary amount of this oxygen-stuff; and by means of this, when underneath the pressure of the snows the husk broke, the seeds were able to support themselves and develop into plants away from the vital air.

It was evident that these alfarene nuts were treasure-houses of oxygen; and soon they were tried by the Limanorans themselves when they flew into the upper regions of the air. At first they broke the nuts into powder, which was made into a hard but soluble paste: a small piece of this held in the mouth till it melted enabled them in their flights to breathe freely in rarer altitudes than they had ever reached before. The Floramo afterwards brought out the oxygen-storing power of the shrub more strongly by careful cultivation and selection. Within a few years they made of it a vigorous, large, and comparatively handsome tree, and its nuts grew larger and more oxygenated, so that they became a necessity for all flight into higher atmospheres. More attention was also paid to the floronal or tree of life and to the germabell or tree whose fruit produced elasticity of the muscles and cartilage. The development of all three in the direction in which they might be useful to the race quickened; the energy stored up in their fruits came to be more and more concentrated; selection of the plants, cross-fertilisation of them, special soil and feed for their roots, and special surroundings, were all-powerful in the hands of the Floramo for changing plants and trees to any purpose they had in view. They studied the tissues and habits of the species that they wished to adapt, not as an abstract and merely scientific investigation, but as one of the practical problems of their own life; they turned the clirolan on its inner and outer tissues, as they anatomised it; they watched its inner processes with the lavolan as it grew or decayed; they chemically analysed its sap in all its stages, and the various soils at its roots; then they experimented with new elements in the soil in the direction of the qualities they wished to encourage; they tried it with various degrees and hours of sunshine by day, and various amounts of moisture by night, at different stages in its growth; if they found some of the qualities that they desired in its fruit or tissues more vigorous in some other species, they fertilised its blossom with the pollen of this second plant, and from the seed raised a new species, which would fully realise their purpose. The whole of vegetal nature was plastic in their hands. And every year saw hundreds of new species.

The Floramo were the forerunners of the Sidramo or chemical families, and experimented in materials and juices and essences, which would be useful to the race in its ever-quickening advance. Often would vegetal nature reveal a compound that shortened some route through the future, and the Sidramo would then analyse the product, and find the secret of its special efficiency. The Floramo were indefatigable in that department of their work which experimented with the application of plants and their fruits and tissues to useful purposes, and every day saw some process accelerated by the results of their labours. In fact they classified the vegetal world not merely according to the structure and methods of growth and propagation, but mainly according to the particular utility of the products. The one classification was more essential to their creation of new species, the other to their discovery of purposes for which new species might be created. Like all their sciences, botany was nothing if it was not creative.

Having discovered the oxygen-storing shrub, the Floramo gave a new bent to it, applying their energies to strengthening its vitality and its vitalising powers, and to finding out the most convenient form in which to use its treasured energy. Aided by the Sidramo they were able to combine the juice of the fruits of the floronal and the germabell with the paste of the nut of alfarene into minute, to my eyes almost microscopic, globules, each of which would support one of their couriers in the ether outside of our atmosphere for several hours. At first they lost one of the vitalising elements in securing another; and even after they had been able to bind the three essences together in one form, it gave air and sustenance for only a few minutes when they tried it in a complete vacuum. But after experimenting for many months, they were able to concentrate these essences under enormous pressure and by the aid of electric stimulus into a form which would not volatilise except in the saliva of the mouth and under electric stimulus. They were also able to give their globules such electric power as would utilise the streams of magnetic energy that filled the ether. Thus the ether-couriers found them far more strengthening and sustaining just above the earth's atmosphere than in it. One globule lasted several hours longer in a vacuum, and made breathing and the other vital functions more easy and enjoyable. Thus was opened up to them by this discovery a long vista of investigation. The new type of sustenance and oxygenation was so concentrated that the couriers into the sky could carry with them enough to serve through months.

During the next great period of discovery the Sidramo superseded this use of alfarene by a more rapid method of concentrating air. As usual they followed up the steps of the Floramo, and created what the botanical families had found in nature. The use of great pressure in the manufacture of the sustenant globules in their final form suggested the track they should take; and the immense accumulation of energy in Rimla and the rapidly increasing faculty of concentrating it on any point or purpose gave them the requisite power. They came to reduce air to liquid, and finally to solid and permanent, form. And, following up the lead of this discovery, they applied greater and greater pressures, and were at last able to transform with ease and without danger any element into gaseous, liquid, or solid form. They contracted the slow processes, that in terrestrial nature covered myriads of ages, into a few minutes or hours, and thus again multiplied indefinitely their vast treasures of power in Rimla.

A pioneering production, the book of elemental transformations, foreshadowed the discoveries to which this would lead. Ether, it was shown, would be transformed into any desired substance, as soon as its constituents and formation were found out. Even modes of motion, like sound and light and electricity, would, with this vast expansion of the possibility of compression, and the growing power of amalgamating and concentrating forms of energy, come to be bottled up in liquid or solid form for any required period. A block of latent sound or latent light or latent electricity would be as common as a block of ice. Another pioneer, the book of abbreviation of geological time, opened up a second vista of power that the discovery pointed out. Nature took geological ages to perform most of her processes; but in great passions she accomplished as much in a few minutes. The safe imitation of these creative and destructive paroxysms was certain to be one of the conquests of Limanoran posterity. For the actual concentration of power in Rimla was as nothing compared with what it would be in the future. Now they were able to contract the work of years into minutes; then would they be able to leap in one moment across geological ages. Time was the inertia of realisation and creative power. The whole drift of their civilisation was towards the mastery of finite periods of time. Years were to them what minutes had been to their ancestry; to their far posterity geological ages would be as brief as years were to them. Swifter and more swiftly would they eliminate from their creative processes the reluctant element of time, and feel that they were pacing in the footsteps of eternity.

As it was, they soon put the liquefaction and solidification of the elements to countless uses. A few of these were the cooling of their buildings by concentrated air, the use in the arts of its corrosive power and of its power of rendering most metals easily plastic, its amalgamation with other elements into an explosive matter so destructive as to supersede the use of the leomoran in earth-perforation, and the storage of their faleenas with supplies for expeditions that would take years in interstellar space.

A minor use to which they put alfarene was the production of vacuums. They had long had mechanical air-pumps, that gave them the vacuums they needed for their experiments. But they now found it much easier to enclose one of these snow-stunted shrubs in an air-tight vessel of transparent irelium, and watch it absorb the air within the walls. The energy formerly spent on the making of air-pumps was saved, and devoted to some other useful purpose.

What was still better was the continual experimentation on the human system carried on by means of these so easily accessible vacuums. The alfarene vacuum became the daily plaything of the Limanoran, and he took pleasure in finding out the needs of his body in it, and the length of time he could endure the pure ether. It was not long before they knew every difficulty they would be likely to encounter in crossing from star to star. The minor defects of the body were easily met after a few years' study of them by the various scientific families. But two gave them long pause.

One was the intense cold they were sure to experience. Where there was no terrene matter or moisture or air to retain the solar or astral heat that travelled through space, the diffusion of the streams of thermal energy would render any far voyaging from the earth impracticable. The experiments to meet this difficulty took three directions. One was physiological—to make the body capable of resisting as great a degree of cold as they would be likely to encounter; this attempt was only partially successful, and that by slow steps. They brought themselves to live with pleasure in any cold that could be found in or around the earth; but it would take many centuries, perhaps geological ages, to bring endurance up to the pitch of interstellar cold; it would in fact mean such a sublimation of their bodies as would make them like spirits. Another direction was chemical—to produce a regular atmosphere round the body as it flew, so that it might retain some of the streams of heat that swept past it; the use of the essence of the oxygen-plant helped them in this direction to some extent; but the amount of it that would be needed to keep up such an atmosphere for years, concentrate it as much as they liked, meant so huge a cargo that none of their winged cars would be able to bear it above the earth. The third direction was physical—to produce as much heat around the body as would act as a shield against the cold of the ether; this was the most successful; for there were such torrents of energy ever moving through interstellar space that it merely needed its utilisation to solve the problem. One plan, that, when carefully developed, would ensure success, was a magnetic garment which would cover the whole of the body and draw to it all the electric energy within a large radius of it, to be transformed into heat by minute engines distributed all over the envelope. Another was, to combine the mechanical collection of electricity from the ether and the full development of the magnetic powers of the body. Already they had been able to flash lightnings around them as they flew through the night; and it would need but small mechanical manipulation to increase this display and to turn it into heat. Like meteors, they would blaze across space, wrapped in a mantle of flame.

But this difficulty in the way of flight through the ether was but slight as against the other defect that their systems had in common with all terrene bodies. They could develop heat easily enough; but how were they to keep intact and consistent in a vacuum constitutions which had been developed under the pressure of an atmosphere? How would the tissues and the organs of their bodies adjust themselves to the absence of atmospheric conditions? As they rose above the clouds, they had long felt as if their limbs and even the molecules of their bodies were without due subordination and apt to assume individual independence, even when the spirit grew boldest and most concentrated in its energy. Their own wings and faleenas that were intended for upper and rarer altitudes had to be made tougher and more elastic than for common flight close to the earth. They had to make them at last in a vacuum, and subject them to all the conditions that met them in the ether. But it would take myriads of generations, if not of geological ages, to bring their own bodies into such a state as to bear vacuum around them for years; and then in their terrene life with such a new constitution they would be unable to endure so great a pressure as that of the atmosphere near the earth. The only contrivance that seemed feasible was a farfaleena enclosing the traveller round, large enough to hold alfarene supplies for the long voyage, and strong enough to stand the pressure of an atmosphere within it. This they might manage after some years of experimentation.

But enclosure within such a narrow space for so long a period, without the possibility of free movement into the ether, did not attract them; and any little accident in their machinery or to their supplies might make their faleena their tomb. Some other line must be taken by investigation and invention, if stellar migration was to become a possible and desirable thing.

This line was indicated by discoveries of the Sidralmo or bio-chemical families, and the Ooaromo or psycho-physiological families. The Sidralmo had long been investigating the ultimate constituents of living matter; and again and again, when seeming to be on their track, they were baffled by the escape of some element, and left with only the *caput mortuum* to analyse. Under their clirolans too, powerful though they were, the principle of life showed itself in many ways to their senses, and yet evaded all attempt to isolate it. The lavolan, which showed the inner structure of living bodies as they lived and moved, brought them nearest of all to the veil that hung over the secret of vitality. Plants and stationary animal organisms allowed them full scope for their investigations. In them they could see the life ebb and flow, as death approached or receded; in them they could find every material element entering into their composition, and test with their varied and minute meteorological apparatus all the forms of energy which moved them; they checked the current of life, and watched in the plant or animal the elements and energies that remained comparatively stable and those that deteriorated;

they let it die out, and watched the throb and struggle of the various constituents and forces as they collapsed; then, when it seemed to have surrendered all life or hope of life, they brought it back, by their knowledge of its existence, to the upward struggle again and no feature of the return escaped their notice; most watchful of all were they on that dim borderland between life and death, where dawn is sunset and sunset dawn. In every stage were they able to isolate each strand of the thread of life; yet the essential secret of all escaped them. Once the organism had shrivelled into a bundle of dead fibres or fallen to dust, no effort of theirs could give it the throb of life again. They could reproduce every element and tissue and fibre, and under their clirolans place them together in the forms of life with marvellous art. One thing was still wanting to make it all it had been. They could even mimic the flow of life through it by means of their command over the sources of energy; but the result was only mechanical; they had not supplied it with the never-failing spring of vitality.

At last, during the period of this great illumination there was thrown a beam of light on the right path for solving this problem. One of the Sidralmo was experimenting on certain substances to see how they behaved under the rays issuing from a lavolan or revealer of inner mechanism. They were chiefly new vegetable substances the properties of which it was his duty to discover and tabulate. He was also mingling one or two new minerals with the plant-products in order to see what modification the blending would cause. One metal had lately been found issuing from the deepest of their lava-wells in the form of vapour; when cooled, it had assumed a crystalline character, and acted to some extent like a magnet; yet it was sensitive to energies that an ordinary magnet ignored, as, for instance, the passage of exceptional nerve-force through the human body. Lightly hung, it quivered when near anyone who happened to be greatly excited. But it paid no heed to the normal currents of energy along the nerves. There was also a species of plant recently evolved that had shown itself singularly sensitive on the approach of any living thing; it shrank not merely from the touch of a hand or of any animal, but from the proximity of life, whilst it remained unmoved when touched by any falling leaf or stone. The experimenter had taken a number of these plants and made of them a basketwork, in which he hung a piece of the new magnetic metal by a slender thread. This he placed above his lavolan to see how the rays from it would affect, or be affected by, the new combination of influences. There seemed to be little or no effect, but he continued his experiment to make sure. Through some imperfection in its walls his vacuum failed; he tried to pump the air out again, but, this failing too, he substituted an alfarene-vacuum which happened to be near him. The result was most striking. The metal, lightly hung in the basket, became agitated at once, and its movements grew more or less active as it approached or was drawn off from the vacuum. After a time it began to show less sensitiveness, and at last became almost quiescent, even though the vacuum remained efficient. On examining the alfarene plant under a magnifier, he found a minute slug, that had evidently escaped the notice of the maker of the vacuum; this had been the source of the agitation of the metal in the basket during its last spasmodic efforts to hold on to life; and, when death, through the lack of air, had overcome it, the agitation had ceased. The plant itself had by the presence of its life kept the test from becoming completely quiescent. The influence of the life of the experimenter himself seemed to be largely neutralised by the surrounding air; it was only when he came very close to the test that it indicated his presence.

Here was revealed to the Sidralmo the path they had to follow; a wide vista into the darkness had been suddenly opened. It was not long before they had taken full advantage of the discovery. They invented the most helpful of all their instruments, the sidralan or biometer; they hung the combination of life-sensitive plant and nerve-sensitive metal itself in a vacuum, directly in the path of an electric current; the details of its mechanism they rapidly improved till it measured with accuracy the degree of vitality in any plant or animal. But they soon found that it was differently affected by vegetable and animal life. The energy of the former moved it but slightly, and only in certain directions; the latter seemed to surround it and agitate it from all sides; it quivered as if with subdued excitement. Yet there were degrees in both; some plants moved it more than the most primitive unicellular animals, although the movement was less pervasive. Thus were they well on the way towards the isolation of the life-principle from its constant concomitants.

The biometer came to be of as much importance to the medical superintendents as to the Sidralmo; it abridged the labour of their weekly inspection; for it told in a moment whether the vitality in any member of the community had fallen or risen in degree, whether it was below the proper average, in short whether all his organs and tissues would have to be minutely examined for the cause, and whether his dietary scheme would have to be revised. The psycho-physiological families found it of some use in their investigations into the faculties of man and their basis in his bodily constitution. They found that the wiser and more intellectual a personality was, the more gently he moved the sidralan; the more of animal vitality he had, the more violently he agitated it by his presence.

But the instrument was too rough and undiscriminating for their purposes. It could not distinguish between the purely spiritual and the purely animal except in this loose way. They tried modifications of it, but without success. It was the Ailomo or astrobiological families that helped them to take the right direction. They were constantly bringing down out of the stratum above the atmosphere vessels full of the seeming nothingness that existed there, in order to investigate it and see whether it was mere vacuum or not; and though the contents appealed to none of their senses but the electric, their various instruments of research revealed different energies and a large amount of life, besides minute forms of matter without life. On several occasions they had noticed that the contents affected their tests differently when the experimenter was near and when he stood at a distance. Step by step they separated the element that acted thus from its various concomitants. And soon they were able to concentrate a considerable quantity of it in a receiver exhausted of air, and to precipitate it in powdery metallic form.

The substance was handed over to the Ooaromo, who saw that it would supply the test they wanted; for it was but slightly sensitive to the presence of animals, and its sensitiveness gradually vanished as they tried it with lower and lower species of animals; whilst it quivered near men, less near young men and women, only slightly near infants, but with quick tremors when near the older and wiser Umanorans, who had suffered and thought through long centuries. They came to the conclusion that this residuum was the essence of some element in the ether that responded to the energy of the higher faculties, as the magnet responded to electricity. They had in fact found at last a true test of soul, that refinement of the higher animal energies which has assumed a new grade in life, the consciousness of itself, and the power of keeping its own form and essence as an entity forever separate from all other beings and things.

It was not long before the Ooaromo had made from it an apparatus which would test the presence of soul and measure its force. In this ooaran or psychometer they were at last furnished with an instrument that would give organic unity and new purpose to their science. They would now be able to watch and measure the growth of soul in the child, and the ebb and flow of its strength in youth; and thus would they give new vigour and life to the creative function of their science. They had now an exact basis for education; as guides of parents and proparents in tuition they would walk in the full day, where before they had groped in dim twilight; in every case would they be able to advise with the same certainty as the medical elders advised on the health of the body. For the mature men and women would they act as true father-confessors, and do what the priests of so many religions pretended to do, but did not do; they would be able to tell everyone, who desired it, whether his soul had advanced or receded in power after any series of sufferings and deeds, or any line of conduct, and thus to give advice as to what should be done or omitted in the future. And when the elders had come near what had before seemed the utmost limit of life, they would be able to tell them whether their nausea of existence was only fleeting and subjective, or whether the roots of their soul were loosening themselves from the soil of the body.

CHAPTER II

AN ACCIDENT

BUT so vast an expansion of science and the unveiling of so many outlooks into the future left no room for the thought of death. The pace of life quickened perceptibly, and the energy of every dweller on the island was strained to its utmost to meet the requirements of the new additions to the force of the country and of all the new inventions. It was impossible to think of anything but the tasks in hand. None had an idle thought, none a leisure moment to waste on mere introspection or dreams.

In fact it became quite clear that the old dream-factory might be closed for a time at least. For several generations it had been the custom of the Limanorans to stimulate invention and discovery by the use of magnetism. When anyone felt his problem insoluble, or an insuperable obstacle in the way of his advance towards some practical goal, he had his dream-consciousness awakened and quickened as he slept. A member of the medical families would attend by his bedside, and apply a magnetic current to the particular point of his brain that controlled the powers concerned in his pursuit, and especially to the parts which were the physical expression of the imaginative faculties. And by day he would instruct the thinker as to what nutritive or medicated chambers he should enter in order to draw the main strength of his system towards the faculties he needed. Day after day the patient nurtured the parts of the brain and of the nervous system that would help him to the solution; night after night he dreamt out the terms of the problem. At last either in day-dream or night-fancy the curtain would be raised, and he would see the path to take; light flashed in on him as if from another world. What in my buried life used to be called inspiration was cultivated, moulded, and directed with as deliberate foresight and care as any feature of the body or the character. Nor were these dream-stimulants ever abused; when the purpose had been served, the goal reached, at once the other faculties and physical parts had equal attention; the strain was unbent, and the symmetry and balance of the whole system restored. Never was the stimulation of dream-consciousness permitted for a mere pleasure or whim; the importance of the aim to the progress of the race had to be proved before it was granted; nay it was only problems the solution of which would lead to extraordinary advances, that were dealt with by narolla or dream-consciousness stimulants. Now the narolla were entirely abandoned; for imagination was preternaturally excited, and discovery and invention seemed to come to investigators almost without effort.

It was indeed a period of accelerated progress, if not of precipitance, in the work of all families. The darkness around existence lifted over the whole horizon, and demanded redoubled exertion, in order that the new regions should be mapped before it fell. The tissues and nerves of every Limanoran felt the stimulus; each worked with a will. Still the necessities of the situation almost ran ahead of their powers. One thing became clear, that they must have more workers; the new generation would have to be more numerous than the last. For the young had to be drawn upon for active nerve- and head-work before their usual time; and these would need more leisure in the next stage of their life to compensate for the loss of it in the period of growth.

It grew evident that parents who had been exceptionally successful in the two children they had brought forth, reared, and launched full-fledged on the career of life should be permitted and stimulated to resume parentage. It was considered one of the highest privileges and honours to be selected as parents again by the magnetic consciousness of the nation. There was needed no formal agreement or resolution; the mind of the race was known without consulting it openly; and every pair felt in a moment that they were selected for reparentage; they required no stimulation, no permission to enter on the patriotic duty. And all considered it a duty of the loftiest kind. Passion in the race burned low; no longer was it a sting or goad that had to be mastered; it was in short no more a passion, such as the use of imagination, the love of the race, or the yearning after advance had become. The animal element in it had grown insignificant, and left it at the bidding of intellect and will. These tried parents had thus no sensuous pleasure to seek in the new task assigned to them. They took it upon them as a duty, and their chief pleasure lay in the honour they had been paid, and in the service they were doing to the race and to the progress of their humanity.

A second necessity of the new position was earlier marriage on the part of the men and women of the community. As soon as bare maturity had been reached, pairing now began. First it had to be scientifically ascertained that all the merely primitive stages of mankind had been passed through, not only the prehistoric, but the historical. It would be one of the greatest of evils to allow the privilege of parenting for the community to any who might have yet to go through a stage of individual life that represented centuries of the past of mankind. Little better would this be than stocking their island with children from their exiles. It was a question of testing every individual; for some passed more rapidly through the life of their ancestry than others; and these were not always the best as parents or even as citizens. Every tissue and faculty had to be tested, after careful study of the records of the childhood and youth. No possible prospect or chance of atavistic taint was overlooked.

The next duty was to review the needs of the race. The tasks and abilities of every family were measured, and the possible expansions of these were estimated; then new sciences, or new divisions of sciences, or new duties that would need the services of a family or families specially selected and moulded for the purpose, were taken into the account. From this elaborate review of the resources and needs of the population conclusions were carefully drawn as to the number and quality of the children that were required. The problem was easy enough as far as mere extensions of the existing families were concerned. But the creation of new types was a question that tasked the abilities of the wisest to the utmost. The special faculties needed for the new science or art or duty had to be discussed and decided; and especially how far existing faculties would have to be modified or newly combined. Then out of the various families those two had to be chosen, a cross which would produce the required modification or combination. But, as this was still largely of the nature of experiment, more than one effort was made towards each new type, in order that, if one child failed, the others might be available. But the wise creators of new types were rapidly getting surer of their ground; their experiments were growing less of experiments; they could almost foretell to a faculty or tissue the result of the crossing of any two families. And where any quality was unequal to the new duty, first creative surgery was called in to modify or add to the tissue of that part of the brain which was the physical equivalent of the faculty, and afterwards education with its various magnetic and dietary aids was brought to bear on its development. Yet there might be some chance of their new type falling short of its purpose and, to guard against this, several individuals of it were brought forth and trained. It was generally found that all of them were needed to carry out the duties of the new position.

After everything had been settled in the programme of the next generation, the task of matching began. Time after time the two who were to be the parents of the new type were thrown together as if by accident in circumstances and surroundings which would touch their imaginations and rouse their enthusiasm for each other. They were put into difficult positions together, so that one might help to extricate the other from them. Alternate debt and service wove mutual bonds around them, till at last neither desired to issue from the network of obligation and love in which they were caught. The magnetism of one was complementary to that of the other; and when separated they longed to see each other. With none in the community was the filammu of either in such communion as with the loved mate. Thus partly wise choice, and partly spontaneity, produced the match. The lifelong bond could never become enslaving for either; for the material of it had been selected not by mere youthful caprice, but by the maturest wisdom of the race, whilst it was spun by the impulse and will of the two friends themselves. Neither the state nor either of the partners could possibly regret the friendship, or wish it dissolved. It passed as naturally into marriage as flower into fruit.

But, whilst the future was thus being safeguarded, the new duties or expanded duties had to be looked after. Seventy-five years of work had to be provided for before the new citizens could be made fit for their duties. Part of this was covered by drawing earlier on the powers of the new generation; the youth must come out of their seclusion a few years sooner than usual. But that was not sufficient. What way was there out of the difficulty? It was a tacit rule of the community that none were to overstrain their energies; overwork was considered as great a vice as indolence; for it cheated the race of some of its advance by demoralising the faculties and tissues, and bringing on the nausea of life earlier than it should come by nature. The biometer was carefully applied to every citizen in order to test how far he could go in work without wasting his energies. And after all had been assigned additional work to their utmost limit, there was still so much unassigned. The only chance of meeting it was the extension of life. The elders must live longer. Happily every condition was now present for managing this. They had new foods and agents for revitalising the tissues; they had new apparatus for discovering internal defects in the human system, and new methods of remedying them; the far vistas opened up into the future gave a new purpose to the life even of the most aged; they longed to see what would come of all the expanded invention and discovery; the enthusiasm of the new age fired the imagination of the oldest. Limanoran life had another century added to it.

In the midst of the bustle of these preparations for the future (if anything the Limanorans did could be called bustle), there occurred an accident that smote them almost with dismay, and brought them as near as I had ever seen them approach to melancholy. The additions to the sources of the energy available in Rimla had entailed more muscular work as well as more superintendence, and it was necessary to assign more physical toil to the now-earlier mature than had been customary. Two scions of the meteorological families, who had been selected for marriage and parentage, were sent to manage a large pirakno, which had been constructed for drawing the magnetism from the air and the spaces just beyond the atmosphere. The great machine had been placed on an isolated spur of Lilaroma, so that if ever through the sudden sweeping of the earth into a supermagnetised area it should become dangerous, it could easily be detached from Rimla and insulated. And there were never less than two beside it to help in its management.

The younger men and women took the night watches in all the physical labour that had to be undertaken. And Tamarna and Omirlo, as one of the youngest and least experienced of the pairs that had to manage this huge pirakno, kept the last watch of the night, the watch that included sunrise and was followed by that of two of the most mature workers. It was thought that, as every Limanoran would be awake and on the alert at dawn, help in any emergency could easily be procured. As it was well known that during that period there was a great increase of magnetism in the atmosphere, provision was made in the machine itself for so regular a change; it was so arranged that, when the sun's rays first touched it, it should automatically increase its capacity for magnetism. But so recent had been the development of cosmic magnetography that the times and seasons of the irregular increase of magnetism had not been tabulated and classified. Had the observations been made for a long enough time to allow of inferring a uniformity or law, then it would have been seen that these supermagnetised spaces, though they may have been entered by the earth during the night, have little effect upon her atmosphere till day dawns; the excess of magnetism seems to lie dormant in the dark; the first rays of the sun act like a fuse to a mine and complete the circuit between extra-terrene space and the surface of the earth. Sunrise, in fact, as they came afterwards to see, was the most critical time for such a machine as the pirakno.

It happened, too, that on this particular night the sarmolan or cosmic barometer had been getting out of order; but its watchers did not think it called for immediate attention; the morning would be time enough to put it right. Its indicator thus lay tongue-tied and misleading, when it should have been violently agitated. Tamarna and Omirlo had no warning of the approaching magnetic tornado. The hour before dawn the pirakno moved as regularly and quietly as at that point of the night when the magnetic tide is at its lowest ebb, the point when sleep is deepest and death is most frequent. They had just seen that every part was moving without friction and fully coping with its work; and Omirlo felt that he could leave his mate for a brief space and consult the sarmolan-watchers. He had been gone but a few minutes when he heard a loud crash behind him, and at the same moment he noticed that the first beams of the sun had struck across the levels of the sea. He turned and saw a flash from the place where, he thought, the pirakno stood. Flying back in trepidation, he found the machine as he had left it, but it had stopped. At first he could not see Tamarna; but on searching he saw her form lying on the ground close to the pirakno, hidden by one of its cranks. He touched her temples and left side, and saw that life had fled. The crank had come upon her as she lay, and bruised her body; the sight of this completed his despair; he felt that the last hope of her recall had vanished.

Yet he knew how much the medical elders could do, and there arose in his mind a flicker of hope. He wasted no time on lamentation, for there moved in him the carefully trained consciousness that all such abandonment to emotion was an offence against the progress of the race. They considered that every occurrence of life demanded as much concentration of energy and thought as a shipwreck, or the incidents of a battle, or anything that we in the West would call an alarming emergency. As grief or despair or fear used up the power that should be spent on action, emotion was strictly reined in at such a moment; the instinct was to call the whole resources of the nature to action.

Omirlo braced himself to the emergency, and sent the whole of the magnetism he was capable of into his will-telegraph. After a few minutes' exercise of it, it seemed to relax, and he knew that he had roused his parents to the danger. Recalling his energies to Tamarna, he followed the few simple rules that he had been taught for the recovery of the seeming dead. He made her lungs and heart imitate the play of life; he switched the magnetism of his own system on to hers. But after all his efforts she lay still inert when his parents arrived. They decided to carry her at once to the medical elders, for they saw that something exceptional had occurred; it was not a swoon, or even death from the bruise dealt by the pirakno. So they took her wings, and making them by means of soft leafage into a couch for her, they bore her through the air swiftly, but just as she had lain when found. Tamarna's own parents met them on the way, and helped them to accelerate their pace with her; and within less than ten minutes after the accident she was in the hands of the sages in the mountain hospital.

The general medical house was Oomalefa. But there were two houses of cure which approached more nearly to what our hospitals are. One was far up the slopes of Lilaroma, not much beneath the winter-line of snow. The other was aërial and movable and was, whenever it was needed, floated upwards to the margin of our atmosphere, where parasitic and microscopic life was reduced to unaggressive feebleness. In it were all the necessities of life at hand; the temperature was kept close to summer heat; and there were lines of communication, so thin as to be almost invisible in the air, connecting it with the halls of sustenance and medication. This hospital was meant for the invalid who was strong enough to be moved up from solid earth; and, as soon as one had been brought back far enough from the grasp of death to bear the rarity of the upper air where it merged into the ether, he was taken up in it. But Tamarna was first borne to the mountain hospital, where the instruments of investigation and cure were ready. When she should have had all the ruptures of her bones and organs and tissues set for mending, and all the tissues that were crushed beyond mending replaced by freshly manufactured tissues, and when she was seen to hold on to life with a tenacious grasp again, then would she be borne into the hospital of accelerative healing high above the clouds.

The biometer recorded the faint presence of life; the spirit had not yet escaped, and before long it grew manifest to ordinary eyes. They had apparatus for stirring any organ of the body into activity; and with the lavolan they soon saw which of Tamarna's functions had been deranged and had suffered syncope. It was her heart that had ceased action; the inrush of magnetism from space drawn by the pirakno, without provision for storing it or letting it pass harmless, had paralysed some of the more important cardiac tissues and the circulation was in many places clogged, whilst a large proportion of the superficial blood-vessels had been ruptured by the fall of the crank upon the body. A European medical council would have abandoned the bruised and discoloured corpse as fit only to be "food for worms." But no member of the community could be spared in such a period of enthusiasm and expansion. The newly discovered agents and methods were brought to bear. Delicate instruments made the heart first mimic and then produce the true cardiac action. Currents of magnetism swept the veins, and cleared the routes for the circulation of the blood, at the same time stimulating the life-fluid. The livid hue gradually disappeared from the face. Another instrument gave action to the lungs, first in mimic and then in vital way. Concentrated sustenance was injected into the veins and soon the breathing grew regular. Yet it needed hours of this recreative work to bring the spirit to consciousness of itself. Out of the depths the soul seemed to be dragged by slow steps back into the reluctant body again. The psychometer was far more slow to give signs than the biometer. But, as soon as it revealed the approach of the soul, the friends of Tamarna were brought near her, all who had magnetic affinities with her, and especially her betrothed Omirlo. From that point the recovery was astonishingly rapid. The magnetism of friendship seemed to draw back the spirit from its desire to escape. The eyes opened, and a look of intelligence and love shone through their vitreous dulness like dawn in a misty sky; recognition quickly irradiated her whole being, then faded out, then came again, till at last the curtain which hid the soul rose, and the very body seemed to become diaphanous to the light of reason. The spirit dwelt again in its old habitation.

The rest was a matter of the commonest medical science. Every tissue was restored to its previous healthy state. Every fracture and bruise and scar was obliterated. Every item of her system which had suffered beyond the possibility of repair was remade and grafted into her body again. Nursing and medicated atmospheres under the wisest medical guidance restored Tamarna to her duties and to Omirlo as efficient and graceful and healthy as before the accident.

In spite of this triumphant success of their medical science, I could see that depression prevailed in the community. Not even what appeared to me to be the almost supernatural power of drawing the life back seemed to console them. For they had often seen still more wonderful displays of medical skill. Men who had been for months to all appearance dead were restored to full vital power, even when the microscopic transformers of dead matter had begun to batten on their tissues. No body that still retained the human form was beyond their skill; the soul could be enticed back after it had accomplished its flight from earth, for it still kept its affinities to its terrene companions, though cosmic distances should separate them. That was the most difficult task, not the recrudescence of life, but the re-enticement of the spirit that had grown happy in its release.

When I observed that the meteorological families were the nearest of all to dejection, even though they had recovered their loved member, I came to the right conclusion. It was the accident that had unmanned them. That they should be taken unawares in a sphere they had mastered preyed on their minds. For one of the immediate objects of their science was to take command of their future, to eliminate the unexpected from life. What was the value of their progress, if they did not see more clearly and farther into the sphere of darkness that bounded life like a horizon? True, the cosmic was still infinite in its night for them, and in the cosmic lay ambushed countless alarms. But they had driven their outposts far into the twilight. The age they were in had seen such an expansion of science that the veil seemed lifted from the face of boundless night. Their sarmolan pioneered before them into space, and foretold them the dire catastrophes that might lie in wait for them. And yet they were at the mercy of accident. What was the use of such an influx of suggestion from the unknown? What was their power over nature, if thus they allowed the fortuitous to drift in upon them? They had not suffered such discomfiture for ages. They abhorred the thought that they should again be the slaves of mere hazard.

But they rebelled against even the appearance of impotence, and would not allow any mood approaching despair to settle on their spirits. At once the Piramo set about the repair of their defences against accident. The pirakno was found to be fused into one mass of metal by the force of magnetism which had gathered into it from the space around. Another, larger and more effective, was produced and in it there was a new arrangement by which the storage was automatically governed; any increase in the magnetism it received was at once provided for; and if at any time the inflow should surpass the capacity for storage, there was a governor which automatically switched the surplusage into the sea, or back again into the air.

A sarmolan too was invented which had greater strength, and at the same time greater nicety of adjustment. It could be left in the space beyond the atmosphere, untended for nights together; for it was self-recording, and as long as its parts were kept clear of extraneous matter or force, it was incapable of derangement. Not that it was to be left to itself for a moment; even though it now regularly telegraphed all its changes to Rimla and to the locality of the pirakno, meteorological observers were near it night and day to watch and interpret its signals. To guard against any possible assault of accident, other sarmolans were ballooned into space whose indications were mutually corrective; where one went astray, the others would be right.

When Tamarna was completely restored to health and it was made certain by the medical tests that every organ and tissue of her system was fit for its task, her marriage with Omirlo was accorded; and the two entered on their career of parentage. Their duties were made lighter, in order that their energy might pass unimpaired into posterity. They still had their round of work, that their tissues might not grow flaccid, or their life tend to excessive solitude. But Omirlo did for both all that needed great exertion of mental or physical faculty.

CHAPTER III

DEATH

THE accident drew the two together, strengthening their affinities into ir-revocable bonds. And now that all was well with them, their sense of the joy of life welled through their whole nature. Those who came near them felt its contagion. Yet there was one in their family who felt it only to smile at it. The aged Amiralno had seen so many centuries fleet past him that the passage of time with its triumphs had grown stale. He was battling with this nausea of life when the new age of discovery and invention had come upon them. And it so far renewed his energy that he was willing to live through it and take his share in the additional duties which it laid upon his generation. He had seen the infancy of the science over which he now presided pass into lusty youth and thence into manhood; and was he to cut his terrene roots before he had seen its greatest triumphs? Meteorology seemed about to take as wide regions of space within its scope as astronomy had; it seemed about to master secrets that would drive mere chance out of its calculations. The curiosity and wonder of youth were again stirred within him. He longed to advance with the new age into spheres that had so long lain under the horizon, only half-guessed at. Before he closed his eyes on Limanora what wonders might not yet be revealed to them? His blood had tingled with the thought, and his organs were filled with the old energy. He would resume the direction of his science for many a year to come.

But the intrusion of accident into his own sphere had palsied his renewed enthusiasms. For a time, whilst he was restoring Tamarna to her old self, and barring out the chance of accident again, he was not conscious of the check given to the vigour of his functions. But, when all was well and the families of the Piramo were busy again at the expansion of meteorology, he knew that the old nausea had returned with redoubled force. The impetus of the new age was beginning to fail; its pace had perceptibly slackened; its best triumphs had been won; and it needed the ignorance of eyes newly opened upon the green earth and the azure vault of sky to peer into the darkness with thrilling hope; it needed the elasticity of youthful muscles and tissues to withstand the weariness and despair that come with the truer perspective of a gigantic future become a pigmy past. What had he to do with human prospects, when a thousand times he had seen them loom large on the horizon, and then fade into commonplace when realised? Here had he outlasted a dozen generations of ordinary men, and shared the triumphs of a people whose progress compared with that of the rest of the earth was as lightning to the pace of a snail; and yet, when he looked at all that they had done in these thousand years, it was as nothing in the shadow of what had yet to be done, a poor hand's breadth beside the voyage of light from a distant star. Where lay the advantage in extending a life that had seen such humiliation before the everlasting future? He might spin the thread of his life out for another thousand years without great effort. But what would that do for his race, or himself who had seen his past, with all the achievements that had each seemed as it came within the range of possibility a marvel surpassing the human, fade into a microscopic speck underneath the sumless stars? The voices of his friends, as they poured consolation and eulogy, persuasion and prayer, into his ears, sounded now like the undistinguishable hum of insects as sleep comes upon a man in the open. What would they not have meant to him in the ambitious time of youth? How strongly they rang out to him at the beginning of the last stage of enthusiasm, when they drove out of him the love of going forever to sleep! But, now, that the longing had come to him again, they sounded idly as the exultant wail of gnats on the evening air. The life of earth was withdrawn and distant for him.

And who could raise a word against his release? He had done more than his share for the progress of the race. He had watched the interests of his science and made it an essential of all advance. He had braced his energies again and again to meet the requirements of a new age, another march ahead into the night. He had time after time molten the Piramo into a new unity by the magnetism of his enthusiasm. More than once he had extended the years of his life that he might serve his race. And now he had skilled men and women under him, who could do all that he had done, and more. The exceptional needs of the new time had found their attendants mechanic or human. The strain it had put on the efforts of the race was unbent. Why should he linger in a world grown so stale to him, a world that needed no longer his guidance or even his help?

There was one question to answer before the mind of the community was made up. It was the final scientific question. Was his vitality great enough yet to bear the strain, were the impulses of another new age to give it enthusiasm? Was the soul already too detached from the body to allow of the two being closely reunited for another great effort? The question was one for their medical science and psychology to answer. The sidralan or biometer abridged the task of the medical elders. It reported a low pitch of vital energy, too feeble to bear up through the labours and watches of another period. But they were afraid to trust wholly to so newly invented an instrument and fell back upon their old elaborate methods of testing; they investigated the state of every organ and tissue of the aged body with lavolans, the heart and brain with especial care. And it was clear from their state that the spirit could not long reside in them and function them with ease. It was at this point that the Ooaromo came in to aid them with their instruments for testing the bond between soul and body, and for measuring the psychic power that still remained ready to use the brain and its instruments the senses. Their older methods and their newest apparatus, the ooaran, all agreed in confirming the conclusion that the medical elders had come to.

* * * *

For Amiralno himself there remained one serious question, which had troubled the race from the time that mere faith had ceased to rule and pilot their creed, and reason had been accepted as the only ultimate guide of life, the final court of appeal in which all questions must be decided. They could not trust to emotion or instinct; for these were but hard-won creeds and habits of past imperfect ages grown unconscious of their origin by transmission from generation to generation. Authority out of the past, tradition, law of nature, had the same taint upon them. They were but the crude conclusions of comparatively primitive times, with the logic leading to them veiled by oblivion, then thrust upon later ages as inspiration. All these dogmatic judges of the present and the future were but the shadows of their own worst and atavistic selves. It was only an illusion, a mirage in the desert of the past, to trust these merely subjective impressions as reflections from the ultimately real, the absolute. A people like this was sure to abandon all such projections of their own dead selves as steps to higher than themselves.

Every man had to settle for himself the problems that his science had been unable to solve, and that he must find some solution of in death. They had longed and striven for absolute certainty, yet every new age had to fall back upon the individual consciousness and hope, which were wholly on the side of belief in personal immortality. They knew that the energy in them could never die, whatever form it might take. Never had they found in the whole round of their investigations anything like absolute death or annihilation; every change that they observed, however far into infinity they had searched, was but a transformation of energy, and not its final evanishment. Matter was only a resting-place, a half-way house, of energy. And even matter was a comparative term, depending on the sensuous point of view of the observer. What was matter to one generation was found by a later to be pure energy, or even a mass of life. What was matter to one sense was to another nothing but energy. And the development of new senses, that gave them full consciousness of some hitherto-unrecognised type of energy, saved them from the dogmatism about the future based upon the idea that all types of energy were known to them. Their wonderful instruments of research revealed to them worlds of energy which might have lain for ages undiscovered, and swept out all stupid trust in the omniscience of the senses or the instincts. They refused to dogmatise about the existence or non-existence of any type of energy or being. Nay, they preferred to accept provisionally the existence of any form that their imagination might sketch out as possible and as consistent with the laws they had found permeating all the known universe. Belief was for them hope waiting for realisation.

Every new discovery pointed more and more definitely to the greater persistence of the higher forms of energy. What appeals to the more primitive and lower set of senses holds to even its inner form for but a comparatively brief time. Touch is the primary sense, and all that it, unaided by the other senses, can discover is apt to keep changing its form. Taste and smell are simple modifications of touch and they report of things in perpetual transformation. Hearing and sight are the highest of the first set of senses; for they respond to types of energy that travel from vast distances. Hearing is the lower of the two, because the lower senses are conscious unaided of the medium in which the energy travels. Sight has as her courier an energy which bridges infinity, and its medium no lower sense can cognise. Light approaches nearer to indestructibility than anything the original senses know. The last-developed of the senses, the firla, takes cognisance of an energy, magnetism, which is farthest of all from the need of a material medium; whilst the filammu or will-telegraph brings soul to soul irrespective of all sense-cognisable means of communication, and proves the existence of a medium more refined than any that either the senses or the reason has yet come to know. This medium, doubtless that of thought itself, as the highest and least material, must be least destructible, least transformable, least unstable in equilibrium of all known mediums. Their ooarans would soon be made delicate enough to measure the faintest presence of soul, and would decide the point whether this medium, evidently spread throughout the universe, was of the same stuff as the soul.

Still were they far from scientific proof of the eternal unity and individuality of the soul. They had reasoned out in accordance with all the axioms of their science the indestructibility of energy, and the rising untransformability of the higher types of energy; they had also reasoned out as certainly that mediums of energy had stability of equilibrium proportionate to the refinement of the energy travelling through them, and that thus the soul was nearer to everlasting persistence as a unity than any medium they scientifically knew. But that on its escape from the body it continued forever as an individuality they could only assume; they could not prove it. They shrank from the idea that it was forever past transformation; for that meant the eternal continuance of the last stage of life. It was indeed contrary to all the results of their scientific investigations to think that any type of energy or medium could at any time cease to change, that is, to improve or degenerate. Perpetual transformation was, as far as they had been able to search, the universal law: it might be into a higher or more stable form, or into a lower or more material form, but onwards must every energy move. The higher it went, the less did it tend to fall back. The law of eternal advance was surer in its action in the higher ranges of existence. And the whole effort of Limanoran life was to purify and ennoble the energy that was in it. For, reasoning on the analogy of all the nature they knew, they had little doubt that the platform they reached by the end of their terrene life was the platform from which their enfranchised energy or individuality, whichever it was, started on its new career.

Whether it was mere unconscious energy or energy conscious of its own unity that escaped from the body, when it was left to the disintegrant power of microscopic organisms, was still a question. The recent discoveries and investigations of the Ailomo or astrobiological families had revealed all space filled not merely with types of energy that were directed and did not guide themselves, but with embodiments of energy which were clearly individualities; not alone the poor microscopic attenuations of life that were waiting for a world to settle on, but highly organised beings, leading a vigorous, self-dependent life in the vast regions of infinitude. This much they knew from the filmy impressions which their air-transcending lavolans brought down from the heights of heaven they scaled. But whence those inhabitants of the ether came they had not yet been able to tell; for their presence affected no existing human sense, but only left on the irelium films certain visible impressions. Whether they were refugees from other stars, or everlasting occupants of interstellar space, and whether amongst them there were any of the emancipate from human trammels were questions they had not yet been able to answer. But they hoped soon to have an instrument which would indicate the presence of personality as apart from vital energy, and as apart from the thought and thought-faculty. Then would they be able to tell in what state the enfranchised energy fled from the body at death.

Amiralno knew not, cared not, whether he would retain consciousness of his past, or would become but a part of the wandering energy of space; what he did know was that he would be released from the burden of his body and the growing weariness that dragged it down. Certain he was that his flesh-emancipated energy would find a career at least as noble as his past. And he believed that its development would not end there, whatever became of it; whether it was to continue the unity it had been conscious of for so many years, or to take another form and individuality, was to him a matter of little concern. One thing he knew, and that was the growing imperfection of the body as an instrument of the energy that functioned it. It weighted to the ground the soul, the spirit, the mind, or whatever name he might give to the fiery stuff which kept it still aflame, and yet chafed to be free. As long as it held this energy in leash, it would live and glow with thought. Nor was this fiery stuff mere vitality, the mere principle of life, though the two were yoked together. It was different in quality from that which merely vegetated in the plant, and that which did nothing but feed and evacuate in the mollusc. Nay, it differed in inner character, not merely from the mind of the savage, but from that of their own highly civilised exiles. Limanoran advance had purified it of grosser desires and passions and made it a thing of ethereal longings and ideals; even the body had been transformed into something more like what the soul of their far past had been, subtle, buoyant, sublimated. Still it dragged the spirit down, whenever the limits of corporeal life became too apparent. Many a long generation of fiery self-disciplined work upon their constitutions would it take even this marvellous people to etherealise their bodies so far as to make them fit companions of their souls.

Amiralno had not the vital energy to bear up against the conditions that harassed their still hybrid system. He had no desire to stay and see the slow evolution of a body that would pace with the soul through infinity. Better to have release and a new and untrammelled career even if the form he should take was unknown to him. It was the nature of all energy to change, and the higher in the scale it rose, the nimbler it became. But in order to rise it had to be yoked for a time with a lower form, which it used as medium and leverage, leaving it as soon as it had accomplished its due development. All things tended to rise above themselves; and it was the greatest of disasters, the very reversal of nature, if ever they should fall back, as they often did. What we call death was but the unyoking of a higher energy from a lower, which it had temporarily made its comrade and medium. It was no misfortune or degradation, but a step higher in enfranchisement. The animate resisted this step, because one member in the lifelong partnership refused to descend into a grosser transformation again. In the human, the nobler the thought-energy, the higher it strove to raise itself before the inevitable divorce from its lower medium and yoke-fellow. But when the time of severance approached, it mastered the reluctance of the lower, and yearned to be set free. And little wonder that the lower resisted; for back it had to fall in the cosmic order, and begin again its slow progress upward from grade to grade; first into the clutches of myriads of microscopic disintegrators of its tissues that would transform it into food for plant-life, and then by weary stages upwards through vegetable and animal tissue, perchance into the sustenance of thought again.

* * * *

This people, I soon found, had overcome the ancient abhorrence of death. For they identified their life and personality with the higher of their energies, and not with the lower and bodily forms. They shrank, it is true, from all that would lead to the divorce of the yoked energies of any animate being before its due time; not so much because they thought this an evil for the victim as because the perpetration would implant in the doer a germ of retrogression. To be cruel, to shed blood, was the beginning of degradation of the soul; it was one of the acts that allowed the lower to take command of the higher in their system. But for a Limanoran himself to approach death became, whenever he saw it to be inevitable, the keenest joy, in spite of the farewells it entailed. He knew that thereafter, should he make effort to live, he would only clog the wheels of progress, he would only be a burden on the race instead of its helper. Amiralno never showed the slightest sign of shrinking from the dissolution of his life-bonds. He was sad to leave his life-long mate, with whom he had done so much for the race; but he knew that she would soon follow him; it was a matter of but a few days or months; her thought-energy would mingle and commune with his again, freed from the material trammels that checked and dulled their intercourse in their terrene life; upwards through the ether their souls would climb, ever becoming purer and swifter in their flight.

But, as I went about my duties, my thoughts would break away to the coming death-scene and sadness would cloud them. I remembered the last farewells of my buried life, and most of all the watch over the fading light in my mother's eyes. Nothing could burn out of my memory the bitterness of at last facing the inevitable. Slowly had I been led by the physician to realise that nothing could save her, and still I hoped against hope, checking my tears lest she should see them and conjecture my alarm. Only when the lips became silent and pale did I at last admit the thought that this was death. How could I stifle my grief longer? Were we not all to each other, this mother, who had clung to me and nursed me through sorrows and misfortunes, I her only child, who had refused to leave her for the seductions of great place and fortune? She was vanishing forever from me, and nothing I could do would bring her back. I was caught and crushed by the iron hand of fate and stood in stony silence, paralysed by my grief and my impotence. There was too much of the man and the stoic in my young blood to cry out; but if only I could give up my own life to bring hers back! In one of her final waking dreams she prattled and wept over me as if I were a child again, saved once more from the clutching breakers. Raising herself with a wild cry from her pillow, she held me in her arms with fierce love; only for a moment; then the cords that bound her life brake; the memory had torn her heart. There she lay, all that I cared for on earth, rigid, uncaring. If but I could have died with her there! Alas, the life in me was too puissant to yield, the nerves too tough to break! The passion came on me to hurl myself into her grave as the clods fell. It was but an insensate impulse. I made no cry or sign till I got into the lonely chamber; and there God alone knows how I survived my hurricane of grief and desolation. Nor could years ever root out the sorrow. There in Limanora, with an abyss between me and my past, and a noble new life around me, I worked and wept. The wound had opened afresh. Was I never to commune with that loving loved spirit again?

There was a touch on my hand, and the magnetism of sympathy and consolation flowed through my system. It was Thyriel. She had felt my deep grief, though then at a great distance from me, and without noise or speech she had come to my side. So absorbed had I been in my past and my sorrow that I knew not her presence till her magnetic touch awakened me from my dream. She had realised in a moment whither my thoughts had gone, and reverenced the holy past. Then, when the mood was growing despotic and paralysing the soul, she stepped into the startled silence. I was myself again, and swept the unmanly tears away.

Yet I could not drive the sadness of farewell out of my system. Here was this sage, who had so often counselled me and guided my faltering foot-steps, about to vanish forever from the scene of his triumphs. Oblivion would sweep his memory and his work into the abyss. We would see him no more; no more hear his grave wise sayings, weighted with the experience of centuries. All his gathered knowledge and skill would lapse; and our civilisation would be the poorer. Up the steep of progress it would have to climb, weaker for the absence of this strong arm, this much-exercised and full brain and heart.

These were the thoughts at the root of my sadness, when I was startled out of them by my companion's voice. She had waited in reverential silence as long as I lived my filial past over again; but, when I returned to my starting-point, and began spending fruitless regrets and pangs over that which neither demanded nor warranted them, her thoughts broke out into loud protest. She could no longer endure such futilities, such waste of tissue, and she met my wailing reflections one by one. Amiralno was glad to leave his chrysalis stage of existence; the energy that was in him would find a freer scope, a nobler sphere, as soon as it had shed its earthly trammels. His counsel and guidance would not be lost to progress; all that he was and had would still be part of what he would become; not one thought or faculty would be left behind; and all would then be spent not on the progress of a little island of a small terrestrial archipelago or its race, but on that of the universe, if not of the cosmos. All of him that could still appeal to our lower senses would remain with us, and would immortalise his memory, as far as immortality would go upon this ephemeral orb. As for his sympathy and love, they were doubtless still with us, or at least with what in us was best and nearest the cosmic. The only thing to regret was that we could not personally feel his presence in the universe. But even this was not for idle regrets. It was mere palsy, if it did not stir us to still further mastery of our conditions. Were we not in the way to feel and know the escaped spirits of our dead? Had we not developed senses in us that were receivers of impulses from the infinite around us, impulses that had been dormant through the uncounted past? Had we not instruments that told us of energies and beings unfelt even by our new-developed senses? And were we to grope in our prison-house, and wail over what we had lost and could not longer see? Were we to sit in the darkness, and weep and wait, hoping for the light? Such feeble conclusions from the past, such futile regrets over the dead, Limanoran progress could not endure. There were new masteries for every generation. Before many years could pass they would get into touch with the spirits and energies that had fled; it might be by means of new instruments; it might be by new senses; nothing but our own dulness broke the connection between our energies and theirs; what we had still to win was consciousness, if not mastery, of that finer type of matter which they now used as medium for their energy. It was only the lifting of another of the myriad veils that hung before our senses dulling their perceptions. This was no more than what they had done a thousand times already. A death was a stimulus to joy and new effort. It taught us the limits of our knowledge and our power; and limits known were limits soon to be overpassed.

* * * *

Her bright activity and banter surprised me into laughter at my own folly and obtuseness. Scarcely had I reached this consummation before I knew that there was gladness in the air of the island. How could I have failed to notice the jubilant strains that were fitfully wafted across my hearing, unless through my dull absorption in my own feelings? I felt thankful to Thyriel that I had been drawn out of my isolation, which seemed to me now little less than disloyalty to the race that had done so much for me.

I wondered what could be the occasion of all this exultation that I was conscious of. Pæan after pæan rose from every part of the island, and, as the moments passed, the many-sounding music seemed to gather towards one centre. The radius lessened, and adjacent masses of melody fused together. Nearer and nearer they came, ever more coalescing and lessening in number; then the jubilance melted into grave and massive harmony, and I recognised some of the world-music I had heard from the cosmophone. The sense of universes creating and dissolving sprang into my mind. It was the diapason of creation that was ringing through the island. Loud, then low, the cosmic symphony swept the atmosphere like a tempest. I knew that some far-reaching event or movement was occurring amongst this people.

I turned to my comrade to confirm and define my conjectures, but she was gone. Away on the horizon I could see the rapid beat of her wings. I followed as swiftly as I could, and, as I rose in the air, I saw company after company soaring like coveys of birds towards a high isolated plateau that stretched from far up Lilaroma and beetled cliff-like over the sea. I had often used it as a flight-platform whence I could spring into the air, and had long known it by the name of Doomalona. I had never thought over the meaning of the word, but now it flashed upon me that it meant the hill of farewells. Thence messengers who were embarking on difficult and important expeditions set out. The elders of the people and the families of the couriers came here to give them their love and benison, in order to make them feel, as they journeyed, that the sympathy of their home went with them like a fire from the hearth.

I had observed that in these farewells this simple-hearted people made little outward sign of the depth of their emotions. Only the magnetic look out of the eyes would have told a stranger what benignity lay underneath. Nor was it merely to show how sympathetic they were that they thus accompanied their foreign couriers to the outskirts of the island. It was chiefly to give them each his contribution of magnetism, to lessen their burden on their far journey, to make them feel how much the spirit of the community went with them. Not one of them would ever allow himself to indulge in so idle an evidence of emotion as tears. There was in this people a vein of stoicism, I thought; they seemed to repress all mere symbols of feeling. A European would have called their farewells dull and emotionless, if not stony-hearted. There was no kissing or embracing; there was not even the shaking of hands or bowing of heads. Without physical contact their spirits could work upon each other with a power that in other civilisations would have been called witchcraft. Through their firlas, through their eyes, rayed forth a keen soul-stirring magnetism. And each assisted the other in preventing the approach of the old wasteful manifestations of sorrow or despondency. Lamentation was a thing of the far, almost prehistoric, past; a sob or sigh or even complaint they knew too well from their physiological knowledge to be mere emotional extravagance, a waste of the energy or the tissue, all of which was needed for the strenuous endeavour towards a higher plane. So it was that they seemed to me stoical in positions where the men and women I had known in my youth would burst into weeping and wailing, or cries and gestures of affection.

But in these scenes of farewell there was needed little energy of repression; the real struggle had occurred many generations before in their history. They had once had a most elaborate symbolism not merely of feelings but of almost every human thought and spiritual attitude. But when the great national repentance was leading to the series of exilings that ultimately purified the race, they became uneasy about this vast system of symbolism; it covered their whole existence from birth to death, from toothache to the salvation of the soul, and seemed to be nature her very self. They had long known it to be the nesting-place of all hypocrisies and untruth. Under its shelter mean things and falsity and even grossness and cruelty could flourish fearless of harm. Everything could masquerade in the guise of anything else it pleased. Of course there were painful revelations and scandals at times; but they were soon hushed up. The system was too much the interest of all who had power or reputation or prosperity, the best of what was then life, to let it get into disrepute, or into risk of revolution or reform. There were various professions which were deeply involved in the retention of it, and they were recruited chiefly from the highest social classes. The lawyers battened on the ambiguity of the symbols, whether expressed in word or deed; the doctors would have lost half their hysterical and hypochondriac patients if it had been abolished; without it the life and pretensions of the military during time of peace would have been a farce and a mockery; and the occupation of the priests would have vanished altogether. Ceremony seemed the very life-blood of an aristocratic state, and especially of its army and its church. It kept the mere workers and plodders at a respectful distance, it fenced off criticism, and supplied topics for the tongue of fame. To abolish ceremony would have been to strike at the heart of all existing institutions.

But, as the purgation proceeded, every occasion for it naturally disappeared. Ceremonial ceased when the church lapsed and the priestly profession went into exile. Ceremony vanished with the expulsion of the militant elements and the professional politicians. The bureau of fame collapsed with its accursed spawn, uncharitableness and evil feeling, servility, adulation, and pretence. The pharisaism of the whole system stood out in all its offensiveness, and the foulness and injustice that were concealed by this constant masquerade in the robes of greatness. It was meant to overawe the unthinking, to make ignorance grovel at the feet of those in power. It had been useful in far past times of savagery in cowing the beast in the human mind and keeping it caged. But a form that has life and meaning and power in the ruder stages of development becomes a curse, if continued into periods of advanced civilisation. They now felt that their elaborate symbolism had been an insult to their intelligence; for they had no brutality in them to be muzzled. To keep up the pretence of greatness or virtue or love or respect or truth, where there was none, was useful as long as most of the community were ignorant, or superstitious, or fierce and intolerant in disposition. But when the race had grown gentle and humane and more and more progressive, it was not merely a farce to retain so much deception and mummery in life, it was a gross outrage on all that was just and noble and spiritual. Why should not the reverence or affection of the human spirit be allowed to shine forth from the countenance without such ridiculous trammels, such coarse humiliations? Forms compelling a show of reverence or love where there is none, are but the trappings of slaves, and soon ingrain the thoughts and feelings of slaves on the one side, whilst bringing out and confirming the nature of bullies and tyrants on the other. Every relic of a past that had harboured and perpetuated such a system was painfully ejected from their natures. They would have nothing in them that savoured of such a death-in-life. All mere forms, all ceremonials and ceremonies had to go. Ostentation and parade became abhorrent to them. Pageant and spectacle, pomp and solemnity vanished from their lives. All formality of manner or intercourse, even etiquette and salutation, was driven out with contumely.

One of the most singular effects of this expulsion of mere symbolism was the disappearance of ridicule and jest. This disappearance was quite unexpected, and yet, when they came to reflect on the phenomenon, they saw how natural it was. The obverse of the passion for applause and influence is necessarily the desire to depreciate possible rivals, to make them seem small, and even to trample them in the dust. And the most successful and least apparently ill-natured method of fulfilling this is to get them laughed at and so contemned. With the ignoble itch for fame went the love of ridicule. The jesters, habitual as well as professional, disappeared with the priests, the soldiers, the lawyers, and the politicians. Not that the Limanorans abandoned the use of humour; they still saw too clearly the incongruities of existence, cosmic as well as human, to cease bringing them out in startling flashes of vivid expression. They never indulged in that boisterous laughter which is so often thought in the West the simplest and most primitive guaranty of enjoyment; for that is as much a waste of valuable tissue as uncontrollable grief. Their laughter was of that low, gentle, tolerant, almost inward, kind, which brightens the nature to its very heart; its only outer mark was perhaps a smile. Never indeed was I amongst a people that looked at existence so cheerfully or enjoyed its little ironies with so light-hearted a geniality. Buoyancy, joyousness, was the most constant characteristic of their spirits. Their intercourse with each other was ever sunny and pleasant-witted, though never jocular. There was no malice or false sense of superiority in their humour or laughter.

But jest they came to abhor as an indignity to the human spirit which was striving to obliterate all traces of its ape-ancestry. The jester implied or produced contempt for his topic, for his victim, and generally for himself. He usually adopted mimicry as the easiest method of bringing about his effect. And so he nursed the ape in him, and pointed back to the vile type from which he had sprung. It was the other kinship of man, his divine relationship, that the Limanorans preferred to acknowledge and nurture. Never did they forget it in their conduct. It moulded their ideals, it directed their purposes, it created their instincts. And to use ridicule was to outrage it, to call up the beast in them, the element, the ancestry that they did their best to forget. Whenever the sense of mutual sympathy crept through the community, the degradation of jest and ridicule, not for the victim alone, but for the jester, became self-evident. They were felt to be inhumane, if not inhuman, and died an easy death with all the vast system of symbolism.

* * * *

It was a surprise to me then to see so large an assemblage winging their way to Doomalona. It seemed as if there was about to be a great ceremonial. And I was not long in doubt as to the occasion. For with music that rose and fell in marvellous rhythm like the waves of the sea there came across the sky a splendid flight-car, more brilliant in opalescent glow, more majestic in architecture, than anything I had ever seen. Its wings flashed fire through the air and seemed to weave the lightnings of heaven into a diaphanous web. It was a car of victory; for around it bands of flying youth raised jubilant harmony, and over its rear rose a canopy crowned with fire. As it floated nearer I could see beneath this a figure resting upon an elevated couch. The music grew more loudly triumphant as it hovered downwards to the central plateau of the hill of farewells. And then I knew that this was Amiralno on the couch; and all the people, except the few who were needed for the essential services of the island, had assembled to bid him farewell, as he sped in front of them into the land of shadows whither no eye could penetrate.

I had without knowing it landed close to Thyriel, so absorbed had I been in the wondrous spectacle. She had been busy with the chorus of acclaim, her thoughts bent on this rare scene of farewell; and she had not noticed my approach. Then a sudden silence, as Amiralno stepped from the faleena, startled the great concourse out of their entranced attitude; their thoughts were set free as by the touch of a magic wand. It was at this that Thyriel became conscious of my presence. I knew in a moment that she had recognised the criticism in my mind. Yet she did not answer or explain the anomaly. She remained perfectly still.

A burst of jubilant music broke my reverie, as the sudden silence had broken it before. It led me back to the symphony of the spheres to which I had been accustomed to listen with rapt attention. I could recognise the harmonious strain that meant the creation of a world. I could almost see the whirling orb of fire, as it flew off from the parent sun, and swept into its glowing round through heaven. Nothing I had ever heard could match the rapturous melody which expressed the approach of life to the surface of the new star. Quicker and quicker grew the pace, and higher the pitch, as the living creation developed and spread over the world. Then came a wild dithyramb, as man broke from his bestial surroundings, and mastered his fellow-beasts by cunning, and drew fire from heaven for his purposes. A nobler strain followed, rhythmically measuring the steps by which he rose out of himself and climbed the steep of heaven. Silver-toned harmonies told of his masterpieces of art. Loud diapasons spoke out his marching armies and fierce battles. Soft involved fugues and dulcet chants expressed the struggles and conquests of thought.

I stood absorbed in the interpretation of this ravishing music, and failed to observe the progress of events upon the lofty plateau. Amiralno had taken up an erect position on what might have been called an altar, had the scene been a religious one. His face was towards heaven. He held his right hand as if waving back those whom he forbade to follow him; for close to him stood the partner of his earthly life, her face set as if she would depart. Around stood his lifelong comrades and counsellors, yet at a lower level, so that every act of the departing could be seen by the concourse. Near him were erected two columns, on the higher of which and above his head I could distinguish a psychometer, on the lower a biometer. Behind him had been built into the rock an elaborate piece of machinery, which I recognised as a manana or petrifier. Often had I seen it transfix almost in a moment a beautiful plant, substituting irelium for its living tissues, and making every leaf and flower of it translucent crystal. By means of electric currents, it sent streams of the atomic constituents of irelium along the sap-channels from rootlet to leaf-tip; it used the living powers of the plant to turn it as it died into undecaying metal. For hundreds of years the flower would live and be a thing of beauty, even if no care was further spent on it; and, if cared for, it would resist the finger of decay for thousands and thousands of years.

At last I was to see the transfiguration of a Limanoran. I had often almost doubted the origin of those lifelike statues that stood in Fialume, and death was so rare a thing among this long-lived people that during my many years amongst them I had never had the opportunity of satisfying the doubt. Curiosity overshadowed my other feelings and made me forget the grief which would keep creeping into my heart at this farewell scene in spite of the jubilant music. I strained every nerve and sense to catch the features of the strange event. Thyriel, I felt, was as eager as I to see all that would occur, and I could see that the younger half of the concourse had their attention closely riveted upon the scene.

The observer of the biometer raised his eyes to the indicator, which had now begun to move in rapid oscillations. Amiralno lifted the forefinger of his left hand as if giving a signal. He looked back a moment with longing in his eyes at his life-partner. From the manana there sprang out an upright groove towards the dying man, and in this he was caught, as his vitality rose to its greatest effort before the final collapse. The indicator of the sidralan shot upwards with great violence, and then fell still. Almost at the same moment the guardian who stood on the loftier column beside the psychometer raised himself in agitation. The indicator had begun the same violent oscillations as that of the biometer. There could be little doubt that the individual energy or soul of the vanished Amiralno had passed near it in his flight upwards.

Through the brief and impressive scene the note of creation rang in the music that filled the air, and never that of dissolution. Then burst forth the chorus of freedom, which was the national song, if anything might be so called. It was the liberation of the energy of their friend and comrade that they united to celebrate, his entrance on a new career untrammelled by lower forms of inert energy. The music rose as if on wings, higher, higher, ever more exhilarant. There were in it none of the undertones, or deeper notes, or mystic subtleties that marked so many of their spheral harmonies. It was a sound of pure joy, ethereal, supernal, unalloyed by any terrene longings. Who could think of grief or the bitterness of farewells, as long as it rang through the sky? Courage, confidence to climb upwards was the only emotion that could live with joy in its presence.

Suddenly the music broke away into a tempest of cosmic melody. Now wailed forth the wild song of dissolution of worlds, again the clashing of conflicting systems, followed by the surge of new life in orbs that were to whirl through space and elevate the existence upon them for thousands of thousands of ages. It was the music of mingled creation and disintegration, of development and decay which we heard once more.

Our thoughts were recalled from the heights of heaven, whither the lost personality of our guide and friend had fled. We were absorbed again in the struggle of a mixed existence; we felt again the agonies of the higher active energies bound to lower and merely latent energies. My eyes came down to the scene of the last farewell. There stood the almost living statue of our vanished brother, erect, eager as for flight, as at the moment when his energy had gone forth. But now it had the clear metallic translucence of the thousands I had seen in Fialume. The transfiguration was complete.

But there was more on the plateau than the figure of what had been. Beside it with rapt, pleading gaze on her face stood yet unmoved the life-comrade of the vanished. The manana was again in position, the observers again stood by the biometer and the psychometer. Another scene of departure and transfiguration was to be enacted. The whole consciousness of the community had granted without words the petition of Amiralno's spouse. Nothing seemed to be so fitting as that the two should leave their trammelled life together, and within the space of a few hundred beatings of the pulse partner had followed partner. The two lives, joined for so many centuries, had come to a close together. Out into infinite space had fled the two intertwined energies, only a few heartbeats apart. Perhaps together they would find their new sphere, their new platform for still higher flight through the diviner stages of existence.

The Limanorans, when they had reached what they considered the limits of their usefulness in corporeal life, gained an instinctive knowledge of the moment when death was certain to come, or perhaps it was an instinctive

power of dying. It is a common thing to see amongst savage or half-civilised tribes a man or woman in full health deliberately lie down, turn the face away from friends and light, and prepare to die. They seem to know when their destiny is coming upon them, and nothing will persuade them to take measures for driving it off. Strong though the currents of life may be flowing in the veins at the moment, it is not long before they have completely ebbed, and left the body a pulseless mass of inert matter. It was this instinct, whether prophetic or suicidal, that the aged amongst this people seemed to resume when they had weighed the vital powers in their systems against the duties that new ages with their progress would bring, and found them wanting. Destiny seemed to speak out to them, when they saw the transference of the minus to the wrong side. Their minds were made up and it needed but a few days or hours to set the imprisoned energy free. In these later and more scientific ages there was some delay, and not uncommonly a postponement of the departure. A careful examination of the system by means of their new scientific instruments revealed some radical mistake in the judgment of the elder as to himself, or the demands of a new age of discovery made the need of more brains and hands imperative. The result was the same in both cases; the reason was persuaded to give up its resolve; life flowed on in the veins with even power again; all the old duties were resumed; and the day of farewells was put off till a more convenient season. But once they were convinced that they were retarding progress instead of accelerating it, the end, they felt, was within measurable distance; they straightway relinquished their grasp of life; they withdrew purpose and power of will from all their vital functions; and the moment of the final collapse was practically within their own choice, as soon as they had the consciousness of the whole community with them.

Here stood two solid memorials to the working of this prescient or devitalising power. The beauty of expression on the two faces was very striking. The attitudes were as natural and noble as life itself, that of Amiralno bidding his partner farewell, hers full of loving petition to follow. That the whole people approved was clear in the heartiness with which they broke into the song of liberation. Everyone was glad that the energies of these two, who had done their full duty by the race, were free to enter other spheres, and follow other than the terrene methods of advance. Reverently, but still with great rejoicing, the family of the departed placed the two lifelike statues in the car of victory, and guided it in triumphal flight to the valley of memories. Then the people as reverently and joyously bent their way to the duties they had left.

* * * *

I stood in a day-dream of the strange but noble ways of life that this people followed, and suddenly awakened to find myself alone on the hill of farewells overlooking the ocean. Sorrow over the departures I had witnessed welled back into my heart; I had not yet got rid of the old attitude of Western civilisation towards death. With the sorrow mingled still the old curiosity; questions sprang into my mind concerning the significance of the ceremony I had seen; or was it a ceremony? I was startled with the answer in the negative. It came from Thyriel, who, knowing my doubts, had remained to solve them. Soon I knew the whole meaning of the scene. It was not premeditated. There was nothing deliberate about it except the deaths themselves. The dulness of my own inner senses had prevented me from knowing the common impulse of the race towards Doomalona. As soon as Amiralno had finally resolved to die, the consciousness of his resolve spread over the island, and stirred the people at their duties to common action. They knew that the hill of farewells would be the scene of the departure, and in bands singing the cosmic music of farewell they made their flight through the air to give a last valediction to the voyager into the unknown and to impart to him in his final effort on earth all the magnetic power they could spare for him on his journey. Every act of what I had thought was a ceremonial was the natural and spontaneous impulse of a people united in spirit. Their music and the changes in it were due to no leader or signal, but to the sympathetic inspiration of the moment. Their creational chant was an assertion of their mood of belief that this scene was one of advance, and not of retrogression, of development and not of decay, that the act was as much an act of cosmic life as the creation of a world. Certain portions of the system were about to become manifestly inert, those which were called bodily and material, but which were as truly forms of energy as the individual energy that was being liberated. They were made unchanging, permanent, for a time, and so were unable to progress or retrograde; they were to retain their energy in latency for a period long or short; but at last they too, when their immediate purpose of remembrance of the vanished was served, would be set free to take other forms. Their creational music was intended, if there was any intention in so spontaneous a thing, to keep before their minds the progressive and evolutionary nature of death, and to quell the old and barbarous attitude of grief which might attempt to show itself when they were bidding the final farewell to a comrade. It was meant to bring into prominence the joy of the spirit freed from the bondage to lower forms of energy, and the delight of all who remained in the progress of the cosmos, even though the immediate act should imply a separation of a loved spirit from them. It helped them to repress any sadness at the thought that they might never recognise the energy of their lost comrade again as an individual and personal thing. Enough for them that the sum of existence should be enriched by the change which was occurring to him.

But was it not a grief to them that the parting was perhaps eternal, as far as personal recognition went? The question rose spontaneously in my mind; and I was answered almost before I had thought it. The doubt was still unsolved whether as impersonal energy they developed into something new at death and forever ceased to bear marks and memories of the phase of existence they had just left, or whether they sallied forth from the bonds of a lower and inert energy into the freer scope of infinity, an individual and complete unity. This doubt, they were certain, would be solved some day by scientific experiment. Meantime there were compensating advantages, whichever alternative was true. If they continued the personality they had already developed on earth without break in consciousness or memory, then would they recognise their old comrades and partners in Limanoran life, and make further progress through existence together.

If, on the other hand, there was a break in the continuity, and only as an impersonal energy they passed forth into the interstellar spaces, then would there be the obliteration of all the animal and barbarous past which they abhorred, as well as of the immediate and Limanoran past which they loved. Any being that has advanced much in its more recent stages must naturally try to forget the lower stages through which it has gone in a more distant past. They were by no means proud of their relationship to their exiles or to the still older and wider humanity existing outside of their archipelago. To remember it was to encourage the lower and less-advancing man in them. To forget it was one of the ethical duties which their progress demanded. It was only as a horror, as a possible hell into which they might fall, if they retrograded, that it was still brought before them.

A race or nation that remains long proud of its past must be but imperceptibly progressive, if it is progressive at all. Its ethical point of view is stationary, its morals and religion are stagnant. The history of a people should rapidly come to seem ignoble to it, if it does its duty to itself and its progress. What is the history of other races but a record of wars, of wholesale slaughters, because of the ambition of a man or a section of men? And as long as we are proud of such a past we can never advance. To have an ancestry nobler than ourselves is an undying disgrace, and to suggest such a thing to a man should be considered the grossest insult. Where a people is developing as it ought to develop in the brief period it has upon earth, oblivion should be one of its foremost duties to all but its immediate past. Man has forgotten his bestial ancestry so effectually that when he comes across the manifest relics of the relationship in his system, he is startled and wildly denies it. If he progressed as rapidly as he ought to do, after there has been implanted in him the divine principle of reason, then would he as surely cast into oblivion his savage and semi-civilised ancestry. Out with the ape and all relics and memories of it is the struggle of thinking men. To be done with the crude undeveloped past is the duty of progressive men. The ideal of today should be the commonplace of tomorrow, and the disgrace of next week. It was useful to study the immediate past in order to get perspective for the present, and to decide on the rate of progress for the future. But it was becoming doubtful to this people whether they should perpetuate in the valley of memories so much of the past after it had faded into insignificance. They had come to think that to forget was as necessary to the advance of man as to remember, and that a universal rubbish-destructor for the now poverty-stricken achievements of their far past would one day become essential. As it was they still preserved records of them lest some historical question might grow to be of importance to their future.

It was little wonder then that they had no great abhorrence for the obliteration of the past from their energy at death. If the other alternative were the true, and if, as so many religions teach, they were to be herded with the criminal and besotted and undeveloped souls that have passed from the earth, then might they bid farewell to true progress beyond death. And what is the meaning of continuity of existence and memory, unless it be the intercourse of terrene souls in the life outside of life? To be rid of the flesh and its inert energies is still to be enslaved to worse evils, the possibility of contact with the foul beings that inhabit the human form, even the noblest and most belauded human form. The Limanorans would gladly abandon the delight of recognising and loving again the souls they knew and loved, if only to be free from such a horror. Better almost annihilation than enslavement to the retrogrades of earth in another sphere. Whence the terror of discontinuity of memory, if the burden of the past were to be lifted off us, and a new and more progressive career given to our energy? The Limanorans believed that when unyoked from the inert forms which had come from their animal past, their higher energy would enter on a progress that would make all they now did seem almost stagnancy; and the power of remembering any past would only mean shame at its having been theirs.

It never gave them pause to think that what came after death was still unknown. They had passed a happy bright life upon the earth, free from the pangs and agonies as well as the fierce pleasures, the snaky involvements as well as the passionate amours, of other civilisations. But, when the effort to live had come to be so great as to overbalance the compensations and utilities of their life, then was it no pang for them to leave it; for they were scientifically sure that death would be no break in their progressive existence; if anything, it was certain to be an intensification of the progress which they loved most.

* * * *

One of the last of their great series of exilings had been to cast out of their midst a number of men and women who never did anything but long for death, and advocated early suicide with religious fervour as the true and only panacea for all ills. Their doctrines would have done little harm to the community, if they had not been rooted in practice, and often led to tragic results. For they came from languid, low-strung temperaments, that felt disinclined to face the strain of life or to help the advance of the race. The current of energy in their ancestry had gradually run more and more feebly, till it was in them at its lowest ebb. It was against their grain to work, and they did their share in the tasks of the community with the most patent reluctance. This alone would have been reason enough for their exile, inasmuch as they gave evil example to the youth around. But they were subtle in the use of the tongue too, and could with skilful jesuitry show how indolence was the noblest life. And worse still, when they were left to their own devices, they soon made a violent end to their feeble lives, and gave a tragic and ghastly appearance to death. Out into Thanasia or the isle of death they were one and all deported, with enough goods and provisions to keep them and their descendants alive, if only they were industrious, for thousands of years. But none of them would work, or till the soil, or even cook their food; and one by one they gave themselves up to death. The more ingenious invented a method of leaving life which had a certain grace if not nobility. They erected great funeral pyres and connected them by a slow fuse to a huge battery that sent up its rod into the heavens. When a tempest threatened, they laid themselves out on these, and when the lightning began to flash, the electricity ran along the wires, lit their fagots, and in a few moments swept them out of existence. It was not long before the isle of death was again left to its silences, nothing but the ashes of its former inhabitants upon the tops of numerous mounds being left to tell that human life had once been there. No one from the rest of the archipelago seemed to care for life upon it; none ever landed there. The only things that marred the mortuary stillness of the isle were the screaming seabirds, and the tempests which drove them thither.

It was better for the cosmos that these emasculate weaklings should as soon as possible submit the relics of energy in them to other conditions of being. But it was not well for Limanoran immaturity to have the spectacle of self-slaughter before them, or the contagion of their death-pyre romance and eloquence touch the spirit of youth. Moreover they took some time to resolve on death; and, in the process of forming their resolution, it was the natural habit of these tame triflers with death to put all the energy they had into their tongues. As long as they could talk heroics to anyone about the deed they contemplated, they were certain not to accomplish it. And romantic chatter is catching where youth is still unbridled by reason, and in the young who had robuster wills, the results might be more prompt.

It was different with the death-scenes of men and women who had done their duty by the race and by human progress, and had worked out the best possible results from the yoking of higher and lower energies. Theirs was a true liberation from exhausted lower forms. It was not the languor of the loftier element in them, but the exhaustion of the lower, that brought the nausea of their hybrid life. They could feel, as they looked back, how far their higher or spiritual energy had risen since their entrance into earthly existence. Every year had seen them climb upwards; nearer and nearer had their inner energy come towards touch with that divine medium which was in and yet above all life and which in youth they were conscious of only in lofty moments of inspiration. Such were the supreme ascensions of life, when they were capable of the noblest actions and the noblest moral resolves. These moments became more and more frequent as they grew older and more progressive, till towards the close of life they were almost habitual. Limanoran youth snatched at these supernal moments by the help of imagination. Limanoran age dwelt habitually in these moral altitudes that lay far above mere passion or instinct. It was the old amongst them who were alone capable of great creative spiritual life. They seemed to feel the tiding of the subtlest energy in the universe, and gave the impulses to most spiritual advance.

Here and there in other civilisations was bred a nature that had fitful consciousness of this divine medium, at times through great creative imagination, but oftener through noble life. Such a nature is spoken of as inspired; and so far is it true in that it has come into communication with the most refined and most creative medium of the universe, that through which what we call the divine seems to work; but only through patient self-moulding and development has it reached such a height of nobleness. Oftenest in past ages these natures have found shelter in religion; for in the world ambition must make use of the coarsest tools and the grossest energies to reach its aim; and the growth of a loftier spirit is at once checked, and noble aspiration stifled. Peace and the shadow of devotional thought were the only conditions allowing such a nature any scope in a world based upon war and guided in its search for the right by might alone.

It was different with Limanoran civilisation. There it was the rule, and not the exception, to raise the spiritual energies to sympathy with the diviner media of the cosmos, and every condition favoured the pursuit. Life began with but a fitful consciousness of it, but it grew more continuous and surer. The young could scarcely distinguish its impulses from those of their own lower energies. But the old had seldom any hesitation as to when they were inspired; they seemed to keep in touch with all that is divine in the world. They needed no retreat, no religious shelter, to nurse the magnetic sympathy with the divine. Their affinity to it grew more and more the essence of their being, without ever having to leave their daily routine of duties. It was this that gave them their wisdom and character, and that made the young feel them to be almost a type apart from the ordinarily human. They became more distinct and striking in their personality as they grew older and felt this affinity. It had come to be a common observation of daily life that the nobler the aspirations and the closer the intercourse with the ethical media of the cosmos, the stronger and more distinctive was the character; and science was not far from the conclusion that on this intercourse depended persistence of individuality, and that the higher they reached in their sympathies with the more refined media of the universe, the less need was there of change in their personality at death, of making alliance with other lower energies when they shed their inferior and earthly forms of energy.

There was, they felt, a noble isolation or apartness of spirit in their old men and women which raised them above common humanity, and made the human body seem an incongruous garment for their soul. They lived above the demands of their corporeal energies rather than in them or by them. In the young the two seemed blended together; it was difficult often to distinguish in them the movements of the two types of energy. But in the old, though the corporeal had been raised and etherealised, it seemed to hang on the skirts of the spiritual and try to drag it down; it bore its earthly origination more manifestly on it in comparison with the nobler refinement of the spiritual. And the longer they lived, the stronger the contrast became, till at last nature herself seemed to demand their eternal divorce. Euthanasia at a certain stage in the development of Limanoran life came to be not so much a privilege as a holy duty. To liberate the higher energy from its alliance with the lower, to die, was but the next and most natural stage in the evolution of the life. Even the family, who would feel the bereavement most in the loss of their wise help and guidance, acquiesced gladly, feeling that the liberation must mean a nobler career for the released spiritual energy. Thus it was that on Doomalona they used the music of creation; they gave utterance to their feeling that death was not dissolution but creation, that the retrogression of the body was an advance for the higher energy, the truer self. The sense of decay or degeneration was quite absent from their thoughts. It was a triumphal farewell; for they were convinced that for the liberated it was the noblest deed of all to die, the very crown of all their life.

CHAPTER IV

AN EPIDEMIC

THOUGHT by thought I ejected my old view of death from my mind. I could not forget the scene of triumph which had been enacted on the hill of farewells; and the chanting that rilled through it haunted my imagination, bringing a sense of satisfaction, if not joy. I got into the habit of winging my exercise-flights towards Doomalona. I was there with Thyriel when dawn struck the world into gladness and music. There were we together to see the flaming picture the set of sun drew on Lilaroma. No platform on the island so caught the inspiration of the coming or departing orb. None, I came to feel, was so fitted for the hegira of earth-weary souls. No such launching-ground was there for the voyage through infinity. As I frequented it in my leisure moments, there grew into my system the sense that death was not so much an end as a beginning, not a dissolution, but a birth and perhaps a forgetting. More and more was the idea of it a nucleus of delight; and the old melancholy and sorrow, making it a burden and a terror for the mind, disappeared.

As a proselyte to the new feeling I was eager to talk of it and make much of its surprises. Not with Thyriel and my proparents alone did I discuss its varied aspects; I could listen by the hour to their teachings. But it brought me into intercourse with many whom I had scarcely seen before except in the course of my education as I wandered through the various halls. I was astonished to find how often they sought opportunity to talk to me. They drew me aside as if they had important business with me, and confidentially imparted their views of death which I had heard a hundred times from others, until I grew weary of their chatter, for I wished to talk myself. But they would not allow me to break in on their everlasting torrent of babble; even Thyriel could not endure my interruptions. Though I never grew weary of her talk, I could not restrain the desire to have my say, too. There was no subject on which we could not soliloquise by the hour, but we preferred to talk of death, the freshest and most joyous of topics. And every other youth was just as eager to deliver his opinions to me and to everybody else. However busy they might be with the task in hand, off they would break from it for colloquy, which soon spun itself into the soliloquy of the stronger lungs and the most enduring tongue. Everyone seemed to comport himself as if his views were of the utmost importance to the world. They all seemed bursting with the obvious; out it must come or they would die. In every other corner I would find two or three debating with faces all aglow, sometimes in the most confidential whispers; approaching to listen, I would find their topic trite and stale as last year's gossip; the speaker was pressing home on his hearers in a voice of portentous awe what no one would think of disputing.

The elders interfered and tried by patient advice to stop this tempest of loquacity. Hurrying from post to post they tried to keep the young at their work, but it was an endless task. On would go the glib current as soon as their attention was turned elsewhere. Matters began to look serious, for the work of the community was being neglected. The ordinary services of life were barely performed. Little or no progress could be made in such a state of affairs. Indeed, it became manifest that the main aim of the race, progress, would soon be forgotten, and retrogression supervene. The faces of the elders became graver every day; their advice was unheeded, their example unfollowed. Babble, babble, babble, on rolled the fluent river of talk, as if the island had been in the midst of Western civilisation. When I closed my eyes so loud and empty sounded the magpie babel I could easily fancy myself back again in my native land, and believe that I had dreamt my recent years and wakened again in Christendom.

The ominous gravity of the elders dispelled the fancy. They looked as if doomsday were near, and were often heard to say that something must be done. For the talkativeness was bringing other vices in its train—vanity, flippancy, carelessness, and want of reason. The torrent of eloquence was spreading wider every day and seemed to have broken down the pales of their long centuries of civilisation. No one was capable of stopping it either by precept or example.

At last in their despair the elders appealed to the medicants. Nothing like the phenomenon had occurred within the memory of the oldest; nothing in the records could be found that in the least resembled it since the series of exilings had been completed. At the periodical inspection, the medicants made a more minute investigation of the systems of the youth and turned their attention especially to the left side of the brain, which is the great originator and controller of speech. In a few they could see evidences of inflammation and morbid secretion in the brain-tissue of this region; in most cases nothing out of the common revealed itself to their most recent lavolans. So they took careful electrographs of the left side of the brain of most of them, and when they put these under their strongest clirolans, it became plain that all of them were in a diseased condition.

The elders were now convinced that they were on the right track of investigation, and all the young people who had shown symptoms of the passion for eloquence were isolated and brought hourly under the inspection of the medicants. Moving electrographs of the thought-processes in the diseased parts were taken daily by means of modifications of the lavolan; and under still more powerful clirolans, made for the purpose, these revealed a microbe of extraordinary minuteness at work in the tissue. Having found the source of the mischief, they set themselves to remove it. At first they put the patient into profound sleep, and, trephining the skull, they cleansed away under the clirolan all traces of the parasite and its débris. What they removed they carefully preserved and analysed; then, having found the chemical elements of the mischievous spawn and their débris, they reproduced the mixture as a cure of the new and singular disease. For a time this was administered as an internal medicine; but finding that it injured other nerve-centres besides those that they intended to affect, they resolved to apply it only locally, and soon learned how to avoid the necessity of trephining the skull. They invented an electric syringe and injector, which caused the mixture to penetrate through the skull into the part of the brain affected, thus sterilising the tissues that had to do with speech and making them unattractive as a feeding-ground for the microbe of loquacity.

The plague soon vanished and the babel ceased. There was comparative silence throughout the island. Only such words were spoken as were essential and relevant to the business in hand. It was, indeed, accepted as the surest mark of the sanity of a nature that it was never betrayed into speech unless that which conveyed necessary information, forceful reasoning, or fresh thought. The trite was avoided as mephitic vapours or an exhausted atmosphere would be. The utterance of truisms immediately led to a microscopic examination of the brain of the speaker in expectation of finding disease there. The habit of expression merely for its own sake and not for what it expressed, for its beauty or wit or pungency, was considered a sure indication of a diseased or morbid condition of the brain-tissue, and the sufferer was at once isolated for treatment, lest he should spread the contagion.

For the whole phenomenon was scientifically investigated, and precautions were carefully taken against a return of the plague. It had been noticed that, after any age of exceptional progress, there generally occurred some epidemic connected with the brain-tissues or nerve-centres, sometimes appearing in excess of emotion, sometimes in various forms of feebleness of thought. It was due, they found, to the comparative exhaustion of the brain and nerves by exceptional strain upon them. As long as the enthusiasm of the new ideas and rapid advance inspired the people, they worked with a will, nor ever thought of sparing any part of their system. The more mature amongst them knew how to bridle this passion for work, and took the necessary precautions against its evil effects; from experience they had found out that they needed more sustenance and more sleep in such periods, and they knew almost by instinct when to rest and how often, and what halls of sustenance and medication they should frequent. The young had not their instincts checked or confirmed by experience, and carried even the best of movements and impulses to abuse. In spite of inspection and superintendence they ignored the rules laid down for their guidance, and took their inspiration to work as better than the wisdom of their elders, knowing that progress was the ideal and law of their race, and thinking that everything done for progress was right.

It was thus the young and immature who generally suffered from these epidemics. The impulse of their enthusiasm carried them far beyond the limits of fertility of their tissues, and the ebullience of their delight, as they saw the work grow before their eyes, obscured from them the gradual exhaustion of their powers. They grew oblivious to everything but the end they had immediately in view, and thus became short-sighted in their enthusiasm for progress; they sacrificed the demands of the future for the sake of the present, and it was difficult for even the elders at the medical inspection to get at the real state of the case, such an appearance of new vigour did the impetuosity of their passion and the tumult in their blood give to their systems. Only when the wandering germs of emotional disease had fixed on the exhausted tissue did the result become apparent.

The wide area and serious effects of the plague of verbosity awakened the medical elders to the necessity of special precautions. A section of them was organised as a medical police to guard against the invasion of such pestilences, and to prevent such exhaustion of youthful tissues as would invite the vagrant germs or fail to repel their attacks. A science was specialised for this purpose—the pathology of epidemic emotions; and a special art grew up to correspond—the hygiene and therapeutics of emotional infection.

The elders who attended to this periodically made careful examination of all the tissue of the immature that had to do with emotion or with any crude spiritual moods inapt to the control of reason and will. And it was astonishing how rapid was the growth of the new science and art in their hands. Delicate instruments were invented responding to the presence even in the air of deleterious germs that tended to settle in the nerve-centres. Still finer instruments revealed the state of the tissues underneath the skull. The symptoms of every disease of the emotions were classified, and the means of checking each was investigated scientifically. Before the next period of exceptional florescence and harvest arrived, the hygiene of all the epidemics that had been known to follow on ages of great exertion was completely organised; and it was chiefly an art of prevention rather than of cure. Precautions were taken by the new section of the medicants against the abuse of the enthusiasm natural to such a period; they examined the nerve-tissues of the immature almost daily, and pointed out everyone that was getting overworked, and the remedies that should be adopted for checking the evil. The result was that no abuse could proceed for longer than a day, and no moral or emotional epidemic unless of the mildest type could settle in the community.

What roused them to such a step as the foundation of a new science and art was the seriousness with which they viewed the last plague, that of loquacity. In the series of exilings no evil had given them such trouble as that of oratory, and they were afraid lest it was about to return in all its virulence. At first they feared this plague to be a case of atavism; for those whom it attacked earliest were descendants of ancestors, or closely related to families, that had been famous in the far past for power of expression. But it soon spread to strains of blood that had been marked by great reticence, if not taciturnity, and ultimately it was completely impartial in its choice of victims. It was manifest, however, that those who had ancestral oratory in the blood were first open to the attacks of the plague and were most difficult to cure; and the phenomenon sent alarm to the very heart of the community. All the mature citizens and especially the elders looked graver than I had ever seen them look, even at the prospect of Choktroo's invasion; they came nearer to the appearance of dejection than I had imagined they could come.

* * * *

The whole matter drove my thoughts to work. When I reflected on the occasion, the attitude my mind had been accustomed to in my forgotten life returned, and it seemed to me as if there had been a storm over nothing. Talkativeness had been one of the commonest features of the men and women I had known in Europe; and loquacity was as little noticed as a red head or a pug nose. Indeed the chatterbox was ranked among the innocents who did little harm except to their own reputations. It became a complete puzzle to me, when I saw the horror with which the Limanorans looked on oratory. Had it not been one of the greatest of the arts of Christendom? Were not the great orators of my own nation looked upon as little short of inspired, and their statues placed in the noblest niche of our temple of fame? Did we not rush by the thousand to hear any one of them, when he was about to perform, and stand breathless by the hour, laying up for ourselves fatigue and faintness and asphyxia, merely for the delight of hanging on his lips? In life he roused hurricanes of enthusiasm; and when he died thousands who had never known him personally followed him mourning to the tomb, and on the most revered page of our literature was his name written. What could be the meaning of so hearty a detestation of so noble an art on the part of this progressive race?

As usual I had not long to wait for a solution. My bewilderment had already stirred the curiosity of my proparents and Thyriel; and they had been watching my thoughts for some time before I put my questions, simple enough for my young comrade and betrothed to answer. She spent a whole afternoon that was devoted to flight-exercise, in discussing and solving my difficulties, and the struggle ended in strengthening my admiration for this noble people.

Their abhorrence of the vice of oratory was not the growth of any sudden revolution, or the unreasoning prejudice often originating amongst a long-established nation in some great personal hatred or fear now buried in oblivion. It was the result of ages of the most patient scientific investigation. And it found its way into practice so slowly that the steps up to the final one are scarcely noticeable on the pages of their history. It had an inborn prejudice in favour of oratory to combat, all the deeper that it could not explain itself or its origin. The reputation of some of the ablest and most influential sections of the community was based upon the art. The orators of the nation had acquired a fame almost greater than that of the soldiers. They had been its leaders and founders; they had developed and mastered its politics; they had moulded the people at certain crises in their history into a unity. Their art had been enrolled for ages amongst the noblest they had. It was the only civilised force which could move great masses to enthusiasm, or fuse their varied purposes and thoughts together to form a single ideal and aim. It was the only means their statesmen had had for accomplishing their schemes, the only stepping-stones by which their lawyers and preachers and politicians could rise to fame. It seemed for ages a hopeless task to unseat it from its place in their civilisation, or eradicate the prejudice in its favour from the people's minds.

The wisest Limanorans had watched its evil influence through many ages; although they had often themselves to make use of it for their purposes of reform and although some of the best men had been successful in its employment, yet they were certain that it sapped the finer sense of truth. So easily could the orator persuade a crowd to accept all he said as true and noble that he came to think there was little difference between the true and the false, the noble and the ignoble; his own aim was all that was of significance, and it was, however selfish or mean, just as good as anybody else's aim. He needed as little to persuade himself of the justice of an evil cause, provided it was his own, as to persuade an assembly. He had but to isolate certain facts and phases, and what were antagonistic to them fell into shadow; the unjust course began to appear just, and those who opposed it were the enemies of justice and of the orator. It mattered not what side he took, if only it stirred his interest; he could rouse thousands to enthusiasm for it by touching their emotions and awakening the passions that were connected with their own self-interest. This power of moving great masses to whatever tune he pleased gave the orator a sense of omnipotence; after a stirring speech he felt like a Jove who held in his hand the destinies of the world. Happily for the welfare of the state, the tongue-doughty was hopelessly incapable when he turned to practice; he could not organise the crusade he had preached; everything he did with his crowd of followers tumbled to pieces as soon as he had to do anything further than speak; a few days or even hours of cool action revealed the hollowness of his cause or his power; the omnipotent Jove of yesterday appeared the skulking slave of today. The only crusades that ever prospered under his influence were those which aimed at destruction; for the work of destruction is brief and sharp; it needs but the passion of the moment to accomplish it; and the love of demolition is the most primitive of all savage desires, and the most unbridled when let loose; its own action as it proceeds kindles into a conflagration the fires that give it strength. Creation is a calm and gradual process, the last conquest of the human mind, as it is the highest function of the energy of the cosmos. The wrecking Omnipotence of oratory is parted from this by the eternity of cosmic development; it is kin with the clashing of worlds and systems that may come before the birth of a universe; but it is as opposite in nature to the slow building up of a world and the slow evolution of its life-energy as hell is to heaven.

The barrenness of the art in all that would develop humanity struck even the less mature minds of Limanora forcibly as soon as vast schemes of reform like socialism began to be discussed. These schemes meant the devastation or the dismantling of existing institutions and systems of life. A plague of demagogues spread throughout the nation. Hitherto orator had neutralised orator as in a debate. Now it was the idle and indolent who grew most tongue-valiant. They, who had before been so discredited, now found themselves on the way to fame. They, who had before been able to gather only a few embeggared discontents at the street-corners to listen, and perhaps to sniff at their eloquence, could now stir masses to action. They had been despised even by their out-at-elbows followers for their impotence in face of the problem of making a bare living for themselves. Now they saw before them place and power, fortune and fame, and all through this poor member of theirs that had not been able to earn enough to lick. Beggarly grovellers, none so poor as not to scorn them, they were now omnipotent, with all the work of devastation before them that these new vast political schemes implied. When the revolution was in full blaze, they were at their best, they thought. But it was just at this point they found their limit. The conflagration they had kindled their eloquence failed to control or even guide; it swept past them through institutions and sections of the community that they specially favoured; and at last even they, many of them, fell themselves victims to its undiscriminating ravage. And, when it had burned itself out, not one of them but skulked away in fear, unable to face the task of building up again. Then it was the man of action that stepped in, the silent, masterful disciplinarian, moulded in war and accustomed to no other means of solving human problems than war; he it was who reaped the dragon's-teeth harvest sown by tongue-bravery: he seized all the glory and place and fortune that the mob-spaniels had thought within their grasp. Some of their ancient folk-maxims embodied this experience: The breath of the demagogue blows the warrior to his fortune; The mouth of the orator is the banqueting-chamber of the soldier; Tempests of eloquence and torrents of blood; Spout, vain tongue, you invite your tyrant; Sow a country with the teeth of haranguers and they will come up the swords of despots; Loquacity is eaten up by her son pugnacity.

In spite of the fear of the art indicated in such folklore, it continued to flourish; for the upper classes, who delighted in war, flattered themselves that they would ever be the best orators, and it is the inevitable tendency of human nature to run to tongue. Not till the age of unbridled freedom of speech did they begin to change their opinions. Then were they easily outfaced and out-harangued by any idler of the poverty-stricken districts. Even in their own assemblies they were no match for the spouters from the slums; with all their high-toned irony and scornful superiority, they were beaten into silence at the public palavers; they were mere stammerers beside the glib orators of the unwashed. This age of tongue-exploits was naturally an age of single ideas, too. When their energy had gone into speech, they had none left for thoughts. One-idea crusades became the order of the day. Every tongue-quixote had his scheme wherewith he would sweep all evils out of life. He was so enamoured of his own that he could not bear to listen to any other. And therein lay safety.

But there came a time when the wordy bravos joined forces; one vast socialistic scheme included all theirs. The institutions of the island were to be wiped out, and something undefined that was to make men equal and prosperous and happy was to be put in their place. Their tongues now wagged in unison with wonderful velocity. Each was still for his own special constructive scheme, but they were at one in their scheme of demolition; they must have a clear space to build on, and their ideal was the same, to make all equal and happy. The babel of eloquence drowned the sounds of other industry. Another revolution was almost within earshot.

Some of the wiser hearts of Limanora anticipated the danger, and saw that it would be better to give the discontented all than to let destruction ravage unmuzzled again. The whole of the property of the island was estimated, land, houses, furniture, and luxuries; and money equivalent to its full value was handed over to the malcontent socialists to divide amongst themselves, provided they migrated to another island. The offer was readily accepted; for it was clear that nothing would then be left in Limanora worth plundering. The ships landed the enraptured equalisers of human goods with their belongings on the shore of their new Eden, and returned.

When the decks were cleared, and a census was taken of all that remained, it was found that the island in purging out the socialists was rid of the plague of orators. The price they paid for their deliverance was small indeed, they felt. They soon recreated the wealth they had surrendered. Everyone grew ashamed and afraid of anything that approached to oratory. Eloquence became a word of evil omen. To prate was now the greatest offence against the commonwealth. And for generations there reigned comparative silence and complete peace over the land.

In the series of purgations every remaining trace of tongue-ambition was swept out. Much of the flattering kind was found to have migrated with the lecherous; much of the haughty kind with the aristocratic warriors; but most of it went with the liars. There remained a horror of all prating and tongue-valiance, and this repressed every atavistic tendency in that direction that appeared.

CHAPTER V

LITERATURE

ALL mere word-mongering was to this people an immoral thing, a shameless waste of the tissue and energy that were needed by the evolution of the race, an offence against its aim and ideal, its progress upwards through the cosmic grades. They were persuaded that it was a base substitution of the shows of life for the reality to make an art of words which should absorb the imagination and the skill of hundreds for their whole lifetime. They would have nothing to do with attention to the appearance and ornamentation of a subject to the neglect of its true spirit. Into the very heart and purpose of life every worker must penetrate. His relation to the progress of the race must be clearly shown. No work that took up any of the time or energy of anyone of the community was to be useless or unfertile.

But this did not mean that language was allowed to take care of itself. It was one of the most diligently tended blossoms of human capacity. No word or phrase, whether spontaneous or invented, was allowed to take root without the fiat of the mature community. Language was more a public institution than even government or justice in a people whose every member was able to be a law to himself. It was not only the great channel of communication; it was the medium and garment of every thought. If it became corrupt, how could the mind itself be saved from its contagion? If it acquired a false tone, how could the falsity fail to enter into the very spirit of the men and women? It was the guardian of law and truth; it was the key to the human heart; it was the ether, the medium, in which the human mind lived, moved, and had its being.

How could such a potent factor in human progress be left to the caprices of accident, or of single persons, or even of a family? It had more influence over the spirit than all their sciences put together, for it was more universal in its use than any one of them; and it subtly tinged all of them, whilst it was almost the breath of the mind which dealt with them. It might be the life or the poison of the whole race. He who was the sole guide of language would be the master of Limanora, not in the shallow sense of a ruler, but in that of the complete arbiter of its destinies. He would be the despot of the Limanoran mind and might subtly throw it back centuries, if it pleased him.

A people so experienced and wise as this would have ruined the whole ideal of their existence if they had allowed the most public of the functions of their civilisation to move at the caprice of individuals. As soon as the purgation of the race had been completed it became plain that their language must be purified too. Hundreds of words and phrases and idioms had had soaked into them the infiltrations of the evil minds which were now banished. Worse than all, language had been the commonest and safest ambush of malignity and deceit; it had been a perpetual trap for the innocent and unwary; it had been a labyrinth, in which even the ablest and purest-minded often lost their way when following the lead of some great and noble thought.

The first aim of the elders was to clear it of coarse or vulgar suggestion. But, as they proceeded, they found their horizon widen; and the intricacies, ambiguities, and pitfalls showed themselves the most serious evils of all. It became absolutely necessary, if they were to have a clear and unrefractive medium of expression, to give a definite meaning to every word, and to have one word for every meaning or shade of meaning. The task extended itself through years. But then they knew that, until it was thoroughly done, their science would be like shifting clouds, and their progress would be over quicksands. If their language was treacherous, their civilisation was but a mirage. So they toiled on sustained by the hope that they were making sure their footsteps in the pursuit of truth.

When their work was done, they found it was only begun. For it took a generation to make the new and purified language the natural medium of the whole people, and by that time new sub-meanings had crept into most of the common words, and new shadings had discoloured most of the everyday phraseology. The new and less used words, and the purely technical and scientific words stood where they were. Everything that lived had shifted ground. Everything that was purely artificial and had taken no root had remained as it began, had been in short petrified. It was clear that with living language there must be perpetual vigilance and superintendence. And the whole people had to become a council for the preservation of its purity and translucence. Every citizen set a watch upon his words, as he used them from day to day or as he heard them used, and reported any drift in the sense and any new shade of meaning; and after deliberation in council and careful consideration by the elders a new form was moulded for each new signification. This form had to pass the ordeal of universal use for some time, and if it stood the test, it was finally accepted as part of the language.

Nor was it ever forgotten that the ear and the sense of harmony had as much to do with the acceptance of a word as its fitness to express an idea. Harsh sounds wasted valuable tissue as much as unmeaning syllables. The verbal atrocities of Western science would have made the Limanorans shudder. Dissonance was an offence against the spirit of harmony which pervaded the cosmos; it was as easy to form a melodious word or phrase as one that was grating or stridulous. Euphony, it seemed to them, was one of the first essentials of a language; and it was much pleasanter to be silent than to talk unmusically. There had grown up an instinct in them that moulded their sentences into what Europeans would have called poems. The barest statement of fact ran with a liquid sweetness that drew the ear like a piece of beautiful music. The strictest scientific discourse sounded to me as majestic and melodious as some of the greatest passages in our Western poets. Their most ordinary conversation had the liquid harmony of our finest lyrics without the monotonous rhythm, the jingling rhyme, or the mincing gait. It never struck them that there should be a special art of words apart from that skill which all had by instinct whenever there was a thought to express. If it were a perfectly new thought, a discovery or invention that was still unnamed, then it was the duty of the whole people to make or approve of a word which would exactly fit it. Loose-fitting language soon meant loose, shambling thought, and it was one of their foremost responsibilities as a race to see that no one of them was driven into that. The appearance of a special literary art, for which some were specially gifted, would have told them at once that their language was disorganised and that the first great public need was its reform.

For a time after my arrival in the island I was accustomed to speak with admiration of the great literatures of Europe, one of the few features of our Western civilisation which I felt it no shame to mention. I would launch into glowing praises of the beauty and aptness of the expression, the nobleness of the music, and the majesty and harmony of each work. When I spoke of Homer and Æschylus, of Dante and Milton, of Shakespeare and Goethe, I was unbounded in my admiration of their lofty genius in the management of their material. Questioned as to the character of their thoughts, I contended that there was no need for these to be absolutely new; the greatest merit of such poets was that they took the wisdom of their age or country, or the wisdom of all ages and countries, and expressed it in a way that was inimitable. Their material they had gathered from books or from the experience of their time; and most of their great poems had been analysed by admiring commentators into their original elements; the source from which almost every idea had been taken could be pointed out. But this was only to enhance the value of their work, to increase their greatness. It was one of the commonest observations amongst literary men in the West, when defending themselves against the charge of plagiarism, that there was no such thing as absolute originality of idea or material; the great merit in literature, the test of its lastingness, was the originality or freshness of expression; the rest belonged to the age or people in which it was produced, or to mankind of all ages and nations. And young men and women were encouraged to learn foreign languages, and especially the classical tongues, at all hazards, because translations missed what was distinctive in the great authors; if they would enjoy the true flavour of their originality, they must learn and study the language of the great books for themselves.

I found my efforts to communicate my enthusiasm all in vain. I was met by a look of pity in the eyes of my listeners, and soon came to know the source and meaning of the emotion. They were sorry that I should continue to admire that which was the symptom of a diseased condition, and they commiserated the retrograde state of so many millions of the inhabitants of the globe, who could spend some of the best moments and feelings of their lives on what was merely superficial. They sympathised with the effort to live in a world of thought, a spiritual world, a nobler existence than that of eating and drinking; this was a sign of a yearning for advance. But they grieved that it should take such a mistaken direction, that their fellow-men in the West should glory in what was an evidence of disease. Language was singularly disordered, when only a few could be found throughout the ages with the capacity to use it aptly and musically. Where was the wisdom that guided the people, if it could let this greatest instrument and medium of thought remain so chaotic and infirm that whosoever was skilled in fit and melodious use of it was held to be inspired? Surely it was the first care of the elders and governors to see that the universal means of communication was at least unambiguous and explicit. The highway of thought was left a jungle, primeval and inarticulate as the intercourse of animals; and one who made a clear track through any part of the labyrinth was lauded as divine. The literature of Europe was evidently but the outcome of the incapacity of its people for proper self-government. That only a few should be able to write or speak in so clear and fitting a way was a disgrace to the civilisation. To honour them so greatly as the people did revealed the depths of incapacity into which all had fallen, and the corrupt state of the language.

I urged the marvellous power of suggestion that European words had in the hands of the poets. They bore so many sub-meanings and branches of meaning that the full depths of a poem or great prose work were never sounded. Age after age of students could go on studying it and still find in it new significance, new inspiration. Commentary after commentary had been written on the *Iliad*, the *Divine Comedy*, and Shakespeare's plays, without exhausting all the meaning they had in them. Vast libraries of interpretation of them had accumulated, and yet every new age found opportunity for additions to them. This was due to the subtle under-meanings that touched innumerable keys in the soul, and played upon a vast variety of emotions. An able writer could bring words together so aptly as to affect different minds in different ways. A nebulous significance gathered round his phrases and sentences, and out of this a hundred scholars would make each his own discovery. Mystically lay the thoughts in the depths of his words, ready for the profounder students to fathom. And so every great poem inspired age after age in a thousand different directions. Would this have been the case, if every word had been made to serve but one purpose, if every phrase had been unequivocal in meaning, and every sentence unshaded and perspicuous? It was the play of meaning, the opalescent glimmer of light in language that rendered European poetry so beautiful and undyingly suggestive. It was the twilight of words that gave such majestic and shadowy forms to the ideas and characters and scenes of the great poems of the past. And what would the generations of scholars and teachers have done without these hidden meanings to reveal in their literature, without these intricacies to disentangle, without these dim allusions and adumbrations of sense to make clear? Where would our youth have found their intellectual training, if all our great literature had been transparent and precise in meaning?

I thought I had made out a splendid case for our European tongues. But a glance at the face of my querist served to scatter my vanity to the winds. There was the same inscrutable look of pity in the eyes. Everything I had pleaded, as I thought, so eloquently had only deepened the Limanoran view of the shameful waste of talent which the undefined and perpetually shifting sense of European words produced in the West. There must the ablest minds of most generations wrestle all their lives with the loose-jointed languages they had to employ, and try to get their benediction and inspiration into form for the ages to wrestle with. There must thousands of capable men and women waste their best years in searching for recondite meanings in the works these have produced. There must all the immature minds spend their youth on the hated, barren task of trying to grasp the mirage of sense in the books they learn. What progress would there not have been in Europe if all this talent and energy and time had been saved for the real work of life, if all the best thinkers she produced had been set to the labour of true discovery? It was little wonder that her civilisation was practically unprogressive, when so much of it was built on the quicksands of her language. All the shades and suggestions of meaning were but pitfalls wherein most of her men and women foundered on the journey of life. It was with mere shadows and shows that her greatest minds fought; they were not conquering the unknown and undiscovered that their fellow-men might advance in their footsteps. The night encircled them as deeply as before their preternatural efforts. How could the blind lead the blind in a land covered with mists and full of pitfalls?

I had still a few arrows in my quiver, I thought. No one could deny the beauty of the literary art and the training it gave to the sense of what was fair and noble. Where will one find anything so melodious as our great poems? Where anything so harmonious as the prose of our finest stylists? A beautiful lyric can hold a nation entranced. A fine piece of prose can stir thousands to admiration. What could be more ennobling than the effect of our greatest poems on the youth of our nations, what more refining than the study of our great prose-writers?

Again I knew how far beside the mark I had shot. Style was but the effort of a language to throw off its diseases, an acknowledgment of the gross imperfections that burdened it and made it a clog on the progress of thought. If a language were what it ought to be, a precise means of intercourse between soul and soul, a true medium of intellectual energy, then ought the race that uses it to be completely unconscious of anything like style. We never know we breathe, or how we breathe, till some stoppage makes breathing difficult; we never realise we have a heart whose pulsations are essential to life, till it beats irregularly, and alarms us with the prospect of disease in it. So it is with speech, the instrument of communication among men, the ether of thought; did it perform all its functions in a healthy and perfect way, we should pay little or no attention to it; were words unambiguous and precise, every man would speak and write in the best of all styles, that natural and transpicuous method of expression which fixes the whole mind of the listener or reader, not on the means of conveyance, but on the energy that passes through it. Speech should be no more than one of the unpremeditated, unguided functions of our system; as soon as it calls for attention, it is deranged; as long as we are unconscious of it, it is healthful and strong, acting in every way as it should, without shadow or broken light, without indefiniteness of meaning or mistaken suggestion.

Nor should a language even in its commonest thoroughfares be devoid of music. How false must be the rendering of a thought, if for the sake of melody he who is called a poet should have to reject all but musical expressions in a language which has little music in it! How artificial must be the labours of this professional word-monger, when he must sit amongst the débris of his vocabulary, and pick and choose with weary exertion the words that will fit into his poem! With most of his language unsuited to his purpose, as being invented or moulded by unmusical people, he is like a mosaic-worker who has to make his work out of common stone, or out of fragments of pottery thrown into the rubbish-heap of the ages. Most languages sound like the rasping of a file over iron, or the shooting of débris over a precipice, or at best the crackle and hiss of fireworks. And it is not surprising; for their individual words are made out of anything that is ready to hand by men who care nothing for the sound of them, whether it is harsh or melodious. Now and again if a word or phrase becomes current out of the range of literary products, it will get its harsh grating syllables ground off, or rounded and polished in the torrent of common speech. Thus are prepared the only elements of the language that are fit for the fine mosaic-work of Western poets. They rescue these time-smoothed pebbles from their gross or vulgar surroundings and place them in a setting that will make them seem beautiful for a time.

It is only for a time; again the fair structure they have made falls into ruin, and fragments are whirled into the eddies of everyday speech and abandon their beauty of form and meaning for something their original maker would never recognise. Then begins the old process; the débris of forgotten works, rounded and smoothed in the current of time, serves as the rubble to be concreted into the artistic works of a new age. Alas for the artists who have such a task before them! Out of the rubbish heap of the past they must mould what will please the new times. And where is there room for true harmony in the result of such a process? The materials depend for their form on the caprice of chance; the artists depend for the form they give on the caprice of the age in which they work, certain to be antiquated by the next new fashion. As long as a literary product depends on its form for its lasting effect, it must be comparatively ephemeral; for form is nothing if it does not suit the fancy of the age to which it appeals, and the fancy of one age conflicts with most others. Artificial means may seem to keep it alive, an ecclesiastical or political movement, the aid of an extraneous art, or the ambition of scholars and critics; but the life is only galvanic, and not from the heart of the people. No true music can come out of that which is essentially unmusical.

CHAPTER VI

INSPIRATION

I ABANDONED the effort to defend the literature of Christendom, and came to the conclusion that a people that so scorned all word-mongering could not have any literature. I was soon disabused of the idea. One day, after my education had advanced into the final stage of its earlier course, and my loyalty to the race had been tested in many ways, my proparents bade me accompany them to the production of a new book. After what I had heard in depreciation of literature such as I had been accustomed to in Europe, I was somewhat startled at this invitation. But they said nothing to explain the anomaly, although they knew well the nature of the discussion I had had with Thyriel.

I had thought that, during my long residence in the island and in my countless flights over it, I had come to know every public institution existing on it. But I was mistaken again. In our course we chose a direction that for a space was one I had several times taken. But soon we bent out of the usual track up Lilaroma, and turning one of its western spurs, made for a deep valley which was concealed from view, except to voyagers towards the sunset. Here we found the air filled with wings and airships streaming onwards. It was a beautiful sight, this navy of the sky fleeting across the snows of Lilaroma, or winnowing the depths of the azure. We had been on the adjoining coast of the island, and had not to strike far upwards in order to reach our destination. So the air-fleet moved far above us, most of it having to round the heights of the gleaming mountain. Nothing could surpass the grace with which they took their way through the heaven, now to this point, now to that; and after a time I could hear the movement of their wings, like the rustle of silken sails.

In gazing dreamily upwards, I had allowed myself to drop too near the earth, and in order to reach the goal of our flight exactly I had to take another long rise. Thereafter my gaze was bent earthwards on a still more beautiful sight beneath me. A broad valley narrowed coastwards to a deep gorge and mountainwards into a rift in the rocks. The river which had sculptured this singular amphitheatre had been deflected by an artificial channel into the centre of force, but was allowed at times to sweep its old bed free of the débris of rocks and vegetation. Up each side vibrated in the air tier upon tier of their automatic rests, enough to accommodate a nation. All lay open to the sky; yet there was a subdued light down in the hollow of the vale, that soothed the eyes tired with the gleam of the blue and snow above; and this twilight deepened into gloom towards the head and the exit of the valley. Only in the afternoon, as the sun westered, it shot its level rays through the chasm at the entrance, and mellowed the gloom even of the ravine at the upper end with its golden light. And at sunset the concentration of the many-coloured rays through the gorge had a striking effect upon the whole amphiteatre; it was as if a theatrical artist were lighting it up for some supernatural scene.

The afternoon sunlight indeed soon revealed to our eyes, as we settled on the slopes, an immense stage that shot out of the ravine on the mountain-side. It was, I could see, the natural theatre of the island, cut out by other than human powers. And from side to side the gentlest whisper would carry, yet without recoil; while the sound of the moving stage, as it rolled forth, rose along the tiers and without break or repercussion died away into the open sky above our heads. It must have been here, I thought, that the architects of Limanoran buildings had learned the acoustic secrets of nature. Never a sound was lessened or confused in passing to the farthest corner of any of their vast halls. Nor was it from any mechanical contrivance underneath the roof, but simply from the shape of the enclosure. Nature had formed this valley into a perfect theatre, in the highest tier of which not one listener could miss the smallest sound. Yet by a singular contrivance, by means of which a globe of irelium was kept over the stage, every sound was tenfold magnified lest the merest whisper should escape, whilst every hearer had at hand a margol, which would soften sounds that carried too loudly to the ear. Another strange effect of this irelium shell was that it magnified to the eye everything upon the stage a hundredfold; it acted as a powerful microscope, so that each spectator was far nearer to the inner structure of any object than mere human eye-power could bring him.

We had not to wait long for the purpose of these preparations. There entered upon the stage two figures that underneath the globe seemed gigantic beside the bodies of Limanoran men and women. They had Limanoran outlines, but transmuted into something more ethereal than aught I had seen. There was a grace of form and a beauty of face beyond any of those around me on the slope of the hill. And even to my eyes, untrained and limited as they were in their powers, there was a transparency in the tissue of their bodies which revealed the movements of their organs; I saw their hearts pulsate, and the currents of the blood move quicker or slower along their veins as they walked or stood still. We could even watch the effect of their emotions in their systems, and the excited or tranquil movement of thoughts in the tissues of their brains. The impulses that travelled along their nerves from brain to hand or foot, and the reports that kept journeying from the various senses to the nerve-centres, seemed all to be made plain to us; and seemed the work of a magician, so marvellous was it, so far above mere human achievement.

But still greater marvels were to follow. These two beings or automata or moving shadows of beings, or whatever they might be, enacted a scene, the significance of which I comprehended only after many days' thought. My immediate impressions and my subsequent conclusions and knowledge have so amalgamated that it is difficult to separate the two elements. These two beings were chosen friends, the complements of each other, with tendencies and tastes and loves all in unison. Such perfect fitting of nature to nature was not as yet to be found even in Limanora. Thought sprang to thought, and emotion to emotion, and yet there was a spontaneity and origination in both that made each a separate fountain of life and action. How independent the characters and powers, and yet how mutually adapted! The scene was meant to picture a friendship that was a true and perfect marriage.

The two had grown year by year closer in harmony till at last the mutual sympathy had culminated in a yearning to see an individuality that would combine the best peculiarities of each and perpetuate the combination. We could see the thought flame into a passion in the two systems, and then we could hear the friends talk around the longing till it grew definite, into a common project. We saw them gather the materials needed for the formation of the body. With intricacies of furnace and crucible and machinery they moulded these into the skeleton of a man, flawless and strong in every part. They tried every bone with numberless tests, till they found it all to their satisfaction. Then they started on the cartilages that kept the bones in place or moved them, giving permanence and life to each, as they made it, by the magnetism they communicated to it. Tissue by tissue they built up the internal organs, modelling them with loving care on those they saw at play beneath their own eyes, and testing them to see that they performed their functions perfectly. What delicate artistic energy they spent upon the upper tissues of the body, upon the brain and ear and eye! Each created and developed the quality loved and admired in the other. There was nothing they omitted to make the new being complete and happy in all his functions. On the minute nerves and tissues they worked under powerful microscopes, and the minutiæ of every sense and organ and function were examined and tested again and again with the same magnifying power turned on them. The figure they made most noble and symmetrical in proportions and outlines, the face they made as beautiful as human face could look. The stuff in which they worked was ethereal in its texture and constituents. It was difficult to discern it with our senses even under the great magnifying globe. It seemed to be of air or some product of the ether; for it flowed underneath their guiding fingers almost invisible. And the result was a body more transparent than their own. It was a marvel of refinement and strength combined; they experimented on every limb and sense, every nerve and muscle and tissue, and they corrected every defect in it before they reached the final act.

At last the work was completed to their satisfaction, and they braced themselves for the most exhausting task of all. How were they to make of this image a living creature? I smiled as I thought of the impossibility of what was evidently before them. Yet they seemed perfectly calm in their preparation for the final endeavour. Only there was a subdued volcanic energy in their systems that seemed to show that they considered it a task almost superhuman. They encouraged each other, and we could see them infuse new magnetism into their bodies by means of machinery of great power. Their faces were filled with the glow of a rapturous appeal to heaven. They were putting themselves into connection with some being they adored invisible to us, some impalpable fountain of life. They took the hands of the image they had formed, and raised it; they placed it between them, so that it should be in the path of all energy that passed from one to the other. They laid their hands upon its head and nerve-centres, and at the same time the pleading rapture on their faces rose almost to trance. Their spirits seemed to go out from them. They looked like two in dream. A faint flush came upon the cheeks of the image between them, and died out. Again their souls seemed to return to full consciousness, and the rapture grew upon their faces. Again the signal of life dawned on the countenance of the image. Throb by throb they gave of their own souls to his, meantime drawing from some fountain of life and spirit unseen by us. Slowly the eyelids rose, and the lips moved. There was true life in the image. The three walked as in trance, yet with the joy of creation pulsing through them. The child of their imagination was like both, yet independent, and more beautiful to look upon. Love broke through the new being and theirs in wild pulsations. The three awoke to a new life. And then the scene vanished, and I seemed to have but dreamed.

Yet there was the deep valley with the sunset rays shooting through it; and up the slopes rested thousands of flesh-and-blood Limanorans beside me. A few thoughts, and I knew that it was no dream. Was it magic? I could not believe that such a people would indulge in mere trifling with life and the powers above life. My spirit of enquiry stirred my guardians, and I soon knew from them that this was the first publication of a new book, called Human Sculpture. The deep valley with its apparatus was the theatre of futurition, where every imaginative foresight was first put into a form that would appeal to the whole people. It was called Loomiefa or the display of pioneering.

Their literature was all science, and that the science of the future. Romancing about the past or the present seemed to this utilitarian people waste of the noblest faculty of man, shameful squandering of imaginative wealth on that which is naught. Mere retrospection for its own sake without reference to subsequent advance was thought by them the most pernicious of madnesses; they diagnosed it as a kind of ethical blindness, that could neither see the right nor do it. The state of peoples who looked at nothing but the past with admiration was one of the lowest circles of their inferno; another was that of nations that saw nothing good outside of themselves and their immediate surroundings. In such unprogressive national or racial attitudes they saw all the evils of inbreeding; the weaknesses and intellectual and moral diseases of the past grew despotic in their power over the human system, till they came to seem the only virtues; even what had been once virtues grew inveterate and routine, or monstrous and overpowering in their excess. The past served only as the soil for the better growths of the future. And an exhausted soil became barren, if not poisonous, for all but weeds, or growths that needed and deserved no attention or cultivation.

To spend imagination on the past, therefore, was to them a crime against the future. What was dead and needed invention to bring before the mind again was better in its grave. A literature that turned back to the past for its progress clogged the wheels of progress, unless it belonged to a race that had fallen back centuries behind the natural advance of the world. For a progressive nation to give of its best for the resurrection of a dead past was to confess a strain of barbarism in it, and to prophesy its own rapid decay. The imagination was the faculty of the future; it had its eyes set in front, and not behind like memory; it was meant to investigate the horizon before us, and to interpret the lights and shadows thrown from below the rim of vision, and not to look back, whether with regret or adoration, over the region that humanity had beaten hard with its weary footing. The future is infinite; the human past covers but a few centuries, and a narrow track through them. It is not for want of scope that the faculty of futurition is driven back on the ground already trodden; it is through a grievous and incurable malady, the malady of preterpluperfection, that twists the face round to the back of the neck, and rots or petrifies the tissues of the brain and the heart. They counted it the saddest of all spectacles on earth to see a race, that by its nature could be rapidly progressive, waste its highest energies in retracing again and again the footsteps of its own ancestry or of the ancestry of some other race. Nothing would persuade them to permit any study of the past that was not meant to be wholly relevant to the future. They tended to be, I thought, almost negligent of the value of history and historical study; for, as our Western commonplace goes, history repeats itself; and however new and ameliorative an age may be, it may obtain lessons, and still more warnings, from ages past.

Their literature was all of the future. There were two of the largest families of the race devoted to it, and their numbers were ever being recruited by adoption into them of scions of others, who revealed exceptional imaginative faculty. They had the generalised training of the island; but their particular training was more completely specialised than that of any other family. Nothing was omitted that would tend to make them of imagination all compact, or to give them such ease in their command of language as would bring them the exact word without effort. Next to these points in their education stood tutelage in all that pertained to scenic art and music. For they had to give their ideas a staging that would at once appeal to the imagination of the whole people. Loomiefa was in their province. And the literary form into which they were to put their communications as to the future had to be as perfect as it could be in their language, exactly expressing all they had to convey, and at the same time appealing to the ear by its melody and harmony. As far as histrionic art was allowable in the island they were the artists, whilst in the linguistic conventions of the people they were the leaders and suggesters in the making of words, and in the choice of words made. They had, I could see, the finest heads in the community; the brow was broad, full, and shapely; the eyes were large and yet deeply set under the brows; the base of the skull was of great width; every section of the brain that had to do with imaginative and poetic power was well developed. Yet their faces and features showed no difference from the common Limanoran type; they had no more beauty or regularity of outline. It was clear that all children of a certain shape of skull and development of brain were selected for training and adoption by these two families, whenever they needed recruits.

From the first the youth of these two families were educated in the sciences of the day in order that they might know what gaps in knowledge had to be filled, and what laws should guide and limit their imaginative prospecting. For the literature they produce is science in embryo. Science lays the foundations of literature, and literature prepares the way for science. These families by their imaginative productions based on all that is already known pioneer the scientific investigators into the new regions of the future. They keep in touch with the leaders of science, and act as allies to them, finding out the track of what these are trying to discover or invent, and suggesting methods of supplying their wants or reaching their aims. They provide working hypotheses for the scientists to apply and test and they map out roads for the whole race into the darkness of the unknown or the twilight of the half-conjectured.

Thus their literature is fiction; for tentative fiction, they hold, is the only unstagnant truth. The productions of the pioneering families have all to be submitted to the national test. What the race disapproves of is promptly cancelled and forgotten. What meets with the approval of the elders or of the leaders of any one of the sciences is handed over to them for experimentation, even though it should not attract the rest of the people. What strikes the fancy of the nation as a whole is adopted as the map and guide of the future;

it is the sacred book of the time, and the citizens study it daily for the purpose of reaching the goal it sets before their life.

But every new age antiquates one or more of these sacred books. For the region they have mapped out in the future is reached and travelled over, the advance they anticipate is made, the ideal they paint is realised and rapidly becoming commonplace. It puzzled me for a time to guess what they did with their superseded books, knowing as I did how superfluous they counted all researches into the past and all imaginative pictures of the present. My question as usual was not long unanswered. I was shown the library of antiquated fiction in the valley of memories. It was used in the very earliest stages of education. The children read the books or heard them in order to see, when they reached years of maturity, what the race had come from and how much it might yet advance, to gather enthusiasm from the spectacle of the progress made, and to learn lessons for their own future. Beyond childhood and early youth every minute was counted lost that was not spent on the future and its possibilities; and for a man or woman of mature years all forms of antiquarianism were counted idleness.

They never permitted themselves to lay too much stress on any sacred book, or to adore it too passionately, however much they might be guided by it for a time; for they knew from experience that it would soon be worked into the nature of the race and the system of the individual, and another would take its place. The sacred book of today was bound to be transcended tomorrow. The foresights and ideals of this year would be the truisms of next. The real desecration, they thought, was to rest too many ages over a sacred book, its precepts unworked into the life, its pictures and ideals unrealised; to adore its words and deny its spirit by failing to advance beyond its point of view. A book too long held sacred is a charge of stagnancy and barbarism against a race and an insult to its intelligence. It proves that the civilisation has become stereotyped, or worse, retrospective; to eat, to sleep, to fall prostrate before a dead ideal, to propagate and die, sum up the ultimate duties of existence at its highest level.

Every book was sacred to the Limanorans which threw light upon the track ahead into the darkness; and so long as it still gave light where light was needed, it remained sacred. Whenever its light became the common daylight around the race, and especially if they had to look backwards in order to see its waymarks, then was it promptly committed to the valley of memories. Not a moment was wasted on its precepts after they had become the laws of everyday existence. They had known from their own history what a terrible engine of oppression a book might be when once it had become antiquated without losing the adoration of the people; its prophecies, which had become mere tales of the past, had to be projected again into the future by mystic interpretation; its precepts, embodying the spirit of a generation long dead, had to be galvanised into life by casuistry; and innumerable methods had to be extorted from its overstrained text to prevent the human mind moving on past its own stage of morality and civilisation. How many ages in their own history did their ancestors live with their dead! Into the warmest feelings of their hearts had the grave-clothes of the past intertwined; and what torture to love and the noblest feelings, what bloodshed and horrors it cost them to be able to stand off from their dead authority, and look at it with unprejudiced mind! It had become a part of their best selves, and it seemed like suicide to cast it from them, and relegate it to its true home, the graveyard of the past.

That long experience was burned into their natures; and to lay too much stress on any new book or idea gave them an instinctive pang. They could not bear to linger over it, once the light had died out of it and its leading had become a highway-mark for the passerby. To utter or admire the obvious or commonplace was counted one of the gravest offences against the common-weal; it awakened a look of pity in the eyes of the listener as for one who was smitten with an incurable disease. A repetition of the offence would lead to drastic measures with the victim. He was haled before the medicists, and his system was minutely examined for the source of the malady, and for weeks was he kept under medical supervision; no labour or watching or remedial pain was spared till the source of offending was scourged out of the constitution of the sufferer.

As a rule it was found on investigation that the infection had come from some book, whose spirit and precepts had become incorporated in the past of the race and could give no more vitality to it. It was good enough for children and youth, who were passing through the primitive stages of development; to them it was fresh and new for a time, and was even the source of life and vigour. But once out of the valley of memories the men and women who could read it with any pleasure were considered unhealthy and atavistic, and were sent to hospital for treatment. The symptoms of the malady of the commonplace were well known and most patent—loquacity, fondness for confidential communications and mysterious suggestions under solemn conditionings, or even oaths of silence, bustling idleness, feeble smiles of impotent superiority, jocular dogmatism, assumption of wisdom, and excessive vanity. If the disease had not been so infectious and stealthy in its spread, it would never have been treated so seriously and so promptly; for it was seldom malignant, in its earlier appearances at least; only when it became morbid, and took the shape of injured feeling at unrecognised genius, resulting at times in jealousy and slander, or conspiracy and rebellion, or when it grew masterful and acquired a sense of its own infallibility and omnipotence, resulting generally in petty spite and persecution, was there any deadly virus in it. It was its epidemic character that made it most formidable, and necessitated a system of moral quarantine. Special precautions were taken in permitting the use of the sacred books of the past, and of antiquated or superseded ideas. They were only useful for teaching the young reverence for great thoughts and great thinkers, and for leading the mature to estimate their own achievements modestly, when they saw the rapid antiquation of even the most striking books.

One evil that arose from the study of past literature, the over-valuation of literary work, they tried to obviate. They placed noble deeds on the same footing with noble words and thoughts, and saw that they were as carefully recorded and described. It was the duty of the young to report, and give permanent form to, anything that was done greatly. With their enthusiasm made more glowing by their ignorance and inexperience, they acted as the historiographers of the race. The youth of a family went with the elders whenever any difficulty offered itself, and with their recording instruments, inasans and linasans and idrosans, they took flying pictures, electrographs, and reports of the scene for deposit in the valley of memories. If any emergency arose and was nobly met when the youthful remembrancers were not present, they wrote the annals of it none the less, and reproduced its scenes in moving representations after interviewing all who witnessed the deed. There was as much inspiration, this people held, in a great action as in a great book, provided it illumined the darkness of the road ahead of them.

For to them the true test of greatness and inspiration was the power of fore-illumination or of stimulus to progress. Whatsoever flashed light over the unknown in front must have come from a higher point of view than their own immediate surroundings. Word or deed, it was to them all the same, if it had this divine characteristic; the one was as worthy of chronicling and preserving as the other. But they ceased to look upon it as a source of stimulus to action as soon as it failed to throw light upon their future, or to hold up an ideal that they had not yet attained. Inspiration, like all other things and beings in the universe, was progressive. No idea or deed, no word or book could be permanently inspired. And the quicker a race progressed, the sooner it sterilised its sacred thoughts and deeds. All noble human advance was a process of deinspiration; a step upwards makes the climber capable of looking down upon the previous point of vision, and of looking up for a still higher, and to gaze downwards is to encourage retrogression. Whosoever or whatsoever caught the first gleam of a peak above them was to them inspired. But it was the duty to reach that peak in their march upwards as soon as possible; and once it was reached, where was the inspiration? It was itself far below with the age that supplied it.

Some new deed or thought or book was certain to take the place of that which had for a time been considered sacred. And, if that did not come, then woe to the race! Progress must stop and darkness must close in on their purblind leaders, who, in order to retain their dominance, must elevate the past, immediate or distant, into a divinity, and its best book into an oracle. After a time so obscured do the pages of this book become with cobwebs of interpretation that at last they must spin new cobwebs out of their intestines. The dread of light from without becomes a horror. If a new teacher or prophet should come, down with him into the dust; his teachings are false, for they agree not with the devotion-cobwebbed book. If a reformer sees light above and ahead, he is banned as a messenger of hell; and what he sees is nothing but a diabolic marshlight. All through the race spread the awful diseases of spiritual inbreeding, inability to distinguish the true from the false, love of delusion, unwholesome and insane pursuits and ends, and the madness of cruelty and intolerance. Nothing but fierce revolution could save a race from such a plight. And the germs of revolution must come from without themselves and without the world.

CHAPTER VII

PIONEERING

IMAGINATION, corrected by racial instinct in the assemblies of all, was the seeker for foregleams of what was to be. And a people that had organised its civilisation into a disciplined advance was not likely to leave its scouts and vanguard unorganised. Its destiny was largely in the hands of those who went before it into the night, or who ascended the heights above it, and told of the region to be traversed next, and the best routes through it. There was no service that needed so much the best powers of the race and its best organisation.

Into the pioneering families were gathered their most powerful imaginations. For imagination is the only clairvoyant of the faculties; it can see what lies below the horizon of knowledge; it can forecast the world as it might be and as it is to be; and it can draw the human mind onwards by the splendours of this forecast. This people had early realised the sibylline character of the faculty, and the great part it might play in their devotion to progress. And they resolved to save it from all waste. They refused to have it become the mere slave of luxury or of popular amusement, such as they saw it was in most other civilised nations. Even where it conjured up the past in magnificent literary pictures, what else was it than the pander to tastes and habits that were overworn, the encomiast of deeds that had better be buried in oblivion? It frequented the palaces of kings and licked the dust off their feet, or it played the buffoon to the indolent, sensuous crowd. At rare times it isolated itself, and, heedless of the babbling world that offered it so many prizes, it wrestled with the powers of darkness and ignorance. But what could a poor recluse do against the infinite night? If it were to help the forward march of humanity, it must be disciplined and organised to a definite aim.

All other peoples have left imagination to struggle for itself. This people recognised it as the most unschooled and shiftless of the human faculties, whilst they felt it to be the most divine and fullest of promise. They determined that amongst them it should lose its reeling gait and wandering, aimless eye, and become the pioneer of their march onwards; instead of fixing its eye on the past or on the favours of the great, it should skirmish before the main army into the region of the unknown; it should report on the difficulties and the enemies to be met, and map out the world as it was to be. What would be thought of the shipmaster who let the keenest-eyed of his crew lounge round the ship looking into the pockets of his comrades and making them laugh, or lean over the stern watching the track left behind, if darkness and cloud and a broken sea ever lay on the horizon ahead? What else were the nations doing with their lookout faculty, imagination, but allowing it to waste itself on providing amusement for the luxurious, or on figuring the problem of the past?

It was one of the first duties of the Limanoran elders, after the great series of purgations of the race, to organise and develop the imagination they had in their midst. They had observed that there were two great types and uses of the faculty; one was short of vision, and could see with great distinctness the regions that were hidden in twilight immediately in front of them; the other was far-sighted, and could descry the features of wide regions that lay in darkness under the horizon. There happened to be amongst them two families distinguished from all others by their great imaginativeness, and from each other by pre-eminence in one of these two kinds of imagination. The task therefore was easy. It only needed care in disciplining the members of these to the main purpose of the race, in developing the faculty of each, and in recruiting their numbers from the most imaginative children of other families. The Loomiamo or pioneers of the immediate were recruited chiefly from the scientific and technical families; for their duties lay most of all in supplying hypotheses for experimentation, in suggesting methods of solving difficult problems, and in tracing out paths that invention should take; invention in fact was what they were oftenest engaged in. But there was a subordinate function, that was, however, of equal importance for the forward movements of the race; it was to take the far-reaching conceptions of the other imaginative family, and show how they could be attained by the civilisation and means they already had. They accepted the scientific ideas and apparatus of the time as they were and out of them and their development they engineered a highway through the intervening twilight to the ideal that the Fraloomiamo or pioneers of the distant had pictured and set up ahead of the race.

I had not known of this division of pioneering work when I flew back from the marvellous spectacle in the valley of futuritions. As I thought over it, I became more and more sceptical of the realisability of the scene. It had the inconsecution and absurdity of a dream. I said to Thyriel, where was the possibility of ever substituting artificial for natural propagation of the race? It was completely out of the line of evolution, and could lead to nothing but what was unnatural and evil. They could modify nature to an indefinite extent, I knew; but what was the use of attempting to supersede nature? And suppose it were possible to supersede it in this respect, where would be the advantage? They could already modify and guide nature so as to produce the type of children they desired for the progress of the race; what more was needed?

Thyriel gave no answer, partly because she thought that the elders were more capable of answering, partly because she knew that the publication of the book on human sculpture was by no means finished. Next day my sense of community with the immediate yearning and aim of the Limanorans drew me unconsciously to Loomiefa again; and on my way the streaming wings through the sky showed me that my impulse was not purposeless; there was a general movement towards the same goal. Soon the whole amphitheatre was filled from height to hollow with spectators enriched in colour by the rays of the afternoon sun.

I had scarcely settled in my rest and surveyed the scene when I knew that all eyes were fixed on the hollow of the valley. The platform had again run out with the globular magnifier covering it. But the succession of scenes upon it was almost too swift for my observation, untrained as I still was in my senses, and a certain confusion still rests over the spectacle in my memory. Many of the links in the chain were so amazing as to bewilder me, and yet the general purpose and effect of the scene as a whole rise above the confusion in my mind.

I knew before it was done that it was a complete answer to my questions and scepticism. The Loomiamo were enacting the various stages in the evo- lution of the race which would connect its actual state with the possibility of artificial human propagation. One scene enacted what they had long been able to do, the production of animal tissue of all kinds; even the most subtle nerve was spun, and under their microscopes they could examine it like a rope. Another showed animal creation at work on the combination of tissue into one of the lower types of animal. One after another in a long series we saw the creative power rise in its ambitions and efforts through the animal creation up to the human. But the most striking scene was to come. It was the application of the newly discovered biometer to the search for the principle of life. We saw the creative artists investigate with the instrument plant after plant and animal after animal, and fail in their attempts to isolate it or pro- duce it. They modified the biometer in innumerable ways. Then we saw them fly though the atmosphere, and set the new life-measuring apparatus afloat in space. After repeated attempts, ever pulling the faleena back empty, they at last showed by the joy on their faces that they had attained the goal of their quest. In the delicate test-tubes of their new biometers was found something that kept agitating their indicators. Soon they had it in their laboratories, and were experimenting with it. Again and again they gathered it from the vacuum above the atmosphere. At last by means of it they were enabled to find it in the plants around them, and in the animals of the surrounding islands. A series of scenes as amazing showed how they came at the discovery of the principle of soul by means of the psychometer. Step by step (and each step, I came afterwards to feel, represented a Limanoran generation) they traced it back to its secret. Most of all were they aided in their researches by investigations outside of the atmosphere; there they captured in the tubes of their psychometers the form of energy that constituted human soul. And in their laboratories they were able to study it at leisure.

For long I felt that these pictures of the future were unlikely to be realised. Yet the steps in the process were so gradual, and the scene representing each so vivid that I came in after years to accept it as well within the range of Limanoran possibilities; for I realised at last how far into the future imagination could pioneer, and what a vast number of ages one of these predictive dramas would cover. My sense of time was crude and weak during my earlier years in the island, and it was difficult for me to appreciate the passage of cosmic periods, such as were often implied in the scenes representing the publication of a book by the Fraloomiamo.

I afterwards listened to the book of Human Sculpture itself, as it uttered itself from a loud-sounding linasan or reproducer of speech. This automaton-reader had the long strip of irelium constituting a Limanoran book fed into it off the cylinder on which the book was kept rolled. It gave the sound and every intonation of the author's voice, so that there was no difficulty in following his every thought as it found expression. I never came to be able to read those books on the irelium rolls themselves under a microscope, as the Limanorans could, and preferred to use my hearing instead of my eyes. There was no possibility of ambiguity if I listened to the words as they came hot from the thinker's own lips.

A new and more esoteric kind of book tended to supersede this at a later period. It consisted of an electrogram of the author's thoughts, as they developed and shaped themselves, flashed on to long moving strips of labramor or electricity-sponge by his active magnetic sense; this placed in an idrosan or electrograph affected the firla of the receiver so that he followed the whole process of thinking. Such a permanent record of creative thought in its process of creating was of measureless value to such a people as this, for every economy of time and intelligence meant a quickening of their march into the nobler future. But for many ages the effort of electrographing the thought was too much except for the most powerful of mature creative minds; and that of receiving the flash of the electrogram through the firla was within the capacity of none but those who had developed their magnetic faculty to great refinement of power.

The book of Human Sculpture was the first of the recent imaginative productions that I became acquainted with. Thyriel and I joined a party of youth who, under the guidance of our proparents, were to listen to it, as it sounded through the linasan in the valley of Loomiefa. Hour after hour we followed the melodious periods, as they echoed up the slopes; at brief intervals on the rocky curtain at the head of the gorge there would flame out for several minutes a moving picture of the scenes we had witnessed the enaction of on the stage; and a still more striking illustration of the text of the book was a magnetic communication to our minds of the originating impulse which moulded each thought and scene in the imagination of the author, and the creative enthusiasm he felt as each idea burst in all its light upon his soul. By the time we had finished the book we knew its whole conception and history, its purpose, and its probable effect upon the civilisation.

It answered all my questions, and rooted out all my scepticism. The whole object of their unending labours was to take command of nature by finding out her secrets and abridging her processes, so as to make them serviceable to their advance. I felt how absurd had been my objections; for where would this people have been, if they had left nature to herself? What else was barbarism but leaving nature to herself, so that the more cruel animal part of her became dominant? Nature included an infinite range of gradations of energy and life from what we call dead matter to the subtle and elevated organisations that fill space and evade the finest perception of our senses. Within our own systems are to be found many of those, from the débris of our bodily tissues and organs to the noblest thought we can conceive; the precept to let nature alone is fraught with inextricable ambiguity; and if we let the myriad natures within us fight it out, it is not difficult to see which would have dominance, for it is easier to level down than to level up. Every interference with the lower nature in order to bring it under the sway of the higher, every new mastery of our systems as a whole by our creative thought, is a step upwards in the scale of existences. Three fourths of the process of human propagation belonged to the sphere of our lower nature, so that civilised men and women were ashamed to speak of it, and tended to become gross and coarse if they did freely speak of it. Every act seemed to drag them back again to the level of the animals, and it took them years of effort to drive the thoughts and traces of it into oblivion. They had as a people painfully fought their way up out of the slough of passion, and mastered the emotions that tended to overbalance them by their excess, and to plunge them back again into it. Guard themselves as they might by all kinds of precautions, and spiritualise the act as they ever tried to do, its necessary recurrence never failed to embrute the nature for a moment, whilst it still kept open a path for retrogression. To shut out this possibility of re-descent into the beast would be one of the greatest services to their race.

As useful for their advance would the command of human propagation be in another direction. The only fear of deterioration that still haunted them arose from atavism. Nature had still a trick of returning on her own footsteps. The child of the noblest pair had at times traces of far-back ancestry resurgent in evil or retrogressive traits; and it wasted the time and the best energy of parents and proparents to obliterate these. In every germ lay dormant the potentialities of its whole ancestral past; and any one of them might assert itself as master during the dim unguided life of gestation. With all their precautions something evil might still lurk in the systems of the young to be developed in full maturity of life. But if they moulded every tissue and organ and faculty for themselves, this retrogressive tendency that nature treasures up in every germ and child would disappear. There would be nothing to watch or obliterate in the immature.

A still greater economy of time and labour would result in the abridgment of the earlier processes of education. Education, it is true, never ceased throughout life. But the education of the mature was self-conducted; the citizen was his own schoolmaster, and his surroundings were his instruments and assistants. That of the earlier stages used up the labour and wisdom of two other personalities for the long period of discipline; they were ever on watch and guard lest the past that lay in the youthful nature should suddenly rise and master it. For all education is a wrestle with the superseded past, which becomes evil as soon as it grows superfluous or obstructs further advance. Every form of vitality that has played its part on the stage of existence leaves it with reluctance; it clings to the new, that it may have a little more of life, and impedes its advance. The obsolete most survives in the tissues of the young and immature; and to educate is to struggle with the obsolete or obsolescent. The labour and thought needed to make the struggle end in the success of the new and progressive have never been understood so well by any as by the elders of the Limanorans. No effort of their civilisation was so exhausting as the educative. To enter on parenthood or proparenthood made them pause, for all acknowledged that the assumption of this duty was the greatest sacrifice a man or woman could make for the progress of the race. They knew that for half a century their individual vigilance could never cease, and that the strain would come on all their faculties, and not on one or two alone, as it would in most of the other duties they owed to the race, even invention or discovery. Whatsoever would commute or abolish this heavy service to the nation was sure to be welcomed. So vast an amount of the best time and wisest ability of the island would be set free that it would be difficult to calculate the acceleration of progress it would effect.

All this and a thousand other considerations passed through my mind, as I listened to the book of Human Sculpture and drank in its inspirations. The doubts that its dramatic publication had left in me were all laid. I now knew that this would be a new sacred book, which would hold up for ages an ideal for Limanora to struggle towards.

* * * *

This book of Human Sculpture made clear to me the meaning and purpose of another publication that I soon witnessed. It was the book of Asexuality, which showed us dramatically how sex and its results belonged to a lower and more physical stage of personal development. It revealed to us the nature of the beings that flit through sidereal space just outside the ken of our senses, centres of energy less inert and more ethereal than any terrestrial creatures. Into them flows more freely than it flows into us the divine energy that is above all. Out of themselves they give as freely to their fellows as they receive. They need no such inequality and unstable equilibrium as sex to teach them such bounteous benignity. Living in the precincts of the fountain of life as they do, not imprisoned within local and temporal limits, but free to move whither they will and to drink unstintingly of supernal existence, they know how essentially all nobler life consists in free bounty; the more of themselves and their energy they give, the higher the energy they receive in its place. Sex is only the rude beginning of this higher law, the principle of antagonism to stagnation, of giving lavishly in order to have room for receiving from higher sources. It supersedes and antagonises the law of parasitism, which governs the crude beginnings of life on a new world. The lower microscopic creatures that live a famished jejune life in space ready to pounce upon any orb their shoals encounter, propagate by mere self-division; they have nothing to give. A new star cooling down on its surface sufficiently for life to settle on is their great opportunity. There they may parasite and feed to their heart's content, propagating by the myriad every infinitesimal fraction of time. And, as long as they live in such primeval luxury, they never move one step higher in life. Over-supply of food, indeed all luxury, damns a being to stagnancy. The full-fed parasite is unprogressive, and, though multiplying teemingly, is practically sterile; his generations are on a level with himself; he is immortal by mere fission; the only function of his life is to grab, till his gettings make him too big for his microscopic unity, and he has to break up. In the higher stages of life, even in human life, this infecundity attaches in the same way to luxurious living, whilst the sycophant is sterile of purpose and existence. All take and no give is a monstrosity above the lowest bacterial life. The more of dependence or flattery there is in a people, the lower their natures; a tyranny is the lowest political organism; and of tyrannies the worst is the socialistic; for there, there is no inequality to antagonise and overcome the lethargy of parasitism.

Even when bacteria begin to feel the pinch of scanty nutrition or malnutrition, they start on a new career, and show the first traces of an advance in life. They incline to give as well as receive, and here are the primeval beginnings of sex. Ill-fed bacteria tend to propagate by means of special cells or spores. Instead of steeping themselves in food till they burst, they now begin to nurse within their systems a germ, to which they give of their best till it is able to launch out for itself; they cease to reproduce by fission, and reproduce by spore-formation. This is the first step upwards on the long road to human morality. The beginnings of sex are the beginnings of unlikeness of individuals, and the beginnings of unstable equilibrium and of overflow of energy from one being into another. This is the organisation of the policy of give in a new star, ultimately meant to drive out, after a world-long struggle, the antagonistic policy of mere get. Sex first introduced into our world the eagerness of one being to give of its best for the good of another being. Conjugal love in the human era is the first noble form of sexuality; and parental love is its still nobler offshoot.

The development of parenthood is the knell of sexuality. For it is a new and higher phase of the policy of give, and antiquates the mere mutuality of sexual love. It gives of its all expecting nought in return. And into the place of the energy that has gone out of it flows an energy that is nearer the divine and raises towards the divine. It is at this point that sex becomes a lower stage, seeming almost to mingle with brute life. Out of it must humanity struggle in order to progress. "In the spirit there is no sex." This I had heard as a meaningless echo from wise lips in the West. Now I saw its significance. The higher, the more spiritual we become, the less we permit sex to dominate, and the less difference there is between the sexes. It was in the world of imagination and intellect that the first idea of equality of the sexes arose. And the more intellectual a people became, the less it insisted on the difference between man and woman. Emphasis on sex in a civilised people was a sure sign of approaching decay.

For the goal towards which the human race is advancing is asexual; not that that will be the main characteristic; but it is the most striking compared with our present phase of being. The more highly organised existences that fill space and hover just outside the range of our grosser senses have reached the stage in which the stimulus of sex or even of parenthood is no longer needed in order to save the benignant instincts from dying out. And the higher a centre of energy climbs in the scale of existence, the more eager does it become to overflow into other centres, to give of its highest and best. What we call life, or the spontaneous rejection of stagnancy, begins on its lowest fringe with a tendency to take all and give none, with appetite. Below this are inert centres of energy, that resist all receiving as well as all giving, that exist only in persisting, in keeping what they have and what they are; this stage is usually called dead matter in contrast to energy, although it consists of nuclei of energy as truly as any living creature. Between the two stages of mere keep and mere take seems to lie a great gulf fixed; but there are minute evidences of transition to be found all through nature. We ourselves, the human race, form the transition from the stage of take all to the stage of give all. And sex is the chief impetus to progress in the earlier history of human evolution.

Parenthood takes its place in the upper levels, where the human is rapidly approaching the supersensuous. The very fact of our nature being so heterogeneous and complex reveals that we are making for something higher; and, as our appetites imply a stage behind us, in which our systems were fitted for nothing but taking, so our loves, our benevolences, our self-sacrifices, point forward to a stage in which the whole of existence will consist in giving. I remember, whenever an average man in Europe quoted the phrase, "It is more blessed to give than to receive," he meant it as a jest, or in a sinister sense; even the priest, when he had to preach the doctrine as one of the foundations of his religion, had incredulity in his heart if not in the smile on his lips, as he spoke the words. Amongst the Limanorans it was a truism that was implied in all conduct and need never be explicitly stated. And the book of Asexuality revealed the inner and scientific significance to me. The highest state of any centre of energy in the cosmos was to be eagerly, lavishly, and perpetually giving out of its best. For thus was it ever kept in unstable equilibrium, towards which flowed higher and higher energies from centres above it; thus it kept its life unstagnant and immortal. That which only received and was eager only to receive, suffered the maladies of the luxurious, soon reached its utmost capacity, and fell into stagnancy and decay. Above the human rose the hierarchy of sexless, supersensuous beings, who peopled infinite space; but into their ranks rose the human by means of struggle, by means of the effluence of their energy into others, by means of sex, and still more of parenthood. The purpose of sex is to attain to the higher asexuality.

Not that monasticism is good for the human race. It is on the contrary the greatest of evils in the sexual stage of progress. It counts as wicked and harmful that which alone prevents self-absorption and the beginning of decay and death. Sex is the provision of nature for drawing the animal outside of itself so that it may introduce into its generations the seeds of development. It makes it as a centre of energy feel the need of other centres, to which it may give, from which it may receive. It is her chief means of keeping any vital centre from falling back into stagnancy and the desire of stagnancy. And, as long as man is still animal, sex and its resultant parenthood must continue to play the main part in development. To attempt to reach asexuality before the animal is ejected from his system is to balk progress and invite stagnancy and decay.

The book of Asexuality showed how the family must remain the unit and lever of advance till sex should be superseded by individual creation. Then friendship or the bond of contrast in community will take the place of the bond of heredity, or of that bond which is based upon sexual passion. The mutual choice will be completely rational and in the will of the choosers. There will be nothing instinctive or mediate or unconscious about it. It is indeed one of the indignities of this present sexual stage of evolution that we are thrust on in spite of ourselves, that we have little command over the stimulus that is urging us on the road of progress.

The Limanorans had got rid of some of this indignity inasmuch as the elders and wise men took command of the instinct of sex, and bent it in the direction of their own line of advance. In other peoples, and especially in the West, it stumbled blindly on, led sometimes by the love of youthful beauty, sometimes by the love of money, sometimes by the necessities of position and diplomacy, most frequently by ambition and the love of power or social influence, seldom or never by the deliberate intent of producing noble posterity. As a consequence retrogression in health, physique, morality, or intellectual power was seen in all ranks far oftener than progress. Over the whole there might be a slight advance in centuries; but in most families it was one generation forward and the next back. This people had by their purgations become the assistants of nature; and since the era of the exilings they had wisely piloted sex to serve the highest purposes of evolution. The young were still driven half-blindly by the sting of sex, and might by chance accelerate progress; but the elders without revealing their art wisely controlled the instinct, and by the governance of proximity and opportunity, companionship and circumstances, amongst the immature made it the guardian and keeper of past advance and the prompter of still renewed advance. The final step was pictured by this new imaginative book, the supersession of sex and the deliberate creation of posterity. This would relieve the elders of their anxious task of match-making, and put into the hands of the pairs themselves the control of the parental instinct and the power of improving their posterity.

Even as it was, I could see, from the axioms and postulates of this book of Asexuality, and the impression it made on my friends and companions, that the sex-instinct was already to a large extent under the control of those whom it impelled. It had become, like their appetite for food, saturated with intellect and deliberation. It was no mere goad that drove them on in the dark stumbling towards some object that would gratify the passion. They knew its physiological and psychological working, and understood how the destinies of the race waited upon the wisdom or folly of its guidance. Not even the youngest of them would allow it the caprice and perverse whimsicality that was considered its native prerogative in the West. The passionate whim of the moment for "a grey eye or so" was no more to them than toothache or the pangs of indigestion, an aberrancy from healthy nature, to be checked and healed as soon as possible. I found that I was far in the rear of their advance in respect to love. My Western heroics and amorous transports were discounted and yet curiously watched as the antiquated manners of an age long gone by. Nothing gave so keen a shock to my self-approval as the smile that played upon the face of Thyriel when I first broke into the raptures of adoration for her which are the natural expression of passionate love in my native

Europe. Romeo-and-Julietism had been consecrated by centuries of the traditions of Christendom as the true attitude and conduct of lovers. And here was I, only fulfilling the instinct and bursting into the appropriate transports of passion, reined in by what I thought at first the cynicism of my Juliet. The smile would have been cynical on the lips of a young European inamorata. In Thyriel it was no more than the amused recognition of manners which she had laughed at in studying the ancient history and literature of the island, as if I had seen a comrade in the commonness of European daily life adopting the language and attitude of Homeric or Ossianic heroes.

I grew ashamed of the amorous ardours of the West, and, when I felt the tendency to erotic idolatry come upon me, I kept it to myself. Even then I knew that I was centuries behind my Limanoran coevals in the rational guidance of the sexual instinct. Nothing brought this so clearly to my mind as the reception of the book of Asexuality. During its dramatic publication I looked round to see the shock of unnatural innovation on the faces of the audience, or the shrinking of modesty, or the sense of outraged religious or traditional instincts. But there was none of these to be found there. The ideal was accepted at once as the proper and possible goal of the race, and the book was treasured amongst the sacred literature of the time.

* * * *

It soon flashed upon me, too, as I frequented Loomiefa, that their art had all a far higher purpose than I had conjectured from my European experience. It was not meant merely to stir or to satisfy the sense of beauty and harmony, but to implant in the emotions and the imagination the love of the future and the passion for rising in the scale of existence. I grew ashamed to think that I had attributed to this wonderful people the frivolity and even lowness of aim that I had so often seen in European art. Here was a drama that the West had not even a conception of. At its best the stage of Europe professed to educate by representing heroic scenes from the past, by evolving from them lessons for the audience, and by stirring their enthusiasm for great deeds of history or myth. In its commonest mood it reproduced in mimic form some scene or action from contemporary life. At its worst it was but a pander to the survivals of a gross and animal past. What I now thought of as the Limanoran stage was wholly occupied with the future, so far as it was a possible evolution from the present. The noblest ideal that the imagination of the race could shape was brought dramatically before the people that their thoughts and ambitions might be fixed on something beyond themselves.

For this high purpose and not for luxury or personal enjoyment their sculpture and painting and music had been developed, and the newest discoveries and inventions of science had been brought to their aid. There was no objection to what gave pleasure; but to spend the thought and effort of the fully developed human mind on that alone was, they held, a degradation. Strenuous endeavour towards a higher and better future was the note that characterised their pursuits. But, if they could add attractiveness to the prosecution of the aim, the task was all the easier; if they could make the path ahead beautiful and pleasant so as to decoy the reluctant senses onwards, the pace would be all the swifter.

Even with this high aim, I could not understand how this people, who loathed all pretence, could condescend to their dramatic art; for on this stage of Loomiefa were members of their community representing in their persons what they were not and could not be for many ages. And I had heard them often decry the histrionic art as one that encouraged in the actors a habit of delighting in mere semblance and superficial show, a habit that is the basis of hypocrisy and deceit; whilst the love of mimicry and pageantry, I had been led to believe, had vanished from the island at one of the last purgations of the race.

The seeming contradiction was afterwards explained. As one of the necessary steps in my initiation into the privileges and duties of the mature citizen I was led behind the scenes. Through the gorge at the upper end of the valley I passed into a great hall that seemed to me a combination of a museum and workshop. Here were the youth of the Loomiamo and the Fraloomiamo at work upon automata and the elaborate machinery that would guide their motions. Had I kept at a distance from them as they worked, I would have thought that the play of human sculpture was being again enacted, such exact reproductions of the human system were the figures that grew under their hands. In one section stood thousands of what I would have called statues, which had served in the publication of former books. In another the puppets were going through dramatic scenes by way of experimentation, and in many the illusion was complete; I should have said that human beings were talking and acting. In others there was some imperfection, and there one could see that they were all mere fantoccini galvanised into life. In a third section the tissues and parts that were to make mimic men and women were being manufactured; the workers and artists could draw on Rimla for as much force as they needed, whilst the advice of the scientific families was at their command. The machinery of the great workshop was bewildering in its complexity and refinement. The finest tissue or nerve of the human brain could be here imitated so that under a microscope I would have said it was part of a living body.

After all it was only the acting of marionettes that I had seen upon the stage in the valley. But it was greatly aided by another department where the pioneering families cultivated the art and science of illusions. They could imitate the human voice at any point in the valley measured to the fraction of an inch; they could reproduce any scene of history, of contemporary existence, or of futuritive fiction so exactly, making it so full of the lights and shadows of life and of the developments of all advance, that none of the senses unaided by the reasoning and analytic faculties could assert that the men and women were not living, and that their actions and words were not real. Even the electric sense could be deluded by the impulses manufactured by these machinists and illusionists; it would take the magnetic thrills it received for genuine enthusiasm and sympathy from the mind of a man or from a crowd. This department was even more important than the factory of puppets; for it made the play of the marionettes look still more human on the stage. After all it was not the puppets themselves I had watched with such breathless excitement, but a mere illusory picture of their proceedings; the illusion was far more lifelike than the play of the marionettes themselves. So much stress did they lay on stirring the imagination and emotions of the race in favour of the ideals of the future that half the work of these two families consisted in the dramatic publication of their books.

The next sacred book I saw produced in Loomiefa would have of itself persuaded me that this people could have nothing to do with the histrionic art or any art that would encourage the habit of pretence and show in the individual nature. It was called the book of Human Transparency and described the various methods by which the inner working of the human brain could be made patent to Limanoran senses. The tissues could be clarified; the significance of every fibre and nerve could be made familiar to all as an essential part of their education; the eye, the ear, and the firla could be made more subtle and acute in their perceptions, till at last they were able to tell in a moment everything that was proceeding beneath the skull and within the heart. What was done slowly and painfully by the medical elders with the help of their instruments, their hypnotic powers, and the interpretation of dreams, every man would be able to do instantaneously, and without extraneous aid, exceptional wisdom, or occult powers. The general drift of a neighbour's emotions was known to everyone through his magnetic senses, but not the particular intention or thought; this would be known only after the long course of training and development mapped out in the book of Human Transparency.

One of the chief ethical purposes that had in recent times been fixed in the mind of the community was to eject from the human system all elements and processes that were offensive to the finer feelings and senses, everything in fact that a man or woman might be ashamed of or wish to conceal. The new book of the time aimed at extending this to the operations of thought and emotion. To get clear of the waste products of the mind in a way that would be inoffensive to others was an ideal they had not yet been able to entertain. They had learned with much pain and self-denial the habit of concealing the crude processes of thought that lead to what is worth saying or doing. It was one of the things they were most ashamed of in looking over the history or the memorials of their far past to see the vast amount of the raw digestion of thought and of the refuse of emotion that was made public, and even put into literature meant to be permanent. Most of the orations and magazine articles, and ultimately most of the books that had been produced in past ages were much the same as if the stomach and intestines of the speaker or writer had been anatomised and laid open with all their offensive processes to the gaze of spectators. One of the most beneficent events of their later history had been a conflagration in their valley of memories; for it had wiped out of existence the libraries and art accumulations of many centuries, of which they had come to be ashamed. They could not understand the long-past stage of their civilisation, in which men, and especially young men, had been so proud of displaying the mere débris of their worst and crudest processes of thought; it had actually been the case that most of the literature and art had been produced by youths under fifty years of age, who had not yet begun to appreciate the difference between the processes of thinking and the results of thinking; and one of the most extraordinary features of that period was that the most applauded literary and artistic productions, those that were supposed to be most distinctively the outcome of what they called genius, were the work of boys and girls, mere children under twenty-five years of age. Natures that should still have been in the nursery for many a year were stimulated to address the public and seek applause with work that was merely tentative and disciplinary. The result was that, on the one hand, one half of the most original and promising minds racked themselves to death years before they should have faced life, whilst on the other a juvenile ideal was set before literature and art, and boys and girls became their chief audience and most powerful arbiters. They felt heartily ashamed of that singular stage in their development, and were glad to have accidental fire come to their assistance in huddling its products out of sight.

One of the first instincts they evolved after the series of purgations was the desire to conceal within their minds what was crude or mere process in thinking, and, still more, what was mere waste product and refuse of the mind. Instead of being eager to speak out or publish all that came into the thoughts, bad or good, they grew shy of public exhibition of their projects and schemes till they had been shaped by long years of thinking and experimenting, and criticised and checked by the caution and wisdom of their fully matured nature. Publication became the last resort of the mature and old instead of the first ambition of the young, so afraid were they of exhibiting what might be crude or offensive. Even in the give and take of conversation and social intercourse they preferred long periods of silence to the utterance of truisms and commonplaces. The trivial and conventional in speech, as in life, was what they abhorred, as revealing an intellectual nature on the road back to the infertility and childishness of barbarism, the elaborate mechanism of thought whizzing round without connection with what represents work.

But now the book of Human Transparency proposed as an ideal to eject from the system every process of thought and feeling that they might blush to let others see. If the nature was made transparent then would it become a self-preserving instinct to develop their natures in this direction. Everything crude or false or offensive, that might begin to show itself in their minds, would be at once suppressed before it got headway, instead of having to be slowly reasoned out of existence with the aid of the moral instincts. This accomplished, the race would be able to take another great leap forward. The advance of their processes of thought and feeling to the level of the former results of them would give them a higher point of view from which to look forth into the future.

* * * *

A mediate book, soon afterward produced by one of the Loomiamo, supplied one of the steps towards the consummation of this ideal. It was the book of Ethereal Nutriment. It took as basis a former discovery, the liquefaction of air, and showed how, by similar methods, the medium that filled interstellar space could be made available in the halls of nutriment and medication, and how it could be manufactured in such a concentrated form as to allow of its being poured along conduits and imbibed by the human organs through the mouth and nostrils, just as air was. For some time the atmosphere had been distilled in liquid form, and supplied to the houses of the citizens absolutely rid of all impurities. Nay, it had been made a fountain of power, transmissible to long distances, and available in a form that was easily carried. Compressed and liquefied, it rapidly returned to the gaseous form as soon as the pressure began to be removed. And the re-equilibrising of the liquid to the expansion of the surrounding air had been made to supply vast quantities of power in the centre of force. The new book proposed to find in the compression and liquefication of the ether an infinite fountain of force that would enable their civilisation to progress at an ever-accelerating pace.

But the most immediate effect proposed by the book was to enable the Limanorans to etherealise their bodies by introducing the liquefied ether into their dietary. The result would be that the tissues would grow more diaphanous. They had already been able to transport some of the universal medium in their anchored vacuum faleenas from the outer margin of the atmosphere to their laboratories, and now they had been able to find it in their manufactured vacuums. With the enormous power they had in Rimla they could easily compress it into forms that would touch the senses, and enter into the blood and the formation of the tissues. As the medium of light and magnetism it was almost certain to make the human body more translucent than it had ever been. All the tissues, even the osseous, had always been pervious to light, but many of them not apparently so to the untrained human eye. Recently their lavolans had shown that by means of certain kinds of luminous rays the human system gave up its most hidden secrets to the human eye. But once they were able to chemicalise and compress the luminiferous ether into palpable form, and to mingle it with the volatile food that could be taken into their bodies as they breathed, there would be no need of lavolans or other apparatus to see the inner movements of the human system.

The sanitary effects of this advance would be no mean result. The medical council would have much of their time set free for their ever-pressing investigations; they would not be needed for the diagnosis of deteriorative symptoms in the tissues; each individual would be able, by the aid of magnifying mirrors to examine for himself what was going on in any part of his system; and every man had sufficient physiological and medical knowledge to understand the beginnings of all the ordinary diseases, and, if he recognised them, to prescribe for himself the hall in Oomalefa that he should frequent in order to check them. Now it would be only the symptoms of obscure or new diseases or deteriorations of the system that the medical elders would have to diagnose. And thus they would have great tracts of their life to devote to new discoveries, and medical science was certain to advance more rapidly.

Another sanitary effect of the new permeability to light would be to render the human body less open to diseases either known or unknown. For it had long been a commonplace of medical science that sunlight reduced the vitality, and therefore the virulence, of all noxious microbes; after nightfall their power increased tenfold. Wherever the sun's rays could not reach by day, there diseases multiplied and festered. And one of the chief reasons why, in their far past history, incurable maladies were generally internal, was that sunshine could not get to the parts affected except in a feeble and straggling way. The fact that they had fixed themselves deeply in the tissues before they could be observed, and that it was difficult to get at their roots without cutting a passage in to them had been generally accepted as the explanation of their frequency and deadliness. But it had been one of the most important discoveries of the new era after the purgation period, that pure oxygen and pure sunlight were the most medicative of all things, and that the nearer any affected part could get to them the sooner it healed. The new book of Ethereal Nutrition pointed out that one of the results of rendering the human system easily pervious to light would be to rid its internal parts of all trace of immedicability; sunlight, permeating the inner organs and tissues, would make any noxious microbes that might lodge in them innocuous.

* * * *

The reciprocity of suggestion and discovery was never more saliently exemplified than by one of the less immediate results pointed out by this book as likely to flow from the attainment of its ideal. Volatile ether-food, gradually introduced into the halls of nutrition and gradually increased, would, step by step, bring the human organs to adapt themselves to existence outside of the atmosphere of the earth. For a long time they would be amphibious, with organs adapted to both aërial and ethereal life. Even as it was, the human body revealed in it traces of having already passed through an amphibious stage. There were in the neck glands that were the remains of gills, which must have once belonged to an aquatic habit; besides, there was the last vestige of an eye in the back of the neck still extant in the pineal gland, and this could have been of use only when the ancestor of man was passing through the stage of a water-animal which must watch his enemies from the surface, his body being submerged and out of sight. Step by step he abandoned the water for a littoral, and even at first arboreal, habit; the result was that the gills came to be unused and closed up, and the upward-looking eye was useless in a head that was held upright and could be turned swiftly in all directions; still man retains the memory of the aquatic stage of his ancestry in the ease with which he learns to swim, and in his love of a life on the sea; whilst an occasional birth in more barbarous tribes with the webbed toes of a water-animal still showing reveals his ancestry atavistically.

What was to hinder him, now he had the mastery of himself and his destiny, becoming again amphibious in a new way? Without guidance of his own, driven only by the forces of nature, he had risen out of the waters that once covered the earth, and taken to dry land; for a long period he had been able to live at will in either of two elements, air and water. Where lay the difficulty in making himself again capable of living in two elements, in air and in the luminiferous ether? In prehistoric times nature had worked her evolution in his system by long and slow stages. But in Limanora progress had become lightning-swift, and would again and again increase its pace. For there man had taken command of nature, and made her accommodate her step to his stride. She was his willing servant, nimble as her own electric flash. He could now compress the work of centuries into hours by his concentration of power in Rimla, and by his countless ingenious contrivances. Thought was the lord of time as of space, and thought was now his essence and characteristic. He could, if he wished, contract the process that used to cover geological ages into a generation. There was no reason why he should not become amphibious again in a less grovelling sense than of old within the few centuries of a lifetime. This was the purport of another production of this time, the book of Amphibious Existence.

It was a mediate book, one bridging the gulf between things as they were and the far ideals held out to the race by the Fraloomiamo. It helped to point out the steps towards the realisation of one of the most cherished productions of the age, the Book of Emigration. It had been many years in the maturer minds of the community before I was introduced to Loomiefa and its wonders, and it had recently been much modified by the discoveries of the new outburst of energy that followed Choktroo's attempt at invasion. Its ideal was to enable the Limanorans of that or some future generation to travel throught space and reach other stars.

* * * *

Long ago a publication that had prepared for, and demanded this, was the book of the Destiny of the Earth. It had made a profound impression on the people when first produced; for it dramatically painted the horror of death that would settle on this globe. It had been proved by both astronomers and physicists that our orb was gradually losing its heat by the same process which had brought its originally glowing surface to a state that would allow of life settling upon it. First, vegetation and animal life were found at the poles, where the lessened heat of the sun made the terrestrial heat endurable; then they crept their slow way onwards to the equator, till the whole surface of the earth teemed with vitality, at first developing towards vastitude in the warm vapours, in later periods towards concentration of energy in special points of the animal body, and especially in the head. Round the poles at last settled the ice-sheet, advancing at long intervals towards the tropics, now in one hemisphere and again in the other, according as the one or the other was farthest in winter from the sun during an extensive period. The hyperborean powers shepherded the growing life of the earth down into her central belt. But the brumal shepherds of the one side of the world receded as those of the other advanced with their arctic winds and fleecy drifts. Within measurable time this alternation would cease, and the glacial fences would move forward together north and south, and pen the overcrowded human life and energy with all its enemies into the narrow equatorial belt.

It was the drama of these boreal limitations that the book of Terrestrial Destiny pictured. The teeming life weltered over sea and land alike in search of foothold and nutrition. No inch of tropical earth was sacred from brute appetite. Animal and man fought with venomous passion for dear life. Not animalculæ alone but beasts, and even man, became parasitic. Creatures that had loved a free existence in vast prairies or forests learned to nest and hibernate in the folds and hollows of larger animals. Life swarmed over life till for lack of food it began to fail. Man crept with loathsome beasts of prey into caves of the earth, and grew as loathsome in his troglodytic habits. On moved the brumal prison walls. The sun shrivelled in the sky and withdrew his heat. Nothing lived that was not arctic not even amongst the still-free birds of the air. Man finally ceased to have faculty enough to notice the shrinking of the already narrow enclosure that was soon to be his grave. Feebly the last remnants of the race stole forth into the struggling rays of daylight and killed everything of life they could find. Only in the sea still lived their possible prey and food, and thither they dared not go beneath the gloom of the thick ice. The cannibal habit came upon man again and no relationship or love restrained his appetite. The last scene of the drama was the death of the last man, the grave of the remnants of his race; where he fell, there he lay embalmed; and his tomb was the earth's own winding-sheet. The meagre relics of terrestrial life soon followed him into silence and darkness, and through the sunless night the dead orb wheeled round the extinguished cinder which had for so many geological ages given it light and life.

The publication of the book would have frozen the hearts within them, had not the Limanorans known that that was not the end of all. They saw that the alternations of death and life were not confined to the vegetal and animal species around them. The same pendulum swung through the whole cosmos. The universe which was dead now would live again in blazing rounds of vapour that would solidify and cool till life could settle on the new orbs again. Dead it only seemed. For it never rested but revolved round some centre revolving also, and too distant for man to see or feel. Out of these motions would come resuscitation. After millions of ages, that are but as moments in the history of the cosmos, it would encounter another exhausted universe, and from the collision would a new system of glowing worlds arise, ready for another series of vital colonisations from the limitless life of sidereal space.

It was this knowledge that took the sting out of their sadness over the new book. Yet the fate of man, age by age more closely penned in by the walls of his glacial-coffin, and drawn back by the eddy of time into his primeval savagery, left a loophole for despair and palsy to enter into their lives. Were they to let their descendants fall back again into the beast, whence their ancestors had come? Was this glacial prison and tomb to remain a possibility and a shadow on even the distant horizon of their race? Once before had their ancestry evaded such a fate, penned between the invasive glaciers and the sea; once before had the race committed their fates to an element they feared and hated, lest the encroaching ice-sheet should smother their civilisation and reduce their vitality to the level of barbarism and at last annihilation. Better to let the race die out at its noblest than leave it to go down into such an inferno. Nothing now so made them shudder as the prospect of retrogression, however slight. But to think of their civilisation ebbing away from their posterity before the waning power of the sun and the earth, to think of the lapse of their own intellectual mastery of nature into decrepitude and putrescence, was to turn their hearts to stone.

* * * *

Under such a prospect they could not sit in intellectual paralysis. For years the imagination of the race worked feverishly towards its rescue from such an appalling destiny, and every new scientific advance brought forth a new book of Emigration. Their one thought of escape was taken from their old migration out of the reach of antarctic glacial advance. To sail out from the earth and commit themselves to the strange conditions and uncertainties of a new element seemed no more hazardous to them now than in their primeval stage of land-civilisation to launch out with their lives in their hands upon the unknown and terrifying ocean. It was urged that there was precedent and basis for their marine adventure in that their ancestry had been amphibious, and that one of the primeval species out of which they had come had been aquatic. The reply was that the case was parallel and not antagonistic. The original vital germs that settled on the cooling surface of the globe must have come out of sidereal space, and must have lived in the element that they would have to cross in emigrating from the glacial orb again; and from these vital germs they, and all living terrestrial things, had evolved. It was only one stage farther back in the history of life; the precedent was the same, though the training and modification of the system would have to be more strenuous and drastic than they had been before the former leap was taken from land to sea. Preparation had already been made; for they had learned aërial navigation far more thoroughly than they had ever known the mastery of the sea. Their airships had ventured right up into the ether, whilst on wings they had themselves coasted the earth's atmosphere. Nothing was impossible to intellect which had mastered the art of evolution.

Recent discovery had led them far on the difficult ascent towards safe departure from the surface of the world. It only needed ingenuity and development to give them a concentration of aërated sustenance, which would enable them to journey for ages outside of an atmosphere such as they had been accustomed to inhabit; they had the germ of this in the nuts of the alfarene or oxygen-shrub; recently their chemists had been able to reproduce the essence of them, and to compress it into microscopic globules. Not till a later age of discovery did they supersede this by the liquefaction and solidification of air. They were rapidly adapting their own systems to the vacuums they could produce and to the rarefied atmosphere high above the clouds. They were introducing the quintessence of the ether into their halls of sustenance and medication, and thus accustoming their organs and tissues to conditions which they would meet continually on their voyage through sidereal space. The next generation would practically be amphibious, able to live in the luminiferous ether with occasional return to an atmosphere such as surrounds the earth. Every new age would enable them to make longer and longer excursions away from the bosom of mother-earth out towards the influence of other planets. Every new generation would have more elastic and adaptable tissues and organs, which would fit varied pressure and varied mediums of vitality. And with all this the Limanoran body would grow lighter at the same time as it would grow more consolidated, coherent, and indissoluble. But most important of all was the new command of gravitation given them by the discovery of the varying sensitiveness or nonsensitiveness of certain rays to magnetism and gravity according to conditions that were in human hands. There were limitless possibilities in this for sidereal migration. And already out of it had come the lavolamma or gravitation power-machine.

The new book of Emigration brought all these discoveries and thoughts into bearing on its problem and harmonised them, and developed them by means of imaginative suggestion. The drama of its publication drew the bulk of the people to Loomiefa. There we saw a representation of Lilaroma itself, piercing the sky in pure and lonely grandeur. Near its top lay moored a fleet of faleenas of strikingly new form and material; they were as light as foam-bubbles, and as opalescently transparent; within each of them we could see stored quantities of alfarene globules, that seemed enough to serve a people for thousands of years; in each we saw a new anti-gravitation engine, ready to deal with every form of attraction and repulsion in the wide ether and turn it into available power. Men and women in Limanoran form, but as transparent and as imponderable and buoyant as their new ships, floated round the ethereal fleet. Now and again a flash of artificial light would dart across the scene, and along it, as if impelled by it, ran with lightning-swiftness one of the rainbow-flecked faleenas, bearing its full freight. We could see the lavol-amma work, and we concluded that there was a new form of it that could take advantage of beams of light to travel with them, as an electric impulse travels along them. Innumerable evolutions with the ethereal fleet took place. The sublimated Limanorans of the future seemed to have complete command of the new ships and of the new power over light and gravitation.

Suddenly came tremors in the framework of the great mountain. It rocked like a buoy in the uneasy surge of a reef. Its snows fell in huge avalanches. Then the conical top was ejected into the sky like a shot from a cannon. The air was thick with dust and stones. But when it cleared and great flames shot forth and licked the face of heaven, we could see far above their reach the rainbow-coloured fleet speeding aloft, filled with their tiny diaphanous sailors.

The scene changed, and we saw universes set in the vault of heaven, and across the space between them we could discern minute specks of light flashing mercurial as thought. Behind them in dim eclipse sped the noctam-bulant earth, still eddying round the central spot of light; now it broke forth in ragged coruscation, only to sink back into pitchy gloom. Yet a thread of light stretched forth to the luminous atoms that flitted on through the night. Nearer they came and, one by one, grew more distinct and larger. At last we could see that it was the fleet on its way from the top of Lilaroma. Within each ether-ship we could make out the movements of the sailors as they bent its way this side and that. The light from a brilliant star in the new universe made play upon the surface of their faleenas. They had caught in its rays, and were speeding as swift as light towards the now-definite goal. The luminiferous current bore them steadily on, their little engines palpitating with the impulse of the new light and the new gravitation.

Again the scene changed, and we looked upon the surface of a new orb, more advanced in vital development, more highly organised than the earth with which we were familiar. We saw the inhabitants in crowds, face upwards into the night, all eyes upon some distant star. The excitement was rising like a tempest. It seemed as if the object on which they gazed were swiftly approaching them. And in a flash there swept within our sight the fleet of prismatic ether-ships, like rainbows in the light of another sun. They stopped and hovered above the atmosphere. We saw their crews breathe in the elements in which they floated. Lower and lower they came, still sounding the atmosphere and testing its effects upon their organs. The absence of commotion and the steady descent showed that nothing alien to their systems had yet been encountered. Out of their faleenas they gazed as wonderingly down upon the new star as its sea of up-turned faces watched their slow descent.

The scene was brought still nearer to our eyes. Instead of microscopic foam-bells floating in the sky, and microscopic crowds resting on the surface of the other world, we felt present at the meeting of these creatures of different universes. They seemed to feel conscious of this great event in the history of the cosmos. The dwellers of the new world were almost paralysed at first with wonder at these beings so like and yet so unlike themselves; they could recognise, we could see in their friendly faces, the divine community of spirit; their eyes, as soon as they recovered from their waking dream, flashed welcome in magnetic fire; there was no need of community of words for open intercourse; the dwellers of the new star had the same development of electric sense as the Limanorans had; their souls could speak without a sound from the lips.

Step by step their mutual sympathy grew more definite, more cordial, and approximated to the communication of thought and fact. Within a brief period they knew enough of each other's language to tell out their whence and whither. But in the people of the new star the language was that of feature and not of tongue. Over their faces flashed the signals of thought as well as of emotion, astonishing the newcomers at the rapidity with which expression flitted over their features. Equally astonished were their hosts to hear the countless variety of tone and accent come from the throats of the strangers. They covered their ears as if shielding them from the assault of some thunderous report. Even the voyagers shrank from the voice of their own spokes-man. And, tone it down as he would, still was it too loud for any delicate ear to endure. They were in a new atmosphere that bore sound so quickly and clearly as to make a whisper reverberate like thunder. So did it make the eyes of the dwellers in it as keen and far in sight as if armed with the most powerful microscopes and telescopes. The slightest adjustment of them and their lids changed them back and forth from distant observation to near. And the same translucency marked their tissues as made the inner movements of the newcomers' heart and brain apparent. There was needed no sound to in-terpret the magnetic messages of the brain along its nerves. Hosts and guests were seen at one, familiar as lifelong friends and thrilling each other with the strange new experiences of their history. The voyagers from earth soon knew why the use of the tongue and throat had been abandoned by their hosts as means of communication; the uncontrollable volume of sound offended their hearing, and drove them to develop the language of eye and feature; the sight grew more powerful and adaptable as voice and ear gave up their share of the energy and sustenance of the system; their tissues, too, had ever been to a large extent transparent because of the rarity and clearness of their atmosphere, and by selection and training they had been able to make them pellucid as they now were.

The gleam of question and answer showed as clearly on the stage of Loomiefa as the movement of the figures themselves. And, when the collo-quy had ended, and the strangers had gained all the information they needed for their farther journey through space, we saw them enter their faleenas and rise above the eager, penetrating gaze of their new friends. Across the face of the heaven we followed the ethereal fleet as it faded again into insignificance. Another scene showed us their landing upon another planet of the universe they had entered. The drama thus bore us with delight from system to system throughout the cosmos, and revealed the ease with which stellar voyaging could be accomplished, once the initial difficulties had been overcome.

****

A mediate book, dramatically published in Loomiefa just before, pre-pared the way for this. It was the book of Sidereal Intercourse. They had always held that the other universes in the cosmos were as much inhabited by life as theirs was. It had ever seemed to them the absurdest of arrogance for the dwellers on the earth to assume that theirs was the only orb out of the countless myriads on the face of night that had life upon it; that it monopo-lised the vital energy of infinity, and the attention of its divine intelligence. The wider they had ranged with their sidereal sciences, the more they smiled at the primitive thought of their remote ancestors that they were the cynosure of the cosmos. It had come to be used as the readiest and most striking example of infatuation and conceit. That the poor earthlings were as microscopic in their importance compared with the vastitude of existence, as the bacterial swarms of a wayside pool compared to the denizens of the great ocean, was assumed in every movement and act of their minds.

And, wherever life was, there was the chance that highly developed intelligence existed. They were not so sure that this was yet the case on the farthest of our planets. It might be that the inner and smaller bodies of our universe had passed the stage in which they could support the higher life. The others, they thought, were rapidly evolving a life of their own, most of it still in a low grade; when the earth had passed its climax and begun to decay, they would probably, one after the other, be attaining to a loftier type of life and intelligence. Whilst they were running their course of progress the earth and her inner sister planets would be waiting in their frozen silence the time when the whole of their universe would be exhausted. Nearer and nearer would the whole solar system be approaching some other system that had run its course; and the encounter of the two would evolve a young universe, full of heat and energy enough from the collision to make a new cosmic career.

They had little hope then of stirring reply, if ever they were able to send an embassy of thought to any star of our own system. All their hopes of astral intercommunication were pointed to other stars and other universes; and, as they looked up into the eyes of night, they seemed to feel magnetic answer to the impulses of their souls, not from Mars or Venus, from Saturn or Jupiter, but from the stars that throbbed in far more distant depths. They had ever believed, of course, and they had now scientifically shown, that the centres of light flashing in the nightly sky were not the true sisters of earth but only suns, round which the unseen universes circled. They tried to find the dim worlds which drew their heat and light from these poignant watch-fires of heaven; and their more recent instruments had revealed the dark outlines of many of these twilight wanderers which hung on the radiance of the visible stars. The magnetism that came with the rays from some of those far distant luminous points had shown striking aberration early in its course; and nothing could explain this but the existence of rayless planets revolving round these lambent sources of light. Step by step had they homed these aberrations, till they knew the courses of the dusky satellites of many stars, and they could tell the moment when a circular shadow would cross the face of any one of these suns.

The eyes of the astronomical families had become so accustomed to the times and places of such obscurations that their firlas acted with them and searched for magnetic impulses from the dark sisters of the star they were watching; till at last they could tell by their electric sense the place of many dim planets in the nearer universes.

It was on this that the book of Sidereal Intercourse based its forecast of the immediate future. Since the definite discovery of varied types of life in the spaces beyond the earth's atmosphere, the last suspicion of mere fancy had vanished from the belief in the existence of high intelligence on the universes of infinity. And now their faces were set towards communication with some of this intelligence on distant worlds. The new book assumed that the electric sense, or something equivalent for the perception of the great cosmic force, had been developed in the inhabitants of some invisible worlds; and it laid down as an axiom that there were vast stores of magnetic material in these orbs, just as there were in the earth and in the sun.

What they must first do was to sweep the range of a universe with an electric impulse on which the whole force of Rimla should be concentrated, and to keep their delicate indicators all set in the same direction. At the publication of the book in Loomiefa we saw gigantic engines slowly moving their long arms this way and that athwart one of the most brilliant stars of night, and scientists eagerly scanning the numerous magnetometers that surrounded the huge electric machine. We could see the air thrill and undulate with the mighty impulse, and the very light of the star seemed to flicker and wink before the penetration of the intrusive force. At last a flash of hope came over the faces of the watchers; the pendent beam of one sarmolan began to quiver. It was a message from the world they sought. Again they turned the whole available power of the island—millions of millions of horse-power—into the electric engine, the arm of which they had at once brought to rest. Fierce lightnings again played through the atmosphere, marking the line of the new despatch. And again the luminous tongue of the magnetometer told of its reception by intelligences like ours. Then came the astronomic families who marked the exact position of the sensitive spot in the sky. And thereafter their sentry stood with sarmolan directed thither, ready to announce the slightest sign of astral impulse or response.

The scene changed, and we saw a new type of electric engine placed in position on the stage. On its long arm was a singularly crooked cage of transparent irelium, flat and sharp like the blade of a sword yet bent into a right angle in the direction of the edge. Within it were placed recording magnetometers. We could see the directors fix them towards their responsive universe. Then Rimla concentrated its tremendous power upon the machine; the arm swung right and left, and finally with a jerk shot the crooked cage like lightning through the air. We followed its luminous track far into the sky, till it seemed nothing but one of the countless stars that silvered the night. Suddenly, like a rocket, it bent back on its course, and as swiftly retraced its flight. I thought to see it shattered into dust as it struck the earth, but there was a deep pool ready to break its force. Its sharp edge cut the water and it vanished, but slowly rose to the surface unhurt, and on the faces of the observers we could see how successful had been the experiment with the limotar, or new boomerang vehicle of electric indications. It had shot far up into space along the true electric impulse that travelled away beyond it towards the sensitive point of sky they had discovered. Before it bent back from its headlong course, the response, speeding more freely and more swiftly through the untrammelled ether, imprinted itself upon the face of the sarmolan. It was this answer, more decided than any they had yet received, that filled the eyes of the observers with joyous light.

There was another change of scene. The gigantic engines had disappeared and in their place we saw the ether-courier families floating on the outskirts of the atmosphere with strata of clouds far below them. On the back of their necks, where the electric sense had its special seat, they bore a singular apparatus, not unlike a small telescope. On their chests they had strapped a small engine of irelium, a miniature of those we had seen in former scenes. The one was a magnifier of electric indications, and the other was an electricity catapult. The couriers could not only draw upon the electric resources of the spaces around them, but upon those of the centre of force. And we could see them converse with distant stars by means of these apparatus. Through unobstructed space they could send with ease their electric impulses to limitless distances, free from the atmospheric retardation which before had demanded immense power to overcome its inertia. And with their new electro-telescopes they could magnify ten-thousand-fold any electric ray for their firlas to receive, although it might have travelled a thousand times the distance between the earth and the sun. They might have to wait days for their answer; but again and again were they rewarded with it. With the dim stars circling round the nearer suns they were able to hold comparatively rapid converse. But they were going farther afield through the cosmos, and they had often to watch and wait for weeks or months or years for any indication of response.

The book awakened little enthusiasm compared with the publication of some of those that I had witnessed. For, though the authors had been rapid in the composition of it, they had been somewhat forestalled by one of the ingenious inventions of the last great age of discovery. This was the modification of the lavolan which brought them records of the life of extra-aërial space. Amongst the luminous impressions that their combination of lavolan and faleena had brought down out of the ether, they had found evidences of highly organised systems which frequented the vacuum outside our atmosphere. They were satisfied with the knowledge of this new-discovered teeming life, and they believed that before many ages they would have developed, first their apparatus, and next their senses, so far as to open intercourse with it. And if they could come to converse with nobler intelligences near the earth, they did not need to go so far afield in the cosmos as the new book suggested.

Their own filammus would serve to bring them into close sympathy with the best life that was to be found in space until they should know the conditions of such life and aim at fulfilling them.

It was one of the subsidiary studies and ideals of the book that drew most attention and produced most result. It pictured an apparatus and method for tapping the thoughts of men as they travelled along the nerves, an adaptation of their huge electric engines for sidereal intercommunication. For some ages they had been able to send emotions and impulses through the air, or rather through the medium that interpenetrated the air, and recently they had developed this into the despatch of thoughts through long distances. The combination of great magnetic power and sensitive sarmolans, this book showed, would draw off thought at any point along its line of flight whether in the body or in the air; and underneath an electric magnifier and interpreter the indicator would reveal the meaning of the thoughts. Thus would they be able to find out the intentions of men, however distant. But this was only a minor result of the ideal. They would be able, with the aid of the apparatus, to tap the torrents of thought speeding through the ether, and so drink of the highest intelligence and imagination which approached the earth. Much of it would be too intricate and abstruse for them to follow or understand. But they already knew that most of their greatest inspirations had come from this ocean of tremulous energy, bordering the shores of our world; and development of their faculties and of their sympathy with this extra-terrestrial thought would gradually lead them to the interpretation of its more complex and deeper elements. All their civilisation had been an attempt to know the thoughts that lie in the structure of our universe, in its complicated energy and minute life. By this new means they would feel the throb of the very heart of our system, perchance of the very heart whose beats are the life of the cosmos; at least they would get to know the intelligence that flashes through space around our world, the wisdom and the inspirations passing between the inhabitants of the ether beyond our grosser senses.

* * * *

Had it not been for this minor issue and ideal, the publication of the book would have been completely overshadowed by that of the book of Immortality. This took as basis the great expansion of life they had been able to produce and their ideals of ethereal nutrition and amphibious life, and pictured the posterity of the Limanorans able to join the inhabitants of the ether without any violent transition or death. We saw a Limanoran on the stage in Loomiefa passing through the new transmutation from mortal to immortal. His transient elements were atom by atom sublimed away in a new hall of medication, where magnetic energy took the place of more material nutrition. His tissues became diaphanous, till only the light and the magnetism he emitted marked the place where he lay. It was what he thought and felt rather than what he was that told us he was still there. His lower and more stagnant centres of energy had vanished; and gravitation seemed to have little or no influence upon him. Whithersoever his thought willed, thither he floated, rather the luminous reflection of a man than the man himself. To our grosser senses he seemed as impalpable and evanescent as a perfume or a mist on the morning hills. Yet there he stood or moved an inexpugnable centre of the highest energy, whither flowed the sympathetic force of other centres, and whither nothing hostile could approach. Storms passed effectless over his head; the deadliest engines shot their darts at him in vain; poisonous fumes, lethal showers, armies of pestilential microbes, swept round him and through him innocuous. All the evanescent centres of energy that had laid him open to the attacks of these, had dissolved and left him fit to be a dweller in the infinite ether. There might be other noxious elements, to whose assaults he was yet vulnerable; but these we could not discover. He was immortal as far as terrestrial enemies were concerned, immortal without the sudden collapse and dissolution of the lower centres which we call death upon our world. By the most natural of processes he lost the substance that awakened our grosser senses and became the mere halo of what he had been, fit only to make himself felt by our centres of thought and imagination. With our firlas we could feel stream from him great currents of magnetic influence, unobstructed by any of those terrene or aërial media that make spiritual intercourse so difficult upon this world.

Such an ideal, when attained, would spread what is now called death over the greater part of our terrestrial lifetime, instead of massing it into a few moments of farewell. It would be difficult to fence off the immortal from the mortal, so many stages would there be of transmutation. The intercourse between the immortalising and the immortal would then be continuous and there would be no sudden break in existence, no great gulf fixed between the spiritual and the material.

With the same corporeal and mental faculties which their ancestry had had in primeval ages, and the bulk of men had in their own day, they would have counted immortality as the gift of a friend. Even with their existing development, noble though it was, they would never think of longing for such a fate; for the lower centres of energy, forming what is called the body, still demanded an amount of attention and sustenance that was burdensome. They had great delight in their life; they energised so purely and continually that they often forgot the corporeal system and its claims. Yet the time came in all men's lives when they felt their still-mixed constitutions advance too slowly for their spiritual ambitions; and then they longed for change, perhaps rest, such as the dissolution we call death accomplished. If, however, they could get rid of the inferior and clogging elements of their systems and float free of terrene forces and conditions like gravitation, then might immortality be an object of desire.

* * * *

A publication that delighted them even more than this was one that had a cognate theme, the dimension of time. It seemed to me the most fanciful of all the productions I had witnessed in Loomiefa. Yet it did not seem to strike the Limanorans as beyond the bounds of possibility. It was called the book of Time-focussing. So fantastic and utopian did I think it that I paid little attention when it was dramatically published on the stage. Yet I remember some of the chief features of the new book.

It counselled the development of the imagination on its prospicient side till it should count æons as moments and take easy flight through eternities. It was the real time-faculty, and had already in the productions of Loomiefa forerun the civilisation of the race by long periods. It had become true prophet not merely over months or years, but over centuries. Trained to use the data of the past and the present, it had been able to forecast the evolution of the future with a certainty that made its art almost a science. What was to hinder extending its range of vision beyond the immediate horizon, and taking in at a glance the course of the future as it did the page of history? And as it reached higher and higher points of view, it could paint eternity as it now pictured the past. There was no limit to its previsional powers, as there had been none to its penetration into the prehistoric and primeval darkness. Prescience should be as organised and exact as any science. In fact all their sciences had become presciential, those that were merely retrospective or synchronous having gradually fallen out of notice. And the families that had been devoted to them were one by one absorbed into other services. No study was counted of much value that had not one eye on the future. Their whole intellectual system was thus becoming futuritive, and all the faculties looked up to and centred in the greatest and most predictive of them all—the imagination.

They had already been able in the valley of memories to focus the past into the view of a few moments or days or months. The time stretching behind us into the darkness was underneath one glance of the intellectual eye. Only greater certainty in their imaginative methods was needed for the eternity that stretches in front of us to flash before the soul in a single picture. Only develop the prophet-faculty as rapidly in the next few generations as it had been developed in the past few, and we might move at will from age to age of the future, as we now move from age to age of the past, living at any moment in any period we pleased, or in a thousand periods at once. From past to future would be as easy a leap as from hell to heaven for this great time-and-space-focussing faculty. Eternity would be as focal to imagination as infinity. It was an eye towards which radiated all time and all space. Post-historic pictures would be as vivid to it as prehistoric. Even now interest was fast leaking from mere recorded history before the romance of eternity past and future. What was the history of the race upon earth, compared with the periscope of the cosmos? Then would their posterity be able to stand on a watch-tower in the heights of heaven, and view the whole arena of existence as it stretched through time and space. There is no faculty so close to the divine as imagination.

I felt that this publication was like all their work, singularly self-regard-less. It clearly recognised that the realisation of its proposed ideal would mean the doom of its art. Pioneering, all of theirs which we in the West would call literature, would be superseded. Loomiefa would then become an institution of the past, less and less interesting as but a rapidly receding item of history. Self-effacement for the sake of progress was the dominant note of Limanoran civilisation. And in this book it seemed to me to rise to its highest pitch; for it held before the race a goal, which, when attained, would render literature and its publication unnecessary to its advance.

CHAPTER VIII

ANOTHER THREAT

WHEN the island was absorbed in the productions of this new literary or pioneering era, its attention was suddenly called to its immediate surroundings. Out of eternity they were jerked into the passing moment to defend their own little plot of earth. Mere existence was endangered if they did not at once withdraw their powers from their march through the future. It had been the result of their humane and lenient policy towards their exiles that every few generations rebellion and menace rose in the archipelago against their mysterious isolation. Fear of the isle of demons awed the imaginations of the other islands for a century or two, and then foolhardy prosperity, or conquest, demanded a new lesson.

Half a century had not passed since the romance of Choktroo's rise and fall; and unaided and unstimulated, the other inhabitants of the archipelago would have grovelled in helpless fear and hate of the central isle. The discipline applied in the repulsion of Choktroo's fleet would have sufficed for several centuries, but for a new power which had insinuated itself within the circle of mist.

One of the days when the book of Emigration was holding the stage of Loomiefa, the spectators were startled by realistic transference of their drama to the sky above them. Just as the opalescent faleenas were about to land on the new star, every eye was suddenly drawn away from the stage to the blue spreading above the valley. Across it was passing a strange airship of huge proportions and ungainly structure. I recognised it as a development of the balloon, with which I had been familiar in my European experience. There was the immense inflated globe, or rather pear, with the car hung underneath; but there was something new in the motions of this balloon. It seemed to be dirigible, for it tacked this way and that across the direction of the wind. And still more strange, the car was filled with implements of war; I could see their great muzzles pointed over the sides.

The Limanorans were startled by this anticipation of their science, but only for a moment; and as soon as the apparition sailed out of sight, they bent their senses as eagerly on the spectacle before them. They knew that their sentries were at their watch-posts on Lilaroma, and nothing hostile to the interests of the civilisation could occur in air or sea or upon earth without stirring their attention, and so placing the whole island on the alert. They waited till the publication of the book was finished and then streamed off to their various businesses and pursuits. As we flew across the upper slopes of the mountain we found out that the aërial stranger had settled upon one of the lonelier heights of the island of Broolyi. No action was taken by the Limanorans against the singular invader of the archipelago, except to set a special watchman who should observe his movements through the idrovamolan, and should report to the elders anything out of the common that might occur.

The stranger had evidently been disabled away to the east of the circle of fog; his steering-gear had ceased to act, and before a tornado he was hurried away from the great continent over which he had hovered. The impetus bore him helpless above and across the ring of mist, and within its calmer sphere the steering-gear was again adjusted. It was then that the watchers on Lilaroma saw his purpose to make for their island, and they sent through the lilaran a blast which would carry him away from their shores, not rude enough to harm him, yet sufficiently strong to defeat his intention. Feeling himself borne again farther away from his home he tacked for the nearest peak that he thought he could reach. This was evidently Klimarol. But the blast of the lilaran was too much for him; and to save himself from drifting still farther west he grappled one of the heights of Broolyi as he passed over it, and settled there.

It became one of the amusements of the younger Limanorans to observe the behaviour and the fate of the newcomer in the isle of peace. The crew of the airship was numerous; they were taken prisoners not long after they had descended from their car, and their captain was hurried off to the court of the new ruler. Before long the balloon was brought to the capital and carefully guarded; and, anchored firmly to the earth, it made ascents with the royal engineers under the direction of the balloonist. His every movement was watched lest he should release the captive by cutting the rope that bound it, and sail off with the officers of his Broolyian majesty. But as the months and years passed on, the newcomer with his strange new ship came to be trusted by the king and his advisers. He saw an arena for his ambitions and talents, and bent his whole energies to his new purpose.

We could see him from day to day and week to week add to the aërial fleet, which he at once began to build in imitation of the balloon he had brought with him. His original subordinates and companions were at first his only assistants, but the Broolyian engineers and mechanicians afterwards joined in the work in great numbers, and became as deft at it as the strangers. Every new balloon that was made was tested in the air. At first there were accidents, which for a time prejudiced the court and the people against the aërial monsters. But by carefully selecting his men from the army the director was able at last to furnish every airship that he made with a complete and efficient crew, able under the leadership of one of his companions to manipulate the vehicle and every implement on board of it. It even became the favourite pastime of the court to make voyages across the island in these swift frigates of the sky.

Ultimately the king so thoroughly trusted the master of this new style of transportation that he abandoned himself to his guidance and allowed him free use of all the resources of the island. He came to see the marvellous possibilities that lay in warfare carried on by such a navy. Though the Broolyians had, after Choktroo's deportation, lost one by one all the conquests that that audacious warrior had made, and had at last been confined again to the limits of their island, they never gave up their ambitious dreams. And the monarch who could fulfil them would be certain to fix his empire in their hearts. The new king looked round for some means to gratify this passion for conquest. But their old methods were now comparatively useless; for the other large islands, warned by their past experience, built fleets as large and formidable as the Broolyian, and the smaller groups confederated for the purposes of defence. It was vain then to think of re-mastering the archipelago in any attempt by sea.

With extreme delight then did the monarch watch a demonstration of the warlike possibilities of the new air craft. The director had some old hulks moored out at sea in sight of the king and his court. Then he entered one of his new balloons, well provided with guns and explosives and well-manned, and bade the crew let go. They sailed straight out till they rose high over the remains of the antiquated navy. As they approached their prey, several guns belched out their fires from the car, and their shot struck and sank three of the ancient ships. But two tough old hulls resisted all their attempts. So the balloon rose straight over them, but much higher in the air. Out of the car was seen to fall two packages, which made for the decks of the old tempest resisters. In the twinkling of an eye, before we could realise that the packets had reached their destinations, there was a thunderous roar, and the air was filled with jets of water and with the flying fragments of the shattered hulks. When the commotion settled, nothing but floating planks and spars and shreds of the vanished ships was to be seen on the surface of the water. And away out of reach of the fierce convulsion rode the airship majestic and unharmed in the blue.

The monarch need no further demonstration. He gave up to the master of the new power the use of his whole army and navy. Before many months were over a vast aërial fleet was equipped and manned ready for the first emergency, and this emergency arose at once. The sullen jealousy which ever smoulders and rankles between two powerful and neighbouring empires took substance and outward shape between Aleofane and Broolyi. The old enemy knew nothing of the new instruments of war which had been forged, and prepared with cheer and good hope for the struggle. Her fleet was in excellent order, well equipped and manned, but within a few weeks it had completely vanished before the wrecking terror of the air. Continuous torrents of lead and iron streamed from above onto their decks, making those of their gunners that survived helpless and inert. And when their captains invented methods of pointing their guns at the aërial ships and of floating fire-kites against them to set them on fire, then the most tremendous engines of the navy in the air were brought into train; and with appalling explosions the Aleofanian ships and their crews vanished in atoms.

No such destruction of a nation's war material had ever occurred in the history of the archipelago. The Aleofanian marine force was swept from the face of the sea. One or two other islands were bold enough to attempt the struggle with the new power, but with the same disastrous results to themselves. Over the whole archipelago except its central island the air-fleet passed, inspiring terror and reducing the peoples to servitude. It was the same all-conquering story as was told under Choktroo's leadership.

And now the Broolyian army and people were willing to worship the maker and manipulator of these balloons as a god. He had plenty of ambition; but he was by nature and acquirement only a mechanician and not a born leader of men. He had none of the self-confidence made monstrous by success, or of the unscrupulousness, that forges the masterful will. He did love power, but he hesitated before those audacious measures which give a conqueror the highest vantage-ground. He yearned to rule widely. But he had not the self-mastery and the leavening imagination which secure command over the minds of human aggregations. He was but an average nature with complete mastery over the newest and most masterful invention.

The Broolyian monarch saw the peril of his too great success, and set the stranger and his balloons aside in time to let the popular enthusiasm cool. Alone with his fleet and his army the king completed the round of conquests. He knew that when the power of Aleofane and one or two other chief islands was broken, there was nothing to fear from the others, and his task, though brilliant, was easy. He took care that there were several great and sanguinary battles that put heart and pride into his soldiers and sailors. Thus by the time the war was finished, the newcomer and his appalling fleet were almost forgotten.

But the monarch himself did not forget them. He knew that the climax of this new era of national conquest and pride was certain to come soon. Never had the Broolyians been continuously successful in war without losing their traditional fear of the isle of devils, and demanding its subjugation. He set his house in order against the day of vainglory. He would develop his new method of warfare. He made the stranger again his commander-in-chief, urging him on towards the increase of the aërial fleet and of its terrorising weapons. Then, fearing from his knowledge of the past that there was little chance of success, he gave him complete command of the expedition, so that all the blame of failure should be on the shoulders of another. In order to complete the contrast, he kept rebellion smouldering in one or two of the adjacent islands, and took care that it broke out simultaneously with the attack upon the isle of devils.

Ignorant of the conditions he had to meet, and puffed up by his past successes, the stranger thought that all he had to do was to add to the number of his fleet and the deadliness of his weapons. We saw him set out with banners flying amid the applause and enthusiasm of the people, whilst the wily king led off his own forces, quietly to embark from an opposite shore of the country against the rebels of neighbouring coasts. Success seemed to follow the aërial navy, for favouring winds bore them swiftly and majestically over the horizon out of the range of Broolyian vision. For myself, as I sat at an idro-vamolan, I feared the strange new torrential guns and the showers of deadly explosives that would rain down from these aërial ships, and my heart sank as I saw them sail like great vultures nearer and nearer to their prey.

But my compatriots were tranquil and free from all anxiety. Everything was really in readiness and they were only awaiting the exact moment for action. It came, and the huge balloons fell suddenly away before the blast from the lilaran, like a flock of storm-beaten birds. I could see them struggling, many of them half disabled, to stand up to the wind. But it was vain; they whirled like snowflakes before an arctic tempest. Their helms became entangled in their snapped cordage, and I could see their guns roll and pitch with fatal effect upon the crews, till from many the suicidal weapons were tumbled overboard into the sea below.

Yet the expedition by no means acknowledged itself defeated. Guided by some experienced Broolyian adviser the admiral of the fleet changed its formation. Evidently from knowledge that the blast from Lilaroma could play upon only one point at once, he divided his air-navy into three squadrons, and making the central face the blast, he sent the other two in different directions round the island. He thought that these two would be able to bring their explosives and guns to bear upon the lilaran by this flank movement. It was as unsuccessful as his other efforts. Both sections came almost within firing distance of the shore, when suddenly their gaseous spheres were seen to collapse. A slight and silent flash was all that told whence the disaster had come. Electric rockets had issued from magnetic ejectors of great power and almost invisibly punctured the spherical supporter of each airship.

It seemed as if the whole of the three squadrons would soon be in the sea, and with the weight of their war material they were certain to sink to the bottom and carry all their crews with them. But the invaders promptly threw overboard their weighty cargoes, and with their usual humanity the Limanorans now did their best to save their enemies. The punctures in the balloons were so minute that it would take some time to exhaust them. So the lilaran sent its blast underneath them and buoyed them up like thistledown, at the same time blowing the three sections of the navy off in different directions. It was amusing to watch the alternate rise and fall of the various airships as it turned its blast from one squadron to another, like a game of battledoor and shuttlecock played by giant jugglers. The warriors in the cars kept crouching in panic and holding onto the cordage, as they rose or fell in the air upon the billows of wind. Their cars danced and leaped and jerked like corks in an eddy where currents meet, and they were too panic-stricken or too paralysed with terror to see that with all the tumult of their movements they were gradually approaching solid earth. We saw each squadron land on the shores of a separate island; and after their terrible voyage the crews threw themselves upon the earth and seemed to clutch it, in fear lest they should be torn again from its sweet anchorage into the warring whirlpools of the upper air.

After a few days they collected their wits and the shattered fragments of their air-fleet, and, hiring boats from the islanders, sailed homewards. As they entered the main harbour of Broolyi crestfallen and dispirited, the army and fleet of the king were returning from their victories with triumphal music and with banners flying. The contrast was striking, and set the monarch more firmly on his throne for another generation.

Yet matters could not remain where they were. The defeat of the new methods of warfare stirred hope in the breasts of the conquered peoples; and muffled sounds of rebellion came from many of the islands. The king knew that he must make some other move, and held long councils with the defeated balloonist.

The result of the conferences soon became manifest. The stranger had seen that his aërial fleet was useless against tempests and electric missiles, such as the isle of demons had command of, and he willingly handed it over to his superior to use against the threatened revolts. With the blind obstinacy of the average mind placed in a position greater than its powers, he ran counter to the traditions of the archipelago, and uttered loud resolves that he was not to be beaten; he would show them how fertile he was in resources; he had no fear of their bag of winds.

The king again gave him free scope with all the material and forces of the country, and the ingenious mechanician forged huge guns that would throw their projectiles enormous distances, and built great ships to hold them. As he launched one vessel after another, he practised his crews on board of it, and taught them how to handle the marvellous artillery. The people stood in awe, as they heard the thunder of their fire dozens of leagues away, and saw their missiles fall in the sea miles and miles from the ship whence they had issued; and they shook their heads wisely and said to each other: "Now, we shall see at last an end to this isle of demons."

When the great armada was all ready after long years of work, and the ships lay at anchor in the harbour, their magazines filled, their guns in train, and everything prepared for the final expedition, the people were so over-joyed at the sight that they organised a festival to the sailors of the wonderful fleet. They had such confidence in the destructive powers of these ships and their guns that they resolved to pre-celebrate with magnificent pageantry and feast the triumph they were so assured of. And as the monarch had already defeated the incipient rebellion by his aërial fleet, and the mutterings of the subjugated were stifled or unheard, there could be no danger in inviting all the sailors on shore to take part in the festivities. So the great fleet lay peace-fully at anchor unmanned, whilst their crews were being lauded to the skies for their intrepidity and the certainty of their success.

The night was moonless and deep darkness was flecked only by the oc-casional blaze of sky-daring illumination. Everything had gone off with bril-liancy, and the banquet to the sailors was nearing its climax and close. Sud-denly the hubbub of jubilance was hushed; there was a series of appalling detonations, shaking the banqueting edifice to its foundations; many thought that the world had come to an end so terrifying and ear-deafening was the continuous roar. The people in the streets at first fell on the earth and prayed to their gods. But they soon saw what had occurred. There out on the har-bour the pyrotechnic display overshadowed anything they had ever seen or even thought of. The great ships were all of them in flames; the magazine of each had exploded, and sent decks and fittings and armaments sputtering in fragments against the black of the sky. The brilliancy of the spectacle over-came the natural alarm and regret. Such titanic catherine-wheels they had never seen, such rending of the heavens, such flame-lit jets of water rising in columns above the doomed ships. But the spectacle was brief. Ship after ship rose high above the scene of its devastation, its banners of fire all flying against the darkness, and then plunged into the extinction and gloom of the depths. The breach in the side close to the magazine sucked in the waters most swiftly, and sent the bow-end of each first to the watery assuagement of her fires. In an hour after the first deafening paroxysm all was still and dark again on the face of the waters, but for a flaming fragment here and there, hissing and sputtering against the night.

Then came terror again. The Broolyians, jubilant over the invincibility of their marvellous fleet, knew not whence the disaster had come or who had been the enemy. And they now crouched in fear, or ran for shelter, lest the invisible foe should take advantage of their palsy and reap his harvest of blood. But no enemy came. No carnage followed the strange catastrophe.

The morning dawned, and the waters of the bay shone as peacefully in the level rays of the sun as if no fleet had ever been there, as if no conflagration had occurred. Not a boat or sign of an enemy was to be seen. Out crept the soldiers and sailors from their shelters, the people in their rear, and soon the harbour was alive with craft, seeking relics and explanation of the disaster.

But no explanation could be found in all the babel of theories that chattered and echoed over the water. A council of the royal advisers was called; they consulted and questioned every admiral and general; but all in vain. The stranger, who had brought the fleet and its equipment into existence, failed to account for the occurrence. He refuted all charges of negligence, and appealed to the desire of the people and the command of the king as his warrant for withdrawing the crews from the ships for the night. Treachery there must have been; there were a thousand conjectures, but no sure knowledge as to whence it came. With the irrationality and ingratitude which mark all panic in nations or other aggregations of men when unexplained disaster has overtaken them, they broke out in fury against the very hero of the night's festivities. They had to find a scapegoat and his figure was foremost in every man's mind; the destructive magnetism of the crowd gathered round the name that was on every lip, and the cry arose that he was the traitor. The mob howled outside the council-room for his blood. He had to be bundled off by a secret passage to the outskirts of the city and thence into the mountains, and to appease their frantic passions the king had to proclaim his exile, and to promise that no such engines of war should again be forged in the royal armories. Fear of the isle of demons again crept over the superstitious hearts of the people. As they brooded over the mystery, they felt that somehow or other it was connected with that inexpugnable centre which had defied all their efforts at its invasion.

And this was right. For the Limanorans had watched the long preparation for the assault, and made calmly ready to defeat it. They knew that, if they ever allowed the fleet to sail, they could not well beat it off without loss of life amongst its crews. It could lie in the shelter of an island some miles distant from their shores and rain great projectiles upon them. The repulse must be accomplished long before this had been reached. They therefore waited till the ammunition was on board each ship. Then, in order to avoid the destruction of life, they sent into the air of Broolyi the exhilarative magnetism required, and into the minds of the inhabitants the suggestion that the whole fleet should be fêted. When the ships had been deserted and not a human being was within reach of them, they launched through the air in its direction a series of electric shocks, which, as soon as they came in contact with the metals of the magazine, ignited the ammunition. Most of the ships were set on fire in this way, the rest by the falling fragments and sparks from their exploding sisters.

Thus was the new threat to Limanoran civilisation frustrated without loss of life or breach of the mystery that sealed the central isle. But the waste of time and progress upon such threats by the withdrawal of so many Limanorans from their ordinary pursuits was an evil not to be tolerated. Something must be done to prevent the recurrence of these expeditions. It was generally from Broolyi they came, the result of warlike ambition. It would be a service to the whole archipelago to reduce this military people to insignificance and silence. There was no security in their subjugation by the people of another island, for the war-fanaticism would surge up again in a later generation. The conversion of them to a religion of peace would mean no change in the blood; it would only transform the method and cue of attack.

What was needed was the elimination of the ambitious and military natures from the Broolyians. For only the aristocracy and the descendants of the original conquering exiles had set their hearts on military pursuits; the conquered and many of the families that came to the island at later dates than the great purgation, were not unwilling to keep to their own bounds, and preferred possession to dispossession. There was no need of extermination of the people, but only decimation. Nor would the Limanorans endure any shedding of blood in the process. It must be gradual, peaceful, free from torture and bloodshed, and almost unobservable.

The physiological and physicist families worked out a scheme that would fulfil all these conditions, and yet finally eject the disturbers of peace from the archipelago within a generation. The scare they had just suffered and the exile of the balloonist ensured to Limanora freedom from their attacks for some years. But they aimed at permanent immunity and this could be secured by nothing less than the sterilisation of the warlike element in Broolyi.

The end was accomplished in the next aggression upon a neighbouring island. The expedition was formidable, and included all the bellicose males of the offending people. After landing, it lay encamped in the open air; then a band of Limanorans set out on wings by night, armed with a new surgical instrument, called the idlumian, which could give an electric shock to any part of the human system and paralyse it either for a time or permanently, according to the power put into it. They approached the whole army as it lay asleep, and by the whiff of a soporific which they diffused through the air, they steeped the systems of the sentinels in lethargy and by the same means ensured the depth and continuance of the slumbers of the embattled host. Before a single soldier had awakened from his deep sleep, the whole Broolyian army was defertilised without being in the least conscious of any loss of vitality or manhood or enjoyment of life. When the sentries awoke and the troops began to move about in preparation for their struggle, the medical embassy had winged its way back to Limanora. Not till twenty or thirty years after did it strike the Broolyians that the fountain of their military power was dried up, and soon they began to attribute the strange infecundity of their aristocratic and warlike families to the witchcraft of the isle of demons, a belief that finally sealed that centre of the archipelago as with walls of adamant against aggression on the part of their neighbours.

My Western instincts, in spite of all my training, would reappear at intervals—which happily became longer and longer—and for a time I could not repress my instinctive disapproval of the use of this idlumian or electro steriliser. Yet my reason told me that it was the only effective method of permanently stopping the horrors of war in the archipelago. Heredity and circumstances would have circumvented any other bloodless attempt at relief from the Broolyian nightmare. A few discussions with my proparents made this rational view of the matter dominant over the conservative instinct in me, and before many years my instinct was quite the other way; it became the ally of the reason; and I had no need to argue with myself on the point or confirm my faith by arguing with others who knew better than I.

There was another Western instinct of mine which gave me frequent though lessening trouble and came into conflict with the reason of the community at this time and on this topic. It was my approval of propagandism. Into my blood had grown through the centuries of Christendom the feeling that a faith could not well prove itself unless it spread out amongst new and alien peoples. It is the prerogative and principle of belief to yearn for universality of acceptance amongst human beings. And it urges on the devotees of any faith to spread it through the world at all costs. After centuries of propagandism the habit becomes an instinct, and it seems to be a dictate of nature to attempt to convert the world to the tenets which have grown up in us from infancy and been incorporated into our very life. The Christian has ever been from its outset a great missionary religion, and it is difficult for one brought up in Christendom to get rid of the missionary attitude of mind which assumes every alien to it to be sunk in wickedness and unprofitableness, and certain to lose all the future blessings promised to true believers.

I could not obliterate this instinct wholly from my nature, and whenever I reflected on the wisdom and nobleness of the Limanoran civilisation, or noticed the marvellous progressiveness of some new phase of it, I found myself longing to go back to the Western world with my knowledge. Thus I often drifted into appeals to the propagandist spirit which I assumed to exist in the breasts of my friends and fellow-citizens, but I was not allowed to rest long in such dreams. Each time I uttered or even thought over my missionary desire, I was brought to book with the widest of knowledge and the keenest of penetration into human nature and its history. I felt that it was almost as useless for Europeans to go out amongst the tribes of monkeys and spend their lives trying to bring them up to such a level of intelligence as is implied in the appreciation of the Christian religion, as for the Limanorans to apostolise amongst mankind, and struggle to drag them up to the stage of progress these islanders had reached.

But now, whenever my missionary mood returned upon me, my friends would point with a smile to the new invention, the electro-steriliser; and if pressed by the disapproving skepticism of my thoughts, they would urge in words the omnipotence of this little instrument as the apostle of progress. By this and this alone was the snail-pace advance of mankind likely to be quickened. Without more rapid elimination of the unfit than was afforded by natural selection, sexual selection, and the accidents of surroundings, there was little hope of wise propagation of the human race. The blunders and defects and maladies of every new century were treasured up by heredity in the tissues of mankind along with any feeble tendency to advance that might appear. The struggle was a losing one in spite of the development of science and wealth. And all reforming theories and efforts were but stumblings in the dark till there had been a thorough purgation of traditional and epidemic diseases, moral as well as physical. Nine tenths of the race, as at present constituted, were unworthy to hand on their natures to posterity. Under the régime of propagational license universal among all peoples of the earth, the evil and diseased multiplied at a much greater rate than the sound in mind and body. The progressive element in mankind was dragged back by the dead weight of the criminal, the diseased, the habitually pauper, and the naturally incompetent. Some religions even set themselves to encourage the vitalisation and propagation of the last. It was noble and good to assuage the evils that heredity had accumulated in their systems; but it was anything but noble and good to encourage them to perpetuate their misfortunes throughout a wide posterity. "Multiply" should be the last word of an advancing civilisation instead of the first, unless there be added to it the condition "only the best." And who cares or dares to preach this true gospel of progress, when it touches a theme that all are ashamed to mention? If ever there was a sacred mission upon earth it would be that of the man who should go to the wise and good men of all nations and put into their hands the secret of the idlumian, or who should himself pass round the world and sterilise all the morally or physically diseased amongst rich and poor, amongst gentle and simple. Within two generations the races of humanity would take such a leap into light and noble vitality and love of progress as would make the most brilliant civilisation of the past seem barbaric. Then would they take command of their own destiny, and look unflinchingly into the future for the path they should take. Advance in material or in the accumulation of force is vain, unless it goes hand in hand with such universal moral and intellectual advance. It is progress in the human system through all its parts that should be the aim of every race.

I gradually came to understand the importance they attached to this new instrument as the most humane and effective of missionaries. Had it come before their great series of purgations, there would have been little need for the expatriation policy. If they had had to eject, they would have taken care that the different sections of exiles should vanish in a generation. They shrank from extinguishing the individual life that had already been brought into being. They would have had no scruple in giving euthanasia to an evil race or a section of a race; for this meant only preventing a posterity coming into existence to take up their burden of evil. And even now it was a question to be seriously discussed and answered whether they would not sweep out the pollution from the rest of the archipelago by the help of this humane little doorkeeper of posterity. Would it not prevent the lifelong evil of thousands? Where lay the humanity or love in allowing a retrogressive and unhappy race to hand on to myriads to come the evil they had received from their ancestors?

CHAPTER IX

POLITY

I WAS privileged to hear, or rather to be conscious of, the discussion that the question of idlumian-missionaryism underwent. I had now reached the age and stage of my training which gave me the entry as audience to the councils of the race. It would not have been wise to admit to the treatment of difficult and advanced themes natures that were still hemmed in by the limits of long-past ages of history. They could not have sympathised in, or even followed, the attitude taken up by the elders of the people; and they would have gone back from the meeting with minds perplexed and bewildered by questions too complex and futuritive for them to fathom. Many of them would have suffered a warping of their natures from the strain, and this would have meant years of additional training and care to set it right. The exclusion of the immature from the national councils was a matter of educational policy rather than of political necessity.

It was evidently for my own benefit that I was present at the discussion of the sterilising embassy. This was somewhat difficult for me to follow, for my magnetic power and faculties had not been developed enough to interpret the silences between the rare speeches. As I sat, my mind ran back to a Quakers' meeting to which I had been taken by my mother; then much self-control had been necessary in order to restrain the expression of my amusement; now I felt as if in the presence of gods who needed none of the babble of human speech to open a pathway from mind to mind. I had sloughed off that singular prepossession of the Western nature in favour of verbal intercourse and had ceased to think that silence, where two or three were gathered together, was a mark of inanity, or incompetence, or at least passivity. I remembered with a shudder the awkwardness that accompanied social lockjaw, even where friends met; each grew afraid of the thoughts of the others; none knew what the silence meant; everyone was frantically searching for something that would break the gag without appearing unnatural. Loquacity, instead of being a bar to ideas, was counted an accomplishment; and freedom of speech was one of the great political watchwords. It was only on rare occasions that reserve was not considered a defect.

Now I felt that there was nothing so powerful as these silences in council. The magnetism of thought and feeling was flowing from mind to mind, all the more that there was not a word or sound to interrupt it. Now and again, when the divergence of thoughts was dominant, one of the oldest and wisest would call them in from their different tracks to a common centre. Speech was rather a method of focussing thoughts than one of chasing and criticising them. The speaker would review all the mental discussion and concentrate its lines, so that everyone present might have a view of the whole field from a high point. It was marvellous how rapidly they went though the business in hand by means of these noble silences, broken by occasional reviews. There were no displays of mental or stylistic legerdemain, no appeals to common feeling, no captious criticisms, such as form the staple of a debate in a Western assembly even of the wisest men. Every fallacy that crept into the discussion was unmasked in a gentle, fair, and kindly way. There was no partisanship, no war-whoop of prospective victory, no lash of sarcasm, and they abhorred above all things the sweetness of harangue.

Yet, the absence of Western methods of beating out a subject was a disadvantage for me, who had as yet little of the magnetic penetration or sympathy needed for the appreciation of their meetings. But my deep reverence for the humanity of the elders, and great sympathy for their aims, made up in part for the lack of magnetic interpretation of their thoughts. At the close of the council I talked the matter over with my proparents, and eked out my own observations and reflections on its proceedings and thus came to a just view of the whole discussion.

They were strongly impelled by their love of the human race to the missionary course, which would now be so simple and effective. Missionaryism before meant the hoisting of every separate alien and barbarous nature up to a higher platform, and continuing the process with generation after generation, a gigantic task. There was more chance of the missionaries levelling down to the civilisation of their converts than of accomplishing their original purpose, while the arguing, preaching, and persuading implied a Niagara of babble for centuries. Where would lie the compensation for such abasement of the mind? Now there was no need of condescension; it was a mere matter of common professional work for the physiological families. The glib energy of the old process was evaded and in its place came the need of wide practical knowledge and keen judgment. For tongue-force and subtlety of reasoning were substituted physiological exactness and selective talent. The process was now eliminative rather than directly creative.

But such pleading ignored the true difficulty, the acquisition of so large a knowledge of local and temporal conditions as would enable them to foresee the full effects of the step. How were they to be certain that only the nobler natures would hand themselves on in each race? Streams from the barbarous and evil past might flow through the mothers. Who could guarantee that the reduced numbers of the next generation would be able to accumulate energy quickly enough to keep the mastery of the earth against its unreasoning and unmoral powers? As it was, the peoples were able to fight with the seasons and the forces of climate and weather, and with the exuberance of the plant and animal kingdoms. If their numbers were greatly lessened by the elimination of the coarser natures, would not the balance be destroyed, and the natural enemies of man have the best of it?

Questions like these made them pause. To be able to answer them would need prolonged and minute investigation of the human race and its conditions, perhaps consuming centuries in the task. Meantime their own forward march would have to be abandoned. Omniscience alone could deal with the problem of missionaryism, and as things were, the omniscience of nature was dealing with it. For evolution was proceeding throughout the universe, however slowly. Those races that seemed to be laggards on the upward path were evolving what was needed on their part for the advance of the whole army of creation, and death was ever opening new careers for the vital force of their individuals. It was difficult to tell without complete knowledge of all the conditions whether the spread of a certain faith or phase of civilisation was going to be beneficent or maleficent for the world as a whole. And all missionaryism that was not based on omniscience was striking out a path through a jungle in the darkness. Even the idlumian, unless amongst criminals and the morally and intellectually plague-stricken, might do irremediable injury to the prospects of the human race. The problem of propagandism was, as often before, abandoned as too complicated and too far-reaching for limited knowledge and brain power.

****

But the discussion gave me an insight into what I had long been curious about, their polity and methods of guiding the course of their commonweal. I had not dared to inquire into the subject lest I should meet with some rebuff, or find that I had been too inquisitive where reverence was needed. Nor had I been able to see much evidence of government or legislation, and had almost come to the conclusion that there was no such thing in Limanora as sovereignty or state. Though everything moved with the harmony and smoothness of perfect organisation I could never find the organising hand.

At last I discovered part, at least, of the machinery of government. There was one assembly or council to which reformers could appeal with their schemes. The whole community often assembled; but it seemed to me that it was more for training, for the reintegration of some faculty or feeling, or for the purification and elevation of the life, than for legislative purposes. The only trace of any approach to selection and decision in these national gatherings was to be found in Loomiefa and in the linguistic assemblies; in the one they practically accepted or rejected some proposed revision of their ideals placed before them in a new book; in the other they decided whether a new word, or the adaptation or application of a word was worthy to live or die, whether a new sense deserved to be kept alive in a form set apart for it, or whether a new distinction was real or merely verbal. I could see that these were the two great functions of a national assembly, to accept or reject a new departure in life or in language, to see that the path into the darkness of the unknown was the right path, and that the verbal armour and weapons they bore allowed of no enemy near. Discovery and advance had their own pitfalls and risks; but the language they used in investigation and research was the most natural ambush of fallacies and the scientific work of a generation might be rendered nugatory by an ambiguous word or phrase. In past time they could point out many ages, which had prided themselves on the marvels of their progress in science and were now regarded as barren and unprogressive; their advance had been apparent and not real, a mere change of nomenclature and not a change of ideas or a discovery of facts. It was natural then that the community, as a whole, should, from the mere instinct of self-preservation, keep the most watchful eye on this unguarded frontier of language, and almost as eager an eye on the regions that lay before them, the ideals they were about to adopt.

I had now been led to see that there was a council for the decision of foreign questions, for it was this that rejected the new idea of the idlumian mission. I soon came to recognise its domestic functions as more important than its policy abroad. The latter occupied its attention only once or twice in a generation. Monthly, almost weekly, it met to agree on questions and schemes which had no connection with the world outside of Limanora. Now that I was inspired to attend its meetings, I felt that it safeguarded the march forward. It never passed a law; and yet its decisions were as clear, as valid, and as universal in their effects as if they had been written out, proclaimed, and printed in a statute-book. All the parents, proparents, and guardians were members of it, and along with them were associated as silent, inactive members the young men and women who had matured and had shown sufficient of the wisdom and virtues of the race to warrant such a privilege. These latter were in training for full and active membership many years before their spirit and influence were felt to have bearing on any decision. On this basis I had been admitted to the meetings.

The scheme of every new book came before this assembly prior to its publication in Loomiefa. Every new departure on the part of any family was brought up by its heads to be tested by the feeling of the council. But it rarely happened that any scheme was rejected; it was, as a rule, only revised and modified. In fact, every parent or guardian was so keenly in sympathy with the spirit and genius of the race that it was almost impossible for any proposal or idea to come from a family in antagonism to the general welfare and feeling. One feature that struck me as marking their meetings was the absence of those searching, flaw-finding criticisms we would have considered absolutely necessary to progress in the West; every modification suggested was an improvement or addition readily welcomed by the author and his family. The council was there to help and develop, and not to be hypercritical or censorious. Every thinker or inventor was eager to bring his work before it; instead of fearing its criticism as an ordeal he knew that his creation would have its true spirit appreciated, and if there was genuine and original work in it, it would meet with its due; whatever was likely to aid the race in its forward march would be welcomed and aided.

Another branch of its duties was the preparation of practical problems and difficulties which were likely to obstruct the national progress till they were solved. The council thought over these as they came up in their minds, and tried to get at their fundamental form or principle. After having ruminated over them for months, or perhaps years, it indicated the family in whose province they lay, and handed them over to it as part of its duty thereafter. In fact, the debatable borderland between family and family was evidently one of its most important spheres. Not that any family ever desired to evade what might be included in its functions or offices, but, on the contrary, was eager to do all that in it lay for the benefit of the race. Often, however, spheres overlapped, so that two different families or individuals were doing the same thing; and it was necessary to define and apportion the duty of each.

* * * *

In all the meetings and discussions I came gradually to feel that there was a dominating spirit that influenced from behind the scenes. I could see no overt mastery or guidance of the proceedings, yet there was manifest an organising power within its organism. Schemes and problems came before it in lucid order and a definite shape leaving no room for mere idle conjectures. As the treatment of any one proceeded, I could feel the magnetism of strong, harmonious spirits moulding and bending the thoughts. I knew that I was in tutelage, although there was no open dictation or even guidance.

After a time I began to trace the vigorous currents of influence that swept us on with such force, to the oldest men and women in the council, those who in Europe would have been thrust aside as incapable of good advice and as on the borders of second childhood. I could see a tendency on the part of most members to look to them for the cue, when thoughts had begun to wander and part company. They did not claim superior authority, but the deference to their opinion and instincts was spontaneous and palpable, and often grew into the deepest reverence. This would never have awakened the notice of an unsympathetic stranger, so little was the feeling expressed in open word or act.

In this way I learned, before many years' experience of the council, that there was an inner council or cabinet, consisting of all the elders who had proved themselves able and wise by centuries of discovery, or invention, or penetrative and far-reaching advice. I could discover no formal election to it, everything in the shape of definite constitution or government being manifestly avoided. Age did not form the qualification for this senate although all the senators were men and women who could count their years by hundreds. Many who were older than they still remained outside the charmed circle. It was rather weight of experience, and the fulness of development resulting from it, that admitted. Whosoever by living long had made the most of life in the line of greatest progress was singled out by the reverence paid to his lofty character and expansive wisdom, for the duty of piloting the race. It took years of massive growth in personality and influence to make the community or the man certain that he had been selected by the national spirit. The responsibility was so onerous that the wisest shrank for years from it, fearing they had not developed sufficiently. It was only with reluctance that they at last listened to the call of their fellows and entered the noblest of all senates. None sought the honour, but once undertaken, none attempted to shift the burdens of it onto other shoulders till the nausea of life, indicating the approach of their mortal liberation, came upon them. No one was jealous of their authority or influence; for all knew that these they would have had by virtue of their nature and advance, even if they had no seat in this inner assembly. And every type of family had its representative there, the ablest, the wisest, the noblest, generally the oldest of the group, whether man or woman. For there was great need in its councils of someone minutely familiar with the practical functions and duties of every science and art in the island. Sex made no distinction in the choice; sex was a mere accident in the realm of reason and wisdom; sometimes the greater brain-power and greater moral and intellectual development belonged to the male head of the family, sometimes to the female; and it never entered the minds of this strange people to discount position or influence because of sex.

In all differences of opinion their decision was final. For everyone felt that the race could not possibly at that particular stage of its progress attain to any clearer light upon the subject than this areopagus had attained. The upholders of the clashing views received the decision as coming from a tribunal, the most impartial and the farthest-seeing that could be found on earth. But it was seldom that any division of view came as far as a controversy which needed the influence of the elders. Where two individuals or families began to feel their opinions on any common topic drawing apart, they each made eager efforts to understand the other's point of view; and their neighbours, recognising a discord in the mental atmosphere, came in with reconciling magnetism and reason. Everyone was too anxious to have the light of others' thoughts thrown on the matters he had to investigate or consider, to reject in haste a view that differed from his, or to let his own view become unreasoning prejudice. I never perceived among them any of that bickering or heat which so commonly attends a misunderstanding in Europe. Long after arriving in the island I still wondered where their courts of law were; and thought there must be some secret tribunal that dealt summarily with all disputes. I came at last to see that there was no need of courts of justice, for there was never any approach to jarring or litigation; and, most of all, there was no written law to appeal to. It was one of the primary principles of their life that any law that needed committal to writing was either artificial, and so beyond the necessities of the community, or implied a flaw in the nature of the race demanding instant attention. Written law, like overt authority, was an evidence of elements in a community which were alien and had better be eliminated. Hostile individuals or factions made a body of recorded laws, backed up by force, a necessity throughout the nations of the world, and rendered most of them practically unprogressive. Since the great series of purgations the spirit of the Limanoran community, working through the electric sense, had been the master of its unity and progress, and it appeared idle to make or write laws. Every advance it achieved made every individual at once debtor to it; all moved up to the new level. The laws, if those principles which were continually being revised and constantly progressing could be called so, were written in the hearts and natures of the race; every new amendment of them was the natural demand of the racial spirit and passed at once through the elders, the parents, and the guardians into the conscience of all the families and individuals. Every man was a law to himself, in that he knew and fully recognised the aim of the community and the part he had to fulfil in its advance. Those who were still in a state of pupillage had each two elders as their guarantors and sponsors, who watched the instillation of the common spirit into them, and any flaw or discord rapidly made itself felt.

Reason was at the back of every word and act of the Limanorans; a new feature or thought or discovery had to prove itself worthy and real before it was accepted. There was no such thing as an appeal to authority. Everyone knew that he would have to reason out and make clear the nobleness of what he expected others to believe or agree to. It was one of the main functions, the most urgent duty, of the two councils, therefore, to revise the axioms and postulates in which the national reason found its leverage and to see that they never became mere prejudices. Every new advance antiquated some principle that had been taken as axiomatic, or revealed the fallacy that lay in some pivot-word. Any difference of opinion or of point of view generally set the inner council on the alert. Not infrequently they found that one investigator had been misled by a verbal fallacy or a mistaken axiom, whilst the other had in searching laid his mind open to the light of truth. They never rejected as trifling or insignificant any divergence in the views of a common topic, but rather welcomed it as evidence of some long-hidden flaw in the foundations of their reason.

Another striking feature of this inner council was that their meetings were open to all but the young and immature. They would have nothing to do with the secret conclave, which, they held, was the beginning and principle of despotism. Away from the sunlight of truth and open thought the most ghastly spiritual diseases of humanity sprang into being and flourished; thoughts and feelings, otherwise healthy and unashamed, became sickly, morbid, and often venomous. Resolutions passed in secrecy need have no assigned reasons, and are soon passed without discussion and without any reason but the lower private feelings and prejudices of individual members. A mystery is attached to the proceedings of such conclaves that gives well-nigh omnipotence to the terror they instil. Hence until their doom is near they are by nature and of necessity despotism. To every meeting of the inner council all active councillors of the larger assembly were welcomed. But, when present, they kept silence, and preferred to keep silence. Nay, it was considered a special privilege for one of the senate to withhold his thoughts from the discussions; silence for a year or two was the hard-earned reward for years of painfully guarded responsibility in debate. Not one of them but looked forward to such a breathing-time for relaxation, so heavy was the care of the future of the race. To speak was the burden; for speech must be weighty, and the recording linasans automatically treasured it up for future years to shed light and criticism on it.

* * * *

In fact their senate-house was arranged so as to be a vast linasan itself. Nothing was needed at the end of a meeting but to touch a spring, and the moving irelium-strip, on which the proceedings imprinted themselves, was securely fixed on its roll and transferred to the valley of memories there to be laid past in the archives for future reference, and a fresh strip took its place ready for the next debate. Knowing this each senator weighed his every word with the utmost care. Whatever building was used as a meeting-place for discussion by either the whole of the people or any section of it had its dome constructed in such a way as to serve as a collector and magnifier of sound, so arranged that the sound should not echo back but pass instead into the receiver of a great linasan and at once indelibly record itself, thus making every member of the community set a watch upon his lips and allow only the maturest wisdom to pass them.

The memories of the Limanorans were marvellous in their precision and tenacity. They could ransack the records of any man's brain in sleep with the greatest minuteness, though they did not care to use this process on anyone beyond the stage of probation and pupillage; it implied something not unlike prying into the secrets of the nature. They knew, too, how inexact the senses are in their reports of what takes place in the world without. Refined and trained as they were, there was always a liability to error. Whenever exactitude of record was required they used machine-reporters which never made mistake except when their gearing was out of order. At all important assemblies and gatherings they had an instrument called an idrolinasan which recorded in permanence not merely all that was said or done, but the electric currents which passed from man to man. Whenever they needed to verify a memory of the past, the irelium-strip of the particular occurrence was brought out of the historical archives and placed in the reversible idrolinasan, and the whole scene flashed vividly before the senses. Doubtless this custom of machine-recording made the Limanorans so watchful of all they said and did and thought; and it was perhaps this as much as any of the wonderful features of their civilisation that quickened the pace of their personal development in more recent years. They made every effort their natures were capable of to think and say and do what was worthy of themselves and their people. Nothing retards the progress of Western civilisation so much as the relaxed habit of life that even the best men and women fall into, when others are not likely to see or hear them. Religion invented the all-watchfulness of God in order to provide a substitute for the consciousness of the eyes and ears of others. But it is too distant and incorporeal to strike a highly materialised civilisation as real; and the belief acts only for a brief period after it has been impressed upon the mind. The economy of breath in churches and of evidence in law courts would be so great if some of those instruments were introduced into the West, that Europe would not know itself within a few years, it would develop and progress intellectually and morally with such rapidity. But the most striking result would appear in politics and legislation. The machine would influence the speech and action of the legislators as powerfully as if they believed every moment that the omni-watchfulness of the deity were as real as the presence of the Speaker in the chamber. There could be no revisal of its hansardisings; every politician would be as true, as reverential, as weighed down with the responsibility of his duties as if he were before the final judgment-seat.

These machines had had a wonderful effect even upon the advanced Limanoran polity. Not even a gesture was wasted in their assemblies. Everything done and said was relevant and weighty. The result was they acted as if they were one man and their meetings were brief and effective; where a Western legislature would discuss a scheme or proposal for years, a few minutes would suffice a Limanoran assembly to get at the heart of it, and accept or reject it. They seldom had to retrace their steps; if they did, the error was due to some mistaken principle accepted in past ages as an axiom, or to some undetected fallacy in a pivot-word. The proposer of the scheme had the responsibility of making every feature and consequence of it clear; he must not, and would not, conceal anything that might militate against its acceptance; he had discussed it fully with his family, and seen in their criticisms and suggestions everything that might be amended. There was, therefore, not a minute lost on defective arrangement or statement.

* * * *

It was astonishing how rarely the councils had to meet, and how brief their meetings were. And this was the reason why I had been so long in discovering any trace of constitution or polity in their midst. One of their favourite maxims was that an organism to be healthy must work without calling attention to itself. And this is truest of all in politics. The government that is never seen or heard or felt, and yet has no secrecy or need of secrecy about its proceedings, is the most efficacious and wholesome. Those loud democracies which occupy most of their time in discussing themselves and their systems are corrupt already or on the road to corruption. And monarchies that have to parade abroad in threats or expeditions are diseased at home and afraid to become too conscious of their disease. "The minimum of government attains the maximum of development," was another of their favourite sayings. To keep this sentiment living, they led their youth back to the study of certain periods of their past that they were ashamed of, called the stagnant ages. Some of them had been republican, others monarchic, some religious or superstitious, others rationalistic or sceptical, some warlike, others peaceful. Their one common characteristic was that the state did everything for the subjects; the island was a nursery, the citizens were infants; no one ever thought of taking the initiative in any scheme; whenever anything was needed, the state had to look after it; the chief duty of a citizen was to talk and hold meetings and criticise; to act was beyond his province; the state had to feed and clothe him at last, and to drive him to his work with the lash. It was the lash that disciplined the army, and urged it on to battle. The state had within it or in its service the few who retained activity or energy; and these few knew how to fill their own coffers better than those of the country. Then came disgrace and disaster. Prosperity and patriotism and courage vanished in decay before the universal corruption on the one hand and the senile helplessness on the other. And all that remained fell an easy prey to the first ambitious marauder who invaded the island.

There grew up in the breasts of the Limanorans an instinctive fear of all encroachments of the state on the duties and functions of the family and the individual; and those who formed the inner council were as deeply imbued with this feeling as the rest of the citizens. One of their chief duties was to draw the line with care between what could best be done by the separate units of the state, and what by the state as a whole. They safeguarded the independence of the individual, and encouraged his initiative in order that every tendency to originality should flourish, and that the capability of meeting emergencies should grow stronger and stronger. Every man on the island knew that he must act for himself in innumerable circumstances without waiting for help or counsel. And the women were trained to be similarly self-reliant. Readiness of resource, confidence, and courage were universal characteristics of the people, and they knew from their study of history, as well as if they had mastered it by experience, that dependence on the action of all and interference on the part of the state would gradually destroy these.

It was, of course, the elders who were most keenly alive to this fact. In their councils they defined with the most exceeding care what might be done by them without injury to the habit of presence of mind and spontaneity of action on the part of the individual citizens. What they had chiefly to look after was the future of the race; and everything done by the citizen or the family that endangered this had to be reviewed and corrected by them. But so powerful a private influence had each elder over every individual of his family that interference in this respect was seldom needed. The ideals held before the race sank into the nature of every citizen and guided him in all his actions, if not now in all his thoughts. The matters that needed most deliberation were the revisal or expansion of those ideals, and the selection of pairs for marriage and parenthood; they knew that a mistake in either of these would lead to incalculable evil, and would necessitate, in retracing the step, long years of thought and labour besides the most drastic remedies. The guidance of the great public institutions needed little counsel or interference, but was almost automatic; everyone concerned knew by instinct what he had to do and had its interests so completely at heart that he required no reminder of the details of his duty. The inspection and review of the various departments were rather the task of the expert families, and chiefly of their elders, than of the elders as a whole.

* * * *

But there was one department for which the inner council or senate was wholly responsible. This was Rimla, or the centre of force. Mechanical power was the one thing, they had all along felt, that must belong to the state and be controlled by the state. All other possessions (wealth, property, reputation) were mere symbols of it. To let it drift into the hands of individuals, who might grasp more than was good for them or even monopolise it, was to endanger the future of the race. Only the wisest and best and the most imbued with Limanoran ideals were ever allowed to control the concentrated force of the island. In fact no one but a member of the inner council could be the master of force, and his term of control was limited to a few hours at a time, for which period he was chosen from day to day from amongst the oldest and most experienced of the nobler-natured. It was the greatest honour the race could bestow. To be trusted by the whole people with the management and distribution of that which was the fulcrum of all progress was to be marked out as one worthy to be divine. When I came to understand this, I saw the meaning of the reverence, almost awe, with which the master of force was pointed out to me on my first visit to Rimla. I had not measured the greatness of his power, or seen that it was far more real and comprehensive than that of any monarch or despot that had ever ruled.

Where would their civilisation or their ideals or great future be without this marvellous concentration of naked energy? What would have become of the race, had a base ambition or an insane caprice entered into the thoughts of anyone of their masters of force while he held the reins of dominion in his hands? It was the duty, therefore, of everyone who was elected to the office, however often he had held it, however noble he had proved himself, however trusted he might be by all, to submit himself the hour before he entered Rimla to the tests of the inner nature and thoughts that the race knew, and this in presence of the oldest of the senate. The workings of his brain and heart were stringently investigated, and after that he was sent to sleep, in order to have his dreams read and interpreted. If any of the tests gave dubious answer, he resigned his office and another was chosen in his place. For almost a generation this had never occurred, yet the precautions were as rigidly enforced as if the tests had often revealed defects. For the master of force held in his hands the key of their civilisation and progress. To the elders all private ends and honours seemed trivial beside the aim of the race, the only divine thing, they thought, that they held in their hearts. To have been able to substitute anything on earth for it even for a moment was to them so absurd and insane as to appear impossible for any Limanoran. All this safeguarding of the probity and the sanity of the masters of force was therefore counted rather as a tribute to the importance of the office than a slur upon the individual.

* * * *

It was not that private motive or stimulus had been annihilated. On the contrary they considered that the chief spur to progress was the struggle of the individual in competition with his fellows. He who could attain most rapidly to the ideal set immediately before the race was a marked and striking personality. To level all means of advance so as to make them the same for all was to destroy this stimulus to development. To be respected and at last reverenced by his neighbours was longed for by every man in the community, and everyone had his own special faculty and means for gaining such respect and reverence. At the great purgation of the island's socialists and thieves, private property had not been abolished, but only disgraded. The socialists had been willing to erase all other methods of civilisation and progress for the sake of the impossible dream, the equalisation of property; the thieves had been willing to do the same for the sake of the swift acquisition of their share of it. They kept up an abnormal and morbid appetite for property which raised it completely out of scale and proportion, compared with the other symbols of power and means of advance. It became a disease that perverted their whole view of life, and nothing wholesome could be done till they were expelled. After their expulsion it was found that property lost its importance, and the word "fortune" ceased to be identified with its acquisition. It fell to its natural and true position in the scale of means of development.

The motive that the socialists had most prominently put forward for their schemes, the benefit of their poverty-stricken and starving brethren, had long become too artificial to hoodwink the wiser patriots. Not since the barbarous stage of their past had bare subsistence been a struggle and aim in the race. They had become too provident to allow population to outrun means or demand. There never had been for centuries anyone who needed his neighbour or the state to aid him with food or clothing or other of the vital necessaries. If there had, he would have been too deeply ashamed of his mismanagement of his life, or his improvidence, to allow anyone to know of it. The arrangements of the state and the carefully proportioned size of the population left no room for him to throw the blame on others. The body of the people laughed at the socialists for the patent absurdity of their pretext, and helped the wise leaders to drive them out. Even if this motive had been the real one, to disorganise the whole political and social system, and to throw overboard the aim of the race for the sake of securing a beggarly pittance for feebler folk who ought not to have been brought into the world, and ought not to be allowed to perpetuate their kind, was a monstrous waste of vital power. There had become deeply implanted in them a racial instinct that no step should ever be taken which could in any way weaken or endanger the sense of individual responsibility. They knew that no amount of self-sacrifice, no kind of guaranty of certain subsistence on the part of the workers in the state, would ever make true and good citizens of those who had lost this.

Even when they had come to have a far more comprehensive and scientific command of the problem of population, and when the communising of property would have led to no evil results, they refused to think of such a measure. Every man was allowed to accumulate as much wealth as he desired. But none had now the ambition to accumulate it. And as soon as communication with the neighbouring islands was cut off, commerce ceased, and with it all opportunity for growing opulent. Everyone had enough for his needs, and these were great in a country so rich in resources and devices and so rapid in its development. The family safeguarded the solvency of every member of it, as it guaranteed his capacity to do competent work for the state and for himself. The state demanded nothing that could be called taxation from the citizens; part of their time, ability, and work was all that it required. But it was one of the methods of showing patriotism to give freely to the state.

It was indeed one of the chief reasons for the retention of private property that it allowed of an easy and ever available means of cultivating benevolence. Personal work was a limited thing, and could be given in aid of others only at fixed places and times and in defined quantities. But if it could be concentrated in private possessions, then there was ready at all times and places and in any quantity the power of helping others. Without it generosity and self-sacrifice would have to mourn their petty limitations. With it benignity was ever in exercise, and remained an active and vital habit in the community. If the state possessed all and demanded all, then the citizens were little better than slaves; their virtues had no freedom, no exercise, and were bound to disappear. To get as much as they could, to sate their appetites as fully as they could, was the only competition amongst neighbours in such a condition of affairs. The blessedness of giving help spontaneously would never be experienced and would vanish from the community, and in its train sympathy, beneficence, humanity.

The competition in Limanora was in giving, not in getting, though getting was one of the conditions and bases of giving. It is true that the advance of the race had almost superseded this palpable method of revealing the bounty of the spirit. In former ages, when hypocrisy was still possible, and language and smiles were too cheap and ready a treasury to be wholly trusted as evidence of kindly intent, private property enabled a man to give a trustworthy guaranty of his generosity; the only other things he could sacrifice, work, liberty, life, were too personal and too limited in opportunity to be symbols of a bounteous heart. Now men and women needed no outer symbol to interpret and pledge their thoughts and feelings. Everyone knew the soul of his neighbour as he knew his own, and hypocrisy was a lost art, having been long ago stripped of its motive.

This singular people retained the institution of private property, fearing the apathy and languor that fall upon the energies of a socialistic people. They had far higher stimuli to competitive vigour in the devotion to progress and to the aim of the race, but they were not so foolish as to abandon the more material stimuli. Everything that would contribute to progress they retained, everything that would tend to quicken the pace. Nor were they yet so far away from the more animal stage of their civilisation as to be wholly rid of the fear of its return. Should it return, the other motives, even that of patriotism, would be so shadowy as to be impotent against the deluge of appetite and indolence if the material competitive principle, the system of private property, had been abolished. To avoid the risk of such a doom as had fallen on Tirralaria, they refused to communise possessions. And a certain sweetness of imagination, of memory, and of harmless romance had hallowed the system in their minds; without it they would have felt a distinct depreciation of life that would not have found compensation in any advantage its abolition might have brought.

The evils that seemed to attach to the system in other times and nations attached to all other symbols of power as well: birth, position, influence, reputation, character, talent, opportunity, luck. All that tended to differentiate one man from another and raise him in the scale of the use of power was open to the same charge as the institution of private property. But early in their reforming career the Limanorans had discovered that the evils that seemed to attach to these features of human life were not inherent in them; they arose from the passions of envy and jealousy. As long as these had possession of men's hearts, the levelling process could never be final.

Communities that made the attempt to plane down human society to a common level, and to equalise all symbols and opportunities of power had an infinite task before them. They really began at the wrong end and struck at the accidental consequences of what they thought an evil, instead of getting to the root and source. The Limanorans had wisely set themselves to bleach their natures of envy and jealousy; and once this was accomplished they found that inequalities amongst them were, instead of being an evil, the greatest good, the keenest stimulus of progress. They smiled at the farce that went on in Tirralaria, a farce that at intervals culminated in tragedy. They saw the inherent futility of all efforts to do away with the occasions of envy and jealousy, instead of eradicating the passions themselves. They compared socialistic and equalising schemes to bailing out the ocean with a sieve.

The disadvantages and abuses of private property and of all inequality in the symbols of power vanish with the opportunity and the desire to flaunt them in the faces of neighbours and rivals, to use them as appeals to envy and jealousy. As a rule it is in small communities and circles and narrow localities, where every man in almost every movement kicks up against some neighbour, that envy and jealousy reach their most virulent development and acquire the greatest refinement in the use of their weapons. But that is in small communities that form parts of wider arenas of ambition, and so learn arrogance and scorn of their surroundings. Where a limited society lives, isolated from alien and ambitious neighbours, a simple and unambitious life, it is generally found to be almost free from the meaner emotions, envy, jealousy, and their counterparts, disdain, pride, and insolence. Amongst them there is little need of coercion or law or government; the more primitive virtues of honesty, truth, loyalty, courage, come to them by nature; the family eradicates or conceals all symptoms of lapse from them, all rebellion against the interests of all. The great drawback to such commonweals is that they are not progressive; they remain centuries in one stage of civilisation, and seem to travellers from larger and advancing nations mere savages buried in filth, and enslaved to the despotism of the seasons. But this people considered such superficially embruted communities nearer to ultimate salvation than the highly refined nations that exhibit a medley of wealth and starvation, militarism and religion. The maximum of government, they held, implied the minimum of progress; for the essentials of spiritual advance are ignored by external administration.

* * * *

A long experience of all types of body politic, and a minute knowledge and study of the history of the world, had made this people antagonistic to every form of great empire. In their own far past they had known the ambition to incorporate other peoples, and extend the bounds of their dominion over the world. But that was in periods that were stagnant or retrogressive in the essentials of a noble civilisation. Great empires are able to concentrate vast resources; but they spend them all on pomp, administration, and war. Wherever the world is parcelled out into huge nations, there is no chance of freeing them from the slavery of omnivorous armaments. Each is a threat to the freedom of the others, and none dares disarm, or spend her wealth on the arts of peace, lest the others should take advantage of her unwarlike attitude. The only progress continues to be in the size and the equipment of the armies, and in the ingenuity of the instruments of destruction. And, should two or three absorb the others, the military vigilance has to be all the greater. Even if the impossible should occur, and one great empire should absorb the world, the internal militarism would be none the less; half of mankind would have to be employed in keeping the other half from rebellion against the central power. Huge empires, instead of being guaranties of peace, are direct incentives to war, or at least to a permanent warlike attitude.

What has most obstructed human progress on its civilised levels is an inevitable tendency at a certain stage to mass into large aggregates; that is, when there has been considerable accumulation of wealth or an exceptional development of commerce, and protection is needed by the wealthy or the merchants. Then the military element gains the mastery of all natural power, and whilst there occurs a rapid evolution of all forms of aggression and defence and of all the virtues connected with them, there is real retrogression; the spirit dwindles as the outer integuments bloom. Militarism only perpetuates itself and protects nothing but its own ambitions. It is in its last analysis a subtle fusion of histrionicism and savagery; it attracts the same tastes as the prize-ring and the theatre. Everything that encourages it or develops it stands in the way of the true advance of the human race.

There is, they held, no hope for mankind in general, unless this stage of imperial ambitions and aggregations can be overleaped. Back must the world recede from vast empires if it would attain to any nobleness of aim, or any development of the higher elements in man. Its sole salvation lies in small communities covering its surface and remaining free from the taint of imperial effort and militarism. Only when the nation has complete command of the numbers within it through the family, that is, when the nation is small, will patriotism become commensurate with humanity, and the true goal of the human race be the aim of the individual.

The family is the natural unit of administration in a community; and, as long as the heads form the common council that watches the interests and aim of all, it can never come into conflict with national unity and progress. The house and its goods belonged to the household in Limanora; and, although the members of it had equal rights to the livelihood that was counted fullest and best by the community, the individual, if mature, had freedom of action that would surprise a Western freeman; he was the equal of all members of the state; within the aim of the race and the path of its progress he had complete personal initiative; his destiny, it is true, had been shaped for him during his pupillage, but the fulfilment of it was his own; his aims and desires had been implanted and developed and pruned whilst he was passing through childhood and youth, so that he would not in full manhood spontaneously change them, but when he became an independent citizen his methods of fulfilling these were all his own. He had to contribute to the family treasury what was needed to keep it level with Limanoran affluence, and he was generally eager to give more; but all the rest was at his own disposal. The family had many buildings in common; but each full-grown member, whether male or female, had a separate house to retire to. Originality in the family, one of the chief methods in the race for encouraging progress, could never be attained without cultivating originality in the individual. It had a track laid out for it through the future, carefully related to the march of the nation; but it might adopt what means it liked to make that track sure, and it might explore on all sides of it for new ideas and methods and resources. It was the same with the individual within it; he was encouraged to find his own means, and to use his imagination and his other faculties fully and independently, provided he kept his eye on the goal of the family, which was involved in the goal of the race.

All the families were equal in their relations to the state, whatever their occupation or wealth or origin might be. This prevented the family from passing into the rigidity of the caste. All work was alike honoured, and personal worth was the test of the man and of the respect paid him, irrespective of external symbols and representatives of power. And to prevent the supersession of this by any other principle, all the physical forms of toil that might at one time or other be considered offensive, were gathered into the hands of the state, and all men and women had to take their share of them. They were the duties connected with the various public institutions, and especially with the centre of force. It was recognised as a good thing that every man and woman should have physical exercise every day in order to keep the basis of the spirit in the best possible condition, by working off the débris of the various organs and functions of the system. This fitted in with the principle that all force should concentrate in the hands of the government. The most severe physical toil was certain to be that which collected, divided, and adapted the vast accumulation of energy in Rimla. The duties in the centre of force were therefore portioned out day by day and week by week; and every man and woman of the community had to spend a certain portion of time each day in this vast forge of energy. But the lighter work was given to the less muscular, and the youthful had to bear the chief burden; whilst the older, as their share, were occupied chiefly in superintending it. Besides this, every citizen had to take daily part in the work of some one of the public institutions that were not assigned to special families, or in the mechanical and unskilled toil of one of those that were under the care of special families. Thus two or three hours of every citizen's twenty-four were impounded by the state, much to his bodily and spiritual advantage.

The only contribution in money or kind that the state made compulsory was that which each family exchequer gave for the support of the medical, architectural, and other public professional families. No valid system could have estimated the value of their services either to the state or to the individual; and it was considered impracticable to valuate the benefits received by each family from their work. An amount was fixed, which each had to contribute to every family that had the care of a public institution, or the performance of a public duty. But over and above this amount the voluntary gifts to them were very large. The result was that the treasuries of public and professional families were oftenest the fullest; and they were as ready and as able to give as any. If there was any rivalry amongst the families and individuals in Limanora, it was in the delight of giving.

CHAPTER X

THE MANORA AND THE IMANORA

WHAT would have been considered taxes in another state were looked on by the people of this land as voluntary contributions. There had been no formal resolution or written law fixing necessary imposts, but they came rather from the heart of the people, and expressed themselves in what would have been called in other nations public opinion. It was opinion which needed no verbal communication and might be called rather the public magnetism of the race, that unified its customs and feelings, and made a body of written law superfluous.

One feature of their civilisation that puzzled me for many years was the seeming immobility of their public relationships. When a man or woman got into a certain family with its professional duties and prospects, there was no means, it seemed to me, of changing. Once in a certain groove, a Limanoran was in it forever. His destiny was irrevocable. It is true that the elders took every precaution to choose his parents and ancestry for such a goal, and to mould his tissues and educate his faculties to it. Yet some inspiration might reveal to him a vista into a future better suited to his powers than that which had been fixed for him. It is true that this feature gave great stability and strength to the state. But a people that believed so firmly in liberty, originality, and progress should surely have adopted some more plastic system for their permanent relationships, some status less rigid and immutable for the individual members. It seemed to me more like the iron system of caste than the flexibility of an advancing civilisation.

As usual I was mistaken in my criticism. I had not looked deeply enough, or observed long enough to know the marvellous fabric of their polity, a full knowledge of which meant an experience of several centuries. The immutability was only in appearance and not in reality.

A few years after I had been admitted to some of the privileges of mature citizenship, I began to feel that we were approaching an exceptional time. There was evident a bustle of preparation, a rare quickening of the pace of all work, and an expectancy that pointed to some unusual event. The flight-exercises and the leisure-time were somewhat curtailed, and as much work was put into four weeks as was commonly put into five. Before the year was half over, I began to understand what it meant. The word Manora occurred too often on the lips and in the minds of my neighbours and friends to escape my observation and on inquiry I found it meant the decennial review. Every ten years, one quarter of the year was devoted to a census of the civilisation of the period.

With all the other newly matured citizens, I had to be instructed in the part I was to take in this census. Each day for months I had to devote some hours to tracing out the progress I had made both in character and in works, and in putting it into graphic and easily observed form. I was taught to draw up comparative statistics of the stages I had passed through from year to year for the decennial period, though they considered this a poor and misleading mode of reviewing the past. It was the mere skeleton of the census.

I was supplied from the valley of memory with irelium-strips, whereon had been recorded automatically without my knowledge my thoughts and feelings and words in the various important scenes in which I had taken part. How surprised was I often to observe the mistakes my memory had fallen into! As a witness of some act I had seen, or some discussion I had heard, I would have sworn confidently to the opposite of the truth. As to my own deeds and words and even thoughts and feelings, I was ashamed to see how completely my subsequent life had distorted the record of them; the likeness was often unrecognisable. And I knew well which was wrong; for the machine-reporters were infallible as far as their report went. After my perusal of these automatic records of my life I came to the conclusion that common history must be a tissue of fiction and error wherever it has had to depend on the senses and memory of men for its details. I grew less and less inclined to add anything from memory to my decennial biography, which I drew from these machine-reports. It was as refreshing to study them as if I had been examining pictures and memorials of another's life. By the time I had done with them, I seemed to know something real of my past; and side by side I was able to place my review of what I had become, and the account of my various stages of growth during this period, with the definiteness and accuracy of one who was analysing scientifically half a dozen different evolutionary specimens of a species. My personality stood out at each different point of its growth as clearly as if it had been that of another man laid under the microscope and in these records I lived my life over again.

But I was still further aided in these researches into my development by the accounts of the weekly inspection of my tissues and faculties kept by the medical families. These were not merely statistical and verbal, but pictorial. The appearance and electric state of every part of my system had been made to impress themselves indelibly in picture-records; and these were now submitted to me for comparison. From the different records set side by side with the electrographs and radiographs of all my animal economy, I was taught how to produce an evolutionary picture of my faculties and organs and tissues.

This was one of the most striking advances in their art. They could combine the pictorial representations of various stages in the life of a growing being in such a way that, when placed in one of their lightning-swift representers, the growth would flash before one's senses as a continuity. A child would grow as by magic into a matured man or woman as we gazed. A seed would grow into a great tree in the space of a few minutes. The brain or heart or lungs of a Limanoran would pass like a flash through the stages of development that had taken generations to achieve. For spectacular study of the history of any living thing nothing could surpass the imataran, or focusser of history, as the new instrument was called.

From the archives of the medical family I was able to make such a series of pictures of my whole constitution and system as revealed the growth of every faculty and organ and tissue. The rapidity of my development astounded me as I looked over these graphic records of my past. It was like a full-grown man inspecting the photographs and annals of his infancy and childhood. I could not have believed the story of it, had it not been engraved so indubitably on these irelium-strips by the machine-reporters. My own memory had become so foreshortened by the consciousness of my present, and by the disproportionate importance of recent events and conditions that I could have no more implicit trust in its representations of the past. But, when I placed the various series of evolutionary pictures in the imataran, the effect was so magical that I was half-inclined to believe in preference my backward-looking faculty again. In the twinkling of an eye the transparent reflection of myself had grown its ten years' growth, and I had developed out of an alien into something not unlike a Limanoran.

All that I had done in the period, or rather all that I had done productively, I had similarly to picturise in series, so that every feature that had been in any way developed might reveal itself, and everything that showed stagnation or retrogression might be observed without trouble.

My proparents and the elders of the family superintended and tested my review of my past, and taught me to be unbending in criticism of myself. No feature that seemed to count against my advance was I to shrink from representing in all its nakedness, nor was I through false modesty to depreciate whatsoever stood to my credit. I scarcely needed the precautions; for I had learned during my sojourn amongst this rigidly sincere and ingenuous people to respect the naked truth above all things. Indeed I had come to feel that it was useless to act otherwise than as if my whole system were open to the gaze of my neighbours.

Every mature member of the community had this drastic valuation of his work and strict criticism of himself to make and all were occupied for three months in reducing the annals of their past ten years to focus. For the young and those still under tutelage the proparents and guardians were responsible, and they picturised for the imataran the decennial life of their pupils as well as of themselves.

But over and above this personal work, the elders had to review the growth of the families, institutions, sciences, and arts of which they had the guidance. This they knew well how to do from long practice, and had carefully prepared the records of each separate year of the decennium, and the pictures of the new features and new growths in the departments they superintended. During these three months all they had to do was to focus the growth of the years and arrange the various records in series in such a way as to reveal the development.

When all was ready, each family gathered in its public spectacular hall and viewed the growth of every member of it in the shadows thrown by the imataran. I thought at first that the effect would be too monotonous to be interesting. But, as the spectacle of the Leomo proceeded, it proved to be a marvellous revelation of the vast variety of types in one family, and of the amount of growth that had gone on in the tissues and faculties of every member in different directions.

The growth of the family as a whole was taken first—its power of coping with new problems and of suggesting difficulties to come, its additions to the treasury of force and to the civilisation of the race, its attitude toward the aim of the nation, its pace on the forward march, its comprehension of the Limanoran ethics and of the general problems of the race, its command over its individual members, and its relationships to the other families and to the state as a whole. The decennial development of the Leomo was graphically focussed in pictures that told their story in a flash even to the least mature.

Massed thus, the advance was felt by all to be surprising, for each had been watching throughout the decennium his own special work or set of faculties, and had been unable to abstract himself sufficiently from his own sphere to gain a just view of the whole family progress. As we saw the science and the art develop before our eyes, the moment's glance intensified the ten years' work into a marvel. From a hundred different points of view we watched the advance of the Leomo, and we felt proud that we belonged to such a family; we knew that taken as a whole it had not been wanting in its duty to the race and the aim of the race. A magnetic thrill went through us, especially when there unrolled before us the living picture of the preceding decennium; the contrast between the two in pace of development was striking. Here and there of course we recognised flaws in the work accomplished during our recent period, when seen against the design of the whole. But we gathered from the spectacle fresh hope and energy for the future, and renewed determination to increase the pace still more during the next period.

We shrank a little perhaps from the next stage of the spectacle, for it meant the decennial confession of every one of us all. The family as a whole acted the priest, and before it we each laid the story of our failures and successes, our deeds of virtue and our sins. The ordeal was less trying than I had anticipated, for the critic was lenient and sympathetic. If the lapse was slight, the source of it was tenderly pointed out by the elders and the remedy indicated; and the stronger members formed resolves to lend their strength to the lapser to master his weakness; everything that was possible, he felt sure, would be done to help the laggard faculty or tissue to recoup its powers and bring itself even with the march of the family. If the lapse was great, the case was sympathetically placed before the council of elders, which investigated the question whether it was due to their mistaken choice of a career for the youth (it was generally a youth that failed strikingly), or whether it had come from some changed faculty or tissue in him; if it were the former, he was aided in deciding what change in his career would be best for him; if the latter, he was dealt with as an invalid, and in the hospital for spiritual diseases the curative powers of the nation were applied to his case. Sometimes his disease originated in atavism, and then the most drastic remedies, both physical and spiritual, were brought to bear; sometimes it was found to come from a new microscopic parasite that had floated from some far atmosphere into the Limanoran arena; and then all the wisdom and science of the race had to be brought into requisition to investigate the conditions of the new foe and the possible means of driving it out.

This indeed was the time for anyone who had made a mistake to retrace his steps. Here it was that the seeming rigidity of the system was tempered and rendered flexible and plastic as nature herself. Ten years was but a point in the continuity of the force in a man, in the great expansion of Limanoran life. But it was enough to make sure that a mistake in the choice of a career was real, not merely apparent, and that the longing for another was not a mere caprice. A shorter period would not have been test enough; and the review of all careers prevented undue proportion being given to any individual failure or mistake. It was not infrequent for youths who thought that they had mistaken their career, to change their minds at the Manora, and acknowledge that, all things considered, the wisest course had been chosen for them; they came to see that their work was not so defective as they had imagined, and that they had contributed their due quota to the advance of the family and the race; against the background of the whole science or art in which they toiled, they recovered tone and hope, and the pride they felt in the progress of all stirred them to new exertions in their own special work. It was as much the aim of the elders in these Manoras to give new enthusiasm in the careers that had been chosen as to revise the scheme of careers. The primary aim was to remove the sense of bondage that might grow up in the breasts of any from the feeling of inevitableness and unchangeableness in the development of their lives. It was rare indeed that a real failure ever occurred. But none the less a sense of failure might seize upon a timid or self-depreciative mind, and then the knowledge that there could be no turning back would send it rankling home into the soul. Circumscription to a course, if irrevocable, is none the less incarceration that it is a course selected by ourselves. A Limanoran never felt enslaved to his career. He knew he had made his choice, and that he might make it again if he showed sufficient reason. The result of this atmosphere of complete freedom was that not once in a generation was any career, once deliberately selected, changed. The elders were fully justified in the elaborate choice of ancestry and parents, and in the still more elaborate pains taken in the choice of surroundings and in training. Misgivings and hesitations all disappeared in the full light of the decennial review.

It was marvellous how the magnetic sympathy of the family, as the spectacular confessional spread life after life before the gaze of all, eradicated timidities, and strengthened each member in the path he had chosen. Instead of having his little defects emphasised or exaggerated, all the merits of his work were brought out. I took new courage and hope, as I felt the air of impartial esteem over the excellencies of each member's development and of sympathetic sorrow and condolence over any evidence of failure or retrogression. Not a sign was there of censorious or captious criticism. Nor was there anything of that barter of laudation and panegyric which makes mutual-admiration societies so unwholesome in their effects. All was subdued, gentle, reasonable, wise, and sympathetic, and the most healthful and invigorating of all tonics to everyone. From what I had looked forward to as an ordeal I came away refreshed and strong, determined to amend everything that could be deemed faulty in my life, and to quicken my pace in marching towards the goal of the race.

The national review of every family's progress was somewhat similar, except that the larger arena and the greater volume of magnetism in the audience stirred a deeper thrill in the natures of the individual members. It was held in Loomiefa, and it took many days to view the whole spectacle of the nation's decennial work. Nothing have I ever seen so varied, disciplinal, and impressive. It was as if ten thousand years of the whole world's progress had been focussed in this valley. Science after science, art after art, graphically displayed all that it had achieved during the period. To me it seemed a universal education; and it strained all my faculties to follow the marvellous array of inventions and discoveries, whilst my neighbours and comrades drank the whole spectacle in with an ease that in other circumstances would have made me envious. It was not the fault of the masters and makers of the display that I followed it with difficulty, for they had made every feature clear even to the least mature. What puzzled me was the logical sequence or interdependence of the various parts of the spectacle. Everything had been worked out so as to reveal its relationship to the whole system and to the aim of the race, and to comprehend it tested all my powers. I felt as if I had to study a great encyclopædia in a few days, or rather its pictorial representation of every feature of the most advanced and intricate civilisation. But even this analogy is inadequate, for the phases of the many-sided progress were not mechanically arranged, but grew out of the central system by a natural and rational magic. The work of every family revealed its central principles and their connection with the advance of the race. It looked as if some master-mind had sat through the years, and watching the nation's work as it was being accomplished, kept it all in system. We felt that there was one design in the progress of the whole period, and that any feature that stood out in independence marred the symmetry, and needed correction.

I remembered the waste of energy that took place in all intellectual spheres in Europe, and felt ashamed of the contrast. I could have told this people of the futile skirmishings and endless controversies of the men of science and learning, of their duplications of each other's work with the consequent clutchings after fame, of their assumptions and merely verbal distinctions, of their thickets of abstruse definitions and ambiguities, of their everlasting substitutions of theory for fact. I never felt so conscious of the shortcomings of the civilisation which had nurtured me as during the array of Limanoran decennial progress in sciences and arts.

After the spectacle was over, we returned to our usual employments. But I observed that there were now more frequent meetings of the elders for several months, and at last we had as the result of their discussion of the review and its aspects a considerable rearrangement of our work, and of our positions in the family and in the state. Most proceeded on the path they had been taking during the previous period. But many found themselves now at work more congenial to their temperaments and destinies, and were able to put into it their whole energy rid of the friction that the artificial application of will had meant. The changes occurred almost naturally and spontaneously; each elder returned to his family from the final meeting of the senate over the Manora, and it was known without effort or command or waste of time who had to modify his position and work, and how the modification was to be accomplished.

The impetus given to the civilisation by this loosening of any bonds which had been begun to be felt sent it on with exhilaration and vigour for years. There was an air of buoyant freedom and alacrity, even of mirth amongst the younger, as they spent their best skill and capacity upon the work they had in hand. The pace perceptibly quickened, and at times the nation seemed to advance with the volume and swiftness of a torrent. Discovery and invention became fuller as well as more minute, and the outlook began to take in regions of which they had not thought before.

I soon came to know that there was a more comprehensive and far-reaching evaluation of the resources, the faculty, and the personnel of the race ahead of us. Every tenth decennium there occurred the event of the century, the Imanora or prospicient review. Ten years made too short a period to give a bird's-eye view of the future as contrasted with the past. Even a century was short enough for the perspective of past and future progress; but it was considered wise to make the period fixed and of regular recurrence, and ten decenniums formed a space symmetrical with the shorter Manora. The Imanora was thus a centennial review. Tendencies that might be ambiguous in their character under a decennial criticism would proclaim themselves evil or good in so long a stretch as a hundred years. Faculties that would still be but in embryo after a course of ten years would be in full maturity when a century had passed. Young men and women, who might still hesitate within a decade as to whether they had chosen their best career, would have found by the Imanora what was their true bent beyond the possibility of mistake.

But it was not meant merely as a review of the past and a rearrangement of positions, as the Manora was above all things. It was rather a revision of aims and destinies, a futuritive evaluation of the powers of the race. Not merely the elders but the whole people were led up to a mount of vision whence they could see their future for hundreds of years spread out before them, bounded by the lines their past had drawn. There they could view in picture the solutions of the problems they had been working at and the final outcome of the lines of development they had been following. They had to decide there and then how far these agreed with the ultimate aim and destiny of the race, and how far they had better modify them, or modify the general aim. Then they had to choose whether their path should turn to the right or left, or should continue onwards as it had continued for a century. The spectacle of their future spread out in living picture and symbol must have been a deeply impressive sight. Every family had prepared a series of tableaux of their possible destinies and the possible developments of their sciences and arts, of the problems they would have to solve, and of their possible solutions, and these were passed in detail before the whole people for criticism and appreciation. It was as if a nation were led to the cave of some great and true prophet, and were shown all that lay before it, whatsoever path it should choose. The Limanorans had before them the choice of a destiny for a hundred years. It was the care of the elders that no ambiguity or disproportion should be admitted into the map of the possible routes that they might take through the future, and that there should be no obscurity in the relationships of these to the ultimate goal.

During the last decade of the century the Loomiamo and the Fraloomi-amo were the busiest of all the families in the island. Their exceptional development of imagination made them essential to the preparation of every map of the future. They seemed to be able to see where others found only night and darkness. Each science and art often awoke to perceive its way barred by some hill of difficulty, round or over which they could discover no way; then the members of the Loomiamo who had made special study of its path were called in to point out the possible tracks that might lead past the obstacle. Or again a family would find the way of its science or art untraceable; they would grope blindly about for it and yet see no farther than the facts and methods immediately before them. Here the help of the Fraloomiamo was indispensable; a thousand different way-marks would soon be apparent, and the route of future development would grow plain.

The pioneering families were the heroes of the Imanora, although most of the hard work belonged to those who watched over the individual sciences and arts. Nothing could be done without them, and the exhilaration of trust in them and need of their services gave extraordinary vigour to their special faculty. The close of a century was one of the great autumns of their literature; their harvests at that era were marked by fulness and wealth, and the pace of their work gave it exceptional fervour and glow. In the West we should have called the passionate ardour with which they threw off scheme after scheme, inspiration of the highest order. But they knew the working of their faculty as well as any of the inventors knew the intricacies of their machines. There was nothing mysterious about it. Their clear knowledge of its constitution and of the conditions that favoured its growth made it easy for them to predict when its pace and volume would be torrential, and every preparation was made by the pioneering families to meet the exceptional drain on their energies at the close of every century.

Loomiefa was then the scene of the most striking prefigurant displays that the human mind could conceive. The resources of Limanoran skill and ingenuity were brought to bear on it, and nothing was left undone to impress the event upon the imaginations and memories of the younger, for the elders expected that it would thus mould the natures of the coming generation through the minds of the prospective parents. The world as it might be, if certain lines of development were followed, was pictured in the most impressive way possible; and to this people, it seemed to me, everything was possible. The Imanora had the sublimity and transcendent consecration of a great religious departure, whose significance was fully foreseen.

CHAPTER XI

ETHICS

I AFTERWARDS found that Imanora necessarily differed from Imanora as widely as age from age or man from man, it being as it was the universal outlook of so progressive a people. What one centennial mount of vision foresaw as a possibility the next viewed as an accomplished fact. What one century peered into the darkness to descry, another brought into the daylight of achievement, and a third antiquated.

But there were other and wider differences than this I have stated. Though all phases of the civilisation were reviewed in relation to the future, generally one phase took prominence and gave character to each Imanora. In the earlier periods, after the purgations, the physiological and biological sciences and arts predominated; for the elders were most anxious then to bring the physical basis of their life up to the level of quickening progress. Then came the periods specially devoted to advance in chemistry and physics and the other sciences and arts that gave them new power over the outside world. One century was the great astronomical period, when the imagination of the race stretched out with yearning to other stars. Another was the great inventive era, when it seemed as easy as a dream to make new machines which should open out wide prospects of additional conquest over nature and humanity.

In the more recent centuries ethics had again come to the front, new points of view having been shown by the great discoveries and inventions of many centuries. The first Imanora after the series of purgations was complete had been predominantly ethical. The race had bent its attention so exclusively upon the crimes and vices which had hindered their advance for ages, that they could think of almost no other development than the ethical. The elders had been investigating for years little else than the defects in the moral nature, their bases in the physical system, and the methods of remedying them. They had come to the conclusion after all their researches that nothing could be done for the cure of the minor vices till the most vicious and defective characters had been cleared out. A systematic purification of the commonweal must precede attempts at moral reform. Most of the purgations were managed by wise and cautious diplomacy; the bait of more than their share of the wealth of the island in portable form, and the chance of a new country in which to indulge their vice to license, induced them to ship off to a distance. Only a few needed forcible measures to make them remove. The lying and hypocritical, the licentious, the envious and jealous, the boastful and the epicurean, the religiously intolerant and superstitious, readily seized the opportunity of seeking a country where they might make their own laws and shape their customs to suit their special weakness. The warlike and murderous and the thievish and socialistic thought they could force a still better bargain; they had strong inner doubts whether they would be likely to have as fine an arena for their talents in a new country, and whether they would make the best companions for one another. An increase of the inducement had little effect on them; they felt that their special vices would lose half their attraction when removed from the presence of the contrasted and shrinking virtues. Much of the pleasure of a murder or a theft lay in the necessity for its concealment, and the ingenuity required to evade punishment. The occupations ceased to be fine arts as soon as they became the occupations of the whole community. To these criminal sections of the race force had to be applied before they left the island; it had to be a policy of deportation.

It was little wonder that for a century after absorption in such work the civilisation of Limanora was essentially ethical. To rid themselves of every trace of the detestable vices of which they had just seen the worst specimens deported over the horizon, became the one aim and ideal of the now-expurgated people. Development seemed nothing more than greater ease and habitualness in the virtues. To be purer, truer, more tolerant, more generous, more gentle and modest and loving, was their one idea of progress. The outlook from the first Imanora was towards an ideal of such benignity and kindliness as would make all personal relations easy and happy beyond the conception of other nations.

The first few decades of the next century gave them exhilaration in the pursuit of this aim. They took the greatest delight in eradicating the seedling ferocities of their savage past. Spite, rancour, disdain, pitilessness, vanity, surliness, ingratitude, partiality, want of candour, acerbity, meanness, and all uncharitableness were rigorously checked, and every thought or energy that might, when abused, tend in these directions was finally mastered. It was a delight to help one another in the crusade against these petty defects. Nothing seemed so noble or progressive as to spend every leisure moment on cultivating the generous attitude towards one another.

But they soon saw the limits of such a progress. The virtues became easy and common to all and it grew difficult to find new ethical worlds to conquer. Most of them indulged too eagerly in introspection and some turned morbidly self-critical, finding defects where there were none. Imagination became a factory of petty faults and vices. The result was new and real faults, which threatened to maim their civilisation and bar their further progress.

They were painfully self-conscious, fearing lest the eyes of a neighbour or comrade should discover in them germs of moral disease which had escaped their own microscopic criticism. They shrank from beginning any enterprise; they feared to come to decisions or make resolves, lest they should be wrong. They tolerated and even encouraged faults and defects in their friends which they would have drastically eradicated from their own natures; they nursed in pity and generosity weak characters and diseased systems into length of life, and shrank from forbidding them parenthood and posterity. They strained at gnats and swallowed camels and indulged in constant casuistry. In short, the whole race fell into a chronic spiritual invalidism and many of them were afflicted with moral hypochondria. They felt the pulses of their souls daily and hourly, and were ever haunted with the fear of the old vices returning on them, so losing their masculine grit and self-command. Finally they threatened to become a race of sinewless effeminates with nothing but spiritual collapse and palsy before them.

It was clear that this microscopic introspection and moral unrest must cease, if there was to be any real advance. They had already recognised that ethics developed by stages, and that any attempt on the part of a race to force it beyond the intellectual point of view which they had reached only ended in temporary failure and retrogression. No new moral outlook can be attained unless reason has ascended a higher mount of vision. Revelation can never come without new achievement. A fixed quantity of ethical knowledge in a nation is moral death, and to systematise ethical maxims into an absolute code for all time is to enslave the reason of the world. For what is the almost unattainable ideal of one stage of racial development is the antiquated truism of a later stage. Savage man compares ill in polity and moral code with the republics of the bee and the ant, just as his engineering and architectural skill are infantile beside those of the beaver. How unprotective and even cruel he is to his aged and women and children, compared with many animals! How unadvanced even the most civilised are in truth and loyalty compared with the dog! How weak in the reasoning that is based on the reports of the senses are men in general compared with the wild animals! There is evidently an infinite variety of stages in the ethical and intellectual development and vision of man, as there is in those of the animals. The most advanced human beings, just like the least advanced, are, in some points, lower than the beasts. But man can, if he will, have mastery of his circumstances and conditions, inasmuch as he can examine himself by reflection, and tends to examine himself through self-consciousness. The power and tendency, however, are only fitfully taken advantage of, and it is therefore at long intervals that even the best races accelerate the pace of their progress beyond that which nature herself indicates.

The elders, and through them the people, were persuaded that this absorbing pursuit of ethical improvement must be abandoned. The development of the physical system was the first distraction that they thought of; and their bodies grew in muscular power, in grace of form, and in litheness of movement. It was during this athletic period that flight through the air was achieved; then, too, physiology and medicine grew into real sciences and began to direct the evolution of physical man, and the struggle against the hosts of microscopic parasites that over-populate the elements and have to seek pastures in the human body. It was in this era, too, that they mastered the secret of prolonging life and began the series of experiments in food and other forms of sustenance, and in heredity, which ended in giving them centuries instead of decades to live.

It soon came to be noticed, however, that a new but analogous hypochondria began to seize even the youthful athletes of the race. There was too much direct attention paid to the state and development of the body to be wholesome. Athletic egotism became rampant, and as a result of it a scorn of intellectual pursuits. It was as truly a diseased state of the human system as the moral invalidism with which they had been afflicted in the previous era. Thews and sinews were measured and examined with scientific minuteness. Muscular development was appraised and applauded as moral qualities had formerly been. The spirit began to be impoverished; the brain decreased in weight and fineness of convolution. Athletic introspection was coming to be as painful and masterful a disease as moral introspection had been. Diet and exercise became the absorbing topics of daily conversation and nothing was invented but machines for training the body. Most palpable of all the consequences was the growth of arrogant gait and rough manners, and this was the first symptom to call attention to the new malady. It became clear to the elders that the worst form of atavism, return to the savagery that is just above animalism, was about to reappear, and with it would come weakened heart and lungs and disordered digestion; for the new training overstrained all the organs, and threw them into disrepair.

The conclusions drawn from these two experiences were that variety of occupation was one of the first essentials of mental and bodily health, and that absorption in the improvement of any part or section of the human system induced disease both of mind and body; morality and health are better cultivated as indirect aims of individual existence; they defeat their own ends when they become egoistic or introspective. In order to remedy the evils which were threatening the life of the state, its framework was completely reformed. To every family and individual was assigned an external work that would draw the thoughts away from self for the greater part of the twenty-four hours; every mature member of the community was expected to achieve something unconnected with himself every day. Exercise merely for amusement was cut down to a minimum, and in order to keep the body in full vigour, the centre of force was organised, where every man and woman had to do so much useful physical work in the round of the clock. The care of the health, both mental and bodily, was handed over to the medical elders, who were, first of all, the healthiest and healthiest-minded of the older men of the nation. Watching for symptoms of disease in one's system, whether moral or corporeal, fell into oblivion, and the great era of external achievement began. Specialisation of work was its chief principle and the source of its success, but no one was allowed to fall into excessive specialism, such as would atrophy all but one set of faculties and energies. No part of the body or mind was left without daily or weekly exercise. The elders mapped out the various types of intellectual and physical work from which a man or woman might select to fill leisure time. Everyone had a large choice within a limited number of kinds of work, generally kinds of work which were dissimilar to his special employment. If it were left to a man to choose his own type of distractions, he might select that which would feed high the sides of his nature he most used, and atrophy those that most needed development; for ease of application is an important factor in his choice of exercise and amusement, and might become too dominant.

* * * *

It was not in order to assimilate the bases of the natures of the community that this limitation of leisure employments was adopted. On the contrary, one of the subordinate aims of the elders was to introduce as great a variety as possible into the talents, faculties, and tendencies of the race. Equality, and still more similarity, of members of a community, they well knew from the laws of nature meant stagnation if not complete national death. Throughout the cosmos it was the unequal degree to which various bodies and existences shared in different types of energy that produced the unstable equilibrium we call life. The disparate masses of the planets induced those currents of influence we call gravitation, one of the greatest sources of power in our world. The differences in temperature between the sun and the planets make it of such vast importance as a source of heat and energy to them, and it is the difference of two bodies as to electric state that induces currents of electricity between them. As soon as there is equilibrium of all the atoms or bodies or existences within a certain sphere of influence there ceases to be movement in it and death supervenes; and if all bodies and existences in the cosmos had an equal and similar share of all its elements and forces, it would be dead. The Deity himself, the sum and source of all life, must, as an eternal existence, have unending variety.

The law of the universe is the law of the political and moral world. There can be no life where there is complete stable equilibrium, that is, where every member of a community is exactly similar to every other member in privileges. Currents of influence cease. Impetus and motive vanish. Desire and yearning and love disappear with passion and ambition. The socialistic ideal is social and political death.

The everlasting flow of influence or power from point to point is the essential condition of vigorous existence in a community or race, therefore one of the chief subsidiary aims of the directors of Limanora was the creation of variety and inequality of nature and position. This made them adopt the family as the unit in the state, for in the family there would be shelter for any new individual talent, and heredity would cherish and increase it as it handed it on. In the Western states the influence of the family over its children ceases not long after boyhood or girlhood, and the world soon puts them into the same moulds as its favourite men and women; individuality and originality in most are planed down by the recognised conventions. A longer continuance of family life and influence would secure and strengthen any new variations in a talent or tendency, till the character was strong enough to stand by them as its own and defend them against the criticism of aliens and strangers. Diversity in unity was the ideal of family life in Limanora. The elders of a family watched with eagerness for any modification of the special faculties or powers, and nursed it with the most anxious care, if they decided that it would assist the advance of the race, and the medical elders were ever suggesting the proper cross for producing a new variety of the old talents. Indeed, one of the most responsible duties of the council of elders was to decide as to the matings and parenthoods of the community; in this lay, they felt, the guidance of their destiny, the real germ of the future. Thus and thus alone were they able to keep up that divergence of new species which would ensure an ever-quickening flow of life in the race.

They had cut off by their policy of complete isolation most of the stimulus that comes from alien rivalry. Such rivalry, they thought, would be worse than none; for it would at last drive them to adopt the means and weapons of their rivals, which they considered wholly retrograde and evil. It would be not unlike a competition between man and the wild beasts. Any kind of communication with those who were below them in civilisation and deliberately unprogressive, was certain to taint and drag down, and the strong consciousness of this fact checked the natural tendency of such benignity as theirs towards missionaryism.

At the same time they knew well that no people would ever advance without competition and the struggle that ensues on competition. They greatly encouraged variation and inequality within their state, but were certain that this was not enough. There must be the knowledge, if not the immediate presence, of another type of being, similar to their own yet higher in some features, in order to stimulate advance. To get this was the object of their system of couriers into space, both mechanic and human. They were never weary of gathering in all possible indications of higher intelligences in extra-terrestrial elements and regions. For a long period they had been satisfied with the reports of their idrovamolans, and other recorders of events which occurred on the earth, out of reach of their unaided senses. But it gradually pressed itself home upon them that the comedy of terrestrial existence gave no stimulus to progress; it stirred their laughter, or scorn, or indignation, or disgust too often to edify. Rare, indeed, was it to witness a deed or phase of civilisation that gave them a new model, or inspired them to higher life. It was, as a rule, degrading to watch beings in their own shape waste their noble faculties on the cruelties of war, the meannesses of commerce and industrial-ism, the pettinesses of social intercourse, and the gross deceits and pretences of politics, diplomacy, and public life.

Year by year the racial energy was drawn off from the spectacle of ter-restrial history. It grew less and less attractive, and the elders came to the de-cision that it had almost better pass unnoticed by all but the most mature and experienced. Thus it became the more necessary to open up other spheres of stimulus and inspiration. The thoughts of the race gravitated, first to other stars, then to the exuberant life they found in interstellar space. For a time they thought that only in other worlds could be found intelligences like their own to stimulate them by their competition; and their intellectual energy was set upon opening up intercourse with the inhabitants of these. The imagina-tive families published book after book on the possibilities and means of stellar intercommunication, and afterwards of stellar migration. Astronomy and its subsidiary and allied sciences and arts for several centuries outpaced all others in development. The world began to seem narrow and prison-like, so eager was Limanoran thought after stellar flight. All the conditions of voyaging through space were investigated, all available means experimented on, all the possible routes and their laws discovered. It seemed as if within a few centuries the round of the earth would be spurned, and the nearest star colonised by terrestrial beings.

The discovery of the varied life inhabiting the ether gave pause to all such speculations and schemes. It was manifestly possible to find stimulus from intelligences nearer than the other planets. Infinite space, instead of being a desert strewn with the wrecks or embryos of stars, is as full of life, and of the elements and nuclei of life, as any world which spins through it. They had ever counted it as unlikely that the life and the life-energy of the cosmos should be confined to the star-dust strewn over it, or that its vast in-terstellar spaces should be given up to nothing but the passage of rays from star to star, cold and inhospitable to every form of existence. They felt it to be more in accordance with the lavishness of nature that these spaces should be life-crammed instead of life-proof. Why should life be unable to adapt itself to the conditions of space, when it has been found to adapt itself to the bewildering variety of conditions existing on the surface of any one world at different stages of its development, and even to the infinite variety of conditions that govern the countless stars?

On the first discovery of life beyond the atmosphere they were led by the medical investigators to think that it was merely embryonic, waiting to colonise the worlds that pushed through it. But recent reports and researches showed that the existences of interstellar space were far beyond the rudimental stage. Beings as intricately organised as themselves left impressions on their supra-aerial lavolans. They grew more and more convinced that the senses which had evolved in them, amid the gross atmosphere of the earth and with the gross feeding that alone would suit terrene constitutions, were fit to detect no other creatures than those developed under similar terrestrial conditions. Their more recent and more refined developments of sensuous perception, and still more their latest mechanical inventions, had brought them within range of an infinity they had not dreamt of. Daily came in from above the atmosphere reports that confirmed their old belief in the vast and varied population of space. Beings, so constituted as never to impress sight or hearing such as men had, yet fit to hold their own with the noblest spirits that earthly imagination had ever conceived, swam close to their atmosphere, close enough to leave their impress on the sensitive films of their courier-instruments, close enough for their own later-developed senses to perceive, if only these were more exquisitely trained. What a vista of new stimulus the knowledge opened up to their imaginations!

There was no more need of projects for stellar migration. Here were beings loftier than themselves at the very gates of their senses, possible sources of exalted, if not divine, influence. Out of them would flow into this little island energy that would give measureless impetus to its inhabitants. Who could place a limit to the nobleness of the existences they might find in the ether, once they were on this track, and were refining and ennobling the perceptive power of their senses? There was no conceivable end to the ethical elevation and development they might reach, now that they had pierced the prison walls of the earth. The sublimer amongst their old beliefs were, indeed, coming true in the fuller fruition of scientific discovery. These they had long laid aside, lest they should be mere fancies based upon illusion and delusion, when they saw the evil that the perversions of them by churches and priests worked amongst men. Till they discovered a sounder basis for them than faithmongers asserted for their crude superstitions, they felt they must not entertain them seriously or found action upon them; and over they threw them till they should find their way to them again upon the solid ground of scientific reason.

****

Now that they saw so wide a horizon before them they knew that they need no longer seek stimulus in the races of men that they had left so far behind them, and they rejoiced. For, though there were ever noble and wise individuals to be found here and there throughout the masses of the nations, and though they knew that these set the standard of morality to the world around them, the bulk of men lagged far in the rear and often, when unnoticed, sneaked into the barbarity and vice which they had been persuaded to abandon. The moral law of a nation, or race, or period is voluntarily carried into practice only by the few best of the mature men and women; in fact, their lives and characters are the makers and arbiters of the moral law. Their fellow-countrymen and contemporaries feel the ideal thus held out practically before them as a mysterious influence that surrounds and shepherds them into the path of right. Sometimes, if the age or nation has degenerated, the mystery comes from the best men of the past through books, or still more powerfully through tradition and instinct; this unaccountable influence they call conscience, or the sense of duty, or the voice of God, or some other name that indicates its mystery, its directing power, and its superior standpoint. Priests and primitive legislators try to formulate its commands in definite codes, and at a later stage thinkers and philosophers attempt to reason out its maxims, and find a unity and universality in them. But the influence defies such codification and rationalisation; with the growth of the ages it overflows and antiquates the primitive attempt at its petrifaction, and the variety of codes in different races or in different periods laughs to scorn all efforts at finding a universal basis for them. As soon as a code is proclaimed or a philosophical system worked out, it begins to be antiquated; the best find a better ideal in front of them and, striving after it, reveal the flaws in the life they have hitherto lived, or they resign themselves passively to the drift of circumstance and degenerate into luxury and license; in the one case the influence overflows the code or system, and makes it seldom necessary or apparent to the view of the race; in the other it ebbs from it and leaves it high and dry, the flouted, neglected wreck of an age gone by.

After all, moral law is nothing but the example and character of the best of them working dimly upon their yearning and capacity for advance; and their best are limited by the point of view of their time and surroundings. A progressive race or age soon discovers the flaws in its accepted codes or systems and throws doubt on their authority. It is only in a stagnant or retrograde period that there is no scepticism or free thought; sufficient unto it is the law that has come down out of the past; so satisfied are its people with it that they never live up to it, and never feel any qualms of conscience or entertain troubled thoughts about its neglect. Developing civilisation means developing ethics; the best of a race advance to higher points of view, and soon come to be astonished at the narrow and primitive moral law their forefathers have handed down to them. As they advance in ideals, the conscience of the mass of their countrymen or contemporaries advances too; what is the rare virtue or heroism of the noblest of one age becomes the commonplace of the next; what was the weakness or vice of all becomes the crime of the outcast and atavist. Injunctions not to kill are soon superfluous to all but the criminally inclined; addressed to a whole people, they imply an age of the greatest rudeness and ferocity.

I realised this more and more clearly as I continued to live amongst this wonderful people, and to see into their lives. The criminal and grossly atavistic had been long ago swept out of the island and vicious tendencies against the moral law of past ages had vanished before selection, crossing, and training. They would have laughed if they had been enjoined not to kill, or steal, or lie, or commit adultery. It would be like telling the civilised Europeans not to eat each other, especially when uncooked, or telling the latter-day Englishman not to enslave his brothers. The proud tribes of wild men counted it as one of their noblest prerogatives to banquet on their slain foes and even on their dead relatives, and the fathers of the present race of English and Americans, sensitive as these latter are to the crime of enslavement, held their slaves with no feeling that they were outraging the moral law, whilst their grandfathers winked at the horrors of the slave trade. The best protested and gradually their opinions, and still more their characters and lives, sank as a mysterious influence into the hearts of the race. The next generation felt the protest as a moral law and a conscience, stinging them to advance to the standard of their noblest. The Greeks and Romans describe and applaud in their finest literature vices that modern men are ashamed even to mention. And it will be the same with acts and conduct that nineteenth century society condones and even boasts of; if the European world advances, in a century or two respectable men and women will be ashamed to hear them spoken of.

The Limanorans repudiated scorn of their lowly kin, the animals; they had long ago shed that blind and false shame which rejected the affinity of universal nature; man was as truly kin in his lower representatives to the mammoth as the mammoth to the mollusc, or the mollusc to the microbe. It is true they desired close proximity to the non-human animal as little as they did to undeveloped or degenerate man; intercourse with a lower stage of life and intelligence, they had long ago proved, leads ultimately to adoption of some of its features and much of its standard, even where there is in it the aloofness of the master to his slave, or the tamer to his beast; they desired no masterdom over lower natures and so they exiled all animals and all degenerate or undeveloped men from their island. They welcomed, however, every indication of approach to human traits or human intelligence in any section of terrestrial life; it was to them no bewilderment that they found most species of animals more courageous and many more provident and keen in their outlook than most men, some of them more tender and humane to their fellows, and some infinitely more loyal than the most advanced races. It is difficult to deny, not merely the higher emotions, but the more difficult processes of reasoning to many of the animals. The cunning of man is often outwitted by them.

Facts like these, instead of driving them to find subtle methods of explaining them away or denying them, urged them on to greater effort in their own evolution. They saw in them evidence that the whole creation was striving upwards, and they resolved to obey the universal law more and more fully and to quicken their pace. Any new observation of animal intelligence or advance only confirmed their faith in the rational spirit that was working but half seen throughout the universe, and gave them greater impetus on the path of development they had chosen.

Every new age had seen them rise above the possibility of some old vice or evil tendency, reach some new and higher mount of ethical vision, and descry some nobler ideal ahead of them. They were far out of reach of any return to the fierce vices or defects of a lawless or militant past. Never since the exile of Noola had they observed any tendency to belligerent atavism; and his return, purified and elevated, had finally buried in oblivion that dead and degenerate preterition. Thieving had vanished with such warlike means of destroying and restoring the balance of political power, and its possibility ceased with the devaluation of all property but time, talent, and character. Once time was taken as the standard of everything of value instead of any dull dead stuff like gold or jewels or land or houses, the whole view of property had changed: for time is a living, moving entity that becomes great or little, valuable or valueless with the method of using it; the life of a man limits it in quantity as far as existence on the earth is concerned; and as soon as a race realises this, it is the rarest and most highly prized commodity in the world; nothing can take away its value but the heedlessness or indolence of its possessor; no man can steal it from us but ourselves. For many ages then it was in terms of time that the Limanorans had expressed everything of value; even talent and character were thus expressible, for their chief value lay in their development; they were estimated according to the rapidity with which they could advance a definite and measurable stage. Thus theft became an impossible crime in this island, the true standard of all value being inseparable from the life that possessed it.

Lying and hypocrisy and all the crawling vermin that spawn from them had long ago been ejected from their systems; and wherever atavistic symptoms of them had appeared in any child they were cauterised by every known method, gentle or drastic. The task of cleansing the community of insincerity and artifice had by no means ended with the exiling of all known liars and dissemblers. Open untruth and fraudulence vanished when the development of the intelligence and observation of the people made it easy and universal to divine motives and inner thoughts quite apart from the word or the act. Yet there was still in some a tendency to evasion, or equivocation, or overstatement. The rags of the old conventionality still hung about them, and unawares there would check them in their utterances an old fear lest candour should be ill-manners, lest their freedom should hurt the feelings of their auditor, or rouse the sleeping tiger in him. Year by year was all this getting eradicated; but the process was quickened by the evolution of the magnetic sense and by the clarifying of the tissues of the body. The more transparent the human system became to the senses and the keener the senses grew, the less cue and the less chance was there for concealment of emotion or thought. They were all thoroughly trained in the anatomy and physiology of the body and the brain, and in the science that taught the physical equivalents and accompaniments of each type of thought and emotion. Even without their preternaturally keen senses they could tell from their practical knowledge of the human system the natural results of any word or act, and their eyes and ears could detect signs of emotion or motive which seemed to be non-existent. It was, however, their magnetic sense that was the greatest foe to all deception or concealment. They could read the feelings that stirred in the heart of a neighbour, and were even conscious of the definite thoughts passing in his brain.

* * * *

The physical equivalents and symptoms of certain emotions and passions, that used to be common before the exilings and are too common in all other races, were scarcely ever to be found in any mature Limanoran; they had to be studied in the bodies, and especially in the faces, of children. Jealousy, envy, hate, malice, anger, lust, had become obsolete in the race, and only the young were afflicted with them now; they were classified as mild spiritual diseases that might, if neglected, risk the permanence of the child in the community; they were the record of a stage through which the race had long ago passed, and they were treated as no fault of the child itself but its legacy from an ancestry it could not be made responsible for. Great pains had been taken with these moral childish maladies in former periods with the result that their appearance was now seldom virulent or dangerous and never fatal, and that every household knew by heart the simple rules and specifics for checking their development. The worst characteristic of them was that they were infectious; but the solitary system of education rendered this inoperative; in fact this epidemic nature of the moral disorders of children made the adoption of the one-child household and the one-pupil school seem an absolute necessity. Occasionally, through some strong atavistic taint in the nature, the appearance of one or more of these maladies in a child threatened its whole spiritual life; then all the science and wisdom of the island were brought to bear upon it; the nerves and tissues of the part of the human system affected, whether in brain or heart, were isolated and powerful electro-magnetic instruments were applied to them so as to atrophy them and render them inactive; the most successful educators of the island were joined to the parents or proparents in the effort to get rid of the evil; and the child or youth was constantly brought into intercourse with the noblest natures who exercised to the full their morally healing powers. If the malady still tainted the nature up to maturity and outbalanced all the good in it in spite of such continued curative efforts, then were the elders sadly driven to the ultimate step of deporting the diseased personality. But this had not occurred for generations, and it was hoped that the necessity for drastic remedies would cease in a few years. Already the virulence of these childish ailments had almost disappeared and they had grown so mild in their attacks that few but the guardians observed their approach. They were generally confined to fixed periods of childhood or youth, periods that corresponded to the ages of past history in which they severally raged in the natures of their ancestors. But every new generation saw these periods shortened and driven farther back towards the beginning of life.

The sense of shame that attaches to some or all of these emotions in the best of advanced races is a sign that they are recognised as moral maladies and that with farther advance they will be forced back into the earlier stages of life. But, as they are, the need to conceal envy and jealousy, malice, anger, and lust and their symptoms, is felt, and this induces and confirms widespread habits of insincerity and deception in most civilised peoples, Western as well as Eastern. This desire of concealment has seated the habit of dissimulation so widely and so deeply in the breasts of all that the bolder and more roughly practical openly avow it as a means necessary to their advancement in life. It had been felt ages before in Limanora that as long as these hateful emotions lurked in the hearts of men and women, there could be no final expulsion of the still more hateful insincerity. Now that they were relegated to childhood, concealment of the inner emotions had vanished and the habit of petty evasion and dissimulation had been entirely eradicated. Even the histrionic in manner and gesture and facial expression had disappeared after having been subjected to drastic treatment; it had been criticised and derided whenever it showed itself in any youth; for it was only by the young and immature that so crude an artificiality could ever be adopted.

One of the last refuges of insincerity was artificial self-abasement. As soon as humility before the daily marvels of the universe came to be a common attitude amongst them, its ape, spurious self-depreciation, appeared. Young men and women would grossly understate their achievements or claims, chiefly in order to set up a reaction in the minds of their friends and companions, and tempt them to overstatement. Ridicule soon put this habit of poor and common natures to rout. The Limanorans were now proud of anything they had done well or nobly and were not ashamed to acknowledge it. They were willing without vaunting or mock-modesty to talk of any invention or discovery or any good or courageous deed, but in that simple, ingenuous way which revealed nothing but anxiety to enlighten others as to the methods of success and to stir them to advance beyond it. They needed none of that self-advertisement which is the bane of advanced and ambitious civilisations; everything of merit in their conduct and labour and its products was valuated, they knew, with an exactitude that left no room for misacceptation by their friends and companions. Everyone was so eager to find an advance in his neighbour's work or system that no effort was needed to explain or commend it. When done its merits would be recognised to the full. The elders in their periodical reviews of the work and the progress of the community would estimate it at its full value, and it was one of the most important parts of the training of the youth to appraise the value of every deed and step with a strict impartiality of judgment. To mete out justice to everything in life was impressed upon the young nature as one of the foremost of duties; and to see every feature of history and existence with a dispassionate and unerring eye was one of the chief aims of Limanoran education.

Thus it was that for a time they enjoyed the comedy of life as it passed in other regions of the world, for they could see very clearly the exact merits of every man and every deed, and the credulity and infatuation which made them unrecognisable in popular estimation. Delusion reigned supreme and the best of the comedy was the ease with which some masters of the art of self-advertisement could swell their puny proportions into the appearance of colossal amplitude; they knew every stop in public opinion, and could play on its gullibility with consummate art. The Limanoran was taught to place every human achievement in the perspective of the future, and as he looked and heard through the idrovamolan, the whole of life, as it went in other nations, seemed one continued bathos, ridiculous disproportion between what it appeared to be and what it was.

But they ever saw a darker side to the spectacles they witnessed through this singular instrument, and their laughter was softened and modified by indignation and sorrow. There was a counterpart to the gullibility and applause in the deep-rooted habit of detraction and slander. If any had the power to see conduct and men as they were, impartially and clearly, they were not allowed to use it, so busy were the tongues of traducers and parasites. All human deeds were either underestimated or overestimated, generally underestimated if the doer or possessor had no favours to bestow and no power or influence to exhibit. Aspersion and backbiting were common habits; for the majority were undistinguished and only in courts and the circles of the great did that of overestimation find any headway.

A trivial, yet pathetic, phase of the comedy was the excessive self-esteem that ran parallel with the torrent of detraction. In Limanora the fountains of both had dried up together. For vanity is the effort of a man's emotions to compensate for the fraud that others constantly commit upon reputation. Robbery of material things is sternly repressed in most civilised communities; thus far have they attained in their hostility to socialism; finally one or two have begun to be uneasy about fair fame as a possession more valuable than any wealth and have attempted to formulate the crime in some crude law of libel that is found yearly as inadequate and as primitive as one of the codes of ancient legislators. But the petty robberies of good fame rather than the open brigandage of it make none feel safe. Tongues will keep wagging, and as long as they wag, the conduct or character of some will surely be undervalued. The consciousness of this, that none but the great or distinguished will get their due or more than their due, keeps self-esteem alive in the breasts of all, and self-approbation an unceasing attitude. Men feel that they must recoup themselves out of the unwilling feelings of others for the perpetual fraud upon their reputation. Self-overestimation is the natural complement of the consciousness of detraction. Commonly the sensitive organisation refuses to rest under the unending injustice and will try to set itself right with the world; but most sink after a time into sullen endurance of the wrong and cease to speak of it, thinking it irremediable.

Nothing so greatly astonished the Limanorans as the concomitant disappearance of detraction and vanity from their midst. One of their earliest crusades was that against evil speaking; it was easier than they had thought, for already the principle of generosity to others had begun to work and reputation was counted more valuable than any property. When magnanimity had eradicated the habit of disparagement, the training in impartial use of the judgment prevented the nature swinging into the opposite extreme of shouting hosannas over the nothings of daily life. As they gained clear-sightedness in estimating human actions and character, they found that the cues of vanity had disappeared. They had no need of crusading against the vice; it had been vanquished.

Another defect that seemed to have vanished without effort was immodesty. The lustful had been exiled and it was easy to eradicate from the natures of those that remained all trace of sexual passion, and with it all pruriency. The chief purpose of sex in nature, that of propagation of the family, became its sole purpose; and this, by the control which the elders exercised over posterity, grew as rare as death. Its other ends, the development of self-sacrifice and the growth of love and friendship, had been completely detached from it and rationalised. Procreation with the extension of the race into the future was counted so tremendous a responsibility that most preferred to postpone it as far in life as the instinct of the people would allow. The sexual passion thus died out of their minds as out of their natures, just as the mere appetites of eating and drinking had died out. They had become parts of the rational nature when they were thought of at all.

There was, therefore, nothing to be ashamed of and nothing to conceal. Immodesty vanished with the cue and motive for modesty. They wore irelium draperies more to temper the power of heat and cold and the rigours of the upper atmosphere, and to aid them in flight, than to hide their bodies from the eyes of others. For the draperies were gossamer-like and semi-diaphanous and emphasised the beauty and grace of the body as an expression of soul. It was not the face alone that interpreted the mind, or attracted by its radiance. Magnetism rayed from every limb; and none of the surface of the body was lost under masses of garments; it all came into play as expressive of the life within. They shrank at first from the unhealthy pallidity of my body as it appeared when I first donned their raiment, but under the transparency of my new garments it soon lost its ghastly whiteness and acquired the ruddy, healthy tints of the face. For a time I shrank from the eyes of my comrades, but as I grew accustomed to their absolute purity of thought, I lost all consciousness of my body. There can be no modesty or immodesty where there is nothing to conceal. It was one of their subordinate aims to simplify and purify the functions of the human system, so that none of them should be offensive to any of the senses, new or old.

By this semi-diaphanous exposure of most of the surface of the body there was far more space of skin for the development of sensations and new types of senses. In their pre-purgation ages, when the greater part of the corporeal system had to be muffled in opaque garments for the sake of what was called decency, the finer modes of perception came to be concentrated in the head and the hand; one sense crowded another and blunted its observations. Now every inch of the corporeal surface was open to the influences of sunlight and magnetism and the other energies that so freely permeated space, and new forms of perception began to develop over the body, chiefly refined modifications of touch. The region of the shoulders became especially sensitive to magnetic indications. The arms and chest monopolised the finer sensations of muscular force, and especially of strain and push. Their feet came to gauge with great subtleness the strength and direction of currents of the wind as they flew through the atmosphere. The spinal region tested the temperature of the surrounding space better than any other part of the body, reacting at once to the slightest change in heat or cold. Another advantage of the half-transparent raiment was the ease with which the slightest change of emotion or thought could be seen, making concealment and hypocrisy an impossibility. A third was the aid it gave the medical elders in their periodical inspections of the health of each member of the community; with unstrength-ened senses they could detect the smallest obstruction in any of the organs or tissues, so that a mere passing notice might be enough to report on the health of the people.

* * * *

But if the sex-problem had retained its old obtrusiveness, this seemingly superficial but really important reform in dress would have been impracti-cable. Amongst the earliest questions that the Limanoran scientists faced was the place of sex in the universe. After minute and wide research they came to the conclusion that it was but an accident of existence on some worlds. It was not an essential of the propagation of life; for some species, like bacteria, multiply by mere fission, so that part of the individual is immortal, and oth-ers, like the medusæ, and ferns, and mosses, alternate asexual with sexual re-production. It was manifestly no characteristic of the first and lowliest forms of life that settled on the earth; in fact large sections of vegetal life retain the older habit parallel with the new or sexual habit; any piece of many plants and trees cut off and thrust into the earth will become a new plant or tree of the same kind without the intervention of a seed or germinative stage. But the change in habit must have been introduced into the world not long after the appearance of animal life upon it; for it is only in the least-highly organised animals that parthenogenesis appears in any form. Their conjecture was that sexuality originated from the meeting of the germs of two worlds on which life had not gone far on the path of evolution. The newcomers would be un-able to adapt themselves and their mode of generation to the new conditions they had to meet; and where members of the two types settled side by side in a position isolated from their kind, the instinct of propagation would evolve out of their proximity a new mode of generation, that would, from the cross-fertilisation of two worlds and the combination of the vital energy of both, make a progeny more vigorous and a development easier and more rapid. The species that remained faithful to parthenogenetic propagation, and those that adopted the new mode only partially, fell behind in the evolutionary race. Sexual generation, uniting in itself the vital principles of two universes, swiftly improved the qualities of the species that adopted it and made them dominant upon the earth. Asexual propagation, the easier and more primi-tive, gave the advantage in numbers of individuals to the vegetal and lowly animal species that clung to it, but left them almost incapable of evolution. On and upwards have passed the dominant species through the invertebrates and the mammals up to man, guided by that bi-sexual principle which has in it the stimulus of two types of life and two universes. Nor did it seem to them contrary to the analogy that some worlds should have in the life upon them a tri-sexual or even a quadri-sexual mode of propagation, according to the types of vital principle which have settled and continued upon them. Wherever multi-sexual generation holds sway, there life is rarer but swifter, and evolution carries it into those higher reaches where localisation of it upon an orb is unnecessary.

It was out of sexuality, they acknowledged, that all the higher phases of existence upon earth had come, love, friendship, self-sacrifice; this, too, had given to humanity in its nobler developments the irrepressible yearning for another and extra-terrene sphere and another life. A vital principle issuing from a different universe seemed to have kept within it the memory of its first home if not of the free existence of space. And in man, at least, this had come to consciousness of itself and led him to religious reverence and devotion and the expectation of immortality.

They considered none the less that sex had almost finished its task in many worlds, and would, in no very distant age, have accomplished all it could do for the Limanoran race. When a principle of life has done its task it must retire and give place to something better; else it would become retrogressive and wholly evil, a mere despot selfishly stopping all progress. Every race that meant to quicken the pace of its evolution had to take command of it and guide it to its own higher ends. It is the prerogative of the nobler types of man to raise nature above her lower needs; the Limanoran ideal was to develop the creative power of the human system so far that it might master all the secrets of life and be able to mould human beings and breathe the breath of life into them, and thus they would be able to supersede the sexual mode of propagation.

As it was, they had gone far towards the complete mastery of the sexual principle, and could mould and guide it to any purpose that the future of the race demanded. They knew the conditions that would govern any new human variety they needed in the state just as well as they could produce new modifications of trees and plants and flowers. They read the nature of each individual on the island as easily as they could read a book. But besides this they had in the pedigree-annals in the valley of memory a complete account of all the possibilities of any family or any branch of it. From the developments of recent years and the outlook that they ever kept up far into the future they judged when some new type of nature would be needed for some post in the community and gauged exactly the qualities that would have to be blended in order to produce it. Then turning to the valley of memories, they studied the characters and possibilities of the various families that had one or more of those qualities exceptionally developed. By the aid of the physiological and biological experts they were able to fix the two out of which the individual parents would have to be chosen; and from their knowledge of the character and history of every member, the elders of these two families along with the medical elders were able to indicate the man and the woman who would exactly fulfil the purpose of the state. Years were spent on maturing the pair in the directions required and in entangling their imaginations and affections mutually. None were allowed to assume the responsibilities of parenthood till they were matured to their fullest possibility; for they held that all the essential characteristics of the two natures had to be developed before the embryo could be produced in its fullest and most virile form.

One of the most singular features of this moulding of posterity was that they did not always choose the most highly developed to become the parents of the commonweal. For it had often been found in the past that the individual who had brought his peculiar faculties or qualities to the highest state of refinement in his own life had exhausted the natural wellspring of them, and that he handed them on in most diminished degree to his children. They often preferred in their selection of possible parents a member of a family who exhibited no exceptional energy in the use of its special talent; sometimes the least active and the least conspicuous were selected. In them individual work had never overstrained their faculty; it lay fallow for a generation and was likely to spring forth with exceptional vigour the next. To this I attributed their acceptance of my own imperfect nature in their midst and my selection for mating with Thyriel.

When a pair had bred the child that was required, if they were not conspicuous for wisdom or self-control, it was taken from them and given to a new pair who became its true parents and trained it in the direction it ought to take. These proparents were generally more successful than parents in educating and moulding a character; they never allowed the bias of natural affinity to affect the future of the child; the parents, besides being swayed by the pride of parenthood and the vigour of their affection for it, were too closely akin to it in qualities and character to view it from an impartial and independent standpoint; and the proparents were as a rule selected on account of their contrastive qualities, qualities which would form the complement to its own.

Though so much care was spent on the choice of the stock, they considered it far more important to have the citizens of the future properly trained, and were quite unbending in their insistence that every child should have the most suitable natures in the community to educate it, whether these should be its own parents or proparents. Nor for ages had more than one child been permitted in a household at one time. If a pair had proved themselves exceptionally successful in the production and moulding of the two children they owed to the community, they were allowed to adopt for a lengthened period the profession of parent, by far the most important, if not really the only, profession in the island. But they must bring one child up to maturity before they undertook another. For, they held, there was no problem so complicated, no duty so responsible, no task so exhausting for every faculty, as the training of a human being in its earlier stages; to sculpture a new and noble nature was considered the greatest creative work that a Limanoran could achieve for the state; the greatest talents that ever appeared on earth could not be better spent than on the parental profession. Another and as important reason for the unitary basis of the household was the moral contagion imperfect natures bring to bear on each other. Children were never allowed together except under the strictest supervision; for they soon undid all the work of their guardians, and confirmed in each other the retrogressive savagery through which they were passing. Before the Limanorans had come to their full heritage of scientific knowledge and wise experience, they had allowed for a few generations households of three or more children together, in order to keep up the breed. But they soon discovered this feature of their domestic life to be at the bottom of the slowness of their development, and abandoned it. After long experience they decided that it was better worth the while for the race to devote half a century of the life of the wisest and ablest to the training of one nature than to do any other work to be found in the universe. The greatest book, the most illuminating discovery or invention, was as nothing compared with a living centre of development and progress. Parenthood and proparenthood well done were considered the greatest claims to gratitude and love, and to everlasting memory if there were such a thing. For a man and a woman to have given to the state by fifty years' work a better trained, more nobly moulded character, with larger possibilities than they themselves had was to have done more than if they had discovered and mapped out a new sphere for science and thought. It was one of the greatest honours therefore that the community could bestow upon any pair, to select them a third or fourth time for parenthood or proparenthood.

That the two sexes were both needed for the training of a young nature to maturity was one of the most unhesitating conclusions from their experience. In spite of the obliteration of all demarcating lines between the sexes as to privileges and duties in the state, there was nothing more clear to them than the permanence of the distinction in their natures, as far as life upon earth was concerned; it had grown less and less marked as the ages went on, and as maternity came to be a mere episode in the long life of a woman, yet it remained as real as it ever had been, passing into every phase of the nature, imaginative and intellectual as well as emotional and physical, and becoming salient and striking in the procreative era of life. As the animal part of the nature fell into greater subordination, it needed keener powers of observation to note the difference; yet it had left its permanent mark upon the spirit.

To women was assigned work which required slow continuous effort; for although they are more emotional, they are also by nature more passive. The temperature of the female in all species is lower than that of the male, and in human beings this means less energy and less explosiveness; the woman is ever building up her system by storing sources of energy, the man is ever using up his stores of energy in impetuous outbursts of work. The generations of active employment in which Limanoran women had been engaged, and the complete cessation of the warlike pursuits that used to fill the lives of the men, had not obliterated these distinctions. The women were still best at sedentary occupations; whatsoever needed continuity and singleness of purpose was given to them; for they have more unity of nature, and can settle down for long periods to an investigation that would be monotonous to a man, and are on the whole longer lived. So any investigation that was uninvolved, but needed intensity of application on the part of one mind for more than an average lifetime, was handed over to a woman; and where the work of several was required for a generation or two, a woman was always one of the workers in order to preserve the continuity.

In the imaginative families it was generally the men who did the most striking work. Their bursts of energy enabled them to go by leaps. They pioneered best into the future; they found the new principles for advance in invention and discovery. The women gathered the material for the sciences; the men invented and applied the great hypotheses leading to new laws and new advances; they also showed the way in progress, and tended rather to revolution than to rest. Whatsoever needed artistic talent was theirs to do. In physical work, wherever rapidity of movement and fitful application of torrents of energy were required, the men took the lead; for they were small and active, having now no distinctively muscular employments, like war and hunting, to develop their muscle and bone exceptionally. The women, as naturally accumulative instead of prodigal of energy, were larger and more passive, and took up departments of labour that needed long and gentle persistence. In counsel they were the conservative element, and in all the assemblies but those that superintended investigation into the future, invention, and discovery, that is, in all councils of judgment, they slightly predominated in numbers. If they had wholly guided the community, it would have stood still or moved at a rate that would not have been noticeable in the generations of men. Happily the masculine imagination dominated the civilisation, and hence it was ever quickening its pace. But the women were no less useful in preventing revolutionary progress, and in making the men wait and meditate over the leaps they thought of taking.

It was not so much sex-function itself, as the impress it had left upon the natures of the people that supplied a rough-and-ready classification of types. A few of the women who were especially fitted to be mothers were assigned to the maternal profession; their natures seemed moulded to bring forth strong, healthy, unexhausted offspring, fit for the duties of a new advance. There were other women who because of their nervous vigour and inclination to exhaust their best energies in work were not the most suitable for the production of children, and yet by their sympathy and wisdom and love of the young seemed especially created to bring up children as citizens; these adopted the proparental profession. A third type of women were, on account of their quick, irritable vigour and their super-emotional temperament and lack of self-control, considered incapable of either function except on rare occasions; and they formed the largest class, the worker-women, rarely generative and always uneducative; they were engaged in the sedentary, acquisitive, and continuous employments that demanded no great strain on the imagination or the creative powers or the muscular vigour. But none in the community were wholly freed from daily active work both of body and of mind, not even those whose lives were given up to the profession of maternity. Amongst men all were eligible as fathers; for though there were always a special diet and training for prospective paternity, these might be enforced simultaneously with the usual work. Not all, however, were called on to exercise paternity; it was a rare and little-noticed duty, and left small impress on the community. But there were some who on account of their great wisdom and self-control and lofty character were specially fitted for the rearing of youth, and these formed the male proparental profession. These had their other duties to perform in the family and to the state as well as to attend to their individual households, but they were dedicated to the guidance of posterity; their eyes were more on the future than even those of the imaginative families. The rest of the men formed the class of male workers at creative and imaginative work, and at muscular work that required agility and concentration of force.

Of the numbers in these different classes the elders had full control. They knew all the physiological laws governing the proportions of the sexes and types, and by their dietary and training and medical precautions they could fill the exact number of vacancies to be anticipated in any class. For instance, if one was needed for the profession of maternity, almost all the energy of both parents was spent for a time in nutrition; they were isolated from most activities, surrounded with what in other civilisations would be called luxuries, and encouraged to spend their time in resting. So, if a male worker were required, the man and woman selected for parenthood were active workers themselves; and during their generative period their nutrition was reduced to the minimum for sustaining their energies, whilst they were encouraged to put all the activity they were capable of into their daily work. Their manuals of guidance in the difficult work of filling prospective vacancies in the community were full of minute detail which was based upon long experience carefully recorded and classified, and still more upon scientific experimentation in human embryology and physiology.

It was one of the earliest conquests of the future that they made after the great purgation, this guidance of the sexual and other characteristics of embryos. They knew the exact stage at which any new organ or function appeared, for they had first of all studied the moulding of embryos in animals; and afterwards, by the aid of their new photographic and microscopic apparatus that revealed the minutest detail of any part or movement within the living human body, they were able to study the effect of changes in exercise or diet or mode of life upon the development of the human embryo. Nothing was neglected to make the knowledge complete and scientific, nothing that might help to turn the science of embryology into a creative art. The invention of instruments which could take the senses of the investigators close to any internal item of the living system had made an era in the history of physiology, and cancelled the necessity of anatomy as its handmaid. The most microscopic change in the structure of any tissue in the innermost part of the body became patent to the eye or the ear or the electric sense of research. Embryology had thus become almost an exact science; even the physiological side of it had attained to such exactitude as to make it practically an art. The medical elders could investigate the health of the embryo and guide its development as well as in the case of the full-grown child.

They were thus able to formulate a complete art for the moulding of the unborn to the purpose the elders indicated as best for the future of the race. Training and education in the truest sense of the words began long before birth. Of course it had begun with the father and mother, if not with the ancestry; but the directly plastic art of fashioning the character began with the first appearance of life. The elders would have blamed themselves if any sign of gross atavism had shown itself in a youth, now that they had full command of his prenatal history, and for generations retrogression had become an impossibility in the race. In former ages it had been one of the most difficult moral problems to fix the responsibility of a man's crimes; somewhat was due to his own choice; but part, they saw, was due to his ancestry, and still more to his parents, not only in their training of him, but in their prenatal preparation if they were not careful to exclude gross or criminal ideas and emotions from their systems whilst he was in process of formation. Now they were able to apportion the blame with ease if anything went astray in the character of the child. They were therefore minutely careful in the precautions they took not only in the half-century of education, but in the choice of ancestry and in the guidance of the prenatal development. To prospective parents the character of the future offspring was as a conscience to their daily conduct and method of life. Every thought, emotion, act, was guided by a sense that it would affect the embryo of the coming citizen.

* * * *

The newest addition to their list of sciences, the physiology of ethics, put into their hands one of the most effective aids to this plasmic art of character, prenatal and postnatal. With their instruments of investigation into the human tissue ever advancing in refinement and power, they were able at last to localise the physical centre and equivalent of each emotion; and thus having mapped out the brain and the nerve-centres, they were able to watch with their new modifications of the lavolan the palpitating life and movement in each part with the strong manifestations of its special feeling. Step by step they found their way towards the nosology of these centres, and classified every disease that turned an emotion from right to wrong. Whenever a Limanoran child became afflicted with an evil or retrogressive passion, he was hurried off to the ethical laboratory, and the nerve-centres of his emotional and moral nature were microscopically photographed as they worked; a complete history of his tissues was recorded on irelium-slips, and, after he had gone, the investigators could run these through the recording instrument and study the phases of the feeling or passion at leisure. The bursts of mistaken emotion were livingly photographed with the greatest care, and afterwards the records were watched through their most powerful clirolans. Then experiments were made in finding remedies which would check the growth of the disease in the tissue. At first the therapeutics of morality were merely empirical; they tried the remedies which had been successful with the common physical ailments of humanity, and found most fail, a few succeed. By degrees they discovered that the most powerful antidote against the moral poison lay in the character of the operator; wherever the ethical investigator had led a nobler life, the cure was more rapid and effective; wherever the attendant had more development of intellect than of lofty moral principle, the patient lingered and often relapsed. Yet there were other prophylactics of a more material kind that greatly aided in the recovery of the patient. Hygienic measures and courses were prescribed for preventing the recurrence of the disorder; and at last something not unlike a science of the art of moral healing seemed to emerge out of the empiricism and chaos.

This culminated in the establishment of an ethical sanatorium, which was in reality a children's hospital for obstinate moral diseases. No mature or half-mature Limanoran had for ages shown symptoms of a relapse upon any ancestral or barbaric ethical code, and the mild moral ailments lasting for only a few hours or days were easily managed by the parents or proparents. Gentle influence, or at most gentle discipline, was all that was needed to dislodge the evil spirit, or if that did not succeed, magnetic remedies were applied to the part of the nervous centres affected.

Should the moral defect still hold out obstinately against all remedies, the patient was removed to the hospital for treatment. There were collected together as moral physicians and nurses the wisest and noblest personalities of the race, who applied all their therapeutic power to the centre that was supposed to be the source of the disease. But the centre had been scientifically examined and fixed by the ethical investigators, who reproduced the parts affected and their symptoms in greatly magnified forms, and suggested the various physical remedies that would aid the sanative influences of the physicians and nurses. The child was isolated from circumstances and conditions tending to reinforce the moral poison; and his better nature was invigorated and encouraged, so that it might be able to throw off the germs of the malady.

Within recent times the ethical investigators had made great advances in their science. The immediate stimulus of the progress was accidental, as so often had been the case, or in other words it had come from outside their recognised spheres of causation. An epidemic of deceit had almost simultaneously seized upon the children of the community, in spite of the solitary method of training adopted. Boys and girls who had not seen each other for months were on the same day impelled to habits of concealment, even when they were in the stage of development that corresponded to the ravening fury and open warfare of the barbaric past. Nothing in their ordinary methods of research could furnish a cause for the outbreak. They searched the general condition of the previous moral health of the children, and found it excellent. None of the patients had come near each other for long periods; none of them had shown any symptoms of the disorder before the epidemic had appeared.

They were driven to some hypothesis quite outside the limits of their usual sphere, for they saw that there was something uncommon in the occurrence. Beginning to suspect that the germs of the disease had come from other regions, as had so often happened, they increased the powers of their magnifying apparatus by means of photography, and invented more delicate aids to the investigation of the nerve-centres than they had ever used before. On watching the part in which they had localised the physical equivalent of deceit, they found signs that the presence of the minutest foreign life was disturbing the nerve-tissues. In the moving microscopic photographs and electrographs of the centre they could detect the growth of a new type of microbe, inflaming and interfering with the nerves of the part. Afterwards they found some specimens of the disturbers in the atmosphere, and were able to cultivate them for investigation and experiment. Soon they accumulated a large enough quantity of the débris to apply to the cultures themselves, and in every case it seemed to prove a steriliser; what the minute life had used up and thrown off acted as a poison and destroyer. By means of the medicine that they manufactured from it they were able to annihilate or eject the disturbers of the nerve-centre of truth in the patients. But in curing the part affected the moral equilibrium of the children was upset. The bio-chemical families applied themselves to the problem, and soon succeeded in isolating the medicative elements from the injurious.

Thus a new and efficient method of treatment was introduced into the ethical sanatorium. Chambers were reserved for sublimating the drug, and thither children were sent if any obstinate form of deceit appeared in them.

And by means of the sterilised form of it they fumigated the child's quarters in any household, whenever signs of a return of the epidemic appeared. The ethical investigators proceeded on the new path thus opened up to them and were in time able to describe and classify the microbes of moral epidemics and their antidotes. After some years' toil they supplied the ethical sanatorium with a complete scientific pharmacopœia, for at least all the grosser forms of vice, all the offences against the moral codes that had been atavised or thrown into the ancestral past.

The nerve-centres concerned with these offences were easy to find and localise; so the minute life that interfered with such centres was studied till it yielded its secrets to science. But it was a more difficult task for the new scientific art of therapeutic ethics to trace out the physiology of the newer moral codes and to discover a cure for the maladies which hindered their complete adoption into the Limanoran human system. The moral offences they had now to deal with were sluggishness of the higher faculties of man, acts that dragged the thoughts downwards, dominance of a physical need, concessions to mere nature as against the highest knowledge of nature, excesses of emotion or disturbances of the mental equilibrium by passion, devotion to the past, superstition, stagnancy of belief, efforts to base belief on unreason or ignorance, faith in a moral code as the terminus of human ethics, or in a state of human scientific knowledge that was omniscient. Step by step the ethical investigators found their way to the nerve-centre that was disturbed when any one of these faults appeared in a man; and after long years of research and experiment they were able to add to their pharmacopœia the antidotes to these maladies or weaknesses.

* * * *

They would have thought the basis of existence irrational, if they had persuaded themselves that ethics was unprogressive, whilst all other things in the universe were subject to the law of evolution. A moral code could be as easily superseded as a polity or a type of society. At one time no race could see beyond the moral codes of barbaric life that recognised no evil in treachery or revenge. Some at last advanced to the moral code of the warrior, which based every rule of life upon the idea of honour. Later still the civilised races of the world adopted the moral ideal of the priest, which could find nothing good beyond the limits of its special ecclesiastical forms. One by one these had been antiquated and Limanoran civilisation had now found as the basis for its moral code the principle of the cosmos, that of evolution. To advance, to raise his system higher, to evolve its possibilities, was the first duty of man as understood by the Limanorans of this later age. To see beyond their present horizon was their ideal. They would rather march forward into the darkness than stand still or retrograde in light. To know clearly and definitely the possibilities that lay before them, and to be able to choose the best of them was the primary and fundamental maxim of their ethical code. All others were corollaries of it.

If they had any unreasoned, unreasoning, and authoritative monitor within them making for all that was right, in short any conscience, it was now the prophetic voice of the ideals that they were still to reach. Ages before it had ceased to be a voice out of the past. Before the great purgation of the island half of their education and literature had been based upon the literatures of two ancient peoples, to whose conquests and legacies of energy and thought they had fallen heir. They now shuddered at the pollution that these used to communicate to the minds of their youth. The ethics running through them belonged to a stage of civilisation that had been long antiquated, and embodied ideals now far beneath them. The heroes and wisest men were recorded in them as having done deeds with applause that the most atavistic of their children would be ashamed to mention. Whatever wisdom or nobleness they might otherwise teach, it would be completely neutralised by the taint of vices which were approved or counted as venial peccadilloes. To submit their youth to such pollution for the sake of the problematic refinement they might gain from the books was to do the greatest wrong a civilisation could commit, to prostrate its own ideals before those of a vanished and barbaric past. Out with the exiles went every trace of those old literatures; and the isle of liars and the isle of lechers had taken them to their bosoms, with the result that they had to adopt lying and impurity as their standards of life. To return upon any past was to reject with recklessness the advantages that it had gained and handed on to the centuries between. But to adopt with deliberateness a past steeped in the grossest impurities, and honouring intrigue and hypocrisy, was to commit moral suicide.

It was only in the immature that conscience, or the future invisibly shepherding the present, was either needed or existent. They had pitfalls and dangers out of the savage past to avoid, and an unreasoned instinct was an essential to their development as an ever-present guide, authoritatively bending their steps this way and that. This moral and instinctive anticipation of the future, though mysterious in its origin to the young whose conduct it moulded, was in reality no mystery; it came from the magnetism of the wisest and best of the elders; the ideal these saw in front of them and held out as the immediate goal of the race, passed sympathetically and magnetically into the moral and intellectual atmosphere of the island. The mature knew whence the influence came, and grasped it rationally. But it was round the young as a subtle inspiration and halo that came they knew not whence; nor dared they question it or disobey its injunctions, lest some evil should entrap them. When they came to maturity, they learned the origin of the mysterious voice within, not to disregard its monitions, but to reason them out and revise them by the light of the advancing ideals of the race and to know that it changes and grows like everything in the cosmos.

One of the first aims and maxims of their polity was to let their citizens on reaching maturity think all through their lives for themselves. The first guaranty of this freedom was rationality, the power of tracing back every act and feeling and thought to the primary principles of existence, combined with the sense of responsibility for the future of the race. There was no repression, no prohibition; the prerogative and duty of every man was to make himself fit to be a law to himself. In former ages their ancestors used to talk of the innocence of childhood; all that they meant was unconsciousness of conventional emotions, ideas, phrases, and habits, and superiority to them. They smiled at it as a temporary stage from which they would soon pass into the restrictions of manhood and womanhood; and only the greatest sages were able to work themselves free again from conventions so far as to be moral and noble and yet to have the innocence, the unperturbed vision and candour of the earliest years. But now all men and women retained the naïve openness of childhood and its artless simplicity; for they had no conventions to trammel the freedom of spiritual movement, no prohibitions to make the will shrink from origination or action. Even when childhood or youth was checked in some mistaken career, the check was veiled in persuasion and reasoning and a vision of the truth. The atmosphere of freedom was an absolute essential for the full development of individuality; and the guaranty that this freedom would never pass into license was the fact that every mature man and woman had a noble aim, and that the magnetism of the race was around everyone. None had to obtrude the claims of his personality upon others; and none was abashed by a sense of despair, or the feeling of insignificance. Humility was a virtue needing no conscious cultivation; there was no occasion for its appearance, for the place and merits of everyone were accurately gauged and acknowledged by all. It was only the insignificance of all humanity against the infinite, of the life of this world against cosmic periods, that deeply impressed them, and rendered them weary of efforts so feeble as those of human life. But the mood was brief in such sanguine temperaments and agile natures. Action they knew to be exhilaration and health and the building up of tissue and faculty.

All they wished to be sure of was that the action was to lead forward. The test of its morality was this: did it make the human system progress? How far did it tend to make the future better than the present? Whether a thing was pleasant or not for the moment, had no influence upon their choice of courses of action. That had been the motive and guide of the barbarous past, the artist of its conduct, the creator of its character. The civilisation of other periods and races had meant only the development of needs. And the pure savage is ever superior to civilised man in this sense; with his minimum of needs and the wherewithal to satisfy them wherever he may find himself, he is not so localised as even the wealthiest and most cultured man of the most luxurious civilisations who is tied to his property and investments, and is miserable unless in the one or two cities where he can indulge his taste for luxury to the full. There was no such thing as luxury in Limanora; everything that was brought into being was essential for advance, for the final aim of the life. Not needs but ultimate ends gave them their point of view, not desires but means, not rights but duties. If there was anything that could stir them to greater eagerness, it was the prospect of more work for the good of others; if anything could be looked upon as a luxury amongst them, it was a surfeit of work that contemplated a widening of the racial horizon. To serve the future of all was their deepest longing. Far into the savage past had faded the idea of servitude; and, as they looked into history, there was nothing they were more thankful for than the disappearance of such a necessity; for they considered the servant, especially if slave, the despot of his master in moulding and pandering to his needs and whims, and an evil despot too, as less advanced and less cultivated.

Among the things they most deeply abhorred was despotism. And the worst despotism of all, they held, was the social, that which is exercised daily and hourly, and from the vantage-ground of proximity; the narrow scope and limited horizon make it all the more intense. The most accursed of despotisms is the system of espionage; it wrecks every chance of freedom and crushes originality, turning the race back into crawling venomous things. It is a vain attempt at complete spiritual repression and feebly assumes omniscience and omnipresence on the part of the despots. Its only chance of success is a spiritual society disciplined like an army and ruled by nothing but loyalty to its superiors who base their authority on the assumption of intercourse with supernatural omniscience and omnipresence; and its only chance of continuance is grovelling prostration of all its subjects and possible critics, in abject fear of unknown terror and of spies in the very precincts of the heart, who can hear and interpret its every beat. That was one of their hells, which they occasionally brought before their imaginations in order to warn them against minute supervision and interference. It was this that urged them on to complete transparency of nature, so that their inmost thoughts and feelings might be open to all. Ever since the liars had been thrust forth, one of the immediate goals of their civilisation had become absolute truthfulness. Now that this had been attained, a further goal was complete limpidity of the human system. The wise elders had already been able to interpret what passed in the heart or brain of a Limanoran; now the aim was to make the sensuous garment of the soul diaphanous to the magnetic sense, if not to the eyes of all. Of nothing in his whole system must a man be ashamed, before he could endure such continuous confessional to his fellows, and it was towards this goal that every Limanoran was now consciously working.

The constant inspections and examinations by the elders might seem to conflict with this horror of espionage and spiritual despotism. But these were voluntary on the part of mature Limanorans; it was one of their recurring pleasures to be able to submit their tissues and faculties to the wise observation of the elders, and to gain the advantage of their experience. Had it been felt as a despotism, it would have been abandoned at once. With children and the immature it was a matter of discipline; they were in the pre-purgation stages of Limanoran history, and had to be in pupillage and under authority. As soon as they were able to keep step with the advancing civilisation, or in other words to be a law to themselves, they were allowed to walk alone and without the trammels of guidance. It was the strenuous aim of the elders and guides of the community to keep the atmosphere of thought free. They were constantly reviewing and revising the end and aim of existence in the light of the new developments of thought and science; hence its form never became a hard dogma. They believed in ultimate truth, but knew that nothing short of omniscience could attain it. They were now and again getting glimpses of it, but fought shy of expressing it in words, for everyone would know it to be only a provisional expression. Language itself was a shifting mirage of the mind, dependent on the point of view for its meaning and even existence; and one of the most constant duties of the community was to define and clarify it, and to free it from its ever-growing opaqueness or nebulosity, and the fallacies that haunted it. One thing they never hesitated about, but grasped with unerring instinct; and that was the goal that they kept before them, or in other words the advance they were eager to make. They hated all jesuitry, knowing that it meant the suppression of spiritual freedom by what merely professed to be progressive and good, and the obscuration of spiritual truth in clouds of subtlety. Nothing that was evil, they held firmly, could lead ultimately to good; nothing that was retrograde could in the end be progress.

* * * *

They had learned from the revolutions of their past how snaky and tortuous are the ways of deceit; and the first sure sign of its triumphant success is the bold adoption of the doctrine that good men may do evil, provided their aim is good. Under this the liars sheltered themselves for ages before they were exiled. The era of the history of the island that filled them most with shrinking and loathing was that of the struggle with the various forms of deceit. The first lesson in the valley of memories was drawn from this division of their annals; they filled their youth with hatred and scorn of untruth and hypocrisy; no firm step could be taken in education till this had become a deeply rooted feeling in their natures, and nothing awakened it so well as the study of this struggle with the liars. But they never taught any subject merely from books or records; everything, even history and its lessons, was made practical and living. Deceit, for instance, was traced back to its sources in nature, and the difficulty of getting rid of it was revealed by finding it so wide spread in the lower ranks of life. Mimicry or involuntary deceit was investigated all through plant and animal life, and it was found to be more prevalent the lower the investigators went in vital organisms. Their loathing of it as a deliberate adoption amongst human beings grew deeper as they saw that in the animal world it belonged either to incompetence or rapacity. The prey mimicked the form and colour of another species that was loathsome to its enemy in order to avoid his grasp; unconsciously the mimicry spread, for only those members of the attractive species which were like the repellent species escaped and propagated. Or the spoiler mimicked the form and colour of a species that was friendly or neutral to its victim, and only those members of the species similar to the unfeared kind succeeded in catching enough of their favourite food to survive and hand on their nature to a posterity.

It was the same in the higher life of human self-consciousness and will; only here intention and deliberateness entered in and turned mimicry into deceit. Wherever hypocrisy existed it was a sure sign of a vast number of incompetent and feeble, who made an easy quarry to the villain, and of the vigour of a cunning minority, who often found it difficult to entrap. Diplomacy and convention are the deliberate mimicry of the predatory section of a race or of its gullible section. When once the Limanorans had purged the island of the liars, they had to prevent the propagation of the feeble and incompetent; for they knew that, as long as these existed in a community, there would persist the more futile forms of deceit. After that first purgation, the weak, though retained in the island, had to abandon family life; they were provided with the means that made existence easy and pleasant in order that they might not resort to their only method of survival; and in a generation the problem of hypocrisy had disappeared.

It was then that the idrovamolan was invented and came into use in education. Having driven out the hated vice, they found that there was still the need of impressing its evil results upon the minds of the maturing youth, just as it was necessary even yet to study the diseases that had disappeared for generations from their midst in order to be able to cope with them, should they ever be reintroduced through their communication with other atmospheres. But they knew the unreality of teaching anything in a merely theoretical way; they felt that lecturing and sermonising and the mere reading of history would give them no such grasp of the vice and its evils as would living, acting things. The idrovamolan with its telescopic, telacoustic, and telemagnetic powers came to their assistance in this difficulty. By its help parents and proparents were able to bring the youths into the very presence of the loathed deceit without submitting them to the chance of contagion. They turned the object-tubes of the wonderful instrument upon Aleofane and its society; and through them they saw and heard and felt men like insects mimic and like stinging worms crawl and diplomatise, lie and cheat, still with the worship of reality and sincerity and truth upon their lips. There they noted the growth of the most offensive form of the vice. The weak learned it for protection, flattering the great and grovelling in the dust before them whilst they cursed them in their hearts, and all in order that some favour might perhaps be flung like a bone to a dog. Having learned the vicious art in this cringing fashion, the feeble were seen to march off with the proud gait and the conceit of adepts and use it like brigands on the still feebler. This combination of incompetence and unscrupulousness was the final curse of a civilisation that had taken deceit to its bosom. The whole of the energy of the race was spent in simulation and dissimulation. Every vice simulated its antagonistic virtue; even virtue simulated the vigour and arrogance of vice. The Limanoran youth needed no more teaching on the evils of hypocrisy. They rose from the idrovamolan with an intense loathing for all forms of deceit, so impressive was the drama they saw enacted in Aleofane. Even what seemed innocent mimicry they shrank from, seeing it universally employed as the means of cheating in that island of liars; mimicry they were encouraged to eschew; for as surely as the art was mastered, it was used for mean or foul purposes at some time or other, either for envy and jealousy and scorn, or in order to lay traps, sometimes for the strong, but chiefly for the weak. Even in art all mimicry was avoided, for there it betrayed feebleness or lack of individuality. The existence of mimicry in the animal world was the mark of degeneracy upon terrestrial life. It argued the wide domain of feebleness and rapacity, and the dominance of the passion for mere existence. Wherever it was wide-spread, it meant the abeyance of progress and of eagerness for progress. Mimicry is the sterilising process of faculty and power. Origination is the principle of fertility, of stimulus to progress.

Whatsoever dallied with an outgrown principle or element was immoral. Mere copying of what had been already attained and was about to be left behind or used as a stepping-stone to something better was neighbour to evil. Morality is the effort to adapt conduct and ideals to the new vistas opened up into the future by an advance already achieved; and it is ever being bribed or throttled by what is outworn. Evil is the past which has become so obsolete and is yet so living as to be obstructive. What has been outgrown has ever its allies among living elements, and its advocates in every mixed and unpurified race. Especially is this the case where there are fixed codes or creeds, and along with them professions organised to preserve and continue their sway. The world is constantly seeing the spectacle of a nation or race or species coming to a standstill after centuries of brilliant progress, and getting fossilised in a certain stage of its advance; there it remains for generation after generation as if alive, yet practically dead for all purposes of development, like a fly in amber. This dead stop is due to the dominance of some code or creed that seemed to embody the spirit of its greatest success; the nation or race sought to secure forever to itself the advantages of the ethical or spiritual methods that had achieved for it its most brilliant results, by fixing them unalterably for all time, with their official guardians to protect them from change; so that which had given such vigorous life and development for a time became a prison-house and grave. Only the most tremendous revolution and cataclysm could burst the walls of the tomb, tear off its grave-clothes, and release its spirit for new conquests. Sometimes a nation seems to fossilise the creed or polity that first gave energy to its life, yet at the same time grows and develops spasmodically. It has only made pretence of having fixed this code for all time, whilst the living spirit of it escapes and follows its own course in freedom; it has periodically to return to its pretended prison and tomb, and to reconcile by jesuitry and in makeshift way the two methods of life which have come to differ so widely. Then it flees again into the struggle of existence and gradually ignores even the new versions of the old code, till the divorce becomes too obtrusive to escape attention, and the process of reinterpretation of the antiquated creed begins again. This has been a common enough mode of advance in the history of the world. But it is fraught with incalculable risks. It induces a habit of self-deceit and hypocrisy, and the nation or race ultimately makes a tomb and prison-house for its spirit out of its own falsities and self-delusions.

* * * *

Advance like this, the Limanorans held, was no true advance. They would have no part or lot in fixity of methods or codes, for whatever became fixed grew thereby evil and obstructed development and advance to higher points of view. They had only to look into their history to see how every new step antiquated some universally accepted belief or maxim. Not so many ages ago a crudely philanthropic spirit was considered one of the surest signs of advancing virtue, in fact one of the noblest of the virtues. Now it was considered distinctly immoral to philanthropise without taking care to foresee the results of the philanthropy. Limanorans used to go out into the archipelagos and try to convert the barbarians to the special code or creed then in vogue. Instead of helping on the human race, it actually stopped the development of a section of it; for the adoption of a creed and its symbols and rites and phrases far in advance of any possible civilisation they could reach only made the savages—whose virtues had hitherto been at least genuine—conventional, false, and hypocritical; whilst the apostles left thousands of their own countrymen at home stagnant or retrogressive. It soon came to be acknowledged that intercourse with inferior civilisations, even for the purpose of raising them, lowered the moral standard of the missionaries, whilst failing in its original motive. Much of the philanthropy that began at home was found to be no less obstructive and immoral. It fed and clothed the poor and improvident, and thus helped to slay and bury the only habit that could save them out of their slough, the habit of measuring every step they took, and seeing whither it led; and it helped to perpetuate the evil; for the ready yet limited supplies combined with the improvidence to make them breed like the lower animals, and the race of paupers and unprogressive was inordinately multiplied. The same feeble and immoral philanthropy opposed all attempts to stop the multiplication of the diseased and semi-criminal, and had to increase the armies of doctors and guardians of the peace every generation. It did well to nurse the feeble in mind and body, and to reduce the penalties under which heredity had placed them; but it failed to see that it was doing endless evil by letting them penalise an increasing posterity with their own punishment. Not till it was branded as the worst of immoralities was such philanthropy ended. This had been a distinct advance and a true virtue, when it had taken the place of cruelty and neglect, and when there was unmeasured space on the earth for the expansion of population; but, once this stage had been passed, and the purgation crusade was proceeding, it became a real plague and vice.

Another immorality that had once been a virtue was the pursuit of beauty for its own sake. Men gave up their lives to the production of beautiful things which served no other purpose than their own glory and the entertainment of idle and leisured people. Others made fortunes and devoted them to the purchase of such works of art, in order that crowds might collect and admire them, and for a time there was something of truth in the assertion that it educated the taste of the people. But this was only when the bulk of the race was unenlightened and unprogressive, and anything that softened their barbarity, anything that drew their thoughts away for even a brief time from sordid cares or cruel projects or mechanical and conventional habits, implied progress or a chance of progress. When the race had been purified, and every eye was bent on the future, and every nerve strained toward some advance in human civilisation, beautiful things became the commonest features and necessities of life, and beauty ceased to be noticed as anything remarkable. Then to spend energies on producing what was artistic and beautiful without serving any other purpose than pleasing was reckless extravagance, and by wasting what should have been expended upon the progress of the race was condemned as immoral. There was no virtue in doing what everyone did by instinct. There was positive vice in making it the sole and deliberate purpose of expenditure of energy.

Another instance of a former virtue having become a vice was statesmanship and political patriotism. At one time half the conspicuous talent of the race went in this direction, so greatly was it admired. And, when there were other races and nations to diplomatise or struggle with, and one half of the race had to provide for or keep watch on the other half, it is no strange thing that to enter into the domain of politics was considered the noblest thing a man could do, and love of the welfare of the country was considered the noblest sentiment a man could entertain. The most difficult problems, involving, some of them, the very continuance of the race, occupied the attention of the statesman and politician; what to do with the vast pauper class and the still vaster fringe of the poverty-stricken and improvident, how to deal with the criminally inclined, how to educate the half-savage denizens of hovels in cities and even in the open country, how to prevent the deadlocks in industry, how to regulate the labour market and how to check the recurrent plagues and famines, were questions that tasked the finest intellectual energies of the nation. What complicated the answer was the fact that the themes of the discussions, the pauper, the criminal, the improvident, the employer, the labourer, the plague-stricken, and the starving had all a share in the government of the country, and had to be persuaded that any scheme proposed was to their individual interests. The virtue of political patriotism was streaked with loquacity, conceit, self-seeking, hypocrisy, corruption, and intrigue, long before it came to be recognised as a vice. The statesman and politician had to make his principles as interchangeable as his coats, had to be a master in the art of making the worse appear the better reason, had to be skilful in lying without seeming to lie, had to rob whilst putting on the guise of self-sacrifice, had to cringe and fawn, bully and overbear, by turns, had to be an artist in bribing men and in taking bribes, in short had to be the most expert of the criminal classes. By the time the end came, none in the list of virtues had become so like a vice as patriotism. The great purgations swept out all occasions for politics and patriots in exiling all the subjects of statesmanship. Where there were no paupers or criminals, no masters or servants, no uneducated or savage except young children, and no chance of plague or famine, the occupation of the statesman and politician vanished. Where every man was taught to be a law to himself, legislation had no place. The problems of most inchoate civilisations had gone into exile with all the isms that were proposed to solve them, and all the charlatans that proposed their solution. Patriotism was now, like breathing, the organic and unconscious process of every mind, and not the exception upon which anyone could plume himself. No longer was it the safety of the country, or the continuance of the race, or the sustenance or justice or criminality of part of the people that demanded conscious effort, but the advance of the human system in all. To propose and argue legislative schemes for the benefit of any section of the race would have been accounted immorality, if it had not been taken as a symptom of atavism or mental disease. A hospital was the certain fate of anyone who indulged in political projects or political eloquence; the old virtue had passed beyond the stage of obstructiveness and vice, and had become one of the tests of insanity.

This disease of politics rarely appeared except amongst the youthful and immature and the methods of driving out the evil spirit had recently grown scientific and unfaltering. The old plan of exiling, it was now felt, had become cruel and pitiless. For in recent generations the pace of evolution in the race had so quickened that now even its laggards and the breakers of its moral law were centuries ahead of the most advanced citizens of the most advanced nations on the face of the earth; and no longer could they, if expatriated, find any to consort with. They would have to live with men who, in their eyes, were vicious and criminal. Noola had been the last to be exiled; the system was finally abandoned as inhumane and unscientific; and science soon found methods of treatment that were prompt and efficient in their cure of all such mental diseases.

My final instance of the old virtue grown vice is of a different kind. It belonged more to the intellectual sphere than to the practical, and seemed to me at first rather a mistake than a defect of the nature. It was the common error of taking a verbal originality or advance for a real, a mere change of name for a change in essence. In the old times it had been counted as a great merit to a man, if he manufactured a new nomenclature for any wide spread phase of civilisation, and so gave the race the sensation of dealing with something novel. Some of the greatest heroes of philosophy and science in the pre-purgation ages of the island had owed their fame to the substitution of fresh phraseology for what had grown outworn and trite, and most of the great writers had done nothing more for their fellows than re-illumine a linguistic world fallen dull and dark. Men grow sick of ideas that have worn the same verbal dress for a generation or more, and hail as a discoverer and benefactor anyone who tricks them out anew; they delight in feeling them to be familiar old friends, whom they have to make no mental effort to know. Even to dye the old garments in new imaginative tints is a service they will not readily forget; whilst the great discoverers and pioneers of the human race have had years or ages of oblivion according to the newness and difficulty of their ideas and the distance beyond the common horizon they have looked into the future. The Limanorans of old, like most other men, abhorred having to think out again their creeds and ideas, and especially having to reform them; and so they stood out lustily against every real advance proposed, and shouted it down as irreverence or blasphemy in overturning the old barriers and old altars. The maker of a new nomenclature and the tinter of the old phraseology pandered to this intellectual indolence.

One of the most striking results of the new point of view after the great purgation was the transformation the fame of these old scientists and philosophers and writers suffered. They began to be execrated as dealers in illusions, as men who fed the passion of the human race for stagnance or retrogression to monstrous proportions. They were thrown down from their lofty pedestals, and cast into oblivion for their sins against truth and reality. To seduce men from the pursuit of truth by mere verbal jugglery was now counted no mere mistake, but a heinous offence against morality. To take as a real discovery what was but a new name or set of names revealed a vicious obliquity of mental vision, that needed attention from the ethical physicians. This was especially easy in the domain of ethics, and the Limanorans were constantly on their guard against the delusion of accepting a change of nomenclature as a moral advance. The elders carefully reviewed every stage of progress, lest it should have been in words and phrases. This was the main purpose of the Manora and of the Imanora, and every month linguistic councils were held to revise the language, and to throw out any fallacies and illusions it might harbour. Every new nomenclature and phraseology was searched and probed, and torn off the ideas that they were meant to express, in order to see if there was anything new underneath them. Delusion, they had resolved, they would have nothing to do with in any shape or form. For delusion blinded the eyes to the route they were taking, and made them march in a circle or back over the old roads under the belief that they were advancing to what was new. It was the greatest foe to true progress, and any man who fell into it revealed vicious tendencies, which needed the ministrations of the physicians and nurses in the ethical sanatorium. To take verbal ingenuity for true pioneering was the most grievous offence against the future of the race.

* * * *

The great standard and test of morality was progress. How far will an act or habit aid the true development of the race? This was the crucial question in Limanora; and in order that it might be answered satisfactorily and easily by any member of the community, the council of elders was careful to accommodate the ideals of the race to every advance made. It had been a rare thing in their history to change or add to the cardinal instincts of morality. But this they knew was by no means impossible; and indeed they were buoyed up with the hope that the moral cosmos was still to open up new marvels like the physical cosmos, that in fact the two would ultimately be found to be one when looked at from the final and divine point of view. There was the strongest conservatism in the ethical phase of life; for it is the last, highest, and most complex development of vitality. The lower we investigate in the animal world, the more revolutions and transformations we see the individual go through, the more enslaved is it to circumstances, to locality, to season, to the moment. The higher we go, the greater we find the conservatism, and at the same time the greater the origination and the adaptability. In man these two conflicting powers grow stronger side by side as he advances in civilisation. He retains features and forms that are outworn and useless longer than most of the higher animals; and yet he originates and adapts himself and his surroundings with far more ease and swiftness. In ethics, his last evolution, the conservatism dominates the origination and the advance, obscures them or makes them simulate its own features, and produces the belief that the final maxims and cue of morality have been reached from the first. Ethical progress has naturally been slow, and it is only the student of vast periods of history and of many nations and races who becomes fully persuaded that there has been any change in the point of view. Because there is not complete transformation, as in the case of the minuter and lower animals, it is assumed that there is no evolution, and that morality and conscience have remained fixed quantities, from the beginning of historic times at least. And the close bond between ethics and religion has assisted this dominant and delusive conservatism in its task. Each great step in ethical evolution has been claimed by religion as its own, and as resulting from its own special revelation from heaven.

The Limanorans were quick to recognise that morality must be subject to growth and development, not only in the individual, but in the race, and that man must gain higher ethical points of view as he progresses. They knew that many of the finest impulses and inspirations towards progress, and especially ethical progress, had come from beyond the earth and the earth's atmosphere. But that any age or race could have caught the ultimate ethical light from the central sun of the cosmos seemed to them after their experience the height of absurdity. There could be no spiritual eye trained and developed enough to receive it. As the bodily eye of man is capable of taking in only a limited range of rays of light, whilst an immense range of them above and below its faculty either blind it or pass unnoticed, so his spirit at any given stage of its development can understand and accept ethical ideas only within certain limits; but, as it progresses, it is able to see beyond, and appreciate ideas that were non-existent to it before. There is as much difference between the ethical comprehension of the modern Limanoran and that of the most highly civilised European as between that of the latter and the savage's, or as between the savage's and the pig's; and if they could have brought themselves to believe that they had attained the fullest and the final light upon morality, the thought would have struck their very hearts to stone.

It was this that kept them from formulating their morality or ethics in any definite code. They knew that a code would soon petrify morality and itself become a fetich ignorantly worshipped, and, gathering to it through the ages the self-interest of its officials and the irrational devotion of its worshippers, attain a despotism that could never be broken or controlled. A code issues in a series of prohibitions which become a boundless slavery, and prohibitions develop the sense of rights which dominates and obscures all sense of duties; this keeps men hanging between savagery and true civilisation. The growing dominance of duty with its complementary obscuration of rights is the first symptom of the approach of rapid ethical progress. To insist on one's rights imprisons the soul in the living sepulture of selfishness. To think of one's duty is to admit the self-revealing and future unmisting light of self-sacrifice. Once prohibitions become the order of the day, especially in a limited community, the spirit of intolerance is abroad; every man yearns to confine his neighbour and put him in moral and intellectual leading strings. The origin and meaning of the "Thou shalt nots" are forgotten; the spirit of them dies rapidly, and the letter binds and petrifies the souls that must obey them. Progress in ethics is finally stopped, and it is accepted as a law of nature that there never was any development of conscience and never can be any other ethical point of view. Moral stagnance is taken as the rule of human life, and nothing short of a new impulse from spheres outside the world can liberate the race, thus blinded, from its vicious circle of thought.

Advance of the human system to higher points of view is in Limanora the moral test and standard of actions and conduct. In all that is, nothing has ever died, nothing is dead; what seems dead and fixed forever in permanent form is suffering change as truly as the flitting aurora of the north; the rock, that seems the same in our old age as when we saw it in infancy, is in process of transformation no less than we ourselves are; it is made up of particles that are groups of molecules; and these molecules, moving with varying degrees of rapidity round and across each other's orbits, consist themselves of still more minute atoms that are but points of living energy. Send another form of energy, like heat, through this apparently torpid mass, and it stirs palpably to our senses; what was dormant to us before has awakened, and, as the supply of the foreign energy increases, the rock moves and changes beneath our gaze; not that the long-torpid mass has not an energy of its own; it is a store of energy, every atom of it waiting but for the touch of another kind to awaken from its age-long sleep, and to send most of it free and a step higher into the wandering sphere again. The difference between solid and liquid and between liquid and gas is only a question of time. In the solids the molecules take longer to move through the same space than those of the liquid, which in their turn take longer than those of the gas; for solids flow under the influence of gravitation or other force just as truly as liquids or gases flow.

It is the same with energies; one differs from another in pace; time is the only essential difference between them. The pace of vital energy is so distinctive in its swiftness that it forms a new order of existence. Thought is the swiftest of the vital energies that we know, and to rise in the scale is to quicken the pace. The civilised man thinks as much more rapidly than the savage as the savage thinks more rapidly than the mollusc, if the last may be said to think or feel at all. And there are heights above existing human thought for man to climb. Higher and ever higher the scale of energies in the cosmos must go, till time becomes what would seem to us but a vanishing point; immediately above us lies the vital energy to which a thousand years are but as a moment. To the microbe, if it could think, human life would seem an eternity. To creative thought, which is the Limanoran ideal, eternity, future as well as past, is focussed into a moment.

Up through the scale of energy the whole cosmos is ever climbing, with occasional lapses and falls, time being the only differentiating quality. To quicken the pace of development is the one immediate aim of Limanoran civilisation, and the morality of an action is measured by its contribution to this aim. The higher they climb, the nobler, the more ethereal, becomes their energy; the less governed and clogged by animal conditions, the more easy to quicken the pace of development. For the cosmic law of influence is that the closer in quality and degree the spheres of energy, the more likely is the higher to mould the lower and raise it near to its level. The source of the everlasting movement and life in the cosmos is the unstable equilibrium of all nuclei and stores of energy. Every world differs from every other world in its capacity for various forms of energy; and so does everything in it differ from everything else in the amount of any particular form of energy it can contain. Comparative proximity sets up a current between any two nuclei of energy that thus differ. Whenever the two reach stable equilibrium, that is, whenever they come to have equal shares of the energy, the current of influence ceases, and they are dead to each other. The socialistic ideal is political and social death; when all the members of a community are equal and alike in their share of its privileges and products and capacities, its rights and duties, it ceases to grow or develop; stagnation is the law of its being, especially if there are no neighbouring communities differing from it on which it can react. The Limanorans deliberately strove to keep up and strengthen the differences between not only families, but individuals, in rights, duties, capacities, aims. The differences were an everlasting fountain of renewing life. The law of political and social life is exactly the same as that of gravitation and of all the other cosmic forces. Two sources of energy will continue to influence each other, till they reach equality, the greater giving of its share of energy a larger proportion than the less. What keeps the cosmos eternally alive is the complexity of the mutual influences. There are no two bodies or centres of an energy so isolated or so simply constituted as to remain forever dead or unchanging, once they have reached stable equilibrium towards each other in respect to their special form of energy. And so it is with men; the socialistic ideal is an impossibility in this universe.

In the human sphere this cosmic law has farther-reaching issues than the merely political. The Limanorans were willing to do much for the advance of mankind, but they had come to see that apostolism is a case of this law of mutuality of influence as truly as any other phenomenon; the higher must not only give voluntarily of his influence and character to the lower, but the lower must give of his to the apostle; and if the proximity continues long enough, this mutual give-and-take will end in the missionary coming nearer to the original moral standard of the convert than the convert comes to his patron's original standard. Where the grades of the two civilisations are widely separated, though the process of assimilation may be long, extended over even many generations, it will be most disastrous to human progress. It is better, they concluded from their long experience, to isolate an advancing race that is far ahead of all other races, and thus to give it the chance of coming within the sphere of still higher intelligences.

Most advanced religions have begun with the impulse towards this, yearning for a loftier sphere than that in which they are hedged. They try to isolate their followers from the lowering influences of the world around, in order that they may reach the ideal and influence that are just above them. But, as they apostolise and expand, the worshippers become mere parasites of their God; they try to batten upon Him with their lower natures, and thus drag Him down to their level. After the first noble impulse and inspiration, it is seldom that a religion does not become as truly an instance of parasitism as the meanest bacterial life. The lower all through the universe is eager to parasite on the higher; minute organisms try to lodge in the tissues of those that are larger and more developed. As long as host and parasite can pursue their functions unhindered by their intimate relationships, little harm is done; but as soon as the débris of the lower clogs the organs of the host, what we call disease results and the minute guest becomes a hurtful parasite. As long as the religious impulse sends the nature higher on the path of development, so long does it give of its best to the Deity, so long does it fail to clog the advance of the cosmos. But when it extends its conquest to mean and unprogressive natures, the common, unenthusiastic natures that are saturated with envy and jealousy, then does it become mere parasitism; the religion has grown into a disease. The warm, humane, and generous natures which are touched by a new inspiration, rise to an exceptional pitch of fervour under its influence, and develop at a pace that stirs the alarm and envy of their neighbours; whilst the resultant persecution continues unabated, there can be no degeneration, the worship can never be parasitic. But as soon as the persistence and progress of the early worshippers and their propagandist enthusiasm begin to invite the commonplace, cowardly spirits of the mass, who can never appreciate what is above them except to envy it and drag it down to their level, its era of development is past. The cosmic law of reciprocity never fails to act, and the united influence of the meaner majority is greater in its power over the whole than the fervour of the noble few; down falls the worship to the level of the many.

It was on this cosmic law that the Limanorans based their refusal to go out and attempt to convert and raise the rest of mankind to their standard. They knew from the nature of the universe that the attempt would end in corrupting themselves and dragging them down farther than they could drag up their converts. They preferred to give of their best to the unorbed existence which filled space outside of the world, and to make their best still better. Thus they knew they were serving most truly the great end of all being, the development of the cosmos, the elevation of the energy in it towards more and more spiritual and progressive grades. They strove to perpetuate and strengthen their consciousness of what was above them, and to break the yoke of the lower self, the self that at death amalgamates with what is material and stagnant, although the latter was needed as a stepping-stone as long as they remained upon the face of the earth. In seeking the proximity and influence of the higher energies and existences that seldom touched the earth, they anxiously guarded themselves from all parasitism which might drag these down in the scale of being; and this led them to abandon attempts to personalise the relationship to them. They would have no part in worshipping or prostrating themselves before these beings in order to obtain their protection and patronage; for this, they knew, becomes merely sectarian, the outcome of envy and jealousy, the cause of bigotry and intolerance, persecution and revenge. They did not desire the exclusive influence of a higher being, nor to become obstructions to its further development; to rise to its level was their active spiritual ambition in striving to gain proximity to it.

As their senses, especially their inner senses, developed, they were getting more and more certain of a vast universe of being just outside the merely terrestrial, and new inspirations and senses were ever awakening in them; nobler ideas and impulses pressed in upon them, they scarcely knew whence. They were afraid to define the source, lest they should humanise the idea of it and pollute it. What they were sure of was that infinite space was filled with unorbed life and energy, rising in higher and higher grades, as it receded from the terrene. The energy of the worlds and of the other nuclei of force was gradually rising through the grades of being, thanks chiefly to the measureless existence which hovered round them, yet settled upon no centre of fixed energy. Out of this unorbed life came the impulses and inspirations that made such epochs in the history of a world. Their magnetic sympathy with this they were strengthening and elevating every generation, as they strove to rise higher and higher amongst these existences in order that into their spirits might come nobler and nobler influences. As long as they were conscious of qualities and degrees of existence above them, so long would they be stimulated on their upward development. They had no fear that they would ever reach a point from which they could not see heights beyond. That, they knew, would be complete spiritual death. But they knew too that there was no such thing as death, or entire annihilation, in the whole cosmos. What seemed to us death was but the final parting of two grades of being or energy, the lower to coalesce with some fixed form of energy and attach itself again to some more rapidly developing form, the higher to range itself with the unnucleated energies of space, still to rise by proximity to some higher life. They were scientifically certain that there could be no end to this process of development upwards. Aspiration was the duty and true function of all existence. To quicken the pace of the evolution, to range themselves more and more swiftly with the higher life of the cosmos, this was the prerogative of vital energy that had gained consciousness of itself and its purpose.

Their conscience and morality were based upon this quickening ascension. The test of an action was this: does it help in raising the humanity higher in the scale of being? Nothing could be good that stopped their ascent; nothing could be bad that compelled them to rise more quickly. The elders generally saw at a glance all the bearings of an act and knew whether it contributed to this general aim or not. Where they hesitated on account of the complexity of the problem, they met and discussed it, calling in all the accurate science they had to their aid; if after all they had to lay the question aside unanswered, then was the act left in that neutral zone of conduct which the Limanorans might or might not enter as they saw fit. Such acts carried no moral discount or credit with them for the time. But often the advance of an age, or even a few years, would remove the act from the neutral zone into the bad or the good; a higher point of view generally solved their doubt. From the opinion of the elders there rayed out magnetically into the young and immature the sense of what was right, to act as conscience where they were incapable of reasoning out the position.

There was thus no feature of their lives but came within the range of morality. Even the habitual and automatic movements and actions, which form so large a proportion of the life of the other terrestrial races had been reduced to an almost inappreciable proportion in theirs and were ever being questioned and tested to see if they harmonised with the newer points of view that had been reached. There was nothing in their whole existence that had not its moral relationships. Their sciences and arts, their experiments and inventions, were as much a part of their moral life as their character and their conduct towards each other. Morality was the relationship to the ever-developing, ever-advancing, aim of the race, and nothing in the whole range of their life was indifferent to that.

CHAPTER XII

A WARNING

EVER and again there overshadowed the spirit of the race a cloud, a fore-boding, that contrasted deeply with their usual exhilaration. The intervals between its appearances were often long, occasionally brief. At first I could not understand the cause of it; for I was still in pupillage and had not yet developed the sympathetic magnetism that ultimately made me a member of the race. But, when it recurred once or twice, I began to see that it followed the passions of Lilaroma, and that the families of the Leomo were least affected by it and most active whilst it lasted. Another concomitance was the subsequent importance of the questions connected with interstellar migration.

The discovery of the infinite and invisible life of unorbed space, not only infinitesimal but highly organised, lessened the gloom of these beclouded periods, and made the Limanorans less feverish in their astronomic and volitational researches. They felt that the divorce of the higher and lower energies of their human system, commonly called death, was no annihilation of their entity, no closure of their career of development, but only an incident in it, that took the further history of their higher energies out of the reach of the grosser terrestrial senses. They had no need, they felt, to reach out frantically towards some other world. They had lost all fear of death, and all thought of it as the end of their evolution. Still upwards would they climb through higher stages of existence, in spite of the loss of that grosser stepping-stone which we call the body. Knowing how full the interstellar infinities are of vital energies and organisms, and knowing too how the body began a new, though perhaps lower, career at death, they were certain that the vitality and spiritual energy that left it on dissolution, a far loftier and more highly organised entity than the divorced terrene elements, would still exist and still develop. The whole encyclopædia of their scientific knowledge was opposed to its annihilation, and the discovery of the vital fulness of space left no other alternative than that it was thither the spiritual energy of the human personality escaped at death.

Yet there lingered a tinge of gloom at the time of any overwhelming spasm in the heart of the great mountain; and the Leomo bated not a jot of their activity at such periods in combating the once-dreaded catastrophe. For they had no definite knowledge of the future pace of their evolution, once the two types of energy in them should be divorced; and they had as a firmly grasped fact their development as they existed upon their island, and the increasing swiftness of its pace as the years went on. They had ever been a people readier to accept a bird in the hand than two in the bush, although they might be fairly confident of their skill in bird-catching. This very preference for facts had helped them to abandon the promises of faith that their old religion had so lavishly held out to them, and to accept the attitude of patiently waiting for light. So now, when their science had found the light and they had every prospect of opening communication with the intelligences that lived just outside of their unaided ken, they would rather wait upon the solid earth till they saw as solid fact to rest on in their flight from the earth.

They were eager, therefore, to postpone for some generations or ages yet the catastrophe they feared. They had had far back in their history a dim sense of the wrecking power of Lilaroma and its connection with the volcanoes in their old antarctic home. Their more recent earth-science had made the twilight prophecy into a clear fact. In an early geological age of the earth the continent round the south pole had sent a broad outlier far north through the southern ocean; it had indeed stretched close up to the equator. This they knew as soon as they began to study the natural history of Limanora and of the archipelago around it. Not merely were the birds of the same or kindred species with those of their old home, but many of them had long preserved the memory of the former bridge between the two; as the ancient expedition that brought the ancestry of the Limanorans sailed across the intervening ocean, flights of the birds they were familiar with were seen making for their new home, and some of them fell on the decks or settled occasionally on the rigging of their ships. Their unscientific and superstitious ancestors took this as an omen of success; they thought that these birds had been sent from heaven to direct their course, and they steered straight in the line of their flight. The successful result confirmed them in their superstition for many ages after they had landed on their tropical isles.

But the careful observation and the science of later times cleared up the mystery. For a period they had taken it as a proof of the similarity of nature all over the world, when they found so much of the fauna and flora like those of their old home. But at last it began to strike cautious observers that certain birds disappeared during their summer season and reappeared in their winter. Classification soon separated the migratory from the localised, and the modifications of the species that they had been accustomed to in their old home from those that were quite new to them. This passed from the birds to the other animals, and thence to the flora. After the observer had done his work of classifying all the animal and plant life, scientific thought entered in and found the causes of both the similarities and the dissimilarities between the new or tropical and the old or antarctic. After many ages the migration of birds lessened; for few returned in the winter, and as the climate became cooler through process of time, most species preferred to remain the summer long. Then, when an expedition went back to the ancient home of the race in the south, all trace of cultivation and cities had vanished underneath the everlasting snows, and the southern summer was found to be as severe as their ancient winter had been. The increasing rigours of the new climate to the south had reduced the mass of the bird-migrations.

The expedition followed the long-charted route of the feathered travellers, and on its return sounded the depths and tested the seas and their fauna the whole way. When the investigators had reached the close of their labours, it became patent to them that their voyage had been along the coast of a buried continent that had had its northernmost point not far to the north of Lilaroma. Their soundings along the line of bird-route were ever the shallowest, and at points on it, if they left its direction, they suddenly dropped into the deepest of oceans. A mountain-range, sometimes broken into immense precipices and forested along its slopes, had evidently margined the lost continent on its west and had stood the siege of the encroaching ocean through geological ages, till the slow catastrophe of subsidence had sent it under the victorious march of its enemy. Here and there it left a barren rock or a volcanoed isle like a buoy to mark where its wreckage had been submerged. Everywhere on the bird-line they found a shallow-ocean flora and fauna; if ever they sounded or dredged or fished or dived at any distance from it, they passed into a deeply pelagic belt of life, or rather belt of death.

It dawned upon them that their old home and their new formed the extremities of the vanished continent, and that their height was one of the consequences of the submergence; the deeper the great submarine range sank, the higher Lilaroma and the lofty torch-mountains of their ancient home rose. But repeated visits to their old snow-coffined land, and the expansion of their earth science into an art, gave them farther-reaching views of the causes of this vast subsidence. The old bird-route was one of the most ancient fissure-lines in the crust of the earth. Out of it along its whole length had flowed in the earliest geological ages the oozes of lava that formed the backbone of the old continent as it rose from the sea, its most lasting bastion against the encroachments of the watery element. Here and there along the great chain of mountains, as they rose denuded of their softer rocks and stood wrinkled into canyons and gorges by the rivers that swept them clean, blazed at long intervals of time huge vents for the smouldering fires underneath. As the mountain-barrier sank and the ocean flowed over its forests that had graved into the winged species the memory of their ancestral feeding-grounds, and finally closed all the breathing-spaces of the fiery Titan beneath, his passion sought vent more and more through the torch-cones of the snow-buried southern land and through the lofty crater of Lilaroma. Expedition after expedition to their ancient home revealed the simultaneity of volcanic action in the two regions; but the greater the titanic paroxysms in the one, the less they were in the other. They were the two pulses and breathing-vents of the buried giant.

For many ages after some unknown submarine catastrophe had hedged them into their archipelago by the untraversible mill-race and the dark belt of mist, they had been unable to test the connection between their own fire-mountain and those in their old home. But they could easily imagine during the paroxysms of Lilaroma what was occurring far off in the southern snows; and when they had mastered the art of aërial flight, they resumed their expeditions to the glacial regions of the south. Every few years might have been seen, had there been mariners there to see them, the strangest of all flying things, beings in human form, winging their way through the air southwards or northwards. At first the bands were large and well equipped in order to guard against all risks. But in time they grew bolder, and companies of half a dozen, or even three or four, ventured on the long flight to the south. At last the families of earth-scientists were entrusted with the task, and sent their messengers to report on the conduct of the antarctic volcanoes.

These reported that, if ever those southern vents should close, no application of the art of Leomarie could save Limanora, or indeed the archipelago around, from disastrous explosion. The circular current with its belt of mist had shown that this was the thinnest crust and the weakest point on the whole line of fissure; and if the sea broke into the volcanoes of the other extremity, the steam generated from the percolating water would make for the archipelago and blow it to dust. Recent messengers to the south had found dangerous developments in the regions of snow and ice. Where it lay in the line of the ancient fissure, the land was rapidly subsiding; and that was exactly the locality of the southern volcanoes. If the walls of their craters should sink so low that the waters of the ocean could make breaches in them, then would the final catastrophe occur to Limanora.

Whilst the last decennial review was proceeding, and high hopes were rising in the breasts of all that a few generations would see the race independent of the fear of terrestrial cataclysms, their minds were jerked from the future into the present. Our torch-cone suddenly broke into a great column of steam, and a fine dust fell upon the island. There had been no preliminary warning and little had been put in readiness, although the Leomo had been uneasy for weeks as they noticed the spasmodic action of their earth-sensors. The heat and the magnetism in their lava-wells had been rapidly changing their degree every few hours. But this had occurred in previous periods without any recorded effect above the surface of the earth. They had therefore only kept more zealous watch without resorting to more than the usual relieving action.

Now the whole people were called to their assistance, and the concentrated power of Rimla was turned on to the boring of vents. On every side of Lilaroma leomorans were busy, and soon the imprisoned lava and steam escaped by a thousand exits. But a new method was adopted by the Leomo. They shipped in huge faleenas of the newest and most powerful type a number of earth-perforators, and along with them a large quantity of machinery that would enable them to use the wasting energies of the southern elements. Amongst others Thyriel and myself had to manage and steer one of the great aërial cars, for it was chiefly members of the Leomo that manned the expedition.

High we rose above the archipelago, before we attempted to cross the mist-ring. Below us we could see the Limanoran houses and buildings gleam rainbow-hued like bubbles on the beach of an ocean. Higher still, and the various isles of the archipelago crept closer together in the perspective, a handful of emeralds cast upon a plain of azure. Our eyes wandered over the scene and saw how it was set in its dull-white milky ring, a narrow and impenetrable hedge that cut this little world off from the sight of its fellows upon earth.

Through a cloud we shot that drenched and freshened our gleaming car, then followed the fleet southwards across the circular thread drawn round the nest of islets. We were out in the wider spaces of the world again, and our home receded into a speck on the horizon. Over the waste of waters we sped, a great grey plain flecked with white. At first I lost my cool confidence in this trackless wilderness; but fearlessness returned to me as I saw the face of Thyriel bent now on the Limanoran modifications of the compass, and again on the rest of the fleet to the right and left of us. The lumona or sun-compass and the ularema or sun-chart were our trusty guides by day, even if we had lost sight of our companions at any time; our track had been marked out for us on our sun-chart of the heavens and we could not fail to know where we were, even if clouds should obscure the face of the great orb. If only a few straggling rays managed to reach the face of the instrument, indistinguishable though they might be to our sense of warmth or of light, they affected its delicate apparatus; it told us their exact direction and angle, whilst another face told us the exact point of the day, and of the north and south line. There was needed no calculation to find the region where we were, the lumona did it for us; and it kept tracing our course, as we accomplished it, by means of an indicator on our ularema or day-chart.

Once I had been instructed by Thyriel in the management and guidance of the airship, she lay down to rest; and I was alone beneath the oppressive paleness of the vault. I dared not look over the side lest the sight of the grey wilderness far below me should make my head swim. Only once did I look up; and the sense of limitlessness numbed me. Now and again I glanced quickly at the rest of the fleet. But I was too fearful lest something should go wrong to turn my eyes away from the tracer of the lumona as it moved upon the sun-chart, or to take my nerve-power from my hands as they grasped, the right the governor of our flight-power and the left the rod of the steering-gear. As the hours flew and nothing untoward occurred, I relaxed the tension of my system and enjoyed the glide of the ship and sang to the beat of its wings. The sense of solitude passed as I felt the magnetic sympathy of my comrades in the other cars thrill me and my spirits rose with the exhilaration of the heights through which we travelled.

The sun had reached the western round of the sea, and swelled into a vast ball of fire. Thyriel awoke as his rim dipped into the ocean and at once prepared for a change of methods. She taught me how to turn on the power of the engine into the rows of huge lamps that were meant to search the darkness of the night. Then she brought out the alumare or star-compass and substituted it for the lumona; she removed the day-chart and put in its place the manularema or night-chart, adjusting the indicator of the star-compass to its tracing.

Night fell and brought out the lamp-jewelled sides of the other airships. They looked like a fleet of gigantic glow-worms sweeping through the air. What we showed like to any wandering ship on the ocean beneath us it is difficult to imagine. I myself had traversed those solitary levels in the *Daydream*, and I tried to think how I could have explained the strange phenomenon had I seen it from my deck. The superstitious amongst my sailors might have taken it for a portent, some as one from heaven, others as one from hell. The scientific would have concluded it to be a series of fireballs travelling before an upper current of the winds. I should have recorded it in my note-book among the observations of meteors and other similar phenomena, and have waited further illumination. By day we were too high to attract the attention of anyone but the investigator of cloud-changes and weather-signs, and we saw no sign of human life during our long aërial voyage to the south. But away beneath us we could just descry floating brown specks swiftly tracing their zigzag course over the grey plain and knew them for the broad-winged albatrosses, whose flight the Limanorans had so carefully studied for the construction and navigation of their faleenas. For by an automatic arrangement which brought the currents of the wind to bear upon the steering-gear, our car now gracefully rose, and again as gracefully fell when the wind was against it, now swept to this side, now glided to that. All that I had to think of was the main course. On a later voyage even the steersman was superfluous, except in a storm or violent change of winds; for a chart was invented on which the course of the voyage was traced in the shape of a metal groove, and in this the end of the steering-rod was made to move. The two automatic movements governed the manipulation of the winds and the course of the car. It was the same with the engines that achieved the beat of the wings; the slightest change in the opposing medium communicated itself to the electric power and modified it. All that was needed from the occupants of the faleena was a little attention now and again to see that the machinery was working smoothly and solidly, and to ensure that the steering-rod adjusted itself to the caprices of the wind.

On this, our first long aërial expedition, one of us had always to be at the helm, although I found after a few watches that there was needed but little tension either of muscle or nerve to keep the ship to her course. Thyriel took the first half of the night and of the day, and I took the other two sections. When I awoke in the middle of the first night and took my place at the helm, the sight bewildered and dazed me; I felt as if I had gone back again into the region of dream. The stars seemed to throb close in upon me; I felt as if in a cosmic confessional with myriads of world-eyes wide open to see into my heart. I was not afraid; yet my veins throbbed in awe before this palpitation of the cosmos. But I settled down to my task and grew conscious of the surrounding fleet of fireflies, that even at their great distance from me numbed my eyes with the flash of their lamps and paled the light of the stars. Beneath me, as I looked over the bulwark, there was nothing but the solid blackness of midnight; never had I felt so isolated. Thoughts wove as unceasingly in my brain as the wing-beats wove upon the loom of night. Now and again was I stirred from my meditation by the swoop of our faleena as it breasted some great billow of wind. So precipitous were some of those waves that my heart leapt in my bosom, as we rose before them or slid down them. I never passed a night of such intensity of exhilaration and thought. There was my lifelong comrade peacefully sleeping as I watched; the infinities above magnetised me with their sympathies, as their eyes searched me to the heart; below me the midnight brooded silently over what I knew to be the untracked ocean.

Day after day, night after night, we sped on, the air growing rapidly colder, till, for the sake of my unadaptable system, we drew the transparent oval roof over the faleena and fixed the radiator which kept the temperature at an even level. Thereafter the stars were not so omnipresent in their gaze; there was more of a limit to the space in which we dwelt; and the movements of the faleena impressed themselves less upon my senses.

At last as my watch was ending one moonless night I could see a dim flare in the southern sky which I took for the aurora australis. But when Thyriel gazed at it and then at the agitation of the fireflies abreast of us, she knew it was the reflection of the great antarctic torch-mountains. I rose at dawn and could see below us the white glacial cliffs of the polar continent. Thyriel seemed stirred by some emotion that I was ignorant of, but soon knew to be the recognition of the original home of her race; there seemed to move in her blood the ancestral yearning for the land from which they had come. She did not shrivel up in the excessive cold as I did, but looked forward with ecstasy to moving amid the snow and the ice, though she had seen little of them in her own short life except around the crater of Lilaroma.

Bred though I had been in the rigorous winters of Scotland, I could not bear the bite of the wind and had to put on one of their cold-repelling garments. This consisted of two layers of flexible irelium-woven cloth, one of which was a conductor of electricity and the other a resister of it. The outer or conducting layer was connected with some labramor which carried a store of electricity and this combination produced a warm, healthful glow all round the body. I had gloves and cap and mask of the same construction and, when fully equipped, I could defy the most bitter cold that the upper atmosphere of the earth ever experienced.

With this armour on I looked forward with delight to our sojourn in the region of snow and ice as I watched our approach to the rough ocean-like surface of the new country. For Thyriel took the helm, now that there was needed more delicate manipulation of the faleena, and I stood in the bow and gazed at the rest of the fleet rising and falling on the wind-waves. Now and again I interpreted a signal from the faleena of the guiding elder, whilst my comrade was busy adapting the course to the caprices of the wind. But as a rule her own magnetic sense was alert enough to know what were the intentions of the other airships.

Round the group of great fire-cones we coasted, keeping clear of their smoke-brush and dust-vomit; for the wind was off the land and bore their ejections miles out to sea and high into the air. Across the icy plains, ridged and hummocked by pressure from the higher land beyond, we flew, once rising high enough to get a glance over the passes of the great mountain-barrier, whence the torrents of ice slowly found their way to the coast. Beyond I could discern, even with my undeveloped eye-power, level plains stretching to the horizon, plains which indicated water underneath; and upon them the direction of the furrows and hummocks revealed whither the mass of the sea beneath flowed towards some narrow exit, overlapping and playing leapfrog in its eagerness to escape the pressure from behind.

But the habits of this almost land-locked sea had no immediate interest for us, and we soon turned and made before the wind for a valley that lay sheltered between the mountain-chain and the group of torch-cones. Within a brief time we had all our faleenas secured, and the multitudinous rings of the leomorans they carried deposited in caves ready for the coming operations. Then the elder who led the expedition took his airship, and with it we saw him circle round the individual volcanoes and reconnoitre the inroads of the sea. He had, we knew, already seen the dangerous proximity of one new crater to the low coast that divided the group of fire-hills from the galloping waves.

Manifestly expedition was demanded. For he returned with great swiftness; and all was soon bustle and preparation in the camp, although it had settled down for a rest. The word was passed round that, if the wind changed and whipped the racing billows to their raid, a high tide might find its way into the new crater and undo the local work of Limanoran civilisation. The fleet was at once in the air with the engines ready to be placed; and within two hours the winds and the waves, the magnetism of the earth, and the electricity of the air had been yoked to the great power-machines. Then the rings of the leomorans were attached, and the stores of energy brought to bear on them; before long we could see at a dozen different points high up the side of the cone brushes of black smoke bending before the wind. Between the new low crater and the old lofty one a score of new vents for the explosive energy of the fires underneath had been worked into the crust of the earth ere the wind had changed round into alliance with the waters. The molten rock which had oozed from the dangerous cone at the edge of the sea had sealed its mouth before the ocean leapt into it. In order to make the seal more secure a sluggish river of lava was directed down the slope from several leomorans, and sent over the lips of the exposed crater. After every sign of the offending cone but a low hummock had disappeared under the molten invasion, bastions were drawn all along the coast beneath it in the manner familiar to Limanora.

When this fortification of the mountain was finished and the strain upon our muscles and nerves, and especially upon our eyes, was relieved, we had leisure to look about us. The sight that met our view, as we looked down the slopes of the mountain, was deeply impressive. The flow of the red-hot rock from the mouths of our lava-wells had melted the glacial concretions for hundreds of yards beyond the margins of the molten currents, and laid bare the ruins of a great city that had evidently been buried in ice and snow since the lowering of the temperature had made the climate unbearable by men of civilised nurture and habits. The steam rising from the neighbourhood of ice and fire had covered the disentombed secret from our vision whilst we were working, and as the wind fell that had swept the veil aside for a moment, the marvellous sight was again curtained over, and we began to think that it had been but a waking dream.

Some days after, when the lava had sufficiently cooled to leave portions of the defrosted slope open to the light of heaven, we revisited the scene. Several broad streets and great squares had been unburied; and the architecture revealed how artistic and how advanced in mechanical contrivances the people that built them had been. A thick covering of volcanic dust and ash had plastered them over, so that it was difficult to move on foot amongst the ruins now that the moisture of the melting ice had mingled with it. After clearing the débris from the doors we entered some of the houses that had not lost their roofs, and there was evidence of hasty flight; on the floors and couches were strewn pellmell the contents of boxes and cupboards and wardrobes, half of them still stiff with the ice that the adjacent streams of lava had been unable to melt. The evacuation of this luxurious city had evidently occurred during some great outburst of the volcano which had threatened its existence. But the climate had grown rigorous before the catastrophe; for in every house and every room there were elaborate apparatus for heating, and most of the clothing lying about was of fur or of thick, warm stuffs, and when we dug beneath the coating of volcanic ash, we found in places accumulations of ice which must have taken years to freeze. Layer after layer of dirt and rubbish had been embedded by the preservative frost; and, had we cared to cut through the stratified ice, we might have counted the years, or perhaps centuries, through which this heap had accumulated.

For several visits we could find no human body, though we came across one or two carcasses of emaciated animals that had evidently lived amongst the ruins till the last vestige of fodder had disappeared under the volcanic layer or the accumulating ice. But at last in a back lane, probably inhabited by slaves, we penetrated into a low house whose roof had crashed in under the weight of the falling dust, and there we saw a scene that moved us to tears. The mummied body of a little child prepared for burial lay upon a bier and over it was stretched the corpse of the mother; she could not tear herself away from the last relics of her dead baby, and in returning to rescue it, or to weep over it, had been overwhelmed by the falling roof; the frost of centuries had kept off the finger of decay, and this Niobe and her child had remained like sculptured stone. We covered the bodies gently with the volcanic mud there as they lay, and left the frost to work its petrifaction again, for we had not the heart to disturb the scene. Here amongst the proletariate of this luxurious people there was evidence of that maternal transport which had showed the path of ethical development and exaltation to the Limanorans, and was destined to raise the energies of our world into higher and higher forms. This, we knew, was but the terrestrial type of an altruistic law which was working throughout the cosmos, and making every centre of energy that had more than the average give of its more to those centres that had less.

All in our power was now done to relieve the pressure of the subterranean fires that were threatening to burst the ancient fissure; and all too that could be done to ward off the batteries of the ocean. Then were we sent in different directions to inspect and report on the state of the ice-cliffs that beetled over the waves. We hovered for days about the rocks and their glaciers and the universal observation was that the coast was rapidly subsiding; since the last visit of the Limanoran messengers its line had sunk many yards; marks that had been made far above the reach of the waters were now washed by the break of the higher billows. Thyriel and I were sent to a loftier bluff which extended for almost a mile between shelving beach and shelving beach just underneath the site of the buried city.

After inspecting the higher parts of it for days and measuring the height of the old marks above the farthest reach of the waves, a windless day, on which the ocean lay as if frozen, gave us opportunity of following the cliff at its lowest sea-margin. For half a mile or more nothing exceptional met our eyes. Then suddenly we came upon a great chasm in the rock where a soft intermediate stratum had mouldered away into sand before the everlasting battery of the waves. Over it a great dome of ice was stretched, which was ever being thickened by the climbing spray of the billows as they broke into it. The entrance into this cave was somewhat low and narrow, and a jagged rock in the centre of it churned the angry waters into milky foam. We saw that this feature would make the opening invisible under its veil of spray on all but days of perfect calm.

We were afraid to enter lest the sea should rise and imprison us, so we called some comrades to our aid, and they brought a light faleena that was made to serve the double purpose of air-boat and water-boat. Then Thyriel took flight from above, and with the impetus we bore ourselves and the boat through one of the passages past the jagged tooth of rock. As we settled upon our faleena and looked up, the sight that met our eyes took our breath away. The sun was shining brilliantly, lighting up the dome of ice with such power as to make its whole thickness transparent. Through it in every direction thick as motes in a sunbeam were strewn human bodies, wrapped and mummied as in death. Some lay on their sides with the head pillowed on the arm; and as the face was uncovered, we could see the features as clearly as if we stood in the chamber where they lay. The frost had kept the flesh and the tints of it uncorrupted. We could almost have sworn that they breathed as they slept, yet in the case of most it must have been the sleep of thousands of years.

This was the cemetery of that ancient people which had built the city lately found. Doubtless this ice-crust in which their graves had been cut had once stood securely miles away from the coast; and in it they thought that their dead would be safe for all time. But, as the shore sank, the glacial crust ceased to be a plain and slid downwards along the increasing slope to the ocean; and, before many years could pass, this hyaline resting-place of the dead would be launched into the sea and be swept by the storms and tides into warmer airs and currents, which would release the bodies from their beautiful petrifaction, and give their elements to the ravening powers of the waters, or the microscopic corruption of invisible life. In fact on our return voyage we flew over several icebergs that were floating catacombs. On the surface of one we discerned the pallor of a mummied face, just released by the strong rays of the sun from its ancient rigidity, and the still stony garments shining through their pellucid covering.

We could almost decipher through the milky blueness of the ice-dome, when the sun shone most brightly, the inscriptions on the tablets lying beside these forgotten dead. But the winds began to dirge within this strange diaphanous mausoleum; and even the waters seemed to move around the cave with suppressed sob. We thought the sounds ominous, and, rising high up into the roof of the cave, close to the dead that had slept there so like life for so many centuries, we poised ourselves and, taking aim, dashed through the narrow entrance, while our comrades without drew the faleena out by the cord with which they had held it securely. Later in the day, as the calm continued, the guiding elder sent others into the cave and they secured one of the most elaborately hieroglyphed tablets. Those of us who had most recently studied in the valley of memories were able to trace much resemblance between the language of the inscription and the ancient Limanoran tongue; and when we returned to our island, it afforded one of the clues by which we were able to unravel the history of this ancient antarctic people. They were the descendants of those whom the northwards migration had left to their fate amid the growing rigours of the southern winter. After the departure of these who founded the colonies of Riallaro and became the ancestry of the Limanorans, the wealthier classes had evidently abandoned themselves to pleasure and luxury within their splendid and superheated dwellings, whilst the proletariate, though growing more vigorous, and venturing far out upon the ice and the ocean on fishing and furring expeditions, fell deeper and deeper into the contempt of semi-slavery. Loyalty to their masters and ignorance still kept them unrebellious in their growing embrutement, till the volcanic catastrophe solved the problem of their future relationships. Whither the survivors had gone, when the outburst of the subterranean fires drove them forth, no one could say; doubtless the peasant fishermen and hunters took the effeminate caste in their rough boats over the sea to some warmer climate; probably, if the expeditions survived the storms and billows of the broad ocean, they landed on the coasts of South Africa or on those of South America and introduced an alien civilisation and more complicated problems amongst the primitive peoples of those isolated regions.

Before we left, we had to investigate the shores of the inland sea for evidence of subsidence, resting on them for a period whilst we punctured the slopes of the mountains, in order to give a new direction to the pressure of the fires upspringing from below. When all the leomorans that were needed had been placed in position and got into working order, not more than half of the expedition were required to attend to them. The others, and amongst them Thyriel and myself, were allowed to wander over the shores of the gulf or sea, everywhere finding abundant evidence that the whole neck of land which divided it from the ocean, high though it still was in the lofty mountain-barrier, was rapidly subsiding, and would ultimately succumb to the batteries of the besieging elements. This might take many centuries, but that the huge volcanic range would be submarine within measurable time was obvious. Had the rate for even a decade of years been constant, we could easily have calculated the number of centuries that would elapse before the great catastrophe; but the amount of subsidence varied from period to period, increasing and then decreasing. The most alarming change had occurred since the last visit of the Leomo to their old home. Square miles that had been low-lying land some few years before were now encrusted with marine ice; and lofty precipices were perceptibly lower.

The most striking proof of the rapid subsidence was not observed till the day before our return. The shoulder of an outlier of the range pushed its way as a lofty promontory right into the gulf, its whole length and breadth being covered with glacial concretion. Some recent tempest had broken off the end of its river of ice, and at the same time a sudden subsidence of the land had left the face of its cliff a complete new section, as if shorn by a microtome. The sight that revealed itself to us as we flew round it was most impressive. City after city had evidently been built upon the broad bluff, its pleasant position overlooking the inland sea and its proximity to easy harbourage ever attracting the population back again after each cataclysm. Time after time the city had, we conjectured, been overwhelmed by the ashes of some great volcanic outburst from the range. There we could see in section the various strata of buildings one above the other, each filled with ash and dust and preserved by the power of frost. Hundreds of years must have elapsed between the destruction of one city and the building of the next, a period long enough in fact to obliterate the memory of panic and anguish from the traditions of posterity. In some houses we could still discern the signs of the stampede that had occurred one day thousands of years ago. Articles of value were half-torn from their treasuries and then abandoned; jewellery and dishes made of the precious metals were here and there held in place upon the mosaicked floors by the frozen mass of earth above them; they had evidently been seized at the first warning of the coming catastrophe and then thrown away as alarm made life dearer. In one chamber we saw the outline of the body of a man across its threshold, his hand out beyond his head clutching some receptacle of precious metals. In the space between the outer walls of two houses the body of a woman was exposed, face downwards, and beneath the bosom the form of an infant child.

How many long-forgotten tragedies might be unearthed we could not stay to discover. A little labour and we could have penetrated into these cities; the application of a leomoran would have melted the dust and ashes and brought to view the stratified life of ages before. Had we been interested in following out the existence of these far-distant relatives of the Limanorans, we could have begun with the lowest layer, and followed the evidences of civilisation up through each successive entombment, till finally the people were driven from the site by frost, a force more rigorous and potent against culture and luxury than fire. But the Limanorans had enough in the records of their own ancestry to tell them all the history that might be illuminated by such excavations. They knew that after an advance in the two or three lower strata, there would be found no progress except in luxury and the arts that contribute to luxury. And they had enough of such development in their own archipelago before their own senses, to allay any eagerness for viewing illustrations of it in ancient and dead history.

The sight was interesting and impressive, but we all had learned its lesson too well to desire further acquaintance with it. In Fialume we had studied similar histories during our pupillage; and daily could we watch through the idrovamolan the enactment of similar life in the islands around Limanora. A little apparent advance was followed by as much retrogression; the generations were as like in essence as two species of the same genus, the difference being merely superficial and unvital. It was enough to make the Limanoran heart stop in its beating to see the dreary sameness of the ages in the history of a people, as far as development of spiritual character and power were concerned. The changes and revolutions were but changes of lay-figures under the official dresses and ceremonials, or at best an expansion of the sphere of luxury. What mattered it to men that were panting after ideals they ever saw above and beyond them who were masters and who were servants or subjects in those unprogressive levels of humanity, who or how many sated their appetites or covered their skins with the rich and ceremonious raiment of dominance? The heroisms and romances, the striking turns of fortune, the world-renowned victories that made the eyes of other races blaze with wonder were all histrionic to those who knew what real development was.

This section cut through the history of ten thousand years would reveal but the same old story that they had read so often in the annals of their own far past. We turned away sick of heart, knowing the countless griefs and agonies, struggles and combats, that had gone to the making of this human stratification, and the complete futility of them all. The best that could be thought was that oblivion had buried them, and that the energy set free at the deaths of so many thousands of generations had perchance a better opportunity of rising in the scale of vitality as it wandered into other spheres than the human or the terrestrial.

It was not then without deliberate intention that our departure from the old home of the race occurred soon after the discovery of this strange frozen museum of forgotten peoples. After everything was done that could be done to divert the upward pressure of the subterranean fires from vents close to the margin of the sea, the faleenas winged their way back to the north as rapidly as they had come. No incident took place to mar the return voyage, and we were soon back at our old employments in Limanora.

CHAPTER XIII

RELIGION

AFTER a few days' reflection and observation, I felt a change in the spirit of the people. There was less of that serenity which had struck me so often as one of the distinctive characteristics of themselves and their actions. Every family seemed to hurry in its efforts at development and the pace of their advance might almost be called feverish now. This was especially the case with all who were engaged in the more spiritual investigations into the nature of the cosmos. Next to them in increase of eagerness and enthusiasm came the astronomical families, the astrobiological, and all whose researches bore upon stellar conditions and interstellar migration. The gaze of the whole race was more distinctly outwards and extra-terrestrial.

I had conjectured the cause of this acceleration and impetuosity and soon definitely knew it to be the result of our expedition to the south and the reports we brought back. The elders on considering them saw that the safety of the island as a resting-place and arena for their progress was not to be depended on for many generations more. The increase in the rate of subsidence of their old home meant a transference of the destructive power of the subterranean fires to the other end of the ancient fissure within a measurable period. The volcanic vents on the antarctic coast must be closed beneath the ocean before many centuries were over; and the rushing waters in quenching their fires would find their way in uncontrollable steam towards the weakest point of the crust, which they knew to be their own archipelago. Ere many generations could come and go this terrestrial home of the race would be blown to dust, and new lands would appear at some other point on the line of fissure.

Where could they settle on the round of the earth? There was no land except their old home to the south isolated enough to admit of their following up their ideals. All the remote islands in other oceans were already fully occupied, and were impracticable for them unless at the sacrifice of human life, a condition that would outrage their whole idea of development. The globe was closed for them except the region of everlasting ice where their remote ancestry had dwelt; and that too might at any moment flash into dust before the explosive forces beneath the crust. The alternative of seeking a home on another star had seemed to them the only one for many generations, and they had been preparing for it by inventions that would enable them to float clear of the terrestrial atmosphere for many centuries, and by explorations in interstellar space. But many discoveries and thoughts had thrown a new light upon this stellar migration. They would have to exist in their circumscribed faleenas as they travelled through the ether for many generations of even their long lives, and these ships would be their cradle and their tomb. They would have to resign for many centuries the conquests of the elements and of the forces of nature, that they had achieved in Limanora. The broad movement which these past ages of history had given to their life, would be narrowed into a space no larger than one chamber of their own mansions. They would live imprisoned, and their imprisonment would lay its brand upon their natures and still more upon the natures of their descendants. The proximity of so many in so small a space would breed physical and, still worse, spiritual disease, that would haunt their posterity for generations after they should settle in their new stellar abode. Their offspring would have the habits and ideas of the savage reared in the wigwam of the rover or the hut of the slave. Even if they could achieve individual flight through the ether, they would have to keep close to their storeships and return every few minutes to the exhausted atmosphere of their swiftwinging faleenas.

If every condition of their interstellar voyage were the same as their life in their own Limanora, what disappointments might not they encounter in their comparative ignorance of the biology of the heavens? Would not most stars that were fit to be inhabited be already choked with life and life at a different stage from that they had attained? If they struck upon a lower grade of existence it would be useless to attempt to raise it, and contrary to their own morality to obliterate it. If they met with a higher type of being, they would be repulsed by it as likely to degrade it. It would be a wretched existence to lead a life of interstellar vagabondage, poor beggars of the cosmos, seeking a star whereon they might rest the sole of their foot. Not more than one world in each system could be at the stage that would fit their life-evolution; most stars would be too young and fierily crude or too old and exhausted to give them the conditions they sought for. In many the life they would encounter would shock and repel them by its monstrosity. What was to hinder some such gigantic form as, the Leomo knew, had existed on the earth in its earlier geological ages, some tremendous winged saurian, having the place on one or more of the stars they visited that man held upon earth? It only meant the development of a brain proportionate to the hugeness of the bulk, and some swiftly moving, deft, and adaptable limb, like the human hand, to give it complete dominance over all the forms of life around it. The elephant needed only the mechanical faculty of the beaver or of the ant to outstrip man in the struggle of life; he had the delicate manipulator in his trunk, he had the long life, and he had the capacity of skull to transform him into the dominant race of the earth. In order to the mastery of his conditions, he had only to make the step from using anything that came ready to his trunk as a weapon into shaping it to his will. Circumstances, accidents, opportunities, pilot the evolution of life upon a world, and the accidental condition of an element or an energy or a locality might have transformed some terrific monster into the master of the first star they visited. It was merely a matter of more or less intricate convolutions of the brain. But perhaps the most terrible thing of all would be to land on a world whose inhabitants had developed the purely intellectual faculties and the section of the brain corresponding to them, at the expense of the nervous centres that have to do with the control of the passions and with the subordination of the animal nature; what a horror it would be to find a star full of Calibans with more than human cunning, and none of human emotion or morality!

The thought of chances like these gave them pause in their migratorial quest. They began to feel that even life amongst the ruder of their fellow-men might be better than landing amongst monsters unstirred by pity or compassion, reverence or tenderness for highly developed life, to whom bloodshed was nothing. It was true that there were in most nations men who were so constituted. But they were, except when they got the command of huge armies and became conquerors, bridled by fear of the punishments that the laws of the country meted out to criminals. It was better to live in proximity to beings amongst whom this moral and emotional neutrality is an exception, than in a world filled with such monsters. Perchance, when their island-home was shattered to dust, their true path lay along the surface of their own globe. They might settle on the slope of some sky-piercing mountain, round whose feet lay untainted tribes of primitive savages; there they might preserve their isolation as perfectly as in Limanora by a hedge of fear around them, which their exceptional power over the forces of nature should forge.

But they knew that before many ages could pass civilised man would penetrate amongst the awed tribes with his potent weapons and his unscrupulous cunning; then would they be unable to avoid bloodshed, or hypocritical ambush, or diplomacy; ambition and hatred would enter in and turn their paradise into a hell. On the whole, they inclined to the other alternative that lay before them when the great catastrophe came; that is, to let it do its worst on their physical or lower elements. Out of their shattered bodies would rise the energy of their systems to follow its career of development untrammelled by any slow-moving matter that was half inert whether living or dead. Death so sudden as that, death under any circumstances or conditions, was no stop or misfortune to the highest that was in them; it was the swiftest way to achieve migration into the interstellar spaces. As it was, they were narrowed and localised in their development, thought (the higher thought) alone finding its way unchecked to any point or sphere in the cosmos. At death they would all be freed from the almost vegetative functions of human existence; they would be released from the prison of locality and their whole being would have the ease of thought in winging from infinity to infinity, and in disregarding the limitations of time and space. Together the whole of their race might find coalescence if not companionship in following out their career of development, unburdened by alliance with a lower type of energy, and in more swiftly attaining a higher and higher goal in the scale of energies.

* * * *

When this conclusion had been reached by the consciousness of the people, the old serenity returned to them. They were ready to meet whatever came, not caring whether their ascent through the grades of being was trammelled by terrestrial forms of energy or set free in the infinities of ether. But I dimly felt that there was a sublime looking upwards in all they did or said added to their former serenity that transformed it into what approached to the noblest forms of devotional ecstasy I had seen amongst men. They never allowed themselves to fall into the moulds of thought that his bodily and terrestrial needs so freely supply to man. Though recognising the practical demands of the physical nature, they satisfied and then dismissed them as rapidly as was possible; and with all their marvellous machinery and inventions and their accumulation of power, the time occupied in this satisfaction was so abbreviated as to be scarcely noticeable in the labyrinth of daily pursuits.

I had been greatly puzzled during my long period of training to see no trace of religious worship in this noble race. Growing up with the instinct in me that of all manifestations of human possibilities religion was the most sublime, yet I had come to know before I left Europe how degraded, gross, and foul even a lofty-minded religion might become. But the best men and women I had known there had ever been stirred with the spirit of religious reverence and love. I could not account for these, the noblest and ablest beings I had seen on earth, ignoring the claims of what is the highest of all, and I watched eagerly for any indication of acts or moods of worship. Early in my residence on the island I had discovered that there were no temples and no priests; that was patent to the most casual glance of the stranger. Amongst all their public buildings there was none that could be taken as devoted to the worship of a deity, and there was no family or caste or set of men whose chief functions were to superintend such a worship. But perhaps their religious acts were private or even secret and I was on the alert many years for any sign of such a thing in the house of my proparents or in that of Thyriel. Finally discovering nothing that could be construed even in the most distant way into a ceremonial attitude or word, I gradually abandoned any expectation of such a thing.

My attention was now aroused by the new halo around their serene acceptance of the conditions of life. There was rapture and there was longing in their halcyon view of the world; yet the rapture and the longing never withdrew them from immediate pursuits and duties, never gave them the ennui of life that transport and passion generally entrain. They seemed to have the vision and the upward glance of the seer without his brooding and apartness. It was rather an intensification of their usual feelings and attitude to life. This was nearer than anything else I had experienced in Limanora to the unperturbed faith in a higher being and the yearning for proximity to him that I had witnessed in those whom we used in Europe to call, for lack of a less trite term, saints. At the next Manora or decennial review the predominating interest was the theopathic side of human nature, and I discovered more of their views of religion in the few years preceding it than in all the decades I had spent amongst them.

So devotional did I think the magnetism which ran through the community, that I plucked up courage to ask about the religion. My question was dealt with in the calmest and most rational way possible amongst human beings. There was no immediate reply, except an elevation of the finger to the brow and then to the wide vault of the sky, but I was led to a part of Fialume I had not visited. It lay in a region of the valley that I had carefully avoided as full of gloom, and damp with the vapour of a tumbling waterfall; I had never noticed any one enter it, and my curiosity had never been awakened about it.

Here were stored the records that illustrated the evolution of religion, records made by light, sound, and magnetism. It was intensely interesting for me to see so complete a museum of the natural history of worship. Every faith in the world had its due place, fixed according to its inner spirit and development. So graphic was the map of the whole that in a moment I saw the common kinship of all, and the differentiating qualities that made one worship higher and more advanced than another. My guide flashed living pictures of the ceremonies of each, and then let me listen to the speeches and talks of the officiants and of many of the worshippers. The magnetographs struck into me the feelings that pervaded the masses in the temples, and those that filled the breast of the solitary priest or devotee during the most solemn and enthusiastic act of worship. I could feel how much or how little the religion introduced into the life of the people. Day after day I returned with eagerness to the sight and the study of this absorbing phase of human nature, and seemed to get to the very heart of every faith and its influence. The mere accidents of its history were felt to be non-essential; its inner development stood out as plainly as if written in letters of fire.

My guide did not need to teach me the lesson. I knew it as well as if I had learned it from infancy. I knew why there were no temples, no ceremonies, no hierophantic families, no outward sign of faith, amongst this far-seeing people. Their own early endeavours to purify and develop the faith handed down to them from their forefathers were there as vividly pictured as any faith from the world outside. They had had temples as splendid as any I have ever seen or heard described; their ceremonies were artistic, noble, and significant; their music was as nearly sublime as earthly music can be; and the priestly profession attracted many of the ablest and some of the best natures in the community by its princely salaries, drawn from the gifts of former ages of the faithful, and by its high prerogatives.

At first I wondered how it had been possible to uproot an institution that had evidently grown out of the most intimate instincts of the race. The higher dignitaries were so lordly and influential they might easily control even by their private alliances and social dominance the powers of the state; and the poorer hierophants had ingratiated themselves with the middle classes and proletariate, from whom they came. Reverence, fear, love, ambition, pride, self-interest, all the commoner emotions and passions of humanity, were engaged and intertwined with the worship. How could such a widely ramifying profession allow itself to be overthrown?

When the exilings were over, it was found that there was not a member of the priestly profession left on the island; nor was there anything of the wealth of the church, except the solid walls of the temples. The dignitaries and most of the transferable riches had found their way to Aleofane; the bulk of the poor clergy landed in Tirralaria, and smaller bands drifted away to smaller islands like Coxuria, establishing there communities marked by some extreme eccentricity of faith. All the vestments and altars and ornaments of the temples had vanished before the last expedition left the shores of Limanora; even the huge bells that had rung to service, and the baser metals for making the roofs water-tight, had disappeared. Nothing but the stones and mortar were left to indicate where the great faith of the past had housed itself. One or two expeditions even were seen to set out from Tirralaria and Aleofane to fetch the very temples away stone by stone. To prevent the cupidity of the exiles from wasting itself on futile attempts against the island, the edifices were tumbled into the sea, and helped to make the bastions which guarded the shores.

Having thus got rid of all the outward property and signs of their former worship, they had to count the cost and consider how they were to meet the situation. It had been inculcated by the officiants of the church for untold generations that all morality, and in fact all civilisation, would vanish with faith. Religion was the foundation of everything in life that was worth preserving, and most of the people trembled if any change were proposed in the national worship. They feared that the object of their devotion would withdraw the light of his countenance from them, should the slightest feature of it be modified. Even the scientific and cultured thought that religion acted as an excellent watchdog or policeman, keeping the uneducated within the bounds of the laws and traditions of the nation. Changes had crept in unobserved by the worshippers, and had been sanctified by time; then open proposals for change gave the shock and the alarm, and made the whole fabric seem to shake and totter. The unperceived changes were far greater and more revolutionary in their ultimate effect, for they were generally changes of degeneration which ended in decay and ruin. But everything that was deliberately intended to fit the old institution to the new times was looked on with horror, as sacrilege never to be forgiven.

It was therefore with a certain tremor that they demolished the ancient temples, and put their stones to new and seemingly secular uses. But once the transformation was accomplished and no great catastrophe followed, even the less bold gathered courage. As time went on and the old faith was forgotten and no definite new creed took its place, it began to be felt that the terror of religious change and the belief that religion alone gave the guaranty of all morality and civilisation were alike baseless. After a decade or two, when they began to reflect on their past and analyse their new states of mind and public feeling, they discovered the most striking effect of this abeyance of ecclesiasticism to be the attainment of the ideal of all true religion. Into their very life had soaked the inner spirit of devotion. Every act was done with a reference to something far higher than itself, to which the doer looked up with reverence yet with the sense of its possible attainment in the future. Every piece of conduct, every item of character was moulded as if for all time. All their work they laboured at with an earnestness, enthusiasm, and care that evinced the consciousness of its everlasting issues. In short, they found that the surest way to exclude religion from the life was to assign to it a special section of time, a special profession, and special edifices. These acted as a conduit that drew it from the true business of existence. Men and women came to feel that, these once being set apart, all was done that could be done for the object of their worship, and that the rest of their life upon earth could be given up to whatsoever pleased them, be it irreligious, wicked, or even vile. The religious section of their lives threw its consecrating and protecting shadow over the worst they might do or say or think. Thus came about the strange paradox that the vilest of criminals were often the most devoted to religion when they went into the temples. The specialisation of what should belong to the whole life and conduct lessens its value. If there is a particular channel for religion it will be confined to that channel, except in rare seasons of enthusiasm, when it floods the adjacent regions and does universal havoc.

Formerly the most religious had been the least trustworthy in the ordinary business of life, and they had not been able to understand why; for the deity they worshipped was a compound of all the noblest virtues they could conceive, and honesty and truth and constancy were three of these. Now they perceived that, having given a tithe of their civilisation and energy to the object of their worship, they had shut him and the virtues he embodied out from the rest; he had no claim on that. It was vain for the creed or the priests to insist that the faith should be carried into the life, as long as there was a special part of life dedicated to it. Once the pales were down, and there was no distinction between time and time, between place and place, and between act and act, the nesting-place of hypocrisy disappeared. Every day was sacred; every place was a sanctuary; every act was holy; every moment of their life, every action was a prayer. For they were ever looking upwards and forwards towards the ideal and believed that the noblest reverence they could pay to the cosmos and to the presiding spirit of the cosmos was to raise their own natures ever higher in the cosmic scale. Everything that withdrew them from this cultivation of the special plot assigned to them in the universe, from the development of their better selves, was delaying the true purpose of existence; even acts of reverence and ceremonies of faith were but waste of cosmic energy. As long as they kept raising their struggle for existence to a higher plane, so long were they truly reverencing the greatest being of all, the spirit that gave and was the palpitating life of the cosmos.

They acknowledged that every religion in its origin was a recognition of unknown elements or beings far above the plane of the worshippers. But it rapidly degenerated into mere parasitism upon its deity. The more spiritual faiths in their earlier stages express the yearning for higher scales of being in true efforts to bring the life of the worshipper nearer to that of the worshipped. But soon the curse of religion comes upon them; they try to include races on a lower plane than that of their first worshippers and moulders and to these they must adapt themselves; for it is the mass, the numbers that form the ultimate mould of a faith; the noble natures, for whom they originally came into being, are left neglected and undeveloped, and the whole worship goes lower and lower to fit the needs of the increasing numbers of converts.

Insignificant though the Limanorans felt themselves to be against the infinity of the cosmos, they refused to formulate their worship lest it should fall into parasitism, the source of most of the evil and retrogression in the universe. They knew that it was possible for the lower being to try to rise to the level of existence of the higher and worshipped, and, in advancing, to help his advance. But they had seen too much in history and in contemporary life of the symbiosis of worshippers becoming mere parasitism to trust themselves to anything definite and outward in religion. In daily intercourse the lower and weaker natures cling to the higher and stronger; and if they fail to reciprocate the benefit they receive, and cease to attempt to elevate themselves to the level of their hosts, then they suck the life-blood from them and degrade them. The same holds in religion. The mean worshippers (and the majority in mixed communities are mean) make no effort to better themselves; the higher ideal that they are taught to reverence as a god, they batten upon for favours; they pray to him and yearn for him, not that they may be like him but that he may be like them, and become their active and efficient partner in material things and their accomplice in their mean or evil deeds. The Limanorans conceived that all the higher beings of space struggle to keep clear of such parasitic religionists as the majority of men are. There is no road up the steep of being but by patient self-development through generations and generations. Almost all religions, after their early and enthusiastic stage, are royal roads that seem to lead to the heights of heaven, and are but descents to hell. They only delude men into thinking that there are other ways to divine happiness than that likeness to the divine nature which is to be attained by nothing but slow, gradual, inward change.

* * * *

They had seen so much of the degeneration and immorality of faiths, not only in their own history but in the history of the world, that nothing would persuade them to formulate or define in words what they meant by religion at any stage of their development. For, once they had defined, there was a platform of self-opinion and self-interest to fight for, a nucleus of petrifaction. Rites and outward worship would follow, and a priesthood whose interest it would be to teach that what they profess as a creed is absolute truth. Right well the Limanorans knew how false such teaching is. No age can have a view of life that is not moulded by contemporaneous circumstances and capacity of thought and feeling, and the farther the people pass in time and spirit from the primitive age of the founders of their religion, the more stoutly will they uphold every word of the creed and every feature of the institution. Nothing but a sanguinary revolution will avail to undo the tragic knot with which the spirit of man has thus bound itself. However good for progress the enthusiasm of a faith might be in its early stage, it inevitably became the tomb of the human spirit. Occult explanations of statements that did not tally with acknowledged facts or laws were bound to appear, as soon as the mind of the people began to move and develop; and the Limanorans knew that their marvellous progress had been largely due to the early resolve to have nothing to do with the occult or merely mysterious. Their pioneering books dealt with what still lay under the horizon of the future; but they started from recognised facts and principles and attempted to supply working hypotheses for the men of science. There was nothing of magic or superstition in them, nothing that did not appeal to the laws of reason and ascertained scientific data, nothing that was not meant to be tested by the methods of daily practical life.

Not that they never thought over the problems that are commonly called religious, or yearned for communion with existences nobler than their own.

But their thoughts and feelings were kept out of the sphere of definite expression, through fear that their temporary solutions might crystallise and become permanent. Their faith was purely individual and inward. Yet, when some great step was to be taken in the onward march of the race, as for instance, when a new type of child or enterprise was preparing to be born, the whole community yearned silently towards the living spirit of the cosmos; all their being thrilled with one magnetism that seemed to quiver upwards through the ether, and return again to strengthen and console them in their work. Their ideal seemed to pass as by an inspiration into the child or the enterprise about to be born. The universe, they felt, echoed to their thought; but it would have been desecration to put their seerlike longing into any form of human expression.

This was the nearest they came to what is called worship in other nations. It was difficult to get them to speak of it, for what they would have called their religion was their whole life, their pressing forward and upward in development. Their religion was what Europeans would have defined as the discovery of God, rather than the worship of any idea of Him. It was based on the knowledge that the world had advanced from insignificant life to comparatively noble self-conscious life, and it held firmly that no finality could have yet been reached, that there was nobler life beyond still to achieve. Ever, as they climbed upwards in development, they had descried new ideals on the far horizon that threw into shadow what they had been aiming at. On and on would they still climb, nearer and nearer to the ultimate ideal of the cosmos, which is God.

Not to progress was to be irreligious; even to look back and make an idol out of a superseded ideal, a hero out of a past saviour, was to sin. There had been revelations of the ultimate spirit of the cosmos, but they were ever superseded by the advance of the race; for every advance to a new type was a revelation; all true and developing life was a revelation. No revelation could be other than for a time; it was sure to lose its illuminating power as the years or the generations progressed. Many sacred books they had had, books that were no longer sacred, only retaining the reverence for that which had once aided in their development. As long as it continued to hold a beacon ahead of the race, a book remained sacred, but once its ideal had been overtaken by the national progress, light died out of it. For a dead book that retained its sacredness became a fetich and obstructed development. Not only did they reverence their sacred books; every noble utterance, every noble act, that held out an ideal for men to strive after was as sacred; but as soon as the sentiment or thought or morality was seen to be merely of the past, it was set aside. Nothing could possibly be final in a universe that was ever developing, with faculties and powers of observation that were ever getting more capable of comprehending new phases and energies of the cosmos. To accept a book or a faith or an ideal as finally sacred was to offend against the ultimate, the free spirit of the cosmos which was ever leading onwards to new heights and new outlooks into the future. There was no outer worship except life and all its works. All other worship was waste of time and effort which might have been used to raise the worshippers in the scale of being. Every attempt to conciliate God or imagine Him or model Him was blasphemy against the effort to rise towards Him. But every man had his own religious thoughts in silence, and there was welding the whole race to a common purpose, a magnetic sympathy which was deeply religious; it was the sympathy with every thought that tended to advance. But all vain contemplation or self-reflection not leading to a progressive purpose was waste of life and therefore evil. For evil, they held, is the rebellion of the past against the future; and though a new religion is an effort of nature to make alliance with the future, it soon, by reason of having reached or seeming to have reached its ideal, crystallises and becomes the ally of the past. The spirit of stagnancy and retrogression, what we in Christendom would call the devil, laughs at new religions and counts old religions as its best allies; so ran a common maxim of theirs. They would have nothing to do with what would withdraw any current of their life energy from the great work of advance.

If there was any division of their race that could be said to approach to a priesthood, it was the men and women of science, especially the pioneers, or the imaginative amongst them; for they had their eyes bent unflinchingly on the future. Theirs it was to see that the race was ever advancing. They never suffered the present to interfere with the development that was to be. They stirred their fellow-Limanorans to the enthusiasm of anticipation, and watched with unfaltering jealousy every glance turned upon the past. The moments spent upon history and antiquarian research they counted lost, unless their aim was to throw illumination upon the future. Mere students of the past were backsliders, whom they had to chide for their offences against the evolution of the cosmos. They held up to the eyes of their countrymen the nobleness and beauty of the ideals that were to be soon attained, or, if need were, the sublimity of those that lay just under the horizon in the dimness of twilight.

They would have nothing to do with mere mystery, the basis of all superstition. They never lost sight of the margin of the half-known that was ever receding before the advance of investigation into the dark infinitude, but they would have no dealings with it beyond the gaze of scientific imagination as it planted itself upon the heights of already achieved knowledge. Such dealings led to gross superstition and charlatanry, to pretence of more intercourse with the unknown than was warranted by the knowledge of the time; there was no standard by which they could be measured or checked, and, if once they were allowed, they would give unlimited scope for self-deceit and imposture. Faith was a matter for silent meditation and for dream; speech or act would only bring it down to the dull level of memory. The faith they spoke of was faith in the great future of man, and the pioneers were encouraged to sketch out and foreshadow its possibilities by way of dream; but that dream was ever the best which traced the whole faith through practice to complete achievement.

One of the great imaginative books of the time mapped out the route of self abnegation; it described the denial of the lower or material self, and the reduction of it to insignificance in the human system. It showed how by such means and by meditation a man of lofty thought might comprehend the whole range of the universe, and, passing from spiritual height to spiritual height, at last be capable of gathering infinitude within the scope of his soul. Thus could he approach to communion with the heart and soul of the cosmos, with the sun of all things. Not in one generation would this be accomplished. But, by the selection of parents who had wrought such a habit of thought and life into their constitutions, they might have in a century of generations beings who were all spirit unhampered by physical modes of thought and feeling.

Not even this ideal man of the future would they worship. For he would still be man, infinities short of the highest he could be in the cosmos; and nothing short of absolute perfection should be the object of so intense a concentration and prostration of the soul as worship. To accept any mere embodiment of humanity as the centre of adoration was antagonistic to their great ethical maxim that the ultimate object of every action or desire should be higher than the highest existing human life. To worship even the idea of humanity, were it possible for a spirit with its feelings and imagination limited to human moulds, would lower the aspirations of thought; apart from the difficulties of its abstractness, it would be open to the objection of obstructing progress by setting up a deity who was but an amalgam of all the failings, as well as all the virtues, of mankind. The Limanorans smiled at the ineptitude of making so imperfect creatures as ourselves the chief elements of godhead, when there were such infinitudes around us and above us, and such eternities before us. Even if it should be possible to eliminate from the human idea of deity all but progress and the noblest virtue, it would be obviously absurd to worship an ideal that was soon, with the earth it dwelt on, to vanish in the dust, vapour, and heat of cosmic collision. All open worship was inevitably hampered, they held, by the limitations of human nature; and anthropomorphic it must be, despite all efforts to bar out the human from it, and as anthropomorphic, certain to be antiquated by any real progress on the part of the worshippers.

These elements in religions make them the enemies of all advance except perhaps advance in luxury. Their guardians feel that they are sure to be superseded if the spirit of man should rise above the conditions in which the worships were moulded. It is one of the strongest yearnings of life to remain as it is; only there are forces material and spiritual ever goading it on the path of advance, threatening inferiority or defeat or death, unless it goes on. But so infinitesimal is the progress thus made under the sting of natural law that it is scarcely noticeable in periods short of hundreds of generations; few or no nations or races have retained historic dominance or even historic consciousness of their past so long.

This unconscious meliorism was considered by the Limanorans as little better than the development of animals, when left to themselves. Only deliberate effort on the part of a state and its members can produce advance that is to be felt, or that acts as a stimulus to farther advance. It is seldom that unconscious progress is other than material, whilst it inevitably entails reaction into stagnancy or retrogression. Nay, the whole human race at times takes a run forward, and then stumbles and falls, only to slide back into its old footprints. Some new impulse, sweeping through the ether, has stirred men in each race, whose enthusiasm, or, as it is commonly called, inspiration, awakens the spirit of progress in the era.

Conservatism is the native or fundamental attitude of every being, the tendency to make the rest of the adjacent world give way that it may perpetuate its existence or that of its brood. Selfishness is thus the very texture of life, and it is difficult to see how it can engender its opposite, self-sacrifice. The sexual and the parental instincts are the crude material of the latter. But the fire of thought and enthusiastic impulse is needed to refine this material into a love that stretches beyond the immediate object of these instincts and takes in the interests of the race and last of all those of mankind; something higher and more alien to the instincts of man is demanded for the comprehension of his nobler development. In the valley of memories was shown me at one stage of my education a complete elucidation of the prehistoric phases of evolution; first came the struggle for life amongst the innumerable claimants for the mastery of the new earth, those elementary forms that, coming out of space, will settle on any world new or old that they may encounter, the advanced organisations seeking only orbs well-fitted for their progress. Across the geological ages I could see this competition raising the minute cells of the primeval creatures into elaborately organised beings. I saw sex save the new existence from the dominion of mere brute appetite. But from outside the world came the transformation which made it the saviour of man, the ultimately dominant animal upon the sphere. This transformed instinct expanded by slow steps love of children into love of race, then into philanthropy, at first bland and crude and often unreal in the presence of the old sensual and family love, but finally strong and noble and able to embrace the progress of man as a spirit. The last stage overleapt the prehistoric, and came to be limited, except in rare and isolated instances, to Limanora. Enlightened philanthropy, I could see, held the attempt to reform all mankind as vain as to convert the lower animals into the human form and nature. Once more I went back into Fialume and studied the panorama of evolution, and I recognised the full meaning of it; the great impulses upwards and forwards had come from outside the world, and chiefest of all the longing to evolve a human nature to which death would be but an insignificant step from life to life, and which would recognise in itself more and more affinity to the highest life of infinite space.

But this section of Fialume only gave a bird's-eye view of the elevation of life upon the earth. None were allowed to linger after they had drawn from it the lesson and the force it could give them for marching forward. Minuter study of the past might lead their youth to think ignobly of life and to accept "Might is right" as its fundamental maxim. Nature, as seen amongst the ravening beasts or amongst the naked cruelty and injustice of primitive men, might be taken by them as dominant through all human evolution. If any history was to be studied minutely, it was only the more recent history of their own race, where the old laws of nature that were opposed to justice and charity and self-sacrifice have been sublimated and transcended, where new senses have opened gateways for a new knowledge which would once have been called supersensible. What could this people learn from the study of lapsed civilisations, that had risen out of childish savagery only to fall back again? The sole aim of these was happiness, and this ever degenerated into the pursuit of pleasure, ending sooner or later in brutal selfishness. It had been one of the earlier instincts from their post-purgation life, that they have least happiness who think most of it. Happiness, or even pleasure, might be made at times the test of successful actions and pursuits; but it never should be made an aim in itself. Higher civilisations were less happy than savagery or barbarism; their advances in commerce and even in science only added more consciousness of misery to the many, and more eagerness for new luxury to the few. Most civilisations, as they advance, merely add to the desires and thus more effectually enslave human nature to locality and time. The newer types produce no greater intellects, no greater imaginations, than those that have lived and fallen, whilst their masses have greatly receded in happiness and in simplicity of virtue. The changes of what is commonly called progress only bring new evils that have to be cured, and the energetic minority who have produced the changes and suppose themselves to benefit by them at first refuse to see the evils, and after a time are driven to attempt their cure by drastic remedies which bring universal ruin all the quicker.

The Limanoran horizon was too rapidly widening to allow of more than the most cursory survey of the degenerate past or of the contemporary present, even had it been to their interests to study them more minutely. Their own future was expanding in so many directions as to demand all their energies. World after world, star after star, universe after universe, were revealing their character and stage of development to Limanoran science. New marvels every year impressed upon them the wisdom of avoiding all denial and scepticism with regard to what imagination or faith should suggest, of holding neutrality towards all that was unprovable or even contrary to their knowledge of the laws of nature. They ventured only in the safe track of facts, whence they shot their flashes of conjecture into the dark. But from past experience they learned to distrust denial or even scepticism in regions where knowledge could not venture yet. Imagination had been found a trusty pioneer, and one of their recent books held out the hope that before long the suggestions of faith might be but the messages which flew through the ether over what might be called a cosmic telegraph, and that, where these touched the souls of the noblest, they came from the central spirit of the cosmos.

Already they were far on the way along several lines towards such a consummation, and modifications of their ooloran or sonarchitect had been employed in many channels of cosmic investigation. They had long ago conjectured that the earth's atmosphere, acting as a gigantic ooloran, gathered the sound-waves that travelled through space and used them to shape the things of the earth, as they came into being; and recent discoveries had almost turned the conjecture into fact. Sometimes the vibrations came from an inchoate or a degenerate world; and then, as in the earlier or saurian stage of animal life and development, the terrene creatures took monstrous shape under the resonator of the atmosphere. Sometimes they came from orbs that knew only beauty and grace of form; and then, as when the plants and trees and flowers and shells of the earth were branching into new species, few terrestrial things but fell into graceful moulds. And now, having struck this far-reaching and fundamental thought, they turned it to noble use. They produced a huge modification of the ooloran which would fix upon the shape of a flower or fern or shell, and translate it into the music that had originally moulded it. Nothing earthly but would yield to them through this reversed sonarchitect the sonant or other vibrations that had at first shaped it. Step by step this new art which interpreted the moulding influences of the universe advanced into an organised and scientific division of the duties of the race. Step by step it mastered the harmony of form, and gave the people the music that rang through interstellar space at the shaping of the beautiful things of the world.

A great book of the time showed how far the art could go in leading their religion from the silent to the sonant form. There were vibrations throughout the cosmos that came from no one of the worlds or their inhabitants. They emanated from the centre of all existence, whence they had mysteriously moulded the spirits of great reformers and sages; they were the voice of God ringing down through the aisles of creation. It was now not only possible, but within the limits of the practicable, to find by the aid of one of their new sonarchitects the cosmic harmonies that had moulded the souls of the great enthusiasts and sages of the world. They might translate the voice of God into the vibrations that would appeal, if not to their ear, to their higher and more recent senses. The seemingly fantastic groupings of stars would send into their minds the divine secret guiding their movements. Nearer and nearer would they creep under the great dome of heaven to the centre of energy, whose voice these vibrations were. True religion though this might be, never would they consent to fix it in creed or ceremonial. On and on must their art of musical sonarchitecture go, keeping pace with their ever-advancing science, but never reaching finality in interpreting the voice of God.

Nothing in fact could be nearer to what other men call religion than Limanoran science; it was never weary of listening to the voice of God in the cosmos and ever looked upwards and onwards to a wider and loftier creation. It refused to look back, unless the retrospect was to assist its march forward. Every discovery was the truest act of devotion, a step nearer to the centre of being; and anything that would obstruct such discoveries or the advance they stimulated was retrogressive, a sin against the being who was drawing all things into the path of development. Fixity of beliefs was the surest obstruction to progress, and, along with all superstition, the grossest immorality.

* * * *

There was no evil inherent in matter or any of the lower forms of life. Evil lay in returning to one of these after knowing and fulfilling something higher. It is this against which the human spirit girds when its lower elements at death go back into the grave. For, the Limanorans held, matter is not to be rigidly divided from spirit as something contrastive and antagonistic. They saw none of the strict divisions in nature that Western science and philosophy knew, arranging terrene things into matter and spirit, man and beast, and cosmic things into God and the world. Matter was vital and moving, as spirit was, though not in the same degree. Animals were ever on the same path of evolution as man was, though most species of them were far behind most of mankind. The worlds were the speech of God, methods of manifesting Himself and of making His lower manifestations evolve into higher. There were gradations throughout the cosmos, and the boundaries between them were difficult to discern.

Man is the highest grade that man knows definitely; for human personality is the amalgam of the knowing and the known. The animal as higher than the vegetable knows the world as separate from itself, but it does not know or study itself as a world apart; nor can it be conscious of the general being or purpose of the universe. Man is the first animal on earth, so far as we know, that has gained self-consciousness, and, through self-consciousness, a glimmering vision of what God might be. Only by love of retrogression or sin can this higher element in him return into the ocean of decay again. The other parts and elements of his system have to suffer reformation like exhausted worlds, in order that they may rise higher than they have been.

This was one direction their science took in finding its way towards the highest of all grades of being. But it had other lines of as truly religious investigation. For example, it had found as it proceeded more and more subtle mediums of energy in the universe, mediums which had long evaded the rude cognisance of their primitive senses but which now yielded the secret of their presence, first to their imaginations, then to their refined apparatus, and last of all to their more recently developed senses. The energies that came through them were impressed upon their senses before the mediums themselves were; and not till the senses were touched would the reason be finally persuaded of their existence. It took long ages to refine their senses or develop new senses up to the power of detecting new energies or the mediums through which these travelled. Imagination led the way; but its lead could not be trusted unless guided by scientific fact and method. Its most trustworthy henchman was invention; for this supplied apparatus that increased the perceptive powers of the senses a thousand-fold. And, as their senses grew in refinement, the instruments they invented to aid them increased in subtlety and magnifying power, so that they were ever able to keep well in advance of their own unassisted perceptive faculties.

Their sciences too had grown subtler and farther-reaching in their methods every generation. To their older chemistry, for instance, the atoms had but a speculative existence. The newer, with magnetism and electricity as its main agents and the clirolans as chief aids, dealt with them directly; and a still more marvellous analysis was developing which, adding will-force to magnetism and electricity as reagents, could find the mediums of nervous energy and classify its various kinds and modes of action. By means of this analysis they were able to get at the physical basis of reflex action, desire, appetite, and the various other semi-spiritual phenomena of humanity.

A book of the time pointed out a science as far beyond this as this had been beyond the older chemistry, for there were far subtler and higher media of energy to be discovered and analysed than those of appetite and desire. Subtlest of all must be that in which the energy called soul moved. It appeared predominantly in none but the higher types of the human race, the men and women of wise creative power. Others had it as a faint aroma which asserted itself only in moments of great enthusiasm over the gross powers of appetite and passion and at other times seemed almost to vanish. In the Limanorans it had grown to be dominant over all the faculties and powers of the human system. The book foresaw that the medium of this noble energy would be found akin to that of the central energy of the cosmos, the great being whose phases and manifestations were stars and universes. And the loftier the mind, the more of this medium did it possess, and the clearer affinity it had with the creative power of infinitude. Not far below this was the medium in which the energy of morality moved; and the higher the morality the more sympathetic was its medium with that of creation. The new science foreshadowed by the book would display to the advanced race of the future the movements of these finer media, and the modes of action by which moral energy and spiritual and creative energy worked through them.

Then would they see their way to such continuance of their life as would seem to other men practical immortality. They would be able so to refine and sublimate the energies of their systems and the media through which they acted, as to be free from any of the transformations called death for almost measureless periods of time. For the subtler the medium, the more self-existent is the energy that moves in it, the less is it subject to change and the less it needs change in order to fulfil the purpose of all being. The nearer to creative power an energy comes, the less it needs alliance with grosser and more perishable media in order to rise in the scale of existence; decay and death become rarer and rarer incidents. As yet Limanoran science had not discovered absolute immortality; nor did it seem likely to discover it. Its experience of the cosmos pointed to change as the most widely spread of all principles; whatsoever is allied with any lower media must shed them, or in other words suffer death, if it is to continue its march upwards; the whole history of the earth was a continual record of these transformations. The Limanorans had taken this aim of terrestrial existence into their own hands, and by gradually rejecting the grosser and shorter-lived elements of their system, they had been able to extend their life, at first to hundreds, and afterwards to thousands of years. They now saw before them a limitless vista along which the necessity of death or transformation would be hunted farther and farther from birth. And the same story they saw written all over the cosmos, energy as it becomes purer and subtler and less dependent for evolution upon lower forms approaching nearer and nearer to what would seem immortality from the human point of view, coming closer and closer to the creative energy of the cosmos. To them therefore all their life was religion, and science was its true hierophant.

If the analytic sciences like chemistry revealed a path that led the minds of men towards God, the wide-ranged sciences like astronomy, astrobiology, and astromagnetism might themselves be called the highways to God. The embodied energy and life of the earth on this side of death seem to the human mind self-explanatory and self-involved; but the enfranchised life and energy that fill space have no human philosophy to account for them and have generally been denied by men. The Limanoran sciences had found space, as far as they could investigate it with their senses and their instruments, no less full of energy and life than the world itself, not merely the infinitesimal and attenuated life that they thought the débris of other worlds and systems, but the enfranchised life of highly organised beings, most of it so subtle and noble as to evade even the new senses of the Limanorans. It was the life of such beings that the science of this people aimed at knowing intimately. On some stars, they were certain, existed inhabitants subtly enough organised to cognise this interstellar life without aid of instruments; and they seemed themselves to be on the verge of attaining such a power. When they gained it, they might hold intercourse with that disembodied energy which perchance has close affinity with the soul of God. Towards this higher, enfranchised energy they laboured and struggled incessantly. They believed that its existence could be accounted for only on the assumption of some perennial fountain of free energy in the cosmos; that there must be some great centre of completely enfranchised energy; the course of cosmic evolution pointed that way, and every so-called death or dissolution was but the enfranchisement of some higher type of energy from the lower forms with which it had been for a time allied. Even the fixed nuclei of energy, what were called matter and the atoms, were ever aiming at liberation of the energy that formed their essence. Every dissolution, every step higher in the gradation, implied an ultimate energy that was free from all the trammels of lower forms. This must be the life of pure thought that sees time past and time to be as clearly as time present, that takes in the cosmos at a glance, that needs no sustenance from lower energies, and suffers no birth or dissolution. Towards this the whole cosmos strives; and perhaps there may be a time in the history of existence when all the fixed forms of energy shall have evolved into the free form, till at last there is nothing but space and disembodied thought which is universally perceptive and creative without the aid of mediums of energy or senses. Vast systems of worlds have come and gone in the infinite past only to distil the energy that was in them through living beings up into the final and immortal form that needs no process of dissolution or migration to purify it.

When they turned back from these heights to view the history of the earth, it seemed to them that creative thought was written all over it; could there be any clearer manifestation of the vast intelligence informing the whole than this marvellous elaboration of genus and species raising terrestrial life step by step upwards from the microbe to the highest type of man? Their astronomical sciences pointed still more unmistakably upwards to the fountain of creative thought. The evolution of stars and systems and of life upon them seemed to them but the history of the intelligence of infinitude. They deliberately avoided all conventional idea of the thought of the cosmos, yet were ever tempted through desire of firm ground to use the analogy of a living terrene thing. Just as the body of a plant or animal is ever decaying, ever renewing itself, so is this cosmos, the material existence, the body of the spirit we call God, ever decaying, ever renewing itself, ever raising its energies into higher and higher forms. The universes and systems are molecules, the stars the atoms, of the infinite body of the cosmos, and each one of them is moving and developing in strict relation to all the others and to the abiding spirit that is their aim and master. There is law or thought guiding the history of every one of them and nothing of them is lost; the energy of everything that seems to die has but distilled elsewhere, or transmuted into something higher and less localised. What seems to us decay is but the liberation of an energy from the less refined forms with which it has been allied. Every process moves in rhythm to the pulsations of everlasting thought that is, and realises all that was and is and is to be. Nothing falls by accident. All is transformation, growth, development towards self-subsistent thought, which moves through all the processes, conscious of itself and of them all. To this final spirit of the cosmos ten thousand ages are but as a moment. The myriads of millions of years that some stars live, and that crush our puny thoughts with their vastness, are but one heartbeat of God. The whirling universes are but molecules looked at from the view-point of the final spirit; our telescopic is his microscopic.

Thitherwards all their astronomy pointed. Round our sun move our planets without failure of harmony, and ever round some still farther point moves our sun and his satellites, as thousands of other suns and systems do. Nor did the epicycloidal movement cease there; great systems of universes have still more inward centres. But all this infinitude of concentricism points to some ultimate centre which is again the pivot of the cosmos. Following their analogy from man, they occasionally allowed themselves to think that this was the brain of God, the concentration of His thought-energy. But they refused to let the analogy master them; they threw it off as but a metaphor and waited for clearer and farther-reaching light. To define what lay so far beyond their horizon was to falsify; and they knew too well from their own past history into what labyrinths of error a single untruth will lead a race, especially if it is planted and watered by religion.

* * * *

Only where science flashed its light forth into the darkness would they dare to define any feature or form of religion. God, they felt, was the infinite conservation of energy. Up an infinite scale it ever climbed towards the ultimate, the purest of all energies, the divine, the goal to which creation groaned and struggled. The grosser forms of energy were the *caput mortuum* of former mixed beings and worlds, after the sublimation of their purest elements. Out of this residue in its new period of probation were distilled again energies that swept upwards. If such lapses from the universal progress of the cosmos occur in self-conscious forms, as in the soul of man, then are they breaches of morality, or, from the point of view of the all, sins. Conversion is the entrance of consciousness of the universal law and of willing obedience to it into the nature. Religious and moral codes are strivings after it and, unfortunately, attempts to define it that soon falsify its spirit. Miracles are fore-glimpses of this law of progress half-understood, intrusions of an energy loftier than the sect or circle or star has been accustomed to. Every new faith is a miracle to its early believers; for it is a prevision of the universal law which is so far beyond their natural powers that it surprises them into enthusiasm; its miraculous quality makes them accept it as the final revelation, and their descendants, after they have advanced to a natural view of its truths, still uphold the tradition that it is divine, and strain every word and feature of it in order to find the divine in it.

A pioneering book of the time attempted to point the way of biological psychology towards the goal of religion. It showed how the plant has a dim sense of its being moulded from without, chiefly by the grosser forms of energy; and how the animal though subject to them is yet capable of moving amongst them and rebelling against their power; whilst the human is attained when this rebellion rises into capacity to rule them and mould them to its will. It emphasised the Limanoran distinction between the grossly human and the wisely human, and held that there were geological ages of development lying between these; for the one is conscious of the self as merely allied with the grosser forms of energy like the animal; the mark of the other is the consciousness of self as a part of the all, as allied with the law of the all. It conceived that the next grade was the divine, distinguished by consciousness of the all as created and guided by the self. The wise amongst men in its view had thus in them a share of the divine. There was it is true in all men the possibility of this, though in most it was latent. The loftiest kind of energy they had yet discovered had as its distinction the sense of continuity of existence, the power to think back through the past and forward through the future; this is perhaps what is meant by personal identity in Western philosophy, the capacity to keep the self from being merged in the mass of energies that fill space. Men have attained it in but a fitful and shadowy way. In savages and in those of the civilised who fall away from the universal law of progress it is obscured or buried by the dominance of the lower and transitory forms of energy. The book imagined that when the wise die this highest energy is so strong in them that it cannot amalgamate again with those they have been accustomed to upon earth; it seeks higher alliance and higher spheres than it has hitherto known; and, once having found its new and sublimer affinities, it can move amid the grosser forms and elements untainted, unsubdued, unrecognised, by them. Gravitation and heat and electricity have no power over it and come into relationship to it only when it wills to use them; for they are the mediate forms of energy that move the molecules and atoms; and they are moved and piloted by still higher forms, that are perchance the will-power or spirit of God; these higher forms come not yet within the range of human senses, but are inferred by human reason and conceived by human imagination as conscious of themselves, evident every where by their results, the marks of intelligence throughout the cosmos. But this book imagined that the disembodied energy of the wise knew and felt them, and thus came nearer to the spirit and fountain of all. Once our universe has distilled its best energies into space and has accomplished the best it can, our swarm of firefly worlds "paling their now ineffectual fires" encounter in their natural epicycloidal course round unperceived centres the systems that they have encountered myriads of geological ages before; and the collision of the two again sends them on their career of the evolution of their lower energies into higher.

But the Limanorans were chary of claiming anything that they discovered or conceived as the ultimate or the absolute; so many absolutes of the past had after a time yielded points of view into infinities beyond them. Hundreds of their scientific highroads led manifestly towards one centre; but they could not say that that was the final centre or God. Just as their sun with its satellites moved round another centre, which was itself in revolution, so might the common point to which their various sciences seemed to converge be but on the outer rim of a series of sciences that had a still more inward centre. Their highest faculties might have above them faculties belonging to other beings in the cosmos as superior to reason and imagination as reason and imagination were to the sensuous perceptions of the animals. The savage had no power to comprehend the results of the reasoning capacities of the civilised man; and the soul of the sage, when disembodied, might begin to perceive the heights of development in faculty he had still to climb. All their recent experience bade them wait further light and refuse to accept any revelation of being as ultimate, and in the rejection of all dogmatism they attained the true religious attitude for imperfect seekers of knowledge like men, the attitude of waiting for light. The book had embodied in it an apologue that put this belief concretely.

If the parasite of a microbe in the body of a flea were able to examine and analyse its conditions and surroundings and had the faculty of reverence, its first religion would have as its object the host on which it battened, and would endow its deity with its own parasitic faculties and desires. But as its horizon widened and it found its host but the dependent of another vital centre, it would contemn the mediacy of the microbe, and fix all its reverence and adoration upon the flea, which would seem to it a miraculous and omnipotent edition of itself. With its vision and all its powers of observation fixed upon the host of its host, it would soon come to see how its deity was not self-subsistent but ricochetted from spot to spot, and the human body with its comparative infinitude would afterwards take the place of the flea in the reverence of the microbe's parasite, and be accepted as the vastest and most etherealised edition of itself the parasite could conceive, having no means of ascertaining the real limits and faculties of its new deity. As soon as it was able to measure and define these, it would undeify man and substitute for him that which man inhabited, and endow it with all its own parasitic powers and limitations.

Following the analogy, the new book saw an infinitude of pitfalls and disillusionments before the religious faculty of man, and refused to accept man's similes and metaphors as in any way accurate representations of the truth. Similes and metaphors they must remain marked by all the narrowness of human limitations. Scientific discovery must be the only guide of religion; and the more they advanced in their sciences, the nearer they came to the true God. For this reason it was that they felt it to be sin to withdraw any portion of their energy or time from scientific pursuits and investigations. To know the cosmos better was to approach nearer to the spirit of the cosmos, to grow more truly religious.

The last decennial review that I witnessed, occurring as it did just before I set out over the circle of mist, impressed upon me the provisional as well as the fundamental character of their religious ideals. Most of the books dramatically presented in Loomiefa at that period had the final aim of cosmic life and energy as their theme; to me they struck far beyond all that the most idealistic of Western religious books had ever attempted to foreshadow; and yet they were wholly based upon the indications that recent discoveries had given. In a still more startling way, they were taken as but temporary satisfactions of futuritive yearnings; they bent the highest energies of the Limanorans into paths that led beyond what they could see from their actual standpoint in science; but they knew from past experience that the full blaze of noon would before long fall upon these dim regions now lit up only by presciential imagination. These books they now reverenced for their pioneering power; but as soon as scientific advance should wither them into the trite and commonplace, nothing could ever make them again guides into the darkness of the unknown, nothing in short could ever restore their sacredness.

CHAPTER XIV

THE LAST FLIGHT

THOUGH this Manora seemed to me so solemn and almost sacramental in its spirit, there was no withdrawal of any of the families from the duties of their daily life. They were as eager for the advance of their special sciences as they had ever been. Nay, the progress seemed to me more and more rapid. The faculties were whetted to their utmost keenness; their energies were buoyant and free. I had expected at this religious review of the whole of their life to find a relaxation of their intellectual temper, a languor in their wills, such as I had often noted in periods of great religious outburst in the West. I had been accustomed to look for an aloofness from the common pursuits of life and a prostration before the great ideals of faith, whenever a wave of worshipful enthusiasm broke over any community in Europe.

This people would have thought a religion that thus blanched common life of its interests and enthusiasms not merely useless but mischievous. Prostration before the infinities and eternities was the last attitude they would encourage; for they considered it blasphemy against the spirit of the cosmos. If the Manora had in any way withdrawn their energies from their forward march, they would have abolished it. Progress was religion, or the fulfilment of the irrepressible yearning of all things to rise in the cosmic scale of being, and that anything religious should check or obstruct advance was to them the grossest contradiction in terms. Religion was in Limanora the essence of practical life, or rather practical life was the highest religion.

Though the review was an intense pleasure to the whole nation, throwing the thought as it did farther and farther into the future, none neglected for a moment the severe physical labour that was their daily portion in the centre of force. None felt their spirits relax in their eagerness to perform the work of their life. On the contrary, the new religious enthusiasm added a zest to all that they had to do.

To no families did so many or so urgent demands come as to those of the Leomo; for the great mountain had been more than ordinarily perturbed. In spite of numerous new lava-wells, the crust of the whole island had been shaken by frequent earthquakes, and out of the mouth of the crater had stormed far pennons of dust and ashes, showing that something unusual was occurring in the depths below. Then had come a sudden and ominous lull during the latter half of the Manora; the earth had grown quiescent and the whole summit of Limanora stood vivid and clear in the azure.

The Leomo were not deceived by this sudden cessation of subterranean activity. It meant new issues for the volcanic energy amid the antarctic snows, and new dangers from the possible intrusion of southern waters. Most members of the families were needed in the island itself for the investigation of the new phenomena and the sinking of lava-wells, and only two could be spared for an inspection of the volcanoes of their old home. Thyriel and I were chosen to make the expedition. For we had lately been accorded the high privilege of marriage, and comradeship in danger was the usual and natural welder of the new bonds. As soon as the review was over we had to set forth on our venture, and we were instructed to return with all the speed we could manage.

We did not need such instructions; our own quickened enthusiasms were incentive enough. We knew that the reports by the idrovamolan of events occurring so far to the south could not be wholly trusted; for these regions were too often envelpped in mist or blinding snow-storm, and it was difficult to float the observer in the teeth of their furious winds and impossible to send the telepathic line of light to such a distance. Even if electric, aural, and visual records had been gathered by means of the machine-reporters, they would not have been minute enough for the purposes of the Leomo. There was generally needed therefore a personal inspection of the lands away to the south, whenever there were unusual perturbations in the great mountain and its precincts.

To have been selected for this difficult duty was honour so great as to stir us to unwonted effort. A few hours after the duty had been assigned us we had everything on board our faleena, and from the hill of farewells we had started, full of eagerness to do our best for our people. We were too happy in our new comradeship and in our extraordinary task to allow any sense of separation or fear of disaster to cloud our thoughts. So anxious were we to be on our way that we scarcely looked back at our companions and guardians, as they stood watching our flight after giving us of their magnetism.

Nothing occurred to make the voyage south especially memorable. We did notice far below us in the night one or two dark masses that were not identifiable with anything in our maps. But we set them down as great icebergs, borne out of their usual course; and the cap they seemed to bear we took for a turban of mist round their heads. From our later observation of the southern lands, we afterwards judged that they were temporary volcanic islands thrown up on the line of shallow water by the renewed violence of the fires below.

A great storm met us as we approached the ice-cliffs of the Antarctic; nothing could be seen for the drift of snow and hail through the air, and we were forced to rise high into the atmosphere beyond the region of winds and tempests and clouds. For days we could see no break in the massed blackness below us. We chafed at the delay but knew that it was inevitable; for even if we could have landed in safety, we should have been able to see nothing for the thickness of the driving snow-storm, and we would assuredly have imperilled our faleena in attempting to come to earth in the baffling winds.

At last we felt the magnetism of the upper atmosphere lessen in force and caprice, and we knew that the disturbances below would gradually vanish. The sun seemed to gather power, and we saw the cloud-floor rend like an ice-sheet on flooding waters. The fifth morning broke brilliant and clear. There lay the heaving surface of the ocean blue as the sky, and away to the south gleamed on the horizon the knife-edge of far-stretching ice. But there was something new and strange beyond it. Thick smoke trailed heavily above it, and a dozen new points of light made it lurid.

We had drifted far to the north, and anxiously we turned the prow of our airship towards the old home of the race. We seemed to wing our way with inordinate slowness, so eager were our spirits to know the new phenomena and to carry the report back to Limanora. Every league nearer made us more certain that some great disturbance had occurred in the crust of the earth. The sea was covered with the débris of a world of ice. Huge icebergs swam lazily breasting the swell, or clashed against each other in splintering collision; in some of them we could see the dark motes that marked them as portions of the vast graveyard we had once visited. Closer still to them we could see many of the long-buried bodies emerging from their tombs of frost, like Lazaruses still bound in their grave-clothes. It was a strange sight, this phantom-like resurrection at the touch of sunlight.

Over the unguided procession of icy funeral-barges, bearing their century-sheeted dead to burial in the ocean, we hurriedly winged to land. There were still more striking sights in store for us. The appearance of the cliffs and mountains had been completely changed. It looked, as we approached, as if what had formerly been a great plateau had been ridged and furrowed by some titanic plough; and where a dozen smoke-vents had once borne witness to the living fires beneath, hundreds belched forth ashes or sent a red tongue of molten lava oozing and licking down their slopes.

We had to change our landing-place far to the west; for dozens of miles had been added to the eruptive area and the cliffs where we used to land were scarred by explosion or were tottering before the assaults of the billows. The storm that we had encountered had evidently been the companion, if not the result, of this vast upheaval and at the same time had hidden from us, as we hovered above the clouds, the titanic pyrotechny.

We flew along the cliff-line, till we reached a region that seemed untouched by the orgasm of the earth. Our airship we piloted into a cleft or valley which, we thought, could protect it from any showers of ashes or torrents of lava that might approach. But to guard against possible disaster, we adjusted our wings and took with us as much of the minute stores of sustenance as we could carry in our garments. We securely fastened down the faleena, so that no storm might bear it away; and then we rose into the air on our wings above the smoke and steam that hung over this region.

It was with great difficulty and some danger that we investigated the state of the land where the lava-wells had been sunk. For the vents spat out great showers of dust and ashes intermittently, and the pall of smoke brushed this way and that as the light breeze rose and fell. By dint of care and watchfulness we managed to see most of the ridge-side that abutted on the ocean. Its whole appearance had been changed. There was not a sign of our old lava-wells. The side of one hill had been blown away, and a torrent of melted snow and ice raced down the ravine. Vents had been broken out where there had been glacier or precipice or rocky peak. But as yet none of the vents were low enough to let the sea break over their lips. The worst of all had not yet occurred.

We could not finish our investigation in the first day. So we lay down in our faleena to sleep, as the brief darkness approached. We were well content with our day's work; and we would have slept easily and well but for the tremors in the earth beneath us. Its very foundations seemed at times to shake and threaten convulsion. Once we thought of taking to the air again for safety, so billow-like were the movements that tossed us as we lay.

However, morning broke without catastrophe, and we were soon busy at our work of inspection. We flew to the other side of the range of mountains in order to note how the shores of the inland sea had borne the effects of the commotion in the crust of the earth. At first we seemed to see no change, but when we had left our faleena and followed the old line of cliffs, the magnitude of the disturbance impressed us. New precipices stood beetling over the still waters, where we remembered to have seen low shelving bays. We searched for the old sections in which we had seen the stratification of civilised abode; but the strange palimpsest of prehistoric history, a dozen times rewritten by the toil and hope of man, had been again obliterated by the finger of fire. A tongue of lava only just cool had licked out the record of the dead ages. A tawny glacis of rock confronted us instead of the panorama of thousands of years.

Everywhere we flew were marks of the recent volcanic work; and not merely creative, but destructive. Still farther off we found vast subsidences which had suddenly unveiled the secrets of many geological epochs. Some of them had been titanic in the abruptness and extent of their work; but the great ice-planes and ice-harrows had been already smoothing and rounding or levelling the serrated or sharp edges. Only in one new cliff did we see a repetition of the now hidden record. A bold hill had been cut through as by a sword and here had evidently been built and overwhelmed village after village; we could discern here and there traces of their employments suddenly abandoned, their looms and ploughs and anvils embalmed in rock; and once or twice the forms of the workers, tragically surprised at their work by the showers of ashes, showed empty and void, the living tissues having fallen to dust leaving only the shell, like the tunnel of a huge worm in the petrified débris. We lingered over this open volume of human history longer than we would have done had we been older and wiser, so deeply did it touch the fountains of romance, and the dimmer twilight of the brief antarctic night overtook us before our task was done.

When we awoke at dawn, we resumed our investigations, only to find countless signs of renewed subterranean energy. We hurried to the various points of danger and discovered only too clearly that the first storm would send the waters of the ocean breaching into many new volcanic vents. We could have no hesitance as to the conclusion to be drawn and the next steps to take. It would be impossible for us, unprovided as we were with instruments and engines, to guard against the threatening catastrophe. The best we could do would be to return with all swiftness to Limanora and warn the elders of our family. Perchance we should be able to anticipate the approach of any tempest; and if temporary measures were taken, the coming winter might stop the gaping mouths of ruin with her downward-creeping glaciers.

We hastened back to the slope on which we had left our faleena. Even at a distance, as we swept down from aloft, we began to be troubled at the changes in the landscape. Where there had been a great ice-cap crowning a precipitous ridge, there was a gaping chasm; rock and incrustation had been together blown to atoms. A new smoking cone was brushing the azure with its cloud of dust; and, as we descended, we found its streams of lava still licking and hissing their way through the snow and ice that clothed its feet.

We recognised the features of the locality with difficulty, and it was long before we fixed the valley in which we had left our airship. Still we could see no trace of our trusty faleena; it had vanished. After long search we came to the conclusion that it had been swept on by a billow of molten rock and overwhelmed, and the realisation of the calamity cast me despairing to the ground.

How different it was with Thyriel, I perceived, as soon as my dismay allowed me to rouse my consciousness from its palsy. She was exploring the edges of the tongue of fire; and up the side of the opposing hill she found a section of our flight-car unmelted by the heat, broken off by a bold jut of rock and left scarred by the fire and twisted by the force of the sea of lava, yet recognisable in its outlines. Happily it was the part that contained our store of sustenance and all our equipments for a long wing-voyage, spare chest-and-shoulder engines and the apparatus necessary for supplying them with electricity from the air.

We did not encumber ourselves with more than we thought would be essential for the long air-journey back to Riallaro. The minute pellets of sustenance were easily disposed of. But it puzzled us to know what to do with the additional apparatus for so protracted a voyage. My powers of flight were still so crude and undeveloped and my locomotion through the air so clumsy and slow that Thyriel had to carry both hers and mine. I was greatly perturbed over the possible result of so dangerous a venture. But it had to be undertaken, and she had buoyancy and exhilaration enough for both. My sinking heart felt the influence of her magnetism, and I gained confidence after we set out.

The first half of our voyage was marked by singular good fortune. The breeze went with us every day, and at night, or when the muscles of my legs and arms grew numb from fatigue, we sighted an iceberg and rested on it; though it heaved and rocked and on occasion threatened submersion, our minds were at rest, for we had our wings always attached and everything in readiness to sweep upwards from our perch.

The difficulty came when we passed beyond the Antarctic Ocean, and voyaged high above that heaving trackless desert of water which lies between the region of icebergs and the first ring of islets that stipple the tropical seas. How were we to find resting-places at night or during the day, when my wing-achievements grew lame and tardy? Even Thyriel's heart sank, as she thought of the hundreds of leagues we had to traverse unbroken by any sign of land.

At first she kept along the immemorial line of bird-travel from the south on the chance of finding here and there some spot of land thrown up by the growing disturbances beneath the sea. For some days we were fortunate enough to find a nightly perching-place above the billows upon the temporary vents of the submarine fires, dangerous it is true, yet with care and watching safe. Then we came upon a zone of calm water, so strangely still and free from the action of wind and current that the albatrosses basked moveless upon it. Here Thyriel bound our wings together and made a raft, on which we floated as we slept.

But that was only for two revolutions of the earth and was the prelude to a tornado from the north-east, a wind so unusual in those latitudes that the Limanorans never take it into the calculations of their voyages through the air. Just when we were within three days' wing-journey of our home the tempest began and brought us almost to a standstill. We tried to battle against it but our efforts were vain. Then we rose, according to Limanoran custom, into the higher atmosphere where is usually found perfect calm and perfect freedom from cloud and storm, but the fury of the disturbance seemed to be miles deep. The upper air was as thick and turbulent as the lower.

Our troubles culminated in disaster to my wing-appendages. I was never expert in their management, but in the baffling storm I grew helpless and in my despair let them beat almost unguided. The result was irreparable injury to the left wing and such an obstruction to the movement of the right as made it unmanageable. I felt my heart sink; for I saw that I must soon fall into the ocean below and be dashed to pieces or drowned.

Thyriel looked down and saw my peril. In a flash of thought she abandoned all she carried except her chest-and-shoulder engines, and, swooping down towards me, caught me as I fell. An upward sweep of the wind aided her in her efforts, and she buoyed me up till I had recovered energy and heart. Then she told me what she meant to do. For a time I would not be persuaded and prayed that I might be abandoned to my fate, but she would not hear of such a thing. By the force of her will I soon gave way and nestled, as I had often done when learning to fly, in the hollow between her wings.

Before the storm she let herself go; and I could feel we were moving almost as swiftly as if we had been in our own faleena. It was useless for her, she showed me, to fight against the wind, especially after she had thrown away the apparatus for quickly renewing the power of her engines. After a time I saw how much she laboured under her burden, and I sent promptly into the gulf beneath all that I had carried, my broken wings, my engines, and my stores of sustenance. I felt that her spirit protested; but she said nothing, and I was relieved to feel that we were rising instead of falling. She grew more buoyant and was even able to spare magnetism enough to put heart into me.

The course she had taken so promptly was the only one that could have saved both of us. She might have weathered the storm alone, and then found her way back to Limanora. But as it was she knew that the tempest would bear us, if she could keep us both high above the earth, right across the long narrow cloud of New Zealand.

She felt by her bodily magnetism that we were approaching it, and while it was still daylight we came within reach of it. She, seeing that we were evidently coasting its southern shores, but too far off to make them with her exhausted powers, grew afraid that we would be blown far off to the south again and thus miss our resting-place; for we could see the coasts round northwards. Happily at this juncture the wind suddenly veered round to the south-west, and we were swept before it in the twilight into a deep fiord. Our hearts were glad to feel that soon we should touch the earth and rest. I was tempestuously elated; for I felt, by the beat of her heart and the quick short breaths she drew, that she was near the end of her powers.

We were close to a precipice and I was eagerly preparing to leap from her back, when she seemed suddenly to collapse. I fell through the air, and then knew no more till I awakened in your hut. What became of Thyriel puzzled me for long. But I am persuaded that after seeing me drawn by you safely to land she went off before the favouring wind towards Limanora for help. That she has been so long troubles my thoughts deeply at times. But I believe that she will return for me, if only I rest here long enough. I dare not leave the place long, lest she should come in my absence. And the solitude and your gentle silence soothe me in my weary meditation.

EPILOGUE

WE felt guiltily conscious, as he came to this close of his narrative. But we had not the heart to hint what we thought might have become of her.

Almost three years had passed before his narrative reached the point of contact with our lives. He now became restless and jaded and flitted in and out amongst us like a ghost. For days he vanished in the bush, and again and again we thought he had finally disappeared. But he ever returned, more restless and yet more gentle.

We could not bear to see his agony and yearning, and at last proposed that we should hire or purchase a small steamer, and under his guidance make for Riallaro. He was long reluctant, but after months of hope deferred resigned himself to the enterprise.

Trowm and I made for the nearest port and brought our purchase round to our fiord, well-provisioned and equipped for a tropical voyage. Somm was left by our huts and our mine to guard our interests, but still more to watch for the advent of any messenger from the strange land within the circle of mist.

The rest of us set out with our guest in search of his home. Nothing happened to our expedition beyond the usual mishaps of tropical seas. A tornado made us take refuge within an uninhabited atoll; in its harbour our craft was safe enough, but it took all our powers to hold on to the scanty herbage that clung to the reef and prevent our being blown into the ocean beyond. Once or twice we had an awkward incident with sharks, and once we came too close to an island whose shore swarmed with threatening savages. They sprang into their canoes and made for us, but our steam enabled us to outdistance them with ease.

Our stranger knew the exact latitude and longitude of Riallaro. He could point out its place on a map with a confidence that made us feel we were about to enter with him into the mysterious archipelago. We sailed straight for the western side of the ring of mist, but never did we encounter any such feature as he had described to us. Once or twice we thought we saw an extended haze on the horizon and made for it; but it vanished as we approached; it was only the mirage of the ocean. Weeks and weeks we steamed around and over the region, but not a trace of the great archipelago or its nebulous fence did we find.

Even our guide at last fell into silent bewilderment. He could not believe that it had all disappeared like a dream; unless, as we fancied, the subterranean forces had blown it into space. Nor could he mistrust his senses or his knowledge. What to think of it he did not venture to decide. He lay in stupor and silence for days.

But we knew that within a few weeks began the season of hurricanes; and we determined to make back for our shelter in the southern fiord. He reluctantly consented to our persuasion, after making us promise that we should return again to search for his lost paradise. In the meantime he would be able to study the charts of the region, and define the knowledge of it more exactly. He knew by heart its relations to the sun and the stars; and with study he could tell the very place where to follow our search. As it was, he had doubtless made some mistake; and he would rectify it in the interval of rest.

Without mishap or obstructive weather we got back into the shadow of our mountains; and one day of brilliant sunshine we sailed into the fiord. Somm was on the shore to welcome us. He had no news to give. No one had been near the place since we had left. But he had had to make into a neighbouring sound in order to supply his empty larder, and as the wind seemed to favour his trip, he had brought the masts and sails of our boat out of our cave.

Our guest paced up to our hut as in a dream, seeming to hear and see nothing around him. We let him find his way alone, whilst we beached and dismantled our little steamer.

In our bustle of work we had forgotten him. Suddenly a strange, scarcely human cry awakened our attention. We rushed up the steep pathway and found him lying in trance by the mouth of the cave, stretched upon the wings that we had cast into our lumber-hole when we rescued him from the water. Somm had had to turn them out to get at the sails and cordage of the boat, and had forgotten to return them to their place. They were cobwebbed and covered with lichen and mould, yet the transparency of them in spots gathered the rays of the sun upon the herbage underneath.

We raised him from his resting-place and carried him into our spare hut. There we tried to bring him back to consciousness, but our efforts were vain. There was life in him, we were certain; yet there was scarcely a sign of it in movement or breath, only a fragment of the wings held to the mouth showed a trace of moisture. So we left him for the night, remembering that it was long before he recovered from the first trance in which we had found him. We wrapped him round with warm clothing, and placing him comfortably on a soft bed of fern put food and drink near him, so that, if he wakened, he should know we had thought of him and were near.

The next morning at daybreak I rose, and the incident of the previous evening rushed into my mind. I made for the hut, expecting to find him recovered and asleep, but I found no human being there. The wrappings had fallen on either side of the fern-lair. The bowls of meat and drink were almost empty; but there were evident marks of the claws and beaks of birds in them.

We searched for him in the bush for days, but we never found track of him. The only sign of his movements was that the wings were gone. Whether he had adjusted them to his body and flown into the air or buried them in the sea we could not discover. There clings to our thoughts the fancy that he faded away into the azure under the blow of assurance that Thyriel was gone forever. We kept our eyes on the alert for years after, as we went prospecting through the forest; and slowly the thought lurking in our minds passed into assured belief that his ethereal texture had melted into the air at death, that the earth received none of his material atoms when his energy fled from its surface.

It is only now, when we are sure that he has gone from our orb, that we venture on giving his story to the rest of mankind. We know no better memorial to him, and no better form for our gratitude than to let others know what he gave us, to let others feel what has passed into our own lives as an imperishable memory.

—GODFREY SWEVEN.